Melville D. Landon

The Franco-Prussian War in a Nutshell

Anatiposi

Melville D. Landon

The Franco-Prussian War in a Nutshell

Reprint of the original, first published in 1871.

1st Edition 2023 | ISBN: 978-3-38212-679-7

Anatiposi Verlag is an imprint of Outlook Verlagsgesellschaft mbH.

Verlag (Publisher): Outlook Verlag GmbH, Zeilweg 44, 60439 Frankfurt, Deutschland
Vertretungsberechtigt (Authorized to represent): E. Roepke, Zeilweg 44, 60439 Frankfurt, Deutschland
Druck (Print): Books on Demand GmbH, In de Tarpen 42, 22848 Norderstedt, Deutschland

POSITION OF PRUSSIAN ARMY, 600,000 (NEARLY).

NUMBERS, AND CORPS COMMANDERS.

AUGUST 7, 1870.					
BERLIN—HOMBURG	SAAR BRUCK.	SAARBRUCK.	DRESDEN.	WOERTH.	
RESERVES.	RIGHT.	CENTRE.	LEFT CENTRE.	LEFT.	SIEGE.
6th Army, Grand Duke Mecklenburg.	STEINMETZ.	PRINCE CHARLES.	CR. PR. SAXONY.	CR. PR. PRUSSIA.	STRASBURG.
7th Army, Generals Von Canstein and Loewenfeld, 14th, 15th, 16th, and 17th Cps.	1st Corps, Manteuffel. 7th " Zastrow. 8th " Goeben.	2d Corps, Fansecki. 3d " Alvensleben. (2d). 9th " Manstein. 10th "Von Voigts Rhetz	4th Corps, Alvensleben (1st). 12th Corps, C.P. Saxony Prus. Guards, Prince Augustus.	5th Corps, Kirchbach. 6th " Tumpling. 11th " Böse. 2 Bavarian Corps.	Gen. Werden, 13th Cps. Würtemberg and Baden Divisions.
160,000	120,000	160,000.	120,000.	200,000	17,000
AUGUST 14.					
	N. E. METZ.	S. W. METZ.	DRESDEN.	TOUL.	STRASBURG.
AUGUST 27.					
March into France.	N.E. & N.W. METZ.	W. METZ.	ST. AVOLD.	CHALONS.	STRASBURG.
SEPTEMBER 2.					
	N.E. & N.W. METZ.	METZ. 2 Corps with Cr. Prince.	SEDAN.	SEDAN. 2 Corps borrowed from Prince Charles.	STRASBURG.
SEPTEMBER 14.					
VERDUN. Besiege Toul & Soissons.	Relieved from duty. Army joins Pr. Charles.	METZ.	PARIS.	PARIS.	STRASBURG.
SEPTEMBER 27.					
Toul surrenders 23d. Soissons " Oct. 16th.	METZ, 200,000 Manteuffel to Thionville and Rouen. Prince Charles to Orleans.		PARIS, 350,000		Army moves on Lyons.

THE

FRANCO-PRUSSIAN WAR

IN

A NUTSHELL.

A DAILY DIARY OF DIPLOMACY, BATTLES, AND WAR LITERATURE.

With Eighteen Portraits, and Fourteen Maps
FROM OFFICIAL FRENCH AND PRUSSIAN FIELD SURVEYS.

BY

MELVILLE D. LANDON.

NEW YORK:
G. W. CARLETON & CO., PUBLISHERS, MADISON SQUARE.
LONDON: S. LOW, SON & CO.
M.DCCC.LXXI.

TO

MR. WILLIAM HENRY DAVIS,

OF CINCINNATI,

THE TRAVELLED GENTLEMAN, THE COSMOPOLITE SCHOLAR,

THE ACCOMPLISHED VOTARY OF ART, AND THE UNHESITATING FRIEND

OF THE GOOD THAT IS IN A MAN,

This Book

IS DEDICATED,

BY HIS AFFECTIONATE BUT UNWORTHY FRIEND AND BROTHER.

TO HIM

THE AUTHOR CAN OFFER NO TRUER TRIBUTE THAN THAT SWEET SENTIMENT OF HIS FRIEND, MANSFIELD TRACY WALWORTH, TO MORRIS PHILIPPS, OF THE "HOME JOURNAL:"

"His words are bonds, his oaths are oracles;
His love sincere, his thoughts immaculate;
His tears pure messengers sent from his heart;
His heart as far from fraud as heaven from earth."

PREFACE.

"Mr. Melville D. Landon :

"*My dear Sir*, — Can you write a concise nutshell history of the present war, and have it ready by the time peace shall be declared ?

"I would have is as short as you can write it, and have it complete. I would have it in plain Saxon language, and calculated to be of value to the business-man as well as to the man of letters. I would not elaborate on facts, but let the intelligent reader himself do the thinking and make the elaborations.

"A little spice, if it reflects the opinions of a people, or a faction ; or the comic turn, if it reflects the ludicrous side of an existing error, — will help to bring out the truth. Histories are generally dry because of the tedious opinions of the historian. The intelligent reader (and for him we will make the book) can put the facts together himself, and draw his own conclusions.

"The people want ungilded facts, as they actually exist, unobscured by time, prejudice, or theory.

"Very respectfully,

"George W. Carleton.

"Madison Square, *August 1st*, 1870."

REPLY.

"George W. Carleton, Esq. :

"*My dear Sir*, — I think I can. I will cable this evening to Berlin and Paris, for official and unofficial documents bearing on the diplomacy, literature, or battles of the war ; also to a friend and classmate in the diplomatic service, who will forward to me all the official information and maps which can be had in Berlin or Paris.

"I shall not let a single official fact escape a record. I will place a *daily synopsis* of the main facts in coarse print — easily caught by the eye ; while dry history, like the draught of diplomatic treaties, or official reports, I will give, at length, in finer print. I will seize upon rough facts as I find them — in diplomacy, in battles, or in literature ; reproduce them in plain Saxon, and 'let the intelligent reader do all his own thinking.'

"I am, most respectfully,

"Your obedient servant,

"Melville D. Landon.

"Eaton, Madison Co., New York,
August 3d, 1870."

CONTENTS AND INDEX.

THE SPANISH THRONE.

DECLARATION OF WAR.

ARMY AND NAVY OF FRANCE.

ARMY AND NAVY OF PRUSSIA.

WAR.

THE REPUBLIC.

The Franco-Prussian War.

Sunday, *June* 26, 1870.—Ex-Queen Isabella of Spain formally abdicates the throne in favor of her eldest son, Prince Alphonso. This was done at Paris, at the Hotel Basilewski, and was witnessed by Queen Christina, General Lersundi, and other prominent personages.

Tuesday, *July* 5.—Ex-Queen Isabella notifies foreign governments of her formal abdication of the throne in favor of her son. On this same day the fact is made public, that Prince Leopold of Hohenzollern has consented to become a candidate for the vacant throne of Spain. This consent is alleged to have been made with the approval of the King of Prussia.

Prince Leopold is a scion of the royal house of Hohenzollern. Frederick William, the great Elector, born in 1620, was the head of the house. Then came Frederick I. (1657), crowned at Königsberg first King of Prussia. Frederick William I. (1688) followed. Then came Frederick the Great (1712), whose mother was the sister of George I. of England.

He was followed by Frederick William II. (1743), whose son, Frederick William III., succeeded in 1770. The eldest son of Frederick William III. was Frederick William IV., born in 1795, but compelled, on account of his insanity, to yield to his brother William, the present King, in 1861. The present Crown Prince, Frederick William, was born in 1831. The Prince Royal, Frederick Charles, nephew of the King, was born in 1828.

The Hohenzollerns are allied by marriage to most of the sovereigns of Europe. Even the Empress Eugenie failed in an intrigue to marry her niece (the Duchess of Alba) to the present candidate, Prince Leopold, proposed by General Prim for the Spanish throne.

Prince Leopold is thirty-nine years old, having been born in 1831; is a brother of Prince Charles of Roumania, who unites with Russia in breaking the Treaty of Paris; a nephew of the Marquis of Popoli, and grandson of the Empress Josephine. He married a daughter of the late Queen of Portugal and the surviving Prince Consort, Don Fernando, of the House of Coburg. On the demise of the Queen of Portugal, Leopold's father-in-law, Don Fernando, married Miss E. Hensler, an opera singer from Boston, but made a Countess by the Duke of Saxe-Coburg.

Prince Leopold has a charming presence, being much handsomer than the Duke of Aosta, chosen to the Spanish throne before the death of General Prim; and his wife, the Princess of Portugal, equals her husband in personal beauty.

His countenance is frank and open, and his conversation is animate with free and candid expressions. Recently, at Versailles (November 5th), where Prince Leopold was serving on the staff of the Crown Prince Frederick William, he asserted that the Spanish throne was unsought by him. He believed that the crown was offered to him in good faith by General Prim, mainly with the view of drawing Spain and Portugal into closer union for the future, through the Princess, his wife.

"Why Napoleon continued the war," said Prince Leopold, "after I had withdrawn in good faith from the royal candidacy, I know not, unless, as it seems, the Emperor, underrating the strength and unity of Germany, resolved to conquer her, and glorify France by extending her boundaries to the Rhine. I believe Napoleon used the fact of my Spanish candidacy as a pretext in the absence of a cause for war, but after my withdrawal even the pretext vanished."

WEDNESDAY, *July* 6. — Paris agitated. The press and Imperial party clamor for war with Prussia. The Spanish Government notifies European Powers of its intention to propose to the Cortes Prince Leopold of Hohenzollern as candidate for the Spanish throne. The Duke de Gramont sends M. Benedetti, the French ambassador to Prussia, to Ems, to demand of King William his kingly renunciation of Leopold's candidature. Gramont, Minister of Foreign Affairs, receives official notification from Spain of Leopold's candidature, and announces the fact to the Legislative Body, creating intense excitement.

NAPOLEON'S STRATEGY.

The strategy of the war party is to make colored statements in regard to German interference, and create a false public sentiment, so that it shall appear that the Emperor does not bring on war. The Left, led by such sturdy republicans as Crémieux, Favre, Thiers, and Gambetta, are opposed to war, and the duty has been assigned to such Imperial servants of Napoleon as Ollivier, Minister of Justice, Gramont, and Valdrôme, Minister of the Interior, to "whip them into" the Imperial scheme. To-day, Gramont announces Prussian interference in Spanish matters in a very dramatic manner. Many members are so hot-headed, that they cannot see that King William's programme is strict non-interference in the affairs of either Spain or Prince Leopold. The whole ceremony of announcement was played in the Corps Législatif as it had been rehearsed with Napoleon at St. Cloud. Gramont, in stating Prince Leopold's candidature, warned his auditors against Prussia with as much cunning as Mark Antony used in turning the conspirators against Brutus while the cool and calculating Ollivier thus telegraphed the successful result of Imperial strategy to his master :

PARIS, *July* 6.

HIS MAJESTY THE EMPEROR, AT ST. CLOUD.

Gramont's declaration has been received by the House with great agitation and immense applause. Even the opposition, with the exception of a very small number, has declared that it will support the Government. The agitation, indeed, was at first *greater than was intended.* They said it was a declaration of war. I made use of a statement of Crémieux to explain how matters stood. I would not allow of *our* being represented as deliberately hastening on war ; *we* only wanted to maintain an honorable peace. The agitation, too, among the people is very great ; but it is a noble, patriotic emotion. One heart beats in this nation

EM. OLLIVIER.

M. Persigny, the Prefect of Paris, immediately telegraphed to the Emperor :

PARIS, *July* 6.

Receive my most ardent congratulations. All France is with you. The enthusiasm is universal.

To-night, amid the war excitement in Paris, a trembling dispatch is sent over the wires by the Spanish Minister to Madrid ; and Marshal Prim, whose innocent offer of a throne had darkened the fair sky of Europe with the threatening clouds of war, read this dispatch :

PARIS, *July* 6.

To SENOR SAGASTA, Minister of State :

I was very far from overrating the effects of the first impression. Declaration of the Government and attitude of the Corps Législatif may be considered as sure precursors of war with Prussia, provided a Prussian prince shall become King of Spain. [And then in cipher] — As France is only too glad of an opportunity for war with Prussia, would it not be expedient for Spain to remove the cause, or at least smooth it over by explanation ?

OLOZAGA.

FRIDAY, *July* 8. — The Spanish Government notifies the crowns of Europe that the candidature of a Hohenzollern is not planned in a spirit hostile to Erance. France demands that the King of Prussia, as King, shall prevent Prince Leopold's acceptance of the Spanish throne.

SPAIN DENIES PRUSSIA'S CONNECTION.

In obedience to Olozaga's suggestion, Sagasta, to-day, sends the following conciliatory explanation to Paris, hoping to allay the fever of war :

MADRID, *July* 8.

To SENOR OLOZAGA, Spanish Ambassador to Paris :

Your Excellency will contradict that the candidacy of Prince Leopold (Hohenzollern) has been proposed in a spirit hostile to France or its government. You will further contradict that Marshal Prim applied to Count Bismarck to obtain the consent of the King of Prussia. Negotiations were carried on exclusively with Prince Leopold, without our having entered in this matter into any connection with Count Bismarck.

SAGASTA.

FRANCE DEMANDS PRUSSIAN INTERFERENCE.

Gramont officially demands, to-day, through Benedetti, the French Ambassador, an explanation from King William. Gramont demands curtly but respectfully, in the name of France, that King William, not only as the head of the Hohenzollern, but as King of Prussia, shall present Prince Leopold's acceptance. Benedetti arrives at Ems from Wilbad, and receives Gramont's dispatches in the evening, presenting them to King William on the day following.

SATURDAY, *July* 9. — The French Court desires a rupture with Prussia. French troops concentrated in Algeria. King William to be held to the Treaty of Prague.

THE GROWTH OF WAR.

Minister of War, Lébœuf, and Minister of Marine, Genouilly, are closeted at St. Cloud with the Emperor to-day, and an order has gone forth to concentrate the French troops in Algeria. The Paris press to-day are in favor of extending the present question with Prussia to the execution of the Treaty of Prague. The *Moniteur* demands that France shall go to war, unless Prussia *grants liberty to the South German States, evacuates Mayence, renounces all military influence beyond the Main, and fulfils the Denmark clause in the Treaty of Prague.*

SUNDAY, *July* 10. — Negotiations are proceeding between Paris and Ems. A money panic in Paris. Marshal Lebœuf orders reports from arsenals and military depots. Powder and munitions of war going towards the border.

FRANCE FIGHTS FOR TERRITORY.

PARIS, *July* 10. — The negotiations are proceeding between Paris and Ems, but the result cannot as yet be foretold. Rentes are quoted at 69.95.

Noon. — Things look blacker than ever. Rentes to-day went down to 69.50, the lowest price since the panic.

Paris wants war, and would be delighted if the Emperor, in a Bombastese vein, should make the declaration. Peace does not depend upon Prussia "giving way." *It depends on an apology.* That is by no means a desperate expectation. "He has 'caved in' many a time before, and if not utterly demented, must do so now." The ministerial journals, whose diabolical cue it is to preach war, are terribly afraid lest the pretext should be removed by the Prince Leopold of Hohenzollern withdrawing his candidature. The (formerly) reasonable *Moniteur* echoes the incendiary language of the *Pays*, and says that after the pass to which things have come, the fullest concession in the Spanish business ought not to stop war. These organs are now instructed to say, that unless Prussia at once executes the Treaty of Prague to the fullest extent, in the sense of the French interpretation — *unless she evacuates the fortress of Mayence, and renounces all influence in Southern Germany — now is the time for France to extend her frontiers to the Rhine.*

Three, P.M. — M. Benedetti has an interview with the King of Prussia at Ems at this hour. He will demand the interference of King William, as King, against Leopold's acceptance of the Spanish throne. If the King does not at once succumb, the Empire will at once declare war The Empire must have war. Of course there is not the slightest chance that the King will submit to this childish bullying. France, by the rash conduct of her so-called parliamentary Ministers, has put herself altogether in the wrong. Europe, to whom in intervals of fright the Ollivier Ministry piteously appeals, can never sanction a war because a distant relative of the King of Prussia, not belonging to the royal family, may possibly be selected to take the Spanish crown, which has been so long going begging.

Six, P.M. — The Duke de Gramont, after returning from an interview with the Emperor at St. Cloud, spoke as follows to an eagerly expectant group in the lobby of the Corps Législatif: "By Monday we shall know what we have to trust to; we shall either have then a magnificent peace or a necessary war."

THE DOGS OF WAR.

Nine, P.M. — The French Government is at boiling heat. War is the word. "*A bas Bismarck*" sounds out on the streets. Some cool heads, like Jules Favre, the Sumner of France; Leon Gambetta, the Seward; and even Ollivier, dupe of the Emperor, deprecate war. The rest, with the Emperor, would shed blood without adequate cause. The nation deserves a severe lesson, which it is extremely likely to get, if it perseveres in its present bloodthirsty sentiments. All modern wars have been prefaced by strenuous efforts to throw the responsibility upon the party beginning. In this point of view France has a most up-hill game to play, if her rulers are determined to draw the sword. The Emperor, who has no right at all to interfere with the choice of a Government by the Spanish people, has objected to a Republic, has objected to the sovereignty of the Duke of Montpensier, and has notoriously intrigued with the deposed Queen Isabella, in the hope of making her boy Alphonso king. To let loose the dogs of war on account of his vexation at Prince Hohenzollern being proposed for the vacant throne, must shock universal conscience. It is no rational or plausible *casus belli.* That fact is beginning to be perceived even by French Imperialists, and therefore they are reduced to say that the present difficulty is only a good opportunity to reckon up old scores with Prussia.

No great power whatever should give any countenance to this mischievous French freak. The world cannot afford to pet such a strong, spoiled child as France. She must be taught that what M. Ollivier calls her "just susceptibilities" are in this case all nonsense, and if M. Ollivier should be upset by the process, no great harm would be done. Bleeding is good sometimes for a fever.

MONDAY, *July* 11. — The King of Prussia declines to interfere in the selection of a King of Spain. Explanatory and confidential utterances of King William are perverted by the French Minister. A thunder-storm changes the French Minister's dispatch. Duke de Gramont declares that France will never permit a German prince to mount the throne of Charles V. Increased excitement. The Queen of Prussia writes from Ems in favor of peace. Napoleon's war horses reported sent to the frontier. Queen Victoria sends telegraphic messages to Paris and Berlin in favor of peace.

PRUSSIA AVOWS NON-INTERFERENCE.

BERLIN, *July* 11. — The Foreign Office has forwarded a communication to the representatives of the North German Confederation in Germany, stating that the allied Governments, and especially the Government of Prussia, have hitherto, one and all, refrained, and will continue to refrain, from every interference in the selection of a King of Spain, or in the eventual acceptance or refusal on the part of any of the candidates. It is added that the German Governments act thus because they have always regarded and treated the matter as one solely concerning Spain and the selected candidate, and because such is the course which respect for the independence of Spain naturally implies. The note concludes by stating that these views were already known to the French Government, but that explanatory and confidential utterances in reference to the affair had been prevented by the tone which the French Minister had assumed from the beginning.

FRANCE PREPARES FOR WAR.

July 11. — Preparations for War are going on upon a grand scale Marshal Lebœuf, Minister of War, has desired generals of division to send in to him, within three days, a full report of the state of the arsenals, depots, and barracks within their supervision. Circulars calling upon all soldiers on furlough to join their regiments are ready to be posted. Powder and munitions of war are hourly rolling by fast trains towards the eastern frontier. The handful of 150,000 men are all ready to be thrown upon the Rhine at the first signal. Eighteen commissariat officers have been sent to Hungary to buy hay, which, it is said, may be got there for half the price which it now costs in France. Six hundred carriages of the Eastern Railway Company have been engaged to transport forage from Hungary.

In the eventuality of war, the Emperor means to command the army "in person." What misjudged flattery this is! Everybody knows that if the Emperor can get up from an arm-chair to walk for a few minutes on the arm of an aide-de-camp, in a green alley in the garden of St. Cloud, he has made a great achievement, calculated to produce a rise at the Bourse. He is, somewhat prematurely, but really, in his "chair days," and the notion of his commanding an army in the field is all nonsense.

THE PUZZLING DESPATCHES.

PARIS, *Monday evening.* — The prolonged suspense is relieved by a comic incident. The expectation of the French Government, confidently expressed on Saturday, that it would this day be able to state positively whether we are to have peace or war, was not realized; the Duke de Gramont told the Corps Législatif this afternoon that he had as yet "nothing to say." A long despatch in cipher, sent by M. Benedetti from Ems, was received last night, and the Emperor and his Ministers, after *puzzling over it* for two hours, could make out very little of the contents. There was in the despatch (so says Gramont) an extraordinary and inextricable jumble of politics and barrels of wine. The war-papers openly accuse the Prussian Government of having purposely spoiled the despatch, in order to gain time. Some attribute the mishap to derangement of the telegraphic wires caused by lightning. But another version, really not more unacceptable than many current *canards*, is, that the King of Prussia, who — it is now an historical fact — asked M. Benedetti to dinner on Saturday, as a preliminary to business, so plied him with the choicest specimens of that *treacherous Rhine wine*, which in this hot weather slips down the throat like water, but is terribly heady, that the ambassador, after leaving the presence, was not able to draw up his despatch intelligibly. The mess made of this important despatch is extremely unlucky. The accident may, however, turn out well for the peace of the world.

The Ollivier journals take the utmost pains to make the maintenance of peace impossible. They insist that nothing short of the submission of Prussia to palpable humiliation and insult will satisfy France. The *Moniteur* (now just as bad as the atrocious *Pays*) says: "The situation comes to this: either the head of the Hohenzollerns must give way and publicly withdraw from Prince Leopold that authorization which he clandestinely gave him — in which case Prussian militarism will receive a mortal check; or, misled by fatal self-love, King William will refuse the just demands of France, and then there will be war." The utmost pains is taken by the Government press to inculcate the doctrine, that it will not do for the King of Prussia to say he recommends Prince Leopold to renounce his candidature, but only in the character of head of his family. They say he must do it in his character of King of Prussia, and give a positive guarantee. It is because they know the King will not and cannot do this, that they insist upon it. M. Arago, after M. de Gramont's statement to-day that he had nothing to communicate for the moment, asked the very pertinent question whether, if Prussia gave way fully on the Hohenzollern question, France would make a *casus belli of other things.* M. de Gramont made a feint of rising to reply, but convenient clamor — patriotic clamor, as the French, in their present temper, style it — prevented him from obtaining a hearing, and so the grounds of war are left as large as possible.

The *Soir* says that M. Benedetti is blamed for accepting the King of Prussia's dinner, and that a "rude and public refusal" would have been an excellent thing for the dignity of France.

A despatch has been received by the Emperor from Queen Victoria in favor of peace. The Emperor's war horses have gone forward.

TUESDAY, *July* 12. — The negotiations between Paris, Ems, and Madrid going on. Announcement that Prince Leopold has withdrawn from the candidature. The French Government and people not satisfied with this withdrawal. Security against future attempts of the kind demanded. French troops move towards the frontier.

LEOPOLD REJECTS THE SPANISH THRONE.

AUGSBURG, *July* 12.— The hereditary Prince of Hohenzollern, in order to restore to the Spanish Government their freedom of initiative, refuses the candidature for the throne of Spain, and is firmly determined not to allow a secondary family question to grow into a pretext for war.

SPAIN NOTIFIES FRANCE.

MADRID, *July* 12.—The Government has telegraphed to the Spanish representatives abroad to communicate to the foreign Governments the act of the renunciation of the Prince of Hohenzollern.

FRANCE REPLIES.

MADRID (*Evening*).—The reply of the French Government has been received. It is respectful and friendly in tone; it recognizes the right of Spain to constitute herself, but considers that the presence of a German prince on the Spanish throne would disturb the equilibrium of Europe. For these reasons, the despatch says, the French Government would refuse to recognize Prince Leopold of Hohenzollern as King of Spain.

WHAT THE PRESS SAYS.

The press of Europe thus reflects public opinion, after Leopold withdraws his name as a candidate to the Spanish throne:

La France says (July 12): The French Government demands not only that Prince Leopold shall renounce his candidacy for the Spanish throne, but that his candidacy *shall be disavowed by the King of Prussia, both as head of the family and as King of Prussia.*

The *Cross Gazette* (German) says: "Is it not boundless arrogance to demand of Germany that she should, for the sake of assisting the behests of French policy, do gendarme's service for the Prince of the Asturias against a German Prince who is of full age. Does France claim a right to act as the guardian of neighboring nations? If so, it is useless any more to speak of settled peace, for its preservation would only remain a question of time, which at any moment may be broken." The paper concludes thus: "Whoever shall frivolously be bent upon quarrelling with us, will find us ready for defence."

The *London Daily News* says, speaking of Leopold's withdrawing his name:

We may now hope that the peace of Europe will be unbroken. The withdrawal of Leopold's name should end a controversy both terrible and ridiculous. The French Government is wholly responsible for all the mischief which the events of the last eight days have produced.

THE FATHER WITHDRAWS THE SON.

To-day, Leopold's father, the Prince Hohenzollern, destroys all cause or shadow of pretext of war, by withdrawing his son's name from the Spanish throne candidacy. Henceforth, if Napoleon shall demand concessions from Prussia, move troops to the border, or by coloring confidential utterances, push the French people into a bloody war, the responsibility will be upon his own head. A people who pay more for arsenals than they do for school-houses will not think, and when such pride and madness rule a nation, it is the prerogative of divinity to school her in a war of adversity. This little dispatch is the harbinger of peace:

SIGMARINGEN, *July* 12, 1870.

TO MARSHAL PRIM, MADRID: —

In consideration of the diffiulties which the candidacy of my son Leopold to the Spanish throne seems to meet with, and the painful position which late events have caused to the Spanish people, placing it in an alternative wherein it could be guided only by its feeling of independence; being convinced that under such circumstances it could not be of that sincerity and independence, which my son counted upon when he accepted the candidacy, I withdraw it in his name.

PRINCE OF HOHENZOLLERN.

Even after the receipt of this dispatch the war excitement was kept up, and preparations were made for a coming conflict. The author has now before him hundreds of telegrams like the following, dated from July 6 to July 16:

PARIS, *July* 9, 1870.

MINISTER OF WAR TO MARSHAL AND GOVERNOR-GENERAL, ALGIERS:

Give orders to generals commanding in provinces of Algiers to make returns of all corps of infantry under their charge, containing nominations for officers of different grades. The generals will send their reports directly to me, in the shortest possible time.

WEDNESDAY, *July* 13. — Both nations rapidly arming.

GRAMONT SHUNS THE ISSUE.

PARIS, *July* 13 (*Evening*). — In to-day's sitting of the Legislative Body, the Duke de Gramont made the following declaration: "The Spanish ambassador in Paris officially announced yesterday to the French Government the withdrawal of Prince Leopold of Hohenzollern's candidacy for the throne of Spain. The negotiations which we are carrying on with Prussia, and which never had any other object in view than the above-mentioned solution, are not as yet terminated. It is, therefore, impossible for the Government to speak of the subject, or to submit to-day to the Chamber and to the country a general statement of this affair."

M. David, Senator, submitted the following interpellation: "Considering the firm and categorical declarations of the Government, which were enthusiastically received by the country, and considering that these declarations are in flagrant opposition with the ridiculous slowness of the negotiations, I ask to question the Ministry upon their attitude, which imperils the national dignity." The Duke de Gramont proposed to fix Friday for the discussion of the interpellations of M. David and M. Clément Duvernois. M. de Kératry, Senator, demanded, on the contrary, that they should be discussed at once, as every delay that occurred was simply so much playing into the hands of Prussia. The debate was ultimately fixed for Friday.

The *Official Journal* of this evening says: "Public opinion in France and abroad has done justice to the moderation and firmness of the Duke de Gramont's declaration in the Legislative Body on the subject of the Prince of Hohenzollern's candidacy for the Spanish throne. As M. Ollivier said at the same sitting, each time that France shows herself firm, without exaggeration, in the defence of her legitimate rights, she is sure of obtaining the moral support and approval of Europe."

GRAMONT'S VAGUE POLICY.

The Duke de Gramont's statement to-day in the Chambers has been received with dissatisfaction and surprise. It is considered vague and incomplete, and public feeling is again uneasy. Ollivier and Gramont are enemies. Ollivier is naturally a peace man—naturally a conservative, but fear of Napoleon makes him for war. Trochu says Ollivier would be "quite a decent man if he had a barrel of powder in him." He is a peace-war minister.

THURSDAY, *July* 14.—Refusal of King William of Prussia to receive Count Benedetti, the French ambassador to Prussia. Contradictory reports of the affair. The King said that he was willing to disavow any knowledge of, or complicity in, the candidature of Prince Leopold, and was ready to advise against it as head of the House of Hohenzollern, *but not as King of Prussia.* He also announced the withdrawal of the Prince. Benedetti insists upon further guarantees. The King refuses to speak to him. He leaves Ems for Paris. Count Bismarck reported to have telegraphed an account of the affair to all the courts of Europe. Tremendous excitement in Paris. Ollivier, the President of the Imperial Council, accused of corruption. The French fleet sails to blockade Prussian ports.

THE KING'S REFUSAL.

BERLIN, *July* 14. — Yesterday, Count Benedetti, the French ambassador, accosted King William at Ems. He handed the King an extra sheet of the *Cologne Gazette* relating to the withdrawal of Prince Leopold from the Spanish throne. The King said this action of the Prince settled the whole matter. Count Benedetti made a new demand, proposing that the King should pledge himself never to give his consent to a Hohenzollern filling the Spanish throne. The King refused. The Count called again, but the King refused to see him, or to sign "his official renunciation, now and forever, of all pretensions to the throne of Spain on the part of any member of the Hohenzollern family."

ALMOST A DECLARATION OF WAR.

PARIS, *July* 14, 5.55 P.M. — Paris is to-day in a state of extreme suspense. Reports of a curt and unsatisfactory reply from the King of Prussia to M. Benedetti, and the arrival of the Emperor at the Tuileries, have largely increased the apprehensions of war, which have been further augmented by minor incidents, among which have been a conference of Marshal Lebœuf with the Emperor, and the departure of a regiment of cavalry from Paris in full marching order. The probability of war is the sole engrossing topic among earnest groups at all public places. The approaches to the Corps Législatif are thronged by an anxious crowd agitated by various successive rumors, and the expectation of a communication from the Government has caused a full attendance both in the Senate and the Legislative Body. The Ministers remained in council with the Emperor until very late this afternoon, and were then on the point of starting for the Senate at four P.M., in order to make declarations of the gravest possible character, when a cipher despatch of one thousand words arrived from M. Benedetti. This is being still translated, and the communication of the Government to the Legislature is therefore deferred till to-morrow.

Evening. — In the Senate to-day, at the commencement of the sitting, M. Rouher stated that the Government would make a communication; but towards the close of the sitting it was announced that the declaration of the Government would only be made to-morrow.

SUSPECTED DECEPTION.

The warlike preparations are being pushed forward with unflagging activity. An article in the *Journal des Débats doubts the alleged discourteous treatment of M. Benedetti at Ems.* The *Débats* urges moderation, and earnestly advocates peace. The *Siècle* says if France seeks a pretext for conflict after the renunciation of Prince Leopold, she must be considered the disturber of public peace. The *Siècle* points out the change in the tone of the English press, which at the outset so frankly sympathized with France, and adds that if France is not content with the real satisfaction now offered her, she must expect to find public opinion entirely against her.

EMS, *July* 14. — The King of Prussia will proceed to-morrow early by special train to Berlin. The Ministers, Herr Camphausen and Count Eulenburg, have left here. M. Benedetti leaves this afternoon.

PERSONAL CÆSARISM.

PARIS, *July* 14. — The news from St. Cloud is that the Court is *bent upon war*, and that the Ministry — though forsooth a Parliamentary Ministry! — can only follow suit. The coming war, just like the former ones waged by that Empire which professes to be "peace," is declared suddenly, "when heaven was all tranquillity," by the sole will of one man. One New Year's Day the Emperor in person astounded the Corps Diplomatique by making an insulting speech to the Austrian ambassador, and within a fortnight a French army was crossing the Alps. Now the suddenness is just the same. The only difference in form is, that the Government, being reputed to be not personal, but parliamentary, the Emperor makes his shot by the mouth of M. de Gramont, his own especial Minister, who, as ambassador at Vienna, has been confidentially concerting a revenge for Sadowa.

FRENCH CORRUPTION.

The *Soir* contains the following attack upon M. Emile Ollivier:

An unheard-of, unprecedented, scandalous fact occurred to-day in the Corp Législatif. A man enjoying the confidence of the Sovereign, a Minister filling the functions of President of the Council, allowed himself to divulge in the lobby, before a certain number of deputies, diplomatic secrets with the *sans façon* with which he might have talked about his own private affairs. "We have got," he said, "Hohenzollern's resignation from his father, and we are satisfied." When the House met, it was found that the Government had no official declaration to make, and nothing remained of the extraordinary extra-official revelations of the Keeper of the Seals. We submit this fact to the verdict of public opinion.

CONFIDENCE LOST.

BERLIN, *July* 14 (*Evening*). — The official *Provincial Correspondence* of this evening explains how utterly unjustifiable was the demand of France that the King of Prussia should forbid Prince Leopold to accept the Spanish Crown; adding, that it was consequently impossible for the King to comply with the behests of France. Meanwhile Count Benedetti has sent an excited telegram to Paris. The refusal of King William to have the third unofficial interview with him as a private gentleman, has been misconstrued by the Count into a national discourtesy. Prince Leopold has refused the throne. If Paris *should now return* to reason and quietness confidence in a lasting peace cannot be restored. Eight days ago France said she was at peace with Prussia. We believed it then.

Now we do not believe it. It were as well for Prussia to have war, as to live armed, and prepared for an intermittent, Napoleonic explosion.

DIPLOMACY AT EMS.

Mr. George W. Ripley of the *New York Tribune*, and with Mr. Dana, editor of the *American Encyclopedia*, thus writes the history of the meeting between the French ambassador, Count Benedetti, and King William, at Ems:

I make a simple record of the facts. The first audience took place on July 9, at the request of Count Benedetti. It was demanded by him that the King should require the Prince of Hohenzollern to withdraw his acceptance of the Spanish crown. The King replied that, as in the whole affair he had been addressed only as the head of the family, and never as the King of Prussia, and had accordingly given no command for the acceptance of the candidature, he could also give no command for withdrawal. On the 11th of July Count Benedetti requested a second audience, which was granted. In this interview he was urgent with the King to prevail upon Prince Leopold to renounce the crown. The King replied that the Prince was perfectly free to decide for himself, and that, moreover, he did not even know where he was at that moment, as he was about to take a journey among the Alps. On the morning of July 13, the King met Benedetti on the public promenade before the fountain, and gave him an extra sheet of *The Cologne Gazette*, which he had just received, with a private telegram from Sigmaringen, relating the withdrawal of the Prince, remarking at the same time that he himself had heard nothing from Sigmaringen, but should expect letters that day. Count Benedetti replied that he had already received the information the evening before from Paris, and, as the King regarded the matter as thus settled, the Count wholly unexpectedly made a new demand, proposing to the King that he should expressly pledge himself never to give his consent in case the question of the candidature should at any subsequent time be revived. The King decidedly refused to comply with any such demand, and when Benedetti returned to his proposal with increasing importunity, stood by his answer. In spite of this, a few hours after, the Count requested a third audience. Upon being asked what subject was to be considered, he gave for answer that he wished to renew the discussion of the morning. The King declined another audience, as he had no answer but that already given, and, moreover, all negotiations must now take place through the Ministry. Benedetti requested permission to take leave of the King, upon his departure from Ems, which was so far granted that the King bowed to him as the latter was leaving the railway station the next day for Coblenz. Each of the interviews of Benedetti with the King had the character of a private conversation. The Count did not once pretend to be acting in his official capacity,

In the preceding statement, which is sanctioned by the King himself, no mention is made of the rudeness of Benedetti in forcing himself upon His Majesty while indulging in the recreation of a walk on the crowded promenade of Ems. It is generally regarded, however, as a studied insult on the part of the French Minister, and is commented on with indignation by the German press. Such a violation of diplomatic courtesy could hardly have been accidental. Not even the excitement of a sudden surprise could excuse the incivility; but there was no surprise in the case; the Count had received the news the night before, and had at least twelve hours to meditate his course of action. The affair was *witnessed with astonishment* by the numerous spectators of the scene, who drew their own augury of its probable consequences. It was interpreted as a sign of hostility toward Prussia, and two days after came the declaration of war.

THE COMIC SIDE.

In spite of the seriousness of the occasion, the procedure had a certain comic side, which is thus described by an eye-witness: "On Wednesday morning the King was taken his usual walk on the promenade, among the other visitors at Ems, in the company of two or three gentlemen. Happening to turn my head, I saw that the King had been fastened upon by a short, fat figure, who was gesticulating and talking with the utmost animation. I asked the bystanders who was that little man in the light-brown summer dress, with his hair cut close to the head, but could get no satisfaction. His liveliness struck me as very strange, it formed such a contrast to the quiet manners of the King, and I could not help following his movements with my eye. The conversation did not continue much longer; the King spoke a few words mildly to the little Italian, as I took him to be, made a parting motion with his hand and his hat, and pursued his way to the house where he lodged. The little man snatched off his hat in a hurry, turned on his heels, and feeling in his breast-pocket, drew out a paper which he gave to one of the gentlemen that accompanied the King. And this little pepper-pot, as I afterward learned, was not an Italian, but a Corsican, and his name was Benedetti."

The final communication with the French ambassador was through Prince Radziwill, an adjutant in the personal suite of the King, who has since given a detailed account of the interview. "In consequence of a conversation with Count Benedetti on the promenade, on the morning of July 13," says he, "I was commanded by the King, about two o'clock in the afternoon, to take the following message to the Count: 'His Majesty has received within an hour a written communication from Prince Hohenzollern, fully confirming the intelligence with regard to the withdrawal of Prince Leopold from the Spanish candidature, which the Count had received directly from Paris. The King regards this as a final settlement of the question.' After I had delivered this message to Count Benedetti, he replied that since his conversation with the King he had received a new despatch from the Duke de Gramont, in which he was instructed to request an audience of the King, and lay before him once more the wishes of the French Government. 1. That he should approve the withdrawal of Prince Hohenzollern. 2. That he should give the assurance that the same candidature should never be again accepted in the future. Hereupon His Majesty commanded me to reply to the Count, that he approved of the withdrawal of Prince Leopold in the same sense and to the same extent as he had previously approved of his acceptance. The written communication which he had received was from Prince Anton of Hohenzollern (father of Leopold), who had been authorized thereto by Prince Leopold himself. In respect to the second point, assurance for the future, His Majesty could only refer to what he had said to the Count in the morning. Count Benedetti received this reply of the King with thanks, and said that he would announce it to his Government, as he was authorized to do. In regard to the second point, however, he was obliged, by the express instructions in the last despatch of the Duke de Gramont, to request another conversation with the King, if it were only to hear a repetition of the same words, especially as new arguments were contained in the last despatch which he would like to present to His Majesty. Upon this, at about half-past 5 o'clock, after dinner, the King ordered me to reply for the third time to Count Benedetti, that he must decidedly decline any further discussion of the last point, relating to a guarantee for the future. What he had said in the morning was his final word on that subject, and he could only refer to that. Upon being assured that the arrival of Count Bismarck in Ems the next day was not certain, Count Benedetti remarked that for his part he would content himself with the declaration of the King."

THE REFUSAL WARMS GERMANY.

The refusal of the King to accept the humiliating conditions proposed by the French Government, has called forth the liveliest approval and sympathy in all parts of Germany. It has awakened a deep feeling of affection for his person, confidence in his judgment, and devotion to his interests. He is now identified, not only with the rights of Prussia, but with the cause of German unity and the defence of German honor.

THE KING'S TRIUMPHAL PROGRESS.

The day after his final and eventful interview with Benedetti, the King left Ems at an early hour in the morning in a special train for Berlin. He took leave of the crowd which had assembled to witness his departure, with evident emotion. "I hope to see you all once more," said he. "*God is my witness that I have not desired war; but if I am forced into it, I will maintain the honor of Germany to the last man.*"

His journey was like a triumphal progress. The heartfelt greetings with which he was received by the people on the way, indicate the sentiment of the whole population. Never in the history of the world did a sovereign enjoy such enthusiastic approval from his subjects for an official act. The feeling is spontaneous and universal. Upon his arrival at Coblenz he was received by a military corps called the "War Union," with music and banners. He could only say, "My comrades, I rejoice greatly in the surprise which you have prepared for me."

At Cassel, the capital of the new Prussian province of Hesse, he was welcomed by the authorities of the city, and a large concourse of people. In a brief speech he expressed his satisfaction at finding such patriotic sentiments in the new capital, and continued his journey amid shouts of congratulations. He arrived in Berlin, or rather at the Potsdam station, about 9 o'clock in the evening. The streets were alive with throngs of people who had come to bid him welcome home. Every spot in the vicinity was full. Prussian banners and German flags waved from all the windows. Many of the houses were illuminated. The carriages were not allowed to pass in the street, but were drawn up, full of people, in long lines on each side. The waiting-room of the King at the station was covered with banners, and filled with garlands and wreaths of fresh flowers. Among the crowd were many military officers of the highest rank, the civil authorities of the city, the most eminent merchants and bankers, and a host of ladies in full dress. The great mass of the population of Berlin appeared to be present, and the streets were so completely blocked up that it was almost impossible to pass. At 3 o'clock the Crown Prince, Count Bismarck, the Minister of War, Gen. Roon, and Gen. Moltke, had gone to meet the King at Brandenburg. It was there that the King FIRST HEARD OF THE DECLARATION OF WAR, and immediately gave orders for mobilizing the army. The train was signalled at a quarter before 9, and entered the station amid shouts of welcome. As the King left the carriage he gave his hand to Field Marshal Wrangel, who *imprinted upon it a reverent kiss.* He was deeply moved by his reception. Advancing slowly along the platform, he reached his hand to the right and left, bowing to the multitude as he passed, and received the bouquets which were showered upon him by the ladies. He was now greeted by the representative of the City Government, who pledged himself for the devotion and self-sacrifice of the people. The King replied in a few words of good cheer. After a short time, the King got into a carriage, with the Crown Prince, and drove from the station amid thunders of applause. The whole way to the palace was one act of homage. There was not a word nor a look of anxiety among that innumerable host. Not a breath betrayed a feeling of doubt. Every soul was inspired with trust in God and a good cause. All was confidence and congratulation, if not joy. As the carriage approached the palace the pressure became so great that even the stone pillars in the public square broke as if they had been made of wood. The ceaseless hurras roared, like a hurricane, around the place. The King alighted on the steps, and with deep emotion repeatedly expressed his thanks. He could scarcely be heard for the acclamations, but those who stood nearest to him caught the words: "With such inspiration of my people, our victory is secure; we may look forward to the future without fear." The King then entered the palace, but the crowd remained. All at once, the national hymn began to ascend from ten thousand voices. The people stood with uncovered heads. A small proportion only were able to sing; the others wept from excitement; and even those who took part in the hymn could do so only with trembling voice and tearful eye. It was a moment of sublime transfiguration. A little before 11 o'clock, Gen. Moltke made his appearance in the square. He was received with a storm of welcome, and the people could hardly be restrained from taking him on their shoulders and bearing him into the palace. At length, about half an hour before midnight, the multitude were informed that the King had still many heavy tasks to attend to, and begged them to retire. "Home! Home!" was at once the universal cry, and in a few minutes the vast throng had disappeared, and left not a soul in the spacious square.

In other parts of the town the excitement continued till nearly morning.

AN ADDRESS TO THE KING.

An address to the King was hastily extemporized, taken to the nearest printing-office, and soon distributed among the people. It was somewhat to this effect: "In this time of danger, when the honor of Prussia, of Germany, is boldly outraged by French audacity, when security and peace are causelessly and criminally threatened, your people are impelled to express their unshaken fidelity, and their universal enthusiasm for the fight. As in 1813–15, around your Majesty's noble father, every Prussian, with blood and treasure, will now stand around your glorious leaders in the war. Only one thing have your faithful people to supplicate of Your Majesty — never to rest until this French arrogance shall be humbled for all time, and Germany restored to its ancient greatness. Only one word have we to speak: With God for King and Fatherland! Hurrah! Hurrah!" The signatures to this address soon amounted to many thousands.

EXCITING SCENES IN PARIS.

PARIS WILD.

PARIS, THURSDAY, 14th (*Evening*).— There could not be a more exciting day in Paris than this 14th of July, the anniversary of the taking of the Bastille. Rumors of war prevailing from morning to night, have intensified that commercial and financial panic from which there was yesterday a considerable recovery. This time I believe the alarm to be too well-founded. The French Government — *i. e.* the Emperor — *is bent upon war.* In all probability war will be declared to-morrow; and within a month France will either have conquered the left bank of the Rhine, or the Second Empire will be relegated with the First to the limbo of things that were. A great mistake of several French papers is to class the Duke de Gramont with the peace party in the Cabinet. He is the Emperor's chosen instrument *to set French legions in motion* to avenge Sadowa, pursuant to a plan slowly matured between him and M. de Beust at Vienna. Ollivier, whom the proud Duke yesterday publicly insulted, has been made the Emperor's dupe, and will certainly be *driven into ignominious retirement.* The denial of the *Constitutionnel* that there are any dissensions in the Ministry, is one of those stereotyped semi-official paragraphs not worth a moment's consideration. A great point has been made of the fact of the two Ministers having publicly shaken hands yesterday. That is true; but how did it happen? M. Ollivier, on taking his seat, ostentatiously proffered his hand to his colleague. The latter could not well refuse it; but he responded to the overture with marked coldness, and ten minutes afterwards astounded the Chamber by the contemptuous expression, referring to M. Ollivier's conversation with some deputies, which put the funds up three francs, that he had "nothing to do with lobby rumors." Last night, M. Ollivier, M. Chevandier de Valdrôme, and M. Maurice Richard, called successively at the Foreign Office to see the Duke de Gramont. The servant did not know where the Minister of Foreign Affairs was. His three colleagues *kicked their heels for a long time* in a first-class ante-room, and then went to look for him in vain, at the house of his mother, the Duchess de Gramont. Very late at night they found that he had been at St. Cloud in consultation with the Emperor, Marshal Lebœuf, and Admiral Rigault de Genouilly. *It is all a joke* to talk of the Ollivier Cabinet as a "Parliamentary one." The Ministers, with the exception of such of them as the Emperor chooses to take into his confidence, and with whom he concocts plans behind the backs of the others, do not know from one hour to another what are his Majesty's designs. Ollivier went about saying that France had gained a grand diplomatic victory, and was altogether satisfied; and now it turns out that the Duke de Gramont, by the Emperor's private orders, informed Prussia that France did not consider the withdrawal of Prince Leopold of Hohenzollern's candidature by his father, the "Père Antoine," as sufficient, and that the King of Prussia, harassed by France, has finally declared that he "did not think it compatible with his dignity and honor to send any other reply than he had done."

A ministerial circus will burst to-morrow, leaving the war party alone in the Emperor's councils. To day at noon as the declaration was nearly settled the Emperor received a despatch in cipher of one thousand words from M. Benedetti, and resolved to take it to St. Cloud, to con over it this evening.

The telegram comes to-night that King William refused to see M. Benedetti when he last asked for an audience, and that the French envoy has demanded his passports.

DOWN WITH PRUSSIA.

There has been an extraordinary scene on the Boulevard des Italiens. The little Bourse was more crowded than it has ever been since the crisis. There was a wild market at ten o'clock; the last quotation of the Rentes at four was 67.20. The pressure was such as to render it almost impossible to do business to any extent. But for at least an hour, without interruption, the Boulevard resounded with loud howlings for war, which to-morrow the French press will call "patriotic cries." People stood up on the chairs in front of the cafés, and frantically cried at the full strength of their lungs, "*Down with Prussia!*" "On to Berlin!"

I record the fact, that among this people, already half-ruined by the mere rumors of war, and whose sufferings, when war shall become a reality, with the rapidity which it does in these days, are appalling to think of, revelled, with a demonstrativeness most rare in the streets of Paris, in hurrahs for the coming bloodshed. While sadly contemplating this scene, the mail brings one of those French catch-penny publications, the *Paris Journal*, from which I extract a few items of (so-called) "Latest News." "It is true," says this organ, "that the Emperor's war horses have been sent to the frontier; but the Empress, who is most anxious about him (small blame to her), sets her face against the idea of his getting on horseback." I should think she would. The notion of his being able to command an army in person in the field is a *ridiculous mystification.*

Half-past ten. — The *Soir*, just out, opens in this way: "A public affront has been put upon our ambassador. There is not a Frenchman living who will not resent the insult. All hearts will unite to require and obtain ample reparation. The long despatch in cipher from M. Benedetti is not, according to our information, of a character to modify the situation."

M. de Werther, the Prussian Minister, called upon the Duke de Gramont at noon to-day, and was kept waiting till six in the evening before he could obtain an audience. Such are diplomatic amenities when war is at hand.

ROCHEFORT FROM PRISON.

M. Rochefort, who for many weeks has been rigorously prevented from writing, has found mean, to address a letter to his constituents, of which the following is an extract:

"DEAR ELECTORS, — I do not precisely know what to take and what to leave of the recent Ministerial fanfaronade, but if I had been in my place in Parliament when the warlike declaration of the Government was made, I should have certainly protested against the *unjustifiable power* which the Executive takes upon itself of superadding the calamity of war to the famine with which the country is threatened. The dynastic conflict which now produces such a terrible perturbation is in itself a most striking condemnation of the monarchical principle. If, instead of expelling Spanish republican refugees from French territory, the Government had encouraged the establishment of a republic in Spain, we should not now be opposing a king whose dethronement will, perhaps, cost *torrents of blood* and years of misery. Every war not strictly defensive is a series of murders. To restore the empire of Charles V. or of Napoleon I. are seductive dreams for sovereigns; but we, who know what sovereigns cost us, know also what we get by their dreams. This, dear electors, is what I should have said, or rather have tried to have said, in the Corps Législatif; for my voice would probably have been stifled, as usual, by the laughter and cries of the majority, which sent your deputy to prison. But here, as elsewhere, I address myself to you, who look to another future for people than their extermination, and who know, alas! the full value of those crowned philanthropists who take the destruction of the poor for the extinction of pauperism.

"HENRI ROCHEFORT.

"Ste. Pélagie, July 11, 1870."

Eleven o'clock, P. M. — Great popular excitement prevails along the Boulevards, from the Grand Hotel to Porte St. Martin. A column of seven hundred people are marching in the middle of the roadway singing the "Marseillaise," and shouting "*Vive la Guerre!*" "*A bas la Prusse!*" "*A bas Bismarck!*" and "A BAS BERLIN!"

FRIDAY, *July* 15.—France declares war against Prussia. The French Chambers conceal the despatches of Benedetti from the Corps Législatif. The declaration of war is forced upon the peace members, through a Ministerial deception.

French troops pouring towards the frontier. Marshal MacMahon recalled from Algeria to take a command. Great enthusiasm in all parts of France. The "Marseillaise" sung in Paris by authority of the Government, the first time in eighteen years.

Excitement in Berlin. President Grant sends a message to Congress, asking them to look after the interests of American shipping. Congress adjourns without action. President Grant says Napoleon desires an *extrinsic* policy, to kill republicanism, and that the war will be a benefit to America.

IS FRANCE READY?

PARIS, *July* 15.—The Government party met in the committee room of the French Chambers this morning at ten. The following conversation occurred in regard to the declaration of war:

M. de Kératry—Marshal, are we ready?

Marshal Lebœuf—Entirely ready.

M. de Kératry—You give us your word of honor? Consider what a crime it would be to engage France in war without having provided for every possible contingency.

Lebœuf—I give you my word of honor that we are completely prepared.

M. de Cassagnac—One word more. What do you understand by these words, "Being ready"?

M. Lebœuf (with authority)—I understand by that to say that if the war should last a year, we would not have even so much as a button to buy.

One o'clock, P. M.—The French Chambers assembled this afternoon, when a communication was simultaneously made by the Government to the Senate and Corps Législatif, explaining the situation of affairs, and terminating by a

DECLARATION OF WAR

against Prussia.

The following is the text of the communication drawn up at the Council of Ministers held yesterday, and read this afternoon in the Corps Législatif by M. Ollivier:

. . . .

"We believe we can count upon your support. We commenced on the 6th negotiations with foreign powers to invoke their good offices with Prussia. We asked nothing of Spain. We took no steps with the Prince of Hohenzollern, considering him shielded by the King of Prussia.

"The majority of the powers admitted, with more or less warmth, the justice of our demands. The Prussian Minister of Foreign Affairs refused to accede to our demands, *pretending that he knew nothing* of the affair, and that the Cabinet of Berlin remained completely foreign to it. We then addressed ourselves to the King himself, and the King, whilst avowing that he had authorized the Prince of Hohenzollern to accept the candidature to the Spanish crown, maintained that he had also been foreign to the negotiations, and that he had intervened between the Prince of Hohenzollern and Spain, as head of the family, and not as sovereign. He acknowledged, however, that he had communicated the affair to Count Bismarck. We could not admit this subtle distinction between the chief of the family and the sovereign. In the meanwhile we received an intimation from the Spanish ambassador that the Prince of Hohenzollern had renounced the crown. We asked the King to associate himself with this renunciation, and we asked him to engage that should the crown be again offered to the Prince of Hohenzollern, he would refuse his authorization. Our moderate demand, couched in equally moderate language, written to M. Benedetti, made it clear that we had no *arrière pensée*, and that we were not seeking a pretext in the Hohenzollern affair. The engagement demanded *the King refused to give*, and terminated the conversation with M. Benedetti by saying that he would in this, as in all other things, reserve to himself the right of considering the circumstances. Notwithstanding that, in consequence of our desire for peace, we did not break off the negotiations. Our surprise was great when we learned that the King had refused to receive M. Benedetti, and had communicated the fact officially to the Cabinet. Baron Werther had received orders to take his leave, and Prussia was arming. Under these circumstances we should have forgotten our dignity and also our prudence had we not made preparations. We have prepared to maintain the war which is offered to us, leaving to each that portion of the responsibility which devolves upon him. (Enthusiastic and prolonged applause.) Since yesterday we have called out the reserve, and we shall take the necessary measures to guard the interests, and the security, and the honor of France."

DECLARATION OF WAR BY THE COUNCIL OF MINISTERS.

To His Majesty the King of Prussia:

The Government of his Majesty the Emperor of the French being unable to view the project of placing a Prussian Prince on the Spanish throne otherwise than as an action directed against the security of the territories of France, found itself obliged to demand of his Majesty the King of Prussia the assurance that such a combination could not be realized with his consent. His Majesty having refused to give any such guarantee, and having, on the contrary, declared to the ambassador of his Majesty the Emperor of the French that he intends to reserve to himself for that eventuality, as for any other, the right to be guided by circumstances, the Imperial Government has been forced to see in this declaration of the King an *arrière pensée*, menacing in like manner to France and the European equilibrium. This declaration has been rendered worse by the communication made to the different Cabinets of the King's refusal to receive the ambassador of the Emperor, and to enter into any further explanations with him. In consequence hereof, the French Government has thought it its duty to take immediate steps for the defence of its honor and its injured interests, and has resolved to adopt, for this object, all measures which the situation in which it has been placed renders necessary. It considers itself from this moment in a state of war against Prussia.

The undersigned has the honor to be, your Excellency's, etc., etc.

Signed by the Council of Ministers.

An animated discussion followed the reading of the Declaration of War, in which M. Thiers, the Duke de Gramont, M. Jules Favre, and M. de Kératry took part. M. Jules Favre called upon the Government to communicate the documents which passed during the negotiations, and especially the Prussian despatch addressed to foreign Governments, admitting the refusal of the King of Prussia to receive M. Benedetti. M. Buffet opposed the demand for papers, and M. Jules Favre's motion was rejected by 164 votes against 83.

PRUSSIA CHARGES FALSEHOOD.

BERLIN, *July* 15. — It is authoritatively stated that the Prussian circular note, which M. Ollivier refused to read in the Legislative Body, *does not exist as a note,* being merely the transcript of a telegram that appeared in the newspapers, and stating literally: "After the official announcement made to the French Government on the part of the Spanish Government respecting the renunciation of the Prince of Hohenzollern, M. Benedetti had demanded further from the King authorization to telegraph to Paris, that his Majesty bound himself never to permit for the future that the Prince of Hohenzollern should become a candidate for the Spanish throne. The King thereupon declined to receive the French ambassador again, and sent him word by an orderly on duty that he had nothing further to communicate to him." The above telegram was communicated to the German Government and to the North German Ministers at some non-German courts for their information, exactly in the very same words in which it was published by the newspapers, and merely as a statement of the nature of the French demands, and of the firm resolution of the King not to yield to them.

Therefore, it is added, the refusal of M. Ollivier to communicate the text of the alleged note to the House is easily understood, because otherwise the French Deputies would have discovered the frivolous deception which had been practised upon them.

PARIS, *July* 15. — In the Corps Législatif to-day, Marshal Lebœuf presented a bill calling out the whole of the Garde Mobile.

DIPLOMATIC FALSEHOOD.

PARIS, *July* 15 (*Evening*). — War has been declared on garbled telegraphic despatches from a French Minister smarting under a personal rebuke. The Government is ashamed to show the feeble documents on which war has been declared. Gramont, as a servant of the Emperor, conceals the despatches, and Ollivier evades the questions of Gambetta.

In the Corps Législatif, M. Gambetta urged the Government to communicate to the House not only the despatches from the diplomatic agents of France on the Franco-Prussian difficulty, but also the *insulting Prussian note,* and especially the circular sent by Count Bismarck to all the European Cabinets.

The Duke de Gramont said the note had been shown to the Committee of the House, and requested the Chamber to remain satisfied with that partial communication.

The Left insisted upon the note being laid before the House, and great excitement prevailed.

M. Gambetta asked if the note had really been communicated to the European Cabinets, and concluded by stating that if this despatch was of a serious nature, it ought to be laid not only before the Chamber, *but before the whole country*, in order that the war might be a *really* national war.

M. Ollivier said — I am surprised that it should be so difficult to make a question of honor understood by a certain side of the House. A striking and incontestable fact exists, in presence of which no text is necessary. We received this note from all our diplomatic agents.

Several members of the Left exclaimed, "Give the text, then!"

M. Ollivier resumed, and implored the Chamber to close the discussion, on the ground of its being inopportune.

M. Grévy endeavored to speak, but the close of the debate was ordered.

Paris, *July* 15 (*Evening*). — During the debate following the declaration of M. Ollivier, the Duke de Gramont addressed the House: "*If we had delayed longer, we should have given time to Prussia to complete her armaments.* For the rest, one fact will suffice. The Prussian Cabinet has informed all Governments that it refused to receive our ambassador whilst the negotiations were still proceeding. If in my country a Chamber should be found who would suffer this, then I would not for five minutes remain a Minister." After the statement of M. Ollivier, the Ministry presented bills demanding a credit of fifty millions of francs for the war budget and sixteen millions of francs for the naval requirements. Another sitting will take place to-night at 8 P.M. In the Senate the Duke de Gramont made a similar declaration to that of M. Ollivier in the Corps Législatif, and he was received with most enthusiastic manifestations.

There was a late sitting of the French Chamber, which commenced at half-past nine. Count Talhonet, the reporter of the Commission upon the credit demanded by the Government, urged that the Bills presented on the subject should be passed at once, as an expression of the national wishes. An attempt was made by M. Gambetta to retard the progress of the Bills, on the ground that the necessary documents *had not been laid before the members*, and that the Government was desirous of making the Chamber responsible for the war, without sufficiently justifying the motives which had caused it to be undertaken. M. Ollivier said, however, that the Government would take upon itself the responsibility.

Count Talhouet said the Commission unanimously recommends to vote the Bills presented by the Government, as an expression of the national wishes. This declaration was followed by prolonged applause. M. Monpeyroux rose to support the credit demanded, and said the Chamber is impatient, and will at once vote the credit. In conclusion, the speaker said: "The war is a necessity, to *repress the reckless ambition of Prussia*, and to bring about a normal state in Europe." M. Gambetta invited the Chamber calmly and coolly to deliberate, and pointed out that the present policy of France differed from that followed by the Emperor in 1866. He spoke of the responsibility of the vote which he said the Cabinet were throwing upon the Chamber. He acknowledged the necessity of saving the country, but desired that all the documents should be laid before the Chamber, which could thereby come to a decision. The Government was desirous of making the Corps Législatif responsible for the war, but they had not sufficiently justified the motives which had dictated their resolution. M. Ollivier (interrupting the speaker) said: "We take upon ourselves this responsibility." M. Gambetta then pointed out that the *Government had made two contradictory assertions.* After vain attempts on the part of M. Pelletan to address the House, a credit of fifty millions was voted by two hundred and forty-six votes against ten; a credit of sixteen millions for naval purposes was also voted by two hundred and forty-eight votes against one. A motion to call out the Garde Mobile to actual service was adopted by two hundred and forty-three votes against one. Another motion, authorizing the enlistment of volunteers for the duration of the war, was adopted by two hundred and twenty-four votes against one. After this the House rose.

WAR.

On leaving the Luxembourg, the Senators were surrounded by a crowd of students and others, shouting, "Vive l'Empereur," "Vive la Guerre," "A bas la Prusse." M. Ollivier was enthusiastically received by an immense majority of the Deputies, and by the crowd assembled outside. Manifestations in favor of war were made at the Bourse this afternoon. Hostile manifestations were made before the residence of Baron Werther, the Prussian ambassador, and warlike cries were raised. Yesterday evening Baron Werther informed the Duke de Gramont that he should leave Paris to-day on leave.

M. Benedetti arrived in Paris this morning, and was present at the sitting of the Corps Législatif. Herr von Werther left Paris to-day. Previous to his departure, the secretary of the Duke de Gramont expressed the regret of the Government at the hostile manifestation which occurred last night at the Prussian embassy.

The *Temps*, *Débats*, and *Siècle* are silent respecting the declaration of war. The great majority of the papers regard war as the only means of replying to the affront received by M. Benedetti. It is stated that the Emperor signed the declaration of war yesterday afternoon. It is believed that the Emperor will assume the chief command of the army, with Marshals Bazaine and MacMahon as subordinates.

The *Constitutionnel* publishes an extraordinary edition this afternoon, with an article signed by M. Mitchell, announcing the declaration of war. The article says that the King of Prussia has *brutally attacked* the slumbering recollections of 1814, and concludes as follows: "Prussia insults us; let us cross the Rhine. The soldiers of Jena are ready."

PARIS, *Midnight.*—There is intense excitement to-night. A city is mad, and ready for war Blood! is the cry. Peace men are insulted. War, *war*, WAR! The great boulevards are thronged by vast surging crowds, and warlike cries and snatches of the "Marseillaise," the "Chant du Départ," and "Mourir pour la Patrie," are resounding on all sides. Numerous bands of people are traversing the streets, some headed by tricolor flags, enthusiastically singing and shouting. The national spirit would appear to be fully roused, and there is every indication that the war with Prussia will be extremely popular. A sultry, yellowish fog hangs over Paris this evening, giving a murky and sombre appearance to the streets. "Mamma," said a child, "the people outside cry, '*Vive la Guerre;*' but that is a *bêtise*, because *guerre* means killing, and *vive* means living. How can you say, 'Live Death?'" Is it out of the mouth of this "babe and suckling" that the philosophy of the twentieth century is foreshadowed?

THE DECLARATION OF WAR IN BERLIN.

BERLIN, *July* 15.—The news of the declaration of war, which took place at Paris at 2.2 o'clock this afternoon, in the Legislative Body, has reached Berlin.

It is received with fearful solemnity. Every cheek burns with suppressed indignation. There is resolution too.

The King will arrive at 8.40. A considerable crowd has

gathered before the terminus, and inside. The terminus is decorated, and many houses are displaying flags.

The King left Ems this morning. Count Bismarck anxiously awaits his arrival.

The excitement becomes intense. Flags wave from the windows. Unter den Linden and Frederick streets are filled with seething crowds.

Evening. — The King has arrived.

The municipal authorities and all the staff officers in town received the Royal cortege on the platform. When the royal carriage stopped, the King, the Crown Prince, and Counts Bismarck and Moltke, who had gone to meet the King at Brandenburg, forty miles from Berlin, to inform him of the declaration of war, alighted. The Crown Prince at once addressed the public, and told them that war was declared. The news was received with continued shouts by the public on the platform. The salute of the municipal authorities having taken place, and the King having replied, they mounted their carriages, amidst the hurrahs of the multitude on the square before the terminus. There can be no doubt, the war henceforward will be popular in this country, and this means much. It means that everybody will act, and make sacrifices for the country. It will be war to the knife. The mobilization of the whole army was announced by the Crown Prince.

WAR.

The order of mobilization will be published to-night by placards and handbills, as is the custom here in time of war, and it will embrace the whole North German army at once. *The plan of the campaign* is openly spoken of, even by such as really ought to know something of it. But this is always the case here, and can hardly be otherwise, where the voluntary co-operation of the whole people is expected. It consists in a simultaneous advance of the whole army, without the reserves, towards the French frontier. The four main railroads leading from the Elbe to the Rhine will then be altogether stopped for private traffic during the days designed for the conveyance of troops. It is supposed that each of these railways can convey 20,000 soldiers a day. The locomotives and wagons returning next day, 20,000 again may be conveyed on the same railway the third day, when they will have collected at the stations in the East, or will have been echeloned along the line. Thus the 240,000 men of the North German army, now in garrisons east of the Rhine, will be on the banks of that river the fifth day after the commencement of the movement. The reserves will follow as they come in, which, in Prussia, is very quickly. The landwehr, this time not destined to act on the aggressive, will fill up the garrisons. Thus the advance from the Rhine, which will be crossed at Cologne, Coblenz, and Mayence by the permanent railway bridges, will be made with 30,000 men complete, followed by 100,000, who will gradually fall in with their cadres. The advance will be concentric upon Paris, unhesitating and unceasing, until the French are met, Neither an attack from the sea, nor a French diversion in South Germany, will be heeded.

Eleven, P.M. — Amazement has changed to joy. A whole city is intoxicated with gladness. Crowds go singing war songs, arm in arm, down the streets. Some shout, some laugh, and some indulge in witticisms. One man takes another by the throat, and cries: "My neighbor's daughter loves your nephew. He will have nothing to do with her; but if you do not declare that he never shall marry her, I will knock you down." One harangues the public from a form: "Ladies and gentlemen," he says, "you are quite in the dark about what the French want. Are you not? I can tell it you in confidence. I have sown my wild oats in Paris. They themselves want a Hohenzollern. They grudge the Spaniards and us our good luck. And why should they not get a Hohenzollern? If that favor has been bestowed upon the Roumanians to bring them peacefully to reason, why not bestow it upon the French?"

AMERICA.

THE PRESIDENT SENDS A MESSAGE TO CONGRESS.

WASHINGTON, *July* 15. — The President sent a message to Congress to-day, calling attention to the imminence of war in Europe, which, he says, indicates the necessity of legislation tending to increase the commercial marine of the United States, which is at present inadequate to meet the demands the war in Europe will impose. The President supposes that the opportunity should be afforded American citizens to purchase foreign-built vessels. The foreign mail service is dependent in a large degree on the Bremen and Hamburg lines of steamers: if these steamers should be in any way blockaded by the French, great embarrassment to the postal service must ensue. The President recommended that Congress should postpone its adjournment until the exigency has been provided for. The House of Representatives has refused action on the message, and adjourned to-day at five o'clock. A despatch announcing the declaration of war between France and Prussia was read to-day in the House of Representatives by the Speaker, which many of the members applauded.

WASHINGTON, *July* 15 (*Evening.*) — Both Houses have adjourned without legislation upon the merchant marine, as recommended by President Grant. An opportunity to rebuild American shipping, destroyed by the late civil war, is lost. The President expresses great regret at the hasty adjournment.

WAR DECLARED.

And so, blindly, on a telegraphic despatch from a mad diplomat smarting under a personal affront, a Council of Ministers declares war.

Without *even these* storm-garbled telegrams, a *corps diplomatique* is dragged into sanctioning a declaration — yes, sanctioning a war which may yet drench nations in blood.

What a responsibility rests to-night upon the heads of Benedetti, Gramont, and Napoleon III!

THE IMPERIAL LIE.

CÆSARISM IS NOT PEACE.

"The Empire is peace" is the Imperial lie which came with Cæsarism, but which will die at Saarbrück. Cæsarism means big-dog-ism. It means France is too strong to be defeated. It means the impious "God is on the side of the strongest battalions" of Napoleon I. The Empire made Magenta, Sebastopol, Sadowa, and will make Sedan — bloody battle-fields! It has kept a million French and Prussian soldiers in the field for seventeen years, and now it drenches Europe in blood, that the damnable lie may live. The first gun at Saarbrück will be the death-knell of lying Cæsarism and the empire of Napoleon III.

WHO MADE THE WAR?

Napoleon III. says the Hohenzollern — that a feeble scion of decayed royalty, struggling to sit upon a tottering Spanish throne, made the French Emperor go to war. This was *not* the cause. Cæsarism and the ambition of Napoleon III. are the true causes, and the Hohenzollern only the opportunity. France *herself* has not gone to war. Napoleon III. plunged the Empire into the bloody struggle, dragging in the nation.

Wars are always popular. Saarbrück and Sedan will threaten the national existence, and France, *nolens volens*, will espouse the lie of Napoleon. Even Rochefort, as much as he hates Napoleon, will be silent when French blood begins to drip at Saarbrück. There were thousands in our country opposed to the Mexican war, but Vera Cruz made them silent. Governor Seymour said *war!* after Gettysburg.

SAID PRESIDENT GRANT

to the author (published in *The Sun*, August 6th):

"Napoleon makes this war, because, as he said to the Mayor of Rouen in 1866, 'he hates the treaty of 1815,' and to kill Rochefortism at home. France was prostrated by Waterloo, when the Ghent treaty confirmed the Rhine country to Prussia. This south bank of the Rhine is what Napoleon is fighting for, while Prussia is fighting for Bismarck's great idea of a North-German confederation." *

"Then Napoleon needs an *extrinsic* policy to kill Republicanism at home."

"Yes," said the President enthusiastically, "Napoleon III. needs what Alexander H. Stephens suggested to President Lincoln and Mr. Seward, when they thought of patching up a truce at Hampton Roads, in 1862—an *extrinsic* policy to unite everybody on. England knew what Stephens' *extrinsic* policy meant, for Seward's despatches made them open their eyes. It meant North and South join against Canada. It took diplomacy to get this *extrinsic* idea out of Stephens and Jeff.; so it took diplomacy to get the French signature to the secret treaty which would enable Napoleon to gobble up Saarbrück and Landau, and restore Luxemburg to the French. But it took greater diplomacy to reject it. Bismarck did it, and he now hands the rejected proposition over to the other powers, as Seward handed over Stephens' Canada policy to England. The defeat of King William is the squelching of Belgium."

AUTHOR—"Americans generally sympathize with Prussia?"

GENERAL GRANT—"Yes, I don't know but what we do. Our sympathy is the result of commerce, German emigration, and because the Germans took our bonds and stood

WITH US DURING THE WAR.

France didn't. King William and Bismarck sent three telegrams of congratulation to us. Not one came from Napoleon, who, on the contrary, was attacking us in Mexico. Seward let him attack, because his army was all the time eating up the beef and tanning the hides which otherwise would have gotten into the rebel army. In fact, Maximilian was a sort of provision destroyer in Mexico. If we go back of the last war, there is no reason why we shouldn't sympathize with France. She sent us troops, and Lafayette came to help us, while the Prince of Hesse hired out the Hessians to Great Britain.

SATURDAY, *July* 16.—German troops massing on the Saar and on the Rhine rivers. Bavaria, Baden, and Würtemberg summoned by France to state what course they intend pursuing. Twenty-four hours given for a reply.

Italy decides against France and in favor of Prussia. Prussia taken by surprise. The Prussians appear on French territory. The French peace newspapers support the war. The

---

* "You cannot but feel a pride, Count Bismarck, in having contributed so largely to the winning of to-day's victory," said a gentleman standing with General Sheridan to Count Bismarck on the battle-field of Sedan.

"Oh! no, my dear sir," was the mild answer; "I am no strategist, and have nothing to do with the winning of battles. What I am proud of is, that the Bavarians, the Saxons, and the Würtembergers have not only been on our side, but have had so large a share—the largest share—in the glory of the day; that they are with us, and not against us. *That* is my doing. I don't think the French will say now that the South Germans will not fight for our common Fatherland."

Duke de Gramont demands an autograph letter of apology from King William to Napoleon. Bavaria decides officially with Prussia. King William speaks in Hamburg. United Germany enthusiastic for war. President Grant calls the war a "blessing to America."

FRANKFORT FOR GERMANY.

FRANKFORT, *July* 16. — The French Government have sent a threatening message to the South German Governments, demanding that they should forward, within twenty-four hours, a declaration whether they intend to remain neutral.

The sympathy of all the South German States is in favor of Prussia. Hanover, even, has no sympathy for France.

The "free imperial city" of Frankfort, seized by Prussia after the Austrian campaign, is enthusiastic for United Germany.

How they hated King William in Wiesbaden in '67, and now every tongue is eloquent for United Germany!

FRANCE DELUDED.

PARIS, *July* 16. — There is immense activity at the War Office. Troops are going forward to Metz with rapidity. It is expected that the South German States will go with France, or remain neutral. This is a vain delusion.

French Ministers at Baden, Saxony, Bavaria, and Hesse have been summoned to Paris, to give information respecting the attitude of those States in the Franco-Prussian war.

Prussian troops are concentrating at Mayence and Cologne, and along the Rhine.

THE FRENCH PRESS

complain of the tone of the observations of Mr. Disraeli and the speech of Mr. Gladstone towards France. "France demands nothing of England but loyal, sincere neutrality."

The *Soir* (Edmond About) says:

"If France wishes to gain, or at least to neutralize, the peoples whom Prussia has enrolled against us, France should commence by formally disavowing all ideas of conquest. Germany will never allow a single village to be detached from her territory, and Germany is right. Let the French motto be, 'No annexation.' If also we wish England to remain a faithful ally, let us hasten to reassure Antwerp and Belgium by an official declaration. If we wish to gain Italy, let us recall the garrison from Rome. Let us be honest, and we shall be doubly strong."

The *Journal des Débats* says that "while a hope remained that peace might be maintained with honor, it had endeavored to calm passion and secure the triumph of pacific ideas. It now renounces the discussion, and henceforth will associate itself with the patriotic sentiment which should animate all Frenchmen, without distinction of party. It will now as earnestly seek to promote the triumph of the French flag, as it had hitherto earnestly sought to maintain peace."

The Republican journal, *La Cloche*, says that "*France is about to pay with her blood* for the inaptitude of her diplomatists."

La Cloche bitterly reproaches the Empire, which, while promising peace, is incessantly leading the country into war, and says that "it cannot find a shadow of pretext for the war."

The *Rappel* strongly attacks the conduct of the Government from first to last, and says, "The Left (*The Republicans*) nobly performed their duty, and blamed the Ministers and the armed soldiers." The Left is severe upon the faults of the Government, but passionately jealous of the honor of France.

The *Siècle* publishes a similar declaration to that contained in the *Journal des Débats*, and says, war being declared, it must be energetically conducted, and the country must make all sacrifice required by the present circumstances.

The *Temps* deplores the impatience and intolerance of the majority in the Legislative Body yesterday, which approved the policy of the Government, without even wishing for proper information.

The *Patrie* states that France will address to the South German States a manifesto, declaring that the war will be confined to France and Prussia, and that France will respect the rights and independence of Germany.

PARIS, *July* 16, 5.40 P.M. — M. Rouher has announced to-day in the Senate, that the Prussians have entered French territory.

According to private information, the Prussians entered France, near Landau, but returned shortly afterwards into Prussian territory.

The Duke de Gramont has informed Lord Lyons, the British ambassador, and Baron Beyens, the Minister of Belgium, that France will respect, even strategically, Belgium's neutrality.

The Senate unanimously voted to-day as urgent the financial credits voted yesterday by the Legislative Body. The sitting was then suspended for a short time. On the adjournment of the House, the members will proceed in a body to St. Cloud.

A decree declares the Departments on the Moselle and the Upper and Lower Rhine in a state of siege.

A decree calls out 90,000 men, who form the contingent of the class of 1869.

ITALY FOR PRUSSIA.

FLORENCE, *July* 16. — An anti-French demonstration has just taken place, which was originated by the National Democratic Society. Crowds of people, shouting, "Down with France," "Cheers for Neutrality,"

"Long live Prussia," proceeded first to the hotel of the Minister of Foreign Affairs, and afterwards to the house of the ambassador of the North German Confederation.

The people shout, "*Let France go away from Rome and Italy; The Pope and the Church; Victor Emanuel and the State.*"

The French Cabinet has requested the Italian Government to state what attitude Italy intends to assume in the pending events.

BERLIN, *July* 16. — The mobilization of the whole army is ordered.

The North German Parliament is ordered to assemble on Tuesday next.

All the provincial Governors who are on leave of absence have been instructed by the Minister of the Interior to return to their posts immediately.

THE KING APOLOGIZE?

The Duke de Gramont stated to the North German ambassador in Paris, on the 12th inst., that the renunciation of the Spanish crown by the Prince of Hohenzollern was *only a secondary question*, as France would have prevented his ascending the throne. The chief thing demanded was, that the King of Prussia, in an autograph letter to the Emperor Napoleon, should make an apology for what had happened, and that this letter, which was to be made public, should contain no mention of the relationship between the Prince of Hohenzollern and the Imperial family.

PRUSSIA SURPRISED.

Prussia, this time, has been taken by surprise. King William's demeanor is serious in the extreme. It is no secret that he was always averse to another war, and he alone prevented it breaking out on the occasion of the Luxemburg difficulty, when circumstances would have been far more favorable to Prussia, and when the Prussian Foreign Office, and particularly the officers of the general staff, with Count Moltke at the head of them, urged it upon him. The scenes he witnessed on the battle-fields of Bohemia have produced this aversion. The activity of the governmental machinery is visible everywhere, and enormous.

A BAS BISMARCK.

HAVRE. — The declaration of war has been received here with great enthusiasm, and the soldiers in the town were much cheered by the inhabitants.

A hostile manifestation has taken place before the Prussian consulate, amid cries of "A bas Bismarck," "Vive l'Empereur."

DRESDEN. — The Crown Prince of Saxony, as commander of the Saxon Army Corps, has issued an order for the mobilization of the troops, whereby the Saxon Army Corps is placed on a war footing. The mobilization commences to-day.

BAVARIA FIGHTS WITH PRUSSIA.

The organs of the Government confirm the news that the King has decided to consider a *casus fœderis* with Prussia as having arisen, and that consequently Bavaria enters into the war with Prussia against France. The co-operation of the Bavarian army with that of North Germany will commence at once.

The order for the mobilization of the Bavarian army has been issued by the King to-day.

LUXEMBURG. — The Prussians have torn up the railway lines on the frontier of the Grand Duchy. 2,000 men are encamped at Wasserbillig. Communication with Treves is interrupted.

GOD'S BLESSING FOR GERMANY.

HAMBURG. — The following is the King of Prussia's reply to an address received from the Commercial Chamber at Hamburg:

"With heartfelt emotion I receive at this moment the telegram of the Commercial Chamber of to-day's date. No one knows better than I, who had to speak the decisive word, what sacrifices will shortly be required from the whole Fatherland; but the self-devotion expressed by the Commercial Chamber the moment the honor of Germany is at stake, fills me with pride and tranquillity. On God's blessing all things depend.

"WILHELM REX."

The utmost enthusiasm prevails here, as throughout Germany, against France. The whole of Germany is as one people in arms to repel the insult offered to the national honor.

CHEER THE KING.

BRESLAU. — The war news published last night in special editions of the various papers evoked a stormy enthusiasm in all classes of the population.

Crowds of people thronged the streets until midnight, singing national songs, and giving cheers for the King.

AMERICA.

WASHINGTON, *July* 16. — M. Prévost-Paradol, the French ambassador, was presented to the President. The usual speeches were made.

AMERICAN SYMPATHY.

American sympathy is generally for Prussia. Great regret is expressed that Congress should have adjourned without taking some action in regard to the merchant marine. The President, in conversation with the author, said relative to the adjournment as follows :

"Here we have made a great, a suicidal mistake. Before Congress adjourned, we ought to have made arrangements for the

PURCHASE OF FOREIGN VESSELS.

They are in the market now at cheap figures, but we can't buy them. The old Act of Congress provides for the building of ships at home, but prohibits their purchase of a foreign power. By an Act of Congress, we can't buy a vessel which we once owned, but sold to Germany during our war ; that is, we can't change her flag. If we buy and sail under Prussian flags, then France will gobble us up. Our war killed our merchant marine. In the face of the *Alabama* pirates we sold out cheap. England had no Acts of Parliament against buying, and she possessed herself of our ships at half price. Now is the time for us to get even by buying the ships of France and Prussia. This is what

I WANTED CONGRESS TO DO."

AUTHOR. — "What will be the effect of war on this country ? "

THE PRESIDENT — "History will repeat itself. Our war raised values, not only here, but all over the world. People couldn't live in Europe after one, nor one-half as cheap as before. The present war will raise values in Europe. Americans will come home. Iron and leather and coal will advance there. Then we can compete with them

WITHOUT A TARIFF.

The war will be a self-imposed high tariff, imposed on every article of foreign importation. This war [and here the General was enthusiastic] will be the greatest blessing that could be afforded to America. It will raise Europe up to an equilibrium of prices and labor. Our factories will start again. Importations will cease. They will no longer be able to make a coat cheaper in Europe than in this country. Our breadstuffs and bacon will have to furnish their quartermaster's department indirectly. Pork will advance, and general farm produce will bring correspondingly high figures, if the war lasts, as I now think it will. Our bonds will come home at first, but they will be quickly absorbed. They are safe, and foreigners are even now making large deposits of them in American banks. Many are coming back, but few want to realize on them. They make a sure revenue for them, no matter how the war turns out at home."

SUNDAY, *July* 17. — Arrival of King William at Münich. He is received by the multitude with uncovered heads. Gramont says France will respect the neutrality of Luxemburg. Sweden and Norway to remain neutral. Marshal Bazaine goes to the front. Canrobert follows. The French troops are at Thionville; the Prussians at Longwy. The French Legislature, in an address to the Emperor, approves his course. Würtemberg and Bavaria with Prussia.

BAVARIA AND VATERLAND.

MUNICH, *July* 17 (*Evening*). — An immense crowd went this afternoon to the King's palace, notwithstanding the rain, and expressed their gratitude for his most recent patriotic resolutions, and his fidelity to his confederate duties, and gave numberless cheers to his Majesty. The multitude, uncovering their heads, sang popular hymns, and Arndt's song, "Was ist des Deutschen Vaterland." The King, with visible emotion, bowed frequently from the open window.

LUXEMBURG. — According to a telegram received here from the Charge d'Affaires of Luxemburg at Paris, the Duke de Gramont has declared that France would not think of taking the initiative in violating the neutrality of the Grand Duchy. The Chamber has been convoked for Friday next.

STOCKHOLM. — Sweden and Norway will observe neutrality in the coming struggle. All the journals are in favor of the maintenance of this attitude.

BRUSSELS. — The French are at Thionville, near Metz. The Prussians have occupied a French village near Longwy, and an encounter is expected to take place to-day.

VIVE L'EMPEREUR.

PARIS, *July* 17. — The *Constitutionnel* announces that patriotic manifestations have taken place in different towns of France, and especially in Perpignan, Mimes, Lille, Tarbes, Nancy, Amiens, Dijon, and Havre. On each occasion of the departure of regiments they received an ovation from the people.

In Paris fresh warlike demonstrations occurred last night. The crowd sang the "Marseillaise," shouting "Vive la France!" "Vive l'Empereur!"

Marshal Bazaine set out last night to take the command of his army corps. He will have 80,000 men, afterwards to be increased to 120,000. Marshal Canrobert leaves Paris this evening.

40,000,000 VS. FRANCE.

The North German Confederation of eighteen Governments have made common cause with Prussia against France. Bavaria and Würtemberg are with Prussia also. It seems as if France has a great and bloody work before her.

THE WAR GROWS.

REMARK, *July* 17. — Prussia was never so strong as now. The Emperor was to soothe and neutralize South Germany by a proclamation, and then deal with his great rival single-handed. The notion was essentially fictitious, for to attack Prussia is to attack the North German Confederation, whose eighteen Governments have undertaken a common defence of their territory.

Fictions, indeed, are sometimes useful while they can be kept up, but this fancy has vanished. The South German States, who were foremost in the view of political speculators, are declaring themselves. Their resolution is taken, and the whole German people, save six million subjects of the Austro-Hungarian Emperor, will be united for the defence of the Fatherland. Bavaria was in armed conflict with Prussia only four years ago, and it was asked with some doubt whether patriotic German sentiment or jealousy of Prussia would sway its resolution. Bavaria has firmly resolved to stand by the side of Prussia, and her determination will be that of Würtemberg also. The rulers of South Germany have comprehended that in such a war as this they could occupy no neutral position: either they must frankly and unreservedly cast in their lot with the defenders of the common country, or accept the miserable part assigned by the First Napoleon to his German dependents, and take sides with France against their brethren.

There are only two parties in this war — the French and the German nations. The alliance of Bavaria, Würtemberg, and Baden with Prussia at once increases by eight millions the population which was previously committed with all its resources to the prosecution of the war with France.

BAVARIA TURNS THE SCALE.

Until yesterday it was doubtful whether this was to be a war between Prussia and France or between Germany and France. It was possible that the South German States might hold aloof. Many plausible reasons for their abstention might have been urged. They could not be said to have had any share in the candidature of Prince Leopold, nor could they have been fairly called upon to fight merely because the King of Prussia had shown himself reluctant to assent to the demand of the French. The Emperor of the French took all these matters into consideration; he counted upon finding allies, none the less valuable because they were passive, among the States of the South. Nothing could have more thoroughly dispelled this apprehension on the side of Germany, and hope on the side of France, than the conduct of Bavaria. By manifesting a readiness to identify herself with Prussia, Bavaria has done much to prove that the war, so rashly and unjustifiably provoked, is a war with United Germany. Such is the conviction, and it is a belief which is fully warranted by facts.

The Bavarian war army numbers 170,000 men.

PRUSSIA SURPRISED.

The statement that Prussia has been making preparations for war while the negotiations with France were in progress, is a pure invention of French Ministers. If careful arrangements had been made, some token of them would be perceptible in the cities which are certain to bear the first shock of war. In Cologne there would have been seen all that was necessary to resist the attack of the enemy. Up to yesterday, however, nothing had been done here. Yesterday was the first day on which the army in the north of Germany was formally put on a war footing. General Herwarth, who commands the Eighth Division of the army, then issued a summons to the effect that the army was to be "mobilized;" in other words, to be prepared for war. The truth is, that this movement is but one in a series, and it is undeniable that the Germans have been taken unawares. But if this should tell against them in one respect, it is a strong testimony in their favor in another. Had the King of Prussia desired to go to war, he would assuredly have taken more pains to render his army ready to take the field at a moment's notice.

The soldiers who are now being got ready to face the foe have been well drilled. Like English militia, they have served a longer or shorter period every year. Although they have not been habituated to act in concert, yet they are well acquainted with the routine of service, and they are all actuated with the desire to do their utmost *for the defence of the Fatherland.*

MONDAY, *July* 18. — The South German States declare their purpose to support Prussia. Departure of the Crown Prince of Prussia for Münich, to take command of their armies. German mail-steamers cease sailing. Coast lights, buoys, and all aids to navigation on the German coast, extinguished and removed by order of the Prussian Government. Rumors of fighting.

King William arrives in Berlin, and addresses the people. Prussia respects Luxemburg's neutrality. France votes 440,-000,000 francs for the Ministry of War, 70,000,000 francs for the Ministry of Marine, and provides for issuing 500,-

000,000 francs in treasury bonds. The Crown Prince Frederick William to command the Southern army.

PARIS, *July* 18. — In to-day's sitting of the Legislative Body the Government brought forward bills granting supplementary credits of 440,000,000 francs for the Ministry of War, 70,000,000 francs for the Ministry of Marine, and 5,000,000 francs for the Ministry of Finance; raising from 150,000,000 francs to 500,000,000 francs the maximum of the issue of treasury bonds; authorizing the Deputies to take service in the Gardes National and Mobile as officers, and prohibiting the publication of intelligence relative to the military operations. These bills were declared urgent. It was announced that the Ministry would render a special account of the war expenses.

The Emperor came to Paris to-day.

FRANCE VS. UNITED GERMANY.

The French Government has received official notification from the South German States that they will not remain neutral, but will support Prussia in the war. The Prussian Government has removed the buoys and coast-lights from the German coast. General Changarnier desires to take the field with a command.

LUXEMBURG, *July* 18. — Count Bismarck telegraphed here yesterday, in the name of the North German Confederation, that the neutrality of Luxemburg would be respected as long as the French should respect it.

MUNICH. — A ministerial order has been published to-day, prohibiting the exportation and the transit of arms, and the munitions of war of all kinds, over the frontier of Saarbrück, Neuburg on the Rhine, and Landau.

THE KING TALKS IN BERLIN.

BERLIN. — The Town Councillors presented to-day, at noon, to the King, an address, thanking his Majesty for having repelled the unheard-of attempt made upon the dignity and independence of the nation, and asserting that France having declared war against Prussia, every man will do his duty. The address says that, however desirous Germany might be to carry out the work of peace, no sacrifice will be considered too heavy to oppose the present rapacious attack upon the independence of the Fatherland. Prussia enters in unison with Germany upon a war to which she has been provoked by foreign arrogance.

The address concludes by stating that it is presented as evidence of the entire devotion to duty, and of the spirited feeling pervading the nation.

The King, in reply, expressed his gratitude for the sentiments contained in the address, and said: "*God knows, I am not answerable* for this war. The demand sent me I could not do otherwise than reject. My reply gained the approval of all the towns and provinces, the expression of which I have received from all parts of Germany and even from Germans residing beyond the seas. The greeting which was given me here on Friday last animated me with pride and confidence. Heavy sacrifices will be demanded of my people. We have been rendered unaccustomed to them by the quickly-gained victories which we achieved in the last two wars. We shall not get off so cheaply this time; but I know what I may expect from my army, and from those now hastening to join the ranks. The instrument is sharp and cutting, the result

IS IN THE HANDS OF GOD.

I know, also, what I may expect from those who are called upon to alleviate the wounds, the pains, and sufferings which war entails. In conclusion, I beg you to express my sincere thanks to the citizens for the reception they have given me."

At the termination of the King's address, the Assembly, with great enthusiasm, shouted unanimously, "Long live the King!"

CROWN PRINCE.

The King has appointed the Crown Prince of Prussia to the command-in-chief of the South German army. The *Cross Gazette* adds that this appointment is a proof, not only of how highly important the King considers the post, but also of the most satisfactory fact, never doubted by Prussia, that the offensive and defensive alliance would be faithfully adhered to by all the South German States.

TUESDAY, *July* 19. — The French invade Prussia. Prussian uhlans exchange shots with French chasseurs at Saarbrück. North Germans serving in the French army called home.

Minister Washburne accepts the protection of Prussian subjects in France. Order of the Iron Cross instituted. King William opens the North German Parliament with a speech on the Hohenzollern affair and the war. A bill for 120,000,000 thalers, for military purposes, introduced. Metz crowded with French soldiers. Queen Victoria proclaims strict neutrality on the part of England.

FRENCH TROOPS ACROSS THE FRONTIER.

COLOGNE, *July* 19 (*Evening*). — The customs inspector at Saarbrück reports that French troops crossed the frontier to-day, and after searching the custom-house at Solsterhöhe, took two customs officers prisoners.

FORBACH. — The hostilities at Forbach were confined to an exchange of shots between some patrols and custom-house guards. A detachment of Prussian infantry and uhlans, of the garrison of Saarbrück, encountered a body of French chasseurs. After exchanging some shots the latter declined to accept battle, and retired into French territory, followed by the uhlans. No casualty occurred on either side.

DECLARATION OF WAR GONE.

PARIS, *July* 19. —Count Wimpffen has left for Berlin, with the French declaration of war against Prussia. Mr. Washburne, the United States Minister, has accepted the protection of Prussian subjects in France, after having previously requested the assent of the French Government.

FRENCH GENERALS' ORDERS.

At a military dinner, given at St. Cloud, last night, his Majesty evaded all questions on the subject. An orderly officer of the Emperor and an aide-de-camp of General Lebœuf left last night with sealed instructions for Marshal Bazaine and Generals De Failly and L'Admirault, which are to be acted on simultaneously with the public proclamation of the declaration of war.

Within the next four days 350,000 men will be assembled between Strasburg, Metz, and Nancy. Three army corps are now echeloned along the eastern frontier.

FRENCH SHIPPING.

BERLIN. — The official *Staatsanzeiger* of to-day publishes a decree ordering that French merchant vessels shall not be captured by vessels of the Federal fleet, except under circumstances where capture would be justified in the case of neutral ships.

The same decree summons all North Germans now serving in the French army to return home without delay.

In to-day's sitting of the North German Parliament the Government introduced a bill demanding a credit of 120,000,000 thalers for military purposes.

SAXONY FOR PRUSSIA.

In the last sitting of the Federal Council, Baron Friesen, in the name of the Saxon Government, which, as he stated, was entirely at one with all other Federal Governments, declared that it agreed with all the steps hitherto taken by the President of the Confederation, and with the views which Prussia had expressed on the circumstances which have brought about the present position of affairs. Baron Friesen concluded as follows: "*France demands war. Let us hope that it will be carried on with all possible speed and energy.*"

SPEECH OF THE KING OF PRUSSIA.

BERLIN, *July* 19. — The North German Parliament was opened to-day by King William in person. His Majesty delivered the following speech from the throne:

"Honored Gentlemen of the Parliament of the North German Confederation: When at your last meeting I bade you welcome from this place in the name of the Allied Governments, it was with joy and gratitude that I was able to bear witness to the fact that, by the help of God, success had rewarded my sincere efforts to meet the wishes of the people, and the requirements of civilization, by avoiding any disturbance of the peace of Europe.

"If, notwithstanding this assurance, the menace and imminence of war have now laid upon the Confederate Governments the duty of calling you together for an extraordinary session, you as well as ourselves will be animated with the conviction that the North German Confederation has labored to improve the national forces, not to imperil, but to afford a greater protection to universal peace, and that when we call upon this national army to defend our independence, we only obey the mandates of honor and duty. The candidacy of a German prince for the Spanish throne, both in the bringing forward and withdrawal of which the Confederate Governments were equally unconcerned, and which only interested the North German Confederation in so far as the Government of a friendly country appeared to base upon its success the hopes of acquiring for a sorely tried people a pledge for regular and peaceful government, afforded the Emperor of the French a pretext for a *casus belli*, put forward in a manner long since unknown in the annals of diplomatic intercourse, and adhered to after the removal of the very pretext itself, with that disregard for the people's right to the blessings of peace, of which the history of a former ruler of France affords so many analogous examples. If Germany in former centuries bore in silence such violations of her rights and of her honor, it was only because in her then divided state she knew not her own strength. To-day, when the links of intellectual and rightful community, which began to be knit together at the time of the wars of liberation, join the more slowly, the more surely, the different German races; to-day, that Germany's armament leaves no longer an opening to the enemy. The German nation contains within itself the will and the power to repel the renewed aggression of France. It is not arrogance that puts these words in my mouth. The Confederate Governments and I myself are acting in the full consciousness that victory and defeat are in the hands of Him who decides the fate of battles. With a clear gaze we have measured the responsibility which, before the judgment seat of God and of mankind, must fall upon him who drags two great and peace-loving peoples of the head of Europe into a devastating war. The more the Confederate Governments are conscious of having done all our honor and dignity permitted to preserve to Europe the blessings of peace, and the more indubitable it shall appear to all minds that the sword has been thrust into our hands, so much the more confidently shall we rely upon the united will of the German Governments, *both of the North and South*, and upon your love of country; and so much the more confidently we shall fight for our right against the violence of foreign invaders. Inasmuch as we pursue no other object than the durable establishment of peace in Europe, God will be with us, as He was with our forefathers."

The King read the speech in a firm voice, but displayed at several passages much emotion, and was often interrupted with vociferous cheering, especially when he spoke of the no longer divided Germany — a remark which was understood to allude to the co-operation of Bavaria.

At the close of the speech Baron Von Friesen, the Saxon Minister, called for cheers for King William, which were repeated over and over again.

METZ ON A WAR FOOTING.

METZ, *July* 19.— All the ordinary trains are compelled to hang about on sidings, in order to let trains laden with troops go by. Metz is one of the most important military positions in France, and the residence of the commandant of the fifth of the great military divisions of the empire. The town contains 54,000 inhabitants, and is most thoroughly fortified, being one of the bulwarks of France against invasion from the north-east. It will be a base of operations in the approaching campaign. The town literally swarms with soldiers. There are nearly 100,000 men quartered in this town, or encamped just outside the walls. Most of the troops have come on from the great camp of Châlons, which is about 100 miles off, midway between Metz and Paris. The streets are gay with tricolors, which hang from nearly every window. Such a tremendous eruption of the national flag has seldom been seen, not even in the States on a Fourth of July.

ENGLAND NEUTRAL.

LONDON, *July* 19.— Queen Victoria has this day proclaimed strict neutrality in the Franco-Prussian war.

IRON CROSS.

BERLIN, *July* 19.— King William reinstates the Order of the Iron Cross in the following Cabinet order:

Looking to the critical situation of the Fatherland, and in thankful remembrance of the heroic deeds of our forefathers in the great years of the War of Liberation, I recall into existence, in its full value, the decoration of the Iron Cross, founded by my father, who rests in God. The Iron Cross shall, without distinction of rank or position, be conferred as a reward for desert which shall be exhibited, either in actual battle with the enemy or at home in connection with this struggle for the honor and independence of the dear Fatherland. The Minister of State is charged to draw up at once the plan of a scheme for the formation of the Iron Cross. In reference to this I remark:

1. The decoration of the Iron Cross, recalled into existence for this war, shall, as before, consist of two classes and one grand cross. The decoration, and the ribbon as well, re-

main unchanged; only upon the smooth front surface the W, with the crown, and under it the year 1870, shall be added.

2. The second class shall be worn on a black ribbon with white edges, when the decoration has been won in battle with the enemy; and on a white band with black edges when that is not the case, in the button-hole — the first class on the left breast; and the grand cross, twice as large as that of the two classes, about the neck.

3. The second class of the Iron Cross shall be first bestowed; the first class can be gained in no other way than by first winning the second class, and the two shall be worn side by side.

4. The grand cross can be received only by a commander for winning a decisive battle, after which the enemy must have forsaken his position; or else for the capture of an important fortress; or for the stubborn defence of a fortress which does not fall into the enemy's hands.

5. All privileges which up to this time have been connected with the Order of Merit, first and second classes, shall be enjoyed by the first and second classes of the Iron Cross.

6. It is my intention to seek information whether and to what extent the existing war decoration and Military Order of Merit shall be distributed in this war.

WEDNESDAY, *July* 20.— France declines English mediation. The war pronounced in the interests of Catholicism. The Crown Prince assumes command of the South German armies. Count Bismarck notified that Bavaria will be Prussia's ally in the war against France. Saxon Minister recalled from Paris. Hesse Darmstadt stands with Prussia. M. Prévost-Paradol, French Minister to Washington, commits suicide. German mass-meetings in America.

ENGLISH MEDIATION DECLINED.

PARIS, *July* 20.—France has declined the mediation proffered by England in virtue of the Treaty of 1856, on the ground that the present circumstances do not come within the scope of that treaty.

CATHOLICISM *vs.* ORTHODOXY.

The *Monde* of this morning publishes an article relative to the Franco-Prussian war, in which it says that the war is not only destined to decide the preponderance of one of the two powers, but will have a most important influence upon the prospects of Catholicism. The *Monde* considers the triumph of France necessary, in order to stay the progress of Protestantism and infidel German philosophy, represented by Prussia.

GRAMONT ANNOUNCES A STATE OF WAR.

PARIS, *July* 20.— In to-day's sitting of the Legislative Body the Duke de Gramont read the following communication: "In conformity with the law of custom, and by order of the Emperor, I have requested the French charge d'affaires at the Court of Berlin to notify to the Prussian Government our resolution to seek by force of arms the guarantees we have not been able to obtain by discussion. That step has been taken, and I have the honor to inform the Legislative Body that consequently a state of war exists since yesterday between France and Prussia. This declaration also applies to the allies of Prussia who lend to that power against us the assistance of their arms."

The Duke de Gramont's declaration was received with loud cheers.

M. Schneider, the President, said he took official cognizance of the declaration.

In the Corps Législatif the Bill prohibiting the publication of news of military operations was passed by 209 against 19 votes. The extraordinary budget of the city of Paris, with an amendment increasing by thirty-eight millions the sum granted for public works, was also unanimously adopted.

It is stated that all Prussian consuls will be requested to leave French territory.

BAVARIA FIGHTS FOR PRUSSIA.

MUNICH, *July* 20.—The Bavarian Minister in Berlin has been instructed by telegraph to notify to Count Bismarck, that in consequence of the declaration of war by France against Prussia, and the fact of an invasion of German territory having taken place, the Bavarian Government, on the ground of the treaty of alliance with Prussia, and as Prussia's ally, has entered into war against France, in conjunction with all the German Governments.

The Chamber of Deputies has voted the extraordinary military credit of 18,200,000 florins demanded by the Government.

BERLIN, *July* 20.—The Crown Prince of Prussia assumes the command-in-chief of the German Army of the South, and has already made the necessary communication on the subject to the Courts of Munich and Stuttgardt.

DRESDEN, *July* 20.—The Saxon Minister at Paris has been recalled. The protection of Saxon citizens in France has been transferred to the American Minister.

HESSE DARMSTADT FIGHTS FOR PRUSSIA.

DARMSTADT, *July* 20. — In to-day's sitting of the Lower House of the Diet, Herr von Dulwigk, the Prime Minister, made a speech, in which he stated that the German frontier had been violated under frivolous pretexts. He declared that all particularist dissensions must disappear in face of the impending danger to the Fatherland, and he begged the House to sanction unanimously the Bills which he had to submit. The credit for 3,376,000 florins for the Hessian contingent, and a loan of 1,800,000 florins, were agreed to *nem. con.* The sitting closed amid cheers for Germany, the King of Prussia, and the Grand Duke.

AMERICA.

WASHINGTON, *July* 20. — An enthusiastic mass meeting of Germans has been held at Cincinnati, to express sympathy with Prussia.

The German societies in the great cities are subscribing large sums of money for the relief of the widows and orphans of the soldiers who may fall in the coming contest.

The French Minister, M. Prévost-Paradol, shot himself through the heart yesterday morning.

THURSDAY, *July* 21. — Arrival of Prince Napoleon in London. Great naval activity in England. Turkey and Austria declare an attentive neutrality. Circular issued by the French Minister of Foreign Affairs to the representatives of France in foreign countries, explaining the position of the Emperor on the subject of the war. Prussia accused of having fomented the conflict. General Lebœuf declared Major-General of the French army. Prussia declares that Germany will demand peace guarantees from France before the war closes.

The French army will be composed of eight corps, each consisting of three or four divisions of infantry, and from six to eight regiments of calvary. Each division will have three batteries of artillery, one company of engineers, and will comprise from ten to twelve thousand men. The commanders of the corps are as follows :

Guard corps — General Bourbaki.
First corps — Marshal MacMahon, Duke of Magenta.
Second corps — Baron Frossard, General of Division.
Third corps — Marshal Bazaine.
Fourth corps — Count L'Admirault, General of Division.
Fifth corps — De Failly, General of Division.
Sixth corps — Marshal Canrobert.
Seventh corps — Felix Douay, General of Division.
Major-General of the Army — General Edmond Lebœuf.
Assistant Major-Generals — Lebrun and Jarras.
Commander-in-Chief of Artillery — General Soleille.
Commander-in-Chief of Engineers — General Coffinières de Neuwerk.

THE KING ASSUMES COMMAND.

Berlin, *July* 21 (*Evening*). — The King of Prussia has sent the following telegram to the King of Bavaria: "On receipt of the telegram from your Majesty, I immediately assumed the command of the Bavarian army, and I incorporated it with the Third Army Corps placed under the command of the Crown Prince. By an unheard-of presumption, we have been driven from the most profound peace into war. Your real German attitude has electrified your people, and all Germany is now united as it never was at any former time. May God bless your arms in the fortune of war! I tender you my most heartfelt thanks for your faithful adherence to our treaty, upon which Germany rests."

The King of Bavaria replied: "Your telegram has awakened in me a joyful echo. The Bavarian troops, side by side with their glorious brethren in arms, will enter enthusiastically into the struggle for German right and German honor. May the war tend to the welfare of Germany, and the safety of Bavaria!"

FRANCE TO BE CRIPPLED.

The *Official Gazette* at Berlin declares that before the war closes, Germany and Europe will exact from France guarantees for the observance of peace hereafter, and in case of refusal will so cripple France as to prevent her from making more mischief. The French circular explaining the war is forwarded to the diplomatic agents of France. It represents the candidature of Prince Leopold as a scheme of Prussia to humble France. A Prussian fusilier shot the first Frenchman to-day.

Stuttgardt, *July* 21 (*Evening*). — Enormous crowds have assembled in front of the royal palace, to give the King an ovation, thanking his Majesty for having attached himself to the national cause, and joined in the war against France. The King, Queen, and Prince William appeared on the balcony, and thanked the people for their demonstration.

PARIS ARMY GOSSIP

PARIS, *July* 21. — M. Berthemy will remain at Washington to replace M. Prévost-Paradol.

Dr. Bamberg, the consul-general of the North German Confederation, left Paris yesterday.

The Emperor is still at St. Cloud.

The French regiments were most enthusiastically received by the inhabitants of Alsace on their arrival in that province.

The number of volunteers enrolled in Paris amounts now to 15,000 men, and in the rest of France to 85,000. The Garde Mobile is being rapidly organized.

A meeting of the Americans in Paris was held here, to form a committee to act with the International Sanitary Association and the French Volunteer Association, for the succor of the wounded. Dr. Thomas Evans, the chairman, subscribed 10,000 francs.

General L'Admirault, the Commander of the Fourth Army Corps, arrived at Metz to-day.

General Frossard, the Commander of the Second Army Corps, has arrived at his head-quarters at St. Avold. Five army corps are echeloned along the frontier.

Admiral Bouët-Willaumez commands the Northern iron-clad squadron, and will hoist his flag on board the *Surveillante*.

SOUTH GERMANY.

FRANKFORT-ON-THE-MAIN, *July* 21. — The feeling in South Germany, and in the newly annexed Prussian provinces, is entirely on the side of Prussia. France has deceived herself if she expected to find sympathy among the anti-Prussians of two weeks ago. Never was there known such a change of public sentiment as has been seen here before and since the declaration of war on the part of France. Two weeks ago, and this once free city was strongly anti-Prussian; but to-day there cannot be counted a hundred men who do not go heart and soul for the German cause. As regiment after regiment has passed through the city, thousands of citizens have met and cheered them, and on the evening after the news of the declaration of war arrived, many hundreds of the city youth paraded the streets, full of enthusiasm, singing "*Die Wacht am Rhein*," and similar Rhine songs. And the change of sentiment in the annexed provinces is equally marked. France calculated very much on Hesse Cassel, where the feeling against Prussia was indeed bitter; but the reception of King William in Cassel on his return to Berlin shows plainly that the hearts of the people are true. The South German States have not hesitated a moment in declaring their intention to keep their treaty of defence and offence made with Prussia in 1866.

STRASBURG.

July 21.—The defences of Strasburg are low, and the moats can be flooded with water from the Rhine. The bridge across the Rhine to Kehl is a magnificent structure. The authorities of Kehl proposed to-day to blow it up, but they were informed by the commandant of Strasburg, that while he would allow them to swing back the movable portion of the bridge upon their side, he would reduce Kehl to ashes by opening from the Strasburg citadel with his rifle guns, should the Germans presume to destroy an international work. So the bridge remains an epitome of the situation—built to connect Germany and France, for the present useless to develop the resources of either country.

The garrison of Strasburg consists of about 6000 men, but there is a camp without the walls which may hold 10,000 more.

GERMAN UNITY.

REMARK, *July* 21.—Count Bismarck is but another name for German unity.

The resolution of the Emperor Napoleon came with startling suddenness this day week. Europe has gradually become a great camp, and two or three short wars—the war with Denmark, the struggle which ended with the peace of Villafranca, and the seven weeks war which culminated at Sadowa—were all but the preliminary skirmishes of the struggle which has now begun.

This war is a war of ideas, and it has long been evident to every observer that such a war must come at length, unless one of the two conflicting ideas were abandoned. The idea of German unity, of a single and undivided Fatherland of all the German people, cannot be realized without disappointing the French idea—the idea that France is to be the first nation on the continent, the leader of civilization, the arbiter of Europe. Germany one and indivisible would be as great as France. The political centre might oscillate between Paris and Berlin, if Berlin were the capital of united Germany. Yet it is to some such end that the whole movement of European politics has pointed for a dozen years past. The French Emperor himself helped its development when he humiliated Austria at Solferino, and he drew suddenly up in his career, partly because he suddenly saw whither he was going. Austria helped it when she obeyed the irresistible impulse of the German people, and went with Prussia to wrest the German

Holstein and the half-German Schleswig from the rule of the Dane. In 1866 Count Bismarck saw that the German idea was ripe for realization, and Prussia won its championship at Sadowa. But for French jealousy, that victory would have been followed up, and Germany would have been one. Morally it has been followed up, and hence the spectacle we have seen this week. The German people are one, and Prussia is their leader. In declaring war against Prussia, France has declared war against the German idea, and Germany rises as one man in defence of the German Fatherland.

The Rhine cannot be forced in a moment, and meanwhile the stream of soldiers will keep on continually flowing to the west, until the North-German Confederation alone has lined the valley of the river with the 700,000 men which constitute the active federal army in its present organization. These the French will have to fight, and if they lose the first great pitched battle, Metz, Thionville, Nancy, will avail nothing. For, notwithstanding these fortresses, the advance upon Paris would be made. If the Germans lose the first battle, the case is a very different one. That would bring the French only to the Rhine, and there a long and tedious war would have to be begun, which would last into the winter, and still without the possibility of any success being obtained that would bend the will of the German nation.

FRIDAY, *July* 22.—Napoleon addresses the Corps Législatif on the eve of his departure for the army. Pope Pius IX. proposes mediation. The Kehl bridge blown up in front of Strasburg. Five French army corps to the front. The *Siècle* says France should not stop fighting till Saarlouis, Landau, and adjacent cantons are conquered and made over to France. Prussia declares that no conversation on the Hohenzollern candidature has ever been held between the Chancellor and Count Benedetti.

SPEECH OF THE EMPEROR NAPOLEON.

PARIS, *July* 22.—The Emperor received the members of the Legislative Body at two, P.M., to-day.

The President, M. Schneider, addressed his Majesty as follows:

"SIRE,—The Legislative Body has terminated its labors, after voting all the subsidies and laws necessary for the defence of the country. Thus the Chamber has joined in an effective proof of patriotism. The real author of the war is not he by whom it was declared, but he who rendered it necessary. There will be but one voice among the people of both hemispheres, namely, throwing the responsibility of the war upon Prussia, which, intoxicated by unexpected success, and encouraged by our patience and our desire to preserve to Europe the blessings of peace, has imagined that she could conspire against our security and wound with impunity our honor. Under these circumstances France will know how to do her duty. The most ardent wishes will follow you to the army, the command of which you assume, accompanied by your son, who, anticipating the duties of maturer age, will learn by your side how to serve his country. Behind you, behind our army, accustomed to carry the noble flag of France, stands the whole nation ready to recruit it. Leave the regency, without anxiety, in the hands of our august sovereign, the Empress. To the authority commanded by her great qualities, of which ample evidence has already been given, her Majesty will add the strength now afforded by the liberal institutions, so gloriously inaugurated by your majesty. Sire, the heart of the nation is with you, and with your valiant army."

The Emperor replied:

"I experience the most lively satisfaction, on the eve of my departure for the army, at being able to thank you for the patriotic support which you have afforded my Government. A war is right when it is waged with the assent of the country, and the approval of the country's representatives. You are right to remember the words of Montesquieu, that 'the real author of war is not he by whom it is declared, but he who renders it necessary.' We have done all in our power to avert the war; and I may say that it is the whole nation that has, by its irresistible impulse, dictated our decisions. I confide to you the Empress, who will call you around her if circumstances should require it. She will know how to fulfil courageously the duty which her position imposes upon her. I take my son with me: in the midst of the army he will learn to serve his country. Resolved energetically to pursue the great mission which has been entrusted to me, I have faith in the success of our arms, for I know that behind me France has risen to her feet, and that God protects her."

AN OFFER OF MEDIATION FROM THE POPE.

The following is the letter of the Pope to King William, proposing mediation:

"YOUR MAJESTY, — In the present grave circumstances it may appear an unusual thing to receive a letter from me; but, as the vicar on earth of God and peace, I cannot do less than offer my mediation. It is my desire to witness the cessation of warlike preparations, and to stop the evils, their inevitable consequences. My mediation is that of a sovereign whose small dominion excites no jealousy, and who inspires confidence by the moral and religious influence he personifies. May God lend an ear to my wishes, and listen also to those I form for your Majesty, to whom I would be united in the bonds of charity.

"Given at the Vatican, July 22, 1870.

"PIUS."

A postscript adds:

"I have written identically to the Emperor."

The King's reply is as follows:

"MOST AUGUST PONTIFF, — I am not surprised, but profoundly moved, at the touching words traced by your hand. They cause the voice of God and of peace to be heard. How could my heart refuse to listen to so powerful an appeal. God witnesses that neither I nor my people desired or provoked war. Obeying the sacred duties which God imposes on sovereigns and nations, we take up the sword to defend the independence and honor of our country, ready to lay it down the moment those treasures are secure. If your Holiness could offer me from him who so unexpectedly declared war assurances of sincerely pacific dispositions, and guarantees against a similar attempt upon the peace and tranquillity of Europe, it certainly will not be I who will refuse to receive them from your venerable hands, united as I am with you in bonds of Christian charity and sincere friendship.

"WILLIAM."

KEHL BRIDGE BLOWN UP.

STRASBURG, *July* 22. — The Prussians blew up the abutment on the Baden shore of the bridge at Kehl at four, A.M., to-day.

The explosion was terrific. The bridge turrets were destroyed, and the *débris* thrown as far as the French shore.

This bridge is built in three portions, the centre resting upon four piers, and a pivoted portion of either end of about thirty yards in length. These movable ends had been swung back, but the Prussians, not satisfied with thus interrupting the traffic, suddenly blew up their swinging portion, which has fallen into the Rhine. The populace on the French side were for ten minutes greatly alarmed, and there was a complete *sauve qui peut.* Some fifty German cavalry galloped about on the opposite bank, brandishing their sabres. Of course, this blowing up of the bridge shows that the Prussians do not intend to deliver an attack on the Strasburg side, and fear one from the French.

BERLIN, *July* 22. — Large numbers of troops are going forward. The Prussian force will be concentrated into three armies. The first army, consisting of the First, Seventh, and Eighth Corps, is to be commanded by Gen. Von Steinmetz. The second army, consisting of the Second, Third, Ninth, and Tenth Corps, is to be commanded by Prince Frederick Charles. The third army, consisting of the Fifth, Sixth, and Eleventh Corps, is to be commanded by the Crown Prince, Frederick William.

The Crown Prince of Saxony is raising a fourth army, to be composed of the Fourth and Twelfth Corps, and two corps of Saxon and Bavarian guards.

Steinmetz is moving towards Saarbrück. Prince Charles (the King's nephew) is moving up behind Steinmetz.

The Crown Prince is marching towards Weisenburg. The entire Prussian force now organizing, when in the field, will be twelve corps, each of 40,000. Total, 480,000.

PRUSSIAN REPLY TO THE DUKE DE GRAMONT.

BERLIN, *July* 22 (*Evening*). — The following statement has been published:

"In reference to a circular of the Duke de Gramont, published yesterday, and of which a telegraphic summary has been received here, alleging that the Chancellor of the North German Confederation had declared the candidature of the Prince of Hohenzollern to be impossible, and that the Under-Secretary of State, Baron Thile, had pledged his word that such a candidature did not exist, both the Chancellor and the Secretary declare officially and in their private capacity that not a single word on the subject has ever passed between either of them and M. Benedetti, either officially or in private conversation, since they were first aware of the fact that the offer of the Spanish crown had been made to the Prince of Hohenzollern."

TROOPS TO THE FRONT.

PARIS, *July* 22 (*Evening*). — The five army corps echeloned on the frontier consist of 340 battalions of infantry, 140 squadrons of cavalry, and from 90 to 100 batteries of artillery. There still remain in France of regular troops available for service, 160 battalions of infantry, 140 squadrons of cavalry, and 130 batteries of artillery.

The whole Imperial Guard, under General Bourbaki, will be concentrated at Nancy this evening. No troops are now left in Strasburg; it is occupied by the Mobile Guard. Three camps of infantry, cavalry, and artillery are established at Metz, at which place there is also a great concentration of war material. Many regiments have left Paris for Cherbourg. The Sixth Army Corps is in course of formation at Châlons. No headquarters has yet been fixed upon for the Seventh Corps. It is composed of troops from Algeria, and is expected to form either a reserve or a corps for disembarkation on some point of the Prussian territory.

CIRCUMSTANCES ALTER CASES.

The *Siècle* of this evening says that since France has drawn the sword she ought not to sheathe it without having made her frontier perfectly secure towards Germany, *and that the restitution of Saarlouis and Landau, with the adjacent cantons, should be* the minimum of her demands.

About 200 Deputies accompanied M. Schneider to the Tuileries to-day. The speech of the Emperor was received with enthusiastic applause. The Emperor's voice when speaking betrayed some emotion.

FIRST FIGHT.

SATURDAY, *July* 23. — Prussian troops from Saarlouis enter the French territory, and advance a short distance in the direction of St. Avold, where they have a skirmish with the French chasseurs, and retire. Nine or ten wounded, and the first blood of the war shed. French reconnoissance on Prussian soil. Demonstration in favor of France at Dublin. Italian demonstrations in favor of Prussia at Milan, Padua, and Genoa.

PROCLAMATION OF THE EMPEROR NAPOLEON.

PARIS, *July* 23. — The Emperor has addressed the following proclamation to the French people :

" FRENCHMEN, — There are solemn moments in the life of peoples when the national honor, violently excited, imposes itself with irresistible force, dominates all interests, and alone takes in hand the direction of the destinies of the country. One of those decisive hours has sounded for France. Prussia, to whom, both during and since the war of 1866, we have shown the most conciliatory disposition, has taken no account of our good wishes and our forbearance. Launched on the path of invasion, she has aroused defiance, everywhere necessitated exaggerated armaments, and has turned Europe into a camp, where nothing but uncertainty and fear of the morrow reigns. A late incident has come to show the instability of international relations, and to prove the gravity of the situation. In presence of the new pretensions of Prussia we made our protestations to be heard. They were evaded, and were followed on the part of Prussia by contemptuous proceedings. Our country has resented this with profound irritation, and immediately a cry for war resounded from one end of France to the other. It only remains to us to confide our destinies to the decision of arms. We do not make war on Germany, whose independence we respect. Let us wish that the peoples who compose the great German nationality may freely dispose of their destinies. For ourselves, we demand the establishment of a state of affairs which shall guarantee our security and assure our future. We wish to conquer a lasting peace based on the true interests of peoples, and to put an end to the precarious state in which all nations employ their resources to arm themselves one against the other. The glorious flag which we once more unfurl before those who have provoked us, is the same which bore throughout Europe the civilizing ideas of our great revolution. It represents the same principles, and inspires the same devotion. Frenchmen, I place myself at the head of that valiant army which is animated by love of duty and of country. It knows its own worth, since it has seen how victory has accompanied its march in the four quarters of the world. I shall take my son with me, despite his youth. He knows what are the duties which his name imposes upon him, and he is proud to bear his share in the dangers of those who fight for their country. May God bless our efforts. A great people who defend a just cause are invincible. "NAPOLEON."

An Imperial decree, dated July 23, appoints the Empress Regent during the absence of the Emperor with the army.

FIRST BLOOD!

SAARBRUCK, *July* 23.

The French custom-house officer opposite Saarlouis fired upon a Prussian cavalry patrol, and wounded two horses. A company of Prussian infantry has captured the French custom-house at Schrecklingen, near Saarlouis, together with the treasury. The customs' officers were killed or taken prisoners. On the Prussian side one officer was wounded.

SUNDAY, *July* 24. — The Bank of Frankfort loans the Prussian Government five million of thalers. Fight at Gersweiler. Skirmishing at Haguenau. Italy announces her neutrality. The American press sympathize with Prussia.

FIGHTING.

SAARBRUCK (RHENISH PRUSSIA), *July* 24. — A French division is quartered at Forbach. Early this morning a skirmish took place at Gersweiler, when the French troops were driven back with a loss of ten men. There was no loss on the Prussian side. The Prussian soldiers assert that the needle gun proved fully equal to the chassepôt. At the same time a regiment of mounted chasseurs made a reconnoissance on Prussian territory. The Prussians appear to be assuming the offensive.

THE AMERICAN PRESS.

NEW YORK, *July* 24. — The sentiment of the press in the United States is unanimously in favor of Prussia. The New York *Tribune* accuses Napoleon of committing France to the most atrocious of modern wars, and says that this is a contest between the people of Prussia and the Napoleonic dynasty for the integrity of the Prussian nationality. The New York *Times* takes substantially the same view. The *Herald* denounces the action of the Emperor as prompted by purely dynastic considerations, with which the friends of the people have no sympathy. The *World* alone among the leading New York papers is on the side of France. The pens of Mr. Marble and George Wilkes have been no mean supporters of the Empire,* though they have battled almost even-handed. The *World* has been ably represented in the war by the Rev. M. D. Conway, formerly of Cincinnati, while "*Massachusetts*" has contributed able papers on the war to the *Times*. W. H. Russell engaged to furnish war news for the *Sun*, but King William would not permit him to send cable despatches from the field.

The American press are naturally with France, but feel a deep resentment against the Emperor: first, on account of the *coup d'état*; secondly, on account of the Mexican invasion; and, thirdly, an account of his hostility towards the North during the late war.

MONDAY, *July* 25.—The secret treaty between France and Prussia on the subject of Belgium made public. Great sensation in England and on the Continent.

The London *Times* prints a secret treaty proposed in 1866 to France by Prussia. In the first article Napoleon admits and recognizes the late acquisitions of Prussia from Austria. In the second, the Prussian King engages to facilitate the French acquisition of Luxemburg. In the third, the Emperor acquiesces in the union of the North and South German States, Austria excepted. In the fourth, France, finding it necessary to absorb Belgium, Prussia lends her assistance to that measure. The fifth article is the usual one of offensive and defensive alliance between the two nations.

The *exposé* of the treaty shows consummate diplomacy on the part of Bismarck to secure the neutrality of Luxemburg, the

---

* A revolution in American public sentiment came with the first announcement of the French Republic. Prussia's strongest supporters abandoned her to her victories, and held out their hands to the infant Democracy. The "lost cause" of a Republic was better than a king's magnificent victories. The hatchet raised against Napoleon and Cæsarism fell harmless when the young Republic held out her beeseeching hands. Even George Smalley, quick to defend Prussia when attacked, could not forget the triumph of dead Victor Noir and prison-freed Rochefort, but with a splendid frankness he instantly decided for that new liberty for which Victor Noir had died. He was only one among a thousand. The young Republic was born without an American enemy, and she will die (may God forbid!) with an American benediction. The American press—the *Herald*, *Tribune*, *Times*, *Post*, and *Sun*—all joined voices in one warm VIVE LA REPUBLIQUE!

Netherlands, and Belgium. England, the friend of Belgium, alienated from France. Ollivier and Benedetti deny the statement of Bismarck.

THE SECRET TREATY.

REMARK, *July* 25.

This celebrated treaty, proposed by Benedetti to Bismarck, has roused the indignation of Europe. Such a treaty, had it been signed by Prussia, would have destroyed the Governments of Luxemburg and Belgium, and blotted out their territorial lines. The Belgians now see on what a dangerous mine they were standing. Belgium sees now how false were the Emperor's professions of friendship; how, under the guise of friendship, he was even intriguing against her national existence.

There can be no doubt about the authenticity of the treaty. Benedetti himself has acknowledged it, and tried to account for its existence to the satisfaction of Europe. The world stands aghast at this fearful diplomatic intrigue, which Bismarck, in an international quarrel, has exposed. The war has warned Belgium to beware of Napoleon III. England, the champion of Belgium, throbs with sympathy for its threatened ally. The following is a translation of this

SECRET TREATY

which Benedetti proposed to Count Bismarck:

"DRAUGHT TREATY."

"His Majesty the King of Prussia and His Majesty the Emperor of the French, judging it useful to bind closer the ties of friendship which unite them, and so confirm the relations of good neighborhood which happily exist between the two countries, and being beside convinced that to attain this result, which is, moreover, of a kind to insure the maintenance of the general peace, it is for their interest to come to an understanding on the questions concerning their future relations, have resolved to conclude a Treaty to the following effect, and have, in consequence, nominated as their representatives the following persons, viz.:

"His Majesty, etc.

"His Majesty, etc.

Who, after exchanging their full powers, which have been found in good and due form, have agreed on the following Articles:

"ART. I. His Majesty the Emperor of the French acquiesces in and recognizes the gains made by Prussia in the course of the last war waged by her against Austria, and that Power's allies.

"ART. II. His Majesty the King of Prussia engages to facilitate the acquisition by France of Luxemburg; and for this purpose His Majesty will enter into negotiations with His Majesty the King of the Netherlands, with the view of inducing him to cede his sovereign rights over the Duchy to the Emperor of the French, on the terms of such compensation as shall be judged adequate or otherwise. The Emperor of the French, on his side, engages to assume whatever pecuniary charges this arrangement may involve.

"ART. III. His Majesty the Emperor of the French shall raise no opposition to a federal union of the Confederation of North Germany with the States of South Germany, excepting Austria, and this federal union may be based on one common Parliament; due reservation, however, being made of the sovereignty of the said States.

"ART. IV. His Majesty the King of Prussia, on his side, in case His Majesty the Emperor of the French should be led by circumstances to cause his troops to enter Belgium or to conquer it, shall grant armed aid to France, and shall support her with all his forces, military and naval, in the face of and against every Power which should, in this eventuality, declare war.

"ART. V. To insure the complete execution of the preceding conditions, His Majesty the King of Prussia and His Majesty the Emperor of the French contract, by the present Treaty, an alliance offensive and defensive, which they solemnly engage to maintain. Their Majesties bind themselves, besides and in particular, to observe its terms in all cases when their respective States, the integrity of which they reciprocally guarantee, may be threatened with attack; and they shall hold themselves bound, in any like conjuncture, to undertake without delay, and under no pretext to decline, whatever military arrangements may be enjoined by their common interest conformably to the terms and provisions above declared."

This is the proposed treaty which has set Europe in a ferment. Its *exposé* by Bismarck was disastrous to French sympathy in Europe. What was France to do? There was nothing to do but to make a denial. So the pens of Ollivier and Benedetti came out in the following

FRENCH DENIALS.

PARIS, *July* 29, 1870.

TO THE MINISTER OF FOREIGN AFFAIRS:

MONSIEUR LE DUC: However unjust may have been the criticisms of which I was personally the object when the fact became known in France that the Prince of Hohenzollern had accepted the crown of Spain, I did not feel called on to notice them, and, as was my duty, I left to His Majesty's Government the care of rectifying them. I cannot maintain the same silence in presence of the use which Count Bismarck has made of a document to which he seeks to assign a value it never possessed, and I ask permission from your Excellency to re-establish the facts in all their exactitude. It is a matter of public notoriety that the Chancellor offered to us, before and during the last war, to assist in re-uniting Belgium to France, in compensation for the aggrandizements which he aimed at, and which he has obtained for Prussia. I might on this point invoke the testimony of the whole diplomacy of Europe, which was aware of everything that was going on. The French Government constantly declined those overtures, and one of your predecessors, M. Drouyn de Lhuys, is in a position to give on this point explanations which would not leave any doubt subsisting. At the moment when the peace of Prague was concluded, and in presence of the excitement raised in France by the annexation of Hanover, Electoral Hesse, and the City of Frankfort to Prussia, Count Bismarck again testified the most ardent desire to re-establish the equilibrium broken by these acquisitions. Various combinations respecting the integrity of the States bordering on France and Germany were suggested; they became the object of several interviews, during which the Count always endeavored to make his personal ideas prevail. In one of those conversations, and in order to form a thorough comprehension of his intentions, I consented to transcribe them, in some sort, under his dictation. The form, no less than the substance, clearly demonstrates that I confined myself to reproducing a project conceived and developed by him. Count Bismarck kept the paper, desiring to submit it to the King. On my side, I reported to the Imperial Government the communications which had been made to me. The Emperor rejected them as soon as they were brought to his knowledge. I ought to say that the King of Prussia himself appeared unwilling to accept the basis suggested, and since that period — that is to say, during the last four years — I have had no further exchange of ideas with Count Bismarck on the subject. If the initiation of such a treaty had been taken by the Emperor's Government the draft would have been prepared at the Ministry, and I should not have had to produce a copy in my own handwriting; besides, it would have been differently worded, and negotiations would have been carried on simultaneously in Paris and Berlin. In that case the Prussian Minister would not have contented himself with handing, indirectly, the text over to publication, especially at the moment when your Excellency was rectifying in the despatches which were inserted in the *Journal Officiel*, other errors which attempts were being made to propagate. But to attain his aim — that of misleading public opinion and forestalling any indiscretions which we might ourselves commit — he has adopted this expedient, which dispensed him from specifying at what moment, under what circumstances, and in what manner, that document was written. He evidently entertained the idea of suggesting, owing to those omissions, conjectures which, while disengaging his personal responsibility, would compromise that of the Emperor's Government. There is no need to qualify such proceedings; to point them out and deliver them to the judgment of the public in Europe, is sufficient. Accept, etc.

V. BENEDETTI.

EMILE OLLIVIER'S DENIAL

is as follows:

PARIS, *July* 26, 1870.

MY DEAR FRIEND, — How could you believe there was any truth in the Treaty the *Times* has published? I assure you that the Cabinet of the 2d of January never negotiated or concluded anything of the kind with Prussia. I will even tell you that it has negotiated nothing at all with her. The only negotiations that have existed between us have been indirect, confidential, and had Lord Clarendon for their intermediary. Since Mr. Gladstone slightly raised the veil in one of his speeches, we may allow ourselves to say, that the object of those negotiations, so honorable to Lord Clarendon, was to assure the peace of Europe by a reciprocal disarmament. You will admit that this does not much resemble the conduct of Ministers who seek a pretext for war. You know the value I set upon the confidence and friendship of the great English nation. The union of the two countries has always seemed to me the most essential condition of the world's progress. And for that reason I earnestly beg you to contradict all those false reports, spread by persons who have an interest in dividing us. We have no secret policy hidden behind our avowed policy. Our policy is single, public, loyal, without *arrières pensées*; we do not belong to the school of those who think might is superior to right; we believe, on the contrary, that right will always prevail in the end; and it is because the right is on our side in the war now beginning, that, with the help of God, we reckon upon victory. Affectionate salutations from your servant. (Signed) EMILE OLLIVIER.

BISMARCK DENIES AND CHARGES AS FALSEHOODS

the statements of Ollivier and Benedetti, and affirms that Benedetti has *desired to make other secret treaties*, looking to the *destruction* of the *smaller powers*, or their absorption by France. He thus writes to the North German ambassador in London:

TO COUNT BERNSTORFF: BERLIN, *July* 29.

Your Excellency will be good enough to communicate the following to Lord Granville: The document published by the *Times* contains one of the proposals which have been made to us since the Danish war, by official and unofficial French agents, with the object of establishing an alliance between Prussia and France for their mutual aggrandizement. I will send the text of an offer made in 1866, according to which France proposed to aid Prussia with 300,000 men against Austria, and to permit Prussia's aggrandizement by six or eight millions of subjects, in return for the cession to France of the district between the Rhine and the Moselle. The impossibility of agreeing to this course was clear to all except French diplomatists. On this proposition being rejected, the French Government began to calculate upon our defeat. France has not ceased to tempt us with offers, to be carried out at the cost of Germany and Belgium. In the interests of peace I kept them secret. After the Luxemburg affair, the proposals dealing with Belgium and South Germany were renewed. M. Benedetti's manuscript belongs to this period. It is not likely that M. Benedetti acted without the Emperor's sanction. Finally, the conviction that no extension of territory was attainable in conjunction with us, *must have matured the resolve to obtain it by fighting us.* I have even grounds for believing that, had not this project been made public after our armaments on both sides were complete, France would have proposed to us jointly to carry out M. Benedetti's programme against unarmed Europe, and to conclude peace *at Belgium's cost.* If the French Cabinet now repudiates aims, for our participation in which it has uninterruptedly labored since 1864, either by demands or promises, this is easily to be explained by the present political situation.

I enclose to you, for Lord Granville, the original copy of Benedetti's proposed second secret treaty, referred to, presented in his own handwriting:

SECRET TREATY NO. 2.

ART. I.—The French empire again assumes possession of the territory which belonged to France in 1814, and is now part of the dominions of Prussia.

ART. II.—If Prussia pledges herself to obtain from the King of Bavaria and the Grand Duke of Hesse the cession of the territory which they possess on the left bank of the Rhine, and to transfer its possession to France, an indemnification of the two German princes is reserved.

ART. III.—All the provisions uniting the territory which is under the sovereignty of the King of the Netherlands to the Germanic Confederation, as well as those which refer to the rights of garrison in the fortress of Luxemburg, are annulled.

The following letter, referring to the above treaty, is likewise preserved in Berlin in Benedetti's own handwriting:

MY DEAR PRESIDENT: In reply to the communications which I have sent from Nicholsburg to Paris, in consequence of our interview of the 26th ult., I have received from Vichy the copy of a secret treaty, of which I enclose a copy. I hasten to communicate it to you, in order that you may be able to examine it at your leisure. I am at your disposition to confer with you about it whenever you think the right moment to have come. Yours,

Sunday, Aug. 5, 1866. BENEDETTI.

One or two days before the 5th of August,

BENEDETTI DEMANDED FROM BISMARCK

the formal acceptance of the above concessions; adding that, in case they should be refused, there would be war (*alors c'est la guerre*). Bismarck replied, *Alors c'est la guerre;* and added that it appeared to him incredible that France should think of seriously demanding concessions which it was so entirely impossible to carry out. Benedetti replied that he should advise the Emperor to insist on the demands, as nothing concerned him more than the preservation of the Imperial dynasty, for which the extension of the French frontier was a vital question.

TUESDAY, *July* 26.—Continued skirmishing at the front. French troops withdraw from Rome. The Emperor's horses and camp service arrive at Metz.

WITHDRAWAL OF FRENCH TROOPS FROM ROME.

ROME, *July* 26.—The French troops here have received orders to leave the Pontifical territory. In announcing this resolution to the Holy See, the French Government represented the necessity of France having the services of all her available troops at this moment, and announced that the Italian Government, in conformity with the September Convention, would undertake to secure respect for the Pontifical territory on the Italian frontiers.

TREVES (RHENISH PRUSSIA), *July* 26.—This afternoon more than 100 soldiers from the French camp at Sierck entered the village of Schengen, in Luxemburg. They remained there, singing the "Marseillaise."

TUESDAY, *July* 27.—A state of siege proclaimed in Metz, Thionville, Longwy, Bitche, Marsal, Pfalsburg, Montmédy, Verdun, and Strasburg. Day of fasting and prayer in Germany.

THE STRONGHOLD OF EASTERN FRANCE.

METZ, *July* 2.—Metz has been constituted the grand starting-point of French operations. It is not only a first-class fortress, but has a powder factory, an arsenal, and is the grand school for the artillery and engineers. It has often been debated whether the advantages of possessing a place of such vast military importance so near the frontier were not more than counterbalanced by the terrible misfortune that it must prove to France should so large a portion of her fighting resources as are contained in Metz be, either by accident or superior force, wrested from her. But if the war is to be commenced by a panther-like spring, made with the whole of France's concentrated military strength, upon the Prussian right, then the position of Metz, both as a fortress and as a grand factory of warlike material, will prove as valuable as though its exact location had been determined for the purpose of opening this campaign with a clap of thunder.

THURSDAY, *July* 28. — Arrival of the Emperor and Prince Imperial at Metz. He addresses the army. Both armies concentrating on the border at Saarbrück, Bitche, and Weisenburg. Warm skirmishing all day at Saarbrück.

FRENCH AND PRUSSIANS IN FORCE.

SAARBRUCK. — Prussian reconnoitring parties crossed the frontier, and came upon the French troops at all points. In spite of a heavy fire opened upon them by the enemy, the Prussians suffered no losses. In the afternoon the French advanced with artillery, throwing shells, which, however, only hit some of the houses of the town, and inflicted no damage upon the troops. After a short cannonade the French troops retired across the frontier.

THE EMPEROR AT THE FRONT.

METZ, *July* 28, 7.40 P.M. — The Emperor, the Prince Imperial, and Prince Napoleon arrived at Metz at seven o'clock. Accompanied by the Cent Gardes, they proceeded through the town to the Prefecture. The carriage of the Prince Imperial and the Cent Gardes were smothered with flags and flowers. The Imperial party was received at the station by Marshal Lebœuf and suite. The "Marseillaise" was sung by the people. There was no ceremonial reception.

Just before the arrival of the Emperor Napoleon, the following proclamation to the French army was posted over the town:

"SOLDATS — Je viens me mettre à votre tête pour defendre l'honneur et le sol de la patrie. Vous allez combattre une des meilleures armées de l'Europe; mais d'autres, qui valaient autant qu'elle, n'ont pu résister à votre bravoure. Il en sera de même aujourd-hui. La guerre qui commence sera longue et penible, car elle aura pour théâtre des lieux hérisses d'obstacles et de forteresses; mais rien n'est auódessus des efforts persévérants des soldats d'Afrique, de Crimée, de Chine, d'Italie et du Mexique. Vous prouverez une fois de plus ce que peut une armée française, animó du sentiment du devoir, maintenue par la discipline, enflammée par l'amour de la patrie. Quelque soit le chemin que nous prenions hors de nos frontières, nous y trouverons les traces glorieuses de nos pères. Nous nous montrerons dignes d'eux La France entière vous suit de ses vœux ardents et l'univers a les yeux sur vous. De nos succès depend le sort de la libertó et de la civilisation. Soldats, que chacun fasse son devoir, et le Dieu des armées sera avec nous ! Au quartier Imperial de Metz, le 28 Juillet 1870. — NAPOLEON."

[TRANSLATION.]

SOLDIERS, — I have come to place myself at your head, to defend the honor and the soil of the country. You go forth to fight against one of the best armies in Europe; but others of equal excellence have been unable to resist your bravery. It will be so now. The war which is commencing will be long and difficult, for its seat will be places bristling with obstacles and fortresses; but nothing is beyond the persevering efforts of the soldiers of Africa, the Crimea, China, Italy, and Mexico. Once again you will show what can be done by a French army, animated by the sentiment of duty, sustained by discipline, fired by love of country. Whatever road we may take beyond our frontiers, we shall find there the glorious traces of our fathers. We shall prove ourselves worthy of them. All France is following you with ardent wishes, and the eyes of the world are upon you. The fate of liberty and civilization depends on our success. Soldiers, let each of you do his duty, and the God of battles will be with us.

NAPOLEON.

Imperial Headquarters, Metz, July 28, 1870.

WARM SKIRMISHING.

(*Translated from the German.*)

SAARBRUCK, THURSDAY, *July* 28. — A company of infantry and a squadron of uhlans entered the town this morning.

About fifty infantry have gone out to reconnoitre. The report of thirty or forty infantry from Saarlouis discomfiting a squadron of cavalry and three companies of infantry — 250 or 300 men — is confirmed.

The owner of a mill near Ludweilen, where the skirmish took place, came into the town this morning with the intelligence that six French pieces of artillery had appeared on the top of a neighboring hill. This is the first artillery that has been seen.

The bridges here over the Saar have for some time been barricaded with casks filled with large stones, a narrow passage being left for the present traffic. The railway bridge is also not in a condition to be of much service to the French. But the chance of a sudden attack is over, and it would make very little difference to either side if the French were allowed to take possession of Saarbrück. Up till yesterday the weather was very sultry, and the air so thick that very little could be made out of the movements of the French outposts. Yesterday there was a thunderstorm, and this morning it was clear. It is thought there may be a battle about Monday or Tuesday. Prince Friedrich Karl is expected at Kreuznach, and the Crown Prince at Kaiserslautern.

The French band is playing on the top of the hill behind Saarbrück. The French shoot at any one who walks along the Forbach road. One has to look out.

Four P.M. — Four artillery shots this moment.

Eleven P.M. — The drums beat, the population turned out into the streets, and the troops took up their position on the bridges among the barricades. A crowd came along the main street of St. Johann, and gathered round a man *who was bringing in the first shell fired.* It had struck a soft piece of ground, and had not exploded. It is the first shell fired in the war, and it will probably be preserved with honor, and become historical. The little Bellevue Inn, at the top of the hill behind the town, is the spot where the picket is stationed.

It is the *first house ruined by the war.* It was this that the French took as a mark for their artillery, in order to get the range of the town for some future occasion. A shell went through the front wall into the room, exploded inside, broke up both floor and ceiling, and turned it into a wreck of boards, table-legs, and broken glass. Another shell struck the face of the house higher up, and made a great dent, without doing further mischief. Another went through the roof of the stables behind. Nobody was in the house at the time; the inhabitants had decamped at the first sight of French artillery. Only six or seven shells were fired. The artillery firing of the French to-day was very good.

FRIDAY, *July* 29. — The Emperor assumes command of the army. The Departments of the Moselle, Haut-Rhin, and Bas-Rhin declared in a state of siege. French fleet arrives at Copenhagen. The French dig German potatoes.

METZ, *July* 29. — The Emperor assumed to-day the chief command of the army. His Majesty held a conference with the major-generals, and will visit to-day the camp of the Second Corps. The Prince Imperial visited the camp, and was loudly cheered. The sanitary condition of the army is excellent.

SAARBRUCK.

(*Translated from the German.*)

Friday Morning, *July* 29, 8 *A.M.* — All quiet. There has been no attack.

It begins to look like war. The German soldiers are glad and jolly. A good many French are behind the hills, but deserters say they have nothing to eat. They are half-starved, and woe-begone. Some infantry entered Prussian territory at 3 A.M. this morning, to dig up potatoes. They were driven off without any potatoes, and with the loss of two men. The potato-digging has been attempted at intervals all along the frontier.

The plan of the campaign is, that three armies will form at points from Saarbrück southwards — the southernmost to advance on Strasburg, the next on Nancy, and the third to mask Metz, co-operating with the second. The French can hardly have been acquainted with the weakness of the force in Saarbrück during the last few days. The patrols are very active, and penetrate to the extreme right and left of the valley. The badness of the enemy's sharp-shooting encourages them to go within unnecessarily short distances of the French outposts. A party had made their way yesterday along an open, marshy space below the woods which stretch to the French camp, when some *chasseurs burst out of the wood*, within fifty yards of them, shouting. The Germans rode off as hard as they could, the Frenchmen firing at them. If the chasseurs could have remained quiet a minute or two longer, they might have destroyed or made prisoners the whole party. When they had nothing to do but take good aim at the flying horsemen, from fifty yards upwards, they did not succeed in hitting their bodies. Three shots were received in different parts of the men's equipments. Bodies of infantry are continually going out to reconnoitre.

Ten P.M. — To-day has been quite quiet, no one wounded or killed on either side, and very little firing. The French artillery is not to be seen. About four o'clock this afternoon a detachment of French infantry appeared on the top of their hill, and passed some time making surveys and taking distances. When they went down, a company of men in white jackets appeared, and began to dig. The dust occasioned by this was visible.

There are no potatoes to dig there.

By and by, when we get into France, we will dig their potatoes, too!

SATURDAY, 8 *A.M.*—The patrols in the night suffered more severely than usual. One was surprised by the French concealed in a wood, who suddenly fired upon them, and wounded a uhlan and also a fusilier of the second battalion of the Fortieth. Two other men have been wounded in different patrols, one of the 8th company of the above-named battalion very severely, the other slightly. The French are making a bridge over the Saar, between Grossblittersdorf and Hunweiler, near Saarguemines. The work done yesterday afternoon on the top of the hill turns out to be a protected battery. Two cannon have appeared there. Fighting is expected in the course of the day.

SUNDAY, *July* 31.—King William leaves for the front. Napoleon at St. Avold. Proclamation of King William.

PROCLAMATION OF THE KING.

BERLIN, *July* 31 (*Evening*).—The King has issued the following proclamation:

"TO MY PEOPLE,—On my departure to-day for the army, to fight with it for Germany's honor and the preservation of our most precious possessions, I wish to grant an amnesty for all political crimes and offences, in recognition of the unanimous uprising of my people at this crisis. I have instructed the Minister of State to submit a decree to me to this effect. My people know with me that the rupture of the peace and the provocation to war did not emanate from our side. But, being challenged, we are resolved, like our forefathers, placing full trust in God, to accept the battle for the defence of the Fatherland.

"WILLIAM."

AMERICA, BRIGHT DAUGHTER OF LIBERTY!

COLOGNE, *July* 31. — At a mass-meeting held at Cologne to-day, an address was adopted to the King of Prussia, Germany, and the German Americans, and especially those of St. Louis, expressive of thanks for their aid in this impious war. The address rejoices "in the preservation of love for the Fatherland by the Germans in the land great for its deeds, *for the life of Washington and the death of Lincoln*." The address, which has occasioned great enthusiasm, concludes as follows:

You are still one with the Fatherland. Awaken your enthusiasm against Cæsarism, which has extended to Mexico, which protects the hand of revolution, and which drenches the glorious Rhineland with blood. For such love and encouragement we extend our hands. Vive Germany, our common mother! *Vive America, bright daughter of Liberty!*

MONDAY, *August* 1. — The French occupy Gersweiler and St. Arnual. No orders to advance.

PARIS, *July* 30, 6.35 *P.M.* — The following is the official intelligence published this evening:

HEADQUARTERS OF THE ARMY, *Saturday*, 1 *P.M.*

The march forward has not yet commenced, and all contrary reports are false.

NAPOLEON.

ARMIES AND NAVIES OF FRANCE AND PRUSSIA.

THE author, before the commencement of the actual fighting, gives, in a condensed form, valuable statistics, which will enable the reader to follow the daily diary of events with a clearer understanding.

THE FRENCH ARMY AND NAVY.

The present field force of France is infinitely smaller than that of Prussia. The French army looks well on paper, and in the official reports of Marshal Niel; but when actual estimates are made, the figures fall far below the official reports.

On the 1st of October, 1869, the official report of Marshal Niel gives the numbers of the French army as follows:

Troops on duty in France	365,179
" " Algiers	63,925
" " Papal Dominions	5,252
Total (peace footing)	434,356

The French army on a war footing will number 662,000 men, including the reserves. The army has 169 batteries with 1014 guns. A battery of mitrailleuses is attached to each corps.

The army on a peace footing is composed of eight army corps, averaging about 32,000 each. During the war the French have never had, at one time, more than ten corps in the field, inclusive of the garrison of Toul, Strasburg, Sedan, etc. It is mysterious where the troops of certain corps have disappeared to. MacMahon's First Corps of 45,000 has dwindled down to 25,000 on the retreat from Wörth to Chalons. A demoralized army loses more men through "stragglers" than in actual battle. This is especially true of conscripts.

4*

Each *corps d'armée* is composed of from three to four divisions of infantry, and from six to eight regiments of cavalry. Each division has three batteries of artillery and one company of engineers, and comprises in its total force ten to twelve thousand men of all arms of the service.

THE FRENCH NAVY.

The Minister of Marine, Admiral de Genouilly (under the Republic, Martin Fourichon).

The French fleet is commanded by Admiral Bouët-Willaumez.

The fleet is distributed as follows:

First division in the Baltic Sea. Iron-clad frigates — La Surveillante (admiral's ship), La Gauloise, L'Ocean, La Guienne, La Planche. Iron-clad corvettes — La Jeanne d'Arc, La Thétis, yacht Jérôme Napoléon.

Second division, Rear-Admiral Petrouet. Iron-clad frigates — La Savoie (flag), La Valeureuse, La Révanche, La Montcalm, La Victoire, L'Atalante, Le Rochambeau (Dunderberg).

Third division — Iron-clad frigate La Savoie (ram). Despatch boats — Duyot, Castor, Cosmos, Bougainville, Catinat, Château Renauld, Peirin, Bousaque, l'Heureuse, Ariel, yacht Hirondelle (swiftest vessel in the French navy).

The navy employs 7000 men.

COMMANDERS OF THE FRENCH ARMY.

Commander-in-Chief, the Emperor Napoleon III.

Minister of Marine, Rigault De Genouilly.

(Under the Republic, M. Fourichon.)

Major-General and Secretary of War, Marshal Lebœuf.

(Afterwards Palikao and Trochu.)

Assistant Major-Generals, Levren and Jarvas.

Commander-in-Chief of Artillery, General Soleille.

Commander-in-Chief of Engineers, General De Noweck.

Commander of the Army of the Moselle (Second, Third, and Fourth Corps), Marshal Bazaine.

Commander of the Army of the Rhine (First, Fifth, and Seventh Corps), Marshal MacMahon.

Commander of the Army of Paris, troops of the line, Marshal Canrobert; reserves, and recruits, General De Vinoy.

Commander of the Imperial Guards (Eighth Corps), General Bourbaki.

Commander of the Department of Paris (Governor of the city), General Trochu.

(Afterwards became Secretary of War, and finally President of the Republic.)

POSITION OF FRENCH ARMIES (350,000).

NUMBERS, AND CORPS COMMANDERS.

AUGUST 4.

SEDAN.	PARIS.	CHALONS.	THIONVILLE.	METZ.	WEISENBURG.	STRASBURG.
	RESERVES.	RESERVES.	LEFT.	CENTRE.	RIGHT.	
		CANROBERT.	L'ADMIRAULT.	BAZAINE.	MacMAHON.	UHRICH.
2,000		6th Corps, 30,000 Recruits, 10,000	4th Corps, 32,000	2d Corps, Frossard, 32,000 3d " Bazaine, 32,000 8th " Bourbaki, 32,000 Cavalry and Artillery, 34,000 SAARBRUCK. Frossard, 35,000 Bazaine, 20,000	1st Corps, MacMahon, 45,000 3d " De Failly, 32,000 7th " Douay, 15,000 Weisbaden, 75,000 Woerth, 100,000	11,000
2,000		40,000	32,000	130,000	92,000	11,000

AUGUST 16.

SEDAN.	PARIS.	CHALONS.	THIONVILLE.	METZ.	WEISENBURG.	STRASBURG.
	TROCHU.	MacMAHON.				
2,000	Recruits, 45,000	1st Corps, 20,000 5th " 25,000 7th " 20,000 Recruits, 10,000	Joined Bazaine, except garrison.	2d Corps, Frossard, 30,000 3d " De Caen, 30,000 4th " L'Admirault, 32,000 6th " Canrobert, 45,000 8th Guards, Bourkaki, 32,000 Cavalry and Artillery, 30,000	Driven Back.	11,000
2,000	45,000	75,000		199,000		11,000

SEPTEMBER 1.

MacMAHON.						
1st C. McM., 20,000 5th C. Failly, 25,000 7th C. Douay, 20,000 12th C. R'ts, etc. 55,000	Recruits, 25,000	Recruits, 15,000	Garrison, 5,000	2d Corps, Frossard, 25,000 3d " De Caen, 25,000 4th " L'Admirault, 30,000 8th Guards, Bourbaki, 30,000 6th Corps, Canrobert, 40,000 Cavalry and Artillery, 30,000		11,000
120,000	25,000	15,000		180,000		11,000

SEPTEMBER 2.

Captured.	Recruits, 35,000	Recruits, 15,000		Bazaine, 175,000		11,000

JANUARY 27, 1871.

LAON.	TROCHU.	CHALONS.	THIONVILLE.	METZ.	SOISSONS.	TOUL.	STRASBURG.
Surrend'd Sep. 10, 3,000.	Capitulates 27 Jan. 230,000.	Deserted.	Surrendered Nov. 25, 5,000.	Surrenders Oct. 27. 170,000	Surrendered Oct. 16, 4,700.	Surrendered Sept. 23, 2,240.	Captured Sept. 27, 11,000.

COMMANDER-IN-CHIEF.

NAPOLEON III.

The world does not furnish a parallel to the history of Napoleon III.

Napoleon I. had a brother — Louis Bonaparte. This brother was in love with and formally betrothed to Emile Beauharnais, the niece of Josephine. Hortense, the daughter of Josephine, was betrothed to Gen. Duroc. Napoleon broke up these betrothals of love, made four lives wretched and unhappy, and compelled his brother Louis to marry Hortense. This was in 1802.

It was a marriage of disinclination on both sides, but Louis was no more able than Jerome to resist Napoleon's inflexible will. After an equally vain resistance, he accepted the crown of Holland in 1806. The want of harmony between himself and Hortense was no longer concealed, and their married life was virtually at an end, when on the 20th of April, 1808, a third son, Charles Louis Napoleon, was born. King Louis hesitated to acknowledge the latter as his own, and only yielded to the urgent solicitations of his brother. The name of Hortense was at that time mentioned in connection with that of a certain Dutch admiral, whose features many persons believe to be reproduced in a face which certainly has no resemblance to either the Bonaparte or the Beauharnais family. The sons of Louis were the only hereditary princes until the King of Rome was born. The oldest of the three children died in 1807, and Hortense, after the birth of the youngest, continued to reside in Paris as Queen Regent of Holland. Napoleon manifested great attachment to her sons, especially the younger. After his return from Elba, Prince Charles Louis Napoleon, then seven years old, stood by his side on the Champs de Mars, and was one of the last to embrace him at Malmaison, when he left Paris forever.

Hortense, banished from France, settled first at Augsburg. The brothers, during their residence in Italy, became implicated in the political conspiracies of the Italian patriots, and both took part in the attempted revolution in the Romagna, in January, 1831. The elder brother, Louis Napoleon, exhausted by the privations he had endured, was attacked with the measles, and died at Forli. The younger, thenceforth known as Louis Napoleon, also fell ill at Ancona, which city he left, when able to travel, in the disguise of a footman to Hortense, who gave herself out to be an English lady of rank.

They reached Paris in March, 1831, and remained there for a month.

Louis Philippe saw trouble in his presence, and the decree of banishment was renewed.

The death of his elder brother was followed, in 1832, by that of the Duke of Reichstadt (King of Rome), and he found himself the next heir to Napoleon's throne. His restless, adventurous spirit had thenceforth a fixed, inflexible aim, and much of his success is undoubtedly due both to the direction of his studies from that time forward, and to the sixteen years of defeat and exile which were still to come. In his *Rêveries Politiques*, published in 1832, he declared that France can only be restored to her prosperity and political importance by a member of the Bonaparte family — that no other could unite *the development of Republican ideas* with the military spirit of the French people! He also published a work on the political and military condition of Switzerland, and a "Manual of Artillery," which is said to be a work of considerable technical merit.

THE STRASBURG AFFAIR.

Either growing impatient of the changeless current of circumstances, or misled by the representations of his secret adherents in France, he determined to strike a blow at the Orleans rule.

Col. Vaudrey of the Fourth Artillery, then stationed in Strasburg, and M. Fialin (calling himself De Persigny), assisted in arranging the plot. On the 30th of October, 1836, Louis Napoleon suddenly made his appearance in Strasburg, was presented to a part of the garrison by Col. Vaudrey, who at the same time announced to the soldiers that a revolution had taken place in Paris, and was accepted by the Fourth Artillery and a portion of some other regiments. The prompt action of Gen. Voirol and Col. Tallandier arrested the movement; the troops hesitated; in a few minutes more, the epaulettes and decorations of the would-be Emperor were torn from him. He was arrested without delay, and forwarded to Paris. Louis Philippe felt too secure in his place to be vindictive; the attempt, in fact, illustrated its own impotence; and the culprit was dealt with very leniently. Within three weeks he was shipped to New York, without any conditions being attached to his release, and $3000, the gift of Louis Philippe, in his pocket.

He was first taken to Rio Janeiro, where the vessel delayed but a few days, and then sailed for the United States. He was landed at Norfolk in March, 1837, and thence made his way to New York, where he remained until some time in May. His brief residence among us has left behind it only a tradition of a visit to Washington Irving at Sunnyside, and a few others of debts and quarrels with landlords. His uncle Joseph, ex-King of Spain, had a residence near Bordentown at that time, and he had other relatives in Baltimore, but he seems to have had little, if any, intercourse with them. The Strasburg affair disparaged his intelligence and magnified the pretension of his character; his personal habits were reckless, and not always respectable; and the name of "adventurer," thus doubly stamped upon him, was no recommendation to what was then "our best society." What chances were lost to Bowling Green and Bleecker street!

BOULOGNE.

Although in 1840 the Orleanist rule was still firmly established in France, Louis Napoleon, yielding less to the impatience of his small band of followers in London, than blindly and recklessly trusting his fortunes to chance, organized a new attempt. Accompanied by Count Montholon (one of the companions of Napoleon at St. Helena) and about fifty others, he crossed the Channel in a small steamer, and landed at Boulogne. One of the "properties" of the expedition was a tame eagle, which — according to the gossip of the day — had been trained to alight on the Prince's head, by the lure of a piece of raw beefsteak attached to his hat. The landing was made, the bluffs ascended, and the garrison summoned to acknowledge their legitimate commander; but the eagle forgot his lesson, and the soldiers had not yet learned theirs. The first alighted upon a post, instead of the selected head, and the second charged upon their rightful sovereign and his adherents. Plunging into the sea in his endeavor to regain the steamer, Louis Napoleon was dragged out, dripping and collapsed, and forwarded a second time to Paris. This attempt was even more disastrous than the first; for at Strasburg a part of the garrison, deceived by Col. Vaudrey, had actually declared for him; whereas at Boulogne not a single soldier appears to have done him reverence.

Louis Philippe, it must be admitted, acted with great moderation. The life of the usurper, who had a second time abused his forbearance, was in his power. Napoleon was brought to trial before the House of Peers. He was sentenced to perpetual imprisonment in Ham. His imprisonment was voluntarily shared by Dr. Conneau, a physician who had faith in his destiny. During the six years at Ham, however, the prisoner was not idle. He occupied himself chiefly with political studies, and wrote three works — *Historic Fragments* (published in 1841), a comparison between the fall of the Stuart dynasty in England and certain features of French history; an *Analysis of the Sugar Question* (1842), in which he took ground against specially favoring production in the French colonies; and, finally, an essay on the *Extinction of Pauperism*, which was the most important of all, inasmuch as it indirectly favored the communistic theories which were then rapidly taking root among the laboring classes of France. He proposed that the Government should advance funds to establish settlement and cultivation in all the waste districts of the country, and that the profits of the undertaking should be appropriated to the support and elevation of the manufacturing classes. Toward the end of 1845, the ex-King Louis, then ill at Florence, made an appeal to the French Government for the release of the only son who bore his name. After a long consideration the appeal was refused, but the refusal was followed, in May, 1846, by the escape of Louis Napoleon from Ham. With Dr. Conneau's assistance, disguised as a workman, he walked out of the fortress, carrying a board upon his shoulder, easily made his way to the Belgian frontier, and thence to England.

Here he associated with very good people. Lady Blessington received him at Gore House and Sir John Browning took him by the hand.

Now came the revolution of 1848. Napoleon saw the chance. The Bonapartist faction in France was not large at that time, but it was very active. Lamartine, originally a Legitimist, knew the power of a name among the people; and the Executive Committee (in May), probably at his suggestion, laid before the National Assembly a proposal to renew the decree of 1832, and banish the Bonaparte family from France. This was rejected by the Assembly, and Louis Napoleon, who had been brought before the people as a candidate by his followers, and had been elected Deputy from four Departments, was free to visit Paris. Nevertheless, he still delayed, from an apparent disinclination to create trouble. After having announced to the President of the National Assembly, on the 14th of June, that he was ready to perform any duty with which the people might charge him, he forwarded a letter the following day, resigning his place as Deputy in the interest of peace and harmony. This step greatly increased his popularity, and he was immediately re-chosen Deputy by four other Departments.

EIGHTEEN FORTY-EIGHT.

Thereupon he left England, reached Paris on the 24th of September, and on the 26th took his seat in the National Assembly. He made a short address, taking strong ground in favor of the preservation of order and the development of democratic institutions. Gen. Cavaignac, then temporary dictator, and candidate for the Presidency, seems to have greatly under-estimated both his ability and the chances of his popularity. But the Bonapartists throughout the country had already prepared the way for his candidacy, and took skilful advantage of the dissensions among the Republicans to unite the most heterogeneous elements in his support. The attempts of the Orleanist and Legitimist parties to set up popular candidates failed; the Socialists, embittered by Cavaignac's stern suppression of the attempted revolution in June, yet powerless alone, were seduced by the supposed tendencies of Louis Napoleon's political essays; the troops began to yield to the magic of a name, now that the one who bore it might legally become their leader; the millions of the ignorant peasantry were easily manipulated by dexterous agents (a large number believing they were voting for Napoleon I., returned from St. Helena!), and even before the election day arrived, the increasing chances of Louis Napoleon's success carried over to his side a multitude of wavering, politic natures.

The election was held on the 10th of December, 1848, and the result gave evidence of an almost complete union of all other parties against that of the Republic of Order represented by Cavaignac. The latter received 1,460,000 votes, Louis Napoleon 5,500,000, and Lamartine a comparatively trifling number. The new President, with no record of offence, except against the banished dynasty, took quiet possession of the realm which another had made ready for his hands.

PRESIDENT BONAPARTE.

His policy, after obtaining power, was very gradually developed. He only appeared to imitate Cavaignac in putting down the disturbances of January, 1849, and the Conservative and Catholic sentiment of France was certainly with him in sending Oudinot to Rome.

This was in direct opposition to the decision of the Assembly, yet the Assembly afterward confirmed the act. Even the title of "Prince-President" seemed to excite no distrust, except among the now thoroughly unpopular "Reds," or extreme Republicans. The foreign policy of the Government was dignified, but conciliatory. The *Prince-President* steadily followed two objects: he made himself popular with the soldiers and the laboring classes, and crushed in every practicable way the intelligent *bourgeoisie*. In October, 1849, the Ministry was changed for one more inclined to support his plans; the dissensions in the National Assembly were secretly and skilfully encouraged; journeys through the provinces, banquets, addresses to the people, appointments of civil officers, grand military reviews, at which officers and soldiers were feasted (as on the plain of Satory) — all were employed to extend the Prince-President's personal influence, and gradually familiarize the people with the Imperial idea.

In January, 1851, a completely Bonapartist Ministry was appointed, but the Assembly having voted its lack of confidence, another Ministry was substituted. An attempt was then made to change the Constitution in such a manner that the President's term of office might be extended, since an immediate re-election was prohibited, but, after a very fierce and stormy discussion, the proposition failed to receive the requisite majority of three-fourths. The Assembly was soon afterwards adjourned until November, which gave the Prince-President time to mature his plans. His term would expire the following spring; the Prince de Joinville was already named as a candidate; the elements of opposition, although without combination, were increasing in strength. In this juncture he called about him men who were equally cunning, daring, and unprincipled — Gen. St. Arnaud (who was made Minister of War in October, 1851), De Morny, Persigny, and Fleury. All of these appear to have been made acquainted with his plans, and two of them — St. Arnaud and De Morny — were his chief instruments in carrying them into execution. When, on the 13th of November, the proposition to restore universal suffrage was defeated in the Assembly, the Prince-President and his accomplices determined (true to Napoleonic tradition) to imitate the 18th Brumaire.

THE COUP D'ETAT.

But the 2d of December, 1851, was not an imitation; it was original in its horror. Before daylight on that morning, 78 prominent men were seized, many of them being dragged from their beds, the National Assembly forcibly dissolved (220 of the Deputies having been arrested and imprisoned the same day), Paris declared in a state of siege, and the people called upon to elect a President for ten years, with power to select his own Ministry, and a Government consisting of two Chambers, with limited powers. Paris arose against the outrage, and until the night of December 4, its streets ran with blood. Entire quarters of the city were given up to murder and plunder. Men, women, and children, natives and foreigners, were shot and bayoneted indiscriminately.

The blow was so sudden and terrible that the spirit of the nation was utterly paralyzed; even indignation was lost in the deeper sense of horror and fear. The mask was removed, and the Empire, in a nearly absolute form, already existed. When the election was held, few days later, the result was: 7,500,000 yeas, 650,000 nays. As Kinglake says, "He knew how to strangle a nation in a night-time with a thing he called a Plebiscite."

THE EMPIRE ESTABLISHED.

In January, 1852, he ordered the confiscation of all the property belonging to the Orleans family; in February, the last vestige of liberty was taken from the press; in May, the Napoleonic eagles were distributed to the army; and in December the Prince-President, Louis Napoleon Bonaparte, became Napoleon III., Emperor, "By the Grace of God and the will of the French people!" Having assured himself that resistance was paralyzed for a time, his next objects were, first, to allay the distrust of the other European powers by showing that the Empire was Peace, and secondly, to bring about a war in order to satisfy his army. At the same time he did not neglect to provide for the foundation of a dynasty. His mistress, an English woman, was set aside, and the inclinations of various marriageable princesses very delicately and secretly sounded. He made strong efforts to obtain the hand of the Princess Wasa, of the deposed royal family of Sweden; but when these finally failed, suddenly gave up all imitation of his uncle, and astonished the Court circles of Europe by declaring his choice to be the Spanish Countess Eugenie de Teba, daughter of the Countess de Montijo, and granddaughter of a Scotch merchant named Kirkpatrick. Tall, handsome, graceful, and twenty-seven, Eugenie was probably quite as acceptable to the French people as any of the (at that time) inaccessible daughters of royal houses. The marriage took place in January, 1853, and the little girl whom Washington Irving used to trot upon his knee became Empress of France.

The first legitimate success of Napoleon III. was his alliance with England. He led the English Government, in 1853, into an alliance against Russia.

Victoria and Albert sat with him and Eugenie in an opera-box in Paris; *he kissed Her Most Gracious Majesty on the staircase at Windsor*, and her royal hands invested him with the Order of the Garter.

The Empire was not peace; it has always been war — war with Austria, war with Russia, war with Prussia. Still the French liked Napoleon III. After Magenta he was popular; even some Americans looked upon him as a man of genius and destiny. Europe believed in Napoleon.

THE BOY.

An Imperial Prince was born in March, 1856 — an only one, and again a resemblance to Napoleon! Even persons not superstitious began to incline toward the theory of "destiny."

From 1853 to 1861 he was the most over-estimated man in the world. Every turn and winding of his apparently subtile policy, every new disclosure of his seemingly impenetrable plans, was accepted as an evidence of greatness by a majority of the civilized races.

THE ITALIAN WAR.

It would, perhaps, be unfair to say that sympathy for the Italian cause had no part in bringing on the war of 1859. But there were two other equally powerful considerations: he would abolish the relentless determination of the Carbonari, and he would increase the territory of France by the annexation of Savoy. Although Napoleon's Ministry was reported to be unfavorable to the war, it was hailed with great enthusiasm by the masses of the people.

Nevertheless, the declaration of war occasioned great alarm and uneasiness throughout Europe. There was a vague fear — now that belief in the genius of Napoleon III. had been generally established — that this would be the beginning of a course of conquest, in which the career of Napoleon I. might be repeated. The English people were more excited than any other.

After entering Piedmont, the Emperor delayed three weeks, plotting and planning, before commencing hostilities. He had an interview with Kossuth, and agreed with the latter upon a plan for co-operating with the Magyar and Sclavonic population of Austria. Tuscany had already risen, the Romagna was stirring, and there were movements in Naples and Sicily. After a small engagement at Montebello, the battle of Magenta, on the 4th of June, gave Milan and Lombardy to the French and Italian armies. The Emperor's reception in Milan was warm and cordial, but a storm of uncontrollable joy surged around the path of Victor Emanuel.

The Emperor's disappointment, however, was bitter, when all Italy, except the little Roman territory held by French troops, pronounced for a united nationality under Victor Emanuel. Savoy and Nice were acquired, it is true; the names of Magenta and Solferino were added to those of the Alma and the Malakoff; the influence of France was more potent than ever in the counsels of Europe; but more than this was necessary. Napoleon did more. He made commerce for France, built railroads, and kept the poor at work. He beautified Paris, and tried in every way to make Frenchmen forget his usurpation in '52. He was a great *Mayor for Paris.*

MEXICO

was an opportunity. The Rebellion occupied Washington.

The Mexican expedition was a threat, an impertinence, an indirect (and therefore unanswerable) interference in American affairs. It was meant to be the first step toward an intervention on behalf of the rebellious South. The dismemberment of the American Republic would have been the triumph of dynastic ideas throughout the world, and there was nothing which Napoleon III. more prayerfully desired.

Two things baffled this nicely-arranged plan — Abraham Lincoln's proclamation of Emancipation and the steady friendship of Russia. The moral support of the English masses and the consequent caution of the English Government saved the United States from what was, for a short time, a very imminent danger. Napoleon III. hesitated, until the proper time for *his* action had passed; and England had more reason for congratulation than her people are perhaps, even now, aware of. The end of the Mexican business was the severest blow which the dynastic system had received since the French Revolution. The divinity of hereditary rulers, instead of being strengthened, was again tragically shaken; and henceforth another bloody ghost was added to the thousands which already haunted the Tuileries.

The failure of his Mexican plans disturbed the general faith in his infallible wisdom, and first revealed the hollow foundation upon which his imperial power was built. It was a source of profound mortification to the French people — how profound only those can know who have visited France, and discussed the matter there, within the last or three four years.

From this point there seems to be a change in the character of Napoleon III. He began to grow phlegmatic, his eye lost its lustre, he became like an old man in his dotage.

FRANCE AND PRUSSIA.

While he was chafing under the overthrow of his plans in Mexico, but before the last sad act of the tragedy had been performed, there came a second and far severer blow.

The Prussian campaign of 1866 drew a broad black line across his calculations. Bismarck had been Prussian ambassador in Paris (in 1862), and the Emperor imagined that in him he had secured another unconscious ally; but Bismarck is one of those men who, naturally honest, are able to dissimulate for the sake of defeating dissimulation. His plans were concealed for ten times the length of Napoleon III.'s *coup d'état*, but they were realized on an open battle-field, in the sight of the world, not through perjury, darkness, and slaughter.

The Emperor was so completely and narrowly a Napoleonist, that his impressions of Prussia seemed to have been derived from one word — Jena. When war became inevitable, he repeated the blunder he had made in the case of Mexico — trusted implicitly in the victory of the side which was defeated. The issue of the six weeks' war was overwhelming. The world, for the first time, heard the creaking of the shaky props of his throne. Forced to become the convenient go-between by which Venetia was transferred to Italy, now "free from the Alps to the Adriatic," against his will — to hear Europe ringing with a victory which made Solferino tame — to see the map of Germany changed without the slightest regard to the sympathies or interests of France, implied a loss of power which foreboded a growing opposition at home.

His efforts were next directed toward preventing any nearer approach of Bavaria and Würtemberg towards the North German Confederation; but, as he only discovered some months afterward, the military alliance of those states had already been accomplished. Luxemburg, by a secret arrangement, nearly fell into his hands; but here again Prussia stepped in the way, and although she did not win the prize, it was lost to France. The sensitive French people began to grow very restive under the humiliations to which they were exposed by the Emperor's reckless diplomacy.

Throughout Europe the concession was generally recognized as an evidence that the Emperor, although weakened in personal power by his blunders, still retained his shrewdness and his presumed prudence. He had saved Rome to the Pope in 1867, and was still the well-beloved son of the Church. His influence was strong in Spain; he had the friendship of Austria, the subserviency of Italy, and the guarded respect of England and Russia. Moreover, the military organization of France was considered — although without any very definite grounds — to be the most complete in Europe.

THE PLEBISCITUM.

The Plebiscite of May 8th was a fraud. It was this: "Will you have Napoleon with some liberty, or will you have him a tyrant." The people voted, "Yes, we will have you with liberty." The army made the vote, and it stood, "*for Napoleon if we must have him*," 7,336,434; for Napoleon in no shape, 1,560,709.

The disclosures which have since been made show not only how long Napoleon III. had been preparing for a war with Prussia, but also how amazingly he had miscalculated the political elements which he expected such a war to set in motion. The subsequent course of the Spanish Regency justifies us in suspecting that the candidature of Prince Leopold of Hohenzollern was arranged with the secret connivance of France, in order to furnish the required pretext; if not, the Regency is pusillanimous, instead of base. A division between Bavaria and Würtemberg and the North German Confederation was positively anticipated; the alliance of Denmark and Italy, with the later assistance of Austria, was a foregone conclusion.

To the Emperor and the Duke de Gramont, the calculation, doubtless, seemed to be perfect. But they had omitted the one important factor which governed the mathematical result — the very element which a man utterly selfish and sceptical of every unselfish quality of human nature — and none other — would easily overlook. The development of public sentiment in Germany had been *national;* in France the entire education and discipline of twenty years had been directed toward making it one of *personal* attachment. Napoleon III. supposed that Barbarossa (German Unity) still slept; but when the ravens ceased flying around the tower — for they had all gone to Rome to vote for Papal Infallibility — the old Emperor came forth, hung his shield on the withered tree, and it burst into a bloom that dazzled the world!

It was all very well to talk of the *élan* of the French soldier, and to hold before him a thin, wavering phantom of "glory." The German soldier went to war, clad in a panoply of willing self-sacrifice, quietly, and even with a religious solemnity, recognizing the grandeur of the crisis, although he could not perceive the profound universal principle underlying the external form of the struggle. He had been made to feel (and sometimes heavily) the full weight of his duty to the Government; but his independent strength had been exercised, his unselfish sentiment developed, and his watchword was, not "King William," but "The German Fatherland." In France, the development of "personal government" seems to have been carried so far, that it weakened that individual self-reliance which is the strength of an army as of a people. The soldier was taught to depend on the officer, the latter on his superior, and finally everybody on the Emperor. Such a system can only succeed where "The Person" is strong enough to walk freely under such a weight of direction and supervision.

In the case of Napoleon III. it has utterly failed. His energy seems to have entirely spent itself in the theatrical *coup* of his declaration of war. He immediately relapsed into worse than his former vacillation, and blind dependence on destiny. Unable to manage a force so vast, yet persisting in retaining its control in his own hands, he threw away the opportunity for a temporary success. He was bold enough to evoke the spirits from the deep, but when they came at his call, he stood bewildered and astounded. The end was then inevitable. Only the grand dimensions of the catastrophe prevent it from suggesting the farce at Strasburg, wherewith he first took his place in history.

It is too soon to paint his portrait, in all its features, as it shall hereafter stand in the records of the world. Some characteristics, nevertheless, are so strongly defined, that they are not likely to change in a greater perspective. His success was owing to a name, to a succession of fortunate circumstances, and to certain real abilities, developed in a school of severe experience; his failure came through inflated ambition, selfishness, blindness to the forward movement of the world, and an almost insane mania for startling effects. He was the leader of the sensational school in politics. He learned, through many misfortunes, to understand the interests, the appetites, and the temptations of men; but he never exhibited the slightest faith in their power of self-denial, their inextinguishable virtues, their loyalty to any deeper principle. Crowned by a deliberate lie, how could he recognize the existence of truth?

In him "personal government" has experienced another overwhelming defeat. In him, dynastic ideas are disgraced before the world. In him, the impertinent intermeddling of one nation in the special interests of other races, has received its severest check. In him, the flunkeyism of the human race is humiliated as never before. Let us, then, be satisfied with his career as another illustration of that power, "which always *wills* the Bad, and always *works* the Good." To him, more than to any other man, Europe owes two new nations — Italy and Germany; and perhaps the blunders by which he assisted, against his will, in creating them, will partly atone, on the great balance-sheet of History, for the demoralization and shame which he has brought upon the French people.

MARSHAL MACMAHON.

(Commander of First Corps and Army of the Rhine.)

War makes and unmakes a good many heroes. MacMahon is the McDowell of the French army. His place was at the pinnacle of fame when he marched the "Army of the Rhine" from Strasburg. Unfortunate General! Outnumbered at Weisenburg on the 4th of August, overpowered at Woerth August 6th, and captured at Sedan September 1st. *He belongs to the Hooker order of fighters.* Marshal MacMahon, the Duke of Magenta, is not, like Moltke, a strategist; he is a personal fighter. He would make a better division than corps commander. He fought at Woerth as Hooker fought at Chancellorsville. His fighting at Sedan is thus described by a French writer:

"To relate what MacMahon did is impossible. Steel, fire, melted metal, explosive balls, and I don't know what other infernal mixture the Prussians there made use of for the first time, appeared to stream off, or to rebound from him, like hail from a roof. He went to the front seeking death. 'Leave me, my friends,' he said to us all, who sought to prevent him from going forward. 'Let me show those kings, those princes who hide behind their masses of men, that a Marshal of France knows how to fight, and, when beaten, how to die.' And he smiled upon us a sad smile, which made us weep, and redoubled our rage. Ah, miserable! We kill, we massacre, and the living seem to spring up from the dead which we heap around us. We climbed a little mountain of dead in order that we might reckon how long the butchery would last. My sabre, broken and reeking, fell from my hands when I saw what masses we had still to deal with. The plain, the horizon, was black with dust. We were but ants in a huge ant-hill. 'Marshal,' I said, 'we have at least two hundred thousand men before us.' 'No,' he replied, gently; 'three hundred thousand.' At that moment, a cloud passed before my eyes, and we went mad. We regained our senses only when we found ourselves beyond the hordes of uhlans who attacked us. We had been fortunate enough to reach the Belgian frontier. We were safe; but at what a sacrifice!"

This eminent soldier, whose name proclaims his descent from a warlike race, is in the sixty-third year of his age. He received his military education at Saint-Cyr, from which he passed to the Staff-Corps. He took part in the expedition to Algiers, and was subsequently aide-de-camp of General Achard at the siege of Antwerp. In 1833, he returned to Africa, and rose rapidly in his profession, until in 1852 he became General of Division. In 1855, he commanded an infantry division in Marshal Bosquet's corps, in the Crimea. In this capacity he took a personal part in the famous and successful assault of the Malakoff, establishing himself in that work, and holding it, notwithstanding the repeated and prolonged efforts of the Russians to dislodge him. For this service he was decorated with the Grand Cross of the Legion of Honor, and on the return of peace was made a senator. In 1857, he was again in Africa, commanding an expedition against the Kabyles, and was afterwards appointed Commander-in-Chief of the sea and land forces in Algeria. It was, however, the Italian war which first placed his name prominently before the European public. With the designation of Commander of the Second Army Corps, but really by the side of the Emperor, he rendered at the great, and for a time very dubious, battle of Magenta, services so important, that he was named by his Sovereign, and on the field of battle, Duke of Magenta, and Marshal of France. He has now been recalled from the Governor-Generalship of Algeria, to which he was appointed in 1864, to take command of the First Corps and the "Army of the Rhine."

The Duke of Magenta is represented as combining rapidity of judgment with calmness of temper and firmness of purpose in a remarkable degree. He has never been considered a personal favorite of the Emperor, who, nevertheless, highly appreciates his abilities and character. It may be interesting to recall the fact that he was the officer chosen to represent France at the coronation of the present King of Prussia in 1861, a position which he sustained with great pomp and dignity.

MARSHAL BAZAINE.

(Commander of Third Corps and Army of the Rhine.)

The fame of Marshal Bazaine, the heroic defender of Metz, has gone forth to every schoolboy. He combines the elements of the old Marshals of the first Napoleon — courage, tenacity, and unflinching fidelity to his commander-in-chief. Bazaine is a stoic. He hates new things — hates the Republic. He is an Imperialist *nascitur* and *fit*. "Tell them," said he to a brother of Jules Favre, when he brought news of the New Republic to his beleaguered garrison, "tell them I know no Republic. I am keeping Metz for the Emperor." Courcelles (August 14), Mars-la-Tour (August 16), and Gravelotte

(August 18) attest the courage of Bazaine. His adoration for Napoleon III. may be blind, but the world will always forgive a General's devotion to his commander.

The fame of Marshal Bazaine dates from the Mexican war, of which he has himself written a history, He is descended from an old military family, and was born in 1811. He was educated at the Ecole Polytechnique, and in his twenty-first year proceeded to Africa—for so many years the great French school of war. Six years afterwards, he joined the Foreign Legion, and went through two campaigns in Spain against the Carlists. Returning to Africa, he had obtained by 1850 the command of a regiment of the Foreign Legion, and at the outbreak of the Crimean war was appointed to command a brigade of that corps. His name is mentioned several times as that of a skilful and brave officer in the despatches of Marshals Canrobert and Pelissier, and in 1855 he was made General of Division. He subsequently commanded the French expedition against Kinburn. When in 1862, while the civil war in America was raging, the Emperor of the French determined to prosecute his designs upon Mexico, General Bazaine received the command of the first division of infantry in General Forey's expedition. In October of the following year, Forey was recalled, and Bazaine advanced to the chief command. In July, 1863, he led his army into the city of Mexico, and commenced a series of vigorous operations in order to expel President Juarez, whom he drove to the frontier of the Republic, and whom he apparently believed he had expelled. This, at least, is the only assumption on which a number of executions of duly commissioned officers of the Republic, who had been taken prisoners in regular war, can be explained. This return to practices worthier of a semi-savage Hispano-American settlement than of the magnanimous French people, was the more regrettable, inasmuch as it was afterwards made the excuse for the execution of the unhappy Maximilian, whose death was said to be a just reprisal for similar murders committed under the French occupation in his name. General Bazaine did not keep up a good understanding with the Emperor Maximilian, who at length avoided him, to follow a course dictated by a sentiment of personal honor. The tragical end of the enterprise is known. The French marched for Vera Cruz, after Bazaine, who had received the rank of Marshal, had called the Mexican notables together, and told them that it was impossible to maintain the Empire, and that the war against Juarez was without object and without hope. His conduct was severely criticised, on his return, in French journals and periodicals, but the Emperor has constantly protected him. His services in Mexico have been rewarded with the rank and emoluments of a senator, and the permanent command of the Third Army Corps. He is also honorary commander-in-chief of the Imperial Guard.

GENERAL CHARLES AUGUSTE FROSSARD.

(Commander of the Second Army Corps.)

General Frossard, with Bazaine, besieged in Metz, was the first French General to invade Prussia. He ordered the Saarbrück advance on the 2d of August, and was defeated by Steinmetz on the 6th. He was born April 26, 1807; was from 1825 to 1827 a pupil of the Polytechnic School.

During the administration of General Cavaignac, he was made a lieutenant-colonel, and took part in the expedition which put an end to the Roman Republic. Having gained the reputation of being one of the most eminent officers in point of military science, and in particular in the art of fortification, he was appointed in 1852 director of the fortifications of Oran, in Algeria, with the rank of colonel, and subsequently, after being appointed general of brigade, member of the Committee of Fortifications. In 1859, he took part as general of division in the Italian campaign. After serving as aide-de-camp to the Emperor, and member of the Committee of Defence, General Frossard was, by decree of March 15, 1867, made chief of the military household of the Emperor, and Governor of the Prince Imperial, whose military instruction he is said to have conducted with military rigor. At the beginning of the year 1869, he was appointed President of the Committee of Fortifications.

MARSHAL CANROBERT.

(Commander of Sixth Corps and the Army of Paris.)

Marshal Canrobert is well known as a good commander during the Russian war. He was born in 1809, of a good Breton family.

Like MacMahon, he was educated at St. Cyr, and won his successive steps of promotion by hard fighting in Algeria, was wounded in the assault of Constantine, and fulfilling the prediction of Colonel Combes, who fell at his side, that "there was a future for that young man," had subsequently the good fortune to be incessantly engaged in the arduous operations of the next few years. Having thus, by the year 1847, won the rank of colonel, he commanded the expeditions Ahmed-Sghir, against the Kabyles and the tribes of Jurjura, and raised the blockade of Bonsada. Having returned to France in 1850, he soon became known as one of the officers who had identified himself with the cause of the Prince-President, who took him for his aide-de-camp, made him a general of brigade, and gave him a command at Paris, in which he displayed great energy in suppressing the attempt at insurrection which followed the *coup d'état*. In 1853, he was made general of division. When the Crimean war broke out, he was appointed to command the first division of the Army of the East, which, it will be remembered, suffered very severely from cholera in the Dobrudscha. At the battle of the Alma he was wounded, but not severely, in the arm. Two days afterwards, Marshal St. Arnaud, suffering from a mortal sickness, following the previous directions of the Emperor, transferred to him the chief command. The position had become difficult, but Canrobert faced it with patience and perseverance. In the end, however, a disagreement with Lord Raglan about the conduct of the war, led Canrobert to resign his command to Marshal Pelissier, and return to his first corps. Two months afterwards he left the Crimea, and in 1856 was made a Marshal of France. In the Italian war he commanded the Third Corps of the Army of the Alps, and distinguished himself at Magenta by his personal valor, and at Solferino by the timeliness with which he countervailed an Austrian movement which threatened to place the army in peril.

GENERAL PIERRE LOUIS ACHILLE DE FAILLY.

(Commander of the Fifth Army Corps.)

General De Failly was born in 1808, received his military education at St. Cyr, and was, at the time of the revolution of 1848, lieutenant-colonel of a regiment of the line. He took part in the Crimean war as brigadier-general, and greatly distinguished himself at the battles of the Alma, of the Mamelon-Vert, and of Tracktir.

After his return, he was made aide-de-camp of the Emperor, and during the Italian war he commanded a division of the army corps of General Niel, and distinguished himself at Magenta and Solferino. In 1867, he was selected to put down the Garibaldian movement, and in this campaign made the first trial on a large scale of the chassepôt, which, as he said in his report, worked wonderfully at Mentana. In October, 1869, General De Failly was appointed Commander-in-Chief of the Third Army Corps. His command at Sedan was the Fifth Corps, which withdrew from Bitche on the 5th of August, and was overpowered and defeated with MacMahon at Weisenburg, on the 6th. De Failly surrendered with MacMahon at Sedan on the 1st of September. He was wounded at Sedan, but not seriously. He received an assault on that occasion from a squad of common soldiers, who, starving themselves, saw the General eating, and became enraged.

GENERAL DOUAY.

(Commander of Seventh Corps, MacMahon's Army.)

General Douay was one of the bravest of the brave. What wonder that MacMahon gave him the post of honor on his right at Weisenburg? He was the Ellsworth of the war, and met his death in the first shock of battle. His death at Weisenburg on the 4th of August threw dismay into the hearts of his troops, and caused the first defeat of the war. He had learned to fight with MacMahon in Algiers. His African education did not avail him against the organized forces of a civilized nation. He was killed at the front, organizing a regiment of demoralized Turcos. Brave General! He died with his face to the foe, and with his sword raised for France.

GENERAL EDMOND LEBŒUF.

(Minister of War.)

General Lebœuf was born November 5, 1809; received his military education at the Polytechnic Institute, and at the Artillery School in Metz. He was a teacher at the Polytechnic from 1848 to 1850, and on returning to active service in the army, was made colonel of artillery. During the entire Crimean war he held the command-in-chief of the French artillery, and served with great distinction in the same capacity in Italy, in 1859. Succeeding Marshal Niel as Minister of War, he introduced essential reforms in the organization of the army, and his administrative talents also found a vast field for useful activity. Napoleon rewarded him for his manifold services, by conferring on him, in 1866, the highest rank in the Legion of Honor.

GENERAL TROCHU.

(Commander of the Fortifications of Paris.)

General Trochu is a writing, fighting man. Parisians call him "*Ollivier on a war-footing.*" He is Ben Butler with the pen, and Hancock with the sword.

The General is Governor of Paris and Commander-in-Chief of the forces collected for the defence of that city, and is fifty-five years of age. He was a pupil of the military school of St. Cyr and the staff school, and enjoys a very high reputation for military ability, though he has never yet held a detached command. He has served in Algeria, having for some years been employed on Marshal Bugeaud's staff. He was afterwards one of Marshal St. Arnaud's aides-de-camp at the time of the Crimean expedition, in 1854. After that commander's death, he was promoted to the rank of general, and commanded a brigade of infantry until the end of the Russian war. During the Italian campaign of 1859, which was ended by the victory of Solferino, he served with distinction in command of a division. Since that time he has been a member of the Consulting Staff Committee at the Ministry of War, and at the end of 1866 he was specially appointed to consider and report upon plans for a reorganization of the French army, in consequence of the aggrandizement of Prussia. In the following year he published anonymously a book entitled, "The French Army in 1867," which attracted great attention, and passed through ten editions in six months. In it he severely criticised the organization of the French army, and especially the consequences of those changes introduced under the Empire, which tended to render the soldiery a separate and professional caste, severed in interest and feeling from their civilian countrymen. He received no appointment in the Army of the Rhine when the present war broke out; but it is understood that he was to have commanded the land forces which were to have composed the Baltic expedition, but which were recalled from Cherbourg and Brest to defend Paris and Metz.

Trochu has been made President of the new French Republic. His position as Commander of Paris is *de jure* from the Emperor, while his Presidential position is *de facto* from the Republic.

GENERAL BOURBAKI.

(Imperial Guards.)

Bourbaki, like Bazaine, is one of the Imperialist commanders. *His sympathies could never be naturally with a Republic.* In case of an insurrection, Napoleon wanted a man as commander of the Guards in whom he could put the utmost confidence — one who loved him personally, and one who loved Cæsarism and a personal government. Bourbaki is such a man. Placed in command of the Imperial Guards (32,000), he joined Bazaine in Metz after the disasters of Worth and Weisenburg. He fought splendidly at Gravelotte, meeting the charge of the Brandenburg cavalry face to face. He was driven with L'Admirault, Canrobert, and Frossard into the walls of Metz, and stood the siege with them until the 30th of September, when he was permitted to leave Metz on a visit to the Empress at Hastings, England, and afterwards to the Emperor at Wilhelmshöhe.

As there was no longer a hope for the Empire, Bourbaki returned to Metz, but he was not permitted to re-enter the fortifications. Not being able to join Bazaine, Bourbaki visited the new Republican Government at Tours, offering his services to the Republic, not, however, without some suspicion as to his sincerity. He may yet prove a dangerous ally for Napoleon III. It will be a surprise if he shall prove to be, as Bazaine's brother claims for him, "a marshal of France, not of the Empire."

GENERAL CHANGARNIER.

(Accepted adviser of the Emperor.)

General Changarnier is an officer whose political opinions have deprived him of the opportunity of fulfilling the promise of his youth.

When the present Emperor became the Chief of the State, there were not three officers in France who would have been placed on the same line with him. Under the Restoration he served in Spain and Algeria, and greatly distinguished himself under Marshal Clausel against Achmet Bey, in the retreat from Constantine upon Bone. After a long series of brilliant services he was made Commander of Algeria by the Duke d'Aumale. In 1848 he returned to France, whither his reputation had preceded him, and was offered the Berlin Embassy, which he declined. Soon after he was sent to Algeria as Governor-General and Commander-in-Chief. Having been elected to the Constituent Assembly he returned to France, and received the command of the National Guard, and afterwards of the garrison of Paris. Soon after he became the object of political suspicions. He was known to be the enemy of the Republic, and while some thought him capable of attempting to restore the Orleanists, he for two years supported Louis Napoleon. At length he separated himself from that Prince, and was deprived of his commands. In the Chamber he declared against the ambition of "Cæsar," and accordingly was one of those who were seized and shut up on the memorable Second of December. Since then his career has been closed. On the outbreak of this quarrel, he offered his services to his country, but they were refused. After the defeat of MacMahon and Frossard, Changarnier flew to the front, met the Emperor, and became his confidential adviser in his days of disaster. His love for France overcame his hate for the Emperor.

COUNT PALIKAO.

Charles-Guillaume-Marie-Appollinaire-Antoine Cousin-Montauban, Count of Palikao, General and Senator. After the reverses of Wörth and Weisenburg, when Napoleon slaughtered Ollivier, Palikao took the place of De Jean as Minister of War.

He made an active War Minister until Trochu succeeded him under the *régime* of the Republic. The French War Ministers, during the campaign of 1870, have been Lebœuf, De Jean *ad interim*, Palikao, and Trochu.

Count Palikao, born June 24, 1796, went into Algeria at an early age, distinguished himself as officer of cavalry, and was, after more than twenty years of uninterrupted service, entrusted with the command of the Tlemcen Division, and finally with that of Constantine. Recalled to France, he was for some time at the head of the Twenty-first Military Division. In 1860, he took command of the French expedition into China, and had the honor of accomplishing the almost marvellous invasion which carried the flags of France and England to the capital of that vast empire. The destruction of numerous Chinese forts, the splendid victory at Palikao, and the entrance of the Allies into Peking, forced the Chinese Government to accept of a treaty imposed by the Allies. Returning to France in July, 1861, he was made Senator of France, Count of Palikao, and Commander of the Fourth Army Corps. In 1860, he had been 42 years in active service, and had fought in 28 different battles.

COUNT JEAN-BAPTISTE-PHILIBERT VAILLANT.

(Marshal of France and Senator.)

Marshal Vaillant was born at Dijon December 6, 1790, was admitted to the Polytechnic school in Paris at the age of 17, entered the army as second Lieutenant in 1809, and from that moment took an active part in the last campaign of the first Empire. When Napoleon undertook the great expedition into Russia, Vaillant on several occasions gave proof of rare energy and indomitable courage, but was finally made prisoner, and remained in captivity until peace was re-established. At once returning to the army, he distinguished himself by his gallant conduct at Ligny and Waterloo. He studied military works to great advantage, and was soon offered an occasion to show his unusual talents during the expedition to Algeria, and in 1832 during the memorable siege of Antwerp. In 1851 he superintended the siege of Rome, and after taking that city was made Marshal of France on December 11 of the same year. During the Crimean war he was appointed Minister of War, in which position he remained active until the outbreak of hostilities in Italy in 1859, where he participated as Major-General of the Army of the Alps, without finding an opportunity to assist at any of the sanguinary battles fought during that campaign.

COUNT ACHILLE BARAGUAY D'HILLIERS.

(Marshal of France, Vice-President of the Senate.)

Marshal D'Hilliers was born in Paris Sept. 6, 1795, entered the army while yet almost a child. He fought at the battle of Leipsic, where part of his left hand was carried away by a bullet. During the "Hundred Days," he embraced the cause of the Restoration, was assigned to the Royal Guards, and afterward ordered to Spain. In 1830 he joined the Algerian expedition, was appointed to the command of the military school of St. Cyr in 1836, and remained in that position till 1840, when he was placed at the disposal of the Governor-General of Algeria, led several expeditions against the Arabs, and was finally appointed Commander-in-Chief of Constantine. In 1851 he was instrumental in securing the success of the *coup d'état*, and was nominated a member of the Consultative Commission. At the outbreak of hostilities between the allies and Russia, the command of the expedition to the Baltic was conferred on him, when he took the fortress of Bomarsund. During the campaign of 1859 he commanded the first corps of the Army of the Alps, fought the battle of Melegnano, and took an important part in the battle of Solferino.

MARSHAL ELIE FREDERIC FOREY

(Senator),

was born in Paris on January 10, 1804; was admitted to the school of St. Cyr in 1822; took part in the expedition to Algeria, and distinguished himself at the battle of Médéah. In 1840, he was called to the command of a battalion of *chasseurs d'pied,* assisted in four expeditions into the interior of the Kabyle country, and after his return to France materially contributed to the success of the *coup d'état* of the Second of December, as an acknowledgment of which he was rewarded with the cross of Commander of the Legion of Honor, and by an appointment as General of Division. In the Crimea he commanded for a short time the troops around Sebastopol. During the Italian war he gave proof of his superior talent and bravery, and was the first French General who offered battle to the Austrians at Montebello, where, after a murderous engagement, he forced the enemy to retreat. In July, 1862, he was appointed Commander-in-Chief of the Mexican expedition, and led the remarkable attack on the fortress of Puebla, but returned to France in October, 1863, after transferring the command of the army into the hands of Marshal Bazaine.

COUNT JACQUES LOUIS CESAR ALEXANDRE RANDON

(Marshal of France),

was born at Grenoble March 25, 1795, enlisted in the French army at an early age, went into Russia with the grand army, and after the return of that disastrous expedition, fought at the battle of Lützen, where he was severely wounded. After the final overthrow of the first Empire, his well-known attachment to the cause of Napoleon retarded his military advancement, until, in 1838, he was appointed colonel of the Chasseurs d'Afrique, went into the French colony of Algeria, and distinguished himself during ten years of incessant warfare against the Arabs. After his return to France he was appointed Minister of War, in 1851, but handed in his resignation ere long, and returned to Algeria as Governor-General of that colony, which position he occupied at the time of its reorganization in 1858. In 1859 he was again appointed Minister of War, and as such remained in the Imperial Cabinet until he was relieved on January 19, 1867.

GENERAL WIMPFFEN.

(Surrenderer of Sedan.)

Emanuel Felix de Wimpffen, the general who has become famous by misfortune, has gone through the Algerian and provincial career of discipline and army experience usual in the French army. He belonged to the Imperial Guard in the Crimea, and was made general for his distinguished services in the Italian campaign. He was commandant of Algeria and of Oran. By a coincidence, there is an officer of the same name in the service of Austria, now a field-marshal.

General Wimpffen was strongly opposed to the surrender of Sedan. He proposed to cut his way through the Prussians. The timid heart of the Emperor overcame his resolution, and with an air of utter disconsolation he gave up his sword to the victorious Prussians.

PRUSSIA AND FRANCE COMPARED.

Prussia has a population of thirty-one millions, counting the whole North German Confederation, with Hanover, Hesse-Cassel, Schlsewig-Holstein, Frankfort, and the German States north of the river Main. The South German States number nine millions. Total, 40,000,000.

France has a population of 38,000,000.

Prussia has four iron-clad ships — the *King William*, *Prince William*, *Prince Charles*, and *Prince Adalbert* — and six iron clad gunboats armed with Krupp's guns.

France has forty-five iron-clads (11 entirely of iron).

Prussia, on a peace footing, has 480,000 men.

France, on a peace footing, has 434,000 men.

Prussia, on a war footing, has 970,000 men.

France, on a war footing, has 660,000 men.

Prussia has a war treasure of 200,000,000, and 200,000,000 in the government coffers.

France has 1,300,000,000 in the Bank of France.

By putting the finances of England at par —

France's	wealth	would	be	86	per	cent.
Prussia's	"	"	"	17	"	"
Belgium's	"	"	"	63	"	"
Holland's	"	"	"	71	"	"
Switzerland's	"	"	"	47	"	"
England's	"	"	"	100	"	"

As Prussia has now (including German troops) seventeen corps d'armée (680,000 men) in the field, or nearly ready to take the field, she is nearly on a war footing.

The standing army of the South German States is 170,325 men.

BAVARIAN ARMY.

War footing — Officers and men, 69,064; reserves, 25,757; garrison troops, 22,614; together with 17,236 horses and 240 guns.

WURTEMBERG ARMY.

The army in 1868 consisted of 34,405 men, of which 14,150 were in active service.

COMMANDERS OF THE PRUSSIAN ARMY,

WITH THEIR BIOGRAPHIES.

Commander-in-Chief, King William I.

Secretary of War and Marine, Albrecht Theodore Emil Von Roon.

Chief of Staff, and Military Adviser, General Count Von Moltke.

1st Army Commander (1st, 7th, 8th Corps), General Charles Frederick Von Steinmetz.

2d Army Commander (2d, 3d, 9th, and 10th Corps), Prince Frederick Charles of Prussia.

3d Army Commander (5th, 6th, 11th, and two Bavarian Corps), the Crown Prince (Frederick William).

4th Army Commander (4th, 12th Corps, Saxon and Prussian Guards), The Prince Royal of Saxony.

5th Army Commander (13 Corps Würtemberg and Baden Divisions), General Werder.

6th Army Commander (14th and 15th Corps Reserves), Grand Duke of Mecklenburg-Schwerin.

7th Army Commander (16th and 17th Corps Reserves), General Von Canstein.

NORTH GERMAN CONFEDERATION.

THIS CONFEDERATION WAS ESTABLISHED IN 1866, AND CONSISTS OF

PRUSSIA AND THE GERMAN STATES NORTH OF THE RIVER MAIN.

STATES.	AREA.	POPULATION.	RULER.	TITLE.	DATE OF ACCESSION.	GOVERNMENT.	NO. CHAMBERS
PRUSSIA	135,662	24,043,296	William I.	King.	1861	Limited Mon.	2 Chambers.
Mecklenburg-Schwerin	4,701	560,618	Fred. Francis II.	Grand Duke.	1842		
Saxe-Weimar	1,403	283,044	Chas. Alexander.	Grand Duke.	1853		
Mecklenburg-Strelitz	997	98,770	Fred. William.	Grand Duke.	1860	Limited Mon.	2 Chambers.
Saxony	5,701	2,423,401	John.	King.	1854	" "	2 "
Oldenburg	2,470	315,622	Peter.	Grand Duke.	1852	" "	2 "
Brunswick	1,525	303,401	William.	Duke.	1831	" Sov.	1 "
Saxe-Meiningen	968	180,335	George II.	Duke.	1866	" "	1 "
Saxe-Altenburg	491	141,426	Ernest.	Duke.	1853	" "	1 "
Saxe-Coburg-Gotha	790	168,735	Ernest II.	Duke.	1844	" "	1 "
Anhalt	1,017	197,041	Leopold.	Duke.	1817	" "	
Schwarzburg-Rudolstadt	405	75,074	Albert.	Prince.	1835	" "	1 Chamber.
Schwarzburg Sondershausen	358	67,500	Fred Gunther.	Prince.	1867	" "	1 "
Waldeck	455	58,805	George Victor.	Prince.	1852	" "	1 "
Reuss, Elder line }	} 558	} 43,899	Henry XII.	Prince.	1859	" "	1 "
Reuss, Younger line }		88,097	Henry XIV.	Prince.	1867	" Mon.	
Schaumburg-Lippe	170	31,186	Adolphus.	Prince.	1860	" "	1 Chamber.
Lippe-Detmold	445	111,352	Leopold II.	Prince.	1851	" "	1 "
Lubeck	142	48,538	Dr. Roeck.	Burgomaster.	1863	Free City.	
Bremen	112	109,572	Dr. Duckwitz.	Burgomaster.	1863	" "	
Hesse-Darmstadt (Up. Province)		252,451	Louis III.	Grand Duke.	1849	Limited Sov.	2 Chambers.
Hamburg	4,430	305,396	Dr. Seiveking.	Burgomaster.	1865	Free City.	
Total	162,790	29,907,359					
South German States		9,000,000					
		39,907,359					

This Table was arranged by Mr. George W. Bible, who wrote an admirable work on France and Prussia, in August, 1870.

GENERALS OF THE PRUSSIAN ARMY.

SOUTH GERMAN STATES.

The following comprise the South German States:

STATES.	Area.	Population	Revenue.	Public Debt	Ruler.	Title.	Date of Access
Bavaria* (deduct provinces ceded to Prussia).	170,688	7,774,464	Florins. 87,144,606	Florins. 334,405,150	Ludwig II	King.	1864
Würtemberg*...	7,568	1,748,328	Florins. 22,395,981	Florins. 126,860,470	Charles I.	King.	1864
Hesse-Darmstadt† (except the upper province, which belongs to N. Germany).	2,970	564,465	Guilders. 9,407,008	Florins. 2,088,000	Louis III.	Grand Duke	1849
Baden†	5,912	1,429,199	Florins. 28,898,998	Florins. 3,228,003	Frederick.	Grand Duke	1832
	187,138	11,516,456					

* Limited Monarchy; two chambers. † Limited Sovereignty; two chambers.

THE PRUSSIAN ARMY

is composed of 17 corps, each having 40,000 men — or a total of 680,000. There are (except in the corps of the guard) two divisions of infantry and one division of cavalry in each corps, or in all nearly 34 divisions of infantry, 17 divisions of cavalry, 58 brigades of infantry, and 34 brigades of cavalry. The last army corps formed have not full complement of cavalry.

The field army has 1272 guns.

The navy (peace footing) employs 1200 men, commanded by Prince Adalbert, Chief Admiral.

BIOGRAPHIES OF PRUSSIAN COMMANDERS.

KING WILLIAM I.

King William I. was born in 1797. His father was Frederick William III., and his grandfather was Frederick William II., nephew of Frederick the Great, born in Berlin in 1712. The mother of Frederick the Great was the sister of George I. of England. We will not dwell further on the house of Hohenzollern. Sufficient is it for the world to know that King William belongs to a race noted for integrity, zeal, and unflinching courage.

The supreme command of the German armies is exercised by the King. His Secretary of War is Von Roon, and his most reliable companion and military adviser is

GENERAL COUNT VON MOLTKE.

Moltke, Bismarck, and Von Roon are the great men of Europe: Von Roon for military organization, Bismarck for diplomacy, and Moltke for field strategy.* Moltke is the Sherman of the war, Von Roon the Stanton, and Bismarck the Seward. Von Moltke planned the victories of Königgrätz and Sadowa from the telegraph office in Berlin.

Von Moltke is by birth a Mecklenberger, and was born in 1800. He at first entered the service of Denmark, but at an early age transferred himself to that of Prussia, and devoted himself with unwearied energy to a scientific study of the conditions of success in war. In 1832 he became a staff officer, and three years later visited the East, where he was presented to the Sultan Mahmoud, who persuaded him to remain in Turkey several years, and take part in the military reforms of which the army stood greatly in need, and to assist in the Syrian campaign. Having returned to Prussia, he was appointed in 1856 aide-de-camp to the present King, at that time the Crown Prince. In 1858 he was appointed Chief of the General Staff. In this capacity he is believed to have drawn up the plan of an expedition intended to arrest the progress of the French arms in Italy, in 1859. Such at least was the suspicion of the French Emperor, which was supposed at the time to be the real cause of the sudden and surprising conclusion of the peace of Villafranca. In 1864 he accompanied Prince Frederic Charles, as chief of his staff, in the expedition which the former led against Denmark. His high reputation, however, rests on his most skilful direction of the war against Austria in 1866, the plan of which he had previously prepared. Moltke's name was very little heard of during the war, while those of his subordinates were trumpeted abroad. No man ever produced greater effects with less ostentation and noise. Only once, and then at Königgrätz, did he appear in front of the armies. Seated at his desk in the rear, he received through the field-telegraph a continuous stream of intelligence from all the corps, followed their movements on the map, transmitted his orders to the generals in command by the wires, and performed all this with such skill and foresight that not a movement failed, and every combination was made at the right moment. He is said to have worked out with his own hand, and himself calculated, almost every detail of those operations, the consequences of which have astonished Europe. After victory had been realized, Moltke was joined with Bismarck as plenipotentiary of Prussia for the negotiations with the South German States, and when the preliminary peace with Austria had been signed, he received the Order of the Black Eagle, the highest decoration which the King of Prussia has to confer.

* The day after the capitulation of Sedan the King of Prussia gave the following toast: "We must to-day, out of gratitude, drink the health of my brave army. You, War Minister Von Roon, have sharpened our sword; you, General Moltke, have guided it; you, my Fritz (Crown Prince) and Prince Charles of Saxony, have struck the blows; and you, Count Bismarck, have for years, by political diplomacy, brought Prussia to its position of unity and elevation."

ALBRECHT THEODORE EMIL VON ROON,

Minister of War and Marine, was born in the city of Colberg, April 30, 1803. He received his education in a Prussian military school, and was afterward assigned as a teacher to a similar institution in Berlin.

Besides his assiduous studies of everything connected directly with military science, he devoted himself especially to the publication of his now world-renowned topographical charts, and of works on history and geography. In 1831, he entered the Prussian army, and advanced step by step until he was appointed major-general in 1858, and shortly afterward Minister of War, in which position he applied himself diligently to the reorganization of the Prussian army. During the preparations for the campaign of 1866, he had occasion to prove to what point of perfection the process of mobilization had been carried in Prussia; and the number of troops, horses, and pieces of artillery, as well as the quantity of ammunition and provisions, which could be sent forward to the theatre of war at the shortest notice, are really astounding.

To Von Roon is due the credit of organizing the Prussian army. It was he who, in five days, threw 300,000 soldiers from Germany across the Rhine. Bismarck organized the States and made them Prussian, Von Roon organized their soldiers, Von Moltke distributed them in battle, and Prince Charles, the Crown Princes of Prussia and Saxony, and Von Steinmetz, have done the fighting.

PRINCE FREDERICK CHARLES OF PRUSSIA

(The Centre),

who commanded the First Army in 1866, and who won the battle of Gravelotte by his brilliant flank movement on Bazaine's right, is the eldest son of Prince Charles, the second brother of the King, and may be taken as the representative of the modern progressive Prussian officer.

He was born in 1828, has from his youth devoted himself to the military profession, is a general of cavalry, and holds a number of high appointments. He commanded in the war against Denmark in 1864. In 1866, he was placed at the head of the First Army destined to operate against Austria, entering Bohemia through Saxony, and so conducted his forces through the latter country as to make its people friends of Prussia. The extreme rapidity and energy of movement which he displayed in Bohemia disconcerted the Austrian general, Benedek, who had calculated upon being allowed to assume the offensive. In a series of actions he drove the Austrians to Sadowa, and won the great battle of Königgrätz, aided by the Crown Prince, who, bringing up the Second Army, effected his junction with Prince Frederick Charles at the crisis of the day. Prince Charles enjoys boundless popularity with the army. He has a prince's memory for names and persons, and has a kind word for everybody as he passes along. The soldiers know that he takes a strong and practical interest in their well-being, and that he has labored successfully to improve their position. A British officer, whom we have before quoted, and who accompanied the French army during its campaign, says, that with all the dash and fire of a cavalry officer, he can equally well lead his squadrons to pursue the broken enemy, and direct his infantry and artillery with patience in an attack against a firm and steady line. "He has a singular power of making his troops care little for fatigue and hardship; on the line of march he is always with his men, and can, by a few happy words, close up the straggling ranks of a weary battalion, and send the men forward cheering loudly." Prince Frederick Charles has labored strenuously, and with great success, to make the Prussian military system more elastic, giving greater freedom to the officers, and relying more upon moral means than upon rule and method in dealing with the men. The unexpected suppleness and dash which the Prussians displayed in 1866 is in a great measure the consequence of these reforms. He is the leading military man of Prussia.

CHARLES FREDERICK VON STEINMETZ

(The Right),

general of infantry and commander of the Fifth Army Corps, born December 27, 1796, was sent to the military school at Culm at the age of ten years, and soon showed a decided predilection for the army.

He was a little over sixteen years old when he was ordered to Berlin and assigned to the corps of General York. Two years later, he received his commission as lieutenant, was wounded at the battle of Dannigkow, fought with distinction at Königswartha, where a ball took away one of his fingers, while another wounded him severely in the thigh. But such was the ardor of his warlike temper, that, although unable to walk, he insisted upon taking part in the battle at Bautzen, in May, 1813, on horseback. He fought in France in nearly all the engagements of 1814, and entered Paris with the armies of the allies. During the long term of peace which followed, he studied military science to great advantage, and after advancing rapidly to the rank of captain, he was soon after assigned to the staff. During the dispute between Austria and Prussia, in 1850, on account of the Electorate of Hesse, Von Steinmetz was ordered to Cassel, and afterward appointed commandant of the place. Although it was his earnest desire to participate in the second campaign in Schleswig-Holstein, in 1864, he was ordered elsewhere, and had to remain inactive against his will. During the campaigns against Austria, Von Steinmetz commanded the Fifth Army Corps.

His triumphant victory at Skalitz, against a force twice as large as his own, gave him the name of the "Lion of Skalitz." He is the hardest fighter in the Prussian army. The trouble has always been to hold him back. It is said that Sigel took his lessons in hard fighting from Steinmetz. He is the Thomas of the war.

THE CROWN PRINCE (FREDERICK WILLIAM)

(The Left),

of Prussia, who commanded the Second Army four years ago, was born in 1831.

The chief of his staff in that campaign was Major-General Von Blumenthal, and he had under his orders three army corps, under Generals Von Bonin, Von Steinmetz, and Von

Mutius, besides the Guard Corps under Prince Augustus of Würtemberg. The Crown Prince led his army, composed of 125,000 men, from Silesia through the passes of the Sudetic Hills, an operation exposed to great difficulties and to considerable danger. By a series of brilliant operations the army pushed its way through the mountains, fighting severe actions at Trautenan, Nachod, Skalitz, and Schweinschadel. Before he had practically effected his junction with Prince Frederick Charles, General Benedek had made preparations to attack the latter with superior force, and the battle of Königgrätz was the result. The Crown Prince was urgently requested to hasten his advance, and appeared on the field, unexpected by the Austrians, in the middle of the battle, struck the heart of the Austrian position, and decided the fortunes of the day. The Crown Prince has the reputation of being careless of his own trouble, anxious for the welfare of his troops, visiting billets and hospitals personally, but not sparing his men or himself in the hour of trial and duty. His march from Miletin to Königgrätz, and his series of victories on entering Bohemia, are considered to have established his reputation as an energetic commander.

The Crown Prince has been the fighting man of the war. He destroyed Douay at Weisenburg, routed MacMahon at Woerth, pursued him in a scrub race to Châlons, and then to Sedan, where, with the Crown Prince of Saxony, he did all the fighting, and brought about the surrender of Napoleon. In the fighting before Paris he has always led the van.

THE CROWN PRINCE OF SAXONY.

(The Left Centre.)

The Crown Prince of Saxony is another of the fighting men of the army. It was his troops who, with the forces of the Crown Prince of Prussia, brought about the surrender of Sedan. He commands the fourth Prussian army, composed of the Prussian Guards under Prince Augustus of Würtemberg; the Fourth Corps, composed of men from the Saxon provinces of Prussia and from the Saxon Duchies of Weimar, Coburg, Gotha, Allenburg, and Meiningen, under General Von Alvensleben (the other Alvensleben commands the third Brandenburgers); and the twelve corps of his own Saxon troops, who fought with his Royal Highness in 1866, at Gitschin and Königgrätz, in Bohemia, against the army of Prussia.

It again comes to pass that, notwithstanding the former alliances and mutual obligations between Saxony and France, the heir-apparent to the Saxon throne leads a body of his father's soldiers in the present German war.

The Royal House of Saxony is the younger or Albertine branch of the ancient princely Saxon family. The elder branch, called the Ernestine, is subdivided into those reigning severally over the small principalities of Saxe-Altenburg, Saxe-Meiningen, Saxe-Coburg with Saxe-Gotha, and Saxe-Weimar; one of which, as all English people know, has given a husband to our Queen, and Kings to Portugal and Belgium. The story of the two brothers, Albert and Ernest, from whom these two Saxon lines of descent are named, has been told by Mr. Carlyle in one of his most interesting historical episodes. The different political and religious inclinations of their offspring, in many succeeding generations, have brought them into very different relations with Germany and Europe. The Ernestine branch has always been stoutly Protestant and stanchly German; while the Albertine princes, as Electors and then Kings of Saxony, have either intrigued for dominion in Poland or subserved the schemes of France. But the time seems now to have arrived when this long truant member of the German nationality becomes heartily and effectively at one with its neighbors in their common cause of patriotism and freedom. The people of Saxony, who are Protestants, are equal, at least, to the Prussians in their courage, sobriety, intelligence, and skill both of peaceful and warlike arts. They have their common schools, their busy and thriving factories; and, when they turn out to fight, there are no braver soldiers. The present King of Saxony, John I., though a Catholic, is not less popular with his Protestant subjects than was the late King of the Belgians with his subjects of the Catholic faith. He is an amiable and accomplished man, of literary tastes, author of a German translation of Dante, and of other poetical and philological essays. His Queen, Amelia Augusta, was a daughter of the late King Maximilian of Bavaria; and their eldest son, the Crown Prince Frederick Augustus Albert, was born April 23, 1828. His Royal Highness is married to a daughter of Prince Gustavus Vasa. He has proved himself a good soldier, and a worthy comrade of the two royal princes of Prussia.

CHARLES EBERHARD HERWARTH VON BITTENFELD,

general of infantry and commander of the Eighth Army Corps, born September 4, 1796, entered the Prussian army at the age of fifteen, fought at the battle of Leipsic, and took part in the invasion of France by the allies in 1814, where he served with distinction in several engagements and at the siege of Paris.

During the second campaign in Schleswig-Holstein, in 1864, he achieved one of the most brilliant victories over the Danish army, and virtually brought the war to a close by taking possession of one of the most important positions of the enemy, the island of Alsen, and by almost annihilating the troops who were ordered to defend the place. The war of 1866 again called him into active service. He was assigned to the command of the Elbe army, and gave many proofs of his superior talent as a military leader and organizer. His participation in the battle of Sadowa was a glorious one, and his behavior on this and several preceding occasions was such, that he is now considered one of the bravest, most skilful and talented commanding officers in the Prussian army.

On account of his extreme age he has lately been displaced as corps commander, General Goeben succeeding him to the command of the Eighth Corps. Steinmetz is of the same age as Bittenfeld — seventy-four, as is also Moltke. The Crown Prince and Prince Charles are younger men, the former being thirty-nine and the latter forty-two.

THE OTHER COMMANDERS

are Manteuffel, of the First Corps; Fansecki, of the Second; Alvensleben (2d), of the Third; Alvensleben (1st), of the Fourth; Kirchbach, of the Fifth; Tumpling, of the Sixth; Zastrow, of the Seventh; Goeben, of the Eighth; Manstein, of the Ninth; Voigts Rhetz, of the Tenth; Böse, of the Eleventh; Crown Prince of Saxony, of the Twelfth; Werder, of the Thirteenth; Canstein, of the Fourteenth; Loewenfeld, of the Fifteenth; Mecklenburg, of the Sixteenth; and Prince Augustus of Würtemberg, of the Guards.

Tuesday, *August* 2.—The heights of Saarbrück stormed by the French. Napoleon telegraphs the Empress, announcing that the Prince Imperial had received his "baptism of fire." Agitation in England on the subject of Belgian neutrality and independence. Italy arming and preparing for war. The evacuation of Rome progressing. The King of Prussia arrives at Mayence.

STATUS AND NUMBERS OF TROOPS.

First Corps, McMahon, 45,000 men, at Strasburg.

Second Corps, Frossard, 32,000 men, at Forbach and St. Avold.

Third Corps, Bazaine, 32,000 men, at Metz.

Fourth Corps, L'Admirault, 32,000 men, at Thionville.

Fifth Corps, De Failly, 32,000 men, at Bitche and Saarguemines.

Sixth Corps, Canrobert, 70,000 men, at Châlons.

Seventh Corps, Douay, 32,000 men, at Besançon and Belfort.

Eighth Corps (Guards), Bourbaki, 32,000 men, at Metz.

Cavalry, 34,000. Total, 303,000. With artillery and reserve cavalry, about 350,000 men.

The left wing has before it the Moselle and the French Nied, the centre has before it the Saar, and the right wing has before it the Lauter.

The German armies, having been assembled at camps on the Rhine, begin to move forward. The entire German force consists of eighteen corps d'armée, containing 40,000 men each, at their normal strength. The First army, under Steinmetz, has the First, Seventh, and Eighth Corps; the Second army, under Prince Frederick Charles, has the Second, Third, Ninth, and Tenth corps; the Third army, under the Prussian Crown Prince, has the Fifth, Sixth, and Eleventh Corps, and the two Bavarian Corps. The Fourth army, under the Crown Prince of Saxony, containing the Fourth and Twelfth Corps, and the Saxon and Prussian Guards, occupies in the regular advance the right of the Crown Prince; the Fifth army, under General Werder, has the Würtemberg and Baden divisions, engaged in the siege of Strasburg; the reserves are composed of the Sixth army, under the Grand Duke of Mecklenburg-Schwerin, on the Rhine, and the Seventh army, under Generals Von Canstein at Berlin, and

Loewenfeld in Silesia. The defence of the northern coast is committed to these reserves. The advance to the French lines is made by the First army, against the French left wing; Second army, Prince Frederick Charles, against the centre; and the Third army, Crown Prince of Prussia, against the French right wing.

The French forces being scattered over a line of eighty-five to ninety miles in length, MacMahon, after a council at Metz, receives orders to make a flank march toward De Failly, at Bitche. He posts the corps of General Douay at Weisenburg to cover the movement. General Frossard, with the Second Corps, advances on Saarbrück, and after seven hours' fighting drives out the three battalions of infantry, three squadrons of cavalry, and three guns, which formed the German force there. The Emperor was present with the Prince Imperial.

SAARBRÜCK (*August* 2).

NAPOLEON'S DESPATCH.

METZ, *August* 2.

TO THE EMPRESS EUGENIE:

"*Louis has received his baptism of fire.* He was admirably cool, and little impressed. A division of Frossard's command carried the heights overlooking the Saar. The Prussians made a brief resistance. Louis and I were in front, where the bullets fell about us. Louis keeps a ball he picked up. The soldiers wept at his tranquillity. We lost an officer and ten men. "NAPOLEON."

(Translated from the French.)

THE BATTLE, AUGUST 2.

SPICHEREN, *August* 2, 8 A.M. — The troops are moving to the front. Marshal Lebœuf has just passed towards General Frossard's headquarters on the heights of Spicheren. A portion of Bazaine's army in reserve supports Frossard.

Ten A.M. — The videttes of Cartoul's brigade have gone to the front. Artillery and infantry are descending the hill, marching across the plain, and ascending another hill in front of Saarbrück. In the middle of the plain the infantry deploys skirmishers and masses battalions. In their rear additional artillery is placed in position on the heights. The skirmish line advances across the valley, followed by the battalions, and keeping some distance.

Half-past ten A.M. — The heights on the other side of the valley above St. Arnual and opposite Saarbrück are not so easily reached. The infantry halt, and the guns open fire on the Prussians in the village of St. Arnual. Now Colonel Thebaudin carries the village with the Sixty-seventh, and the troops rush up the hill opposite Saarbrück. The Sixty-sixth drives the Prussians from the exercising grounds. Batteries are now planted so as to sweep the Prussians about and in the town of Saarbrück, who return our fire, falling back across the bridge to the height on the east bank of the Saar.

Twelve M. — The Emperor arrives. The Prussians are on the retreat. We fire after them. The *mitrailleuse* is used for the first time. The Prussians are not to be seen. The battle ends.

Two P.M. — We occupy the ground held by the Prussians. The bridge over the Saar has been blown up.

Evening.—The French loss is twenty killed and fifty wounded. We captured a few prisoners, but no cannon. The Prince Imperial has gone back to Forbach with the Emperor.

PRUSSIAN ACCOUNT (*August* 2).

(Translated from the German.)

SAARBRUCK, 10 A.M. — Our videttes have been driven in from St. Arnual. Two large bodies of French troops are advancing toward the parade ground ; and it seems as if the one battalion of German troops will retreat from the town fighting.

Evening. — Our orders are not to challenge battle, but in case of attack to fall back. At ten o'clock this morning the small detachment at Saarbrück was attacked by three divisions of the French army, and a fire from twenty-three guns was opened upon the town.

The Prussian detachment evacuated the heights of the drilling ground at noon, and the town at two this afternoon. A retrograde movement was then made to the next defences. The losses on the Prussian side are comparatively small. According to the statement of a prisoner, the Emperor Napoleon arrived on the ground in front of Saarbrück at eleven o'clock this forenoon. Perhaps a dozen of our men have been killed and wounded.

At one time there was a cannonade from Ludwigswald, a mile and a half to the left of Saarbrück, to the extremity of the forest of St. Arnual. The Prussian forces blew up the bridge over the Saar.

The French division engaged in the fighting at Saarbrück was the second of General Frossard's army corps, and was commanded by General Bataille.

We captured four officers and seventy privates. They had gotten too far in advance, and we cut them off.

REMARK BY THE AUTHOR. — The future historian may make more or he may make less of this day's skirmish. I contend that the first account of battles by actual witnesses are the truest ever written. J. T. Headley has fought on paper battles which would astonish the first Napoleon, though he was the central figure in the fight. This battle of the hero of Strasburg and Boulogne some coming Abbott may transform to a second battle of Sarguntum. Who ever made truer history than George Smalley made at Antietam, Dr. Russell at Bull Run, or E. C. Steadman at Manassas?

SAARBRÜCK.

Most travellers familiar with the Rhine country may remember Saarbrück, with the great castle or château, and its curious Gothic church, on the top of the hill, containing the tombs of the departed Herzoggs of Nassau, and other relics of bygone days. It is on the left bank of the Saar, which, tumbling down from its cool sources in the heart of the Vosges, here becomes navigable. It is a really beautiful spot. The gardens and public promenades of the town are most lovely and picturesque, and the town itself lies embosomed in a valley, at the base of a succession of hills, which enclose and protect it.

FRENCH OFFICIAL ACCOUNT OF SAARBRUCK, AUGUST 2.

(Translation of General Frossard's account to the Emperor.)

SIRE: — I have the honor to report to your Majesty the movements effected this day by the Second Army Corps, in pursuance of your orders — to take possession of the positions on the left bank of the Saar, which command the heights of Saarbrücken. General Bataille's division, supported on the right by that of General Laveaucoupet, and one of the twelve-pounder batteries of the reserve, and on the left by the first brigade of the division of General Verge, with a second battery of twelve-pounders, formed the first line. General Bastoul, encamped at Spicheren, and entrusted with the duty of directing the movement on our right, was ordered to send two battalions to occupy the village of St. Arnual and the heights above it, whilst the remainder of his brigade, crossing the ravine in front of Spicheren, was to make a front attack on the positions to the right of the road from Forbach to Saarbrücken. The other brigade of the Bataille division was to move on to the position known as the exercising ground. Three squadrons of the Fifth Mounted Chasseurs preceded it to clear the way. Finally, Colonel Du Ferron, of the Fourth Mounted Chasseurs, with two battalions of the first brigade of the Verge division, was to push on a reconnoissance to Guerswiller, to connect the movement of the Second Corps with that of Marshal Bazaine. The troops left their bivouacs between nine and ten o'clock. Lieutenant-Colonel Thebaudin, with two battalions of his regiment (the Sixty-seventh), in advancing to the attack of the village of St. Arnual, found it strongly occupied, and defended by batteries of position planted on the right bank of the Saar. To demolish this artillery, General Micheler, whose brigade had come forward to support the movement of General Bastoul, ordered into action a battery of the Fifteenth regiment, which effectually opened fire on the Prussian guns. Supported by a battalion of the Fortieth regiment of the line, and by the company of sappers and miners of the third division, materially assisted by the flank movement of Colonel Mangin, who, with the remainder of the Sixty-seventh regiment, and the Sixty-sixth regiment, descended the heights on the left, Lieutenant-Colonel Thebaudin was able to carry the village of St. Arnual, and occupied it with a battalion of the Fortieth regiment, and the company of sappers and miners. The battalions of the Sixty-seventh, with great *élan*, rushed up the slopes of the hillock of St. Arnual, and established themselves on the crest, opposite Saarbrücken. The Sixty-sixth, with equal resolution, took possession of the heights up to the exercising ground, driving the enemy from all his positions. At the same time, General Bataille rapidly moved his First brigade to the rising ground on the left of the Saarbrücken road, connecting his movement with that of his Second brigade by advancing a battalion of the Thirty-third regiment. Advancing in line, the battalions of the Twenty-third and Eighth regiments, their front covered by numerous skirmishers, resolutely carried the many ravines which run across the ground, which is very difficult and thickly wooded. One battalion of the Eighth regiment, working its way across the woods, followed the railway as far as the village of Frotrany, where it effected its junction with the other battalions of the regiment, and together they attacked the exercising ground of the right. On gaining the heights, General Bataille planted one of his batteries in front of the lines of the Sixty-sixth regiment, and another on the exercising ground, to fire on the railway station and silence the enemy's artillery, which had taken up a position on the left of Saarbrücken. It was unable to sustain our fire, and had to fall back. The 12-pounder battery of the reserve was ordered by me to support the fire of the batteries on the exercising ground; and finally a battery of mitrailleuses of the Second division threw into utter disorder the enemy's columns of infantry, which were evacuating the town. During this artillery duel, the troops were able to

ACCLAIM HIS MAJESTY

the Emperor and the Prince Imperial, on the very ground from which they had just dislodged the enemy. The movements of the infantry were excellently seconded by the Fifth regiment of horse chasseurs, under the orders of Colonel de Sereville. The squadrons, supported by infantry in skirmishing order, searched every nook in the ground, and rapidly gained all the crests of the hills whence they could descry the enemy. The Twelfth battalion of foot chasseurs, and the company of sappers and miners of the Second division, formed the reserve of General Bataille. They joined the troop of the First brigade on the exercising ground. The First brigade of the Verge division, which formed the second line, constantly kept at four hundred or five hundred metres of the first line, and availed themselves of every rise in the ground to cover themselves. The reports I have received up to this time announce the following losses: The Sixty-sixth regiment had one officer killed, M. De Bar, lieutenant of the *francs-tireurs;* Captain Adjutant-Major Privat has a very dangerous gunshot wound; Lieutenant Laramey received a bullet through his shoulder; fifteen or sixteen rank and file were killed or wounded. The Sixty-seventh had no casualty among its officers; rank and file, twenty men killed or wounded. The Eighth regiment, two rank and file wounded. The Third division reports a sergeant killed and a private wounded. I have not received the report of Colonel Du Ferron. I am told that he was engaged, and had about ten men wounded. Neither have I received the report of the commander of the Tenth battalion of foot chasseurs, which has pushed forward on the right, along the road from Sarreguemines to Saarbrücken. The troops are encamped on the ground they have gained. I have had a few entrenchments thrown up in front and flank of their position. Some *épaulements* have also been established, to protect our guns and gunners. I was greatly pleased with the dash and resolution of the troops. They showed great energy in marching up steep ground, and also in action. The heads of the several corps congratulate themselves on the steadiness of their men, their intrepidity, and the growing confidence they show in their weapons. I will make known to your Majesty the names of the officers and men of all ranks who specially merit being pointed out. Our losses amount to six killed and sixty-seven wounded. Receive, etc.,

FROSSARD.

WEDNESDAY, *August* 3. — Skirmishing near Saarbrück and elsewhere. Proclamation of King William to the army. The French Garde Mobile preparing for the front. A levy *en masse* ordered by Prussia for the defence of the seacoast. Newspaper correspondents expelled from the French lines. The French fortify the Spicheren hills back of Saarbrück. First news from American correspondents at the seat of war published to-day in the *Tribune.*

PROCLAMATION OF THE KING OF PRUSSIA.

MAYENCE, *August* 3.—The King of Prussia has issued the following proclamation:

"To the Army:—All Germany stands unanimously in arms against a neighboring State, who has surprised us by declaring a war against us without any motive. The defence of the threatened Fatherland, of our honor, and our hearths, is at stake. To-day I undertake the command of the whole army, and I advance cheerfully to a contest, which, in former times, our fathers, similarly situated, fought gloriously. The whole Fatherland, as well as myself, trusts confidently in you. The Lord God will be with our righteous cause. WILLIAM."

FRENCH STATUS.

METZ, *August* 3.—The day is tranquil. French officers begin to look serious. The Prussian armies outnumber the French, and it begins to look like a bloody war ahead. The hope of being able to detach a powerful corps across the Rhine, or to North Germany, so as to effect a diversion while the main army advanced to Mayence, has well nigh, if not altogether vanished, as the German army is now so strong as to require the whole French army to meet it. French armies hold the fortified towns of:

THIONVILLE, with a population of ten thousand, on our left.

STRASBURG, with its garrison of eight thousand, on our right.

BITCHE, defended by a strong citadel, is in front of MacMahon.

METZ is to be the impregnable centre of France.

THURSDAY, *August* 4.—German invasion of France began this day. The forces of the Crown Prince surprise a French division at Weisenburg, and after a bloody battle, rout it. Five hundred prisoners and a piece of artillery were captured. Loss on both sides heavy. MacMahon abandons the idea of crossing the Rhine.

FORCES.

French — First Corps (MacMahon); Seventh Corps (Douay), 75,000.

German — Second Bavarian, Fifth (Kirchbach), Eleventh (Böse), 120.000.

WEISENBURG.

The Third German army, under the Crown Prince of Prussia, crosses the Lauter, and advances upon the corps of General Douay posted behind the fortifications of Weisenburg. These defences extend from the town of Lauterburg, northwesterly to Weisenburg. After crossing the Rhine at Maxau, the Baden and Würtemberg troops marched against Lauterburg; the Fifth and Eleventh Prussian Corps marched west of the Rhine against the centre of the works; and the Bavarian Fourth Division against Weisenburg. The first shot was fired at half-past eight in the morning. The Crown Prince stood on the Schweigen hill, north of the town. Weisenburg was occupied by the Seventy-fourth French regiment, and on the Geisburg hill, south of the place, were the First Turco regiment, Fifth and Fiftieth line, three light batteries of artillery, and one of mitrailleuses. These troops also occupied Altstadt, on the right of the French position. Altstadt was quickly taken by the Ninth Prussian division; Weisenburg, after sharp resistance, by the Bavarians and some battalions of the Forty-seventh and Forty-eighth regiments; and the grenadiers marched against the Schafenburg hill where the mitrailleuses were stationed. The mitrailleuses did not do the terrible execution expected of them; the German columns steadily advanced without firing a shot, and the position was taken. There was no fight at Lauterburg, which was found to be unoccupied by the French, and after midday all the German troops were concentrated for the action at Weisenburg. The defeat of the French became a rout, which was continued in disorder to Woerth. Thus, in this first combat between the veteran troops of the French and the citizen soldiers of Prussia, the former were not only completely beaten, but showed an ominous lack of steadiness and *morale.* The German losses were over 700 in killed and wounded. The French losses were much greater in killed and wounded, and one gun and 1000 prisoners were also taken from them.

CROWN PRINCE'S DESPATCH.

WEISENBURG, *August* 6, 7 *P.M.* — "We have won a brilliant but bloody victory. The left wing was the attacking body, and consisted of the Fifth and Eleventh Prussian Corps, with the Second (Bavarian). This force carried by an assault, under the eyes of the Prince Royal, the fortress of Weisenburg and the heights between Weisenburg and Geisburg.

"Douay's division of Marshal MacMahon's corps was splendidly defeated, being driven from its camp. General Douay himself was killed. Five hundred prisoners were taken. None of them were wounded. Many Turcos were among the captured. The Prussian General Kirchbach was slightly wounded. The Royal Grenadiers and the Fiftieth regiment of the line suffered heavy losses."

The King ordered the attack upon the French outposts by telegraph.

THE BATTLE.

Prussian Account.

This is the first German victory. Weisenburg, until the 4th of August, 1870, a French fortress of third rank, is an old German town, chartered in the year 1247 as one of the ten free cities in Alsacia, conquered 1673 by Louis XIV.; twice retaken, 1744 and 1793, by the Germans, but ultimately taken possession of by France. Much importance was always attached to Weisenburg, as evident from the fate of Beauharnais, who, having suffered defeat in the year 1793, when he was routed by the Germans under Prince of Waldeck and General Würmser, was beheaded by the guillotine.

The small town of Weisenburg lies on the little river Lauter, which, flowing in the Bavarian palatinate, forms the boundary between Germany and France, and empties into the Rhine at Lauterburg. It lies in a beautiful valley, at the foot hills of the Vosges, five hundred feet above the level of the sea, and is distant but three and a half miles (German) from the French fortress Haguenau, and seven miles from Strasburg. The last census gives the population of the industrious little town at 5570, occupied in the vine culture, weaving, tanning, printing, brick-making, felt, glove, comb, etc., manufacture. It contains a college, two Catholic and one Lutheran church, a synagogue, a theatre, etc.

FORTIFICATIONS.

The present fortifications are of the eighteenth century. They were commenced in 1705, by order of Marshal Villars, and extend along the banks of the Lauter for two and a half miles (over eleven English miles), being an unbroken series of moats, walls, and bastions, which, during the Peninsular war and the war of the French revolution, have repeatedly been the scenes of bloody engagements. These defences, called the "Weisenburg lines," or "*les lignes de la Lutter*," run zigzag, flanked by formidable redoubts, and were considered, prior to the successful storm of the Germans, in 1793, as very strong.

THE BATTLE.

The fight commenced on the 4th inst., at eight o'clock, A.M. It was known that General Douay, with the van, stood in Weisenburg, while the larger part of his division occupied a strong position on the Geisburg, an elevation distant about one and a half English mile south of the town, seven hundred and fifty-seven feet above the level of the sea. Under cover of the fire of the Prussian and Bavarian artillery, the storming regiments were forced to wade through ditches for half an hour. It was the Second Bavarian Army Corps, under Lieutenant-General Count Bothmer, and the Eleventh Prussian Army Corps, under the Crown Prince, both thoroughly combined, and to the number of about eighty thousand, who led the attack. The strong works, which the enemy bravely defended by a murderous fire, were finally taken, Prussians and Bavarians vieing with each other in deeds of boldness, and not halting until they arrived in the centre of the town. Here they were met by fresh French regiments, and it now became a close combat. Previous to it, the Prussian and Bavarian artillery had distinguished itself by excellent firing, throwing thirteen-pound grenades and fifteen-pound shells with the utmost precision.

Considering the great disadvantages of the ground which had to be overcome by the storming troops, their position when inside the town and opposed to fresh divisions of the enemy, was rather critical; but at this juncture they were reinforced by the Fifth Army Corps, under General Von Kirchbach, successor to the celebrated General Steinmetz, who did such wonders with the same troops in 1866, who, instantly surveying and comprehending the situation, threw his forces against the right flank of the French, and with such irresistible vehemence, that soon after the enemy was driven not only from Weisenburg, but from the walls and fortifications in its rear, and thereby forced to retire to the aforementioned Geisburg. The storming of this well-fortified elevation could now take place on three sides. *A murderous fire met the Germans,* whose cavalry, owing to the peculiar formation of the ground, could but little participate in the action. The fighting here was almost as severe as at Königgrätz, but German tenacity triumphed. Position after position was taken by bayonet, and with the cry of "Hurrah!" and "King William," the Germans fought like lions, until, at two o'clock in the afternoon, the whole division of the enemy was routed, and, leaving behind dead and wounded, camp materials, horses, etc., in full flight. At four o'clock, P.M., the Germans were seven English miles beyond Weisenburg, in the village of Betschdorf.

The number of prisoners was eight hundred, and so excellent was the plan of operation, that they found themselves surrounded without the possibility of escape. Many of them belong to the Algerian troops of McMahon's corps, and did not seem sorry at their mishap. Douay, the general of division, was killed. The Prussian General Von Kirchbach received a slight wound in the face.

A Prussian regiment on a war footing has 3000 men, with 69 officers. Of these 69 officers, the Seventy-fourth regiment (Hanoverians) lost no less than 30 in killed and wounded at Weisenburg. The Seventy-seventh (also Hanoverians), on the same occasion lost 25 officers; the Thirty-ninth (Rhinelanders), 26; the Eighty-second (Hessians), 19; the Ninety-fifth (Thuringians), 16; the Eighty-third (Hessians), 14; the Fifty-third (Westphalians), 11; the Eighty-eighth (Nassauers), 9; the Eightieth (Hessians), 8.

FRENCH ACCOUNT OF WEISENBURG.

(Translated.)

While General Douay's division, composed of the Seventy-fourth and Fiftieth regiments of the line; the Sixteenth battalion of chasseurs, on foot; one regiment of mounted chasseurs, and one regiment of Turcos, were engaged, yesterday, in the neighborhood of Weisenburg, they were actually startled by a tremendous discharge of artillery. As the patrols which had been posted all along the frontier had not signalled the presence of any Prussian troops, the men believed for a moment that they were surrounded by the enemy. This was not the case, but Prussians in great force and well supplied with artillery appeared on the heights of Schwergen, occupying the whole of the country near a small Bavarian village.

Our soldiers were at their soup, when they were surprised by the first attack of the Prussians. Most of the Turcos were at that moment bathing. The surprise was so sudden and the call to combat so pressing, that some of them had scarcely time to slip on their pantaloons, while many others, seizing their pieces, rushed quite naked into action. An African colonel, who heard the fact related, said that he had often seen Kabyles in Algeria fight in a nude state. Under such circumstances, the Turcos fought like lions. They precipitated themselves with an indescribable fury on the Prussians, and took nine guns, but as they were hauling them off, they were crushed by grapeshot.

General Douay ordered his troops to advance before the enemy, keeping as much as possible behind Weisenburg, which lay between them and the Prussian forces. But this precaution proved quite useless, because the guns were pouring a tremendous fire upon them, and the troops were falling in great numbers in the town of Weisenburg itself. The French retired from their former position, and commenced marching on the right side of the town. The Prussian guns were firing at a tremendous rate, and their shot and shells fell equally in Weisenburg and among the troops. Several houses were on fire, and a large number of soldiers lay dead or wounded.

General Vohcan's division was beginning to retire at about eleven o'clock, when a new attack was ordered. The Turcos led the way, and, bayonet in hand, threw themselves on one of the Prussian batteries. All proved to be useless, Had the French insisted on attacking the enemy any longer, there would not have been a Frenchman left on the ground alive. As soon as what was left of General Douay's forces began retiring, the Prussian artillery began playing upon them. It was about twelve o'clock when General Douay himself fell, a victim to Prussian artillery. The troops began to run without order, crossing roads and vineyards until they again reached the farthest part of Weisenburg.

The number of dead and wounded must be very large indeed. The remaining troops are eager to avenge the death of their General.

Both killed and wounded were literally hacked to pieces by the Prussians. It was owing to those horrible engines of destruction, and after these savage brutalities, that the enemy remained in possession of the guns, which the intrepidity of our too ardent companions in arms had captured in their ranks. Some companies of Turcos, and notably that in which M. Albert Duruy, a volunteer, had taken service, had, after this heroic combat, only five men left. M. Duruy, son of the late Minister, was one of those miraculously preserved.

FRIDAY, *August* 5. — Great excitement in Paris, caused by the defeat of the French. Skirmishes at various points. MacMahon moves his corps from Haguenau to Froschweiler.

The French defeat at Weisenburg calamitous. Crown Prince Frederick William pursues MacMahon towards Haguenau. The French cease to give news of battles. The Crown Prince and Von Steinmetz proclaim the forward march! Prince Charles issues a proclamation on invading French soil. Three Prussian armies (480,000 men and 1270 guns) marching into France.

PARIS.

PARIS, *August* 5. — The following proclamation forebodes bad news for France:

The Council of Ministers to the population of Paris: Inhabitants of Paris, in the name of the country, in the name of our heroic army, we beg you to be calm, patient, and to keep order. Disorder in Paris would be a victory for the Prussians. As soon as any certain news arrives, whether good or bad, you will know it. Let us be united, and have but one thought, one wish, one sentiment — the success of our arms.

August 6, 1870, six o'clock.

Emile Ollivier, Duc de Gramont, Chevandier de Valdrôme, Segris, Général De Jean, Admiral Rigault de Genouilly, Plichon, Louvet, Maurice Richard, De Parieu.

JOY IN BERLIN.

Dense crowds assembled to-day in front of the Royal Palace, to whom the King's despatch announcing the victory at Weisenburg was read by order of the Queen, causing great enthusiasm. Buildings are generally covered with flags, and there is to be an illumination to-night.

Subscriptions to the war loan already exceed 120,000,000 thalers.

The substantial fruits of the Crown Prince's victory are said to be the destruction of one side of the French quadrilateral, and the cutting off of MacMahon's corps from its northern connections.

The loss of the Prussians was heavy, but they took eight

hundred prisoners and the town. There is the greatest enthusiasm here, and a crowd around the palace is waiting to cheer the King.

THE SITUATION.

SAARBRUCK (*Evening*). — The three Prussian armies are moving.

THE FIRST ARMY, Von Steinmetz, with the First, Seventh, and Eighth Corps of 120,000 men and 250 guns, is at Saarbrück, in front of Frossard's Second Corps (French), reinforced by divisions from Bazaine and L'Admirault, in all about 60,000 men.

This order from Steinmetz has filled his soldiers with enthusiasm:

SOLDIERS, — You will have the opportunity of standing in presence of the enemy. With God's help you will maintain your old fame, and add new laurels to those on your standards of the year 1866, when I had the honor to lead you; and the Fatherland will look with pride upon her sons. Show that you belong to an army worthy of the civilization of centuries, by a calm and friendly demeanor, temperate bearing, respecting the positions of strangers, whether friend or foe. Each one of you bears the honor and the fame of the whole Fatherland.

THE THIRD ARMY, Crown Prince Frederick William, with the Fifth, Sixth, Eleventh, and two Bavarian corps, of 200,000 men and 460 guns, advances from Weisenburg along the Geisburg hills, driving before him the defeated soldiers of MacMahon and Douay, reinforced by De Failly's Fifth Corps from Bitche —110,000 men.

The victorious troops of the Crown Prince are stimulated by this address of Fritz:

SOLDIERS, — By command of the King, you begin to-day the forward march against the enemy. The sons of Prussia have always distinguished themselves in presence of the enemy. On this occasion, too, you will win laurels, so that the Fatherland can look upon you with pride. Show by a calm demeanor toward friend and foe that you are worthy children of Prussia.

THE SECOND ARMY, Prince Frederick Charles, with the Second, Third, Ninth, and Tenth Corps, 160,000 men and 460 guns, is moving towards the front from Homburg.

With the eyes of his enthusiastic soldiers fixed upon the green hills of France, Prince Charles thus addresses them:

SOLDIERS OF THE SECOND ARMY! —You enter upon the soil of France. The Emperor Napoleon has, without any reason, declared war upon Germany, and his army are our enemies. The French people has not been asked if it wished to carry on a bloody war with its German neighbors. A reason for enmity is not to be found. Meet the feeling of the peaceable inhabitants of France with a like sentiment; show them that in our century two civilized peoples do not forget their humanity, even in warring with each other. Bear always in mind how your fathers would have felt if an enemy, which God forbid, overran our provinces. Show the French that the German people confronting its enemy is not only great and brave, but also well controlled and noble-minded.

The Prussians have now ready to throw into the fight (exclusive of Prince Charles) 320,000 men and 710 guns; and with Prince Charles, 520,000 men and 1170 guns. The French have ready for fighting, 319,000 men. Their entire force to-day (reserves and all) is 350,000 men.

The odds in favor of Prussia is startling. I do not wonder that the French Generals begin to abandon the idea of carrying the war into Prussia.

SATURDAY, *August 6.* — Bloody battle of Saarbrück (Spicheren), between Steinmetz and Frossard (Steinmetz, 120,000; Frossard, 60,000). The first Prussian army was engaged from midday until after dusk; spirited and very heavy fighting between Saarbrück and Forbach. Fourteenth German division opened the battle; was supported by three battalions and one battery of the Sixteenth division; three battalions, two batteries, and cavalry of the Second army in succession, against the enemy, who was also constantly reinforced; the heights of Spicheren, south of the parade ground, were stormed, and the enemy thrown back on Forbach and Metz in disorder. The Prussians captured 2500 prisoners, 4 guns, a pontoon train, 10,000 woollen blankets, 40,000 cloths of rice, and $5000 worth of rum and tobacco. The Fifth German division lost 239 dead and 1800 wounded; the Twelfth regiment 832 dead and wounded.

WOERTH.

The same day the Crown Prince attacked MacMahon at Woerth, where he was strengthened by divisions of the corps of De Failly and Canrobert. The French suffered a terrible defeat, and lost 6000 prisoners, including 100 officers; also 2 eagles, 6 mitrailleuses, 35 cannon, 42 wagons and carriages, 200 horses, the baggage and camp tents of two divisions, and two railway trains with provisions; the military chest of the Fourth French division, with 220,000 francs, was captured. General François was killed. The First division of First Bavarian Corps lost 36 officers and 800 men dead and wounded. The Würtemberg corps lost 6 officers and 23 men dead, 10 officers and 225 men wounded, and 118 men missing. The Crown Prince had 200,000 men, MacMahon had 80,000.

SAARBRUCK (*SPICHEREN*).

(AUG. 6.)

At one P.M. to-day, General Goeben advanced Prussian skirmishers from the Eighth Corps (Rhineland), driving the French videttes from the village of Saarbrück. The entire Eighth Corps now formed across the Saar and through the town. A small French force, encamped on the exercising ground (a large even space for holding reviews and fairs), immediately fell back toward Frotrany and Spicheren. The French, after some fighting, all fell sullenly back under cover of the hills of Spicheren, a position of natural defence, besides defended by earthworks bristling with cannon and one battery of mitrailleuses, Gen. Zastrow, of the Seventh Corps, was ordered to move through a series of ravines and make a flank assault from the woods on the French left, while Goeben fought his way over the plains directly in front of the French centre (Spicheren hill).

At two P.M. the Prussian artillery commenced a fearful cannonade, which was replied to with equal vigor by the French.

Position after position was carried along the plain, until the French even abandoned the village of Spicheren. The last Frenchman had fled up the hill in front of Goeben's victorious advance, commanded by Von Kamecke. (Goeben, at this time in command, occupied a sightly position in the rear, while Steinmetz had not yet reached the army, but was hurrying up as fast as possible.) The Prussian army had before it a bloody job. 40,000 Frenchmen were in front. 80,000 Prussians were advancing full of daring — ready to storm Gibraltar itself. They had before them the work of Hooker at Chancellorsville.

THE BATTLE GROWS.

At three P.M. the cannonade was a deafening roar — but it was the roar which precedes an assault. The Fortieth, Thirty-seventh, Seventy-fourth (Hanoverian), Twelfth and Third Regiments, were selected to do the fearful work. It was to be a second Balaklava—"into the jaws of Death!" The brave Hanoverians, whom Napoleon had said would never fight the French, were given the post of honor, and were to lead the assault. The word was given. Amid the deafening artillery roar, ten thousand men throw down their knapsacks, and rush across the intervening plain and up the hill. With a rush the artillery limbers up, following the infantry, with pauses to fire. The French fire from the hill is fearful. Bullets rain down upon the Prussians, leaving a harvest of death behind them. The charge goes on. A few leading companies actually reach the crest, but only to die. The Prussians are repulsed, and back comes a scattered caravan, decimated, but not conquered—

> "All that was left of them,
> Left of six hundred!"

The French begin to find their position in danger. Frossard sends word to Bazaine's advance to hurry forward.

They are not fighting in Italy to-day: they are fighting the victorious soldiers of the "Lion of Skalitz"—fighting men who conquered at Königgrätz.

Again Kamecke with his brave Hanoverians, reinforced by a portion of Manteuffel's First Corps, prepares for the

SECOND ASSAULT.

The troops are eager, and re-form as if by magic.

The force is increased to 15,000. The artillery limbers up, advances, and belches forth a nearer fire. The French reply weakly. They are saving their fire. The second assault commences. 15,000 men file up the foot of the hill at a double quick, and then break into a run. The French fire opens again. The French cannon tear through the Prussian ranks. The whiz of the *mitrailleuse* and clatter of chassepôts have no terror for Prussia. The Prussian advance stops. *It is repulsed!* They are fighting for dear life. Night begins to come on. The Hanoverians are in front of the French, at close quarters. It was a fearful moment. How the *mitrailleuses* mowed a swath of death! It is death to stay, defeat to Prussia to retreat. There are 27,000 Prussians, and 40,000 French.

VICTORY.

Suddenly guns are heard on the left of the French.

A puff of smoke comes out of a wood on the French left

flank, and the advance guard of Zastrow's corps are in the battle.

The French see the new army advancing, and are filled with consternation. Frossard says "Bazaine is here too," but his patriotic falsehood did not save his army. Seized with consternation, as dusk comes on they fall into a precipitate retreat.

As Kamecke's army comes sweeping up with Zastrow's corps, a shout of victory rings over the field, and Gen. Steinmetz rides up in breathless haste, to hear of the final triumph.

Though it is dark, Steinmetz orders pursuit, and the victorious advance captures in Forbach many baggage wagons, and a complete pontoon train. It was a pontoon train, to be used in crossing the Rhine. What a fate if the Prussians should use it to cross the Seine!

LOSSES.

The loss on both sides was very great. On the part of the Prussians 2000 of killed and wounded are reported. The important results of this victory were only ascertained during the next forty-eight hours, when it was found that the French had retreated in complete panic, leaving their killed and wounded — much more numerous than first anticipated — together with ammunition wagons, magazines, and camp materials. Then, too, a large number of prisoners was constantly being brought in, and Forbach, which the enemy had completely abandoned, was taken by the Prussians. On this occasion a pontoon train, consisting of as many as forty wagons, was seized — proof evident of the utter demoralization of the enemy.

Though the official list does not yet extend to this sanguinary encounter, there can be no doubt as to the correctness of the private intelligence forwarded me, which gives the total of the losses as 2297, of whom 811 are dead and 1486 wounded. Accordingly, every twelfth man was killed or wounded. Some companies left nearly one-half of their men on the spot; as, for instance, the fifth company of the Forty-eighth (Rhinelanders), which went with 250 men into the fire and came out with 129, and the first company of the Eighth (King's Own — Brandenburgers), which on the evening of the battle consigned 107 comrades either to the grave or to the hospital.

CAPTURES.

The official list of Prussian captures at Saarbrück and in its immediate vicinity is as follows: 2500 prisoners, 4 guns, a pontoon train, a tented camp, and two magazines containing 10,000 woollen blankets, 40,000 packages of rice, coffee, and sugar, large quantities of wine, rum, and tobacco — the last alone amounting in value to $50,000.

GENERAL GOEBEN'S OFFICIAL ACCOUNT.

Several hundred men of General Frossard's corps were made prisoners. According to their statements, we were opposed by four divisions of the

French army. The fighting did not terminate until dark. The enemy covered his retreat by a heavy artillery fire from Spicheren. General Steinmetz arrived towards evening and assumed the command. General François fell, Our loss is great, especially in officers. The enemy left many dead. GOEBEN.

GENERAL STEINMETZ'S REPORT OF SAARBRUCK.

To-day, from noon till after dark, a severe and well-contested battle has been fought between Saarbrück and Forbach. The Fourteenth division commenced the engagement, and was successively supported against the enemy, who had fortified themselves, by three battalions and the battery of the Sixteenth division, three battalions, two batteries, and cavalry. The heights of Spicheren, to the south of the exercise ground, were taken by storm, and the enemy driven back upon Forbach. While this was going on, the Thirteenth division advanced opposite Volklingen, took Rossein, and by nightfall established the head of the column at Forbach. General François was killed. Very many wounded men, and a large number of prisoners from the different regiments of Frossard's corps. The number has not yet been ascertained.

I have assumed the command. V. STEINMETZ.

WOERTH (FROSCHWEILER).

KING WILLIAM'S DESPATCH.

TO THE QUEEN:

What fortune, this new great victory of Fritz's! To God alone be praise for His goodness. Won some 30 cannon, 2 eagles, 6 mitrailleuses, 4000 prisoners. MacMahon was strengthened from the main army. Our guns shall salute Victoria. WILHELM.

(Victoria is the name of the Crown Princess of Prussia, wife of "Fritz".)

The Crown Prince's despatch is:

Victorious battle at Woerth; MacMahon, with the largest part of his army, entirely beaten; French thrown back upon Bitche. Upon the battlefield near Woerth, four and one-half o'clock, afternoon.

FREDERICK WILLIAM, Crown Prince.

NAPOLEON'S DESPATCH.

METZ, *August* 7.—Marshal MacMahon has lost a battle. General

Frossard on the Saar has been compelled to fall back. The retreat is being effected in good order. All may be regained (*tout peut se rétablir*).

NAPOLEON.

THE BATTLE.

It has been a day of battles — battles from Haguenau to Saarbrück. While Steinmetz was advancing his victorious columns against Frossard, the Crown Prince was engaged in a death struggle with MacMahon. The result has been victory to Prussia.

After Weisenburg the victorious Crown Prince, with the Third army (Fifth, Sixth, Eleventh, and two Bavarian Corps), pushed down upon the French, who were retreating along the Geisburg hills and the valley from Weisenburg to Woerth. Woerth is in the line of retreat from Weisenburg to Saverne and Nancy. All day long on Friday, the Crown Prince had been marching and skirmishing along the valley. MacMahon was falling back for a strong position. Saturday morning found him on the heights south of Woerth (German, "Wörd"), with Froschweiler and the road to Niederbronn on his left. To the right (south-east) of Woerth is the forest of Haguenau. As the battle advanced, MacMahon swayed to the left — the heights of Froschweiler — keeping in view the retreating road to Niederbronn.

The French force consisted of MacMahon's corps, a division from Canrobert's Sixth Corps, and all that was left of Douay's Seventh Corps (General Douay having been killed at Weisenburg on the 4th). De Failly (Fifth Corps), compelled to fall back from Bitche, through repeated delays, did not arrive in time to be of service to MacMahon. So MacMahon's force was in all about 80,000 effective men. The Crown Prince had nearly 200,000 men (five corps of 40,000 each). Forced to fight the impetuous Crown Prince, MacMahon gathered his forces in the positions given in the map.

(MacMahon was in about the position of General Pope at Centreville at the second battle of Bull Run. There was no concentration. Canrobert was like McClellan in Alexandria, while De Failly was as slow to join the unfortunate MacMahon as was Fitz John

Porter to join General Pope. How many battles are lost from a lack of prompt concentration and a unity of action !)

At the commencement of the battle, MacMahon's left was in front of Froschweiler toward Niederbronn, his centre nearly in front of Woerth, and his right rested against the forest of Haguenau in front of Marsbrunen. The Crown Prince formed with his army a line from Gunstadt (the Prussian left) to Guefdorff (the Prussian right), in front of Froschweiler.

The following is the report of three eye-witnesses who surveyed the battle fiom the church tower in Woerth, reporting the affair with almost singular unanimity to the London *News* and *Times*, and New York *Times*:

Three A.M. — We were awoke at half-past three A.M. by a sharp attack of the Prussians on the French outposts; but they retired about an hour later.

From conversations I had before the battle with Marshal MacMahon's staff, I know for certain that it was generally believed the Prussians had about 50,000 men present, instead of which the whole of the Fifth and Eleventh corps d'armée, numbering at the very least 150,000, under the Prince Royal, were there; and to these Marshal MacMahon could only oppose his own corps d'armée, which was minus the division of General Douay.

The Prussians are in great force, about 150,000 strong, and MacMahon has altogether some 90,000 under him. The troops are in excellent spirits.

PRUSSIAN SIGNAL OF BATTLE.

The Prussians have just fired three bombs into the village, and the panic is terrible to see. The village church, about twenty yards from this, is on fire. I believe, after all, the Prussians will attack MacMahon.

The Prussians are now (seven A.M.) entering the village in which we are. A couple of their men are at the door of the inn.

Some wounded Prussians have (half-past eight A.M.) just been brought in and taken to the hospital, where that blessed flag — tl.e red cross on a white ground — hangs out as a sign that there, at any rate, Christian charity is supreme, and that no one should injure the building. Four Sisters of Charity are already busy at work tending the wounded with that wonderful care and charity for which their order is so famous.

MACMAHON'S STRATEGY.

MacMahon has (nine A.M.) got his wish. The whole of the Prussian corps d'armée seems to be upon him. He still holds off, as if to draw them on more and more. Bombs and shells are exploding every minute, the Prussians evidently trying to drive the French army from the position they have taken up. The French game is to fire now and again, and to seem as if their strength did not admit of their doing more than defend their position.

The cannonade upon MacMahon's position is (quarter past nine A.M.) getting hotter and hotter. The smell of gunpowder is fearful; the dull air seems impregnated with it.

As yet the battle is confined to a huge duel of big field guns. MacMahon is answering with batteries the Prussian guns, and will soon, no doubt, make a dash with his infantry. But it is no easy matter to silence the immense amount of artillery which the Prussians evidently have with them. But every hour that MacMahon can delay the main attack improves his chances, for there is no doubt but that the movement of drawing on the Prussian army and then cutting off its retreat except upon the Rhine, is what the Marshal intends to do — if he can. But he has evidently a very tough and a very strong enemy to deal with.

A great part of the Crown Prince of Prussia's corps, commanded by the son-in-law of Queen Victoria, is with them, having arrived last night; an immense body of French Zouaves and Turcos descend the hill, the gallant MacMahon himself leading them, and divide like a mighty stream and take up fresh positions.

THE COMBAT RAGES — FEARFUL WEAPONS OF DEATH.

The battle is raging, but is farther off, near to where the Prussians had their position this morning, at a village called Lieb-Frauenberg, and as I write, the repeated discharge of the mitrailleuse tells a tale that the French are getting at their enemy. It is curious enough that close by here, at a place called Freswillain, General Hoche (who tried to invade Ireland with a French force in 1795) fought a splendid battle against the Prussians in 1791, with one of those famous armies of the French republic.

Another look from the church steeple at half-past ten A.M. The battle is still raging, but the cannon on both sides is heard now and again. The fight is one of infantry against infantry. The French have descended upon the plain, but they seem to find it very hard work to dislodge the Prussian infantry from the position taken up. MacMahon, as I said before, has a stubborn foe to beat. He does not seem to gain upon them, and the danger of this is, that the French, who cannot be stopped either from firing or advancing, may get to the end of their ammunition before the proper time.

10.40 A.M. — The big guns are at work, but chiefly on the French side. General Lartique, with the Fourth division of his army corps, has now come down upon the Prussian flank, and is fighting fiercely with their reserve, that has just been brought up to support the centre of their position. I cannot exactly make out why the French reserve artillery on the heights has begun to fire, for to do so they must fire over the heads of their own people. The hospital already full of wounded and dying men. What devil's work there is, to be sure!

As the battle seems to die off at one point (eleven A.M.) it rages fiercer and fiercer at another. Ten minutes ago there was no firing near the villages, now it is getting hotter and hotter upon every side. A great number of Prussians are being brought in fearfully wounded, but I have not seen anything of the French wounded. The Prussians are brought in by their comrades, fine, stout, well-dressed men, with spiked helmet and blue tunic, so often depicted.

The massacre on both sides has been fearful. In one spot, in a wood about a mile from where I write these lines, the Prussians resisted manfully for a long time, but had at last to give way to the mitrailleuses. I can see with a glass their dead bodies lying there in masses. They fell where they stood, doing their duty bravely. But to what end? And what an end many of them have had!

During the last two hours, it seemed as if hell had been let loose among us. Right and left, front and rear, the street firing of infantry and the mitrailleuses of the French artillery continued to vomit destruction and death. The cries of the wounded were fearful, but no one dared go to help them, for even to show your face at the window was to receive a well-aimed bullet from a needle-gun.

At three P.M. the whole nature of the battle seemed to change. The Prussians became the attacking party, and, much to the surprise of every one, the French gave way and retired to the rising ground behind Woerth. For three long hours the village was the scene of the hardest struggle of the day. A Prussian division occupied it, and the French tried hard to dislodge them, but without effect, by firing from above with shells, and by repeated advances of the French outposts. The Prussian left has driven back the French right, and the bloodiest fighting of the day is being done at Froschweiler.

STILL MORE FIERCE.

Presently the battle began to rage hotter and hotter in the upper part of the town. I felt certain that MacMahon had drawn on the enemy in order to give them battle in the position he had himself chosen. For a time the Prussian infantry continued to pour into the town by the little bridge just before the inn. By companies, by battalions, by regiments, by brigades, and by divisions they passed, all in excellent order, all looking wonderfully clean after having passed the night under heavy rains in the open fields. I never saw finer, stouter, better dressed or better drilled men.

At four P.M.,

VICTORY CAME TO PRUSSIA.

The French silenced their fire, and fell into a precipitate retreat. Presently firing could hardly be heard at all, and then, as I saw the Prussian cavalry and light artillery push through the town and make for the French position, I instinctively felt that MacMahon had fallen back, and the star of France was on the wane.

And I was right. The Prussians commenced to enter the town, not to pass through it, but to remain and establish their hospitals. It has been my fate to see not a little service in the East, but such fearfully ghastly wounds as those I have seen this day, it never entered into the mind of man to imagine. Men seemed literally to be mashed into bloody, shapless masses of gore. In many instances the poor creatures could not be recognized, all their features being utterly destroyed. To get to the French headquarters is utterly impossible, for MacMahon has fled, no one knows where. The local post-office is taken possession of as a hospital, the postmaster has fled in terror, and I have every reason to believe that a long letter which I wrote on Friday, the 5th — giving an account of the defeat of the French the previous day at Weisenburg — will be, or rather has been, lost.

LOSSES.

The French lost in killed and wounded not more than 10,000 men; the Prussians more than that number. The Prussians did not lose more than 200 prisoners: the French lost 100 officers and nearly 10,000 men taken. The Prussians lost no stores or guns; the French lost six mitrailleuses, twenty-five other pieces of cannon, 400,000 francs of treasure, all their baggage, tents, etc., and all their stores; also four eagles, which in the French army take the place of regimental banners.

However, the moral power and experience of the French army is utterly broken, and I doubt much whether it can ever be put on the same footing as before. The very best corps d'armée, under the most renowned leader they had, has been not only defeated, but routed.

Marshal MacMahon's position on the heights above Woerth was a good one — so good, that the Prince Royal, I learned yesterday from one of his staff, hesitated to attack him. But he did so, and this is what the French leader wanted. But when the attack commenced the Prussians believed their enemy to be much stronger than he was, and the French were not aware that two whole corps of the German army, with nearly the whole of a third corps in reserve, were before them.

The French were outnumbered by three to one, at the very least, and they had among them some regiments that had been beaten forty-eight hours before at Weisenburg. The

Prussians were all fresh. MacMahon certainly was attacked in the position he had chosen himself; but then he never knew until late in the day the real strength of the force he had to contend with. He then commenced to retreat, but had taken no precaution to secure his rear; everything in the shape of baggage, stores, and tents was more or less in confusion, and it is exactly in such a retreat as this that French troops always fail. In five minutes the retreat was almost a rout, in half an hour it was completely so, and then came the enemy's cavalry, which completed their disaster and their enemy's victory.

THE ROUT.

At seven P.M. the Prussians are pushing beyond Froschweiler, where was the scene of the most frightful carnage during the day. The name of the battlefield should be Woerth. MacMahon is flying with his shattered army toward the Vosges (centre and left). His right is being captured by Würtemberg cavalry. The remainder of his defeated army is retreating in disorder, by way of Niederbronn, on Saverne, to escape to Metz.

Great heroism was displayed by the corps of MacMahon in the disastrous battle of Woerth. The French charged the Prussian line eleven times, each time breaking it, but always finding a mass of fresh troops behind. MacMahon had no idea whatever of the numbers that were before him on the morning of the 6th. Of his four divisions, one was the remains of the division that had been beaten at Weisenburg forty-eight-hours before. The rest of his men were in excellent spirits the night before, but they laid all that night on the wet ground, in a perfect deluge of rain, and had nothing to eat before they went into action.

AT REICHSHOFFEN.

Among the heroes who fell at Reichshoffen, a mile from Woerth, where the last bloody stand was made, are mentioned Colonel de Vassart, Count de Septeuil, the Marquis d'Espeuilles, and Count Robert de Vogüé, brother of Count Melchior, chief of the ambulances of the society for succoring the wounded.

After the combat, the body of Count Robert was recognized on the field of battle by some Prussian officers who had known him at Baden. The Prince Royal being informed that Count Melchior was not far off, sent for him, and said, in a grave, sad tone,—

"Monsieur, I have to announce some painful news to you. Do you comprehend?"

"My poor brother!" exclaimed the French gentleman.

"Yes," replied the Prince, "he has fallen as a hero worthy of his name. His body is there, Count. You shall have every facility for removing his glorious remains."

The country people seem to be in great consternation. The roads which lead to Haguenau are covered with peasants carrying their goods and cattle with them, and crying over the *sad fate of their humble cottages.*

Item.—The official list of captures by the Prussians at Weisenburg is as follows: 30 officers and 1,000 men as prisoners, 4 mitrailleuses, 22 cannon, 51 army wagons, and carriages of all kinds.

FLIGHT OF MACMAHON'S ARMY.

(Translated from the Vienna Wehr Zeitung.)

I could now (Aug. 6, 2½ P.M.) stay in Haguenau no longer. Despite the warning of my host, I turned out of the northern gate and took the direction of the Haguenau forest toward Niederbronn. The roar of cannon was loud. Columns of smoke rose in the northwest, and even in the direction of Saarburg. I judged the fight to be near Niederbronn, and did not err. At four o'clock in galloped a horse through the town gate with empty saddle slipping under its belly. Directly after, a second; then a third; then followed a cuirassier without cuirass, without arms, his horse covered with blood and foam. Next an artillerist, on an unsaddled horse, his face distorted with inexpressible fright. Some minutes later, a mob of some twenty horsemen hurried past, among whom two Zouaves clinging upon one horse were conspicuous; the others were cuirassiers in every stage of fright and terror, some swinging wildly their sabres; others, most of them without arms, as if out of their wits, flogging their poor exhausted horses, several of them without saddles. One cuirassier halted his horse just before me, loosened his cuirass, threw off his helmet, next his heavy sword, lastly his weighty breastplate, and then, laughing contentedly, rode leisurely on. A pause of some five minutes followed. The townsmen had all fled inside the gates. The field watch and I stood alone at the point where the Niederbronn branch railway intersects the high road. Presently up gallops a field *gendarme*, halts his half-dead horse, and calls out, "Shut the gates instantly; the Prussians are at my heels." The field-watch turned white. I exclaimed, "What madness. Haguenau is an open town. There could be no defence; and if the Prussians really were there, the best thing for the town was to open the gates as wide as possible." His face brightened up. The tumult became greater. Among a crowd of cuirassiers some lancers were mixed up; then came hussar uniforms. The roads are thronged; unmounted horses gallop past as if driven on by panic; on all sides are swarms; artillery men in shirt sleeves; many of the horses, with the traces cut, ridden by infantry-men or artillery. So far I have not remarked one officer. As the mob was thickest, a railway train came screaming along from the north. At the moment a number of peasant girls, with their conveyances entangled in the throng, were close upon the rails. They cannot move forward or backward; they seem lost. The field-watch and myself, seizing the barrier-tree, forced back the distracted wenches, shut the barrier, helped them over, and the train rushed past without mishap. The train ought to have saved the *matériel* accumulated at Niederbronn; it ought to have transported the wounded; it was entirely devoted to flight. They were the first infantry soldiers who saved themselves. All the wagons overfilled — on the roofs, hanging on by the handles, with half their bodies in the air, on the gangway boards, some fully accoutred, some half naked, no wounded! So flashed past us this novel picture of distraction, crossing the current of misfortune in the high road. We let the barrier balk drop, and sprang aside. *Like a wild hunt, the horsemen galloped* into the town, and clattered through it without drawing bridle. By five o'clock the torrent gradually ceased. After a pause came the conveyances. I saw four or five carriages, all completely harnessed, yet without their guns. Then jolted and rattled past a broken ammunition wagon crammed with Turcos; next a peasant's wagon filled with bedding and household gear, but no owner; a Zouave led the horses, two frightfully wounded Turcos lay on the top.

MACMAHON'S REPORT.

SAVERNE, *August* 7.

SIRE: I have the honor to report to your Majesty that on the seventh of August, after having been obliged to evacuate the town of Weisenburg, the First Corps, with the object of covering the railway from Strasburg to Bitche, and the chief channels of communication between the eastern and western sides of the Vosges, occupied the following positions: The First Division was placed with the right in front of Froschweiler, the left in the direction of Reichshoffen, resting on a mound which covers that village. It detached two companies to Neunwiller, and one to Jaegersthal. The Third Division occupied, with its First Brigade, a contrefort detached from Froschweiler, and terminating in a point toward Guefdorff. The Second Brigade rested its left on Froschweiler, and its right on the village of Elsashausen. The Fourth Division formed a broken line on the right of the Third Division, its First Brigade facing Gunstadt, and its second *vis-à-vis* with the village of Marsbronn, which it was unable to occupy from want of sufficient force. The Dumesnil Division of the Seventh Corps, which joined me early on the morning of the sixth, was placed in rear of the Fourth Division. In reserve was the Second Division, placed behind the Second Brigade of the Third Division, and the First Brigade of the Fourth. Finally, further in the rear, was the brigade of light cavalry under the orders of General de Septeuil, and the division of cuirassiers of General de Bonnemains; the brigade of Michel cavalry, under the orders of General Duchesne, was placed behind the right wing of the Fourth Division. At seven o'clock in the morning the enemy made his appearance in advance of the heights of Guersdorff, and commenced the action by a cannonade, soon followed by a lively fire of tirailleurs against the First and Third Divisions. This attack was serious enough to oblige the First Division to make a change of front in advance on its right wing, so as to prevent the enemy from turning the general position. A little later the enemy augmented considerably the number of his batteries, and opened a fire on the centre of the position which we occupied on the right of the Sauerbach, much more serious and more threatening than the first, which continued. This second demonstration was, after all, only a false attack, which was vigorously repulsed. Toward noon the enemy commenced his attack on our right. Clouds of riflemen, supported by considerable masses of infantry, and protected by more than sixty pieces of cannon, placed on the heights of Gunstadt, threw themselves on the Fourth Division and on the Second Brigade occupying the village of Elsashausen. In spite of vigorous charges, many times repeated, in spite of the well-directed fire of the artillery, and several brilliant charges of the cuirassiers, our right was borne back, after many hours of obstinate resistance. At four o'clock I ordered the retreat. It was covered by the First and Third Divisions, who put a bold face on affairs, and permitted the other troops to retire without being too much pressed. The retreat was effected to Saverne by Niederbronn, when the Guyot de Lespart Division of the Fifth Corps, which had just arrived, took up position, and did not retire until after nightfall. I enclose to your Majesty the names of the officers killed, wounded, or missing. The list is incomplete; and I will send it again when I can get it in its complete state. Accept, etc.

(Signed) MARECHAL MACMAHON.

MACMAHON'S CONTINUED FLIGHT.

(Translated from the French of Edmond About.)

SATURDAY (*Evening*).

It was clear that our artillery had been roughly tried when limbers were seen passing without their guns. There were, nevertheless, one, two, three regiments of the line quite firm, sufficiently perfect, their rifles on their shoulders, and their knapsacks at their backs. In their rear was Marshal MacMahon, calm, dignified, almost smiling, and as fresh as a rose. I saluted him in passing, and he responded without knowing me. One of his aides-de-camp, M. d'Abzac, named me to him, and he then stopped and asked for news, listening with fine composure to the defeat of M. Frossard, of which he was still ignorant, and telling me very simply, in few words, of his own misfortune.

"I had but 35,000 men, and I found 150,000 before me. We have succumbed to numbers. They have killed or wounded about 5,000 men, but we will take our revenge. Explain that to the public. But where are you going thus?"

"To Saverne."

"You will get yourself taken; the Prussians will be there in two hours; they are seen."

"I have my wife and my children."

"Then, God protect you! Do not fail to say that the *morale* of the troops is excellent."

We shook hands. I exchanged a few good words with M. d'Abzac. I recognized Prince Achille Murat in his martial guise, but I sought vainly in the état major at a distance for the smiling and sympathetic face of M. de Vogné, officier d'ordonnance. That noble young man was killed by a bullet in the forehead, as General Cólson was by a bullet in the heart, both of them at the side of the Marshal, who was prodigal of his life. Immediately after came a regiment of Turcos, the most solid of the three. *A la bonne heure!* These had thrown away neither their knapsacks nor their arms.

SAVERNE FRIGHTENED.

I found the little town in a tremendous panic. Marshal MacMahon arrived here on Saturday evening, followed by the remains of his army, and preceded by a number of runaways out of breath. In the wink of an eye, Saverne was seen full of soldiers of the First Corps, who the enemy very luckily believed to have retired upon Bitche. They quartered themselves wherever it was possible—the most fortunate among the inhabitants; those who had brought their knapsacks and encampments under tents, many on the pavements of the streets, and in the fields, in the open air. The night was passed in sleep. If the enemy could have profited by the opportunity, they might have made ten or fifteen thousand prisoners at one *coup.* The men were so tired that they had not the severity to send any on vedette. The officers said, "What should we do if we were surprised? We should appear on horseback in a single line, and get ourselves killed before our troops. But after the things which they have done to-day, it would be absurd and cruel to ask them to do any more." The population was only half reassured by our presence, dispirited, discomforted, and hungry. Some families went off by the mail train at midday—the last which could go from Strasburg to Paris. Others regained confidence in listening to the officers, who kept saying, more from habit than conviction, "You have nothing to be afraid of while we are here." But on Sunday, at six o'clock, upon a false alarm caused by the arrival of the Fifth Corps, the Duc de Magenta had the *générale* beat, and Saverne believed itself lost. While the officers and soldiers threw themselves on the road to Pfalzburg, three-quarters of the inhabitants utterly lost themselves, and rushed into the neighboring woods. The example, a sad example, was given them by the gendarmes and the sergeants de ville. They shut the shops, threw their furniture into the gutters; many of the farmers drove their beasts before them, as in the time of Abraham. There was an incredible accumulation of men and beasts in the wood-houses and the ruins of the old country mansions. This morning all is quiet in the town, or rather all is dead. We expect the invasion from one minute to the other, and we shall not dream of defending ourselves against the 150,000 men of the Prince Royal.

SUNDAY, *August* 7.—Official despatches from Napoleon, acknowledging defeat of MacMahon at Woerth and Frossard at Saarbrück. Paris in a frenzy. General Sheridan represents General Grant at the seat of war. Rejoicings in Berlin, and intense excitement in Paris. The Empress Regent issues a proclamation appealing to the patriotism of the people. The Corps Législatif and Senate convoked. Retreat of MacMahon towards Saverne. Advance of the Germans into France along the entire line. MacMahon's army starving.

Haguenau, in Alsace, taken by the Baden cavalry, which overruns Alsace, and, with a loss of five men killed and wounded, captures 103 prisoners, among whom are 39 Turcos. The Germans have now taken more than 10,000 prisoners, immense stores, trains, and magazines, and inflicted three demoralizing defeats upon the French. Pfalzburg (a fortified place in Lower Alsace, on a spur of the Vosges, 2000 or 3000 inhabitants) is beleaguered. Bitche, having only 300 Mobile Guards for a garrison, is merely blockaded by one company. German cavalry near Luneville (on the Meurthe, about sixteen miles from Nancy, with 13,000 inhabitants). Haguenau, abandoned by the French, occupied by the Germans. Saarguemünd occupied. Forbach taken after a slight action. The whole French army beaten and retreating. The centre driven in, the right wing turned and cut off, and Napoleon calls upon France to rise and save the country.

FRENZY OF PARIS.

PROCLAMATION OF THE MINISTRY.

"FRENCHMEN, — Up to this hour we have always given without reserve all the certain news which we have received, and we continue to do so. Last night we received the following despatches:

"METZ, *August* 7, 12.30 A.M. — Marshal MacMahon has lost a battle.

"General Frossard on the Saar has been compelled to fall back.

"The retreat is being effected in good order.

"All may be regained (*tout peut se rétablir*).

"NAPOLEON."

"METZ, *August* 7, 3.30 A.M. — My communication with MacMahon being broken, I had, until yesterday, but little news of him. General L'Aigle informed me that MacMahon had lost a battle against very considerable forces of the enemy, and that he had withdrawn in good order. The battle began at one o'clock, and did not appear very serious until gradually increasing reinforcements came up on the enemy's side, without, however, compelling the Second Corps to fall back. Only between six and seven o'clock, as the enemy became constantly more compact, did the Second Corps, and the regiments from other corps which served as his supports, fall back upon the hills. The night was quiet. I go to the centre of our position.

"NAPOLEON."

"PARIS, *August* 7.—The Major-General of the Army to the Minister of the Interior: After a series of engagements, in which the enemy brought heavy forces into the field, Marshal MacMahon was forced to fall back from his first line.

"The corps of General Frossard had to fight yesterday from two o'clock in the afternoon with an entire army of the enemy. Having held his position until six o'clock, he ordered a retreat, which was made in good order.

"LEBŒUF."

Details of our losses are wanting. Our troops are full of *élan*. The situation is not compromised; but the enemy is on our territory, and a serious effort is necessary. A battle appears imminent. In the presence of this grave news, our duty is plain. We appeal to the patriotism and the energy of all. The Chambers have been convoked. We are placing Paris with all possible haste in a state of defence.

In order to facilitate the execution of military preparations, we declare the capital in a state of siege. There must be no faintheartedness, no divisions. Our resources are immense. Let us pursue the struggle without flinching, and the country will be saved.

Paris, the 7th of August, 1870, at 10 P.M. By order of the Empress Regent.

M. OLLIVIER, Minister of Justice.
DUKE DE GRAMONT, Minister of Foreign Affairs.
M. CHEVAUDIN DE VALDRÔME, Minister of Interior.
M. LEGRIS, Minister of Finances.
GEN. VICOMPTE DE JEAN, Minister of War *ad interim*.

PROCLAMATION OF THE EMPRESS.

PARIS, *August* 7, 3.50 P.M.—The Council of Ministers is sitting *en permanence*.

Messrs. Rouher and Schneider have been summoned to the Tuileries. The Empress arrived at five o'clock this morning. Her Majesty issued the following proclamation:

"FRENCHMEN,—The opening of the war has not been in our favor. Our arms have suffered a check. Let us be firm under this reverse, and let us hasten to repair it. Let there be among us but a single party—that of France; but a single flag—the flag of our national honor.

"I come in your midst. Faithful to my mission and to my duty, you will see me first where danger threatens to defend the flag of France. I call upon all good citizens to preserve order; to disturb it would be to conspire with our enemies.

"EUGENIE.

"The Tuileries, August 7, 11 A.M."

PARIS PLACED IN A STATE OF SIEGE.

PARIS, *August* 7, 10 A.M. — The Council of Ministers has addressed a proclamation to the people.

Paris is placed in a state of siege.

The Chambers are convoked for to-morrow.

The Bourse has been firm and excited on a rumored victory of the French. Rentes closed at 67.70, or one franc higher than yesterday.

General MacMahon is retiring on Nancy.

Three French corps have not been engaged.

MACMAHON'S ARMY STARVING.

On Sunday, August 7th, a special train came into Nancy with some of the wounded. Marshal MacMahon accompanied them. He came "precipitately" to Nancy in search of subsistence for his troops, the enemy having taken all his provisions. His troops had eaten nothing for twenty-eight hours. The Marshal went on foot from the railway station to the Café Boillot, a well-known rendezvous of the officers of the garrison. He was in such a state as to be hardly recognized. He was covered with mud from head to foot, his hands were black, one of his epaulettes had been carried away by a bullet, the skirts of his uniform were full of bullet-holes, his telescope was broken asunder by a ball, which at the same time slightly wounded him in the hand. He had not had time to take off his Hessian boots and long spurs. Everybody in the café, as soon as he was known, respectfully saluted him. He hastily called for some cold meat, for he had not tasted food for twenty-eight hours. He wrote a letter while he was eating, and was very soon joined by an officer, who is believed to be General De Failly. They went into a private room and had a short consultation, after which the Marshal went back by rail with the provisions he had bought for his soldiers. An inhabitant of Nancy, personally acquainted with the Marshal, asked him news of the cuirassiers. His answer was, "The cuirassiers! why, there are none of them left."

When he returned with the provisions, he addressed his men thus:

"SOLDIERS,—In yesterday's battle fortune betrayed your courage; but you yielded your positions only after a heroic resistance, which lasted not less than nine hours. You were 35,000 against 140,000, and were overwhelmed by force of numbers. Under these conditions defeat is glorious, and history will say that in the battle of Froschweiler the French showed the greatest valor. You have suffered heavy losses, but those of the enemy are much greater. Although you have not been successful, you see a cause in your misfortune which makes the Emperor satisfied with you, and the entire country recognize that you have worthily sustained the honor of the flag. Let us show that, though subjected to the severest tests, the First Corps, forgetting these, closes up its ranks; and, God aiding us, let us seize a great and brilliant revenge."

REJOICINGS IN GERMANY.

BERLIN, *August* 7.—Salvoes of artillery are now being fired in honor of the victory of the Prussian arms.

The city is dressed in flags. Hamburg, Dresden, and Breslau are in a blaze of excitement and joy. It is a great day for Germany.

The batch of 500 French prisoners, who have reached Berlin from Weisenburg, were well received by the people, who treated them with the respect due to brave men.

MacMahon is retreating on the road to Nancy.

PRINCE CHARLES MOVING.

MAYENCE, *August* 7.—Prince Frederick Charles proceeded to-day from Homburg to Bliescastel. General Steinmetz is between Sulzbach and Saarbrück. The chief headquarters of the Prussian army are now at Kaiserslautern.

SULZ, *August* 7.—The Crown Prince is here. Upwards of 4000 prisoners taken at Woerth have been brought in. Marshal MacMahon is said to be wounded.

SHERIDAN REPRESENTS GRANT.

WASHINGTON, *August* 7.—The President, after consultation with General Sherman, took occasion to forward to General Sheridan several official documents, which in reality place the General in the position of a representative of the President as Commander-in-chief of our Army and Navy; he also sent some telegraphic messages on the subject to Ministers Bancroft and Washburne, and to General Sheridan.

KING WILLIAM ADDRESSES THE ARMY FROM HOMBURG.

SOLDIERS: The pursuit of the enemy, forced back after bloody fighting, has already carried a great part of our army over the frontier. Many corps will enter upon the French soil to-day and to-morrow. I expect that the self-discipline with which you have heretofore distinguished yourself will be also especially maintained in the enemy's territory. We carry on no war against the peaceable inhabitants of the land; it is, on the contrary, the duty of every honest soldier to protect private property, and not to allow the good reputation of our army to be marred by even *one* example of lawlessness. I depend upon the excellent feeling which possesses the army, but also upon the vigilance and rigor of all commanders.

STEINMETZ ADDRESSES HIS VICTORIOUS ARMY BEFORE PURSUING FROSSARD.

SOLDIERS OF THE FIRST ARMY! By command of His Majesty the King, the First army will to-morrow cross the French boundary. Let us greet this first result of our previous efforts as we enter upon the enemy's territory with a hearty hurrah for our wise supreme war-leader. Of your good conduct in the struggle which awaits us with an equally brave army, I am assured by your love of the Fatherland, your courage, and your just pride, which forbid you to suffer the insults cast upon us by an intemperate opponent to remain unnoticed. But the peace-loving citizen and countryman, as you will say yourselves, stands under the protection of the humanity which is comprehended in Prussian discipline. I trust that you will never falsify either the one or the other by excesses which can never be countenanced by your superiors. When and where the enemy confronts us, I expect that he will be attacked with the greatest determination. For the cavalry, it is already a principle of long standing that it always attacks first. The excuse that there was nothing to be done, I can never allow, when the thunder of the cannon can be heard. On the contrary, each detachment of troops must march toward that direction, and, arrived upon the battle-field, to inform itself upon the condition of the fight, in order to attack at once, in the best way. The same sound must also serve as a sound to each superior commander in a pitched battle. One thing more. What can be done on one day must never be distributed over two days. Only with the greatest energy can great results be attained, and with them the peace which God will give us after victorious combat.

MONDAY, *August* 8.—Meeting of the French Parliament. Preparations for the defence of Paris begun. Marshal Bazaine made Commander-in-Chief of the French army. Arrangements made to call out the entire Garde Mobile of France. The army of the Crown Prince advancing rapidly on Saverne. Prussian official reports of victory. Proclamation of the French Ministry, appealing for unity of action.

Excitement in Paris. General Changarnier offers his services, and is received by Napoleon. The Emperor reports the situation. Paris in siege.

NAPOLEON.

METZ, *August* 8, 10 A.M.—General De Failly is in communication with Marshal MacMahon. The *morale* of the army is excellent. There has been no attack since my despatch of yesterday. In the battle of Froschweiler 140,000 Prussians attacked Marshal MacMahon's corps, numbering only 33,000 men. NAPOLEON.

PROCLAMATION OF THE FRENCH MINISTRY.

PARIS, *August* 8, 5.30 P.M. — The following proclamation, signed by all the Ministers, is now being posted up throughout Paris :

"FRENCHMEN ! — We have told you the whole truth ; it is now for you to fulfil your duty. Let one single cry issue from the breasts of all, from one end of France to the other. Let the whole people rise quivering, and sworn to fight the great fight. Some of our regiments have succumbed before overwhelming numbers, but our army has not been vanquished. The same intrepid breath still animates it. Let us support it. To a momentarily successful audacity we will oppose an union which conquers destiny. Let us fall back upon ourselves, and our invaders shall hurl themselves against a rampart of human breasts. As in 1792, and at Sebastopol, let our reverses be the school of our victories. It would be a crime to doubt for an instant the safety of our country; and a greater still not to do our part to secure it. Up, then, up ! and you inhabitants of the Centre, the North, and the South, upon whom the burthen of war does not fall, hasten with unanimous enthusiasm to the help of your brethren in the East. Let France, united in success, be still more united under trial ; and may God bless our arms !"

PARIS IN SIEGE.

Napoleon, by the grace of God and the national will, Emperor of the French : — To all for whom these presents shall come, greeting. Our Council of Ministers having been heard, we have decreed and do decree as follows : Art. 1. The Department of the Seine (Paris principally) is declared in the state of siege. Art. 2. Our Ministers are charged in their respective Departments to execute the present decree. — For the Emperor, and in virtue of the powers conferred on us by him, EUGENIE. By the Empress Regent. The Garde des Sceaux, Minister of Justice and Public Worship, EMILE OLLIVIER.

TUESDAY, *August* 9. — General advance of the Prussians upon Metz. Strasburg besieged by the South German forces. The French army concentrating upon Metz. MacMahon leaves Saverne, and continues his retreat to Nancy. Overthrow of the Ollivier, Ministry by the Corps Législatif. Intense excitement in Paris.

General Uhrich, with 10,000 men, besieged in Strasburg by General Werder with 17,000 Prussians.

A change of the Ministry in Paris.

THE SITUATION.

Baden troops at Brumath, twelve miles north of Strasburg. Cavalry and artillery close under the walls. General Uhrich, in the city, refuses to surrender. The last French troops at Rome leave Civita Vecchia. Lichtenburg, in the Vosges, bombarded and set on fire. The French army, which from Forbach had retreated to the intrenched line of the river Nied, now abandons that line, and retreats to the Moselle.

GENERAL FROSSARD has retired upon Metz with the Second Corps.

L'ADMIRAULT has joined Bazaine at Metz from Thionville, with the Fourth Corps.

MACMAHON and De Failly are retreating at Luneville, on Nancy.

THE CROWN PRINCE with the Third army is at Saverne, moving rapidly after the flying forces of MacMahon.

STEINMETZ is at St. Avold with the First army.

PRINCE FREDERICK CHARLES, with the Second army, has marched on to French soil, and is now at St. Avold, moving on Pont-à-Mousson, to take a position between MacMahon and Metz.

Bazaine is in chief command of the French army at Metz, and De Caen commands Bazaine's old corps, the Third.

The force in Metz is as follows·

L'Admirault, Fourth Corps	32,000
Frossard, Second Corps	30,000
De Caen, Third Corps	34,000
Bourbaki, Imperial Guards, eight corps	25,000
" Cavalry	5,000

The Emperor is here, at the headquarters of Bazaine.

Against this 126,000 men of Bazaine, the Prussians can bring the First and Second armies of Steinmetz and Prince Charles, numbering 280,000 men. The French are always outnumbered.

FRENCH LOSSES.

Terrible accounts of the losses in the late battles circulate in Paris. According to *La France*, the Eighth Cuirassiers is reduced from 600 to 170 men, nearly all the officers being wounded or dead. The Ninth Cuirassiers lost 35 officers, and had only 220 men left. Out of 65 officers in the Third Zouaves, 47 were dead, wounded, or missing. Of the whole regiment only 500 to 600 men remain.

A German correspondent of the Vienna military paper, *Der Kamerad*, writes from Paris that MacMahon, having fought with 33,000 men at Woerth, was unable to collect more than 18,000 after the retreat. From 7000 to 8000 had fled to Strasburg, and the remainder were killed, wounded, and prisoners, with the exception of a thousand or two who might come in later. A week later this correspondent puts the losses at Woerth at 9000 killed and wounded and 6500 prisoners. To-day Haguenau was occupied, having been abandoned by the enemy. The affair at Niederbronn was brought on by some French troops making a stand during their retreat. They were defeated by Bavarians. Würtemberg cavalry also had a successful action at Reichshoffen, and took four guns, one mitrailleuse, and large booty. Headquarters of King in Homburg; of First army in Saarbrücken; of Second army in Bliescastel; and of Third army in Sulz. The Third army being established in French territory, General Von Werder proceeds with his own corps and the Baden division southward, and occupies Haguenau.

A VOTE AGAINST THE MINISTRY.

PARIS, *Tuesday*, *Aug.* 9.—The Corps Législatif met to-day. An order of the day directed against the Ministry was proposed by Deputy Clement Duvernois, and was adopted by a large majority. M. Ollivier asked for the suspension of the sitting for a few minutes.

STORMY SCENES.

PARIS, *August* 9, 6.40 *P.M.* —The Corps Législatif has declared urgent all the propositions submitted by the Minister of War.

M. Jules Favre demanded the immediate armament and complete organization of the National Guard in Paris and the Departments on the basis of the law of 1831. He attributed the reverses of the army to the absolute incapacity of the General-in-Chief, and therefore demanded that the Emperor should relinquish the command, and that the Legislative Body should take in hand the direction of the affairs of the country. Indescribable agitation followed this speech; the Deputies of the Left applauded it, but the majority protested. M. Granier de Cassagnac declared that such a motion was the commencement of revolution. (Tumult and excitement.)

M. Picard proposed that the regiments now in Paris should be sent to the frontier, and said that if arms are refused to the population of Paris, they would procure them by every possible means. He demanded a change of Ministry.

Baron Jérome David, who was present at the battle of Weisenburg, said: "If our soldiers heard us they would cry out, 'Leave internal dissensions.' Let the army retain the confidence that the whole of France is at its back."

M. Ferry, assuming a threatening attitude towards the Ministry, shouted, "Paris is being fired upon."

Count Kératry *demanded the abdication of the Emperor*, and was called to order.

The discussion was declared to be closed, and the sitting was suspended.

An immense crowd surrounds the Législatif building, and the authorities have been obliged to clear the approaches.

The journals almost unanimously demand the general armament of the population. There was a great display of military forces in Paris yesterday; 10,000 men of the marine and infantry arrived from Cherbourg and other ports on Monday. The people cheered the troops, and shouted "*A la frontière.*"

THE NEW FRENCH MINISTRY.

PARIS, *August* 10.—The Count de Palikao has announced in the Chamber that the new Ministry had been constituted as follows:

General Cousin-Montauban (Count de Palikao). Minister of War.
M. Chevreau .... Minister of Interior.
M. Magne .... Minister of Finance.
M. Clement Duvernois .... Minister of Commerce and Agriculture.
Admiral Rigault de Genouilly .... Minister of Marine.

Baron Jérôme David	Minister of Public Works.
Prince de la Tour d'Auvergne	Minister of Foreign Affairs.
M. Grandperret	Minister of Justice.
M. Jules Brame	Minister of Public Instruction.
M. Busson-Billault	President of the Council of State.

OLLIVIER.

The order came from Metz to turn out Ollivier, the Emperor seeking to propitiate Paris by sacrificing the most unpopular and least responsible of his advisers. Ollivier himself had not the least suspicion of his fate. He came smiling into the Chamber, only to leave it pale, terrified, and ruined.

BIOGRAPHIES OF THE NEW FRENCH MINISTRY.*

COUNT PALIKAO, MINISTER OF WAR.

(*Biography given with the French Generals, page* 96.)

ADMIRAL RIGAULT DE GENOUILLY,

the Minister of Marine, has been in the naval service for forty-two years, and commanded a detachment of marines during the siege of Sebastopol. In 1860 he entered the Senate, and has since distinguished himself by taking an active part in administrative affairs, and in 1867 was appointed Minister of Marine. During the illness of the late Marshal Niel, he was temporarily in charge of the War Department. He is regarded as an able authority upon all matters connected with the naval service, and as practically conversant with the important changes introduced during the last decade.

PIERRE MAGNE,

the Minister of Finance, has given evidence of great administrative ability, and was Minister of France from 1845 to 1860. He was previously in the Constituent and Legislative Assemblies, and was appointed Minister of Public Works in 1851. He did not occupy a leading position as a debater, but his practical speeches were always listened to with attention.

BARON JEROME DAVID,

the Minister of Public Works, entered the naval service at an early age, but afterward joined the army, and served in Africa and the Crimea. He entered the Corps Législatif in 1859, and has since been several times re-elected as a Government candidate. He was Vice-President of the Corps Législatif during the sessions of 1867, '68, and '69. He has been prominent in debate, and when M. Schneider last year resigned the position of President on account of the reappointment of Baròn David to the Vice-Presidency, the Emperor personally intervened, and testified his esteem for the Baron, and desired to have him continue in that position.

HENRI CHEVREAU,

the Minister of the Interior, has been forsome time designed for that position. He has, almost since his entry into public life, been known as an active and ardent supporter of Napoleon's interests, even during the *coup d'état*. He has in consequence been liberally rewarded.

---

* At the declaration of the Republic the Napoleonic Ministry was changed thus: Trochu, War, and President; Cremieux, Justice; Fourichon, Marine; Favre, Foreign Affairs; Gambetta, Interior; Picard, Finance; Magnin, Commerce; Simon, Public Instruction; Dorian, Public Works.

JULES BRAME,

the Minister of Public Instruction, represents a Northern District in the Corps Législatif, and is remarkable as an ardent Protectionist, and advocate of the rights of labor.

CLEMENT DUVERNOIS,

the Minister of Commerce, has been recently conspicuous in French journalism by his servile subserviency to the Emperor, whose views he was regarded as expressing in the *Peuple Français*. He recently retired from that journal. Many political pamphlets have been written by him in the interests of imperialism.

PRINCE DE LA TOUR D'AUVERGNE,

Minister of Foreign Affairs, is a member of an ancient Vendean family, and has been engaged in the diplomatic service for about ten years. He was Minister of Foreign Affairs in 1869, but retired on the formation of the Ollivier Cabinet. He has since acted as French ambassador, and is regarded as identified with the Clerical party.

WEDNESDAY, *August* 10. — The Palikao Ministry organized. Laws passed calling out all Frenchmen between the ages of twenty-five and thirty-five. Napoleon invited to return to Paris. General Trochu appointed Governor of Paris.

THE EMPIRE DEAD!

Excitement and blows in the Corps Législatif. Strasburg refuses to surrender. King William proclaims the war against armed soldiers, not citizens. The Empress sends a secret despatch for Napoleon to return to Paris.

The French army continues its retreat toward the Moselle at all points. The cavalry of all the Prussian armies follow close at their heels. The line Saarunion, Gross Tenquin, Faulquemont, Fouling, Les Etangs, is passed by the cavalry. Great stores of provisions, two pontoon trains, several railway trains captured. The small fortress Lützelstein (Petite Pierre), in the Vosges, has been abandoned with its guns and magazines. Lichtenburg capitulates with 280 men. Commander Uhrich, in Strasburg, issues a proclamation, in which he says that the walls are armed with 400 guns, and the garrison contains 11,000 men, without counting the National Guard; and adds that "if Strasburg is attacked, it will be defended to the last man, the last ration, the last bullet."

THE SIEGE OF STRASBURG.

General Uhrich addresses the people of Strasburg thus:

Disturbing rumors and panics have been spread, either by accident or design, within the past few days, in our brave city. Some individuals have dared to express the opinion that the place would surrender without a blow. We protest energetically, in the name of a population courageous and French, against these weak and criminal forebodings. The ramparts are armed with 400 cannon. The garrison consists of 11,000 men, without reckoning the stationary National Guard. If Strasburg is attacked, Strasburg will defend herself as long as there shall remain a soldier, a biscuit, or a cartridge. The well-affected may reassure themselves; as to others, they have but to withdraw.

The General of Division, Uhrich.
The Prefect of the Bas-Rhin, Baron Pron.

Strasburg, Aug. 10.

STRASBURG,

the old capital of Alsace, is one of the strongest fortified towns in Europe, and the centre of the defence of the French frontier of the Rhine. Besides being the seat of military and artillery schools, which make it a sort of capital of military science, and more or less assure its maintenance in efficiency, it is an arsenal, and contains a cannon foundry, and ateliers for various kinds of military manufactures. It is undoubtedly capable of rendering immense service to France in this war, whether as a depot in the second line, or as a base of operations against South Germany; but there is an essential difference between it and the German fortresses lower down the Rhine: Mayence, for instance, has Kastel for its bridge-head on the right bank, and thus commands the passage of the river; while Kehl, opposite Strasburg, is in the hands of the Prussians.

THE KING AT SAARBRUCK.

August 10. — The cavalry are everywhere sweeping down upon the French. Steinmetz (First army) is at St. Avold and Carling. Prince Charles (Second army) is moving towards Pont-à-Mousson, to cross the Moselle.

King William is here — just leaving for the front. The soldiers cheer him. It is a grand shout of patriotic enthusiasm. The King seems overcome with emotion. He addresses the soldiers in short phrases, as "*Immer vorwärtis, meine Kinder!*" As the King leaves the town, he addresses the following in French to the French people:

We, William King of Prussia, make known the following to the inhabitants of the French territories occupied by the German armies. The Emperor Napoleon having made, by land

and by sea, an attack on the German nation, which desired and still desires to live in peace with the French people, I have assumed the command of the German armies to repel this aggression, and I have been led by military circumstances to cross the frontiers of France. I am waging war against soldiers, not against French citizens. The latter consequently will continue to enjoy security for their persons and property so long as they themselves shall not, by hostile attempts against the German troops, deprive me of the right of according them my protection. By special arrangements, which will be duly made known to the public, the generals commanding the different corps will determine the measures to be taken towards the communes or individuals that may place themselves in opposition to the usages of war. They will in like manner regulate all that concerns the requisitions which may be deemed necessary for the wants of the troops, and they will fix the rate of exchange between French and German currencies, in order to facilitate the individual transactions between the troops and the inhabitants.

THE EMPRESS'S SECRET DESPATCH.

The Empress sent this despatch to-day to the Emperor: "M. Pietri's despatch has been received;" and adds: "Have you considered the consequences of a return to Paris under the blow of two reverses? I decline the responsibility of advising you. If you have decided, would it not be best to have it stated to the country thus: 'The Emperor returns to Paris to reorganize the second army, provisionally intrusting the command-in-chief of the Army of the Rhine to Bazaine.' EUGENIE."

FIGHTING IN PARIS.

PARIS, *Wednesday, Aug.* 10, 1870.

In the Corps Législatif to-day, the project of Deputy Kérâtry, for the calling under arms of all unmarried men of the classes of 1859 to 1864, inclusive, was extended to embrace all men from the ages of 25 to 35 who are not married, and not already members of the Garde Mobile.

THE EMPIRE SICK.

Jules Favre proposed that the Chamber should assume full power to save the country; the incapacity of the Emperor to command the army had been too conclusively proved, *and he should be recalled.*

A tremendous uproar ensued. The voice of the President was heard propounding the truism, that the motion was unconstitutional. He added: "You will never make a revolution with this Chamber." Granier de Cassagnac said, with great energy, that if he were in the Ministry, he would have Jules Favre and all the members of the Left brought to a court-martial, and shot that very evening. Ollivier, in an excited state, said: "M. Jules Simon has asked me whether we mean to have all the opposition Deputies shot." What answer he made, the tumult rendered it impossible to collect.

The Count de Kérâtry *proposed that the Chamber should now treat Napoleon III. as a Chamber treated Napoleon I. in* 1815. The Ministers and Home Deputies actually came to blows, and Chevandier de Valdrôme *had his face scratched.*

THE EMPIRE DYING.

PARIS, *August* 10 (*Morning*).—The Empire is on its last legs, but it will die hard, and involve millions in its ruin. Imbecility is killing it—mismanagement is the poison gnawing at its vitals. An old man in his dotage cannot lead French armies to victory.

DEAD!

Evening.—M. Thiers has just said in the French Chamber, "*The Empire is henceforth out of the question. There can be no Empire without an Emperor.* THE REPUBLIC IS INEVITABLE."

THE FRENCH EMPIRE

has ceased to exist. Napoleon's attempt to appease an angry and threatening populace by sacrificing an unlucky General and a subservient Ministry, is not successful. The people look upon him as the cause of all their humiliation. They denounce him openly. They have no hesitation in asking his abdication. He has no longer the direction of the country. No reference to him is found in the debates on the situation, except a request that he will return to Paris and await the people's pleasure. The Corps Législatif threatens to resolve itself into a National Convention, assumes the entire responsibility of the National defence, and already contemplates the idea of taking the sovereign power away from an incompetent ruler, and intrusting it to a military dictator, who shall be charged, as the Roman consuls were of old in hours of extraordinary peril, to see that no evil happen.

LICHTENBURG.

The small fortress of Lichtenburg, which guards a defile of the Vosges, near Ingweiler, has capitulated; and at Petite Pierre, and other military posts, large quantities of military stores have been taken.

THURSDAY, *Aug.* 11.—The French Minister of the Interior calls on the Prefects to organize bodies of free soldiers, who will receive one franc per day. Gardes Mobile organizing in all parts of France. MacMahon hotly pursued towards Châlons by the Crown Prince.

THE CROWN PRINCE ON THE MARCH.

ADVANCE, NANCY, *Aug.* 11.—We have passed Saverne,

Pfalzburg, Sarreborg, and Luneville, and now the whole army seems to be rushing towards Châlons and Paris. We pick up thousands of MacMahon's and Douay's stragglers, guns, and blankets. His army must be fearfully demoralized. Daily the Crown Prince shifts his quarters from village to village.

Everything is done in perfect order. The carriages are told off in a slow-moving column, with mounted troopers at intervals to regulate the line of march, and when all are placed there is a halt of a few minutes to allow the Prince and his staff to pass. Well may the villagers stare at the show, for they are not likely to see again so many fine horses and bright uniforms. Old and young crowd the wayside as his Highness goes by, and doff their caps respectfully, but without any sign of welcome. It is curious to see these German Frenchmen, or rather these Gallicized Germans, dealing with the invaders. The power of understanding one another makes their intercourse much less disagreeable than might be supposed. Yet, nevertheless, there is a strong sympathy with France among the Alsacian peasants, because they have, thanks to the conscription, such a number of their sons serving in the French army. I notice that the younger folks can all speak a little French, though they answer the question of the soldiers, "Parlez vous chassepôt," with a sententious "nein," which seems to imply utter ignorance of the language referred to. Poor souls! They are very much frightened by this astounding invasion, and make the most of their rough Alsacian dialect as a means of propitiating the new and dreaded invaders of the Empire. This dread of the invaders is founded on a notion of what might be rather than on what really happens. Beyond compulsory service in country wagons to carry wounded men or loads of hay, and compulsory sales of provisions to the military authorities, there is little to complain of. It is as with Wellington's army in Southern France in 1814, rather than as with the allied armies in that memorable year. No invasion can be pleasant to the conquered people, but this one of 1870 is conducted on the humane principles of modern warfare. The Crown Prince of Prussia has resolved to strike only at the French Government, and at the armed forces which oppose him, and to spare as far as possible the unfortunate people who inhabit the scene of hostilities.

FRIDAY, *August* 12. — Great energy of the new Ministry of France. Paris tranquil. Crown Prince at Nancy. MacMahon arriving at Châlons. The French Senate adopt the Bills granting 1,000,000,000 (a billion) francs for war purposes. King William at Herny. Canrobert goes to Metz with the Sixth Corps.

METZ.

(*Translated from the French.*)

FRIDAY (*Evening*), *Aug.* 12.— For some days there has been nothing but marching and counter-marching. The troops are utterly weary. Nearly the whole of Canrobert's corps has arrived, and the remaining regiments are coming this evening. By to-morrow 200,000 men will be in line between Montigay les Sablons, Grigny, and Herny. The soldiers, though complaining of useless fatigue, are full of ardor, and impatient of the prohibition to fire on Prussian scouts.

The Prussians occupy the whole country in front, and use the French railways to bring up troops. The whole country has been abandoned to them. They occupy the villages and towns in parties of one hundred, and even twenty. It is believed here that there is a comparatively small force opposite Metz, and that the main army is getting in the rear of the French. Gen. Frossard is reported to be under arrest. The soldiers are kept constantly in readiness, and are ordered not to take off their shoes. Thirty Prussian prisoners were brought in from Pont-à-Mousson last night. The railway was cut at that point, but is now repaired. Four spies were taken today. The dragoons of the Sixth Corps have just returned from a serious reconnoissance.

MACMAHON.

CHALONS, *Friday.*— MacMahon's extreme advance is arriving. It is composed of runaway stragglers. The main force is at Bar-le-Duc, fatigued, jaded, and demoralized. Disorganized bodies of troops are arriving here from Paris. General Trochu has been placed in command of the Twelfth Corps, a new corps forming here. General Vendez is to command the Thirteenth Corps, forming in Paris. MacMahon's 45,000 men, they say (*on dit*), has dwindled down to 18,000 men; and Douay's 30,000 to 12,000. MacMahon will have to (*lui faut*) incorporate the Twelfth Corps, now forming, into his command. Canrobert has gone to Metz with the Sixth Corps. Provisions and stores are arriving from Paris. The new troops embrace the old troops, and there is great excitement. The fortress of Toul is left with a garrison strong enough to hold it against a large army. MacMahon destroyed the Toul bridge of seven arches over the Moselle when the Crown Prince made his appearance.

Division General Jarras (until now director of the war depot in the Ministry of War) is appointed chief of staff, army of the Rhine, in place of Marshal Lebœuf; Brigadier-General l'Heriller to command the Third division in place of General Raoult, wounded and a prisoner; Pelle to command of General Douay's division; Aymard to general of division, and Vice-Admiral La Roncière le Nourry to division of marines in Paris: Rear-Admirals Saisset and Pothuan to under-commanders of this division.

SATURDAY, *August* 13.— The Emperor proclaims about Sadowa and the Crimea. Steinmetz before Metz. Prince Charles passes Pont-à-Mousson in his flank movement on Metz.

King William proclaims, "The conscription is abolished throughout the French territory occupied by German troops." The French abandon the Nied, and fall back on Metz. General Trochu forming a corps 35,000 strong in Châlons, and General Vinoy a similar one in Paris. King's headquarters at Herny. A French battalion sent from Metz toward Pont-à-Mousson retreated hastily, leaving its baggage, as the latter place was occupied by the German troops. The latter destroyed the railway north of Frouard. Other detachments took forage trains in the advanced posts of the French troops, which were still on the glacis before Metz.

EMPEROR'S PROCLAMATION.

METZ, *August* 13.

SOLDIERS:—To-morrow will be the 14th of August, that anniversary of your triumphant return to Paris after that glorious campaign which decided the destiny of Austrian domination in Italy. On that day, as after your Crimean victories, all France welcomed you with enthusiasm, and Europe dazzled, saluted you as worthy sons of the grand armies of the First Empire. To-day, however, Prussia dares to invade the sacred soil of the country. She launches against you a torrent of men, who have surprised your valor and for the moment triumph over your indomitable courage. Let us march again to encounter them. Soldiers, at Jena, against these same Prussians, so arrogant to-day, your fathers fought as one to three; again at Montmirail, one to six. Is any among you inflamed by that exciting memory, let him set an example to all Frenchmen. The Saxons, the Würtembergers, the soldiers of the Rhenish ex-confederation, groan at being compelled to lend their arms to the cause of Prussia. They know what little respect that power has for the rights of peoples. After absorbing millions of Hanoverians, Danes, and Germans, she will not hesitate to absorb the remains of Southern Germany. Insensates! a moment of prosperity blinds them. The oppression or humiliation of Frenchmen belongs not to them. May they have entered France only to find their graves! Soldiers, we shall have to deliver fierce and bloody battles; but with energy and patriotism the country's honor will be safe. For every Frenchmen with a heart, the moment has arrived to conquer or to die.

NAPOLEON.

WAR PICTURES.

(Translated from the German.)

HEADQUARTERS (between Toul and Nancy),

CROWN PRINCE, *August* 13.

What a sight! a victorious army marching. The brilliant staff comes out of the village in the midst of wondering rustics. The long train of headquarters' carriages and wagons follows steadily behind. Let us pass on through the village, and look round us as we come into the open country. Those men under the trees yonder are lancers, watching the field telegraph. That dark mass of horses and wagons creeping along the road is a column of ammunition moving towards the front. There are the sutlers' carts following the army resolutely wherever it may go, and there are the peasants pressed into the service with their carts and horses. They are not afraid of their invaders—at least, not very much afraid—as we see by those peasant girls who stand chatting with the drivers of the artillery wagons.

Now we hear the squeal of a pig and the cackle of a chicken. The rascals are looking out for something better than black bread and salt. Some soldiers have run on to a bee-hive. The bees swarm around them. The soldiers can charge the heights of Woerth, but they run like Turcos from the maddened bees. There is a shout, and the honey goes from hand to hand.

Forward from village to village, forward from one column to another, we glide to the front, and find the lancer outposts approaching the enemy with care. They look sharply about them. It is no joking matter to be shot through the head; and behind that clump of trees, just in front of them, they have a glimpse of French uniforms. Very cautiously they advance. Now we see the Frenchmen slowly winding their way up an opposite hill, and in ten minutes more the lancers are in the village below. They want food, they want forage for their horses, they ask eagerly after liquor of any sort.

The staff of the Crown Prince of Prussia is made more brilliant by the presence of several other German princes who are serving under his orders. There is the candidate for the Spanish throne,

PRINCE LEOPOLD OF HOHENZOLLERN,

riding beside his kinsman to assert the right of Germans not to be bullied because Spaniards choose to manage their own affairs. He is a jolly fellow—this "bone of contention"—this cause of the death of countless legions! He hands a flask of wine to the Duke of Saxe-Coburg, brother of the lamented Prince Albert of England, and whose little principality is German to the core. To the Fatherland they drink, and Prince Leopold points out the smoking bridge of Toul, fired by the flying MacMahon. There is the young Prince of Mecklenburg, son of the English Princess of Cambridge. He looks like an Englishman, but his heart is warm for the great German Fatherland These and other men of high position in Germany follow the Crown Prince of Prussia as he rides forth from halting place to halting place, always farther on French soil. You should stand at a corner of the village and see the staff go by.

The peasants do not cheer. It would be absurd if they did, for their sons are serving in the French army, though they are of German stock. They do not cheer, but they have a good long stare, hat in hand.

SUNDAY, *August* 14. — The French begin their retreat across the Moselle river. General advance of the German army. Severe fight of Steinmetz, in front of Metz (Pangé). The Prussians pursue the French up to the guns of St. Quentin. Germans expelled from Paris — 400 families. The French army withdrawing across the Moselle is reported to contain 130,000 men:

Bazaine, Third Corps (De Caen)	50,000	
" Fourth Corps (L'Admirault)	30,000	
" Second Corps (Frossard)	25,000	
" Gardes (Bourbaki)	25,000—	130,000
MacMahon, First and Fifth Corps		50,000
Canrobert, Sixth Corps		50,000
Total		230,000

The Prussian army in front of the French is reported to contain:

Steinmetz: First, Seventh, and Eighth Corps	110,000
Prince Charles: Second, Third, Ninth, and Tenth	150,000
Crown Prince: Fifth, Sixth, Eleventh, two Bavarian	180,000
	440,000

The Crown Prince at Toul. Prince Charles at Pont-à-Mousson, moving north toward Metz, and Steinmetz opening his guns on the east of Metz. The King at Herny, and the Emperor flying from Metz, toward Mars-la-Tour. Forty-five thousand men leave Paris for the front. The French army is now formed in thirteen corps, of which Bazaine has the Guards, and the four old corps in his "Army of the Rhine" at Metz. Three others, mixed regulars and recruits, form the "Army of Paris." The Twelfth Corps is the reserve of the Army of the Rhine, and the Thirteenth (Vinoy's) that of the Army of Paris. Fifty thousand men working on the defences of Paris.

DESPATCHES.

LONGUEVILLE, *Aug.* 14, 10 P.M. — The army began to cross to the left bank of the Moselle this morning. Our advance guard had no knowledge of the presence of any force of the enemy. When half of our army had crossed over, the Prussians suddenly attacked in great force. After a fight of four hours, they were repulsed, with great loss to them.

NAPOLEON.

The Queen of Prussia to-day received the following despatch, dated in the vicinity of Metz, Sunday evening:

"A victorious combat occurred near Metz to-day, the troops of the First and Seventh Corps participating. I hasten to the scene of the conflict.

"WILLIAM."

TO QUEEN AUGUSTA: HERNY.

A victorious combat near Metz, by troops of the Seventh and First Army Corps. Details still wanting. I am going at once to the battle-field.

The advance guard of the Seventh Corps attacked last evening, towards five o'clock, the retreating enemy, who took up a position, and called reinforcements from the fortress. Parts of the Thirteenth and Fourteenth divisions, and of the First Corps, supported the advance guard. A very bloody fight spread along the whole line, the enemy was thrown back at all points, and the pursuit was carried as far as the glacis of the outworks. The neighborhood of the fortress permitted the enemy to cover his wounded to a great extent. After our wounded were cared for, the troops withdrew at daybreak into their old bivouacs. The troops are reported to have, all of them, fought with a wonderful energy and gayety not to be expected. I have seen many of them, and have thanked them from my heart. The joy was overpowering. I spoke with Generals Steinmetz, Zastrow, Manteuffel, and Goeben.

WILLIAM.

BATTLE BEFORE METZ.

(PANGE — COURCELLES.)

The morning of the 14th found the advance of the Crown Prince past Toul, moving by rapid marches on Bar-le-Duc, cutting off MacMahon from Metz and filling Paris with consternation. King William was at Herny. Prince Charles, with the Second army, was moving rapidly across the Moselle at Pont-à-Mousson, flanking Metz, and at the same cutting all possible communication between MacMahon and Bazaine. With the Crown Prince and MacMahon it seemed like a race for Paris. Steinmetz, with Goeben and Zastrow, was encamped to the west of Metz, to prevent the retreat of Bazaine from that quarter.

Suddenly THERE COMES A PAUSE. The position of both armies is fearfully tragic. It was a moment big with events. Four armies were marching to carry out great strategetic movements. Two rulers were facing each other — Napoleon at Metz, and King William at Herny. Napoleon first sees the danger of his position, and makes preparation for a hasty flight with the Prince Imperial. Before leaving the garrison, threatened with investment, he holds a consultation with Bazaine. It is decided that Bazaine shall try to cut his way to MacMahon. The Emperor leaves at two P.M. for Verdun. He leaves a tragic proclamation behind.

He says: "On quitting you to fight the invaders, I confide to your patriotism the defence of this great city. You will never allow the enemy to take possession of the bulwark of France, and I trust you will rival the army in loyalty and courage. I shall ever remember with gratitude the reception I have found within your walls, and I hope that in more joyous times I may be able to return to thank you for your noble conduct."

When he wrote those words he thought Bazaine would soon follow him. Alas! for human calculations. Little did he think, when he left Bazaine, that he left behind him a crown and a throne. Bazaine attempted to follow. Canrobert and a portion of the Imperial Guard had withdrawn towards Longueville, following the Emperor towards Verdun, when L'Admirault and De Caen were violently attacked by Steinmetz's First and Seventh Corps near Colombey. Thus began the battle on Sunday. The advance uhlans from Prince Charles' army had espied the retreating force of the Emperor, who was fleeing with the Prince Imperial and an escort of Cent Gardes on the Verdun road.

THE FIRST CORPS (German right wing, Manteuffel) advances from Etangé and St. Barbe, in front of Noisseville and Montoy.

THE SEVENTH CORPS (left, Zastrow) and a division of the Ninth advance on Colombey.

THE EIGHTH CORPS (Goeben) is in reserve near Flanville.

THE FRENCH occupy in the beginning Servigny, Noisseville, Montoy, Colombey, and Borny (the French right, L'Admirault; centre, De Caen; left, Frossard).

The French form a horse-shoe line from Borny through Colombey, Montoy, Noisseville, and Nouilly.

The Prussians occupy the outside line of the horse-shoe, and pour a concentric and well-delivered fire upon the French. The air is filled with cannon balls falling down upon the French position. Covered by the artillery fire, at four o'clock the infantry advances. The French are driven back, and their positions repeatedly stormed.

At five the whole line is engaged. L'Admirault and De Caen show a determined front on the right at Borny, Grigy, and Colombey, and battle obstinately at every point. Zastrow advances impetuously against Colombey from the south. The slaughter is terrible. Every storming party seems to advance into the jaws of Death. The conflict grows hotter. The whole Seventh Corps is engaged — Glumer, Kamecke, and Woynac. Eight batteries pour an incessant stream of shot and shell upon Colombey. Every advance of the Prussians is met with an equally hot fire from the French. Woynac storms the French right near Colombey. It is a fearful advance. The French fire SWEEPS THE GERMAN LINES with deadly precision. These, however, were filled up, as if the North gave out heroes at call. The deep rumbling growl of the mitrailleuse, the roar of the heavy guns from the outworks of the fortifications, the spiteful spitting of the chassepôt, and the cutting ring of the needle-gun bullets, is said by the officers to have been something truly infernal! The attack is repulsed. Again the Germans form and advance over the field strewn with dead brothers. It is the advance of Lee upon the left centre at Gettysburg, but with a better result. Weary and decimated, the brave French give way. There is a shout of victory from the Prussian left, and the Ostend Brigade occupy the wood covering Colombey. The French right is defeated, and L'Admirault falls back upon the guns of Fort Quelen, commanding with 17 guns the south of Metz. De Caen looks with aching eyes towards Noisseville to know the fate of Frossard.

Towards evening, General Frossard decided to make one more attack on the Prussians to the north. This last resort was an offensive movement to turn the Prussian left towards Servigny. The First Corps met the French with sturdy courage, and then Manteuffel ordered a bold advance against Frossard. The onslaught was bloody. It was the last struggle of the giants. Crippled, decimated, and defeated, the French recoiled back upon Nouilly and then behind the guns of Bellecroix. Night threw a veil over the thousands slain, and darkness closed the fight.

In the darkness of night, the Prussians advance through the miles of slaughtered braves before the guns of Bellecroix, one of the outworks of Metz. There was sorrow as well as joy in Steinmetz's army. The victory was complete, but the real cost to Prussia was beyond computation. Few prisoners were taken and few trophies, owing to the activity of the fortress, the heavy fire of which tore through the Prussian masses. General Steinmetz, who came in, was in time to give orders for the night and the following day, and to prepare for a renewal of the conflict.

The Prussian force engaged was about 80,000 men with 125 guns, with 40,000 men in reserve.

The French force engaged was about 60,000 men, with 150 guns, with 30,000 men in reserve, besides troops in Metz.

The battle was a mitigation of disaster to the French, and a fearfully bloody success to the Prussians. In this most savage slaughter the Prussians lost in killed and wounded 4000; the French 2000.

FRENCH ACCOUNT OF THE BATTLE AT METZ (*14th Aug.*)
(*Translated from the Figaro.*)

On taking command, Marshal Bazaine, seeing the country invaded on three sides by the armies of Prince Frederick Charles, Prince Frederick William, and Marshal Steinmetz, contemplated uniting the scattered French troops at Metz, in order to be able to confront the enemy. One point in this movement was at Borny, a small village at the junction of the Boulay, St. Avold, and Forbach roads. There the enemy advanced, confident of triumph.

While, therefore, on Sunday, Aug. 14, the enemy had decided to cross the Moselle and leave Metz behind him, a great movement was taking place in the French camp. Gen. L'Admirault was preparing to turn Metz on the north, and thus separate himself from De Caen, who would enter the city, when the enemy, who was well posted at Noisseville, Montoy, and Colombey, had the boldness to open fire on us. The troops halted. The soldiers of L'Admirault, who had already left by the ravine of Vallière, returned and advanced toward the Prussians. In an instant the fire thus opened from Vallière to Grigy by way of Borny, being a length of nearly six miles. The Prussians never resisted such an attack. The cannonade continued from four to five o'clock. It ceased then for an hour, to allow the infantry and mitrailleuses to do their work, and recommenced at half-past six, ceasing only when the enemy had entirely abandoned their positions. It was one of the most glorious feats of the war. The enemy left 2000 dead on the field, while our loss was scarcely 1000. Rows of men were lying in the order they stood; and the wounded were in some cases under the dead. This was the work of the French mitrailleuses. It must be said, however, that the Prussian steel cannon did us considerable damage.

At three o'clock P.M. the Third Corps (De Caen), the Fourth Corps (L'Admirault), and La Garde Imperiale (Bourboki), were preparing also to leave their encampments, when suddenly the Prussians were seen to prepare for battle, some of their regiments taking positions as tirailleurs, some others preparing offensive movements in front of the woods of Borny, and in the direction of Grigy and Mercy le Metz. The intention was unmistakable. The French troops under the command of Marshal Bazaine, were composed of the Third and Fourth Corps and La Garde Imperiale. They were fronting Borny, Grigy, and Mercy le Metz, the Imperial Guard forming the reserve near the Fort Quelen. At half-past four the attack commenced. A heavy fire of artillery was at once heard in every direction, the soldiers of the Prussian landwehr heading the Prussian corps d'armée. A battery of artillery with a mitrailleuse was making fearful havoc in the Prussian ranks.

At seven o'clock P.M. the Prussians were making a movement of retreat. A mitrailleuse had been twice taken from the French. The brave Colonel of the Forty-fourth Infantry, Second Division, in retaking the mitrailleuse, was the cause of an immense body of Prussians emerging suddenly from the woods, and precipitating themselves as an infuriated torrent on the French divisions; it was only a pretext, for it was expected that the Prussians would follow the same tactics as at Forbach and Froschweiler, which consists of keeping out of sight their masses, their best divisions, and when the result of the battle seems to be in favor of their opponent, to change defeat into victory by that powerful movement of immense bodies of troops plunging suddenly on the enemy; but this time Marshal Bazaine had prepared a match for them. The Imperial Guard, commanded by Bourbaki, had been kept in reserve; their artillery, from a strong position, began the defensive, the grenadiers advanced, and from that moment till a quarter to nine you might have thought you were in the middle of the eruption of Mount Vesuvius. Fort Quelen sweeping with its powerful batteries the flank of the advancing columns, regiments of cavalry charging on the wings, at a quarter to nine precisely the Prussians were retreating, leaving from 23,000 to 24,000 men *hors de combat*. The French have lost close on 4000 men killed or wounded.

One hundred and forty thousand Prussians took part in the fight against 70,000 Frenchmen (positively). Owing to the Fort Quelen slaughtering the enemy, the Guards, except its artillery and a brigade of grenadiers, did not fight. They were kept in reserve to the last. During the combat, the rest of the French army was retiring on the route to Verdun, and at nine o'clock I followed the Imperial Guard, retreating in the same direction, the day's work being over.

THE EMPEROR.

(Translated from the pen-pictures of Edmond About.)

The Emperor, at the commencement of the battle, was at Longueville with the Prince Imperial, Prince Napoleon, and their aides-de-camp, in an inn situated in the middle of the village. The Prussians were certainly not aware of the presence of those illustrious guests, or the house would have been battered with artillery. Two or three shells, however, fell a few paces off, and as the village was in danger of being destroyed by the enemy's fire, the Marshal sent to warn his Majesty of the peril, and orders were at once given for the departure of the Imperial household. The Emperor and his suite mounted on horseback, but the difficulty was great, as the country around was scoured by the German troops. A guide, however, undertook to lead the party by pathways through vineyards, and at a certain moment the Emperor passed within a mile and a half of the Prussians, who, however well informed they usually are, were not aware that such a rich prize was within their reach. After two or three hours march through woods and plantations, which time must have appeared very long to his Majesty and his suite, they arrived at the high road, which they had then only to follow to reach their next destination at Gravelotte. The Emperor rested one day at Verdun, and then proceeded to Châlons by rail in a third-class carriage; the servants at the station, who had not been informed of the departure of the Imperial household, had not even time to clean out the compartments, which still bore traces of the troops who had travelled in them on the preceding days. He was only too glad to find a third-class carriage at Verdun, in which to pursue his way to Châlons. An officer approached him at St. Hilaire, and without much ceremony ventured to say, "Sire, you must be fatigued." "Yes, indeed!" answered the Emperor, "and hungry also."

He is altered astonishingly; looking not only much older, but blotched and puffy. He moves about with an air of helplessness.

CHALONS, *Aug* 14.—The Imperial headquarters present an aspect of melancholy. The Emperor does not show himself, and no one has seen him since his arrival at the camp. In passing along the road near the pavilion which he occupies, I met the Prince Imperial, in uniform, and wearing air the military medal, walking with his equerry. He had the gay and careless of a boy of his age. After following the road for a distance, he crossed a field and went and sat down on the edge of a ditch, where he amused himself in drawing lines or figures with his walking-cane in the sand.

It was on Thursday, the 28th of July, that the Emperor made his entry into Metz, and promised to lead the army beyond the frontier of the Empire. He has remained there just sixteen days, and leaves the city, as he says, "to resist invasion."

FEELING IN PARIS.

The *Moniteur du Soir* publishes an article full of confidence and resolution. The following is an extract, and is a fair exhibit of the tone of the French press:

> The passage at arms which took place yesterday under the guns of Metz is the first act in the new drama. Eight days hence the energy that has marked the first operations of the invaders will have given way to discouragement and exhaustion. Our fortified towns all hold out — Bitsche, Pfalzburg, Verdun, all defended by the army and their inhabitants, answer with their guns to the arrogant summons of the enemy. The national defence commences. It but just commences, and every Frenchman is ready to answer the call of his country. See your National Guards, Guards Mobile and volunteers, who are on the way to the Vosges Mountains! There shall the Prussians find their graves. They have asked for a war of races, and such they shall have.

MONDAY, *August* 15. — Engagement near Longueville. Departure of Napoleon for Verdun. Bazaine leaves Metz, and then places his army in échelon, right and left from Rezonville. Headquarters of the Marshal and Emperor in Gravelotte. The Guards, Second, Third, and Fourth Corps lie between Metz and Doncourt, front toward south, in two lines. The Emperor telegraphs the Empress: "All is prepared for a great battle, and in such a manner that I can now guarantee a victory that will perhaps be decisive."

Prince Charles moves north from Pont-à-Mousson toward Thiaucourt and Gorze. Bazaine reconnoitres toward Mars-la-Tour. There are now eighteen Prussian corps d'armée. Besides the First, Second, and Third armies of Steinmetz, Prince Charles and the Crown Prince, the Fourth army, under the Crown Prince of Saxony, has the Fourth and Twelfth Corps, and the Saxon and Prussian Guards; the Fifth army, under Gen. Werder, has the Würtemberg and Baden Divisions, and is engaged in the siege of Strasburg; the Sixth Army, under the Grand Duke of Mecklenburg-Schwerin, is on the Rhine.

WAR PICTURES.

(THE EMPEROR.)

(Translated from the French.)

LONGUEVILLE, *Aug.* 15.

The Emperor has transferred to this pretty little spot his headquarters, and somehow or other, by dodging about and watching my opportunity, I have been able to follow him.

ON MARCH, *August* 15 (near Genivaux).

Balls and shells, which whizzed at six this morning over my head, killed the commandant of a line regiment, and severely wounded other officers of the same regiment. Six or seven soldiers were also struck, and were borne past me to the ambulance. The fort which commands Longueville, where the enemy surprised us, discharges some twelve-pounders, and dislodges the enemy, who retire. I perch myself on the *impériale* of the post carriage. The road is full of fourgons. We draw up for a moment till our turn comes, before the house where General Changarnier passed the night.

It is half-past seven. The Emperor mounts his horse, with the Prince Imperial and Prince Napoleon. Marshal Lebœuf comes up. General

Changarnier, speaking of the brush that had taken place, says, smiling, to those who surround him, "These are Prussians, who wished to compliment the Emperor on his fête." A bouquet for a sovereign it may be, but a dangerous bouquet, and one which would have been kept far from the Imperial quarters if a better look-out had been kept. But it is always the same story. We keep no watch, and allow ourselves to be surprised by an enemy whose vigilance is extraordinary. Changarnier mounts his horse, not without difficulty, for his right leg seems to be paralyzed. He wears the uniform of a general of division. The cannonade is heard in the distance.

Eight o'clock. — We go forward across the army, ranged in order of battle right and left, and occupying strong positions. I could not be better placed either for seeing or receiving information. At half-past eight, five sharpshooters bring in seven scouts who were taken in a neighboring wood. They were quite proud of their success, and cried out as they passed, "*soyez tranquilles*, we shall nip others."

At nine we pass Moulins-les-Metz. Our troops are posted on the surrounding heights. The cannon begins to sing. At half-past nine we enter Maison-Neuve, and continue by a mountain road as far as Point-du-Jour, where the Emperor has fixed his headquarters.

Ten o'clock. — From Point-du-Jour there is a splendid panorama. Here is Rezonville, with its tufted woods and its rich dale; Gravelotte, commanding the valley of La Mance; and behind us Metz, whose cathedral stands like a piece of lace on an azure ground. The tall chimneys of mills are seen; here and there the spires of churches, and some hamlets lighted up by the sun's rays. The hill we have ascended, and at the extremity of which we now are, is called Des Genivaux. All around this the battle will take place — is taking place, for the Guards are struggling with the enemy along the whole line. The artillerymen catch the fire of battle, and hearing the discharges in the distance, they say in their strong language, "We gave them a smashing yesterday at St. Julien; we shall give them a smashing of another kind to-day." The troops are full of firmness and ardor. One sees that they do not consider themselves beaten, and that, confident in their courage, they are sure of victory, if well commanded.

"I sit on the grass to begin this letter, which will reach you God knows when. It is the first time I have written in the midst of a cannonade, and in a field. Yet it seems as though I was never more comfortably placed. One gets accustomed to everything. Marshal Canrobert leaves headquarters. The Emperor has taken a seat on a stone at the edge of the plateau, and looks down into the valley." He looks so sad — like a general defeated.

GRAVELOTTE, *one o'clock.* — Our troops hold the valley of the Marne, and the surrounding heights. A column of voltigeurs of the Guard which convoys us takes possession of a meadow; they bring in right and left dead branches, and kindle fires to cook their soup. Will they have time to finish their meal? I doubt it, for I am told we are to march immediately. Some cannon shots on our left, fired, no doubt, by the Prussians to bring us to the edge of the wood. But we know their trick now.

The opinion of those who surround me is, that the Prussians will attack towards three or four o'clock, as is their custom, and if they fail, will endeavor to surprise us to-morrow morning, as they did this morning, knowing by experience that we do not keep a sharp look-out. Our mitrailleuses are scattered over a vast extent of ground, and our artillery continues to occupy the most elevated positions. It strikes me that we weaken our lines by extending them too much. Marshal Bazaine has just arrived, and has had an interview with the Emperor. He starts for Moulins or Longueville.

Three o'clock. — An express rides by at full gallop, telling us that Canrobert's divisions have been attacked by Prince Frederick Charles, and that we had the advantage. Supporting artillery has been sent in haste from this side. Line regiments follow. They have a swaggering air — these dusty little soldiers, bronzed by the heat, and heaped together from fatigue. They inquire, "Where is the enemy?" "Down there," we reply. "We long to meet the cowards face to face," is their spirited remark. *Ces lâches-là.* This is the way in which our soldiers speak of the Prussians. No; this war of wolves, this war of trappers, this war of ambuscades, is not ours. We do not hide ourselves in order to fight the enemy; we present our breasts exposed, our heads erect. We can fight, we cannot assassinate.

TUESDAY, *August* 16. — Mars-la-Tour, the fifth great battle of the war, fought. The entire French Army of the Rhine repulsed by Prince Frederick Charles, and driven back on Gravelotte. Sortie from Strasburg defeated. Fortress Marsal captured by Bavarian troops. Pont-à-Mousson the King's headquarters.

The army of Bazaine is in position right and left from Rezonville, a town nine and a half miles west of Metz, with outposts towards Mars-la-Tour, five miles further. His lines cover the two southern roads to Verdun, extending from Doncourt nearly to the Moselle. Doncourt is on the northern branch of the Verdun road, and about fifteen miles from Metz. With the exception of the Imperial Guards, all the French troops have now suffered heavy disaster. The whole army is pervaded with the demoralization of defeat. Southern Alsace is abandoned, and there is no army there to act for the relief of Strasburg. The advance guard of Prince Frederick Charles, which has been hurrying forward by forced marches from the right bank of the river, reaches the southernmost Verdun road, near Mars-la-Tour, and attacks the left wing of the French army. General Von Alvensleben, with the Third Corps, opens the conflict, and a bloody battle, with divisions from all the corps under Bazaine's command, is gradually developed as the troops on each side come up. The Fifth German Division (General Stülpnagel) fought from nine A.M. until three P.M. without supports. Then the Tenth Corps, the Seventeenth Division of the Ninth Corps, and the Hessian Twenty-fifth Division, one after the other, came up, and after six hours more the defeat of the French was complete. The positions they had occupied were in the hands of the Germans. They lost 2000 prisoners, among whom were two generals, and seven guns. The French General Le Grand was killed; he was commander of a cavalry division, Fourth Corps.

MARS-LA-TOUR.

BAZAINE'S REPORTS.

TO THE MINISTER OF WAR: METZ, *August* 16.

This morning (at nine) the army of Prince Frederick Charles directed a spirited attack against the left wing of our position. The Cavalry Division (Torton) and the Second Corps (Frossard) maintained a stout resistance to the attack. The corps, which were placed in *échelon* right and left from Rezonville, appeared gradually upon the battle-field, and took part in the combat, which continued until nightfall. The enemy had deployed heavy masses of men, and attempted several attacks, which were stoutly repulsed. Towards evening appeared a new army corps (Steinmetz's), which attempted to cut off our left wing. We have everywhere maintained our position, and inflicted heavy losses upon the enemy; our losses are also great. At the moment when the battle raged at its height, a regiment of uhlans attacked the general staff of the Marshal; twenty men of the escort were put *hors de combat*, the captain commanding killed. At eight o'clock the enemy was repulsed on the whole line. BAZAINE.

CAMP BON ST. MARTIN, *August* 16.

TO HIS MAJESTY THE EMPEROR, CHALONS CAMP:

The army fought all day yesterday in its positions of St. Privat and Rozerieulles, and has maintained them. The Fourth and Sixth Corps only made, at about nine P. M., a change of front, the right wing in the rear, to guard against a turning of the right flank, which the masses of the enemy attempted, with the assistance of the darkness. This morning I moved the Second and Third Corps from their positions, and the army is again concentrated on the left bank of the Moselle, from Longueville to Sausonnet, forming a curved line passing over the height of Bau St. Martin in rear of Forts St. Quentin and Plappeville. The troops are wearied with incessant combats, and it is indispensable to let them rest for two or three days. The King of Prussia was at Rezonville this morning with M. Von Moltke, and everything indicates that the Prussian army is about to attack the fortress of Metz. I reckon confidently on taking a northern direction, and on pursuing afterwards by Montmédy on the road to St. Menehold and Châlons, if it is not occupied in force. In this case I will go on upon Sedan, and even Mezières, to reach Châlons. There are in Metz 700 prisoners, who will become an embarrassment to the place in case of a siege. I am about to propose an exchange to General Von Moltke for a like number of French officers and soldiers.

BAZAINE.

KING WILLIAM TO THE QUEEN.

TO THE QUEEN: PONT-A-MOUSSON, *August* 16.

The battle took place at Mars-la-Tour. We took 2000 prisoners, seventeen guns, and two eagles. WILHELM.

GERMAN OFFICIAL ACCOUNT.

At nine o'clock Lieutenant-General Alvensleben advanced with the Third

Army Corps westward of Metz, on the road to the enemy's retreat towards Verdun. A bloody fight took place between the divisions of Generals De Caen, L'Admirault, Frossard, Canrobert, the Imperial Guard and the Tenth Corps successively, supported by portions of the Eighth and Ninth Corps, under command of Prince Frederick Charles. Notwithstanding the great superiority of the enemy, they were driven back to Metz, after a hot fight lasting twelve hours. The loss of infantry, cavalry, and artillery on both sides is very considerable; on our side, Generals Von Doering and Von Wedel have been killed, and Generals Von Rauet and Von Grueter wounded.

His Majesty the King greeted the troops to-day on the field of battle, which they had victoriously maintained. VON VERDY.

BATTLE OF MARS-LA-TOUR.

To-day the French Army of the Rhine gave and lost a great battle. For the first time since the commencement of the war the French army proper was pitted against a Prussian force. At Woerth and Saarbrück only the army corps of MacMahon, Douay, De Failly, and Frossard were severally engaged. At Mars-la-Tour the Imperial Guard (Bourbaki) and the three army corps of De Caen, L'Admirault, Canrobert, and Frossard were fighting under the command of Bazaine (untrammelled by the Emperor), from nine in the morning until nightfall.

The battle was fought between the triangle formed by Mars-la-Tour, Gorze, and Gravelotte, and along the road leading from Metz to Verdun *via* Gravelotte, Rezonville, Vionville, and Mars-la-Tour. The hardest fighting occurred between Gorze and Rezonville.

THE ATTACK WAS A MISTAKE.

It was supposed Bazaine had made good his retreat from Metz, and that the troops in front were the rear guard of the French army. Prince Charles was at Pont-à-Mousson, sixteen miles from the battle-field. His advance guard were hurrying forward to the Verdun road. Between Gorze and Mars-la-Tour were marching three regiments of cavalry. Marching behind them at a double-quick were nine regiments of infantry and fifteen batteries belonging to the Third Corps (General Alvensleben). There were also a few regiments of hussars and lancers, and a division from the Tenth Corps (General Von Voigts Rhetz). The French Army of the Rhine was in front.

THE COMMENCEMENT.

At nine o'clock in the morning the Wiehen Red hussars dashed against a squadron of French. There was a hot fire of infantry, and a hundred horses dashed riderless over the field. It came like a flash of lightning, and then, like deep thunder, the French batteries opened on the astonished Prussians. The Prussians faltered a moment, but did not retreat. They did not think that Frossard, De Caen, Canrobert, Bourbaki, and L'Admirault were ready to pounce down upon them—130,000, against 80,000.

With his guns and mitrailleuses posted on the hills commanding the plain on which the Prussians were, the enemy presented an aspect which might well have staggered the stoutest heart. But the Prussians knew their duty, and in their business-like, matter-of-course way determined to do it. Finding themselves

"PITTED AGAINST SUCH SUPERIOR NUMBERS,"

they easily discerned that if they had any prospect of escaping destruction it lay in boldly assuming the offensive. If they could but put themselves in possession of the rising ground on which the enemy had placed his camp, they might perhaps be able to hold out until Prince Charles should come with the Second and Ninth Corps from Pont-à-Mousson.

"Forward, Brandenburgers!" shouted Alvensleben. And 5000 cavalry went clattering in among the French. In ten minutes the first French camp was captured, and with it 600 Zouaves and Turcos. Now came the conflict. It was Burnside and the old Ninth at Antietam bridge over again. The Prussians established themselves in the French quarters. The ground offered an advantage. Thus they stood and battled for nearly eight hours. Six times they were charged by the Imperial Guard; six times they repulsed the attack; and, pursuing the enemy in their turn, drove him from position to position. One after the other, the corps of Generals Frossard, Canrobert, De Caen, L'Admirault, and the Second Division of General

Failly were forced to give way before the Prussian onslaught. But their triumph was dearly bought by the gallant band.

UNDER THE TELLING FIRE

of the enemy, they had suffered grievously from the first. Gradually their numbers were more and more reduced; at last they were so few, and these so tired, that the French could venture to attack their guns. Once more they warded off the charge, knowing they could not do so again. Yet they saw the enemy massing his columns in the distance for a last, a decisive attempt.

The day was growing dark for Alvensleben. Where is Prince Charles? Wellington

PRAYED "FOR NIGHT OR BLUCHER:"

Alvensleben prayed for night or Prince Charles. Thunder! went the Ninth Corps' cannon off to the right, — and a long, glad shout was heard above the din of battle as the puffs of smoke from Prince Charles' musketry were seen to the right. His coming was like the coming of Sheridan at Winchester; for, eager to share the dangers and gain the laurels of that great day, Prince Charles, Sheridan-like, had ridden sixteen miles, from Pont-à-Mousson. He threw two divisions of the Ninth Corps against the French left, and in a moment he stood with Alvensleben and assumed supreme command of the Second German army.

THE BATTLE WARMS.

Von Voigts Rhetz, with the Tenth Corps, had been fighting toward the Verdun road. Alvensleben knew not precisely where, but he could hear his guns. Prince Charles, on his dripping horse, was just giving orders to his brother-in-law, Duke Wilhelm of Mecklenburg, who had led the cavalry charge, when Von Voigts Rhetz and the Tenth Hanover Corps filed into view. They were needed immediately; and off to the French right flank they went at a double-quick. They made a bloody assault towards Rezonville, but the French met their advance without flinching. L'Admirault had chosen a strong position for the French right.

INTO THE JAWS OF DEATH.

To assist the Prussian Tenth Corps, Von Voigts Rhetz called upon the cavalry of General Von Bredow and Von Rheinbaben. It was a case of life and death to storm infantry and artillery with cavalry, but it had to be done. The French position *must be taken.* Von Bredow responded quickly; and with a rush went two divisions of cuirassiers and lancers in amongst the French gunners.* The brave Hanoverian cavalry fought worthy of the military renown of their race, but alas! it was of no avail. Decimated, but not defeated, they were compelled

---

* Count Schmettow, the major in the Halberstadt cuirassiers, has written the following account of the fatal cavalry charge at

MARS-LA-TOUR:

"ETAIN (near Verdun) *August* 22.

"I will give you herewith what I can state as positively certain up to this point. I have delayed, as persons reported dead have in some instances appeared alive.

"The French cuirassiers could only succeed in taking men prisoners after they had been wounded, or after their regiment, in its heroic ride, had broken through two batteries and two infantry columns. I quite agree that a commander would be inexcusable in leading his troops into such a mess unless there were the most urgent reasons. But such was the case in the present instance. Colonel Von Voigts Rhetz, Chief of the Staff of the Third Corps d'Armée, came to our Brigadier, Von Bredow, whom we have on every occasion been accustomed to see in the thick of it, and said: 'General, in concert with General Von Rheinbaben, commander of the cavalry division, the Commanding-general has decided that you must break through at the wood, and you are still standing quietly here.' General Von Bredow replied, 'Am I to understand that cavalry is to break through infantry and artillery here by the wood?' 'Certainly,' was the answer; 'we have already taken the hamlet, but cannot reach the wood; so the issue of the battle depends upon your clearing away everything along the forest. You must attack, and with the utmost energy.' So you see we had got to do it. We formed two divisions, the cuirassier regiment on the left wing along the edge of the wood, the lancer regiment on the right wing and one hundred paces farther back. Our brave General, with his staff of four officers, three of whom he lost, was nearly on a line with the cuirassiers. Before the French battery had discharged its third gun, we were masters of it. The honor of challenging the French commander I could not leave to another, and I rather think I found him. It was clear to me that in this death-ride the object was not to bring home trophies, but to strike down everything between the wood and the road. At the battery all were put to the sword, and then we went in tearing course at an infantry column, which was ridden over, and cut down. Its remnants sent a good many shots after us. At this time the lancers were close on our heels. A second battery was attacked, and all who did not run put to the sword. Then, as many as were left of us made for a second infantry column. Just before reaching it, two squadrons of French cuirassiers wheeled from a woody hollow into the gaps of our little handful, and after the last infantry column had been ridden down, we wheeled to the right and rushed back. By this time we were pell-mell with the French horse. Before the battery I received two shots, which went through my helmet, without, however, touching me. The adjutant, hit by two bullets, fell from his horse; one trumpeter was shot down, the horse of the other wounded. I was just speaking with Captain Heister when he also fell. Lieutenant Campbell was for a while by my side, until, in the attempt to tear away from the French cuirassiers the standard he had seized with his left hand, he was fearfully maltreated. Some one helped him to cut his way out. I never shall forget my ordering the first trumpeter I found, nearly on the same spot where we set out on our ride of nearly a quarter of a German mile, to blow the regimental signal. The trumpets had been bored through by shots, and a sound came out that pierced me to the quick. At my call, three sections out of the eleven (three had been detached) assembled. A gloomy bivouac followed. Two days after, we were again under fire. The regiment lost seven officers and 206 men (of 600). It is authentically reported that all the officers are in our own hospitals. Captain Meyer and Color-bearer Von Stockhausen were buried on the battle-field."

to return. Led by a brave general, who lost three out of four of his staff, a moment victorious, and then to die or return!

The battle now remained stationary *for two hours.* It was the assault of Spicheren hill over again. Then it took 27,000 Prussians to carry the heights.

The wonder is, not that it took the Prussians seven hours to take it, but that they ever got it at all. The woods above Gorze extend to within about two miles of Gravelotte, behind which village the French lay in the morning, as also at Rezonville, another village higher up on the road from Metz to Verdun. Nearly the whole of the Prussian position was backed by the thick woods. The plain on which the battle was fought extends from the woods to the Verdun road, about one mile and a half, and is about three miles in length. On the French right the ground rises gently, and this was the key of the position, as the artillery, which could maintain itself there, swept the whole field. In the centre of the field is the road from Gorze to Rezonville and Gravelotte, joining the main road to Verdun between the two villages.

It was now three o'clock. The Tenth Corps had been under fire since eight in the morning. The French still held that fearful line of hills; yes, even more — it looked as if L'Admirault was about to assume the defensive. The Prussian Third and Tenth Corps began to waver. One impetuous advance of the French might bring on consternation and defeat. The Second Corps (Fansecki's) was expected every moment. What was to be done? In this critical emergency there seemed to be nothing left but to let loose the cavalry again, and send it right into the jaws of the hostile battalions. To be sure, to let cavalry charge against the chassepôt, and that at a distance permitting of several rounds being fired against them, would be to sacrifice vast numbers, without, perhaps, producing anything like an adequate result. In point of fact, it would be doing a thing regarded as absurd, if not absolutely impossible, by modern military science. But necessity knows no law. The attack was ordered and executed. Two regiments of dragoon guards and one regiment of cuirassiers, the whole forming a column of 1900, rode against the enemy, a thundering block of steel. Decimated long before they could flash their swords, their shattered remnants sufficed to cut down or disperse whole battalions. Then, attacked in their turn by Chasseurs d'Afrique, and immediately rescued by their own swift hussars, they again cut a path for themselves into the enemy's ranks, and actually succeeded in preventing his contemplated assault. Shortly after this repetition of the Balaklava exploit, two divisions of the Ninth Corps came into view, and a messenger flew forward with the report that Steinmetz was fighting on the Prussian right toward the Moselle and the wood of Vaux. The "Lion of Skalitz!" *Prince Charles breathed freer.*

BOTH ARMIES ENGAGED.

At four P.M., all the French and Prussian forces were engaged. Frossard, L'Admirault, Canrobert, Bourbaki, and De Caen formed a chain around Rezonville, extending from the Gorze to the Verdun road.

At five P. M., the Prussian line was drawing closer and closer. The battle surged around the lovely little villages that nestled in these valleys, and the long lines of poplar trees that crossed the battle-fields appeared only to grow the gloomier as the dark smoke of battle curled lazily among their branches. The French, feeling that the glory of France and her safety depended upon them, fought like demons. As they were driven back inch by inch, they took cover, and the long lines and heaps of German horse, foot, and artillery told that France only yielded an inch of territory when it was SATURATED WITH GERMAN BLOOD. Nothing but the most desperate resolve on the part of the German troops drove the French from their lines. At one moment it was very doubtful if the overwhelming columns of the German army corps were not being dashed to pieces, like waves against a rock. The fighting was magnificent. France yielded her glories under the same terrific pressure by which she won them.

L'Admirault still held the French right, like serried granite, against the Prussian fire. Prince Charles saw the position must be taken. It was an encounter fearful to undertake. An assault was feigned by the Ninth Corps in the centre, while simultaneously the Forty-fifth, Sixty-seventh, Sixty-ninth, and the other regiments were ordered to advance on the fortified heights on the French right. This was the key of the position, — hence the number of men (15,000) sent against it at once.

VICTORY TO PRUSSIA.

The French, knowing how vitally important it was to keep possession of the hill on their road, as soon as their troops began to fall back in the woods, had thrown up a hastily-made earthwork to shelter their infantry lying down. Behind them the Sixty-second Regiment of the Line lay, with several batteries of artillery firing over their heads. The Prussians came up the slope, but were several times repulsed, and it was not till after thirteen hours' fighting that they drove the French from the heights, and their own artillery was dragged up then. As battery after battery of Krupp guns clambered up the height, the gunners using their spurs and cutting whips freely, it WAS ALL OVER WITH THE FRENCH, and, however bravely they might fight (and the Prussians all allow their enemies fought splendidly), they must ultimately give way. The French batteries, driven from their first position, retired to the hill on their right, and a regular artillery duel took place between their batteries and those of the Prussians on their recently-conquered hill.

The report about Steinmetz proved true. His Eighth Corps had crossed the Moselle at Ars, and was now flanking the French left at Vaux. As Goeben's artillery thundered against the French, hope died with Bazaine. It was no longer an even fight, for 160,000 Prussians were in front!

Not until after six o'clock, when, some Rhenish regiments coming up, the Germans were no longer so very much outnumbered in front, did the scale of victory begin to incline in their favor. Eventually a general charge forced the enemy, already frightened by Steinmetz, to fall back, hotly pursued by the Hanoverian horse and artillery. As usual in a French retreat, confusion now ensued, and rapidly assumed a degree out of proportion to the defeat sustained. But for the vicinity of Metz and the protection it afforded to the discomfited troops, there might have been another disaster like that of Wörth. This was avoided by the nearness of the detached forts; but from a military point of view, retreat to Metz, whence there is no escape, was perhaps even less eligible than flight to Paris, however precipitate and calamitous.

THE DAY OF MARS-LA-TOUR

has cost Germany almost twice as many men in killed and wounded as the day of Königgrätz.

You cannot call this day's struggle "terrible" or "awful." The Prussian captures — 36 officers and 3000 men — have not been great, but more have been killed. There is no word for such dreadful havoc as this day has made. The French losses have been severe; but the most fearful slaughter has been on the side of the Prussians. The ground chosen by the French had many advantages, and their splendid position told fearfully upon the advancing Prussians. Their advance was the "life in death" advance of Lee at Gettysburg.

DETAILS.

Some regiments have fared badly. The Twelfth Infantry (German) lost 61 officers of the 69 it had, and 1500 rank and file of the 3000 forming its full complement. The Forty-seventh, almost equally unfortunate, had 47 officers and 1400 men removed from the ranks; the Sixty-fourth, 41 officers and 1000 men; the Seventy-second, about 30 officers, 13 of whom are dead, and 1000 men. Gloomiest of all seems to have been the doom of the Twenty-fourth, which is said to have been deprived of 2000 men and nearly all its officers. Of the Dragoon Guards we know for certain that one-half the rank and file are dead or wounded. Nearly all their officers are gone, or in a critical condition.

Fearful has been the slaughter of fathers and sons and bridegrooms. In a day or two, fathers and brothers and brides will be leaving in shoals for the front, to fetch the corpses of their beloved ones. The day's battle could not have killed and wounded less than 20,000 Prussians. An official German report shows that there were 626 officers and 15,925 men placed *hors de combat*. Eighteen hundred and thirty-two horses were lost, not including those of several South German cavalry regiments. Alas! at the name of Mars-la-Tour many a heart will ache for many a year to come!

APART FROM THE MELANCHOLY INTEREST

attaching to so fearful a collision, as a historian, the author holds up the records of this battle as affording a standard for appreciating the relative value of the contending armies. At Mars-la-Tour the French, for the first time in the entire course of this momentous war, engaged the Germans in a fair stand-up fight. Until this action, the French, having always had time to choose their ground, had either stationed themselves high on hills or dug themselves into rifle-pits, or, as usual, combining both advantages, lined the upper part of mountainous slopes with successive rows of ditches. But on this sanguinary 16th, being taken by surprise, they were mostly in the open fields, and obliged to do battle free of cover. At first they did not relish fighting under these unwonted conditions, and yielding before their advancing enemy, lost their camp and the position they had originally occupied. But soon getting exasperated at the reverse sustained at the hands of a foe not half as strong as themselves, they took the offensive with the utmost vehemence, and displayed the *élan* for which they have been so long and so justly famous. Met with composure, they eventually succumbed. The regiments who kept them at bay nearly a whole day were Brandenburgers, the descendants of the soldiers of Frederick the Great, and, it seems, as imperturbable as their forefathers.

The Prussians have not alone displayed all the valor. The French have made many brilliant charges, in one of which Gen. Le Grand was killed at the head of his division. Gen. Montaigne is missing. The Prussian Gens. Doering and Wedel were killed, and Gens. Grueter and Von Rauet were wounded.

The battle was a drawn game, but the object of Prussia — let us henceforth say, Germany — has been partly attained, for the Army of the Rhine was crippled, halted, and forced to stand and fight again, to see if Châlons or the fortifications of Metz were to be its resting-place.

STRASBURG.

August 16th.— The garrison have just made a sortie toward Hönheim, but were driven back with a heavy loss of men. They also lost three guns. A despatch from Carlsrühe, the headquarters of the Baden army, dated August 14, says the people and garrison of Strasburg have labored with zeal to arm the ramparts, clear the glacis, and barricade the entrances, but the besiegers have destroyed much of their work.

MARSAL.

Fortress Marsal, a small town a little north-east of Nancy, and formerly fortified, has been captured by a body of Bavarian troops, after a short bombardment. Sixty cannon were captured.

WAR PICTURES.

(From M. D. Conway's World Letters.)

PONT-A-MOUSSON, *August 16th.*— There was never, perhaps, an instance in which a king took possession of an important town belonging to an enemy with so little display as attended the arrival of the King of Prussia at Pont-à-Mousson. An old man in a common coach, such as one may hire in Paris on the street, with a blue uniform, covered thick with white dust — behold King William entering the largest town he can as yet claim as a trophy. There were, of course, certain forerunners — body-guard, trumpeters, etc.—, who gave the occasion, in one sense, some splendor; but when all the impressive scenes had passed, and the music and the cuirassiers in shining armor, it was almost droll to see the dusty King in his plain carriage. However, when the thunderous plaudits of the soldiers rose in the market-place as he passed, and the old man took off his hat and bowed, he showed about as good-humored and frank a countenance as ever belonged to a man throwing a million men upon a foreign soil. I have been sometimes inclined to think with poor Jeannette —

"All the world should be at peace;
And if kings must show their might,
I'd have those who make the quarrels
Be the only ones to fight;"

but, after seeing the honest, rotund, rosy face of King William, I should really say that he would be personally the last man on earth to make a quarrel, and that the last thing that any one could associate with him would be a duel with Louis Napoleon.

Bismarck entered the city *incognito;* that is, there was no parade about his entrance. In truth, it is not absolutely certain in my mind at this moment that it would have been safe for the Count to have shown himself in any very public way. Whatever fears his friends might have had, he himself evidently had none; for hardly had he descended from his carriage than he set out to stroll on the streets. How he came to be recognized, I do not know. I was in a small chocolate shop on a side street, when the word was tossed and caught from door to door — and the people live now outside their front doors — that the huge figure walking along the street was Bismarck.

"Bismarck! Bismarck! Bismarck!"

Men, women, and children half shrieked, half whispered it, and with pallor and agitation, as if they had beheld a man with one flaming eye in his forehead, who drank blood instead of beer (which Herr Bismarck decidedly *does* drink), and was in the habit of supping on at least one baby each evening. With wonder, but also with some anger, they gazed at him, as he moved along in the middle of the street — a sort of European institution. As I looked at him closely, I conceived an impression that the Count has not been unmindful of some recent inventions in the way of bullet-proof underclothing, and that he has not chosen, since the attack of young Blind upon him, to submit the task he has to complete a German Confederation to the caprices of the lead and iron which are beginning to fly about so rudely just now.

MONDAY, *August 17th.*— Both armies exhausted, and resting. Steinmetz and Prince Charles concentrate troops, and prepare for Gravelotte. King William rides seven hours over the field of Mars-la-Tour. Gen. Trochu appointed Commander of Paris. The Emperor and Prince Imperial leave Châlons for Rheims. Emile Ollivier flies from Paris. He is hooted at the station. General Sheridan a guest of King William. Von Falckenstein expostulates with Admiral Fourichon against the capture of Prussian unarmed merchantmen.

ALL QUIET ALONG THE LINES.

PONT-A-MOUSSON, 18th, 11.20 A.M.

Complete calm prevailed during the whole of yesterday. The German army maintains the positions gained by the victory of the 16th. The object of that battle was completely attained. The cavalry of the Third Corps d'Armée attacked in the morning, without waiting for the support of the infantry; after having been rejoined by the latter it fought for six hours, resisting three French corps and a part of the Imperial Guard until the evening, when the Tenth came up to its aid. The cavalry of the Third attacked with great vigor, broke the French ranks with the sacrifice of many lives, and drove back the enemy on Metz. Many prisoners have been taken, including several officers of the Imperial Guard. Gen. Sheridan, of the United States Army, is at the King's headquarters.

(Signed) VON MOLTKE.

TROCHU GOVERNOR OF PARIS.

The General Trochu is named Governor of Paris, and Commandant-in-Chief of all the forces charged to provide for the defence of the capital.

Done at Châlons. NAPOLEON.

STEINMETZ FEELS THE ENEMY.

On the 17th the First corps was beyond Ars sur Moselle; the Eighth and Ninth Corps were at Gorze, while the Second army was marching rapidly toward Metz, on the Verdun road. After the victorious fights at Vionville and Flavigny, the task of the First army this day was to act as the right of all the lines of attack, holding the left bank of the Moselle, while the Second army moved so that the front would extend from the north toward the east, thus bringing the First and Second armies between Metz and Paris. On the 17th no offensive movement was made, the Prussians resting in a sheltered position near Gravelotte; the Seventh Corps contenting itself with repelling a slight reconnaissance near the forest of Vaux. Gen. Steinmetz, reconnoitring at the south of Gravelotte, in the forest of Ognons, discovered the enemy, three corps strong, encamped on the heights north of Gravelotte. Gen. Steinmetz, hearing a cannonade at Verneville, and having been falsely advised that the head of the Ninth Corps was engaged, gave orders to resume the attack. The Seventh Corps deployed on the south and east of the heights of Gravelotte. A formidable artillery practice followed, presenting an imposing spectacle. Fifty cannon, presently augmented to eighty, opened on the enemy's batteries, while advancing steadily along the high-road was a *mitrailleuse*, whence fire was opened on the reconnoitring party. Strong outposts, well sustained, were placed. The enemy made no serious attack that day.

NAVAL MATTERS.

A Prussian ship, bearing a flag of truce, boarded Admiral Fourichon's vessel. Prince Von Hessen, received by Baron de Roussin, announced that he bore a letter for the Admiral. He spoke in German, which the Baron did not understand, and the English language was used in the further negotiations. The Baron, saying that he was authorized to open the letter, did so, and, finding it written in German, requested to have the contents explained in English. After an hour, which the Germans improved in examining the French vessels, the answer of the Admiral was brought. The two letters are as follows:

EXCELLENCY: You have opened hostilities at sea by the capture of German merchant ships, and have thereby forgotten that we are at present in a condition on land to be able to make unrestricted reprisals for such a war against peaceable Germans. In the interest of your countrymen I submit to your Excellency to make war on the sea only against armed forces, just as at present in France war is not made against unarmed citizens. Well, then, let us fight each other as knightly soldiers, show ourselves equally honorable, respect the private property of peaceable citizens. If your Excellency is of the same mind, you can make known your inclination to give back the ships you have taken; you will gain more by that course than these small prizes are worth to you. The bearer of this, Rear-Admiral Prince Von Hessen, is charged by me to deliver this letter, and to conclude terms with your Excellency. With particular respect, your Excellency's to command,

VON FALCKENSTEIN,
General Governor of the Coast Lands.

ANSWER.

ON BOARD THE "MAGNANIME," August 18, 1870.

My interpreter of the German language being at this moment on a cruise in another frigate, I have been able to obtain only an imperfect comprehension of the letter you have done me the honor to write; but the Prince of Hessen, your flag-of-truce bearer, has indicated its object to my chief of staff. Its purpose is to secure to private property upon the sea the respect which the law of mankind accords it upon the land. Your Excellency is not ignorant, that up to the present day the international law and treaties do not agree with that stipulation, and you will readily acknowledge that such a subject lies exclusively within the prerogatives of our governments, and that I have in no way the right to treat of them. Be pleased, Excellency, to receive the assurance of my highest consideration.

L. FOURICHON, Vice-admiral.

GRAVELOTTE, THURSDAY, *August* 18. — Last great battle near Metz. Severe fighting from eight in the morning until nine at night. The French defeated — their centre pushed back by Steinmetz, their right flank turned by Prince Charles, and Bazaine's entire army forced back to Metz. King William sends a despatch of victory. Palikao deceives Paris, by claiming a French victory. Bazaine sealed up in Metz. General Von Werder assumes command of German troops operating before Strasburg.

* At daybreak the First German army, with the First, Seventh, and Eighth Corps, stood on the hills south of Rezonville. The Second army, with the Third, Ninth, Tenth, Twelfth, and Guard Corps, was on the left flank, south of Mars-la-Tour and Vionville. The southern branch of the Verdun road, west of Rezonville, was in the hands of the Germans. The northern branch as far as Cautre was held by the French, whose line extended from Amanvillers, through Verneville and Gravelotte, to the Bois de Vaux. Towards ten o'clock in the morning, after having already spent six hours in visiting the corps in position, the King from the heights of Flavigny ordered the Ninth Corps, in position there, to move toward the woods behind St. Marcel; while the Seventh and Eighth Corps marched against the Bois de Vaux, south of Gravelotte. The latter had orders to push the enemy very slowly, in order to give time to the Guards and Twelfth Corps to make a long detour on the left, by way of Jouaville, Batilly, and Ste. Marie aux Chênes. The Third and Tenth Corps were in reserve, and but few of their troops were in the fight, these being mostly artillery. The principal movement was that on the left. Preceded by

* This synopsis, as well as valuable statistics on other occasions, is taken from the *Army and Navy Journal* (39 Park Row). This journal has shown much talent in its military reports and reviews of the present war. Its writers have shown a power of analysis deserving appreciation, and a military acumen which has made plain many obscure situations. The author only wishes that he knew the individual writers, that he might give them the personal credit due.

Prussian and Saxon cavalry, the Second army advanced, still maintaining communication on the right with the First army. The Twelfth Corps took the direction by Mars-la-Tour and Jarny, while the Guards advanced between Mars-la-Tour and Vionville on Doncourt, and the Ninth Corps crossed the highway to the west of Rezonville, toward Cautre farm, north of St. Marcel. Their purpose was to gain the central and northern roads. They quickly found that the French were not retreating, and moved to the right, meeting at Ste. Marie aux Chênes and Doncourt resistance which was overcome, and after another struggle among the steep hills at St. Privat-la-Montagne, that place was gained. The right flank of this Second army holding the centre of the whole German line, had been earlier engaged with some advanced forces of the French, and toward noon the Ninth Corps was engaged at Verneville. The Guards and Twelfth Corps reached St. Privat about four P.M., and immediately moved south and east against Amanvillers. The fighting here was exceedingly severe. The Germans lay in a long curve, sweeping from St. Privat, where the Saxons fought on the extreme left, through Ste. Marie aux Chênes and St. Ail (Guards), Verneville (Ninth corps), Gravelotte (Eighth corps), and Bois de Vaux (Seventh corps), across the Moselle, on the right bank of which a brigade of the First Corps and artillery from the reserves were engaged. The French army fought with its back to Germany; the Germans had Paris in their rear. Bazaine's entire army was in line, including those troops which had been prepared for the Baltic expedition. On the left wing the flanking column, after meeting with resistance at every point, pushed its enemy back through Ste. Marie, Doncourt, St. Privat, St. Ail, Habouville, the wood of La Cusse, and Verneville, until, toward evening, two small outworks of Metz, lying northeast of Gravelotte, and named *Leipzig* and *Moscow*, were reached. All the roads south of Metz were then firmly in the hands of the Germans.

The right wing had great difficulties to overcome. Early in the day its work was to press the French lightly in the Bois de Vaux. Back of this wood was the strongest part of the French position. It was covered by a deep road with sides fifty feet high, back of which was a plateau 325 to 600 feet in height. Behind this is the Rozerieulles hill, along the slopes of which the highway to Metz runs. This whole steep was covered with rifle pits, in three tiers. Behind these were the infantry; behind the infantry the artillery. The highway as it runs along this hill is only 5000 yards in a straight line from Fort St. Quentin, one of the strong outworks of Metz. But the crest of the hill intervenes between them, and by the road the distance is nearly twice as great. The French soldiers, driven from this last position, and crossing the ridge, would find themselves directly under the guns of their forts. When news of the successes on the left, and the evident abandonment of the retreat by the French, was brought to the King, he moved forward to a hill near Rezonville, and ordered more positive action on the right wing. The French, however, maintained their post with great determination. Driven from it at one time, they retook it by a counter-charge. The King, to whom news of the success had been sent, arrived on the hill back of Gravelotte only to see his cavalry on the wrong side of the defile, on the opposite side of which the enemy stood. The fire of the artillery ceased ; the troops had lost so heavily, that the position seemed to be beyond their grasp. The King, however, ordered another attempt, and after an hour, during which night came on, the troops were re-formed. They were no sooner in motion than the whole face of the hill revealed such rows of artillery and infantry, delivering an extremely rapid and deadly fire, that General Von Moltke sent an officer to recall the troops. Before he was out of sight, the men appeared themselves, returning down the hillside, fully repulsed. Just then the Second Corps, which had been on the march since two o'clock in the morning, came up, and as soon as enough regiments showed themselves, they were sent to take the hill from which their comrades had so often returned in failure. Following the withdrawing storming party came the French in counter-attack. Their success was so great, that the German troops showed symptoms of serious disorder. Some parts of the line began a disorderly retreat, and the moment was critical. General Von Moltke, who had anxiously awaited the coming of the Second Corps, rushed up, and himself gave them the word to advance. They sprang forward after him, and, when the reinforcement was well up the hill, the repulsed troops were again sent forward, going through their terrible experience for the last time, as it proved, with great steadiness and spirit. This attack succeeded ; and at half-past eight the last position of the French was in the hands of their enemy. Bazaine officially reported his wounded at Gravelotte at 18,000 ; and for 18,000 killed and wounded that Bazaine lost, his enemy lost at least 25,000. The Prussian captures were, at Vionville, 36 officers and 3000 privates; Gravelotte, 54 officers and 3000 privates.

BAZAINE'S DESPATCH.

To His Majesty the Emperor, Camp of Chalons:

Camp of Fort Plappeville, *18th August*, 1870.
20 m. past 8 in the evening.

I do not understand the importance of provisioning Verdun. I think it is necessary only to leave there what the fortress requires. I have come in from the plateau. The attack has been very smart. At this time, seven o'clock, the firing has ceased. Our troops constantly remain in their positions. One regiment, the Sixtieth, has suffered severely in defending the farm of St. Hubert. Bazaine.

KING WILLIAM TO THE QUEEN.

Bivouac, near Rezonville, *August* 18, 9 p.m.— The French army, occupying a very strong position to the west of Metz, was to-day attacked nnder my leadership, and after nine hours' fighting was completely defeated, cut off from its communications with Paris, and driven back towards Metz. William.

SECOND TELEGRAM.

About 8.30 p.m. fighting ceased gradually. Without this I should have acted as at Königgrätz. Von Roon saved me this alternative. The troops have performed miracles of valor against an enemy equally brave, who withdrew by inches, resuming the offensive to be again repulsed. I cannot foretell the enemy's fate. I shrink from learning our losses. I had designed bivouacking here, but I find, after some hours, that I am without my luggage. In fact, I have not removed my clothing for thirty hours. (Signed) William.

THE KING'S LETTER REPORT.

To the Queen: Rezonville, *August* 10.

Yesterday was a day of renewed victory, the consequences of which cannot yet be estimated.

In the early morning the Twelfth Guards and Ninth Corps proceeded toward the northern road from Metz to Verdun as far as St. Marcel and Doncourt, followed by the Third and Tenth Corps; while the Seventh and Eighth, and finally the Second, remained opposite Metz. As the former swerved to the right, in thickly wooded ground, toward Verneville and St. Privat, the latter began the attack upon Gravelotte, not heavily, in order to wait until the long flank march upon the strong position Amanvillers-Chatel should be accomplished as far as the Metz highway. This column did not get into action until four o'clock with the pivot Corps, the Ninth at twelve o'clock. The enemy put forth stout resistance in the woods, so that ground was gained only slowly. St. Privat was taken by the Guards, Verneville by the Ninth Corps; the Twelfth Corps and artillery of the Third then went into action. Gravelotte and the woods on both sides were taken and held by troops of the Seventh and Eighth Corps, and with great losses. In order to attack again the enemy, who had been driven back by the flank attack, an advance beyond Gravelotte was undertaken at dusk, which came upon such an enormous (*sic*) fire from behind rifle pits *en étage*, and artillery fire, that the Second Corps, which just then came up, was forced to attack the enemy with the bayonet, and completely took and held the strong position. It was half-past eight before the firing gradually silenced itself in all quarters. By this last advance the historical shells of Königgrätz were not wanting near me, from which *this* time Minister Von Roon removed me. All troops that I saw greeted me with enthusiastic hurrahs; they did wonders of bravery against an equally brave enemy, who defended every step and often attempted offensive attacks, which were each time repulsed. What the fate of the enemy will now be, pushed into the intrenched very strong position of the fortress of Metz, is still impossible to determine. I dread to ask about the losses, and to give names, for only too many acquaintances will be named, and often incorrectly, Your regiment (the Queen's) is said to have fought brilliantly. Waldersee is wounded severely, but not fatally, as I am told. I expected to bivouac here, but found, after some hours, a room, where I rested on the royal ambulance which I had brought with me; and, since I have not a particle of my baggage from Pont-à-Mousson, I have not been undressed for thirty hours. I thank God that he vouchsafed us the victory.

WILLIAM.

FRENCH DENIAL.

In the Corps Législatif, the Count de Palikao, Minister of War, made the following statement:

The Prussians assert that they were victorious on the 18th. *I affirm the contrary.* I have communicated a despatch to several of the Deputies, showing that three Prussian army corps united and attacked Marshal Bazaine. *They were repulsed*, and driven into the quarries of Jaumont. My reserve about this despatch will be understood. I need not mention the small advantage gained near Bar-le-Duc. We are now actively completing the fortification of Paris. In a few days all will be assured.

OFFICIAL REPORT OF GRAVELOTTE.

(Translated from the German War Office Despatch.)

TROOPS LOCATED.

On the morning of the 18th, the First Army, with the Seventh Corps, was posted south of Gravelotte, the Eighth Corps and the First Cavalry Division being south of Rezonville (the First Corps of the Third Cavalry remained on the right bank of the Moselle, before

Metz). This army was first directed to cover, in the wood of Vaux and at Gravelotte, the movement of the Second Army against any sortie of the enemy from Metz. The Second Army advanced in the morning by échelons of the left wing toward the north road, maintaining communication on the right with the First Army. The Twelfth Corps took the direction by Mars-la-Tour and Jarny, while the Guards Corps advanced between Mars-la-Tour and Vionville on Doncourt, and the Ninth Corps crossed the highway to the west of Rezonville, toward Cautre farm, north of St. Marcel. These three corps composed the first line, and if the assigned points were reached, the north main road was gained. Saxon and Prussian cavalry preceded the column as skirmishers.

THE ADVANCE.

As soon as it was found that the enemy did not contemplate a retreat, and could therefore only remain before Metz, it was necessary to move these three corps considerably to the right, and to bring up both armies against the enemy. The Tenth and Third Corps followed in a second line, and then as the last reserve the Second Army Corps, which since 2 A.M. had been marching from Pont-à-Mousson toward Buxières. About 10.30 it was evident that the enemy had abandoned his retreat, and had taken up a position on the last ridges before Metz. The Second Army was thereupon ordered to carry out its sweep to the right, and, keeping up communication with the first, to direct its centre and left wing on Verneville and Amanvillers. The general attack was not to begin till the movement was entirely executed, and till the front of the strong position could be simultaneously attacked on the right flank. The Ninth Corps first threw itself on advanced detachments of the enemy. Toward noon artillery fire from the neighborhood of Verneville announced that the corps at that spot was engaged. The First Army was consequently ordered to occupy the attention of the enemy on the heights by artillery fire from its front.

THE BATTLE OPENS.

About 12.45 they opened a slow and well-directed cannonade upon the eminences of the Pont-du-Jour, to which the enemy replied from numerous batteries. The thunder of the cannon was drowned by the strange noise of the mitrailleuses.

The position was an exceedingly strong one, and its security was increased through fortifications and by ranges of rifle pits; at certain points it had quite the appearance of a fortress. The attack could not succeed until our commanders had achieved the difficult task of so directing their measures that the whole of the troops were ready as well for the battle on the north as on the east, and the latter attack could only commence when it was apparent that the enemy had given up a retreat. It was not practicable, moreover, to completely carry out the movement, which was to envelop the enemy's right wing, and nothing remained but to attack the front of this formidable point. The struggle was long and difficult at various points. On the left wing the Saxons fought, and the Guards near Ste. Marie aux Chêsne, afterward near the precipitous slopes of St. Privat la Montagne, then in that village and in Doncourt. On the right, at St. Ail, and beyond at Habouville, the wood of La Cusse and Verneville, as far as the northerly road from Metz to Verdun, the Guards and the Ninth Army Corps sustained the struggle; at Gravelotte, and in the Vaux wood up to the Moselle the Eighth and Seventh Corps; and from the further side of the river bank a brigade of the First Corps took part in the fight, likewise some single divisions of the Third and Tenth Corps, especially artillery. On the enemy's side the whole of the main French army was engaged — even the troops originally destined for the Baltic expedition, with the exception of MacMahon's divisions not stationed at Metz, and the larger part of Failly's corps.

THE BRAVE TROOPS.

The unsurpassable bravery of our troops succeeded, at the approach of dusk, in storming the heights and driving the enemy from his whole line; the Second Corps, which had been marching since 2 A.M., taking a decisive part in this, on the right wing. The battle terminated about 8.30, when it was quite dark. During the night the enemy drew back into his intrenched camp at Metz. Numberless wounded and stray detachments still wandered in the neighborhood of the battle-field. His Majesty, who had directed the battle ultimately from the hill of Gravelotte, made Rezonville his headquarters.

The losses, as was inevitable in such a combat, must be very considerable; at present they cannot be approximately stated, as just as little can the number of the prisoners and other trophies be reckoned. As to the last, as in reference to all encounters round Metz, a great booty cannot be looked for, as pursuit was not possible in the vicinity of the fortress. The battle formed the conclusion of the previous strategic movements round Metz, and the result is that the hostile army is for the time cut off from all communication with Paris. It is a subject of rejoicing that on this eventful day the brotherhood in arms of the Prussian, Saxon, and Hessian troops has been sealed in blood.

BATTLE OF GRAVELOTTE (AUGUST 18).

All day long on the 17th, preparations were progressing for

to-day's great conflict. Steinmetz, whose advance near Gorze had attacked the retreating French force on the 16th, was now on the west bank of the Moselle, with the First, Seventh, and Eighth Corps, ready to march against the French left. Late last evening, the "Lion of Skalitz" felt the enemy, and he knew there was bloody work for to-day.

The last remnant of Prince Charles' army, with the Second Corps, had been hurrying down all night from Pont-à-Mousson. Three hundred thousand men were preparing the machinery for a grand battle which was to decide the fate of two of the grandest armies of modern time. The King was to command in person.

The bloody conflict of Mars-la-Tour had thrown the French back on the Verdun road, from Vionville, through Rezonville, to the hills around Gravelotte, the little village at the junction of the two roads from Metz to Verdun, about seven miles from Metz. There, on a circle of hills, from the wood of Vaux, by Gravelotte, towards Moscow, stood the Army of the Rhine. There was Canrobert, De Caen, Bourbaki with the Imperial Guards, L'Admirault, and all that was left of Frossard. The French had 160,000 men; the Germans, 280,000 (the First, Seventh, Eighth, Second, Third, Twelfth, Ninth, and Tenth Corps).

Eight A.M.—Morning found Steinmetz directly in front of the French left centre, between Gorze and Rezonville (see map), his left extending in front of Rezonville. Prince Charles was marching his forces, the Twelfth, Ninth, and Guard Corps, directly north between Mars-la-Tour and Flavigny, the Third and Tenth following in reserve, and the Second farther towards Pont-à-Mousson. Steinmetz had orders to remain still until Prince Charles should wheel his three corps to the right toward Verneville, and come against the French right flank. All the morning the Ninth, Twelfth, and Guard Corps marched northward, the left of the line wheeling towards the French right. Twelve o'clock found the pivot Corps ready for action. The Second Corps, coming forward, joined Steinmetz, and commenced an attack on Gravelotte. The corps making the extensive flanking march did not become engaged until four o'clock.

The King commanded in person, surrounded by Von Moltke, Bismarck, Von Roon, Sheridan, etc., his headquarters being on the battle-field of the 16th, on a hill commanding a view of the

French and Prussian centres and a part of their wings. From this commanding position, directly in front (southwest) of Gravelotte, the view was magnificent. On the left was the road to Verdun, for the possession of which this series of actions had begun. It was between the lines of poplars which stood against the horizon on the left; and on, as far as the eye could reach, toward Metz, with military regularity, strung on this road like beads, were the pretty villages, each with its church tower, all of which are really only a hundred yards apart, although they have separate names — Mars-la-Tour, Flavigny, a little south of the road, Vionville, Rezonville, and Gravelotte, which is divided into Great and Little Gravelotte. On the right were the thickly-wooded hills, behind which lie sthe most important village of the neighborhood — Gorze. So environed was the foreground of the battle, which should be called the battle of Gravelotte, for it was mainly over and around that devoted little town that it raged. The area indicated is perhaps four miles square.

The Seventh and Eighth Corps of Steinmetz, and the Ninth (pivot Corps) of Prince Charles, opened the conflict.

The author now follows the thread of the narrative of an eye-witness (with some corrections which time has made), believing, as remarked before, that the testimony of a disinterested eye-witness on a battle-field is the truest history which will ever be written. The description used here is that famous account published in the London *News*, and cabled by Mr. George W. Smalley to the *Tribune*, *World*, *Times*, *Herald*, and *Sun*.

Twelve o'clock, M.—At this moment the French were making a most desperate effort to hold on to the last bit of the Verdun road — that between Rezonville and Gravelotte, or that part of Gravelotte which in some maps is called St. Marcel. The struggle was desperate, but unavailing; for every one man in the French army had two to cope with, and their line was already beginning to waver. Soon it was plain that this wing, the French right, was withdrawing to a new position. This was swiftly taken up under cover of a continuous fire of their artillery from the heights beyond the village. The movement was made in good order, and the position, which was reached at one o'clock and thirty minutes, would have been pronounced impregnable by nine out of ten military men. When once this movement had been effected, the French retreating from the pressure of the Prussian artillery fire, and the Prussians as rapidly advancing, the battle-field was no longer about Rezonville, but had been transferred and pushed forward to Gravelotte, the junction of the two branching roads to Verdun. The fields in front of that village were completely covered by the Prussian reserves, and interminable lines of soldiers were steadily marching onward, disappearing into the village, and emerging on the other side of it with flaming volleys.

THIS SECOND BATTLE-FIELD

was less extensive than the first, and brought the opposing forces into fearfully close quarters. The peculiarity of it is, that it consists of two heights, intersected by a deep ravine. This woody ravine is over 100 feet deep, and at the top some 300 yards wide. The side of the chasm next to Gravelotte, where the Prussians stood, is much lower than the other side, which gradually ascends to a great height. From their commanding eminence the French held their enemies fairly beneath them, and poured upon them a scorching fire. The French guns were in position far up by the Metz road, hidden and covered among the trees. There was not an instant's cessation of the roar. Easily distinguishable amid all was the curious grunting roll of the *mitrailleuse*. The Prussian artillery was posted to the north and south of the village, the guns on the latter side being necessarily raised for an awkward half-vertical fire.

THE CARNAGE.

The French stood their ground and died — the Prussians stood their ground and died — both by hundreds, I had almost said thousands. This for an hour or two, that seemed ages, so constant was the slaughter. The hill where I stood commanded chiefly the conflict behind the village and to the south of it. The Prussian reinforcements, coming up on their right, filed out of the Bois des Ognons; and it was at that point, as they marched on to the field, that one could perhaps get the best idea of the magnitude of this invading army now in the heart of France. There was no break whatever for four hours in the march of men out of that wood. It seemed almost as if all the killed and wounded revived and came back and marched forth again. Birnam Wood advancing to Dunsinane Hill was not a more ominous sight to Macbeth than these men of Gen. Goeben's army to Bazaine, shielded as they were by the woods till they were fairly within range and reach of their enemies' guns. So the French must have felt; for between four and five o'clock they concentrated upon that spot their heaviest fire, massing all available guns, and shelling the woods unremittingly. Their fire reached the Prussian lines and tore through them; and though the men were steady, it was a test to which no General cares to subject his troops long. They presently swerved a little from that line of advance, and there was no longer a continuous column of infantry pouring out of those woods.

THE PRUSSIANS RECEIVE A CHECK.

The attack of the Prussians in the centre was clearly checked. About five o'clock, however, a brigade of fresh infantry was again formed in the wood, and emerged from its cover. Once out from under the trees, they advanced at double-quick. I watched their movement. The French guns had not lost the range of the wood, nor of the ground in front. Seen at a distance, through a powerful glass, the brigade was a huge serpent bending with the undulation of the field. But it left a dark track behind it, and the glass resolved the dark track into falling and dying and dead men. As the horrid significance of that path, so traced, came upon me, I gazed on more intently. Many of those who had fallen leaped up again and ran forward a little way, striving still to go on with their comrades. Of those who went backward instead of forward there were few, though many fell as they painfully endeavored to follow the advance.

I do not know whether, after the vain effort of that brigade, another movement was attempted from within the wood. But half an hour afterward great numbers of troops began to march over the hill where I was standing, and moved forward toward the field where so hard a struggle had been so long protracted. These also were, I think, a portion of Gen. Goeben's troops, who had been directed upon a less dangerous route.

Steinmetz was getting tired and exhausted in front. Every moment he expected to hear the roar of Prince Charles' guns on the French right flank. The battle stood still.

THE FLANK MOVEMENT.

4.30 *P.M.*— The troops of Prince Charles on the Prussian left begin to be heard from. The grand flank movement of the Ninth and Twelfth Corps begins to strike the French right.

The battle from this point on the Prussian left became so fierce that it was soon lost to us, or nearly lost, by reason of the smoke. Now and then the thick cloud would open a little and drift away on the wind, and then we could see the French sorely tried. To get a better view of this part of the field, I went forward about half a mile, and from this new stand-point found myself not far from Malmaison. The French line on the hills was still unbroken, and to all appearances they were having the best of the battle. But this appearance was due, perhaps, to the fact that the French were more clearly visible in their broad height, and fighting with such singular obstinacy. They plainly silenced a Prussian battery now and then. But the Prussian line also was strengthened by degrees on this northern point. Infantry and artillery were brought up, and from far in the rear, away seecmingly in the direction of Verneville, shot and shell began reaching the French ranks. These were the men and these were the guns of Prince Charles, who then and there effected the junction of the Ninth, Twelfth, and Guards Corps with Steinmetz, and completed the investment of Metz to the northwest.

With reinforcements for the Prussians thus continually arriving on both sides of the field, the battle grew more and more obstinate. There could be no doubt that the French well understood the meaning of the new movements of the Prussians, and of the gradual development of their line to the north.

Farther and farther towards Metz the Twelfth Corps fought its way until the French were outflanked, and began to be threatened, as it appeared, with an attack on the rear of their extreme right wing. So long as the smoke from the Prussian guns hovered only over their front, the French clung to their position. The distance from headquarters to where the Prussian flank attack stretched forward was great, and, to add to the difficulty of clearly seeing the battle, the darkness was coming on.

Prince Charles' army was doing its deadly work. Bazaine began to fear that his communications with Metz would be cut off. The Prussian onset became irresistible. The puffs of smoke from the French guns mingled with the flashes, brightening as the darkness increased, receded gradually. The pillars of cloud and flame from the North as gradually and steadily approached. With that advance the French fire every moment grew more slack. It was not far from nine o'clock when the ground was yielded finally on the North, and the last shots fired on that terrible evening were heard in that direction.

ANXIETY AT HEADQUARTERS.

But to go back now to the movements of the King and those with him at headquarters. The King's face, as he stood gazing upon the battle-field, had something almost plaintive in it. He hardly said a word, but I noticed that his attention was divided between the exciting scenes in the distance and the dismal scene nearer his feet, where they were just beginning what must yet be a long task — to bury the French who fell in Tuesday's battle. On them he gazed silently, and, I thought, sadly.

Count Bismarck could not conceal his excitement and anxiety. If it had not been for the King, the Count would clearly have gone forward where the fighting was. His towering form was always a little in advance of the rest.

When the French completely gave up their hold upon the road up to Gravelotte, the horses of the Headquarters' party were hastily called, and the entire party, mounting, with the King at their head, dashed down to a point not very far from the village. Then shouts and cheers arose, and followed them wherever they passed.

A CAVALRY CHARGE.

A little after four o'clock a strange episode occurred. From the location of the flanking army a magnificent regiment of cavalry galloped out. They paused a moment at the point where the Conflans road joins that to Metz. Then they dashed up the road toward Metz. This road between Gravelotte and St. Hubert's is cut through the hill, and on each side of it rise cliffs from forty to sixty feet high, except at the point where it traverses the deep ravine behind the village. When it is remembered that at the time the culminating point to which that road ascends was held by the French, it will not be wondered at that only half that regiment survived. What the survivors accomplished, I do not know; nor could I learn the name and number of that regiment, which seemed to meet its fate under the eyes of the King. The situation hardly admitted asking many questions, but their plunge into that deep cut on the hillside, where next day I saw so many of them and their horses lying, was of that brave, unhesitating, unfaltering kind, which is so characteristic of German soldiers, among whom stragglers and deserters seem to be absolutely unknown.

THE RESERVES ADVANCE.

The army of Steinmetz had been fighting long and hard, and suffering, it was only too plain, heavily. From this army division after division had been taken, and vainly sent against the French centre.

The Third and Tenth Corps of Prince Charles' army had been decimated fearfully in the engagement on the 16th. These corps were in reserve to-day, and were only to be called into action in a pressing necessity. At one time it seemed that every German division, brigade, and regiment would be needed. The losses in the centre, and the massing of great forces for a fresh attack on the French right flank, left the Verdun road itself at one time almost uncovered — the very road for possession of which the Prussians were fighting.

At this critical moment the Third and Tenth Corps, decimated in the fight of the 16th, marched upon the field, occupying ground before held by a portion of the forces of Steinmetz. They passed the point which in the morning had been the royal headquarters. For hours before dark, their dark lines could be seen winding towards the front. It cannot be doubted that the presence of that large body of men made itself felt upon the fortunes of the field. They were visible to the French as well as to us.

Here was another example of the moral effect that may be and so often is exerted in battle by masses of men whose presence is known to the enemy, but who may not fire a shot in the actual conflict. From their line of march it is clear that the divisions were finally posted a little in the rear and on the left of the Prussian centre at the time when the attacks so long directed against the key of the French lines had ceased — in fact had failed for the time. It was possible that the French, having suffered far less in holding their ground than the Prussians in attacking, might have advanced in their turn and have undertaken a vigorous offensive movement. If they had any such purpose, it is not unlikely that they abandoned it on sight of the Prussian reinforcements.

Instead of advancing, the French now contented themselves with the mere occupation of the ground to which earlier in the day they had been driven back. At no time did they seriously strive to regain the westernmost line of hills which had been theirs in the morning. At no time did they recover, or seek to recover, by any vigorous forward movement to the junction of the roads at Gravelotte. From seven to eight the weight of the battle tended more and more to the north of the road. There was a lull, the meaning of which the French failed apparently to interpret. By seven they may have believed themselves partly victorious. They were still perhaps in condition to renew on the morrow the struggle that had gone on all day for that fated road from Metz to Verdun. If they had not gained the road or the battle, they had not clearly lost the latter. Two hours later they had lost both.

A BLAZING HOUSE ILLUMINES THE FINALE.

A little before eight, a large white house on the height beyond Gravelotte caught fire. It seemed through the gloom to be a church. Its spire grew into flames, and a vast black cloud of smoke arose, contrasting strangely with the white smoke of the battle. More and more picturesque grew the whole field. As evening fell the movements of the troops could be followed now by the lines of fire that ran flickering along the front of a regiment as it went into action. Tongues of fire pierced through and illuminated the smoke out of the cannons' mouths, and the fusees of the shells left long trains of fire, like falling stars. No general likes fighting by night in ordinary circumstances, for chance takes then the place of skill; but the flanking movement on the French right had been resolved on by daylight, and it was the necessity of moving troops to a great distance over difficult ground which delayed its execution and brought about what seemed a renewal of the battle after the day was done.

A NIGHT ATTACK.

To leave the French in their positions during the night, would have been to imperil the plan on which the Prussian commander had resolved. So, from eight, or half-past eight to nine, the decisive blow was struck. When the battle of Gravelotte had actually ended, we knew that the Prussians held the strong heights beyond the Bois de Vaux, which command the surrounding country to the limits of artillery range from Metz; we knew that two great Prussian armies lay across the only road by which Bazaine could march to Paris for its relief, or for his own escape; we knew that a victory greater than that of Sunday, and more decisive than the triumph of Tuesday, had been won. We believed that the French army, which had fought as valiantly and as vainly as before, was now hopelessly shut up in its fortress.

As I went back to the village of Gorze to pass the night, I turned at the last point to look upon the battle-field. It was a long, earth-bound cloud, with two vast fires of burning buildings at either end. The day had been beautiful so far as nature was concerned, and the stars now looked down in splendor upon a work of agony and death such as no one could ever wish to see again.

THE KING.

For ten hours the King was exposed to the enemy's fire. He had taken a seat near a garden wall, close to Rezonville. A worsted spinning factory on fire near by illuminated the royal headquarters.

A ladder, one end resting on a pair of scales and the other on a dead horse, furnished a seat for His Majesty. He was accompanied by Prince Charles, the Grand Duke of Saxe-Weimar, Count Von Bismarck, and Minister of War Von Roon.

The deepest silence reigned, when suddenly Gen. Von Moltke, gasping for breath, approached and cried, "Your Majesty, we have conquered!" "Hurrah!" was the response, and the party, all life now, began a frugal supper of soldiers' brown bread.

SECOND ACCOUNT (GRAVELOTTE).

The following vivid account of Gravelotte was written by the Rev. M. D. Conway from the battle-field, for the New York *World:*

GRAVELOTTE, *August* 18. — As I passed up from Gorze, I saw an opening into a beautifully green valley, embowered, and with a soft sward, and thought to myself that it was fit to be the haunt of artists and thinkers, who loved solitude. Shortly after, I found that this very valley was one centre of the bloody struggle. It holds the very "quarries of Jaumont" into which M. Palikao said the French had repulsed the Prussians. Over this country, then, upon which art and nature have united to put the most exquisite finish, I saw scattered already

SOME THOUSANDS OF MASSACRED MEN,

and in the distance the vast din, the shriek, the roar, the mad shout — as the weird, demoniac work went on.

I hurry on to the spot where King William is standing with his military cabinet around him. The old King, stout, and somewhat heavy, looks upon the scene before him with a certain wonder. A herald on horseback dashes in with a despatch in his hand — "for the King!" While it is being read nominally for King Wilhelm, really for General Von Moltke,

THE KING NESTLES

between Count Bismarck and Moltke, like a child. I fancy the old man is getting too aged now for his faculties to be in a very active condition. No one seeing these officers could help remarking how fine-looking they are. Tall, shapely, handsome, richly-dressed, they made a magnificent show on the field, even more as they stood for an hour or so, than when mounted. Count Bismarck stood with his eagle eye piercing to the far confines of the battle-field, as if he would search out every individual Frenchman in the ranks. He paced up and down for a time, speaking to no one. Then he would go and chat a little with General Sheridan. Then he built himself a seat of the knapsacks of fallen soldiers, and sat gazing upon the long line of the French, who seemed to stand as an immovable wall. At length the Count went to a small shelter of canvas, and stretched his great form on the ground, as one who would sleep. His eyes did not close an instant.

There was another messenger. The Count gained his feet by one leap. He glanced beyond Rezonville, toward the road, and saw the French line begin to waver. Then

HIS EYES SHONE WITH FIRE.

He sprang to his horse, the whole party following his example, and they rode to a nearer position, where, with burials of the dead going on all around them, they watched the process of multiplying the already horrible host of the dead. As they rode on, they passed by a point where, on a space of twenty yards square, lay piled thirty-one dead men, and seven horses, French and Prussians mingled and mangled together in a way that I count it a misfortune to have seen.

There are brilliant parties of uhlans dashing forward upon their chargers. A regiment of them has just passed us, shouting "hurrah!" and darting away until they are lost to my eye in the smoke and din about the

VILLAGE OF GRAVELOTTE.

But on the whole, the cavalry seem to me to be at this juncture, in a strictly military sense, more ornamental than useful. The men who are doing the work are those fellows whom I see fighting their way inch by inch, purchasing every yard of their advance with a thousand lives. It was after these brave fellows on foot, with losses such as I shudder to think of, had at last convinced the French commander that to hold on the road by Gravelotte was impossible, and the effort to do it mere sacrifice of life — it was after these with dogged pertinacity had at last slowly forced back the French line, that it alone became safe for the King to go nearer, attended by his officers and lancers.

During all this fighting, I have seen nothing that looks like brilliant fighting, manœuvring, fine and swift combinations — nothing whatever. The men have been set before each other in ranks, and they fire at and kill each other; when one rank on either side is destroyed, another is put forward in the same place. At one o'clock, I observed a large mass of troops midway the village of Gravelotte, standing on this side of it, so still that they seemed to the naked eye like masses of humanly-shaped black rock. Looking at them through the glass, they were plainly fighting, and fighting very hard. The outline of this mass of men hardly changed. Reverting to it from time to time, it could be seen that it was shrinking in dimensions. About five o'clock, it had vanished into the village. About 5.30, about two-thirds of the same mass crept with similar slowness out on the other side of the village. At every other point, something of the same kind appeared, which seemed to indicate that the age of great generalship has made way before the "pegging away" system of warfare.

If war comes to be the mere deciding of which of two nations can hold out longest in losing men, might the same end not be reached by simply comparing the census of each with the other?

The French were driven out of and beyond Gravelotte, that is, at their centre, at a comparatively early period. But all the more did they concentrate themselves on the two sides. On the moment when they (the French) seemed to be inclining to co-operate on their right with those who were contending with Steinmetz, that general

ORDERED A CAVALRY CHARGE

up the great Metz road, at the point where it cuts a deep ravine through from Gravelotte below, to St. Hubert on the height. That was the wildest movement, apparently, of the struggle. The charge was made, I doubt not, with the intention of preventing any co-operation of the French centre with its right, by cutting in between them. It would also for the time have covered the road, hy which the infantry might climb to the height beyond the "carrières" which the French were holding. These ends may have been partially accomplished by the cavalry charge; but if so, it was accomplished by the sacrifice of the large number of them. The French right fought against heavy odds. The whole landscape in front of them was darkened by soldiers; and with all their gallantry and heroism, they gradually (in the course of three hours) lost their hold on the road, falling back to Malmaison, and in two hours more losing their hold even on that point.

A little after four o'clock, there came over the hill across the point which had been the King's headquarters in the morning, a new army altogether. It did not come from the direction of Pont-à-Mousson, nor from the north, but straight from the east. So exactly from the east did this army come, that when their bayonets were seen in the distance against the horizon, there was a sort of panic at the front, where we stood, and a cry that they were French troops just arriving with MacMahon to attack the Prussians in the rear. This, as you may readily judge, was a civilian's panic; but certainly it was a curious problem for many besides civilians to know what corps this was. I asked an officer whose men they were. "It will be known," he replied with a smile, "when the history of the war is written." The current explanation is, that they were a corps from the army of the Crown Prince.

This corps did not go into battle.* It stood ready to crush any victorious French body that should have cut its way through to the Verdun road.

THIS WAS THE HOPELESSNESS

of the French case. Their every army had to confront two armies, their every man two men.

At the same time it should be said, in justice to the Prussians, that the French held the commanding heights of the field. The Prussians had to fight up hill from the time they left Gravelotte at their backs. The French position was equal to an army corps, and nothing but the willingness of the Germans to spend their last man in that one conflict, ever drove them from it.

On the Prussian right, General Goeben had as much as he could do. The French on that side had their artillery in perfect position, and there they held on until after dark. They shelled all the roads, all the woods, along which the Prussian reinforcements were advancing, finally forcing them to abandon that path altogether. The soldiers who were wounded on that side of the battle-field — with many of whom I have conversed to-day — told me that the mitrailleuse told upon their ranks with such effect, that whenever they heard its peculiar sound, they knew that they were weaker than before. Whatever officers may think or say, one who has to-day mingled with the rank and file will recognize very plainly that

THE MITRAILLEUSE

has become to them a terror. So fearful were the wounds made by it — almost always fatal — that a rumor prevailed to-day that the balls were explosive. I picked up many boxes which held their balls, as they lay unused and scattered on the field, and was unable to find one that was not quite as solid as the ball of the chassepôt or the needle-gun.

The King and his party remained on the battle-field until the last gun was fired; they then went to Rezonville to pass the night. But it was no easy matter. The men of the red cross, who alone war against pain and death, had already borne a very large number of the wounded into all the villages, and the always small accommodations of Rezonville were insufficient to afford lodgings to the generals, except the wounded were removed. Of this none of the royal party would hear. A small room was found for the King, but the rest,

MOLTKE, BISMARCK, AND THREE PRINCES,

slept on the floor, on straw. They supped together before retiring, the supper consisting only of black bread, and very fat cold pork.

In any of these houses, one may see Prussians and Frenchmen tenderly assisting each other, and they not unfrequently, when either knows the language of the other, are found conversing upon the war and its causes, without coming to high words.

At daybreak, this morning, new regiments fresh from Germany were still arriving in great numbers. A long train of provision wagons was started westward, on the direct road to Paris. It is plain there is to be no delay in the progress of the army towards that city. The officers and soldiers generally name a week as the longest time it can take them to reach and enter Paris.

The scene to-day has been sad in the extreme. The King has been visiting the wounded, and personally thanking and encouraging his soldiers. Bismarck and Prince Frederick Carl and Prince Carl, and Lieutenant-General Sheridan, have been riding over the field.

Sheridan said: "*The Prussians are winning, but it costs them dear.*"

But just outside of the villages there have been dreary, touching scenes they have not seen. There, young French girls — beautiful girls, of good position — are hiding, crouching, terrified, with nothing to eat, little to wear, their homes smoking ruins, their friends they know not where.

It became plain by five o'clock, that the French could not regain what they had lost — that they were defeated. Yet for three hours thereafter the battle was more desperate than at any other time. Nay, after dark the French tried to cut their way to the road on the right and left

BY A FURIOUS ONSLAUGHT,

but they only added more to the list of killed and wounded on each side. The last roll of musketry was heard far on toward nine o'clock. For ten minutes the bombs darted and burst over the cloud of smoke like meteors. Then all became silent. After a pause a loud shout of victory rang round the German lines, caught from rank to rank, and echoed on

---

*These reinforcements were the Third and Tenth Corps (Alvensleben and Von Voigts Rhetz) of Prince Charles' army, which, on account of having been fearfully decimated in the battle of Mars-la-Tour, had been kept in reserve. The fact that their existence could not be accounted for by the King, proves on what a large scale the battle was fought. They were under the immediate command of Prince Charles, and their evolutions would not be known to the King. The Crown Prince was fifty miles away towards Bar-le-Duc, moving after MacMahon.

the far verges of the vast army, and then again there was a deep stillness, broken only by the groans of the poor sufferers, who could hear the pæan only with dying ears. A few burning houses shot up pillars of fire, which stood as monuments of the day of devastation. Near the little village of Flavigny, I met two young girls, bareheaded. One of them had in her apron about a pint of rice. "*Ah, mon Dieu! mon Dieu!*" one of them exclaimed, "what shall we do?" "Do you live here?" I asked. "We did live in the house at the corner there," pointing to some blackened walls, the interior of which was just sinking into ashes.

"NOW ALL WE HAD IS BURNT UP.

Our friends have run away, and we know not where they have gone. Last night we slept on the ground in the field out there." They then sat down on the side of the street, and wept. "Here is some bread," said a rough German soldier, drawing his whole ration from his haversack. His were not the only eyes that were wet.

The field was covered with rifles, swords, and all manner of accoutrements. They are collected and guarded carefully. An officer permitted me to take away a French sword as a souvenir, for no Prussian will wear a sword that has been raised against his country. No Prussian sword is allowed to be touched under any circumstances. There is a custom of firing off every rifle they find on the field loaded, and they do it rather carelessly. A bullet passed uncomfortably near my head from one of the arms so discharged; and the ignorance of a German concerning the chassepôts which he was collecting to-day, cost a Prussian colonel his life.

I passed to the most advanced line of the Prussian army — not without some nervousness — for it was not known how soon a shell from the French might announce the renewal of hostilities. From that point, with the aid of my glass, I saw the French in their camp on the hill St. Quentin, in front of Metz. They seemed, however, to be busy about other matters than fighting, and their activity was no doubt the preparation for a complete retirement within the walls of Metz. There is nothing whatever left to prevent the Prussians from taking possession of any position they please in the surrounding country. *The French are hermetically sealed in Metz.*

FRIDAY, *August* 19.— Napoleon at Châlons. De Failly reaches Châlons after disastrous losses. Canrobert in Metz. The Crown Prince at Bar-le-Duc and Vitry-le-Française. Metz invested by Steinmetz and Prince Charles. Strasburg bombarded, and twelve houses in Kehl burned. Gen. Von Werder protests against the bombardment of Kehl, an undefended city.

By Imperial order, a Committee of Defence is formed in Paris, consisting of General Trochu, president; Marshal Vaillant, Admiral Rigault de Genouilly, Baron Jérôme David, General De la Tour, General Guiod, General D'Autemarre D'Ervillé, and General Soumain. It possesses the fullest powers.

FRENCH BLUNDERS.

(*Correspondence of Pall Mall Gazette.*)

NAPOLEON UP.

CAMP OF CHALONS, *August* 19.— When Napoleon started from Paris, three trains were hardly sufficient to carry his carriages, furniture, and equipages of all sorts. Even his genérals and aides-de-camp took with them their plate and linen, and every possible comfort. They imagined they were going to war like Satraps. General Frossard, at the battle of Forbach, remained at table having his dinner till four o'clock, while his division was being cut to pieces, and, when his aides-de-camp came in to tell him things were going wrong, he answered them, smoking his cigar, that it would be all right, for he had taken all his measures! Such things are most incredible, but when they are told by eye-witnesses who have been the sufferers of all that abominable system of favoritism, and who still suffer, and are ready to suffer again, and die without a complaint, one must believe them.

NAPOLEON DOWN.

The Emperor, whom I caught sight of this morning, is altered to a degree one could not imagine possible, He is old-looking, but besides being aged, he looks blotchy and puffy, and withal quite impotent and helpless. A gentleman who was with me, to whom I told the change I noticed, answered by a sentence that struck me: "*Il est pourri, et sa pourriture a amené celle de l'Empire.*" As for the Prince Imperial, all he can do is to call out for his papa. He came up to an officer of the Cent Gardes with whom I was talking, and asked us if we had seen his papa. I am told he asks for his papa if he loses sight of him for ten minutes.

FOOLISH GENERALS.

I have met here the officers of the Forty-ninth Infantry, who have just arrived here from Bitche, where they were with De Failly. They have given me several astounding proofs of the more than foolish conduct of that General, and also of the incredible incapacity of French Generals, who were thought for a long time by the world to be the most learned captains of Europe. The day of the battle of Reichshoffen, they say M. De Failly would have been in plenty of time to reach the scene of action. The cannon were distinctly heard ahead, but he kept every three or four miles making halts of an hour or more; and when they retreated they marched for twenty-four hours without lying down. They had no food, and they arrived here marching every day, and sometimes in the night, without the corps having any distribution made to them the whole time. The officers say they do not know how the men lived, for they only had what they begged at the doors of villagers. As to the officers, they only had what they could get from the men. The number of stragglers was incredible, and they say some regiments were 300, 400, and even 500 men short, who are still in the villages through which they have passed. They have remained eating and drinking with the peasantry, who have been heard to say they had rather have Prussians than such guests as these; for those soldiers who have remained behind in that way are the scum of their respective regiments.

BLUNDERS, BUT NO DISCIPLINE.

Discipline is entirely destroyed in that corps. The officer who was telling me this was nearly stabbed by one of his own regiment, whom he was punishing for firing off his rifle in the midst of a village, alarming the whole column, which is a very serious thing. As for the ignorance of the staff, on a night march, the General had to ask his way at the junction of two high roads in France from a peasant. There was not a map or a field-glass among the whole staff, and on one occasion they had to send to a small railway station to borrow one, where they obtained one which concerned only race-horses. They have since sent to Paris for some at the

War Office whence, by mistake they have received maps of Africa, which will not be very useful for the Department of the Meuse.

STARVING SOLDIERS.

The French papers keep on saying the French army is perfectly provisioned, and so it is at Châlons; but all the regiments that have been employed and moving, have but one story to tell, viz., that they have been starved. It is enough to see their faces, to guess what they had gone through; they are gaunt and thin; as for the color of their faces, the sun alone could not give it. They have slept night after night in fields flooded with water; they have lived upon crusts of bread, or potatoes which they stole in the fields; their beards are grown; in short, they don't look like men.

THE EMPEROR BUTCHERS 250,000 FRENCHMEN AND GERMANS.

A distinguished officer, William de Robau, writing to a British journal, thus unmasks the real situation:

It seems incredible, from what we as yet know, that any one man could so deliberately have plunged a country suddenly into war with not one single arm of the naval or military services really prepared, but such is the fact; and it was within my personal observation at the camp lately, that whole divisions went into action in a literally famishing condition, as well as deficient in drill and general efficiency. Of about 450,000 men sent to the front, up to September 1, it is my serious opinion, from ocular evidence, that not over 200,000 were really in a state of discipline or drill fit to face even an ordinary enemy, let alone such an army as that of confederate Germany. "Turcos" and "mitrailleuses" alone were relied on as balancing all and every deficiency, and when the irresistible impetuosity of the Germans demolished those two military fallacies—for such I hold them to be—why, the collapse was fearful, terrible beyond precedent. I believe it quite within the mark to set down the number *hors de combat* of the two armies, French and German, at not less than 400,000, of which fully 250,000 are dead, or badly maimed for life; of the numbers killed outright, it is not easy to speak definitely, as fully fifty per cent of the merely wounded perished on the field where they fell, from want of ambulance and hospital care. I remember seeing one trench fully a kilomètre long, wherein at least 10,000 German and French dead were indiscriminately huddled, many bodies not yet quite cold. People are naturally saddened, not despairing, but quite the other way, though in my humble opinion I believe Paris utterly indefensible under the circumstances, and against such an army as the German; but there is no one to utter the word "surrender," and if the Germans will persist in attacking Paris, why they will only enter it as Sebastopol was entered. I believe there is no gasconade in the determination thus expressed, and I cannot help thinking that Germany will eventually regret a war of extermination against a nation which was literally driven blind-folded into it, like sheep to the slaughter; war is one thing, but this campaign has been butchery, not war.

THE PRUSSIANS CIVILIZED.

France does not suffer what is technically called "the horrors of war." Young girls stand at the cottage doors in the villages, or street corners, to see the soldiers pass, and are not harmed by them. The shops open in the towns are not plundered. Peaceable citizens go about their business without fear for life and limb. It is essentially civilized war in these respects. But fruit and vegetables are taken along the wayside, horses are pressed into the service, soldiers are quartered on the people, and large supplies of food are demanded from the local authorities.

WAR PICTURES.

Murat Halsted thus writes to the *Cincinnati Commercial:*

Those who paint battles are generally sycophants. In Meissonier's "Solferino" there is not much to be seen beside the Emperor and his horse. The galleries at Versailles are disgusting in the everlasting adulation of royalty. Your picture of a battle consists principally of a king, or emperor, or marshal, on a portentous horse in an impossible attitude and incredible situation. So when the Prussians paint the battle of Gravelotte the feature will be King William on his steed, dashing dreadfully at a staggering square of infatuated Frenchmen, and my only consolation will be in making oath that the stalwart and superb old monarch did nothing of the kind. The scene on the hill at three o'clock: The King, with Prince Frederick Charles and Baron Moltke, and a glittering company of princes and highnesses, and great captains and shining staff officers — and Count Bismarck, lying in his waterproof overcoat on the ground, supporting his puissant head in the white cap, with the red band, on a hairy French knapsack — and Phil. Sheridan a few steps aside and ahead, with his field-glass steadfastly on the fight, and the King's carriage with the oriental servant on the right, the slope of the hill toward the battle littered with dead horses — the burial party between the hills (if we may speak of hills in merely a rolling plain) dragging head and heels the fallen heroes into the broad, but not deep trench, where the ripe fruit of ambition is gathered; the next slope facing westward so covered with dead, that the resemblance to a flock of sleepy sheep lying among red rags is striking and obvious. Take this scene, and for a background give us a village with a single sharp stub of a spire, and a burning house, a few dark lines and a great deal of smoke, and if the artist had the root of the matter in him, and did not elaborate the king too much, he might produce a picture not absolutely absurd, as are nearly all the war pictures in the world.

SATURDAY, *August* 20.— Reported attempt of Bazaine to cut his way through the German army. Prussians on short rations in front of Metz. Opposition to Napoleon commences in Paris. Republicans begin to talk treason against the Empire. The King at Pont-à-Mousson. Marshal MacMahon appointed commander of the First, Fourth, Seventh, and Twelfth Corps, General Lebrun receiving command of the last named in place of General Trochu.

MACMAHON TO THE MINISTER OF WAR.

CAMP OF CHALONS, *August* 20, 1870, 8.45 A. M.

The intelligence which has reached me seems to show that the three armies of the enemy are placed so as to intercept Bazaine on the roads of Briey, Verdun, and St. Michiel. Not knowing the direction of Bazaine's retreat, although I am ready to march, I think I shall remain in the camp until I have knowledge of the direction taken by Bazaine, whether to the north or south. MARSHAL MACMAHON.

The Minister of War, in reply, says:

20TH, 3.40 P. M.

The only information I can give you is the following: On the 18th. in the evening, Bazaine occupied the line from Amanvillers to Tussy.

SORTIE AT METZ.

METZ, *August* 20.—Marshal Bazaine, at the head of the French troops, made a most desperate effort, just at daybreak this morning, to cut his way through the Prussian investing line. He was met instantly by the Prussians in great force, and, after three hours of desperate fighting, repulsed with a loss to the French. The Prussians are on half rations, the First Prussian army having now occupied the same region for some days, and the country all about being eaten out; but supplies are hourly expected, and the men are cheerful.

FIRST GLEAM OF THE REPUBLIC.

The Republicans don't care to push things much faster than they are going; they do not, at least, want to declare a republic now. The nearest to a conclusion reached last Friday by about a hundred of them, members of the Left, journalists and others, was to wait and watch the growing chance. At a later and much smaller meeting, or interview, between a dozen Republicans and Gambetta, the latter being asked whether Palikao deserved all the trust he seemed to place in him, answered, "Yes, because he is a traitor."

Gambetta, young as he is, shows more of the quality of a political leader than anybody else in the Chamber, except the Nestor, Thiers. The real trouble is the old one: the party is all heads and no body. As Béranger long since said, "There is no one for Vice-President." But the mill even now has begun to grind Napoleonism pretty hard, crushing it finely and not slowly. The Napoleonists are already bolting, and getting ready to bolt.

You hear treason constantly in the open streets and cafes. Spies, if any still remain, may listen and be welcome. Even the American tourists and residents are cooling in their admiration for the Emperor. As for Trochu, the Parisians have already nicknamed him "*Ollivier on a war-footing.*" Ollivier himself kept his promise to support his successors, by quitting the Chamber. Rarely before has he been so faithful to his word.

PRINCE AUGUSTUS TO THE GUARDS.

The commander of the Corps of Guards, Prince Augustus of Würtemberg, which suffered so cruelly at Gravelotte, issues the following order. His men, numbering 35,000, are said to have lost one-fifth of their force.

SOLDIERS OF THE CORPS OF GUARDS,— In a bloody battle God has given us victory — a victory which we only now see in all its extent and greatness. The Corps of Guards has been able to contribute in a prominent manner to the achievement of that victory. All arms have rivalled in courage and endurance. The artillery by united efforts at decisive points, and by deliberate and correct firing even where exposed to the shots of hostile infantry, has successfully prepared and supported the attack of the infantry. The storming of the villages of Ste. Marie aux Chênes and St. Privat-la-Montagne, each surrounded with stone walls, under the murderous musketry fire of the enemy, has been carried out in a manner which is above all praise. Carried away by the example of their officers, the infantry, with the sharpshooters and pioneers, drove the enemy from a position considered by him unconquerable. Our losses are great with which we have purchased the victory, but Ste. Marie aux Chênes and St. Privat-la-Montagne are glorious laurels which you have added anew to the brilliant wreath of victories of the Corps of Guards.

SOLDIERS OF THE CORPS OF GUARDS, — You have once more justified the confidence which His Majesty our most gracious King has ever placed in his Guards, and this confidence you will also maintain in future. I am proud to be commander of such a corps. Hurrah for the King!

BIVOUAC AT STE. MARIE AUX CHENES, August 20, 1870.

SUNDAY, *August* 21. — General Trochu prepares Paris for a siege. Prince Charles, before Metz, lends the Crown Prince two-and-a-half army corps (the Fourth and Twelfth Corps and cavalry under the Crown Prince of Saxony). The King at Pont-à-Mousson. Metz to be starved out. Crown Prince marching on Paris. The Emperor at Rheims. A decree dated Rheims, August 21, signed by the Emperor, appoints MacMahon Commander-in-Chief of the Army of Châlons and Paris. Blockade of the East Prussian coast declared. Four French ships anchor in the bay of Putzig; and during the night the German corvette *Nymphe* steals among them, and delivers two broadsides, returning safely to anchor.

PARIS MUST STAND A SIEGE.

PARIS, *August* 21. — General Trochu has issued another proclamation, the meaning of which is, that Paris will have to stand a siege. The following is the text:

To the National Guard, to the Garde Mobile, to the Troops and Seamen in the Army of Paris, to all the defenders of the Capital.

In the midst of events of the highest importance, I have been appointed Governor. The honor is great — the peril also. I depend on your patriotism. Should Paris be subjected to a siege, never was there a more magnificent opportunity to prove to the world that long prosperity has not effeminated the country. You have before you the example of an army which has fought one against three. Their heroic struggle compels the admiration of all. Show by your conduct that you have the feeling of the profound responsibility resting upon you.

FORWARD GERMANY.

CROWN PRINCE'S HEADQUARTERS (near Toul). — While there seemed a chance that Napoleon might win near Metz, it was necessary to hold the Third army in readiness to march northward; and so while battles were raging near Metz, this army lay about Nancy and Luneville, half expecting to be ordered up to support the other German armies. Then came news of the defeat of the French by Steinmetz and Prince Frederick Charles. There was no longer any need to hesitate about invading Central France, and the march was begun of which you will soon hear the results.

There is a straight and rapid march westward of the Third army, supported by other troops. Without giving details of the movement, it is to be said that more than 150,000 men, full of confidence, flushed with victory, and splendidly organized, are about to "beat up the quarters" of the French.

Three or four columns march abreast on some roads. Two go by the main road itself, and sometimes two more move through the fields on the right and left; at least one other column makes the adjoining fields — though the marching is a little out of order, it serves the purpose of the moment. Sometimes there are great blockings and crushes of the moving forces, but on the whole it is remarkable how well the columns are directed, and how carefully their routes are chosen through the invaded province.

AUERBACH AT STRASBURG.

(*Translated from the German.*)

Berthold Auerbach, who has been summoned to the headquarters of the Grand Duke of Baden, has commenced a series of letters on the siege of Strasburg. The most recent abound in picturesque incidents and narrative:

August 21. — No Sunday bells rang out in all Alsace to-day; not the less do the villagers stream out from every hamlet towards the churches. The peasants are astonished to see at church so many of our soldiers, and of higher and lower officers, all attending without orders. Wonderful coincidence, the Gospel lesson, tenth Sunday after Trinity, was Luke xix. 41: "And when he was come near, he beheld the city, and wept over it, saying, If thou hadst known, even thou, at least in this thy day, the things which belong unto thy peace! but now they are hid from thine eyes. For the days shall come upon thee, that thine enemies shall cast a trench about thee, and compass thee round, and keep thee in on every side, and shall lay thee even with the ground, and thy children within thee; and they shall not leave in thee one stone upon another: because thou knewest not the time of thy visitation." Is it not strange that upon this day the text should fall? for on this week will events move forward, perhaps even the destinies be decided by Strasburg, the city stolen by the French. And within it stands a hallowed relic of German architecture and German piety. Evil reports fly about. It is said that Commandant Uhrich has declared that when Strasburg can no longer be defended from the German forces, he will blow up the Cathedral and lay the crime upon the Germans. That would be a sad prospect. The enclosing of which the Gospel speaks, fails not. By Lambertheim stand 2200 peasant wagons. Round about, in all the villages and on the roads, cannon of every calibre, up to the heaviest siege, advance, with abundant ammunition. An exchange of despatches hurries to, and fro. Our pulses beat quicker. We have plunged into the whirl of an historic drama. The arrogant governor of Strasburg citadel must no longer feel secure; at least, he is throwing out ballast. This morning one hundred German soldiers, who had served in the Foreign Legion, were thrust out, ten at a time, at all the doors, with the threat that if they turned round they should be immediately shot down. The poor wretches stood between two fires. Some of them wore French uniforms, and were naturally regarded by our troops as Frenchmen. As they neared our outposts who knows how many would get fired upon? I saw two of them brought in. They were born Pomeranians, and fell into the hands of their own landsfolk. The expulsion of these people may be regarded as a symptom that discipline inside the fortress is in a very precarious condition. And yet it is said the commandant, simply because the French arms have suffered defeat in the open field, now declares that they will vindicate their honor in the fortress. But after what fashion? By the sacrifice of a beautiful city and of thousands of its inmates. Is that to be called a vindication of honor? How much effort is made on our side to show forbearance, is evidenced in the renewal of strict orders to spare, even in the minutest details, the property of the Alsatians.

MONDAY, *August* 22.—The siege of Strasburg continued. The course of the river Ill changed. Bazaine holds all his positions. The Crown Prince planning an advance on Paris. The camp at Châlons broken up. MacMahon moving to relieve Bazaine, with 120,000 men. Destruction of the Bois de Boulogne. 480,000 Prussians in the field. MacMahon leaves Rheims, marching in the direction of Rethel and Mézières. Châlons completely deserted.

MACMAHON MARCHES TO BAZAINE.

The following despatch from Bazaine, through Colonel Stoffee, MacMahon's chief of staff, changes MacMahon's course of march:

LONGWY, *August* 22.

TO MARSHAL MACMAHON, CHALONS:

I have been obliged to take up a position near Metz, to give rest to the soldiers and to renew my supplies of provisions and munitions. The enemy is continually increasing around me, and I shall probably take the northern line to join you, and will give you warning if a march can be undertaken without compromising the army. BAZAINE.

Châlons camp is deserted. Rheims is crowded with MacMahon's troops. A part of Bazaine's force which escaped from Metz is coming in. The troops and officers are discouraged that Bazaine has failed to come up. The force here numbers, under MacMahon, 100,000.

Evening.— The whole army is moving towards Ardennes. They take the road to Rethel and Mézières [respectively twenty-four and forty-seven miles north-east of Rheims].

The troops here ordered to go direct to Montmédy [twenty-five miles due north of Verdun, close to the frontier]. The movement is to free Bazaine. Bazaine and MacMahon will both fight the Prussians under Steinmetz and Prince Charles, if they can reach them before the Crown Prince, now towards Bar-le-Duc, discovers the movement. The Emperor is at Rheims. The army has been reinforced from Paris to 120,000. The orders are changed, and the army is now moving on Rethel and Mézières.

PARIS FIGHTING TALK.

PARIS, *Monday*, *August* 22, 1870. — One hundred and sixty thousand men have passed through Paris to the front since Friday morning. It is said that there are now nearly 300,000 good troops at and near Paris. Profound enthusiasm was produced yesterday by the passage through the streets of American ambulances going to the front. Every one remarked the completeness and perfection of all their arrangements. The activity in equipping the artillery regiments has lately been increasing. Several have already gone to the front. One hundred priests, going to the army as volunteer assistants in the hospitals, yesterday marched through Paris, carrying their knapsacks on their backs. The people were deeply moved by the spectacle.

The destruction of the Bois de Boulogne has been commenced. A large part of it, however, will not be touched. Only those positions near the wall of the city will be cleared away. The ramparts are strongly fortified with large cannon. The forts are fully prepared, and the entrances to the city may be closed at any moment by draw-bridges. It is reported that in case of siege all strangers will be compelled to leave.

The Emperor left behind at Châlons his personal baggage and wagon train. It is reported that he is determined to charge with MacMahon's troops in the next battle.

The Prussian army besieging Strasburg caused the people of Ernstein to change the course of the little river Ill, in that neighborhood, in order to stop the supply of water for the city. The Prussians appointed a Mayor for Ernstein.

Amount of national French loan taken, 62,000,000 francs.

PRUSSIAN ARMY.

Eight army corps, which aggregated 320,000 men before decimated by war, are marching on Paris.

"*First*—The First army is commanded by General Von Steinmetz, and consists of the First, Seventh, and Eighth Army Corps. This army is now near Metz.

"*Second*—The Second army is that of Prince Frederick Charles, comprising the Second, Third, Ninth, and Tenth Army Corps. This is also near Metz.

"*Third*—The Third army, commanded by the Royal Prince, comprises the Fifth, Sixth, and Eleventh Corps, as well as the two Bavarian Corps. This army has been directed to move on Paris by way of Troyes.

"*Fourth*—The Fourth army of the Prince Royal of Saxony, comprising the Fourth, Twelfth, and Saxon Corps, is advancing on Paris by way of Châlons, near the Crown Prince.

Fifth—The Fifth army, under General Werder, embracing the Würtemberg and Baden divisions, is now engaged in the siege of Strasburg.

"Besides these, there is the Army of the Reserves, partly under the command of the Duke of Mecklenburg-Schwerin, on the Rhine, partly under the command of General Canstein, at Berlin, and partly under the command of General Loewenfeld, in Silesia."

TUESDAY, *August* 23.—MacMahon at Rheims with the Emperor and Prince Imperial. The Crown Prince's advance checked at Bar-le-Duc. Strasburg holds out; but Auerbach writes, "Strasburg is lost!"

MACMAHON.

RHEIMS, *August* 23.—General MacMahon is still here with the First, Fifth, Seventh, and Twelfth Corps, and the cavalry of Canrobert's Corps, escaped from Metz. The Emperor and Prince Imperial are also here.

CROWN PRINCE.

ST. DIZIER, *August* 23.—The Crown Prince's advance is here. We look Paris-ward. The main Third army is at Bar-le-Duc. There are doubts about MacMahon's position. The Crown Prince of Saxony is coming with the Fourth army, but he has not yet arrived.

STRASBURG.

(*Translated from the German of Auerbach.*)

August 23 (*Evening*).—It is decided. Enough of *pourparlers.* Our patience is worn out. To-night the bombardment opens, at first from the artillery at Kehl. Commandant Uhrich, who requires us to display every species of humanity while he exhibits none himself, requested, yesterday, that he might send the women and children out of the city. Apart from the impossibility of our undertaking this, there is the quartering them or the conducting them away, for neither of which have we the means. Many other inconveniences are obvious; and besides, this is war, and we cannot relieve the Commandant of the difficulties which should force him to a surrender. Want and hunger, the tears and lamentings of women and children, are indeed heartrending—at least, for an army of citizens such as the German army is; for how many thousands of them have left wife and child to stand before the bullets of the foe? But within the fortress the misery of the innocent, maybe, will at length constrain the Commandant, who vapors about his military honor, to desist staking human life upon his gambler's game of glory. The game is lost; no further stroke of hazard will avail. . . . The Commandant further required of us to forward for him a letter to his wife in Paris. This was courteously acceded to. This afternoon, at Mundolsheim, it was strangely quiet. It was like the deep inhaling of one's breath before a mighty cry of alarm was pealed forth. As I returned to Lampertheim troops of Bavarians met me in blue blouses, with axes and shovels, who must work to-night in the trenches. The willows along the road, and far into the thickets, are cut down to make gabions for the trenches. Troops of artillery follow them — fine, sturdy fellows, full of a courage which knows no bounds. . . . At midnight the fire opens. I go to the heights of Mundolsheim, which command Strasburg and all the landscape round, to witness the scene.

WAR PICTURES.

PONT-A-MOUSSON.

HEADQUARTERS OF THE KING OF PRUSSIA, *August* 23.

Finally, after going a mile or two, I saw a French peasant driving an empty voiture. He told me he was going some five miles on my way, and would take me that far. Once seated, gold did the rest; the voiture did not stop until I was at the door of my Figaro in Pont-à-Mousson.

There was no night, none of the repose of night, in Pont-à-Mousson during or after the great battles on the frontier. There was dismay, excitement, hideous confusion. Moaning men, with fearful wounds, walked about the streets begging to be carried to their homes in Germany. To every wagoner or cart that passed a score were crying, "Take me with you." The King had returned to this place, and the headquarters were again here, previous to their removal to Bar-le-Duc; but those headquarters were filled with mourning and consternation, for it was found that from the circle usually gathered there, some of the most important officers were missing. It was hardly any consolation that two or three equally eminent

FRENCH GENERALS LAY STARK AND COLD

on the field, and others dangerously wounded were groaning a few steps away. Count Bismarck sat, grim and silent,

BY THE SIDE OF HIS WOUNDED SON,

whose hand was clasped in that of his brother — a noble-looking, flaxen-haired youth of about twenty years, who, though he had dashed again and again into danger during the battle, had escaped unhurt. Why linger with this group? It is one of many thousands. One man's life seems of too little importance just now to be mentioned.

The excitement of the French in Pont-à-Mousson is tremendous. I feel sure now that if the Prussians had met with a reverse on the 18th, this little city would have been the scene of an attempted massacre. Looking from my window, I see a crowd of French people — peasants, bourgeois, women of all degrees, bareheaded and in *deshabille* — following a wagon through the streets. In the vehicle are four French officers of high rank wounded — two of them mortally, two others dangerously. In the front seat of the wagon sits upright and stately a general, whose name is called out by the crowd as "General Latour." I finer-looking man I have rarely seen. There is a look on his face of dignity, a self-respect which is mastering the agony of his dreadful head wound. When the wagon stops (it is in the street under my window), the street is absolutely blocked by the French, and just as many wounded Prussian soldiers. The women rush out of the houses with wine and other delicacies (hitherto hidden away), and the wounded Prussians begin to grow angry. The people

SEIZE THE GENERAL'S HAND,

kiss it again and again. At the windows are scores of women and children weeping and calling out with expressions of enthusiastic devotion. No attempt at repressing these demonstrations was made by the Prussian officers or men. But one thing, I own, startled me not a little. So soon as the wagon stopped, the French general hastily took out of his pocket a large package of papers, and handed it to a woman with a single word. The woman vanished with them, and no doubt the papers were speedily turned to ashes. That no Prussian interfered with the disposal of papers belonging to a prominent general just picked up from the field, was certainly singular.

Before leaving Pont-à-Mousson I went to take leave of a Frenchman and his wife who had been kind to me. "Ah, sir," said the man with tears in his eyes, "this has long been the most beautiful town on the Moselle, and among the happiest. You see what it is now. For many years it will be a

DREARY PICTURE OF WAR.

But if it be still standing when peace comes, come hither again, and we shall take our coffee and our cigar together, and talk of many things. For me, for my wife there, our lips are now sealed; we know not who is friend, who foe; but we know how to do well by strangers, and shall not forget those who spoke to us in kind tones during this frightful week."

WEDNESDAY, *August* 24.—The Emperor, with MacMahon, at Rethel. The Crown Prince, King William, Von Moltke, and Bismarck in consultation at Ligny (ten miles south of Bar-le-Duc). The abandonment of Châlons known, and the German advance ceases. The Crown Prince halts at Clermont-Vitry, and goes in pursuit of MacMahon. The uhlans capture eighty wagons of war material at Châlons. Ollivier in Switzerland. Jules Favre charges misfortune upon French leaders. Metz is isolated. The citadel and arsenal of Strasburg destroyed, and two French mortar batteries silenced. The Prussian scouts at Sezanne. Seven hundred and thirty-four German prisoners sent out of Metz for exchange. They report that their daily ration of bread, a half loaf, had been lately reduced to a sixth loaf. All old French soldiers from twenty-five to thirty-five years, married or unmarried, to the number of 300,000, are called out; all officers up to sixty years; and all generals capable of service, up to seventy years of age. King's headquarters moved from Pont-à-Mousson to Bar-le-Duc. Headquarters of First and Second armies before Metz. The Crown Prince of Saxony joins Crown Prince Frederick William with the Fourth, Twelfth, and Guard Corps, making the Fourth army.

THE MARCH TO PARIS.

(*Translated from the German official report.*)

The long delay of the French main army at Metz permitted us to fight the battles of the 14th, 16th, and 18th ult. in the immediate neighborhood of that fortress, and cut off General Bazaine from all communications with Paris or any other part of France. But there remained a considerable portion of the French forces ready for further action. In consequence of the introductory operations of the campaign, the two corps of MacMahon and Douay, as well as the corps of Failly, despatched to their assistance from the capital, had been entirely separated from the main army. These troops retreated to Châlons, where the Twelfth Corps was then forming under General Trochu, while another, the Thirteenth, was being organized by General Vinoy near Paris. With its large depots, Châlons was the very place in which to repair the losses of the regiments that had been already under fire, as also to organize the fresh reinforcements sent there from different parts of the country. The command of the new army, consisting of these various bodies, was entrusted to General MacMahon, the Emperor being at his headquarters.

While such measures were being taken by the enemy, those Prussian corps not required before Metz had continued to advance in a westerly direction. The Third army, under the command of the Crown Prince of Prussia, which had been steadily pushing on all the while, now proceeded with greater rapidity. In its onward march it was accompanied by a new army, formed of a portion of the forces under Prince Frederick Charles, and placed under the Crown Prince of Saxony. Both these armies, the latter of which consisted of the Guards, and Fourth and Twelfth Corps d'Armée, marched in the direction of Paris. It would have been decidedly desirable if they had found their way blocked up by the French, and if a battle could have been fought on the road to the capital. Marshal MacMahon might have awaited us in a strong position, or under the very ramparts of Paris. Another course open to him was to assume the offensive, with a view to rescue General Bazaine. As much depended upon our ascertaining the intentions of the enemy as soon as possible, our cavalry were sent far in advance of the army to watch his movements. Up to the 24th of August the Marshal held the camp of Châlons. The two Prussian armies, not allowing their advance to be delayed by the fortifications of Verdun, marched straight on, and had already reached the line Clermont-

Vitry, when, just as they were concentrating preparatory to the attack upon Châlons, news arrived on the 25th which rendered it probable that MacMahon had evacuated his camp. He was reported to have taken the road to Rheims. One of the inferences to be deduced from this was, that, picking his way along the narrow strip of land between the Belgian frontier and the right wing of the Crown Prince of Saxony, the Marshal might possibly attempt to relieve Metz. It was evident that if the proper measures were taken instantaneously by us, the Marshal would find it very difficult to succeed in his enterprise. Accordingly, our advance upon Paris was suspended on the night of the 25th.

THURSDAY, *August* 25.—Vitry surrenders. MacMahon moves towards Mézières. The Emperor, MacMahon, and the Prince Imperial at Rethel. The Crown Prince in hot pursuit of MacMahon. Duke William of Mecklenburg pushes MacMahon, and a skirmish ensues. The Oder closed. MacMahon has the First, Fifth, Seventh, and Twelfth Corps, and cavalry of the Twelfth Corps—about 115,000 effective men. The Crown Prince has 160,000, and the Crown Prince of Saxony 120,000. Steinmetz moves westward towards Verdun, to assist the Crown Prince, if needed.

VITRY SURRENDERS.

Vitry was summoned to surrender on Thursday. In half an hour the commandant capitulated, and the city was occupied. The stores of arms and munitions were great: 5000 guns, 3000 side arms, and 17 cannon. Two battalions of the French Garde Mobile were annihilated by the Prussian cavalry. Seventeen French officers and eight hundred and fifty soldiers were captured. The Prussians had one major severely and three troopers slightly wounded. This capture is of importance, as it secures a passage over the Marne, and covers the bridge of the Nancy-Bar-le-Duc railroad; ten miles east of the place the railroad branches off to Chaumont. Toul, which still blocks the road east of Vitry, is surrounded by a brigade of the Second Bavarian Corps.

MACMAHON'S FIRST ATTACK.

SEDAN, *August* 25.—MacMahon is trying to reach Bazaine by the way of Mézières, Montmédy, and Thionville, but the

Prussians have cut through Varennes and Dun. There is fighting going on between Dun, Buzancy, and Mouzon. According to all probability, there will be an important action before long, not far from Montmédy.

Evening. — Affairs are getting hot. The two Crown Princes are both pushing MacMahon. The Crown Prince of Saxony is marching the Fourth army along the west bank of the Meuse, to cross at Verdun. The fighting to-day was with a portion of his force, the cavalry division of Duke William of Mecklenburg, and fifteen hundred of the Garde Mobile The French were hastily retreating from Verdun towards Sedan. The Duke threw a few shells amongst them, compelled them to halt, and a determined charge of the Fifteenth uhlan regiment was made to scatter them. The Mobile Guards formed a square, and received the cavalry with a spirited fire, but immediately threw their guns away or fired them in the ground. Seventeen officers and eight hundred and fifty men were taken, with a loss of four uhlans.

FRANCE MUST PAY.

The entrance of the river Oder was finally closed on the 25th. Ships are sunk, as well as torpedoes, along the coast. The Paris *Constitutionnel* says "the injury to the commerce of Germany by blockade amounts to a million of dollars a day." The official paper of North Germany, the *Allgemeine Zeitung*, replies: "*That is just so much added indemnity which France must pay.*"

A new division of iron-clads, under Rear-Admiral Baron Didelot, leaves the harbor of Toulon with sealed orders. It consists of the *Magenta*, *Gloire*, *Normandie*, and *Corse.* The frigate *Orinoco* also prepares hastily for sea, under sealed orders. France will pay again.

FRANCE SICK OF THE EMPEROR.

The Paris *Siècle* this morning, commenting on the item of news that "the Imperial headquarters are at Rheims," says:

"Who cares? MacMahon can only have one headquarters — the centre of operations. The 'Imperial headquarters' can only be a superfluity (*superfetation*) — an embarrassment — a pretext for losing battles. The crisis is too dangerous to talk of the 'Imperial headquarters' anywhere near those of the Commander-in-Chief."

STRASBURG BURNS.

(*Translated from the German of Auerbach.*)

A NIGHT OF ST. BARTHOLOMEW.

August 25. *Before Strasburg, Morning.* — Strasburg burns! In this word are crowded all the horrors, terrors, anguish of heart, we experienced in the past night. My eyes yet smart from the fire flashes, my hand trembles still. So was it to be! Again is there a night of St. Bartholomew — for such was the one just passed — with detestation to be graven in history, but not through fault of ours. On those who must needs deck their heads with glory — on their heads alone lies the blame. The worst injury an enemy can inflict upon a man, upon a people, is to force them to acts from which they recoil with aversion. We are in the position of a man who declines a duel, and yet is compelled to shoot down his adversary. Unhappily it must be done. But yesterday we made offers to the commandant of Strasburg to come out, or send a trusty officer, to convince himself that resistance was in vain, and that we could only with the utmost pain bring ourselves to fire even a part of Strasburg. He replied, an inspection of our position would be construed as a first probability of surrendering the fortress. He had, however, resolved to defend it to the last man and the last cartridge. It was said yesterday, and the broad pillars of smoke testified, that Kehl was again set on fire by the French. We kept quiet until the break of evening; the columns of flame in Kehl flared up wide, mounting heavenwards, and incessantly were fireballs hurled thither from the citadel. Now began on our side the fire — flash for flash, blow for blow they were returned with interest. There, the citadel blazes up; the fast-falling night revealed every fire-flame. Bombs soared aloft and descended. Now the city was on fire north from the Cathedral. It must have fallen on inflammable material, for instantly the flames shot heavenward. From this point who can paint the scene? Here and there it blazed up; we saw four, five conflagrations; two united, and presented a vast roaring furnace. The wind blew from the west, and fanned the flames; they darted up forked tongues of fire. A spectator cried out, "See how the Cathedral towers aloft above the clouds of smoke! how venerable, as if mutely threatening and reproving the men who hurl reckless flames against each other!" "If the Cathedral does but remain unharmed," was the cry that ran from mouth to mouth, and meanwhile feelings of deep compassion were expressed for those within the city. In spirit we were transported among those now wailing in vaulted cellars, as they heard the thunder of the guns, ignorant where the fires were raging, perhaps even their own homes. And in the streets the fires must be left to rage unchecked. Who could strive to quench them, while each minute further discharges were falling? How many cry out to their own dear ones, seek them, and are like beings bewildered in their own homes. What shrieking, what misery! If one could but compress together the heart-throbs of the people, far louder, quicker, mightier must be the stroke than the deep roar of the guns, which, incessantly discharged, light up the lgoom, here — there — till the eye could no longer follow. Midnight had set in before we decided to go home. We could see each other as in full moonlight. The fields, the vineyards were lit up. The church of Mundolsheim, with its white gravestones; suddenly the light grows still brighter. Now that we had not seen the flames for a time, they appeared broader, stronger, more voracious. It was difficult to tear one's self away from the fearfully grand spectacle, and yet it must be. The villagers we met professed to know which parts of the city would be saved from the flames. We strove to believe their assurances that the precincts of the cathedral, above all itself, would remain uninjured. And yet for a moment it had seemed to us that the cathedral terrace, which had been made the observatory of the enemy, was on fire. It was, however, an illusion. The flames illumined our homeward way. The sky was overspread with light clouds of a blood red. The fire must have been visible beyond the Rhine, far into the Black Forest.

FRIDAY, *August* 26.— The army conscription law announced in Paris. The Crown Prince commences the great flank movement and change of front of eight army corps (300,000 men). The Crown Prince of Saxony to move north, down the east bank of the Meuse, to cut off MacMahon from Metz, while the Crown Prince of Prussia pushes him in front, on the west bank, and cuts him off from Paris. Both armies crowd MacMahon towards Belgium. The Crown Prince proclaims the war against soldiers, not citizens. The Prince Imperial at Rethel. The Emperor and MacMahon move towards Mézières. The uhlans scour through France, from Vitry to Château Thierry, Soissons, and Rheims. Pfalzburg * continues its defence. A church and twenty-one houses destroyed by Prussian shells. Headquarters of the King removed from Bar-le-Duc to Clermont, in the Argonnes.

PRUSSIAN OFFICIAL REPORT.

(*Translation.*)

On the 26th eight and one-half German army corps, which had been marching west, effected a change of front, and, turning north, prepared to intercept the enemy on his march along our flank.

[These corps were the Fourth, Fifth, Sixth, Eleventh, and Twelfth Prussian, the First and Second Bavarian and Guards Corps, and the Würtemberg, and the Second, Fourth, Fifth, and Sixth Cavalry Divisions — 300,000 men.— AUTHOR.]

The difficulties of this movement were increased by our march lying partly through the Argonne forest. Care was, moreover, taken to prevent the enemy from falling back upon Paris, in case he should find it impossible to penetrate to Metz. Supposing our being able to surround MacMahon, he would be ob-

* Pfalzburg is a stronghold of the third class, with works constructed by Vauban, and was erected under the crest of the Vosges to defend the defile between Saverne and Sarreburg.

liged to fight under the most unfavorable conditions, or to find safety for his army in Belgium.

While this movement was going on, General Von Steinmetz threw a portion of the First army towards Stenay, to feel the enemy. His scouts cut the railway at Lamouilly, between Montmédy and Mézières, but the French appeared in force, repairing the bridge, while the Prussian force fell back on Dun, a few miles to the south.

The Corps Vinoy not having as yet arrived, we had a great numerical superiority over the French, then estimated at about 120,000; but it was not so easy for us to bring up our forces in time to use them. While our troops were approaching from a considerable distance it became certain that MacMahon had really a flank march in view.

In the mean time the siege of Toul was postponed, to throw all our available force upon MacMahon, while the latter was joined by 10,000 fresh troops from Paris *viâ* Rheims.

FLAGS OF TRUCE FIRED ON.

A diplomatic despatch relative to flags of truce is sent from Berlin to Baron Gerolt, Minister of the North German Union at Washington. It says:

BERLIN, *August* 26.

The incident mentioned in the telegram of the 22d has occurred twice since. Captain Rochow, sent by General Alvensleben to Toul with a flag of truce, has been received with shots, and a trumpeter accompanying another flag of truce has been killed. You will lodge a protest with the United States against these repeated violations of international law, and declare that we shall henceforth be unable to send flags of truce to a nation whose soldiers have lost, in Africa, China, and Mexico, all recollection of the usages of civilized warfare.

VON THILE.

MARCH WITH THE CROWN PRINCE.

HEADQUARTERS CROWN PRINCE, *August* 26.— The Crown Prince arrived late to-night at the Châlons Prefecture, after a hard ride all day. His infantry have made a twenty-mile march to-day, and the cavalry forty. The latter are about midway between Châlons and Epernay. This day's march has been the greatest march of the campaign. The men have fairly run some of the way. There is great joy everywhere. The soldiers carry green sprigs in their guns, and shout and sing the national hymns.

The Crown Prince issues this proclamation to the people of France:

"Prussia makes war against the Emperor, and not against the people of France. The people have nothing whatever to fear." The Prince also announces his purpose to instantly restore the lines of travel, which have been interrupted or destroyed by army movements, so that labor and commerce may everywhere be resumed. All the French officials have been requested to remain at their posts, and "their personal safety is guaranteed." The

Prince further says that "only surplus food will be taken for the German troops — that only which is not required by the peaceful French."

SATURDAY, *August* 27. — MacMahon near Beaumont and Stenay, falling back. The Crown Prince drives MacMahon's rear guard from Rheims. The Third Saxony Cavalry defeat six squadrons of the Twelfth French Chasseurs of De Failly's Corps, near Buzancy. The King proclaims relative to the treatment of prisoners. The Bishop of Strasburg remonstrates with Lieutenant-Colonel Von Leczynsky, chief of the Baden staff, against the bombardment. Prussians disagree. The Bishop asks permission to send the people out. Prussians deny. He then asks for a truce. The Prussians will grant it if the French commander desires to talk capitulation. By order of General Trochu, all houses which are in the way of the defences of Paris are to be destroyed.

BISMARCK TALKS.

CLERMONT-EN-ARGONNE, *August* 27. — Count Bismarck, in conversation to-day with a correspondent, gave a résumé of the situation. "The French," said the Federal Chancellor (in excellent English), "had taken up a strong defensive position near Rheims, which we intended to attack without delay. But on Thursday evening we learned that MacMahon, with 120,000 men, had left Rheims, and was marching towards Metz to relieve Bazaine, who, as you know, is shut up there with about 100,000 men. The Crown Prince arrived just in time to stop MacMahon's march, and is now on the short line between him and Metz. The Bavarians have gone to cut off his retreat to Paris, and are already at Châlons." "Then we shall not continue our advance on Paris now?" I asked. "No, not till MacMahon is disposed of; we shall drive him to the Belgian frontier, or into the sea at Calais." "He had better go to England." "He won't find many friends there," answered Count Bismarck, laughing. The Count, who had been writing, now handed me

THIS PROCLAMATION,

which appeared with the King's signature the next day:

"The Commander-in-chief brings to the knowledge of the inhabitants of the arrondissements, that every prisoner who wishes to be considered as a prisoner of war, besides [establishing] his character as a French soldier by an order issued by one of the legal authorities and directed to him personally, has to produce further proof that he has been called to the standard and entered in the lists of a military corps organized by the French Government. At the same time the military rank which he occupies in the army must be made known by military and uniform insignia, which are inseparable from his dress and are visible to the naked eye at gunshot distance.

"Individuals who have seized arms while setting at naught one of these conditions, will not be considered as prisoners of war. They will be sentenced by a court-martial, when they have not made themselves guilty of an act which carries a stronger punishment with it, to ten years imprisonment with labor, and will be detained in Germany until this sentence has been fulfilled."

SUNDAY, *August* 28.—MacMahon's line extends from Stenay to Beaumont and Rethel on the left bank of the Meuse. The two Crown Princes crowd him in front. The King at Varennes, south of Grand Pré. The Crown Prince at Vouziers and Buzancy. The Emperor at Le Chêne, and the Prince Imperial at Mézierès. The French decide to blow up bridges, blockade roads, and destroy railroads, to impede the Prussian advance on Paris. The American ambulance train leaves Paris. Dr. Pratt, with the daughters of Dr. Sims, leads the corps. Bismarck says "*Prussia will insist on Strasburg and Metz before peace, and that Alsace and Lorraine shall be divided among the South German States.*"

FRENCH SOIL TO BE SEIZED.

BISMARCK SAYS PRUSSIA WILL HAVE METZ AND STRASBURG FOREVER.

I found Count Bismarck at a deal table covered with papers, journals, orders, maps, and cigar boxes; busily smoking the cigar, which never seems to quit his lips.

I broke ground by asking what were likely to be the conditions of peace demanded by the King of Prussia's Government.

He answered at once, with great apparent frankness, and in the clearest manner. I suppose I need hardly remind your readers that Count Bismarck speaks capital English, so that there could be no possibility of my misunderstanding him.

"There are three courses open to us," he said, "with regard to peace with France. We must stop the possibility of another so unprovoked and uncalled-for attack by the French nation or the French Government on our common Fatherland. No Minister who failed to do this could hold office for a week, for the opinion of all Germany would be against him. There are, as I have said, three ways of stopping an attack on the Rhine provinces.

"*First*— We might make Alsace and Lorraine a neutral State, like Luxemburg or Belgium, extending from the former country to Switzerland, and so separating France and Prussia by a group of neutral States; but I confess it appears to me that the neutrality of the existing small States is already so difficult to protect, and is at every moment capable of so many and such dangerous complications, that I do not think it would be worth while to make more neutral States, and with them new duties and dangers.

"*Secondly*— We might annex Alsace and Lorraine, and hold them as conquered territory. But I am sure that this would not be looked on favorably by the majority of my German fellow-countrymen. We are all most anxious to complete our unity; but we do not want any people among us who are unwilling members of the German nation. That the Alsacians would be most disloyal subjects of the King of Prussia, in spite of the great majority of them speaking the German language, and being of Teutonic origin, there can be no doubt.

"*Thirdly — There remains to us, then, as a third course, to take Metz and Strasburg, and to keep them. This is what we shall do.* Strasburg particularly is absolutely needful for the protection of South Germany, which is at the mercy of a French army. So long as France possesses Strasburg, there is nothing to stop a French invading army. Now it would be very unfair if we were to leave our South German brethren unprotected, after they have fought so bravely and well by our side in this campaign. Then, again, by holding Strasburg we could always prevent any movement on the Rhine. We should be able, not only to march an army by the valley of the Main on Paris, but to take a French army marching on Mayence or Coblenz in flank and rear. So we have besieged Strasburg vigorously; and when we have got the old German town back again, we shall make a Gibraltar of it."

"But allow me to suggest," I said, "that the cession of Strasburg is not a thing to which France will be easily reconciled; all the more because it is, as you say, 'the key of France on the East.'"

"My dear sir," was the reply, "you have been with us continually since our entry into France. I have heard you constantly talking French. Now, have you not clearly seen that it would be difficult for the French to be more angry with us for our victories over them than they already are? No, not if we were encamped in the Bois de Boulogne itself. And just because they are and will be for many a year to come very sore against us, we must take care not to leave in their hands the means of doing us a mischief.

"When you meet a drunken man in the streets, what do you do if he is mischievous? Call a policeman, don't you? Well, Strasburg and Metz will have to be our policemen, and good stout ones, too."

"It is curious," I remarked, "how much the French do hate the Prussians, and what stories they tell and believe about you. I have lived a great deal in Paris, and I know there are told there as facts some fables which are all but incredible."

"Yes," answered Count Bismarck, "we have taken the place of the English thirty, nay twenty years ago. But as they have come to forget their hatred of 'perfidious Albion,' so they will have to find some day or other that there is some good in us. Also, it seems as if the French nation stood in constant need of a bugbear to vent their wrath upon. For the moment, we are the bugbears."

I ventured then to say, "I see that the people are in a great fright in England lest your Excellency should cast a covetous eye upon Holland."

"Yes, I am aware that is an English idea," replied the Count; "but, like other English ideas, it is not accepted out of the country of its birth. We want nothing in Germany that is not German, and Holland certainly is not German. Already Posen is looked upon with no friendly eye by many of my countrymen as a non-Teutonic province. There is no fear of our taking Holland — as little as there is of the French taking Belgium."

Now, I fancied I saw a quiet twinkle of satisfaction in Count Bismarck's eye as he added the above last word; and perhaps I may as well let it be the last word of my report.

(*Interview with Count Bismarck, published in London Daily News, Aug.* 28.)

MONDAY, *August* 29. — MacMahon's four corps stationed on the two roads from Le Chêne to Stenay (two being *échelonnés* on each). German army extends from Grand Pré to Stenay, the van in front of MacMahon. The Prussian Twelfth Corps, threatens the eastern divisions of MacMahon's army, MacMahon decides to cross to the east bank of the Meuse, and fall back on Sedan. The Prince Imperial is hastily transferred to the fortress of Avesnes. The Paris Bois de Boulogne filled with cattle. The Emperor at Sedan.

PARIS SPECULATIONS.

A law is published in Paris, by which the battalions of the National Guard are incorporated with the active army; and those citizens who take up arms for the time being, and wear the insignia of the National Guard, shall be considered as forming part of that organization. The question is whether the Germans will consider men in blouses, with a cross or other insignia on their dress, as having fulfilled the clear conditions of the King's proclamation yesterday. Senators Bihic and Mellinet, and Deputies Daru, Dupuy de L'Ome, De Talhuet, and Thiers are added to the Committee of Defence. General Trochu orders all people of the unsafe classes, and all persons who cannot support themselves, to be sent out of Paris, and all Germans to leave the Department of the Seine.

March of the Germans on Rethel and Vouziers continued. Bummers (*Plänkler*, a favorite term with the Germans in this war) in the neighborhood of both places; 20,000 men reported in Paris to have passed Châlons, going toward Epernay.

The military drawing for the army conscription of the present year is fixed to take place in all parts of the empire on Monday next, August 29. The call of Government on the nation by this army draft is for 140,000 men — instead of 90,000, the legal quota — in consequence of the exigencies of the present war with Prussia.

TUESDAY, *August* 30. — Severe battle near Beaumont.*

---

* THE EXACT SITUATION of the armies before the battle is thus given in the *Army and Navy Journal:*

MacMahon's army lies between the Ardennes mountains and the river Aisne. His advance having been beaten at Nouart, and his way to Metz cut off, there was danger that he would retreat into Belgium, if not at once attacked. His army does indeed begin to cross the Meuse, though with the intention of retreating by Sedan and Mézières. The German leaders decide to attack it again in the country between the Ardennes and the Meuse. According to the orders given the Third army, the First Bavarian Corps, which on the 27th had been advanced past Vouziers, on the road to Stenay, as far as Bar and Buzancy, was to go viâ Sommauthe toward Beaumont. The Second Bavarian Corps followed behind the First. The Fifth Prussian Corps moved from Bregenay and Authe toward Pierremont and Oches, and formed therefore the left wing of the Third army. The Würtemberg division directed itself from Boult-aux-Bois, via Châtillon, against Le Chêne. The Second Prussian Corps moved on the left of the Würtembergers, viâ Vouziers and Quatre Champs; and a side column of this corps occupied Voncq, on the Aisne. The Sixth Corps was to extend itself from Vouziers southwesterly, or towards Châlons. The Fifth cavalry division marched toward Tourteron, the Fourth toward Châtillon, the Sixth toward Semuy, with advance troops toward Bouvellemont, cutting the road to Mézières. The second division of cavalry moved toward Buzancy. Headquarters of the Crown Prince were moved at half-past eight from Cernuc, via Grand Pré (where the King's quarters were), toward Bregenay, before which place three regiments and some artillery lay in two rows about half a mile long. Precisely at noon came the first shot from the hills before Oches, where some French artillery had posted itself, and was directed against the German artillery back of Buzancy, nearly 5000 paces distant. There was, however, no attempt to make a stand, and the position was deserted so soon as German cavalry approached, The artillery retreated, following the chain of hills on which it lay, back to Stonne, its highest point. Although the ground here was very favorable, the retreat was soon continued toward Beaumont, where the French centre had been driven in, after a sharp fight. The battle here was opened about midday by the Fourth Corps, which, making a sudden attack upon Beaumont, swept so suddenly upon the French, that a camp from which not an article had been removed fell into their hands. This corps was supported on the left by the First Bavarian Corps, placed in the Petit-Dieulet wood, where, being attacked on its left flank, a return attack was made, and the enemy thrown back on La Besace. On the right of the Fourth was the Twelfth Corps, operating against Letanne. Beaumont having been brilliantly seized, the Fourth and Twelfth Corps of the Fourth army moved against the Givodeau wood and Villemontry, fighting at every step, and steadily extending its left wing, in order to occupy the hills which enclose Mouzon. From six to eight o'clock a tremendous artillery and mitrailleuse battle was kept up here, to which night alone put an end. The Fourth Corps then occupied the place. As the bridge here was the line of retreat for a great part of the French army, its crowded columns suffered terribly in crossing. Large quantities of baggage and material were also abandoned. Meanwhile, the western wing of the French army, formerly the right, now the left wing, crosses the river at Bazeilles. Part of the First Bavarian Corps having advanced in a northeasterly direction toward Yoncq, driving back on its way a force that had been withdrawn without a fight from a strong position at Stonne, attacks them late in the day, and in its turn wins guns and prisoners, and inflicts severe loss on the retreating columns. The German army bivouacked on the line Raucourt-Villemontry. The advantages gained during this day were, the winning of so much ground that the passes of the Ardennes remained entirely in German hands, and an approach to the frontier so close that the ground between it and the Meuse could be occupied as a base of operations. In addition, the number of guns and prisoners taken was enormous, amounting to more than thirty guns and 5000 prisoners. The French appeared to have withdrawn toward Sedan, the main body having crossed the Meuse at Mouzon, under cover of heavy artillery fire from the high right bank of the river. Mouzon is six miles north of Beaumont, and ten miles south-east of Sedan.

The first shot fired from the hills of Oches at twelve, M. The Crown Prince of Saxony, with the Fourth and Twelfth Corps, captures the French camp at Beaumont, and pushes MacMahon's left beyond the hills of Mouzon, which village the Fourth army occupied at eight P.M., shelling the retreating forces of MacMahon as they struggle across the Mouzon bridge. The French army faces about, and the right becomes the left. The western wing (left now) is driven across the Meuse at Bazeilles by the Crown Prince of Prussia.

The German army bivouacs at Raucourt, on a line parallel with the Meuse. The passes in the Ardennes in German hands. 5000 prisoners captured, and 31 guns.

The Crown Prince of Saxony commands the Fourth and Twelfth Prussian, the First Bavarian, and some Saxon and Prussian Guards — 115,000 men.

The Crown Prince of Prussia commands the Fifth, Sixth, and Eleventh Prussian Corps, Second Bavarian, and some reinforcements from Prince Charles — 170,000 men.

MacMahon commands four corps, viz.: First Corps, General Ducrot; Fifth Corps, General Göze, in place of De Failly, on the staff of the Emperor; Seventh Corps, General Felix Douay; Twelfth Corps, General Lebrun — with some reinforcements, in all about 115,000 men.

THE KING'S DESPATCH OF VICTORY.

TO THE QUEEN:

VARENNES, *Aug.* 30 (*Evening*).— We have had another victory. The Fourth, Twelfth, and one Bavarian Corps were engaged. MacMahon was beaten, and driven from Beaumont across the Meuse to Mouzon. Twelve guns, several thousand prisoners, and much material are in our hands. I repair to the battle-field to pursue the routes of victory. God help us further! WILHELM.

BATTLE OF BEAUMONT.

PRELIMINARIES.

The events of this campaign within a campaign, up to to-day, are as follows: MacMahon left Rheims on the 24th of August, carrying the main part of his army through Vouziers, 20,000 men at most having been sent by railroad to Montmédy. This movement appears to have become known to the King on the 25th, and on the afternoon of the 26th, his headquarters were suddenly removed from Bar-le-Duc, fifteen miles northward to Clermont, the orders for changing the direction of the march having already been issued. The procession of the Third army toward Paris was stopped, and it was ordered to move northward for co-operation with the Fourth army. The course of both armies was by the right flank, and was accomplished with great rapidity. On the next day, the 27th, the Saxon cavalry had a successful encounter at Buzancy. The first blow struck by the infantry was on the 29th, at Nouart, and on the 30th the marching was so far completed that the two armies occupied a line about eighteen miles long, the Fourth in the right, the Third in the left wing. An attack was now possible, and this was made at Beaumont so brilliantly, that De Failly's corps, which composed the principal French force engaged, was surprised and overthrown. Although the chief part of MacMahon's army remained untouched, it was held fast by this defeat, and the 31st of August was occupied by his enemies in closing around it.

The author gives an account of the battle by an eye-witness, which was published in the *London Daily News* and cabled to the American Associated Press.

START FOR THE BATTLE-FIELD.

On Tuesday morning I started early from Grand Pré, the King's headquarters, to see the battle which was expected to take place on a line from the village of Stonne to Stenay, nearly midway, passing through Beaumont. MacMahon was believed to be trying to push on to Metz, according to his plan of catching Steinmetz between himself and Bazaine. But the Prussians were always just thirty-six hours in advance of MacMahon from the time he left Rheims.

I had not gone far on my road to the front before I fell in with the Crown Prince's staff, his Royal Highness riding at the head of his aides-de-camp, in the plain uniform of a Prussian general, with no orders but the star "*Pour la Mérite*," and the iron cross. For that matter, however, any Prussian officer who wears these two is not permitted to display any others. We rode slowly over the hills until we reached an eminence above the valley of the Bar, a small stream which, on the French map, is honored as a river. On this hill we sat for a terribly long time.

THE BATTLE BEGINS.

But at 12.15 o'clock there was suddenly a puff of white smoke from a hill about two miles in front of us, and before we had fairly time to turn our glasses on the hill, a French battery of six guns opened on the Prussian columns advancing in the road below. So ineffectual, however, was their fire, that it was not thought advisable to send up a Prussian battery to reply; especially as we did not wish to let the enemy know what our forces were, and whether we were a corps d'armée or merely an advance guard. After a little more than half an hour's firing, the French batteries ceased to fire, limbered up, and retired down the hill to gain the high road to Beaumont. Our scouts discovered that the French were in full retreat in the direction of Stonne, where they again took up a position later in the day; and that the cause of their rapid retreat on Stonne was the advance of our right wing, Prince Albert of Saxony in command, between Beaumont and the Meuse, threatening to turn the flank of the French left on the ridge of the hill on which lies Stonne. The enemy made a stand, but the attack from the Prussian right was so determined, that the French could offer no effectual resistance on this hill; yet they had a very strong position, somewhat resembling that occupied by them on the hill above Gravelotte on the memorable 18th of August.

THE ARMY RISKED TO SAVE THE EMPEROR.

They had two mitrailleuses, and fired a dozen rounds or so, with what object it was difficult to discover. They were much too far from our most advanced columns to do the slightest mischief. Possibly they hoped to attract the attention of their own right flank. The Emperor was with them, and they may well enough have been nervous about his safety.

After some time, one of the Prussian batteries advanced up the slope and shelled the Stonne road for half an hour to see if they could get a reply. About five o'clock we advanced rapidly from our hill to that of Stonne. The columns climbing the slope below the village cheered loudly as the heir to the throne passed them. I was, I own, not very much inclined to cheer, as the Prince had been compelled by the nature of the ground to keep well away from any other point which could give us a good view of the right. In that direction we could hear heavy fighting which we could not see.

A FRENCH DIVISION SURPRISED IN CAMP.

However, when we got on the hill above Stonne, we had a capital view of nearly the whole of the right; and one aide-de-camp coming up with the news, we soon learned what was passing there. A whole French division had been surprised near Beaumont in camp, and had fled, leaving all their tents and baggage. When I say "had fled," I mean all fled who could, and whom the Prussians were not too quick for. More than 6000 were made prisoners without striking a blow.

The peasants in the village told us that the Emperor had been there only two hours before the Prussian skirmishers entered it. This was confirmed by some prisoners taken. In the woods on our left, the troops that had been opposed to us had fallen back to the other side of the descent beneath us, and had occupied the sides of a narrow valley leading toward Raucourt. It was most important for the French to defend this valley, as, had the Prussians been able to reach down it, they would have turned the French right flank, getting between its position at Mouzon, whither it had fallen back from Beaumont and the road to Sedan.

THE BATTLE WAS BEGUN TOO LATE.

The French had concealed their skirmishers so well, that we on the hill were astonished to hear independent firing suddenly begin as our foremost *tirailleur*s entered the low ground, and pushed up the Raucourt road. It was necessary for us to act vigorously, for the sun was sinking, and there was hardly an hour more of good light. "It is too late, too late," said one of the Staff to me; "had we got here at 2.30, instead of nearly 5.30, we could have forced that battery, and got down on the valley of the Meuse by Raucourt to Remilly, broken the bridge there, and so caught the French between the river and our troops."

"I wish I could understand clearly," I said, "what the French are trying to do this morning; are they trying still to advance toward Metz, or are they in retreat toward Sedan, having abandoned all hope of relieving Bazaine; in other words, are we fighting their advance-guard or their rear-guard?"

THE FRENCH ADVANCE BECAME A RETREAT.

"Both, my dear sir," answered this officer, who, though I did not then know it, being a stranger at the Crown Prince's head-quarters, was the Count Von Eulenberg himself, "I believe, though no one is certain; for you have probably discovered that it does not do to infer from ordinary rules what the French are doing. For my part, I believe they were thinking of going on toward Metz, when the Bavarians surprised De Failly in camp near Beaumont. Now, of course, they are retreating on Sedan, and what was this morning meant for their advance-guard is now their rear-guard."

Meanwhile the Prussians had put two guns on a rise of ground from which they could shell the French skirmishers in the wood overhanging the valley leading to Raucourt. But soon their own skirmishers got so far forward, that the guns had to cease firing for fear of hitting them. The skirmishers kept gaining ground, the French, however, struggling hard, knowing that they were lost if they let their enemy get down the valley.

BAVARIANS CHARGE ON THE MITRAILLEUSES.

To our right we could see the Bavarians forward of Remilly from Beaumont; but there the valley grew broader, and the French mitrailleuses did much execution, the Bavarians going in with great determination, not waiting for the artillery to silence the mitrailleuses, but themselves dashing at the batteries.

It now became so dark that we could see by the flashes of the guns that the Bavarians were steadily advancing up the valley toward Remilly. At 7, and from 7 till 8, the fire from the mitrailleuses was very hot—not single explosions, but one continuous roar.

FRITZ, HAVING THE RHEUMATISM, RIDES HARD.

Soon after eight the Crown Prince turned his horse's head, and we rode back to a little village named Vaux. As we came down the hillside we had a most picturesque view of the regiments encamped about us. The bivouac fires shone brightly out, the moon not having risen. As we passed through, the men came trooping out, leaving their cooking and their letters to give a cheer for Fritz, who, poor fellow, had the rheumatism, and dreading the night air, took us home at a tremendous pace over wild cross-roads, to the great danger of our horses' knees and our own necks.

WEDNESDAY, *August* 31. — Terrible struggle near Bazeilles. MacMahon wounded. The Bavarians receive a check. Citizens fire on the Bavarian troops, and they burn the town (2500 inhabitants). The Crown Prince of Saxony crosses the Meuse, and advances on Sedan. The King is in command, and, during the day, orders the German forces to march into positions which will enable them to completely surround Sedan in the morning.

PREPARING FOR SEDAN.

Wednesday morning was bright and beautiful. The Crown Prince bivouacked during the night on the battle-field five miles to the south of Sedan, while the impetuous Saxon Prince crossed the Meuse, and pursued MacMahon towards Sedan.

The day was exhausted mostly in marching troops to positions, to surround Sedan in the bloody encounter of to-morrow. The army of the Crown Prince was to surround the south and west of Sedan, while the Saxon Prince was to surround the east and north. During the 31st, the Crown Prince sent the First and Second Bavarian Corps to Remilly; the Eleventh and Fifth Corps proceeded from Stonne to Chenery, the King's headquarters, and had orders to encamp opposite Donchery (three miles to the north of Sedan, on the Meuse). The Würtembergers moved towards the west of Sedan, to fill up the unoccupied space. This completed the southern and western investment of Sedan, the First and Second Prussian, Würtembergers, and the Fifth and Eleventh Prussian, making a continuous chain from Remilly to Donchery.

The Crown Prince of Saxony was ready to move against Sedan from the east with the Fourth and Eleventh Corps, while the Saxon and Prussian Guards were to invest the north.

THE BATTLE OF BAZEILLES.

The Crown Prince had no trouble in marching his forces for the investment of Sedan; but the Saxon Prince met some opposition, which brought on the battle of Bazeilles, and which caused the burning of that village.

While King William was giving an order at Chenery that the French should be pursued on the morrow into Belgium, if they were not immediately disarmed by the Belgian authorities, the Emperor was issuing a proclamation in Sedan, which was posted on all the walls, saying, "that he had confided the command of the armies to the generals whom public opinion had seemed to select as most capable of leading them, and that he himself intended to fight as an officer, forgetting for a while his position as sovereign."

MacMahon, in making his retreat before the Saxon Prince, coming upon a strong position, determined to make one more stand for the Empire and for France. The French line was south-east of Sedan. The right was in front of Bazeilles, and the left ran away towards Bouillon, in front of Douzy. The valleys of the Meuse and Chières were in front of the French line. On the right and left were massed regiments of all arms; but towards the left, on the second line, was a very large force of heavy cavalry, dragoons, and cuirassiers.

The Saxon Crown Prince had pushed his batteries directly opposite the French centre, on a plateau or table-land which terminated abruptly, and made it a very strong position. For some time the cannonading continued on both sides, the Prussians constantly reinforcing.

At two o'clock a force of Prussian infantry advanced across the bridge in the village of Douzy, and immediately there began a very sharp fusillade, lasting, however, not more than ten minutes. The Prussians sprang forward in larger forces, but a battery of six mitrailleuses advanced, and opened fire through the trees. Six volleys came all at once. The Prussians fell hurriedly back, leaving whole ranks behind, which had gone down like those leaden soldiers which children play with.

At three o'clock the Saxon Crown Prince ordered an advance of the Prussian left against the French right, to cut off the French army from Sedan. This led to some terrible fighting, where for hours the positions were lost and won, and where each German wave rolled down the slopes only to give place to a new and more formidable one.

THE BURNING OF BAZEILLES.

While the artillery fire is raging on both sides, a brigade of Bavarians are ordered forward past the village of Bazeilles. Shot and shell are falling thick and fast about them. Their eyes are on the front, when in their rear flash goes a half dozen muskets from a house, and two Bavarians drop dead. Their comrades instantly face about to see the enemy. He is hidden in the house. The Bavarians had been victims to civilian treachery at Weisenburg, and filled with indignation they forgot the foe in front, and with a shout and a rush broke the doors open; but the intending assassins had fled. The house was set on fire, and the inhabitants opened a regular fusillade on the Germans from every window. House after house was burned. It was the madness of a mob. The innocent were the victims. Frantic at seeing their homes in flames, men and women united in massacring wounded Bavarian soldiers in the street, and were to be seen lifting them up and throwing them into the flames. Soon the whole village was in flames, and 2500 poor people are homeless. A thousand smoking ruins and silent chimneys will tell a tale as sad as Pompeii, as mournful as Gomorrah. The wrath of an army is the wrath of God. There is no apology, for it is the fruit of war. It will be pointed at as a barbarism. It was a barbarism; all war is barbarous. A thousand begrimed and silent chimneys stand in Pennsylvania and Virginia, tombstones to our barbarism. I pray God they may be the tombstones of war in America.* Bazeilles is but the Harper's Ferry and Chambersburg of the present war.

THE BATTLE AGAIN.

Four P.M.—How different the picture on the French right! The fighting was splendid; for the fortunes of the hour seemed to balance — now for France, now for Germany. The sun was shining brightly, and everything was plainly visible. The glittering of weapons, the bright and showy colors of the French uniforms, the white smoke curling under the blue sky, or lingering, vapor-like, beneath the trees, the crackling flames rising from the burning village of Bazeilles — the whole scene formed a spectacle which one seldom finds himself in a position to witness.

Five P.M.—The Prussian fire becomes fiercer, the French right is forced sullenly backward towards Sedan, and at dusk, with the forked flames of Bazeilles as a beacon, they withdraw for the night. The battle had swept along the whole line for hours, until night declared again for German arms; and MacMahon, wounded and exhausted, retired within the fortifications of Sedan, and turned his army over to Gen. Wimpffen, his second in command.

* The author appends the sequel to the burning of Bazeilles and the bloody battles about Sedan, as seen, bereft of war's poetry and romance, ten days later.

TEN DAYS LATER.

BAZEILLES, *September* 10. — Three or four miles from Douzy is a heap of blackened timbers, bricks, and ashes. Here was the village of Bazeilles, which was destroyed by the Prussians in the fight that preceded the capitulation of Sedan. When the French troops had been driven back from their position outside the village, and were pursued into its streets, they got into the houses, and fired on their foes from the windows and the roofs. The Prussians could not drive them out; and the Prussian commander, to his eternal infamy, ordered his men to set fire, simultaneously, to every house in the village. The fire spread with almost lightning speed; in ten minutes the whole town was wrapped in sheets of flames, and hundreds of families — fathers, mothers, and children — were

ROASTED TO DEATH,

while the combatants, encircled with fire, died fighting to the last. The Germans did not escape from the destruction they brought upon the unarmed villagers: the fire spread so fiercely and suddenly, that they were themselves hemmed in by flames, and many of them, especially those who were wounded, were burned in the pyre they had kindled. I was told by the *curé* of the village, who was himself saved only by an accident, that out of a population of over 3000 souls, not more than a third were now living. Hundreds were burned to death; hundreds of others were slain by the Prussians, who, maddened at their own desperate straits, attacked every one they met; and hundreds of others who sought refuge in the cellars of their houses, perished there by suffocation. This is not a tale of the dark ages I am telling you — it is the simple story of what took place in a pretty and innocent French village, on Friday, the 22d of September, in this year of grace and of modern civilization.

PESTILENCE HAS BROKEN OUT

in Sedan, and in the neighboring villages of Carignan and Douzy. Before the German army moved away from Sedan, disease had begun to make havoc in its ranks, and every day we hear from those who come hither from the rear of the advancing forces, that dysentery and cholera hourly slay their scores of victims. But the advancing army must be better off than those they have left behind them. The pestilence was the inevitable consequence of what happened after the battles. As usual, no report of the losses in these engagements has yet been suffered to appear; but it is certain that while the number of killed and wounded French was great, the losses of the Prussians were hideous. Around Douzy and Carignan, however, the losses were about equal, and here, for the second and third days after the battles, the corpses lay in heaps. The Prussian grave-diggers use no ceremony in their operations, but the dead were too many for them. The corpses, in great numbers, remained unburied. They putrefied quickly, and the air became tainted with the fearful odor. The battles took place on Friday; on Monday the fields were still covered with unburied bodies of men and horses, and the stench was intolerable. During Sunday and Monday, since the dead could not be buried quickly enough, a new plan was adopted to dispose of them. They were consumed by fire. The plan adopted for the accomplishment of this

WHOLESALE CREMATION

was curious. In various places in the field a deep trench in the form of a cross was dug; a fire was made in the centre of this trench, and the currents of air coming from the four arms of the cross-shaped trench gave to the flames a fierce intensity. Then upon the fierce fire were piled the bodies of the dead, German and French together, and these were left to burn, while the grave-diggers went on with their work of burying the other dead in shallow pits, with only a few inches of earth thrown over them. For the living it would have been far better had all the dead been burned; for from all these thousands of shallow graves a pestilential stench is now arising, and filling the air with the seeds of death. I might fill columns with descriptions of the awful scenes on this battle-field, which covers a space of ten miles. Among the dead were many peasants, and even some women. How they came to be among the soldiers, no one knows; but there were their corpses.

SEDAN AND DEATH.

SEDAN, *September* 10.—***Never before in the world's history has there been seen such a butchery as went on during that great fight.*** I believe it may also be affirmed, that never did a contest in arms result in such terrific consequences to the surviving combatants, and to the people whose country has been made the scene of hostilities. For miles around Sedan ONE SEES NOTHING BUT DESTRUCTION AND RUIN; AND FROM MORNING TILL FAR INTO THE NIGHT PROCESSIONS OF THE MAIMED AND WOUNDED ARE PASSING FROM THE FRENCH FRONTIER INTO THE NEUTRAL TERRITORY OF BELGIUM. Sedan itself is one vast hospital, and between that town and Bouillon, a distance of about ten English miles, there is scarcely a church or a house from which the white flag with the red cross is not waving, to make known that there are wounded inside.

THURSDAY, *September* 1.—Last day of the battles near Sedan. The French defeated, with great slaughter, after a bloody battle. Bazaine also defeated near Metz, and forced to retire into the fortress. 10,000 French driven through Mézières into Belgium, and disarmed. General De Failly wounded. Entire French force surrenders with the Emperor.

SEDAN

THE WATERLOO OF THE SECOND EMPIRE.

THE KING'S DESPATCH TO QUEEN AUGUSTA.

SEDAN, *September* 1, 3 o'clock P.M. — The battle has raged since half-past eight o'clock this morning. Our forces have advanced victoriously. The Fourth, Fifth, and Seventh Corps and the Bavarians were engaged. The enemy was almost entirely driven into the city.

WILLIAM.

PRINCE GEORGE'S DESPATCH.

Great decisive victory at Sedan, wherein the Saxon (Twelfth) Corps has played the prominent part. It has captured trophies and prisoners in great numbers, but lost heavily.

GEORGE.

FROM THE CROWN PRINCE OF SAXONY.

In a battle on September 1, lasting twelve hours, the army of MacMahon has been destroyed by the army of the Crown Prince of Prussia and my own. The Saxon (Twelfth) Corps has behaved splendidly. George and myself are well. I do not know the losses as yet, but I do not believe they are as great as on August 18.

ALBERT.

KING WILLIAM REPORTS THE BATTLE.

(*Translation.*)

VENDRESSE, *south of Sedan, September* 3, 1870.

TO QUEEN AUGUSTA:

You know from my three telegrams the whole extent of the great historic event which has just happened. It is like a dream, even when one has seen it hour by hour developing itself. When I consider that after one great and successful war I could not expect more glorious things yet to happen during my reign, and now behold this historical act accomplished, then I bow before God, who alone has chosen me, my army, and my allies, to perform what has happened, and has made us the instruments of His will; I can only look upon it in this light, and in humility praise God's guidance and grace.

Now let me briefly give you a picture of the battle and its results.

TROOPS LOCATED.

On the evening of the 31st and the morning of the 1st the army had moved in the positions assigned all around Sedan. The Bavarians had the left wing at Bazeilles on the Meuse. Next to them the Saxons in the direction of Moncelle and Daigny; then the Guards still on the march in the direction of Givonne; and the Fifth and Eleventh Corps at St. Menges and Fleigneux. The Meuse making here a sharp bend, no troops were stationed from St. Menges as far as Donchery; but the latter place was held by the Würtembergers, who at the same time covered the rear against sorties from Mézières. The cavalry division under Count Stolberg, in the plain of Donchery, formed the right wing. In the front toward Sedan were the remainder of the Bavarians.

THE BATTLE.

In spite of a dense fog, the fight commenced at Bazeilles, already early in the morning, and gradually developed into a hot engagement, in which house after house had to be taken, last-

10*

ing almost the whole day, and the Erfurt Division, under General Schoeler (in the reserve, Fourth Corps), had to come to the assistance. When I arrived, at eight o'clock, at the front, before Sedan, the great battery was just opening its fire on the fortifications. A huge artillery combat ensued at all points, which continued for hours, and during which, on our side, ground was gradually gained. The villages mentioned were taken. Very deep ravines covered with timber rendered the advance of the infantry difficult, and favored the defence. The villages of Illy and Floing were taken, and gradually the circle of fire was drawn closer and closer around Sedan. It was a grand sight from our position, on a dominating eminence behind that battery mentioned, to the right of the village of Frénois, and forward above Pt. Forey.

The stubborn resistance of the enemy gradually slackened, as we could see from the battalions in disorder, hastily retiring from the woods and villages. The cavalry attempted to attack some battalions of our Fifth Corps, which held out and bore themselves splendidly. The cavalry dashed through the intervals between the battalions, then wheeled and returned the same way, repeating it three times with different regiments, so that the field was covered with dead men and horses. We could see it all distinctly from our position. I have not yet been able to learn the number of that brave regiment.

THE ROUT.

The retreat of the enemy in many places becoming a rout, and all — infantry, cavalry, and artillery — crowding into the town and the nearest surroundings, but still no indication appearing of the disposition of the enemy to save himself from this desperate condition by capitulation, nothing remained but to order the town to be bombarded by the battery before mentioned.

THE SURRENDER.

In less than twenty minutes it was burning in several places; that, together with the many burning villages in the whole radius of the battle, made an appalling impression, and I ordered the firing to cease, and sent Lieutenant-Colonel Von Bronsart, of the staff, with a white flag, as truce-bearer, offering capitulation to the army and fortress. He was met by a Bavarian officer, who reported that a French truce-bearer with a white flag had appeared at the gate. Lieutenant-Colonel Von Bronsart was admitted, and upon his inquiry for the General-in-

Chief, he was unexpectedly conducted before the Emperor, who wanted at once to deliver him a letter addressed to me. When upon inquiry by the Emperor what his orders were, the reply was given: To summon army and fortress to surrender.

THE EMPEROR'S LETTER.

The Emperor directed Bronsart to address himself in the matter to General De Wimpffen, who had just assumed command in place of MacMahon, wounded, and stated that he would send his letter to me by Adjutant-General Reillé. It was seven o'clock when Reillé and Bronsart came to me. You can imagine what impression it made upon me especially, and upon all. Reillé dismounted, and delivered to me the letter of his Emperor, adding that he had no further orders. Before opening the letter I said to him: "But I demand as first condition, that the army lay down their arms." The letter commences thus: "*N'avant pas pu mourir à la tête de mes troupes, je dépose mon épée à Votre Majesté*" (not having been able to die at the head of my troops, I lay down my sword before your Majesty),—leaving everything further to my discretion.

THE KING'S REPLY.

My reply was, that I regretted the manner in which we had met, and requested that a plenipotentiary be sent, when the capitulation could be concluded. I had given the letter to General Reillé. I spoke a few words to him as an old acquaintance, and thus ended this act. I gave Moltke full powers to treat, and directed Bismarck to remain behind, in case political questions should come up, and then rode to my carriage, and drove to this place.

JOY OF THE ARMY.

I was everywhere on the road saluted with thundering hurrahs by the trains moving up, and soldiers were singing everywhere the national hymn. It was sublime. Everywhere lights had been lit, so that now and then we drove in the midst of an improvised illumination. I arrived here at eleven o'clock, and drank with my suite the welfare of the army that had accomplished this great result. No report having reached me from Moltke up to the morning of the second of the result of the capitulation treaty which was to have been made in Donchery, I drove, at eight o'clock, according to arrangement, to the battlefield, and there met Moltke, who came to get my consent to the terms of capitulation proposed, and at the same time inform me that the Emperor had left Sedan at five o'clock, and had come to Donchery. As he wished to speak to me, I selected for our meeting a little castle with a park, which was close by. At ten o'clock Moltke and Bismarck made their appearance with the articles of capitulation, signed, and at one o'clock I set out with Fritz, escorted by a cavalry guard.

THE KING AND THE EMPEROR.

I dismounted at the castle, and the Emperor came to meet me. The interview lasted fifteen minutes. We were both deeply moved at *thus* meeting again. What I felt, having seen Napoleon three years ago in the very summit of his power, I cannot describe.

After this interview, from half-past three to half-past eight o'clock, I rode along the front of the whole army before Sedan. The reception by the troops, the meeting with the decimated Corps of Guards, all this I cannot describe to you to-day. I was profoundly moved by so many tokens of love and devotion. Now, good-by; with throbbing heart at the close of such a letter.

WILHELM.

THE BATTLE OF SEDAN.

(Translated from German Official Report.)

The Prussian Crown Prince invests the north of Sedan with the Fifth and Eleventh Corps, and the Würtembergers, the west with the Sixth in reserve, the south with the First and Second Bavarian, while the Saxon Crown Prince, Albert, invests the east with the Twelfth and Fourth Corps and the Guards Corps, with the Fourth division of cavalry.

The Germans have 240,000 effective men, and 60,000 in reserve.

The French have MacMahon's First Corps (commanded by General Ducrot); De Failly's old Fifth Corps (commanded by General De Failly until wounded); General Felix Douay's Seventh Corps; and the Twelfth Corps (General Lebrun)—in all about 110,000 effective men. The author gives a translation of the Prussian official report, as sent to the War Office in Berlin by the Prussian Secretary of War, Von Roon:

THE ORIGINAL PLAN.

It was originally intended to put off the decisive blow to September 2. It seemed desirable to give a day's rest to the

Saxon army, which had undergone considerable fatigue in their forced marches on the 30th and 31st. But when the King, between five and six o'clock in the afternoon of the 31st, passed Chenery on his way to Vendresse, he held a consultation with the Crown Prince and Generals Moltke and Blumenthal, in consequence of which he determined that the attack of Sedan, and the French lines between the Meuse and the Ardennes, should be undertaken on the ensuing day. Toward one o'clock in the morning of September 1, the Crown Prince of Saxony received orders to advance. Fire was to be opened at five A.M.

LINE OF BATTLE.

Our line of battle was formed in this wise: On our right we had the army of the Crown Prince of Saxony. His van consisted of the Twelfth Corps d'Armée; next came the Fourth and the Guards, the rear being brought up by the Fourth division of cavalry, with their back to Remilly. Those troops of the Crown Prince of Saxony, still on the left bank of the Meuse, crossed at Douzy. To the left of his army was stationed the First Bavarian Corps, and behind this the Second. The Bavarians threw their bridge opposite the village of Bazeilles. The Eleventh Prussian Corps had placed its pontoons during the night about one thousand paces below Donchery. A little to the left crossed the Fifth Corps on another bridge, and still further in the same direction, near the village of Dom-le-Mesnil, the Würtembergers. The Sixth Corps, as a reserve, was stationed between Attigny and Le Chêne. To these troops were opposed the corps of MacMahon, Failly, Canrobert, the remnants of Douay's army, and the newly-formed Twelfth Corps under General Lebrun. The centre of the French position was the fortress of Sedan, their flanks extending from Givonne on the left to Mézières on the right. In the rear of the French position were seen the spurs of the Ardennes.

CROWN PRINCE'S HEADQUARTERS.

The Crown Prince left Chenery in his carriage at four in the morning. Having mounted his horse near Cheveuse, on the road to Donchery, he took up his position on a hill projecting over the valley of the Meuse, near the town of Donchery, not far from a small mansion called Château-Donchery. From this point the whole array of the German army could be surveyed, and the progress of the battle watched in all directions.

SEDAN.

Sedan is situate at one of the finest points of the valley of the Meuse. Hills crowned with forests rise in terraces on either side of the river. On the right bank there is a narrow strip of meadow-land by the water-side; on the left, a little to the left of Sedan, is an open plain, with the town of Donchery pleasantly situated in its centre. The plain is traversed by a slight elevation. To the right the river Meuse makes a double curve, enclosing a strip of land on which lies the village of Iges, with Villette to the left, and Glaize to the right. Between Iges and Sedan there is Floing, and further to the right Givonne on the right bank. The main road between Donchery and Sedan proceeds from a bridge at the former city, and half-way touches the village of Frenoy. Bazeilles, which was opposite to the Bavarians, is southwest of Sedan; Douzy, where the Guards crossed, is on the extreme right.

THE BATTLE BEGINS.

A dense fog covered the valley and the hills. Only at half-past seven in the morning, the sun broke through the clouds, when the day became hot and sultry. The army of the Crown Prince of Saxony began operations a little after five o'clock. At half-past six a continuous cannonade was heard on our right, somewhat in the rear of Sedan, indicating the left flank of the enemy to have been attacked by our troops. But the French were in excellent position on the hills, and could not be so easily dislodged. While the fight was going on in this locality, our left wing prepared to turn the other flank of the enemy. The Eleventh Corps proceeded along the slight elevation in the midst of the plain; the Fifth marched straight on to get to the enemy's rear. According to the plan of the battle, these corps were eventually to effect a junction with our right wing, and, entirely surrounding the enemy, to cut off his retreat toward the Ardennes. The Würtembergers and the Fourth Cavalry division, subsequently sent to their support, were to protect the plain in case the enemy should push forward in this direction, which, however, was not very probable, as he would have found it difficult to cross the Meuse, and indeed, had himself destroyed the railway bridge between Donchery and Sedan. At a quarter past nine the Eleventh Corps d'Armée had so far turned the enemy's flank as to come close upon his position. An increased fire of the batteries marked this moment. The Saxons, who had designedly reserved their strength for this contingency, now attacked with an overpowering shock. Shortly after the right wing of the French began to fall back, but only to find themselves in the iron embrace of the two Prussian corps in their rear. At the point where the Eleventh Corps descended from the hills upon the surprised enemy the resistance of the French sensibly diminished since half-past ten. In some places, especially at Iges and on the fields leading down to Sedan, the fight assumed a desperate character. Being chiefly attacked by artillery, the French sent their horse to charge our guns in flank. The French cavalry made two brilliant onslaughts, some regiments, and, above all, the Chasseurs d'Afrique, behaving with the utmost gallantry. The infantry gave way earlier, the number of those battalions which surrendered without further resistance being considerable even before twelve o'clock. In the meantime the Fifth Corps had performed the long distance to the extreme heights, and after a sharp encounter succeeded in driving back the detachments making for the Ardennes.

FRENCH ARTILLERY REPULSED.

Things now assumed a favorable aspect. At half-past twelve it was announced that the French reserve artillery, which the Emperor had opposed to our Fifth Corps, was repulsed, and that only a few scattered bodies of infantry had effected their retreat across the frontier. Flight being thus rendered impossible, we had to deal only with the central portion of the battlefield — the slight elevation crossing the plains, the hills stretching from it to Sedan, and the fortress itself, which formed the last refuge for the troops driven from the heights.

SURROUNDING SEDAN.

Since quarter of one, the fire of the Prussian batteries on the right and left wing so rapidly approached one another, that it was evident the enemy would soon be completely surrounded. It was a grand sight to watch the sure and irresistible advance of the Guards, marching on, on the left wing, partly behind, and partly by the side of the Twelfth Corps d'Armée. Since quarter past ten, the Guards, preceded by their artillery, had been pushing toward the wood to the left of Sedan. By the advancing smoke of their fire we noticed how fast they were gaining ground.

They were effectively assisted by the Bavarians. After a smart resistance by the French, the Bavarians had stormed

Bazeilles, which was burned. They then took Balan, southwest of Sedan, where a narrow gorge gave them much trouble. Toward noon they posted two batteries in a meadow to the left of the road to Sedan. From this point they fired on Villette, the spire of which was soon enveloped in flames. The French artillery having been compelled to yield at this point likewise, there was nothing to stop the Eleventh and Twelfth Corps from pressing forward in the direction of Sedan. The enemy was now hastening to make good his retreat to the fortress walls. While the fight was still going on, large numbers of prisoners were seen being led down the hills to the plain.

In the meantime the Guards, a little before two o'clock, had effected a junction with the Fifth Corps, on the slopes in the distance. This closed the circle around the French.

COMPLETE INVESTMENT.

Encompassed by a living wall, they found themselves thrust back within the ramparts of their small stronghold.

Here and there villages and hamlets were still burning. Small detachments were continuing the fight in isolated localities, and the roar of cannon had not yet entirely ceased. A little later there was a pause, when we waited for the French commanders to resolve on what they had better do in their embarrassed position. If they determined on prolonged resistance, the fate of Sedan was sealed.

VICTORY.

Toward four o'clock the Crown Prince sent the message "Complete victory" to headquarters. Immediately after, His Royal Highness, with the Duke of Coburg, the other Princes, and the orderly officers, proceeded to the King, who had halted during the day on a hill to the right of the heights of Donchery. As there was no white flag to be seen on the tower of Sedan, we resumed firing at half-past four. The Bavarian batteries sent the first shots into the fortress. Within a quarter of an hour one of our igniting grenades set the place on fire. A straw shed having caught fire, dense black smoke rose immediately to the sky. Upon this the enemy opened negotiations. The Crown Prince was still with the King, when news arrived that the Emperor Napoleon was in Sedan. We now became aware that we had not only crushed the principal army of the French, but also, in a twelve hours' fight, secured a guarantee for the victorious issue of the war.

It is a fact that Napoleon, when he became aware of the probable results of the battle, for four hours stood the fire of Prussian grenades near the village of Iges.

At nine o'clock, when the Crown Prince returned from the scene of victory, a festal reception awaited him at his headquarters. The main street of the village was illuminated, the soldiers sang and shouted, and the band struck up the German National Anthem.

BAZAINE'S BATTLE NORTH OF METZ (*August* 31).

(See map, p. 156.)

Before the defeat of the Emperor at Sedan, he had ordered Bazaine to fight his way out of Metz, and join the Sedan army near Montmedy. To show the concert of action, the author gives Bazaine's reply, which explains his fight on the 31st:

TO THE EMPEROR: METZ, *August* 3.

I received your dispatch of the 19th instant at Rheims. I am moving in the direction of Montmedy, and will be on the line of the river Aisne the day after to-morrow. I shall act according to circumstances in trying to come to your assistance. BAZAINE.

In obedience to this order and reply, Bazaine gave battle to Prince Charles on the morning of the 31st. The assault was furious and the battle was glorious, though it resulted in a French defeat. De Caen died during the battle. General Manteuffel commanded the Prussian forces at the commencement, forcing Bazaine back into the fortress. After his defeat, Bazaine sent the following dispatches:

TO THE MINISTER OF WAR, PARIS: METZ, *September* 1.

After a sortie, executed with all my strength, and which brought on an obstinate fight of two days' duration round St. Barbe, we are again intrenched in our camp before Metz, with little ammunition for our field artillery, and lacking meat and biscuits. The town is full of wounded. The sanitary condition is rather bad. Notwithstanding our severe struggle the army preserves its firm spirit. I continue my effort to extricate ourselves. General De Caen is dead. The wounded and sick amount to about 18,000. BAZAINE.

TO THE EMPEROR: METZ, *September* 1, 1870.

It is altogether necessary that the army should know what is going on in Paris, and generally in France. We are without communication with the interior. The strangest reports have been spread by French prisoners who have been sent back by the enemy. These reports are, indeed, of an alarming nature. It is of the greatest importance that you should supply us with instruction and information. We are surrounded by strong forces. I tried, but in vain, to break through the Prussian line yesterday. (*See Prussian dispatch*, p. 357.)

The 1st and 9th Corps and Gen. Kummer's division (line and

landwehr), and the Twenty-eighth Infantry Brigade, participated in the engagements. The principal fights took place at Servigny, Noisseville, and Retonfay.

THE BATTLE OF SEDAN.

(*French account.*)

THURSDAY, *September* 1.—At seven o'clock the cannonade began in earnest; some slight firing having taken place earlier. The Prussian batteries facing us appeared to me much more numerous. There were batteries everywhere. They roared from every point of the Prussian line, which then stretched nearly parallel in front of the French. I could follow the falling of their shells, which exploded as they touched the ground, and fell with wonderful precision. I noticed also how quickly they changed and corrected their fire. As soon as a French corps took up a position it was instantly assailed by shells. The first would, perhaps, fall a few feet short or beyond, but the second or third was sure to find its way to the troops, and do its awful work among them. The French shells, on the contrary, exploded generally before they reached the ground, and the smoke of the explosion formed innumerable little clouds at different heights, some so high that the shell could do no harm to the enemy.

I noticed some inexplicable movements. A few squadrons of Prussian cavalry made as if they would charge a French force which was toward the left. Immediately

TWO REGIMENTS OF FRENCH CAVALRY CHARGED

in turn upon the Prussian squadrons, which fell back and fled. But at the same moment a Prussian corps of infantry opened a murderous fire upon those too eager French cavalry regiments, and they came back sadly shattered from their rash pursuit. About nine o'clock the Prussians were extending farther to the left; for, on asking whether certain new batteries were French, I was told they were Prussian. The Prussian line was evidently curling around us.

I have learned since that the Crown Prince had crossed the Meuse during the night, about five leagues from Sedan, and that this had not been known to MacMahon. A large force of Bavarians must also have arrived after the commencement of the battle, for it was Bavarian troops who began pounding us from the left. At half-past ten o'clock

THE ADVANCE OF THE PRUSSIANS

was perceptible on both wings at the same time. Some French

infantry, which were close to the town on the east side, gave way, as it seemed to me, rather quickly. Soon afterward shells were coming from behind my left, and it became evident that the French position had been turned, and that a fresh German corps had taken a position in our rear.

The reserves were now necessarily directed against these points. The battery near which I stood was already in action, and I thought it quite time to beat a retreat. The place was becoming as dangerous as any in the field. Among the guns close to me, the Prussian shells began falling with their usual beautiful precision. So I got on the other side of the slope, and made my way toward the town.

THE PRUSSIAN CIRCLE CONTRACTING.

As the road to Bouillon, which crossed the field of battle, was wholly closed to me now, I also perceived that I should be shut up in that circle which the Prussians had been drawing about the army and the town, and which was ultimately completed. I made my way as fast as I could, by the safest paths. When I reached the suburb, before the Porte de Balan, I found it encumbered with soldiers of all corps, hastening, as I was, into the town. It was a defeat, evidently, yet it was not eleven o'clock, and the battle was destined to continue, at various points, for some time longer, though continuing without any real hope of victory.

THE FRENCH ROUTED.

To one entering the town as I did, there was no longer any battle to describe. It was first a retreat and too soon a rout. I thought myself lucky to get away from the field as I did; for an hour afterward the rout of those forces that had been near by me was complete. Already soldiers were crushing against each other in the struggle to get inside the town. Dismounted cavalry were trying to make their way, some even by the ramparts, leaping down from the counterscarp; others forcing their way in by the postern gates. From a nook of the ramparts, where I rested a moment, I saw also cuirassiers jumping—horses and all—into the moat, the horses breaking their legs and ribs. Men were scrambling over each other. There were officers of all ranks—Colonels, and even Generals, in uniforms which it was impossible to mistake, mixed in this shameful melée. Behind all came guns, with their heavy carriages and powerful horses, forcing their way into the throng, maiming and crushing the fugitives on foot.

TERRIBLE SCENES IN SEDAN.

To add to the confusion and horror, the Prussian batteries had by this time advanced within range, and the Prussian shells began falling among the struggling masses of men.

Bazeilles, Daigny, Givonne, Iges, Frenoy, and the woods of Donchery formed a wall of fire around Sedan. From every side the terrible fire rained down upon the French.

On the ramparts were the National Guards, manning the guns of the town, and replying with more or less effect to the nearest Prussian batteries. It was a scene horrible enough to have suited the fancy of Gustave Doré himself. I could form but one idea of our unhappy army: that it was at the bottom of a seething caldron.

I hurried back as best I could to my hotel, following the narrow streets where the shells were least likely to reach the ground. Wherever there was a square or open place, I came upon the bodies of horses and men quite dead or still quivering, mown to pieces by bursting shells. Reaching my hotel, I found the street in which it stood choked like the rest with wagons, guns, horses, and men. Most luckily at this moment the Prussian fire did not enfilade this street, for a train of caissons filled with powder blocked the whole way, itself unable to move backward or forward. There was every chance that these caissons would explode, the town being then on fire in two places; and I began to think Sedan was a place more uncomfortable than even the battle-field over which a victorious enemy was swiftly advancing.

THE EMPEROR UNDER FIRE.

From friends whom I found at the hotel, I learned that the Emperor, who had started early in the morning for the field of battle, had returned about the same time that I did, and passed through the streets with his staff. One of my friends was near him on the Place Turenne when a shell fell under the Emperor's horse, and bursting, killed the horse of a general who was behind him. He himself was untouched, and turned around and smiled; though my friend thought he saw tears in his eyes, which he wiped away with his glove. Indeed, he had cause enough for tears on that fatal 1st of September.

Meantime, shells began to fall in the direction of our street and hotel. We all stood under the vaulted stone entrance, as the safest shelter we could find. I trembled on account of the caissons still standing in the street, and filling all the space from end to end. It was at this time when we waited watching painfully for the shell which would have sent us all together into another world, that General De Wimpffen came past, making

A VAIN EFFORT

to rally and inspirit his flying troops. He shouted, "*Vive la France! En avant!*" But there was no response. He cried out that Bazaine was taking the Prussians in the rear. News which had been current all the morning at intervals, coming now from the mouth of Gen. De Wimpffen, seemed to be believed, and a few thousand men were rallied and followed him out of the town. People began to have hope, and for one brief moment we believed the day might yet be saved. Need I say that this intelligence was a patriotic falsehood of brave Gen. De Wimpffen? Mad with anguish, and in direct opposition to the Emperor's orders, he had resolved to rally what men he could, and make a stand. He could not have known that he was bound in the grasp of at least 300,000 men.

A DESPERATE SORTIE.

The bugle and the trumpet rang out on all sides. A few thousand men hearkened to the sound. My friend Rene De Guiroye, of the Chasseurs D'Afrique, whom I have just met, after losing sight of him for ten or twelve years, got on horseback again and joined the General. The sortie took place thus: They went out at the Porte de Balan. The houses of the suburb were already full of Prussians, who fired on the French out of every window. The church, especially, was strongly garrisoned, and its heavy doors were closed. The General sent off De Guiroye to bring two pieces of cannon. These soon arrived, and with them the door of the church was blown in, and 200 Prussians were captured and brought back with the French, who, in spite of all efforts, were themselves soon obliged to retire into the town. It was the last incident of the battle — the last struggle.

While this took place at the Porte de Balan, the Prussian shelling went on, and the shells began to fall into the hotel.

SHOCKING SCENES

followed. A boy, the son of a tradesman around the corner of the street, came in crying, and asking for a surgeon. His father's leg had been shot off. A woman in front of the house met the same fate. The doctor who went to the tradesman found him dead; and returning, attempted to carry the woman to an ambulance. He had scarcely made a step when she was shot dead in his arms. Those of us who stood in the gateway and witnessed such scenes must have got beyond the feeling of personal fear. Any one of us, I will venture to say, would have given his life to spare France on this dreadful day. Yet we stood pale and shuddering at the sight of the fate which befell the poor people of the town.

I care not to dwell upon horrors, which, nevertheless, I shall never be able to forget. I can mention more than one brave officer who did not fear to own that he shrank from the sight of what had become a mere massacre. Those who were safely out of the way as prisoners, whether officers or men, needed no pity. When, after a time, it became clear that there was no sign of Bazaine, the hopes of the French again departed. A sullen sort of fight still went on. The guns of the town answered the Prussians. An aide-de-camp of the Emperor went by on foot, and I heard him ask the officers near by to help him in putting an end to the fire. Such being the Emperor's wish, at length

THE WHITE FLAG

was hoisted on the citadel. The cannonade ceased suddenly about half-past four. Eager as we were to know the cause, we cannot leave the house, for the street is impassable, and we have to be content with learning the mere fact of the surrender. As night drew on, the crowd a little diminished, and by some effort it was possible to make one's way about the town. The spectacle it offered was more horrible than war. Dead were lying everywhere; civilians and soldiers mingled in the slaughter. In one suburb I counted more than fifty bodies of peasants and bourgeois — a few women among them, and one child. The ground was strewn with splinters of shells. Starving soldiers were

CUTTING UP THE DEAD HORSES

to cook and eat, for provision had again failed us, as everything has failed since this campaign began. I was glad to get away from the sight of our disasters, and lose their remembrance in a few hours of sleep.

NAPOLEON A PRISONER.

The next day we were told that the Emperor had gone to the King's headquarters to treat for a surrender. At eleven his household and carriages left the town, and we knew that he was a prisoner and the Empire no more. About the same hour there was posted in the streets a proclamation from Gen.

De Wimpffen, saying that, notwithstanding prodigies of courage, the army having no more ammunition, found itself unable to respond to the summons of its chiefs and force its way to Montmédy; that being surrounded, he had made the best conditions he could — conditions such as would inflict no humiliation on the army.

These conditions prove to be the surrender of the whole army, not less than 100,000 men, as prisoners of war, with all their arms, baggage, horses, standards, and guns. The officers who sign an engagement not to serve against Prussia during the war, may return to their homes, the remainder to be sent to German towns in Germany. Many officers refuse to sign, preferring to share the captivity of their men.

BAD FAITH OF THE FRENCH.

On Saturday the whole force laid down their arms. Not a few soldiers, in their rage, broke, rather than give up their arms, and the streets were littered with fragments of all kinds of weapons broken — swords, rifles, pistols, lancers' helmets, cuirasses, even mitrailleuses covered the ground; and in one place, where the Meuse runs through the town, the heaps of such fragments choked the stream, and rose above the surface. The mud of the streets was black with gunpowder. The horses had been tied to the houses and gun-carriages, but nobody remembered to feed or water them, and in the frenzy of hunger and thirst they broke loose and ran wild through the town. Whoever liked might have a horse — even officers' horses, which were private property — for the trouble of catching them.

EMPTYING THE MONEY CHEST.

When the Prussians came into the town they were very sore and angry at the sight of all this destruction and waste. What must have pleased them still less was the state in which they found the military chest. As soon as the surrender was resolved on, the French officers were told to make out the best accounts they could, present them, and receive payment. Naturally, the statements thus brought in soon proved sufficient to empty the treasury. I know of officers who demanded and received payment for horses that were not killed and baggage which had not been lost. Demoralization showed itself in every way. Even the standards were burned or buried, an act of bad faith not to be palliated even by the grief and rage of a beaten army.

GEN. DE FAILLY.

Their rage is greater against no one than Gen. De Failly. He had a room in the hotel where I was staying. On Friday, a great multitude of soldiers gathered before the house, the doors of which were closed, demanding Gen. De Failly with such shouts and menaces, that the landlord thought it prudent to hurry him out of a back window. The soldiers, could they have reached him, would have torn him to pieces. Since then, I have heard the report that he was shot by one of his own men; but no such event had happened on Saturday, and could not well happen later.

FRENCH ANNOYANCES AND PRUSSIAN COURTESY.

It was a relief on Saturday when the Prussians came in and occupied the town, and restored order. I am sorry to have to acknowledge, that all through the campaign the French have acted much more like a conquering army in a hostile country than the Prussians. All the annoyance I have experienced personally came from my own countrymen; from the peasants, who, above all, saw a spy in every stranger. When I fell into the hands of the Prussians, I found them courtesy itself. On leaving Sedan, and thence to the frontier, in passing through the Prussian posts, I was stopped often. I had but to say, "I am the correspondent of an American journal," and I was at once sent kindly forward. On the back of my military pass the Prussian staff had endorsed a Prussian safe-conduct. Often I was not obliged even to show my papers: my word was taken; and once out of Sedan I was speedily through.

When I left Sedan on Sunday morning things were rapidly getting in order. The streets were cleared of dead horses and men. The indescribable filth of the town was swept into the river. The shops were opening again. Discipline had taken the place of disorder. I saw enough of Prussian organization and energy to change, if the grievous defeat of a noble army had not already changed, the opinion I have so often expressed, that ultimate victory for France was sure.

WHY THE FRENCH WERE SO OFTEN SURPRISED.

I have followed MacMahon from the day when I found him reorganizing his army at Châlons to the fatal day at Sedan, when he surrendered the last organized force in France, save the remnant of that which is shut up in Metz. Certainly, when I was at the camp of Châlons, and then at Rheims, I had observed that the number of stragglers was enormous, and I continually met soldiers who did not know where their regiments were. I had seen men and officers disabled by wounds which French soldiers of other days would have despised; I had remarked how untidy and careless the men were allowed to be about their dress and equipments. These things, slight, but significant to a military eye, had caused me, no doubt, some misgivings as to the rapidity of the success we had a right to expect. I saw also how prone French officers were to avoid the fatigues of long marches and the discomfort of bivouacs. I remember how often I have traversed the French lines at dead of night and at early dawn, and never heard a challenge, never came across a French vidette, never have fallen in with a party of scouts. On the other hand, I have seen officers spend the time that ought to have been given to their men, in cafés or in poor village inns. Often even officers of the staff seemed to neglect their duties for paltry amusements, showing themselves ignorant sometimes even of the name of the Department in which they were; so that I have known a French General obliged to ask his way from peasants at the meeting of two roads. I struggled long against all this kind of evidence, but the end is only too clear. Painful it is to me, but I am bound to declare my belief that any further effort France may make can only cause useless bloodshed, and that a means of escape from her peril must now be sought otherwise than by force of arms.

PUSHED INTO BELGIUM.

During the battle ten thousand officers and soldiers of the French army were forced into Belgian territory, where they were required to instantly surrender their arms.

Last night the frontier guard captured, disarmed, and unhorsed two hundred French on Belgian territory near Sedan.

The French troops who were captured and disarmed have been sent to the camp at Beverloo.

FRENCH LOSSES (OFFICIAL).

The official figures of the capitulation at Sedan are 39 generals, 230 staff officers, and 2095 line officers, beside 500 officers of various grades discharged on parole. The number of privates surrendered and transported into Germany is 84,433; 28,000 were made prisoners during the battle; 5000 escaped into Belgium; 20,000 were killed and wounded—total, 137,000.

Besides the prisoners, 400 field-pieces, including 70 mitrailleuses, 150 siege guns, 10,000 horses, and an immense amount of war material, were surrendered.

CLOSING SCENES OUTSIDE.

While General De Wimpffen, at 2 P.M., was trying to rally his flying troops in Sedan—shouting "Vive la France," and "En Avant!"—a strange scene was being enacted at King William's headquarters without. Just as the brave De Wimpffen was leading the final assault,

A GENTLEMAN ASKED BISMARCK

"where he thought the Emperor was. In Sedan?" "Oh, no!" was the reply; "Napoleon is not very wise, but he is not so foolish as to put himself in Sedan just now." For once in his life, Count Bismarck was wrong.

At 2.45 the King came to the place where I was standing. He remarked that he thought the French were about to try to break out just beneath us, in front of the Second Bavarian Corps. At 3.50 General Sheridan told me that Napoleon and Louis were in Sedan.

BRAVERY OF THE BAVARIANS.

At 3.20 the Bavarians below us not only contrived to get themselves inside the fortifications of Sedan, but to maintain themselves there, working their way forward from house to house. About four, there was a great fight for the possession of the ridge above Bazeilles. That carried, Sedan was swept on all sides by the Prussian cannon. This point of vantage was carried at 4.40. When carried, there could no longer be a shade of doubt as to the ultimate fate of Sedan.

A FLAG OF TRUCE.

About five o'clock there was again a sudden suspension of the canonnade along the whole line. Many were the speculations as to the cause, but nobody seemed to divine the truth. You must judge of our surprise when, five minutes later, we saw a French officer, escorted by two uhlans, coming at a handsome trot up the steep bridle-path from Sedan, to our post, one of the uhlans carrying a white duster on a faggot-stick as a flag of truce. The messenger turned out to be a French colonel, come to ask for terms of surrender. After a very short consultation between the King and General Von Moltke, the messenger was told by the General that, in a matter so important as the surrender of at least 80,000 men, and an important fortress, it was necessary to send an officer of high rank. "You are therefore," said the General, "to return to Sedan, and tell the Governor of the town to report himself immediately to the King of Prussia. If he does not arrive within an hour, our guns will again open fire. You may tell the commandant that there is no use of his trying to obtain any other terms than unconditional surrender." The *parlementaire* rode back with this message. When he was fairly out of ear-shot, his mission was most eagerly canvassed.

At 6.30 there arose a sudden cry among the members of the King's staff—"*Der Kaiser ist da!*"—and then came a loud hurrah. Soon we began to look anxiously for the arrival of the second flag of truce. In ten minutes more General Reillé rode up with a letter for the King of Prussia.

THE EMPEROR'S SURRENDER.

As soon as the French General was in sight, the slender escort of cuirassiers and dragoons we had with us was drawn up in line, two deep. Behind the King, in front of the escort, was the Staff, and ten yards in front of them again, stood His Majesty, King William of Prussia, ready to receive General Reillé. That officer, as we soon learned, was the bearer of an autograph letter from the Emperor Napoleon to King William. The Emperor of the French wrote: "As I cannot die at the head of my army, I lay my sword at the feet of your Majesty."

Why Napoleon III. could not die, as did thousands of his soldiers, sword in hand, with his face to the foe, is not so clear. It seems a Bonaparte has not been born to be killed in battle. The death of Napoleon III. at Sedan would have been practical justice.

On receipt of this most astounding letter, there was a brief consultation between the King, the Crown Prince, who had come over from his hill on the arrival of the flag of truce, Count Bismarck, General Von Moltke, and General Von Roon. After a few minutes' conversation, the King sat down on a rush-bottomed chair, and wrote a note (on another chair held as a table by two aides-de-camp) to the Emperor, asking him to come next morning to the King of Prussia's headquarters at Vendresse.

SHERIDAN CONGRATULATES BISMARCK.

While the King was writing this note, Count Bismarck came up to Generals Sheridan and Forsyth, and myself, and heartily shook our hands. "Let me congratulate you most sincerely, Count," said General Sheridan. "I can only compare the surrender of Napoleon to that of General Lee at Appomattox Court House."

When it came my turn to grasp the Chancellor's hand, I could not help saying, after I had warmly congratulated him:

"You cannot but feel a pride, Count Bismarck, in having contributed so largely to the winning of to-day's victory."

"Oh! no, my dear sir," was the mild answer; "I am no strategist, and have nothing to do with the winning of battles. What I am proud of is, that the Bavarians, the Saxons, and the Würtembergers, have not only been on our side, but have had so large a share — the largest share — in the glory of the day; that they are with us, and not against us. *That* is my doing. I don't think the French will say now that the South Germans will not fight for our common Fatherland."

I asked His Excellency whether Louis was taken with his papa, and was told that no one knew; and I think that no one much cared where that little man was.

When the King had written his letter, he himself handed it to General Reillé, who stood bareheaded to receive it — the Italian and Crimean medals glittering on his breast in the fading sunlight. Queen Victoria's image and superscription have not often been seen on the uniforms of men surrendering without conditions.

At 7.40, General Reillè left for the beleaguered town, escorted by the uhlans.

A DRINK TO UNITED GERMANY.

Then there was a general demand for something to drink, and Count Bismarck's aide-de-camp produced two bottles of Belgian beer. One of them His Excellency shared with General Sheridan, General Forsyth, and myself, saying that he drank to the closer union of the three great Teutonic peoples.

FRIDAY, *September* 2. — The entire army of MacMahon, 90,000 men, surrender. Napoleon III. a prisoner of war. 400 field-pieces, 150 siege guns, and 70 mitrailleuses fall into the hands of the Prussians.

THE CAPITULATION

When the Emperor, who had passed the weary hours of the night, looked out in the early morning, he beheld a forest of steel and iron on the valley and hill-tops, batteries posted on every eminence, cavalry in all the plains, and as far as his eye could reach, the hosts of embattled Germans, his decision was taken. At last, attended by a few of his staff on horseback, His Majesty proceeded along the road from Sedan in a brougham. Count Bismarck was in bed in his quarters at Donchery, when an officer rushed in, and announced that the Emperor was coming to meet him and to see the King. Count Bismarck rose and dressed hastily, you may be sure, in the white peaked cap, with yellow band, dark uniform coat, with metal buttons and yellow facings, and hastened to meet the Emperor. He was in time to stop the cortége outside of the town. As his Majesty alighted, Count Bismarck uncovered his head, and stood with his cap in hand, and on a sign or request from the Emperor, put it on. The Count replied :

"Sire, I receive your Majesty as I would my own royal master."

There happened to be near the place where the interview occurred, a few hundred yards outside the squalid town of Donchery, the humble cottage of a handloom weaver, of whom there are numbers around Sedan. Count Bismarck led the way, and entered it. The room was not inviting. The great Count walked up the stairs. The apartment was filled by the handloom and appliances of the weaver ; so he descended, and found the Emperor sitting on a stone outside. Two chairs were brought out of the cottage. The Emperor sat down in one ; Count Bismarck took the other, and placed it on his Majesty's left hand side. The officers in attendance on their fallen master lay down some distance away, upon a small plot of grass in front of the cottage. The conversation was a strange one.

Count Von Bismarck has made that memorable conversation historic in his report to King William.

BISMARCK'S REPORT.

NO POWER TO TREAT FOR PEACE.

"I had about an hour's conversation with the Emperor.

"His Majesty principally expressed a wish to obtain more favorable terms of capitulation for the army. I completely declined to negotiate on this matter with His Majesty, while the purely military questions were to be settled between Generals Von Moltke and Wimpffen. On the other hand I asked his Majesty whether he was inclined to enter into negotiations for peace. The Emperor replied that, as a prisoner, he was not now in a position to do so; and when I further asked through whom his views in relation to the Government of France were now to be learned, His Majesty referred to the Government then established in Paris."

THE SURRENDER PURELY MILITARY.

"After this point, of which we could not safely form an opinion from the letter of yesterday from the Emperor to your Majesty, had been cleared up, I recognized, and I did not conceal the fact from the Emperor, that the situation to-day, as yesterday, presented no other practical bearing but the military one."

WANTS TO GO INTO BELGIUM.

"The Emperor went out into the open air, and invited me to sit beside him before the door of the house. His Majesty asked me if it was not practicable to let the French army cross the Belgian frontier, that it might be there disarmed. I had already discussed this contingency also with Gen. Von Moltke on the previous evening, and, for reasons already alluded to, I could not enter into a promise of this compromise."

FRANCE COMPELLED HIM TO MAKE WAR.

"In reference to the political situation, I, on my part, took no initiative, nor the Emperor either — only in so far as he lamented the misfortunes of the war, and declared that he himself had not wished for the war, but that he had been compelled to make it by the pressure of French public opinion."

A CHANGE FROM THE NEAREST HOUSE TO THE CHATEAU.

"I mentioned Frenois as the place which I would propose to your Majesty as the place of meeting; and I therefore suggested to the Emperor whether he ought not to go there immediately, as a delay inside the small laborer's house was unsuitable to him, and he, perhaps, was in want of some repose. His Majesty readily agreed to the suggestion, and I conducted the Emperor, preceded by a guard of honor of your Majesty's regiment of body-guards, to the Château Bellevue, where meantime the remainder of the suite and the equipage of the Emperor, whose arrival there out of the town ought to be considered uncertain, had come from Sedan."

GENERAL DE WIMPFFEN TALKS CAPITULATION.

"Gen. Wimpffen had also arrived, and with him, while waiting for the return of Gen. Von Moltke, Gen. Podbielski resumed the conversation in reference to the negotiations for capitulation, which had been broken off on the previous day, in presence of Lieut. Von Verdy and the Chief of Gen. Wimpffen's staff."

THE KING CAN'T SEE NAPOLEON.

"I was just taking part in the introduction of these negotiations by laying before them the political and moral aspect of the situation, as affected by what the Emperor said to me, when I received from Rittmeister, Count of Noslitz, on the order of Gen. Von Moltke, the information that your Majesty would not see the Emperor until after the completion of the capitulation of the army. This announcement extinguished on both sides the hope that any other conditions than those already offered would be agreed to."

CAPITULATION SIGNED.

"I rode after this to Chénery to see your Majesty, that I might announce to you the position of affairs. I met on the way Gen. Von Moltke, with the text of the capitulation as approved by your Majesty, which, after we entered Frenois, was, without controversy, accepted and signed."

A BRAVE GENERAL AND A BRAVE ARMY.

"The conduct of Gen. Wimpffen, like that of the other French generals on the preceding night, was very dignified, and this brave officer could not refrain from expressing to me his pain at being called upon, forty-eight hours after his arrival from Africa, and half a day after his receiving the command, to sign his name to a capitulation so fatal to the French army. But the want of provisions and ammunition, and the absolute impossibility of any further defence, had, he said, laid upon him, as a General, the duty of sinking his personal feelings, since further bloodshed could not make any change in the situation. Our agreement to let the officers depart on parole was received with lively gratitude, as an expression of the intention of your Majesty to spare the feelings of an army which had fought bravely, as far as the demands of our military and political interests would allow. To this feeling Gen. Wimpffen has given emphatic expression in a letter in which he has returned Gen. Von Moltke his thanks for the considerate manner in which the negotiations on his side were conducted.

"COUNT BISMARCK."

ARTICLES OF CAPITULATION.

At 11.30 the following articles of capitulation were signed, as agreed upon by General Wimpffen and General Von Moltke, Count Bismarck taking part in the deliberations:

SEDAN, *September* 2.—By the chief of the staff of his Majesty King William, Commander-in-Chief of the German armies, and the General Commanding-in-Chief of the French armies, both with full powers from his Majesty the King and the Emperor of the French, the following agreement has been concluded:

ARTICLE 1. The French army, under the command of General Wimpffen, surrounded actually by superior forces around Sedan, are prisoners of war.

ART. 2. Owing to the valorous defence of that army, an exception (exemption) is made for all the generals and officers, and for the superior employes having rank of officers in the military list, who will give their word of honor in writing not to take up arms against Germany, nor to act in any way against the interests of that nation, till the end of the present war. The officers and employes accepting that condition will keep their arms and the effects belonging to them personally.

ART. 3. All the other arms and the army material, consisting of flags, eagles, cannons, horses, war ammunitions, military trains, will be surrendered at Sedan by a military commission named by the commander-in-chief, to be given at once to the German commissary.

ART. 4. The town of Sedan will be given up at once, in its present state, and no later than the evening of the 2d of September, to be put at the disposal of the King of Prussia.

ART. 5. The officers who will not undertake the engagement mentioned in Article 2, and the troops of the armies, will be conducted with their regiments, in their corps, and in military order.

This measure will commence on the 2d of September, and will terminate on the 3d; the soldiers will be brought up by the Meuse, near D'Yzes, and put in the hands of the German commissary by their officers, who will then give their commands to their non-commissioned oficers. The military surgeons will remain, without exception, at the rear, to take care of the wounded.

(Signed) WIMPFFEN.
VON MOLTKE.

LIST OF FRENCH OFFICERS SURRENDERED.

First Army Corps—Gen. Ducrot, Commander of Corps; Brig.-Gen. Joly Frigola, commanding artillery; Gen. Pelle, commanding Second Division; Gen. L'Heviller, commanding Third Division; Gen. Lartignes, commanding Fourth Division; Gen. Michel (now dead), commanding cavalry; Brig.-Gen. De Montmarie, First Brigade; Brig.-Gen. Grandil, Second Brigade; and Brig.-Gens. Léfèvre, Paterettre-Court, Fraboulet de Kerleadec, De Belle Mare, and Leforestier de Vaudœuvre, commanding cavalry brigade.

Fifth Army Corps—Division-Gen. Göze; Gen. de l'Abadie d'Agdrin, commanding Second Division; Brig.-Gen. Abbatucci, commanding Second Division; De Mauzières, Chief of Staff; Brig.-Gens. Saurin and Baron Nicolas-Nicolas.

Seventh Corps—Division-Gen. Felix Douay, commanding Corps; Gen. Renson, Chief of Staff; Gen. Louis Doutrelaine; Brig.-Gen. De St. Hilaire, commanding First Division; Gen. Lieberd, commanding Second Division; Gen. Brodas, commanding Third Division; Division-Gen. Baron Ameil, commanding cavalry, and Brig.-Gens. De la Bastide and De Liegard.

Twelfth Corps—Gen. Lebrun, commanding Corps; Brig.-Gen. Gresley, Chief of Staff; Gen. Grandchamp, commanding First Division; Gen. Lacretelle, Second Division; Gen. De Vassoigne, Third Division; Gen. D'Ouvrier de Villegly, commanding artillery; Division-Gen. Bucape; Brig.-Gens. Cambriels, Marquiseau, Reboul, Cadart, Labaske, and Bertrand. Gen. Wimpffen, with his Staff, is not included, because he was accorded the privilege to leave before the surrender was consummated, and Marshal MacMahon is not mentioned, because he, when the capitulation took place, lay wounded in a village near Sedan.

The actual numbers of prisoners from each corps is as follows: First Corps, 32,400; Fifth Corps, 11,106; Seventh Corps, 15,618; Twelfth Corps, 25,309.

DE WIMPFFEN MAD.

De Wimpffen, while he was signing his name, spoke bitterly of having hurried back from Africa only to find such a task as this devolve upon him. It was indeed an ill-omened journey to join a force which he found outnumbered and defeated, one might almost say, before the battle began, and to assist in an act of surrender that would be to his eternal regret.

THE KING TO THE QUEEN.

BEFORE SEDAN, FRANCE,
Friday, *September* 2, 1.22 P.M.

TO QUEEN AUGUSTA:

A capitulation, whereby the whole army at Sedan are prisoners of war, has just been concluded with General Wimpffen, commanding instead of Marshal MacMahon, who is wounded. The Emperor surrendered himself to me, as he had no command. He left everything to the Regent at Paris. His residence I shall appoint after an interview with him at a rendezvous to be fixed immediately.

What a course events, with God's guidance, have taken!

WILLIAM.

THE KING AND THE EMPEROR.

About 2 o'clock the King, with his body-guard and escort of cuirassiers, attended by the Crown Prince and staff of general officers, proceeded to a château outside Sedan, and received the Emperor, who came with his personal followers and staff in charge of an escort, which was ranged on the other side of the avenue facing the cuirassiers. Napoleon remained perfectly calm. In the beginning of the visit he received his guest of 1867 and his conqueror of to-day with grave politeness. The

King and his captive retired into the glass-house off one of the saloons of the drawing-room floor, and they could be seen by the staff outside engaged in earnest dialogue.

What they had said to each other may have concerned the status of the captive Emperor. Certain it is that Napoleon was much affected by the courtesy of King William, and that he expressed to the Crown Prince in warm terms his sense of the generous manner in which he had been treated.

At the interview with the King the Emperor had a few moments' conversation with the Crown Prince, during which he was much agitated when alluding to the manner of the King. His great anxiety seemed to be not to be exhibited to his own soldiers. The result was, however, that his Majesty, wishing to avoid one mischief, was exposed to a great humiliation, for his course had to be altered to avoid Sedan, and thus he had to pass through the lines of the Prussian army.

THE KING TO THE QUEEN.

VARENNES, *September* 2. — What a solemn moment when I met Napoleon! He was bowed down, but dignified. I have assigned him Wilhelmshöhe, near Cassel (capital of Hesse Cassel), as his residence. Our meeting took place in a little castle in front of the western glacis before Sedan.

From there I rode along the front of the army at Sedan. The reception by the troops you can hardly imagine. It was indescribable. At eight o'clock, when it became dark, I finished my ride, which had lasted five hours, but I did not return here till one. May God help further.

WILLIAM.

NAPOLEON'S FUTURE RESIDENCE.

Cassel, which is designed as the future place of residence of Napoleon III., is a walled city of Germany, beautifully situated on both banks of the Fulda, ninety-one miles northeast of Frankfort-on-the-Main. It has a population numbering 40,000. The residence which Napoleon is to occupy is the summer palace of the Elector at Wilhelmshöhe, a suburb on the left bank of the river. It is surrounded by a magnificent garden.

THE EMPEROR'S PRISON.

"I have given him Wilhelmshöhe," says the King of Prussia, in this telegraphic despatch to the Queen, his wife, which briefly but eloquently depicts a great scene in the drama of history. There is, indeed, something highly dramatic in this gift to a broken man. "Where and what manner of place is

Wilhelmshöhe?" many readers will ask. It is the Versailles of Germany. It is a château and pleasure park on the east slope of the Habichtswald Mountains; and it has for the captive Emperor associations of peculiar interest, forasmuch as it was once the favorite residence of his uncle Jerome, sometime King of Westphalia. This palatial retreat and its surroundings are in the luxurious taste of the last century. There are hot-houses on an amazing plan; there are temples of Apollo and Mercury; there are waterfalls, pheasantries, lakes, and a Chinese village. There is a great fountain, perhaps the greatest in the world, for its column of water, rising to a height of 190 feet, is 12 feet in thickness. And lastly, at the farthest and highest point of the grounds, nearly 1400 feet above the Fulda, there is a strange, if not preposterous, building of octagonal shape, with a series of cascades descending from its foot, through five basins, to a "grotto of Neptune." The building at the top of the cascade is named the Riesenschloss, from a colossal statue, which is an immensely enlarged copy of the Farnese Hercules, the club having a cavity in which nine people can sit. Such is Wilhelmshöhe, whose precincts are reached from Cassel by a straight avenue of lime-trees.

SATURDAY, *September* 3. — Proclamation of the French Ministry announcing the disaster to their arms, and declaring that France will resist to the last. General Ducrot, who refused to sign his parole, escapes from Sedan.

Patriotic enthusiasm in Berlin. Wild delight in London. The *déchéance* of Napoleon III. cried in the streets of Paris. Wild excitement at the French capital. The Emperor goes to Wilhelmshöhe an exile. "*I shall return to Paris to exact a reckoning, not to give one.*"

HOW THE WORLD RECEIVES THE NEWS.

BERLIN REJOICES.

BERLIN, *Saturday, September* 3.

The receipt of the news that the Emperor and MacMahon had capitulated, has occasioned the most prodigious enthusiasm here. Thousands of people throng the streets, moving in ranks with arms linked, singing patriotic songs, shouting, and exhibiting every other sign of enthusiasm.

A surging crowd assembled before the palace, when, in response to the cheering, the Queen appeared and made a short address. All the schools were closed, and the children given a holiday. The monument to Frederick II. was literally buried in flags. Demonstrations were made before the residences of Count Von Bismarck, Baron de Moltke, and Minister of War Von Roon. The shops and stores were mostly closed, and the day given up to festivities and rejoicings.

PARIS IN MOURNING.

PARIS, *September* 3 (*Morning*).— A nation mourns. There is a grief too deep for utterance! A proud nation stricken down! A wail of despair goes up from the women, while brave men clench their teeth, and stand motionless and fixed. The Emperor captured? It is not credited. *A bas!* Rumors fly in the air. There is a fearful uncertainty in every face — a terrible foreboding that France is in danger.

Noon. — Rumors fly thick and fast, but no official news. The streets are crowded, and the people move like a funeral procession. "What is it; have you heard?" Only an ominous look.

Evening. — There is dreadful news, but as yet it is locked up in the Corps Législatif. A great caravan of bursting hearts is swaying back and forth in the Place de la Concorde. A stormy scene is taking place in the Corps Législatif. There is no disorder, no violence without. There begins to be impatience. The crowd blocks up the doorway of the Corps Législatif. They cry, "Tell us of MacMahon!"

News at last! A proclamation from the Ministry. A million eyes devour the few words of misfortune, and a murmur of relief, mingled with patriotic exclamations, goes through the crowded streets.

THE GOVERNMENT TO THE FRENCH PEOPLE!

A great misfortune has come upon the country. After three days of heroic struggles, sustained by the army of Marshal MacMahon, against 300,000 of the enemy, 40,000 men have been made prisoners. General de Wimpffen, who took command of the army in place of Marshal MacMahon, badly wounded, has signed a capitulation. This cruel reverse will not shake our courage. Paris is to-day in a complete state of defence. The military forces of the country will be organized in a few days. A new army will be under the walls of Paris. Another army is forming on the banks of the Loire. Your patriotism, your union, your energy will save France. The Emperor has been made a prisoner in the struggle. The Government, in accord with the public powers, will take all measures required by the gravity of events.

COUNT DE PALIKAO,
H. CHEVREAU,
RIGAULT DE GENOUILLY,
JULES BRAME,
DE LA TOUR D'AUVERGNE,
GRANDEPERRET,
CLEMENT DUVERNOIS,
P. MAGNE,
BUSSON BILLAULT,
JEROME DAVID,
of the Council of Ministers.

PARIS, *Midnight.*—What a change! There is no longer despair, but a grim determination seizes every heart.

As the proclamation of the Ministers, announcing the capitulation of MacMahon's army and the capture of the Emperor, becomes known, the excitement among the people is indescribable.

Tumultuous crowds assemble before the Corps Législatif, and shout, "The people will save France. The Emperor has fallen; the people will rise, and chase out the invaders." "A bas L'Empereur," for the first time in eighteen years, sounds out in the Place de la Concorde. Some one demands the *décheance* (the dethronement) of the Emperor. A hundred voices catch the cry, and "*décheance*, DECHEANCE!" is shouted in the street. All night long on the Boulevard Bonn-Nouvelle the surging masses shout "*Vive France!*" "*La décheance!*" and death to the Empire which has betrayed them. The death warrant of the Empire is signed to-night in ten thousand Paris hearts.

IN THE CORPS LEGISLATIF,

when the Count de Palikao announced that the army at Sedan. with the Emperor, had surrendered to the Prussians, Jules Favre declared: "We are unanimous for defence until death.

(Great applause.) It is time that compliances should cease, if we wish to repair our disasters." He concluded by attacking the Imperial power, and proposing to place extraordinary powers in the hands of Gen. Trochu.

There was a breathless silence as that venerable patriot, Jules Favre, a second Patrick Henry, announced the death of the Empire and the birth of a young Republic! With a dreadful solemnity the father of the Republic advanced with these resolutions in his venerable hand: "We move that the Chamber adopt the following resolutions:

"That Louis Napoleon Bonaparte and his dynasty be declared to have forfeited the powers which the nation conferred upon them.

"That there shall be chosen an executive committee, composed of members, the number of whom shall be fixed by the Chamber, which shall be invested with all the powers necessary to repel invasion and drive the enemy from the soil.

"That General Trochu, Governor of Paris, be charged exclusively with the defence of the capital."

The reading of these resolutions was listened to with profound silence. A single voice was raised. It was that of M. Picard. "We have not the power," said he, "to pronounce the *déchéance*."

Like thunder they fell upon the astonished Chamber. There was a moment — a painful moment of hesitation, and then a murmur of approbation. Count Palikao only spoke for the dead Empire.

LONDON WILD WITH DELIGHT.

London is wild with delight over Prussia's triumph. The streets were for two hours filled with excited multitudes. Englishmen congratulate each other as if it were an English victory. Their sympathies with Prussia were never before so strongly manifested. The intelligence of the surrender was first published here by *The Daily News*, in an extra, at about half-past ten o'clock this morning. Other papers soon followed. Placards are everywhere in the streets. Thousands of despatches were sent in every direction.

THE NEWS IN AMERICA.

Telegrams from Washington, Baltimore, Philadelphia, Richmond, and all the principal cities of the Union, state that the news of the surrender of Napoleon and the capture of MacMahon's army caused intense excitement among the Germans, and the event was celebrated by firing salutes, ringing of bells, processions, and other manifestations of joy.

IN NEW YORK,

the startling intelligence of Napoleon's surrender and the capitulation of MacMahon's army fell upon the people like a clap of thunder out of a clear sky. Despite the swift and crushing succession of Prussian victories, from Weisenburg to Beaumont, the public mind had not grasped the possibility that Napoleon's Empire could so suddenly crumble to the dust like a fragile house of cards, leaving him with only the poor refuge of death, a hapless prisoner, sans throne, sans sword, sans friend, sans everything. Even the sturdy Teuton patriots who clustered around the bulletins, or eagerly grasped the extras, scarcely dared put faith at first in the glorious tidings; while Americans, though more than willing to believe in such an overwhelming Prussian triumph, found it hard to fully credit the astounding intelligence.

Printing-House Square was filled with excited crowds. The Germans left their workshops to hear of victory to the Fatherland. Gold fell on Wall street 2½ per cent. The bulls gazed despairingly, while the bears danced with delight. "The Patrol on the Rhine" was sung in the Gold Room, and a hundred wild brokers danced a weird *can-can* around the fountain in the centre of the Stock Exchange.

THE PRESS.

The *Tribune* forms show victory in such headlines as these:

„Der große Sieg!

Ausführlicher Bericht über die Uebergabe Napoleon's und der Armee McMahon's."

The *Herald* rejoices at the speedy termination of the war, and

The *World* alone has a word of sympathy for Napoleon.

LONDON PRESS.

The *Pall Mall Gazette* says:

"The news will be regarded as final. If the Emperor hopes, by a hastily patched-up peace, to find means to transfer the throne to his son, it is the last and greatest delusion of a life of delusions. He may find it easier to begin than to end war. Peace is by no means yet certain. There is no Government to make peace. Imperialism is dead. The substitute is Orleans or a Republic. It can hardly begin by a surrender. France has for the first time to act. Her eyes are for the first time opened."

The London *Evening Standard* says:

"Sedan is the Emperor's Waterloo. The Second Empire is now overthrown." It deprecates exultation, and expresses heartfelt sympathy with the fallen sovereign.

The Echo says:

"The Emperor's last act does what is possible to redeem his fault. The author of the war surrenders himself to the conqueror, admitting his own defeat, that he may help avert that of France."

FRENCH PRESS.

Le Messager Franco-Americain says, with a dreadful irony:

"The Empire! Let us hope that the present is the last time we shall have to speak of the detested thing. The empire has fallen. The empire has capitulated, but France is erect. France never capitulates. Let the defenders of Bonapartism and his government now behold their work and their triumphs. Let the poor dupes of the plebiscitic government and of imperial glory contemplate the abyss of shame in which they have plunged the empire for three times in sixty years. If Bonaparte had the least wish to die, he had the opportunity to do so while wearing his Cæsarean toga. If the first Bonaparte had been killed at Waterloo, his crimes would have been pardoned; and if the second had followed the example of the brave General Douay, and been killed by a Prussian ball, France would have accepted the expiation. But, instead of this, he has surrendered his sword to the King of Prussia, and yielded to the enemy he had provoked, and capitulated the army which accompanied him. Let not King William and Bismarck, with too much audacity, gloat over their mastery of freedom. These men belong to the same band that Bonaparte belongs to. They are enemies of each other, only as pirates and brigands are enemies of each other."

The Courier des Etats Unis sends up a wail of despair:

"The deed is done. France is broken-hearted. One month has sufficed to paralyze her, if not to annihilate the living forces of the most grand and powerful people upon the earth, and at the same time to displace the political axis of the earth. It is useless to dissimulate. The army which has surrendered was the very flower of the military people. MacMahon destroyed! Bazaine powerless! For the rest, France is but a huge mass, fanatical and patriotic — ready enough to strike its head against the mouths of the Prussian cannon. There is no more for us an army. The masses, now so full of faith, can do nothing against military science, against discipline, against new armies. France has been made to bleed, but she is not humiliated. Still she bears a proud front, and she can look fiercely in the faces of her enemies and of the world. All her wounds have been received in the front, and our soldiers are hailed as giants by the very troops before whose superior numbers they have succumbed."

THE GERMAN PRESS.

The New Yorker Journal says:

"Ours is the Rhine. For ever and ever will this German stream flow quietly and uninterruptedly between its splendid shores. The Latin world has gone down, and the Germanic ascends after a brief pause. The spectre of Cæsar sinks in its open grave. The peace-making German Emperor can say, "The German Empire is peace," and this now will be the truth. Henceforth the people of the earth will be required no longer to spend their means in heavy war budgets, but can devote themselves to the mission of cultivating the laws of spiritual and material welfare. But the highest triumph is the German unity. During the first excitement over the wanton attack the German States gave each other the hand, and in a glorious war the new alliance was re-sealed. For ever and ever the dismemberment and disagreement of past centuries is gone, and German Union is no longer an imaginary phantom — a pious wish of honest patriots — but a glorious and powerful reality."

From the *Staats Zeitung*:

"At divers times the *vox populi* of Germany has uttered its warning to France, that should Germany ever be forced to war against the French, she would never sheath her sword until she had reconquered her old provinces of Lorraine and Alsace. The French ridiculed this menace, and said that they would yet not only take the whole of the Rhenish provinces, but also divide Germany. But while the French were dreaming of the line of the Main, German Union has become a fact; and thanks to France, this German Union is now enabled to revenge the wrongs of past centuries on France, but to obtain that position to which, by its brilliant spirit and power, it is entitled."

From the *Demokrat:*

"The question, whether, after the events of the 2d of September, peace will soon ensue, can as yet not be answered. France's best army is used up and disarmed, and the others will soon, if they have not yet surrendered. But we are as yet without an answer to the question. What will Paris say? Will she attempt resistance, or submit quietly? Will she appeal to the once powerful word, Republic?"

THE CAPTIVE EMPEROR.

DONCHERY, *September* 3. — The Emperor, a prisoner of war, passed through the streets to-day. It was raining in torrents. The cortége was preceded by a troop of black hussars in full uniform, and uncloaked. Then came the brougham with the Emperor. He was in the *kepi* undress uniform of a lieutenant-general, with the star of the Legion of Honor on his breast. His face looked exceedingly worn, with dark lines under his eyes, which were observant of what was passing around, for he saluted the Englishmen who ran out to see him, and raised his hat. By his side sat a French officer, Achille Murat. The imperial postilions wore the imperial cockade, and looked as smart as if they were in the Bois, or *en route* for St. Cloud. As the brougham stopped a moment, the people caught sight of the captive Emperor's face. He had his hand to his moustache, which had the well-known points and waxed ends. But there was no nervous twitching, and the emotion which shook him for a moment when he was speaking to the Crown Prince yesterday of the King's manner, had passed away. Then he brushed the tears from his eyes with the gloves he had in one hand, and was overcome for several seconds.

No one cried "God bless him!" no "Vive L'Empereur!" as was wont to greet his ears as he rode in state to the Bois de Boulogne. It was like the journey of the first Napoleon to Toulon, without the enthusiasm. The only sound was the tramp of horses and the inopportune jingling of bells, of chara-bancs and horses; but now and then a chorus was sung by the Würtembergers trudging through the mud, celebrating the victory. Now the mimic "*Chant du départ*" comes from a neighboring hill, as full of dreadful irony as fell the strains of "John Brown's body" on the ears of General Lee at Appomattox:

"Tremblez ennemis de la France,
Rois ivres de sang et d'orgueil;
Le peuple souverain s'avance;
Tyrans, descendez au cercueil."

BOUILLON, *September 3, P.M.* — The Imperial train is passing. The cortége is of great length. First comes the Emperor's own carriage, a travelling berlin; then an open carriage; after these two or three carriages something like prison vans, all marked "Maison Militaire de l'Empereur," and containing members of the staff. Numbers of horses follow, some mounted by Imperial servants in liveries. The horses are magnificent animals, over sixteen hands high. The postilions wear glazed hats, gay coats, and scarlet waistcoats. There are relays of horses for carriages, and hacks, saddle-horses, and chargers beyond price.

At noon the Emperor alighted in Bouillon, and walked to the hotel. The crowd of people was enormous, but was kept off by the Belgian troops. French officers of high grade, among them Prince Murat, strolled about. The Emperor appeared at a window, and the crowd hurrahed. The French prisoners were silent — they made no response. It was impossible to find quarters and food at the hotel. The Emperor dined first, then his suite, and the rest ate what they could get. About two o'clock, the Emperor, accompanied by General Castelnau, came to the door of the railway station. He seemed well, his face showing no emotion. Though he leaned heavily on the arm of the servant who led him out, he walked well. Despatches were handed him, and he sat down out-doors on the platform, and wrote replies. He afterward paced up and down the platform, smoking cigarettes. He returned to the waiting-room, and read the *Independance Belge* until the special train arrived, when he departed.

A friend condoling with the Emperor expressed the hope that his popularity in Paris was not gone. The Emperor replied:

"*It matter not.* I SHALL RETURN THERE TO EXACT A RFCKONING, NOT TO GIVE ONE."

EUGENIE'S FAREWELL WORDS.

The unhappy Empress, pale and quivering, receives the sad news of Sedan. Beautiful becomes her bereavement when in spirit she goes back again to that widowed mother in Madrid, whom she had left seventeen years before, to become the Empress of France. Before the last sad drop of the Imperial curtain comes a beautiful benediction — the daughter to the mother!

MA CHERE MERE: PARIS, *Sept.* 4, 1870.

General Wimpffen, who had taken command after MacMahon had been wounded, has capitulated, and the Emperor has been made prisoner. Alone and without command, he has submitted to that which he could not avert. All day he was under fire. Courage, dear mother; if France will, she can defend herself. I will do my duty.

Your unhappy daughter,

Madame la Comtesse DE MONTIJO, Madrid. EUGENIE.

VIVE LA REPUBLIQUE!

THE SYMPATHY OF THE WORLD CHANGES IN FAVOR OF THE REPUBLIC.

SUNDAY, *September* 4. — The French Republic declared in the Hôtel de Ville. The *déchéance* of Napoleon III. proclaimed. Gambetta declares the new Provisional Government. Rochefort released from prison. Ovation to Victor Hugo. The Tuileries invaded by the mob. Intense excitement in Paris. American sympathy for the Republic. The Prussians continue their march on Paris. The Empress Eugenie in Brussels. The Emperor passes through Belgium a prisoner.

THE REVOLUTION (REMARK).

To-day the world is revolutionized. The Empire — the lie which drenches France in blood, and sends a cry of death and despair over the hills and valleys of central Europe — *is dead!* The ugly form of Cæsarism goes out in darkness. The young Republic is born, and proclaimed where, a month ago, stood the proudest throne in Europe. The Republic *is* strength — *it is peace!* The voice of the young Republic, crying from the tumultuous streets of Paris, rouses universal sympathy. The world is changed. Yesterday it was the struggle of despotism with despotism: to-day it is despotism, Herod-like, at the throat of an infant Republic.

How America, who loved Hungary and Greece, and who weeps, Government tied, for Cuba, stretches forth her hands to-day toward this young Republic! Yesterday she sympathized with Prussia — an insulted despotism: to-day she embraces the mother of Lafayette. Ties of gratitude bind America to France. France was her ally; hatred for Napoleon made America forget France.

Our country nursed her young Republic in 1848. We saw it strangled in the coils of Cæsarism in 1852. The surrender of Napoleon III. frees the Republic, and the cry of the old liberty of '48 comes over the Atlantic again.

The American people would be false to their noblest instincts, they would belie all their generous utterances in the past, and prove recreant to the honored principles of their fathers, if their hearts did not go out in fervent, forward sympathy with a great, heroic nation, their ancient ally, who, in this season of sudden humiliation and sore calamity, courageously holds aloft the banner of free institutions, and places itself in the van of a great republican movement in Europe. Providence has vouchsafed to France a great opportunity, such as seldom occurs in the history of nations; and she has had the wisdom to recognize and improve it. Out of the nettle, danger, she magnanimously attempts to pluck the flower, freedom. Every true American heart, every heart whose pulsations were ever quickened by the spectacle of heroic efforts of patriotism blended with aspirations for liberty, will wish well to France in this hour of trial, of hope, of transition, and possibly of renewed conflict with the invader, who, after having bestowed upon her this great opportunity, may interpose to crush the expanding blossom in the bud.

The whole aspect of this wonderful, this terribly destructive war has suddenly changed, as if by the stroke of an enchanter's wand. Hitherto, it has been a war against the French empire; if it is continued, it will be a war against the French people.

HOW THE REPUBLIC WAS DECLARED.

EXCITING SCENES IN PARIS.

PARIS, *Sunday morning, Sept.* 4.

The Empire is dead, and the Republic has risen from the ruins. The commotion commenced on Saturday. The news of the Emperor's surrender and the capitulation of MacMahon's army were made known to the Empress at seven o'clock in the evening. She immediately retired into her apartment, and refused to received even intimate friends. Toward nine the broad facts were known to a few persons only, but a general uneasiness prevailed, and angry groups assembled. At eleven o'clock on Sunday, while the Mobiles, on their way to camp at Saint Maur, accompanied by a small crowd, were proceeding up the Boulevards toward the Bastille, they sung the Marseillaise, and some shouted "La Déchéance." This cry had been already heard in other localities.

THE NEWS OUT.

The news was not generally known till after nine on Sunday morning, when the Ministerial statement appeared on the walls and in the morning papers. Soon immense excitement was apparent everywhere. By noon, the Place de la Concorde was crowded, and the passage of the bridge interrupted to the public by the police sergeants, gendarmerie on horseback, and the troops on the bridge, and around the Chamber. Popular Deputies were recognized, and met with acclamations and cries of "La Déchéance!" and "Vive la République!" As the day wore on, the crowds augmented. On the passage of companies of National Guards, the people shouted "Vive National Guard!" "Vive la République!" and the Guards reciprocated.

THE CROWD OVERPOWERS ALL RESISTANCE.

At two P.M. the gates of the Tuileries garden were closed, and had remained so since morning, watched by the Zouaves and other detachments of the Imperial Guard. The people on the outside were trying to shake the gates on the side of the Place de la Concorde. At half-past two, a rush was made by a part of the crowd, headed by some of the National Guard. The police sergeants and gendarmes made an armed demonstration of resistance, but suddenly yielded, and the crowd rushed by, shouting, "La Decheance" and "Vive la République." People fraternized with the gendarmes and troops, and these with the National Guard.

THE MOB INVADES THE CORPS LEGISLATIF.

At an earlier hour in the Corps Législatif, the Deputies were returning to appoint a committee to consider the three proposals submitted by Palikao, Thiers, and Favre. A company of National Guards having charge of the gates shouted "La Déchéance," and as the Deputies passed, some few Nationals mounted the steps of the Palace of the Corps Législatif, and signalled their comrades from the Pont de la Concorde. Presently the latter rushed forward, followed by the crowd, all classes intermixed, and shouting "Vive la République!" Once inside the palace gates, the people spread themselves all over the building, except the hall where the sessions of the Deputies are held. The next hall was occupied by troops, who fraternized with the people.

THE PEOPLE CRY "DOWN WITH THE IMPERIALISTS!"

The Right, the friends of the Empire, are not allowed to speak. The crowd hisses them down. Crémieux, of the Left, an influential young Republican, addresses the people. They listen, but demand the withdrawal of the troops. Palikao, Imperial Secretary of War, appears, and promises that the troops shall be removed.

Schneider, led by two officers, crosses the court-yard, pale, haggard, and with tears in his eyes. He disappears into the hall where the sessions are held. Attempts are made to force its doors. Gen. Motterouge orders the National Guards to defend the entry. There are loud cries of "Déchéance" and "Vive la République."

THE CONSTERNATION OF SCHNEIDER.

In one of the galleries somebody begins a speech. A few Deputies of the Right enter, but suddenly, as if panic-stricken, they retreat precipitately.

Schneider, the strong friend of the Right and the Empire, now appears. He attempts to speak against the *déchéance.* The crowd cry, "Down, *down!*" Schneider loses his nerve, and seizing his hat, flies in fear from the Chamber and his Presidential chair. Gambetta, the strong Republican, speaks. The people listen, for it is a voice from the Left. He says, "Await the arrival of the Representatives, and they *will bring in the question of déchéance.*" (Enthusiastic applause.) "The majority must proclaim the *déchéance.*"

THE LEFT TO THE HÔTEL DE VILLE.

It is now three o'clock. Suddenly a crowd of people rush into the hall. The Deputies try to keep them back, but the hall is entirely invaded. The President puts on his hat and leaves the hall, declaring the session closed. As he quits his seat, National Guards and people come crowding in. There are general cries of "Vive la République." The Deputies of the Left mix with the people, and all cry, "To the Hôtel de Ville!" Gambetta and other Republican leaders leave the Chambers, and go in procession down the Pont de la Concorde, followed by the crowd.

Meanwhile, outside the Chambers, men climb up to the statue of Law over the portal, and destroy the eagle which adorns the baton in the hands of the image. Then it is itself destroyed—the head first, then the arms. Gambetta and the procession pass down the Quai des Tuileries. Soldiers applaud, and shout with the crowd. A lieutenant-colonel cries "Vive la République!" the procession stops, and fraternizes. The Turcos and the Spahis at the barracks of the Quai d'Orsay wave their turbans. The flag over the pavilion of the Tuileries is hauled down. In front of the Prefecture there are cries of "Down with Pietri." The Prefecture is closely shut.

THE REPUBLIC IS DECLARED.

Arrived in front of the Hôtel de Ville, the crowd forces its way in. Jules Favre and Jules Ferry go to the further end of the great hall. Two Gardes Mobile, with drawn swords, clamber up the ornamental chimney, and seat themselves in the lap of a marble nymph. Gambetta, Crémieux, and Kératry press in, and take a place beside Favre, followed by Picard, Étienne Arago, Glais-Bazoin, Schoelcher, and others. Gambetta, Crémieux, and Kératry are by themselves at the Mayor's table.

Amid the tumult, Gambetta declares the Republic a fact, and that E. Arago is appointed Mayor of Paris. The people shout approval. The Bureau is constituted. Kératry is appointed Prefect of Police. The Bureau retires to constitute a Provisional Government and Ministry. At four o'clock the Bureau returns, and Gambetta declares the Provisional Government constituted under the title of Government for the National Defence, consisting of Arago, Crémieux, Favre, Simon, Gambetta, Ferry, Glais-Bizoin, Garnier-Pagés, Pelletan, and Picard.

ROCHEFORT.

The people shout Rochefort's name, It is added amid acclamation. The members of Government again retire. There is a discussion whether the tricolor or the red flag is to be adopted. Schoelcher says "tricolor," and it is adopted.

Suddenly a carriage arrives. A number of men are drawing it. Crowds follow and accompany it. There are four persons in the carriage. One is very pale. It is Rochefort. He has just been liberated from Sainte-Pélagie prison. There are enthusiastic shouts on his being recognized. He is borne into the Hôtel de Ville upon the shoulders of the people, who now — men, women, and children — make their way into it. The leaders of the new republic have already retired, but the people visit all the apartments. The revolution is over. An empire has fallen, and a republic has been reared in its stead, without riot, without bloodshed. It has been done in an hour.

THE DEMONSTRATIONS AT THE TUILERIES.

It becomes known that the Emperor is deposed by the Chamber, and that the Republic is declared. The people rush upon the police sergeants, and disarm them. One National Guard has his head gashed with a sword, and is led away. The police sergeants get off the best way they can. The people assail the gates of the Tuileries. The guards, after a menace, consent to a parley. The men clamber up and wrench off the eagles from the gates. The gates are presently opened, and the people flock in, going toward the palace. The flag is still flying from the top of the Central Pavilion. The crowd approaches the private garden. There is a detachment of troops there. The officer is summoned to open the gates. He refuses, but says he can let his men be replaced by the National Guard. This is done, and the officer saves his honor. The people walk in, and immediately invade the interior of the palace. The flag is torn, and handed down. The Empress has left. The Mobiles and people amuse themselves looking at the albums and the Prince Imperial's playthings. They notice that the draperies of the windows are partly removed. The people write with chalk, "Death to thieves." They respect property. Then the Guards, National and Mobile, line the road which leads from the Tuileries to the Carrousel. The people defile through, shouting, "This is our property," and "*a bas volaille*" (down with the poultry). The mob write upon the walls, but disturb nothing. One chalks down this "stanza" :

"Les deux Napoleons les gloires sont égales,
Quoiqu' ayant pris les chemins inegaux ;
L'un de l'Europe a pris les capitales,
L'autre au pays a prix les capitaux."

DESERTED.

On the ground floor there is great disorder. The Empress has just left. Somebody says "*The poor Empress! how her friends have deserted her!*" The Imperial apartments are filled with empty trunks, work-boxes, and the Empress's bed is unmade. The Emperor's room is full of the Prince's things. On the sofa is a child's sword, half unsheathed. On the floor, buried in old newspapers, is a revolver case. Here are cigar boxes, and vials of phosphate of iron.

IN THE PRINCE'S STUDY.

Lead soldiers are strewn over the carpet. An historical exercise book lies open on the table. The last exercise written by the Prince begins thus :

"Louis XV. Bourbon, Fleury (1723-1741). Regency resumed. Bourbon. 1723-1726. Bourbon. — Madame de Prie, Paris-*Duvernois* [*Duvernay* was intended]. At home, corruption, stock-jobbing, frivolity, intolerance. Abroad, marriage of the King with Marie Laczynska. Rupture with Spain, which country displays Austrian tendencies," etc., etc.

A BREAKFAST INTERRUPTED.

In one room a breakfast is prepared. It is simple — only a boiled egg, a little cheese, and some bread. In the Emperor's apartment, several maps of Prussia; busts and statuettes of the Imperial Prince; a great number of little painted figures, representing Prussian soldiers and officers in uniform; also, volumes with annotations. A repast is ordered in the kitchen for the regulars. For the first time in eighteen years, the people go through every room in the Imperial Palace. They own it under the Republic — *and guard it as their own.*

THE END OF THE DAY.

Even now (midnight) crowds of people are still on the Boulevards, and there is still great commotion and excitement, but no rioting. People look as though relieved of an immense load. A large "tree of liberty" is planted near the Bastile, and covered with flags and flowers.

THE ROCHEFORT EPISODE

was as follows: A hundred of Rochefort's constituents met, by appointment, at three P. M., at the Great Market Hall. At a given signal, the leader raised a cane with a flag attached to it, and a shout, "To Sainte-Pélagie!" ascended. The group was joined by other men, who up to that time had been lurking in the immediate vicinity, making in all about 300 when they reached the prison. There were three marines acting as sentries outside. One of them made believe to lower his bayonet. It was raised by his comrade. The third followed his example. The crowd took the guns and broke them, but fraternized with the marines. There was no opposition from the wardens. Rochefort's cell doors were burst in, and he was taken out.

There was no coach at the door. A lady passing in one got out of it, and made Rochefort get in. He was driven to the Hôtel de Ville, arriving there at five, and was carried in triumph to the throne room, where, amid the shouts and congratulations of friends, he learns that he is a member of the new Republican Government.

OVATION TO VICTOR HUGO.

There was a great ovation to Victor Hugo, and a torchlight ovation to Thiers, whom some portion of the people desire to see appointed Minister of Finance.

A number of the Democratic leaders of Paris, including Victor Hugo's sons, M. Rochefort M. Glais-Bizoin, the venerable Michelet, M. Laboulaye, and others, had assembled to meet the exiled poet and patriot.

A hasty arch had been thrown up over the doorway of the station, and wreathed with the flags of France, Italy, the United States, Switzerland, and Spain. Much attention was excited by the appearance among these standards of the flag of the German Republic of 1848.

M. HUGO'S SPEECH.

CITIZENS — I have come back from an exile of twenty years simultaneously with the Republic. The Republic comes to defend in Paris the capital of civilization. Paris must not be sullied by invasion; for to invade Paris is to invade liberty — it is to invade civilization. No such invasion shall triumph. Paris will be saved by the union of all souls, all hearts, all arms in her defence. The defeat of Paris means new hatreds, new resentments, new barriers between people and people. Paris must be victorious in the name of fraternity, for only by making the fraternity of all possible can the liberty of all be gained.

THE AMERICAN FLAG.

Pointing to the American flag, Victor Hugo said, "That banner of stars speaks to-day to Paris and to France, proclaiming the miracles of power which are easy to a great people contending for a great principle — the liberty of every race, the fraternity of all."

The speech was immensely cheered, and the speaker fairly carried by the people to his carriage. He looks well, though aged — his long locks gone, his dark beard white, his eyes full of fire, his voice as firm as ever.

The Minister of the Interior proclaims the following at eight P.M.:

PROCLAMATION OF DECHEANCE.

REPUBLIQUE FRANCAISE, MINISTERE DE L'INTERIEUR.

The *déchéance* has been pronounced in the Corps Législatif. The Republic has been proclaimed at the Hôtel de Ville. A government of national defence, composed of eleven members, and all the Deputies of Paris, has been constituted and ratified by popular acclamation. Their names are:

Emmanuel Arago, Crémieux, Jules Favre, Jules Ferry, Gambetta, Garnier-Pagés, Glais-Bizoin, Pellatan, Ernest Picard, Rochefort, Jules Simon.

Gen. Trochu will at the same time continue in the exercise of the powers of Governor of Paris, and is appointed Minister of War in place of Gen. Palikao.

Please placard immediately, and, if necessary, have proclaimed by the public crier this declaration.

For the Government of National Defence. LEON GAMBETTA,
The Minister of the Interior.

Paris, the 4th day of September, 1870, at six o'clock P. M.

TO PREFECTS OF DEPARTMENTS.

PARIS, *Sept.* 4, 1870.

Gen. Trochu, Governor of Paris, has been appointed member of the Government of National Defence, installed at the Hôtel de Ville. He takes the portfolio of War, and his colleagues have conferred upon him the Presidency.

LEON GAMBETTA.

The offices of the Provisional Government are distributed as follows:

Minister of Foreign Affairs — JULES FAVRE.
Minister of Justice — ISAAC CREMIEUX.
Minister of the Interior — LEON GAMBETTA.
Minister of Finance — ERNEST PICARD.
Superindendent of Public Works — PIERRE DORIAN.
Minister of Commerce — JOSEPH MAGNIN.
Superintendent of Public Instruction — JULES SIMON.
Minister of Marine — MARTIN FOURICHON.
Minister of War — LOUIS JULES TROCHU; also, President of the Committee.

Seals have been placed on the doors of the Corps Législatif.

NEW YORK SALUTES THE REPUBLIC.

American flags were displayed on the City Hall in honor of the proclamation of the French republic. In 1830 there was the grandest procession ever witnessed in the city of New York, in honor of the downfall of Charles the Tenth, and the establishing of a republic in France. In 1848 there was a remarkable display of bunting in honor of the formation of another republic in France. These demonstrations were witnessed by the present generation; but like the illusion of a dream, or the mirage upon the desert or the ocean, republicanism, as a power, was swept away from the soil of France before the French people really had the opportunity to comprehend the situation. Republicanism is the root of the political policy of the French people, but, unfortunately, imperialism has been the blossom and the fruit.

FLIGHT OF THE EMPRESS.

The deposition of the Napoleon dynasty was voted in the Corps Législatif about one o'clock on Sunday afternoon. At two o'clock, M. Pietri — then Prefect of Police — rushed breathlessly into the Empress's apartments at the Tuileries with the startling announcement and warning: "The *déchéance* has been declared. I have not a moment to lose. Save your life, Madame, as I am now hastening to save my own!" Then he disappeared — and with good reason too, for the Revolutionary Government would give something to be able to lay hands upon him now. The Empress found herself alone with her old and trusty secretary and friend, Madame le Breton, and with M. Ferdinand de Lesseps, who both earnestly urged her to fly at once. But her high spirit made this a most unpalatable counsel. It was a cowardice — *une lacheté* — to desert the palace. She would rather be treated as was Marie Antoinette by the mob, than seek safety in an unworthy flight. For a time, all persuasion was useless; but at length Her Majesty's mood calmed, and she saw the utter uselessness of remaining.

Attended only by the two companions we have named, the Empress fled through the long gallery of the Louvre; but suddenly her course was stopped short by a locked door. The little party could distinctly hear the shouts of the crowds who were invading the private gardens of the Tuileries. M. de Lesseps, to gain time, proposed that he should go out on the terrace and get the soldiers on guard to hold back the people for a few minutes, while in addition he would delay the crowds by addressing them. The resort to this expedient was not necessary. Madame le Breton found the key, opened the door that had obstructed their progress, and gave egress to Her Majesty, who, accompanied only by her tried friend, issued into the street at the bottom of the Louvre. There they hurriedly entered a common *fiacre*, not without a risk of detection on the spot, for a diminutive *gamin de Paris*, not more than twelve years old, shouted, "*Voilà l'Impératrice!*" Luckily, no one about heard or heeded him; and the cab got safely away with the two ladies.

They drove to M. de Lessep's house in the Boulevard de Malesherbes, where the Empress sat until she was joined by M. de Metternich, who did what he could to facilitate her departure to a place of safety. Later in the evening, the Empress, still accompanied by Madame le Breton, drove to the Gare du Nord, escaped all detection — thanks to the thick veil which she wore — and at seven o'clock rolled safe and unsuspected away toward the Belgian frontier.

THE FLIGHT TO ENGLAND.

Morning found the flying Empress at Trouville, on the channel, opposite England.

Sir John Burgoyne's yacht was lying off Trouville, when a Frenchman came on board, asking to be allowed to look over an English yacht. Sir John, half suspecting him to be a French spy, allowed him to look about. Soon after this visitor was gone, two French gentlemen came on board with the same request, and after asking many questions as to the sailing powers of the *Gazelle*, begged to be allowed to speak to Sir John alone.

"What! M. de Lesseps?" exclaimed Sir John, the young Crimean hero, when he recognized his old friend.

"Yes, yes, my dear Sir John, but don't waste any time — will you do me the greatest service I ever demanded of any human being?"

"Name it," said the gallant soldier.

"Will you find me three places on your yacht for the passage to England on Wednesday?"

"Is that all?" said Sir John, laughing; "the places will be ready for you."

There was again a momentary pause, during which M. de Lesseps fixedly regarded the young man.

"Do you know?" he asked rapidly, as if ashamed of the doubt which had prompted his scrutiny — "do you know whom you will carry with you as my *compagnon de voyage?*"

Sir John smiled, and shook his head.

"Her Imperial Majesty, the Empress of the French," said M. de Lesseps quietly.

The two men rose, and clasped hands. No word was spoken, but they understood one another. M. de Lesseps was affected to tears, and Sir John was scarcely less moved.

On Tuesday evening, Sept. 6, the Empress came on board privately, and the yacht weighed anchor at once, and set sail for Ryde. The Empress was wholly unprovided with luggage, not having even a comb and brush, or a change of linen with her. The crossing was very rough, the sea washing over the deck, and the Empress was wayworn and exhausted when she arrived at Ryde.

EUGENIE MEETS LOUIS.

Early on Thurday morning, the little vessel cut into Ryde, and the Empress, taking a most affectionate leave of her generous host, made her way to the York Hotel, where she partook of breakfast. She then crossed by the ordinary steamer to Portsmouth, where she immediately took train for Hastings, arriving there at about nine on Thursday night, September 8th.

Leaving the Empress at the *dépôt*, M. de Lesseps went to the Hotel where the Prince Imperial had been directed to put up. The Prince was there, and M. de Lesseps was just leeving the house to tell the Empress, when a veiled figure rnshed past him on the stairs.

It was the Empress, and before her astonished guide could

restrain her either by voice or gesture, mother and son were locked in a close and almost convulsive embrace.

"Mon pauvre Louis! Mon pauvre Louis, maintenant je n'ai que toi."

"And papa," said the child; and before he could continue, the doors of the drawing-room were closed upon mother and son.

Words cannot convey the solemn tenderness of that meeting between the ex-Empress and the child so lately the hope of France!

Both mother and child looked fearfully worn and ill, the child especially bearing evident traces of the effects of nervous excitement. His eyes, naturally large, appeared unusually so, and they attracted the particular attention of the Empress, who was observed to push back the hair from the boy's forehead, and after looking at him long and earnestly, to close each eyelid with a kiss.

The scene proved too trying for the Empress. On Friday she kept her room, and sent for the same physician who had ministered to Louis Philippe on a similar occasion. On Sunday the Empress appeared for the first time in public, at church. As soon as her presence in England was known, the Queen wrote an autograph letter to her, and the Prince of Wales proposed to pay her a visit. The Empress begged to be left *incognito.*

SKETCHES OF MEMBERS OF THE PROVISIONAL GOVERNMENT.

The following are brief biographical sketches of the principal members of the provisional government of France:

LEON GAMBETTA, MINISTER OF THE INTERIOR.

M. Gambetta was born at Cahors in 1838. He made little noise at college, but was a hard worker, although he toiled after his own fashion and when he pleased, agreeing but indifferently with his tutors, and regarded by them as rather eccentric than intelligent. He was self-possessed and vehement in tone, fond of solitude, fairly worshipping his own personal independence, but too precocious and too eminently gifted, perhaps, to be understood by his classmates. He came to Paris, went through his law studies there, and entered the bar as the secretary of M. Crémieux, who gave him his confidence, his friendship, called him his "son" upon all occasions, and predicted for him a brilliant future.

Gambetta soon became known among knots of friends at lectures and at the bar. His rapid advancement has surprised none who were acquainted with him, for his triumphs were expected, and were looked upon by all as inevitable. Occasions for them were sure to arise, and the greatest of these was the Baudin affair, when the Republicans of Paris gathered at the tomb of that orator and martyr of their cause. It was this striking incident which prepared the way for Gambetta's entrance to the Chamber, where his high tone, yet determined Liberalism, and his tact and eloquence combined as a debater, soon placed him among its leading minds.

Let us glance at the physique of the man. His complexion is pallid, contrasting strongly with very thick black hair and beard. He has a masculine and intellectual head, solidly embedded in a stalwart pair of shoulders. His bust is superb, and his frame thick-set and muscular. His walk is brisk, yet firm, and his speech rapid and energetic. His voice, which never seems to tire, is sometimes full of cadence, sometimes stunning in its intonations, and somewhat low, but always powerful. His countenance is a very attractive and sympathetic combination of Italian delicacy — for he is of Genoese origin — and of Gascon vigor, full of commingled thoughtfulness and audacity, frankness and haughtiness. His nose is straight and regular, with strongly marked nostrils, broadly dilated. His mouth is neatly cleft, with fair expansion, and is none the worse for a strongly disdainful lip, that is sometimes brightened by a hearty laugh of Rabelaisian mirth. His arms are muscular, and yet lengthened as though to clasp an adversary; and his hand is broad, firm, solid, and seems made for energetic grasping and setting free by turns.

When Gambetta is in repose, the observer would say that he is just about to leap upward or to take his flight in the air; in other words, that he is going to speak. His large black eye looks upward and far away into the distance. He then seems to be counting the "black spots" on the horizon. Yet this does not prevent his scanning with sufficient accuracy the minor questions that swarm below and on either side. His mind is versatile enough to sweep in at one and the same moment the grandest topics and the most minute details. He can soar aloft or creep below, and is just as much at home amid the intricacies of affairs as on the loftier heights of politics.

Gambetta is, above all things, a popular orator and advocate, and it would be impossible to find one more electrical or more vibratory in the shock and tremor of his words.

He lives in modest appartments on the fifth floor at No. 45 Rue Bonaparte. A few engravings, a good many books, a bust of Mirabeau, form about all the luxuries of these quiet quarters, which have been occupied by the student, the lawyer, and the deputy in the successive stages of his career. Such is, in brief, a hasty picture of the man whom the grand events of the current year have made a conspicuous figure in French contemporaneous history, and who is now called to the front in a decisive hour.

GABRIEL CLAUDE JULES FAVRE, MINISTER OF FOREIGN AFFAIRS.

The name of M. Favre heads the list of members composing the Provisional Government. This distinguished politician was born at Lyons on the 31st of March, 1809, his father being engaged in commercial pursuits. Sent to Paris to receive his education, he was there studying law when the revolution of 1830 broke out. In a letter published in the *National* on the 29th of July, he declared in favor of the abolition of monarchy and the creation of a constitutional republic.

His views, however, were not adopted. Louis Philippe ascended the throne, and the young Republican student immediately after engaged in the practice of law. Returning to Lyons, almost his first public appearance at the bar was as counsel for the workingmen charged with belonging to illegal associations. This affair was the signal for a bloody struggle between the workingmen and the garrison, during which M. Favre narrowly escaped death from a fire of musketry directed at him. In 1835 he defended the revolutionists of April, and began his great speech with the defiant avowal, "I am a Republican." As an orator as well as a revolutionist, he had by this time made a considerable reputation, and was recognized as one of the heads of the Republican party of France.

Until 1848, M. Favre remained out of office, but still a never-ending thorn in the side of the Government. The revolution of 1848 succeeded as much under his leadership as under that of any other man in France. He was at once appointed Secretary General of the Ministry of the Interior, and as such wrote the famous circulars to the commissioners of the Provisional Government instructing them how to exercise their almost unlimited powers. Soon after he was elected a representative from the Department of the Loire, when he at once resigned his office in the Ministry. During the same year he acted for a brief while as Under Secretary of Foreign Affairs, and in this capacity supported the prosecution of Louis Blanc and Caussidière for the insurrection of June. Voting with the extreme Left, he refused to vote the national thanks to General Cavaignac. Soon after he became an opponent of Louis Napoleon, and bitterly denounced the expedition to Rome. He was reelected to the Legislature from the Department of the Rhone, and, after the flight of Ledru-Rollin, became the leader of the "Mountain." The *coup d'état* of 1851 put an end to the political career of M. Favre for six years. In 1857, however, he was elected to the Corps Législatif as an opposition member. As the defender of the conspirator Orsini, he created a great sensation by his denunciations of tyrants. Since then he has remained a member of the Corps, and been distinguished by his bitter hostility to the empire. He is a radical Republican, a brilliant orator, and an author of note. What his capacity as a statesman is, remains to be seen.

LOUIS JOSEPH ERNEST PICARD, MINISTER OF FINANCE.

M. Picard, who has just been appointed one of the Committee of Public Defence and Minister of Finance, was born in Paris on the 24th of December, 1821.

He is a strong Republican politician, and, like many others of the Parisian politicians of the French capital, is a lawyer by profession, being called to the bar in 1844. He was elected a member of the Corps Législatif for the Fifth Circonscription of the Department of Seine in 1858, since which time he has been more or less actively engaged in politics.

JULES SIMON, MINISTER OF PUBLIC INSTRUCTION.

M. Simon is a native of Lorient, where he was born on the 31st of December, 1814. He received a brilliant education, which was concluded at the Normal School.

Selecting philosophy as his profession, he was employed in 1835 in teaching that science at the Lycée de Caen, and subsequently at other places, gaining great reputation by his numerous lectures and writings. In 1845 he was decorated with the Legion of Honor. During the following year he was an opposition candidate for the Chamber of Deputies, and was beaten; but in 1848, when he espoused the cause of the revolution, he was elected by the same Department by 63,000 votes. In the Assembly he voted with the moderate Republicans. He was made a memher of the Council of State in 1849. Refusing to give his consent to the *coup d'état*, he was forced into temporary retirement, from which he emerged when elected an opposition member to the Corps Législatif. He was known as one of the most determined opponents of Louis Napoleon, but was not regarded as an extreme Republican. As a philosopher, M. Simon has achieved a brilliant reputation. His published works are quite voluminous, and rank with those of Cuvier and other eminent writers on philosophy.

MAJOR-GENERAL TROCHU, MINISTER OF WAR.

This distinguished officer, who is now in command at Paris, bears the reputation of being one of the ablest military men in Europe. He is fifty-four years of age, having been born in 1816. He was educated at the military school of St. Cyr, where he displayed marked aptness and ability. On graduating, he was commissioned a sub-lieutenant in the army, and was soon after sent to Algeria. Here Lieutenant Trochu, as is the case with nearly all of the prominent generals of France, first saw military service.

In the numerous campaigns against the Arabs he greatly distinguished himself by his skill and gallantry, and at the outbreak of the revolution of 1848 had risen to the rank of major. Immediately after the re-establishment of the empire he was commissioned a colonel, and for a time served on the staff of the Emperor Napoleon. During the war between France and England on the one side, and Russia on the other, Colonel Trochu was sent to the Crimea as the confidential agent of Napoleon He took part in all the military councils of the allied commanders, and is said to have had more to do with determining the action of the French army than either Marshal St. Arnaud or General Canrobert. For his services he was promoted to the rank of general of brigade. The Italian campaign of 1859, report has it, was planned by him and the late Marshal Niel. Its complete success is well known to all students of history. Subsequently Trochu was made major-general. It is certain that until 1860 he was looked upon as a supporter and friend of Napoleon. Since then it is claimed that there has been a coldness existing between the two, Trochu laboring under the impression that he has been overslaughed by the Emperor, who has promoted inferior officers over him. But it is not true that he was always an adherent of the Orleans dynasty. He may be now, and if he is, his partisanship dates since the Italian war. As regards the present war, the General is not only reported to be a bitter enemy to Prussia and in favor of it, but also to have prepared a plan of campaign, offensive and defensive, and if these statements be true, we may depend that he will continue the struggle to the bitter end. Trochu is a Liberal, and his sentiments in favor of parliamentary government have long been known. He is not a Republican, however. Soon after the defeat of Marshal MacMahon at Woerth, General Trochu was appointed Governor of Paris, a position he still holds in connection with the office of Minister of War. Whether he will remain faithful to the Republic, now that one has been proclaimed, or intrigue for a restoration of the monarchy, time alone can decide.

JULES GREVY, PRESIDENT OF THE COUNCIL.

M. Grévy was born at Mont-sous-Vandrez, in the Jura, in 1810. He moved to Paris when a young man, studied law, and after his admission to the bar became conspicuous on account of the radical sentiments he gave expression to at every opportunity.

After the revolution of 1848, he was appointed a Commissioner of the Provisional Government in his Department, and exercised his powers with much discretion and moderation. He was subsequently elected a member of the Constituent Assembly by a large majority, and became Vice-President of the Assembly and a member of the Committee of Justice. As a representative, he was noted for his conservative sentiments — although he generally voted with the extreme Left — and for his eloquence as an orator. After the election of Louis Napoleon, he went into opposition, and denounced the expedition to Rome. Re-elected to the Assembly, he remained faithful to the democracy, and opposed the coalition between the Royalists and Bonapartists. The *coup d'état* drove him from political life, to which he returned last year, when he was elected to the Corps Législatif.

GARNIER-PAGES.

Louis Antoine Garnier-Pagés was born in Marseilles on the 17th of July, 1803. The double name he bears is owing to the fact that his mother had been twice married. When the revolution of 1830 broke out, Garnier-Pagés played his part, though an unimportant one, in and around the barricades in the streets of Paris.

When quiet was restored, and the machinery of government was again in running order in the French capital, Garnier-Pagés was returned as a deputy of the arrondissement of Verneuil, and took his seat in the Chamber on the Liberal side. From the tenor of his speeches and the course which he pursued, it was evident that he had given the subjects of finance and commerce no small degree of attention. This was acknowledged on both sides of the house, and his remarks on these important questions attracted considerable attention. He became one of the leaders of the organization which was engaged in the getting up of the banquets known as the reform banquets, which preceded the revolution of 1848. His ability was at that time so recognized, that he was chosen Mayor of the city of Paris, and discharged the duties of the office with such marked ability, that he was afterwards appointed Minister of Finance under the Provisional Government. In this more delicate position he proved himself equal to the task. He introduced many important reforms, and had also to deal with a financial crisis. The ability with which he handled this latter duty again won for him an enviable confidence. A system of dock warrants and bonded warehouses were among some of the reforms he introduced while acting in the capacity of Finance Minister. In 1864 he was elected a member of the Executive Commission, and also of the Legislative Assembly. Though his career as a politician has been an active one, extending at times through periods of wild excitement, he has found time to devote some attention to literature. He has written a "History of the Revolution of 1848," a work of considerable merit.

HENRI ROCHEFORT.

Perhaps there is no man to-day living in France whose name is better known than that of Henri Rochefort — certainly none in Parisian Republican circles. His well-known, outspoken, and determined hostility to Napoleon III. involved him in many troubles. An intense Republican, he was ready at all times to express with his tongue and with his pen sentiments which less courageous men would hesitate to pronounce.

This proclivity on his part was the means of bringing him into collision with the Government, and as a consequence he was arrested and convicted, and the publication of his journal, the *Lanterne*, was suppressed by the Government. Rochefort, however, succeeded in making his escape to Belgium, where he again entered upon the publication of his notorious journal. Though proscribed in France, it found a ready sale, the very ban of exclusion which was placed upon it by the Imperial Government doing more to increase its popularity than to prevent its circulation. After a short exile the Emperor extended a full pardon to the noisy journalist, and he returned to Paris. For a time he was the lion of the hour; but he gradually subsided into something like comparative quietness. Yet occasionally he fell into his old habits. As the *Lanterne* could not be revived in Paris, and as Rochefort could not do without a journal to ventilate his opinions, he commenced the publication of the *Marseillaise*. In this paper he again attacked the Government, and so bitter were his strictures on the Executive, indulging in personal slurs rather than discussing the public management of affairs, that his paper was not only suspended, but he himself was imprisoned. Last year, Rochefort was elected a member of the Corps Législatif, but his career in that body is not remarkable for anything which can distinguish him from any member of it possessed of ordinary ability.

PIERRE MAGNE.

It is proper here to notice Pierre Magne, the ex-Secretary of Finance, who remains as good friend and sound adviser of the Republic. He was appointed Minister of Finance on the overthrow of the Ollivier Ministry. M. Magne was born at Perigoux, December 3, in the year 1806. He is a self-made man, being of what is termed an "obscure" family.

In 1831 he was admitted as an *avocat*, or attorney, and was patronized by Marshal Bugeaud. M. Fould noticed his peculiar ability, and soon afterwards took charge of his political fortunes. He became a member both of the Constituent and Legislative Assemblies, in which bodies he was recognized as a practical man, although not much of a debating speech-maker. He retired to private life in 1848, but was recalled to official position as Under Secretary of State for Finance in 1849. April 10, 1851, he was appointed Minister of Public Works, in which office he was very successful during three or four years. He was an able advocate of railroad extension in France, and during the interim inspected all the main lines already laid down in the empire and in other countries of Europe, adopting and suggesting improvements. From 1854 to 1860 he held the portfolio of Finance. In 1860 he was nominated Minister without a portfolio, retired from the Cabinet in 1863, and was named a Privy Councillor in April of the last-named year. He is a Senator, and was commander of the Legion of Honor before he received the Grand Cross in 1854. M. Magne originated and conducted most of Napoleon's great loans. During his absence from Paris at one period the Empress Eugenie visited him, and found him feeding a flock of chickens.

ALEXANDRE GLAIS-BIZOIN.

This statesman, one of the Government of National Defence, was born in Quintin, Côtes du Nord, on March 9, 1800. He was admitted to the bar in 1822, and, at once entering into political life, associated himself with the Liberals against the Restoration.

After the revolution of 1830, he was appointed Councillor-General of his Department, and was subsequently elected a deputy for the arrondissement of Londéac, serving in this capacity until 1848. He voted always with the extreme Left, signed the Compte Rendue of 1832, and was conspicuous for his demand for the complete application of the principles of 1789. He took an active part in the reform banquets, and aided in overthrowing the Ministry of M. Guizot. After the revolution of 1848, he was elected to the Assembly, and adhered to the extreme Left. On Louis Napoleon's election to the Presidency he at once went into opposition, and, being beaten for re-election, retired to private life. In 1863 he was returned to the Corps Législatif as an opposition member, and was re-elected in 1869. M. Glais-Bizoin is regarded as one of the most radical of French Republicans.

EUGENE PELLETAN.

M. Pelletan, who is a distinguished French writer and politician, was born at Royan, Charente Inférieure, on the 26th of October, 1813.

He studied law in Paris, and was elected a member of the Corps Législatif in 1864. He is the author of several works, some of which have attained a good place in French literature.

MONDAY, *September* 5.—King William proposes to continue the war. Great war excitement in Berlin. Napoleon a prisoner at Wilhelmshöhe. Mob continues in Paris. The Crown Prince marching on Paris. The Republic proclaimed in Lyons, Bordeaux, and Marseilles. The Republic addresses the army.

BERLIN.

BERLIN, *September* 5 (OFFICIAL).

The Emperor Napoleon having declared that his captivity prevents him from negotiating the peace, the French Government being at Paris, the war will be continued.

MARCHING ON.

A private despatch from the King's headquarters says the Crown Prince resumed his march on Paris the morning after the victory at Sedan. Camps were broken up, and heads of columns in motion at daylight.

CONTINUED JOY IN BERLIN.

There is a mad, intense, fiery excitement of joy prevailing everywhere, on all sides, in doors and out, in the Prussian capital, caused by the wonderful developments which are taking place momentarily. There are five hundred thousand persons in the streets of the city. There is a most magnificent illumination in every dwelling, from the highest to the most humble. *Wherever an American flag is displayed, the processions halt, and salute it with loudest cheers.* The royal palace is surrounded to its very doors with the joyous crowds. Queen Augusta came out and saluted the people, but in doing so her Majesty was so completely overcome by her feelings, that she burst into tears.

PARIS MAD WITH MOBS.

PARIS, *September* 5, 6.12 P.M.—The mobs continue to tear down signs containing the Imperial arms and medals. In some cases the people have climbed up the highest stories to tear from the theatres the word "Imperial." Extreme care is evinced to respect the arms of other nations. In one of the streets a large crowd, upon the point of tearing down a representation of the American eagle, ascertained their mistake, and *shouted loudly*, "*Vive Rêpublique Americaine.*" The police are no longer to be seen in the streets. The large bronze eagles have been taken down from the new Opera House. Portraits of the Emperor and Empress, seen in the Hôtel de Ville ballrooms, were thrown out of the windows, and the people trod and danced upon the canvass.

"*An Emperor dies, but does not surrender,*" and "*A bas l'Empire!*" are heard; while the people shout, "*Vive la République,*" "*Vive Rochefort,*" and throw a scarlet scarf around his neck.

The following proclamation has been issued to the Garde Nationale:

"Those on whom your patriotism has just imposed the formidable mission of defending the country, thank you for your brave devotion. To your resolution is due the civic victory which has restored liberty to France.

It has not cost a drop of blood. Personal power is no more. The nation entire resumes her rights and her arms. She rises ready to die in defence of the soil. You have given her back her soul, which despotism had stifled. You will maintain with firmness the execution of the laws, and, rivalling our noble army, you will show us together the road to victory."

THE EMPEROR.

At two o'clock to-day, the Emperor passed through Cologne without stopping, the engines having been changed outside the city. The train consisted of ten cars. It left Verviers at eleven o'clock this forenoon, and Aix-la-Chapelle at noon. Another long train with the Imperial household preceded it. The various railway stations were thronged with crowds of people, who were curious to catch a glimpse of the Emperor.

By the order of King William, two Chamberlains of the Court of Prussia are in attendance upon the Emperor.

WILHELMSHOHE, *September* 5.—The Imperial train reached this station at thirty-five minutes past nine P.M., where the garrison officers, General Plonske and resident officials of the province, had assembled. The Emperor, on alighting, passed to Plonske's carriage, saluting the officers of the corps, who drew up with presented arms. He looked serious, not crushed. There were no signs of bloat or unhealthy *embonpoint*. He wore the undress uniform of a general, with a riding cape of the Garibaldian pattern. The crowd was silent, respectful, and sympathetic.

Napoleon is accompained in his exile by General Castelnau, the Prince de la Moskowa, and Counts de Genlis, de Waubert, Reillé, and Pajol, all of his personal staff.

TUESDAY, *September* 6. — King William at Rheims. Bismarck says the North German Confederation must have Strasburg and Metz. Jules Favre addresses the crowned heads. The American Press declares for the Republic. The Crown Prince addresses his army.

THE PRUSSIAN ARMY.

RHEIMS, *September* 6. — The King's headquarters are established at Rheims until the 9th, to enable all the troops to come up. Seven North German corps, beside two Bavarian and the Würtemberg corps, are on the road, unhindered. The German army, with the reserves are coming up, and will number 400,000 men.

BISMARCK SAYS

to-day, that "Prussia will not interfere with France's domestic affairs.

"Our people think we must have those German provinces France took from us many years ago. We must, at least, render France powerless to menace us by the same road. Metz and Strasburg we must have, and we ask no more than is necessary to our own safety.

"We are a very patient people. They have been telling us that if we would not fight, they would compel us. Well, we are like the father of a family, who, after enduring many insults, at last determines to fight a duel, only on condition that the combat shall be decisive and shall be final."

PROCLAMATION OF THE CROWN PRINCE.

SOLDIERS: Through great victories of the armies, the hope of a glorious peace has been won for the German people.

On the battle-fields of France, the nation has become conscious of its greatness and union, and this gain, sanctified by the blood of many thousands of our warriors, we trust, will keep its binding power for all future time. But to the enthusiastic outbursts and emotions of these weeks have come also feelings of deep sorrow. Many of the flower of our youth, many of the leaders of our army, have fallen victims of the victory, and greater still is the number of those who, from wounds, and excessive endurance and exertions, will be unable in future to gain their livelihood by their own efforts. They, above all, and those whom the dead have left behind them, and the living victims of the war, have a claim to the gratitude of the nation. Whoever has shared the enthusiasm of this contest; whoever, from the rising up of our whole people in their might, hopes for a new happy era of peace, and in our victories and the defeat of our foes worships a judgment of God on high, let him now prove his fidelity to the warriors of our people's army, and their families Help from the State alone, however fully it may be given, will not suffice to support the large number of invalids and their families, That help only affords what is absolutely necessary, and unavoidably confined to general normal rules, and cannot attend to the need and wants of the individual. Great efforts of voluntary help will be required this time, for, huge as the successes have been, the losses of the war are enormous. In the same way in which this war has created a uniform and united German army, in which sons of all the German lands fought in brotherly emulation of bravery, the care for the invalids and helpless whom the war leaves behind must become the common business of Germany, the North and South of our Fatherland taking a like share in it. Former experience has taught that it does not suffice with generous hearts to offer donations of money. Nay, not less important and more difficult is the proper distribution thereof—the kind considereration of personal circumstances, and, most important of all, the precaution that the assistance rendered shall not weaken instead of strengthen the power to earn which may still exist, and that it really prove beneficial for the life of those assisted. The "Victoria National Invalid fund," which was founded in 1868, throughout the largest part of Germany, having answered this purpose, and having been found effective in its organization, I hereby authorize the executive manager of that fund to take in hand the organization and management of an "Invalid Fund of Germany," and to call for contributions and the establishment of branches thereof. His Majesty, the King, commander-in-chief of the German army, as in the years 1864 and 1866, has given me his consent to this patriotic enterprise. This time it has been my good fortune to lead an army into the field, in which the Bavarian, the Würtemberger, and the Badenener have, fought side by side with the Prussian, and I may address myself to the hearts of all Germans. May this work of love be a common labor between us for our Fatherland, and may it be the introduction of many united and blessed works of peace.

FRIEDRICH WILHELM,
Crown Prince of Prussia.

Headquarters, Rheims, Sept. 6, 1870.

REVOLUTION — PARIS.

The Revolution in France extends, and peacefully. In all the important towns the Republic has been proclaimed amid enthusiasm, not confusion; and the Imperial officials and agents have retired, and the new administrators of the new Government have taken their places, without collision or bloodshed. The Mayor has issued the following proclamation :

HOTEL DE VILLE, PARIS, Sept. 6.—*Citizens:* I have been called by the people and Government of the National Defence to the Mayoralty of Paris. While waiting for you to be called to elect your municipality, I take possession of this City Hall in the name of the Republic, which was the scene of the patriotic events of 1794, 1830, and 1848. I speak to you now as our fathers did in 1792. Citizens! The country is in danger; rally around this Parisian municipality, defended to-day from siege by a soldier of the Republic. *Vive la République!*

ETIENNE ARAGO.

THE INTERNATIONAL WORKINGMEN'S SOCIETY,

in their address to the Social Democracy of Germany, says :

"Prussia made war against the Emperor, not France, who now asks the withdrawal of your armies; otherwise it will be the universal duty of Frenchmen to rise and re-enact the scenes of '93. Frenchmen make no peace with the enemy on their soil; but they are the friends and allies of all free peoples. We protest against the intervention of the Powers, and implore the Prussian forces to recross the Rhine. Let us, with grasped hands, forget crimes prompted or perpetuated by despots. *Let us form the United States of Europe.* Live the Universal Republic!"

THE MINISTRY TO THE ARMY!

To the Army: When a General compromises his command, he is relieved; when a Government puts in peril, by its own weakness, the public safety, it is set aside. This is just what France is doing in abolishing the dynasty responsible for all our misfortunes. She has done boldly, in the face of all the world, this great act of justice. She executes the decree under which all your conscripts have been summoned, and in the same act secures the public safety. To save itself, the nation needs now but to rise *en masse*, and henceforth to count on two things only: Its own resolution, which is invincible; and your heroism, which has never had an equal, and which, in the midst of unmerited reverses, has astonished the world. Rally round the glorious symbol which eighty years ago drove back all Europe before us. To-day, as at that time, the name of the Republic signifies the intimate union of the army and the people for the defence of the country.

Minister of Foreign Affairs — JULES FAVRE.
Minister of Justice—ISAAC CREMIEUX.
Minister of the Interior — LEON GAMBETTA.
Minister of Finance — ERNEST PICARD.
Superintendent of Public Works — PIERRE DORIAN.
Minister of Commerce — JOSEPH MAGNIN.
Superintendent of Public Instruction — JULES SIMON.
Minister of Marine — MARTIN FOURICHON.
Minister of War —LOUIS JULES TROCHU; also President of the Committee.

M. JULES FAVRE'S CIRCULAR TO THE WORLD.

PEACE — BUT NOT AN INCH OR A STONE TO PRUSSIA.

The Vice-President of the Republic, and Minister of Foreign Affairs, issues this circular letter to French representatives to-day : — (*see Bismarck's reply, Sept.* 16.)

THE REPUBLIC A NECESSITY.

SIR — The events which have just taken place in Paris explain themselves so well by the inexorable logic of facts, that it is useless to insist at length on their meaning and bearing. In ceding to an irresistible impulse, *which had been but too long restrained*, the population of Paris has obeyed a necessity superior to that of its own safety ; it did not wish to perish with the *criminal government* which was leading France to her ruin ; it has not pronounced the deposition of Napoleon III. and of his dynasty ; it has registered it in the name of right, justice, and public safety, and the sentence was so well ratified beforehand by the conscience of all, that no one, even among the most noisy defenders of the power that was falling, raised his voice to uphold it.

THE CRIMINAL EMPIRE COLLAPSES.

It collapsed of itself under the weight of its faults, and amid the acclamations of an immense people, without a single drop of blood being shed, without any one individual being deprived of his personal liberty, and we have been able to see — a thing unheard of in history — the citizens, upon whom the popular voice conferred the perilous mandate to fight and to conquer, not thinking for a moment of their political adversaries who, but the day before, threatened them with execution. It is by refusing to their adversaries the honor of being subject to any sort of repression that they have shown them their blindness and their impotence. Order has not been disturbed for a single moment. Our confidence in the wisdom and patriotism of the National Guard and of the whole population, permits us to affirm that it will not be disturbed. Rescued from the shame and the danger of a Government which has proved itself a traitor to all its duties, each one now comprehends that the first act of the national sovereignty, at last reconquered, must be one of self-control — the seeking of strength in respect for right. Moreover, time must not be lost ; the enemies are at our gates ; we have but one thought — namely, their expulsion from our territory. But this obligation, which we resolutely accept, we did not impose upon France. She would not be in her present position if our voice had been listened to. We have energetically defended, even at the cost of our popularity, the policy of peace. We still maintain the same opinion with increasing conviction. Our heart breaks at the sight of these human massacres, wherein is sacrificed the flower of the two nations, that a little good sense and a great deal of liberty would have preserved from such frightful catastrophes. We cannot find any expression capable of rendering our admiration for our heroic army, sacrificed by the incapacity of the supreme commander, but showing itself greater in its defeats than in the most brilliant victory ; for, in spite of the knowledge of faults which compromised its safety, the army has immolated itself with sublime heroism in the face of certain death, redeeming thus the honor of France from the stain cast upon her by her Government. All honor to the army! The nation looks towards it with open arms. The Imperial power wished to divide them. Misfortune and duty join them in a solemn embrace, sealed by patriotism and liberty. This alliance renders us invincible. Ready for every emergency, we look with calmness on the position of affairs, made what it is, not by us, but by others. This position I will explain in a few words, and I submit it to the judgment of my country and of Europe.

WE LOUDLY CONDEMNED THE WAR,

and, while protesting our respect for the rights of peoples, we asked that Germany should be left mistresss of her own destinies. We wished that liberty should be at the same time our common tie and our common shield. We were convinced that these moral forces would forever insure peace, but as a sanction, we claimed an arm for every citizen, a civil organization, and the election of leaders. Then we should have remained invincible on our own soil. The Government of the Emperor, which had long since separated its interests from those of the country, opposed that policy.

We take it up, with the hope that, taught by experience, France will have the wisdom to put it into practice. On his side, the King of Prussia declared that he made war, not against France, but against the Imperial dynasty. The dynasty has fallen to the ground. France rises, herself free. Does the King of Prussia wish to continue an impious struggle, which will be at least as fatal to him as to us? Does he wish to give to the world of the nineteenth century the cruel spectacle of two nations destroying one another, and, in forgetfulness of humanity, reason, and science, heaping corpse upon corpse and ruin upon ruin? He is free to assume this responsibility in the face of the world and of history. It is a challenge; we accept it.

NOT A STONE, NOT AN INCH.

We will not cede either an inch of our territory or a stone of our fortresses. A shameful peace would mean a war of extermination at an early date. We will only treat for a durable peace. In this our interest is that of the whole of Europe, and we have reason to hope that, freed from all dynastic considerations, the question will thus present itself before the Cabinets of Europe. But should we be alone we shall not yield. We have a resolute army, well-provisioned forts, a well-established *enceinte*, and, above all, the breasts of 300,000 combatants, determined to hold out to the last. When they piously lay crowns at the feet of the statue of Strasburg, they do not obey merely an enthusiastic sentiment of admiration: they adopt their heroic *mot d'ordre;* they swear to be worthy of their brethren of Alsace, and to die as they have done. After the forts we have the ramparts; after the ramparts, we have the barricades. *Paris can hold out for three months, and conquer. If she succumbs, France will start up at her appeal, and avenge her.* France would continue the struggle, and the aggressor would perish.

Such is, sir, what Europe must know. We have not accepted power with any other object; we will not keep it a moment if we should not find the population of Paris and the whole of France decided to share our resolutions. I sum up these resolves briefly in the presence of God, who hears me; in the face of posterity, which shall judge us. We wish only for peace, but if this disastrous war, which we have condemend, is continued against us, we shall do our duty to the last; and I have the firm confidence that our cause, which is that of right and of justice, will triumph in the end. It is in this manner that I invite you to explain the situation to the Minister of the court to which you are accredited, and in whose hands you will place a copy of this document.

Accept, sir, the expression of my high consideration.

The Minister of Foreign Affairs.

September 6, 1870. JULES FAVRE.

THE COSMOPOLITAN PRESS ON THE REPUBLIC.

The London *Times* and other morning papers accept the French revolution with favor, as the clear expression of the national will. They anticipate no disorder. The *Times* has every good wish for the French statesmen now seeking to reëstablish the Government and preserve order. It expects, as a matter of course, that a new Constitution will be made.

The Pall Mall *Gazette* says the Prussians have utterly broken and defeated the Emperor and France, and it would be creditable now to desist. Only one or two strong frontier places, like Strasburg, should be retained as guarantees.

THE AMERICAN PRESS.

The American Press is almost a unit in favor of the French Republic. The *Tribune* calls upon King William to be liberal with a suffering people, who had nothing to do with the Imperial war. Manton Marble and George Wilkes are out in bold leaders for the young Republic Scathing are the Philippics of George Wilkes against the crowned heads, as they were against rebellion in '62; but he does not lead Mr. Dana, the champion of Cuba, who writes to a hundred and twenty thousand readers every morning to stand by France and the new liberty. Theodore Tilton, and George W. Smalley, who has heretofore been a champion of insulted Prussia, have espoused the Republican cause. Outside of the city, the young French Republic can claim among her supporters, Mr. Charles F. Smith of the Albany *Evening Journal*, Mr. Roberts of the Utica *Herald*, Mr. S. H. Gay of the Chicago *Tribune*, "Mack" of the Cincinnati *Inquirer*, and John Gano and Mr. Halsted of the *Commercial.*

The Southern papers, the Louisville *Journal*, Memphis *Avalanche*, and New Orleans *Picayune*, have no sympathy for Prussia against the new Government of France.

WEDNESDAY, *September* 7.—The Prussian march on Paris obstructed. Order restored in Paris, and the city preparing for defence. Garibaldi sustains the French Republic.

PRUSSIAN ARMY.

SOISSONS, *September* 7. — The advance of the Crown Prince is here to-day, consisting of the Fifth, Sixth, Eleventh, and two Bavarian Corps. The Crown Prince of Saxony has the Fourth and Twelfth Corps, with Saxon and Prussian Guards. The French engineers are blowing up bridges, while the Prussian advance are rebuilding them. The Prussian advance will cross the Aisne to-morrow.

PARIS PREPARING FOR SIEGE.

PARIS, *September* 7. — There seems to be but one patriotic sentiment among the people — the defence of the nation. Organization is quietly proceeding. The *Moniteur* says orders have been given to barricade the streets, to render any assault of the enemy more difficult. People are quitting the city with the utmost haste, now that the Prussians have approached so near. The city is very quiet. Singing in the streets has entirely stopped, and as the enemy draws near, the people evince a quiet but firm determination to fight. There is great rejoicing at the practical removal of the rigid press censorship. War news and details are now published without hindrance.

ARRIVAL OF TROOPS.

General Vinoy, with his entire force, arrived at Paris by railroad at four o'clock yesterday afternoon. His division consisted of eleven trains of cavalry, thirteen trains of artillery, and fourteen trains of infantry. The rolling stock of the Northern and other railroads will be despatched immediately to the eastward to bring back other troops. Trains are arriving hourly with artillery, cavalry, and infantry from the front.

DESTRUCTION OF RAILROADS.

The French engineers are destroying the tunnels on the railroad lines running east out of Paris.

GARIBALDI TO HIS FRIENDS.

TO MY FRIENDS: — Yesterday I said to you, War to the end against Bonaparte; I say to-day that the French Republic must be sustained by all possible means. Invalid as I am, I have offered my services to the Provisional Government of Paris, and I hope it will not be impossible for me to fulfil a duty. Yes, fellow-citizens, we ought to regard it as a sacred duty to succor our French brothers.

Our mission will not certainly consist in fighting our German brothers, who, in the hands of Providence, have destroyed in the bud the germ of the tyranny which weighed on the world; but we shall go to sustain the only system which can assure the peace and prosperity of nations.

I repeat, sustain by all possible ways the French Republic, which, rendered wise by the lessons of the past, will always be one of the best columns of human regeneration.

Caprera, September 7, 1870. GARIBALDI.

THURSDAY, *September* 8.—America and Spain recognize the Republic of France. Joyful demonstrations at the announcement. The Orleans Princes requested by Jules Favre to leave Paris. The Emperor is treated like a king at Wilhelmshöhe. The French fleet with the Republic.

AMERICA RECOGNIZES THE REPUBLIC.

Minister Washburne telegraphed to the Secretary of State on Tuesday last that he had been officially informed of the formation of a Republican government for France, the passage of the *déchéance*, etc. This despatch Secretary Fish sent to the President at Long Branch, who at once ordered Secretary Fish to instruct Minister Washburne to recognize the new Government, and extend to them congratulations on the formation of a Republic. Secretary Fish did so at once.

Minister Washburne communicated to Jules Favre the import of the President's instructions, to recognize the sister Republic of France, with the congratulations, etc., in the following note:

SIR:—I have received the communication which you did me the honor of addressing to me on the 5th inst., in which you inform me that, in virtue of a resolution adopted by the members of the Government of National Defence, the Department of Foreign Affairs has been confided to you.

I have, in my turn, the satisfaction of announcing that I have received from my Government a telegram, by which I am instructed to recognize the present Government as that of France. In consequence, I am ready to enter into relations with that Government, and to treat with it on all the subjects that may concern me. In making this communication to your Excellency, I beg you to accept for yourself and for the other Ministers the congratulations of the people of the United States; they will have learnt with enthusiasm of the proclamation of the Republic in France without the slightest effusion of blood, and they will associate themselves with heartfelt sympathy in the great movement which they hope and trust will be productive of happy results for the French people and for the whole human race.

Having enjoyed for nearly a century the numberless benefits of a Republican government, the people of the United States can only watch with the deepest interest the efforts made by the French nation—with which they are connected by so many ties—to found institutions of a nature to insure the general well-being of all.

In terminating, I am anxious to assure your Excellency that I congratulate myself on having, as intermediate between myself and the Ministry of the National Defence, a man whose distinguished merit is so well apppreciated in my own country, and who has devoted all the strength of his intelligence to the cause of liberty and free institutions.

PARIS, *September* 8. WASHBURNE.

On receipt of this letter of recognition, Favre was much moved. He called immediately on the American Minister in person. Grasping Mr. Washburne by the hand he exclaimed: "*I receive the notification with gratitude and profound emotion.*"

Minister Washburne telegraphed the President to-day, that the officers of the Republic were overjoyed at the announcement.

PRESIDENT GRANT AND THE REPUBLIC.

It is a matter of much national importance to state that the President is now openly and avowedly for the maintenance of the French Republic. He said to-day: "*I have hastened to give the new Republic our moral support, and hope that before the week is out she will not need anything further. I think the Prussian King may be induced to stop fighting.*" He talked freely to several gentlemen in favor of the Republic. In his avowed support of the Republic he is warmly supported by Secretaries Fish and Robeson.

THE REPUBLIC TO AMERICA.

The recognition of the French Republic by the American Government led to an imposing demonstration. When the crowd arrived in front of the Legation, several of its members were chosen to convey to Mr. Washburne the expression of its sentiments. Mr. Washburne listened with much emotion to the following address delivered by M. Lucien:

"SIR: In the name of a great number of citizens, certain of the approval of and support by the entire nation, we come to beg you to testify to your Government our gratitude for the spontaneity with which it has answered the announcement of a French Republic. A great part of our thanks belong to you also, Sir, for the generous expressions which your heart dictated when communicating to us the adhesion by your Government. We did not expect less from that great and generous American nation, whose aspirations and principles have always been in harmony with the ideas of France. To-day America and France are sisters—sister Republics; that is, sisters of Liberty. The ocean which separates us is less profound than the sentiment which unites us. *Long live the United States of America.*"

The Minister then appeared at the balcony, and said:

"I am moved by this demonstration. The Republic of the United States has received with joy the advent of the French Republic. I will convey the thanks you have given me to my Government, which I know will be much pleased with this patriotic manifestation."

Along the Boulevard to-night there were many shouts of "*Vive les Etats Unis,*" and "*Vive l'Independance.*" The action of the United States Government is warmly commented on in all parts of the city. Jules Favre called again to-day to reiterate his thanks to the nation and to Mr. Washburne. *La France* (newspaper) recalls the fact that in 1848 the United States was the first country to recognize the French Republic, and she is the first again in 1870.

The *Journal de Paris* says:

America has merited well of the civilized world for addressing France in the hour of peril and misfortune words of consolation and hope. By recognizing the French Republic, America opens the way of peace. It must be that the people of this continent will follow her example.

SPAIN'S RECOGNITION.

A COMIC BLUNDER IN DIPLOMACY.

Spain recognizes the Republic, but all through a comical diplomatic blunder. Its ludicrous history is this: After the declaration of the Republic, Paris was in a whirlpool of excitement. Señor Olozaga, the Spanish ambassador in Paris, was enthusiastic with the rest. Being of a fiery temperament, he, in great haste, telegraphed to Señor Sagasta, the Spanish Minister of State at Madrid, for instructions. Sagasta and Prim flew to Mr. Layard, the English representative in Madrid, and asked him to telegraph to England, to find out what the Cabinet of St. James was to do. Mr. Layard telegraphed. Lord Granville replied: "*Lord Lyons has instructions to continue* OFFICIOUS *relations, and not to show any official recognition.*" As soon as Mr. Layard showed this reply to Señor Sagasta, the latter telegraphed to Señor Olozaga, in Paris, as follows: "*Maintain* 'OFFICIOUS' *relations. Follow the conduct observed by Lord Lyons.*"

THE TELEGRAPH BLUNDERS AGAIN.

When this telegram (a *cipher* despatch) reached Señor Olozaga in Paris, the "*officious*" was changed to "*official.*" Señor Olozaga was delighted, and, thinking he was obeying instructions, immediately drew up this hasty letter of recognition to Jules Favre:

PARIS, *September* 8.—MONSIEUR LE MINISTRE: On the night of the 6th I received your Excellency's circular of the 5th; I hastened to communicate it on the 7th by post to my Government, giving them also an account of it by telegraph. Before I received your circular the Minister of State in Madrid had sent me the necessary telegraphic instructions to enter immediately into official relations with your Excellency, and he manifested his desire to maintain the good relations which fortunately exist between Spain and France. I believe it unnecessary to add, that all my efforts will, as ever, be employed that these relations may be strengthened more and more, to the prosperity and advantage of both nations. Yours, &c. SALUSTIANO OLOZAGA.

Jules Favre replied as follows:

SENOR EMBASSADOR: With lively satisfaction I have received the letter you did me the honor to write me, announcing that the Minister of State of Spain had sent you by telegraph the instructions necessary for you to enter upon official relations with the Government of the National Defence. Very precious is it to me to receive such a testimony of friendship and confidence on the part of the representative of a country which has so recently taught us the road to liberty. By it I hope we shall jointly advance, and become closely united by community of interests and of hopes. This hour, so cruel for France, is precisely the time when with the greater evidence there is revealed the prudence of a policy which unites in one common bond three veritably sister peoples, who, to recover their family titles, only waited the signal of liberty. Permit me, Señor Embassador, to offer you, both in my own name and in that of the individuals of this Government, the expression of my high consideration, and of my complete affection. Yours, &c.

JULES FAVRE, Vice-President
of the Government, and Minister of Foreign Affairs.

PARIS AFFAIRS.

Princes Joinville, d'Aumale and Chartres were in Paris. They called on Minister Favre, and asked to share in the defence of Paris. M. Favre told them their presence might be misunderstood, and appealing to their patriotism, requested them to leave the city, which the Princes consented to do, and they have since fulfilled their promise.

ELECTION PROCLAMATION.

FRENCHMEN: In proclaiming four days ago the Government of the National Defence, we ourselves defined our mission. Power was lying in the dust. What had commenced by a crime finished by a desertion. We simply grasped the helm which had escaped from powerless hands. But Europe has need to be enlightened. It is necessary that she should know by irrefragable testimonies that the entire country is with us. It is necessary that the invader should meet on his route, not only the obstacle of an immense city resolved to perish rather than yield, but an entire people, erect, organized, represented—an Assembly, in short, which can carry into all places, and in spite of all disasters, the living soul of the country.

Consequently, the Government of the National Defence decrees:

Art. 1. The electoral colleges are convoked for Sunday, the 16th of October, for the purpose of electing a National Constituent Assembly.

Art. 2. The elections will be held by collective voting, conformably to the law of the 15th of March, 1849.

Art. 3. The number of members of the Constituent Assembly will be 750.

Art. 4. The Minister of the Interior is charged with the execution of this decree.

Given at the Hôtel de Ville of Paris, Sept. 8, 1870.

General TROCHU.
EMMANUEL ARAGO.
CREMIEUX.
JULES FAVRE.
JULES FERRY.
GAMBETTA.
GARNIER-PAGES.
GLAIS-BIZOIN.
PELLETAN.
E. PICARD.
ROCHEFORT.
JULES SIMON.
The MINISTER of WAR, General LEFLO.
The INTERIM MINISTER of MARINE and the COLONIES, Rear-Admiral DE DOMPIERRE d'HORNOY.
The MINISTER of AGRICULTURE and COMMERCE, M. MAGNIN, ex-Deputy.
The MINISTER of PUBLIC WORKS, M. DORIAN.

PROCLAMATION NO. TWO.

The Minister of the Interior has issued the following circular to Prefects of Departments:

The enemy is advancing on Paris in three corps d'armée, one of which has arrived at Soissons, in the Department of Aisne. The advance guard of this corps has summoned Laon, which shuts its gates and resists.

The interruption of telegraphic communication with Epernay and Château Thierry indicates the presence of the enemy at those points. Communication continues with Mézières, Epinal, and Mulhouse. There is no news from Bazaine. The news of the death of MacMahon has not been officially confirmed. At Paris, order is perfect. The inhabitants received with warm demonstrations of confidence the assurances given by the Government that the city is abundantly provisioned for two months.

The Prefect of the Rhône sends word that harmony has been established between himself and the Committee which took the direction of affairs, and order prevails. M. Esquiros has arrived at Marseilles, where he is received with enthusiasm by the citizens.

The work of revision is actively going on in all the Departments. The Garde Mobile everywhere asks to be led to Paris. Many battalions are now here or on the march hither.

GAMBETTA.

GENERAL SHERIDAN

writes from Rheims as follows:

There seems to be but little of the war left except the siege of Paris, and that will not save France. It is possible that French troops have not done so well as I think they are capable of doing, on one or two occasions which I witnessed, from the fact that the poor fellows found themselves so badly handled by their commanders, that they could see no equivalent to be obtained by sacrificing their lives. All men like to have an equivalent for their labor, and especially is it so with soldiers, who require success where many lives are to be sacrificed. The French generalship put this out of the question in every battle which I have witnessed.

THE FRENCH NAVY.

THE SQUADRON,

hitherto, has done nothing but blockade the coasts, a task involving numberless difficulties. The plan of the campaign has not proved wise; the French chiefs either failed to define their intention clearly or to understand the nature of the sea where the fleet was to operate.

The fleet has no base of operations; no port of anchorage, except by retiring to neutral waters. Not having seized, as it might have, some small undefended islands off the coast of Schleswig, the squadron, in fact, never anchors, and is subject to continued surprises in the night from Prussian gunboats, which, coming out of harbors known only to themselves, appear amid French vessels either to reconnoitre or to blow them up with torpedoes, as nearly happened in the roadstead of Dantzic, when Admiral Bouët anchored under the very guns of the Fort.

The Prussian vessels being small and swift, risk little, but if successful might destroy a French vessel. The squadron can only take in coal on an open sea, and in circumstances of danger. A want is felt of suitable vessels for blockading purposes; ironclads are too slow, and of too great draft. Cruising proves most difficult and perilous.

Admiral Bouët has separated the squadron into two divisions. With the first he blockades the shore from the Russian frontier to Rugen; the second, under Admiral Dieudonné, watches the coast from Rugen to North Schleswig. There has been no important encounter hitherto with the Prussian fleet. Two vessels, the *Océan* and the *Flandre*, are about returning to France.

The news of MacMahon's and the Emperor's surrender is just received. The latter causes little grief, for the fleet is not Bonapartist. After such events the squadron must remain inactive; but if the new Government resolves to continue the struggle, it will wage pitiless war on the German coast.

FRIDAY, *September* 9.—The siege of Strasburg is made a scientific school for Prussian engineers. Houses in the "military zone" of Paris to be destroyed. George Sand and Victor Hugo address the Republic. Prussians advance on Paris.

PARIS.

The inhabitants of all houses within the "military zone" are ordered to quit their habitations forthwith, as the houses are now to be pulled down. The Prefect of Police orders all persons intending to leave Paris to go immediately.

VICTOR HUGO

writes to-day —

"You may take the fortress, you will find the rampart. You may take the rampart, you will find the barricade. You may take the barricade, and then — who knows the resources of patriotism in distress — you will find the sewers mines of powder, ready to blow whole streets into the air. This will be the terrible sentence you must accept: To take Paris stone by stone, to slaughter Europe on the spot, to kill France in detail; in each street, in each house that great light must be extinguished soul by soul! Germans, hold back! Paris is formidable. Think awhile before her walls. All transformations are possible for her. Her indolence gives you the measure of her energy. She seems to sleep. She will awaken. Her thought will leap from its scabbard like a sword; and this city, which yesterday was Sybaris, to-morrow may be Saragossa."

GEORGE SAND

salutes the new *régime* in the following words:

"The Republic! She must have life in her, since she rises again from her ashes by the voice of all, by a will of which she is worthy, without the spilling of blood, without fratricidal strife. Behold the third awakening: it is ideally beautiful! The third? say rather the fourth; for we must not forget that 1830 was republican at the beginning. We have fought for her only to lose her. To-day she rises complete with a single word — *Vive la France*. This, then, is the normal state which the conscience of humanity desires. This is the inevitable end of the prodigious toil of humanity. It is well. It is the law of intelligence. The manliness of man can only develop in the air of freedom. Behold the God of armies! His name is country and liberty. Hail to the Republic! Thou art in good hands, and a great people is now marching under thy banner after a bloody expiation. Thy task is hard. But should it happen to thee to fall once more, thou wilt surely rise again. The rights of man are imperishable."

STRASBURG SCHOOL.

The operations against Strasburg are carried on by a slow but sure rule. Gen. Loewensky (Gen. Von Woerder's chief of staff) recently said: "We do not mean to press the siege in an irregular way. It is a grand study for our scientific engineers, though a trifle stupid to those who do not understand the refinements of the science of war." He expressed the opinion that it was a mathematical certainty that the place would fall about the 24th inst. (It fell on the 27th.)

Gen. Uhrich, the heroic commandant of Strasburg, telegraphs to the Ministry as follows:

STRASBURG, FRIDAY, *September* 9. — Affairs are in a deplorable condition, and are growing worse. The bombardment from the Prussian advanced works is incessant and frightful. *I hold out to the end.*

UHRICH,
the commandant of the City of Strasburg.

SATURDAY, *September* 10. — Laon surrenders. The citadel blows up, killing fifty Prussians, 300 Gardes Mobile, and the Duke William of Mecklenburg-Schwerin. The Emperor talks with the children at Wilhelmshöhe. Frère Hyacinthe thanks Minister Washburne.

SURRENDER OF LAON.

Duke William of Mecklenburg's official report says the

capitulation of Laon took place on the basis of that of Sedan Arms to be laid down, the Gardes Mobile to be discharged on parole, and the line infantry to go under escort to the city. Many officers, including the French commander, remained in the yard of the citadel. When the last man had passed the citadel gate, two powerful detonations were heard in quick succession. The powder magazine, shells, cartridges, and mine, exploded, and all in the yard were buried under the ruins. There was fearful destruction, and the losses cannot be ascertained.

THE EXPLOSION.

TO THE QUEEN: RHEIMS, *September* 11, 10 P.M.

Sad news from Laon, where, after the capitulation and the entry of our troops, the citadel blew up. Fifty of our men and 300 of the Gardes Mobiles were killed, and many wounded.

The Duke William of Mecklenburg-Schwerin is among the latter.

"Unquestionably the disaster is to be attributed to treachery."

THE EMPEROR.

The Emperor at Wilhelmshöhe enjoys entire freedom of action; walks or rides as he pleases. His chief companions are Prince Moskowa and Prince Murat. He disregards the stare of the curious people whom he encounters outside of the gates. It is said he looks thirty years older than he did in 1865, when the writer saw him. He is now bloated, bilious, and yellow. His eyes are faint, tired, and expressionless; his movements are slow, awkward, and mechanical, and his face absolutely devoid of expression. "Apathy" describes his appearance in one word. He retires late and rises early.

His chamber windows are lighted till long after midnight, and at half-past four in the morning the Emperor is seen walking in the garden. He dresses plainly in black, and amuses himself a great deal by talking to the school children, who gather around to see him.

RETIRED TO PRIVATE LIFE.

In the true sense of the word, Napoleon III. has retired into private life; he keeps his hours of rising, lunching, dining, walking, and sleeping as regularly as an old pensioner at Greenwich. The day after his arrival he was seen walking as early as half-past seven, and ever since he has stuck to this customary walk on the gravel paths of the beautiful park.

NOBLE GUESTS.

At twelve o'clock to-day there arrived and drove up to the palace the Duchess of Hamilton, who, having taken up her abode at the Grande Hôtel Schombardt, called on her imprisoned cousin. She stayed in the palace for quite an hour, when she was conducted back to her carriage by the Emperor himself. On her driving off, Napoleon uncovered his head, apparently in some emotion.

AT DINNER.

At the Emperor's dinner table there are assembled about twenty persons, usually including the Governor of Cassel, Graf Monts. What feelings must besiege the heart of this brave and gallant soldier, who only a short time ago was decorated for his fifty years' service, when he is dining on the right of that man whose policy has demanded the life of his only son.

HE WALKS OUT.

The Emperor was, as usual, in his undress uniform — a black coat, red trousers with black strips, and the red cap of a General, wearing on his breast the grand cordon of the Legion of Honor, and four other orders. He walked quite slowly, his step not reminding one in any way of that firmness exhibited on the evening of his arrival. His hands were folded on his back, and remained so until he returned to the palace, half an hour after his exit. It ought to be remarked that Dr. Conneau did not leave his side, though there was a continual change of the Generals on the other side.

AN EMPEROR STILL.

Beautiful Wilhelmshöhe! Sixty-six years ago, Napoleon's gay Uncle Jerome revelled in noisy festivities in this beautiful château. Did he not astonish the ancient inhabitants by superseding its ancient name, and calling it Napoleonshöhe?

There is a warm glow inside the splendid hall. Generals and gentlemen of the royal household are standing ready to do the honors of the occasion. They bow low, and are the most obedient servants of His Majesty. They conduct His Majesty upstairs with the deference due to a Sovereign. They take the commands of His Majesty, and will be happy to execute them. Meanwhile attendants are bustling about outside, and everything is in *gala*. Napoleon is received as a guest, not as a prisoner, by his generous host. The entire palace is placed at his disposal. A numerous suite of some forty persons, with a large retinue of servants, have followed him, and will be likewise entertained by the King. He has brought eighty-five horses and a variety of carriages — greater, almost, than can be stored in the mews of the princely mansion. Royal *valets de chambre* and *chefs de cuisine* have been sent down, and everything will be done to render his stay as pleasant as possible. The movements of the Emperor are apparently without restraint, and if he chose he might drive about in the grounds, see company in the evening, and close the day with a visit to His Majesty's Opera at Cassel. Such is the aspect royal imprisonment assumes in the courtesy of the present age. Times have changed since Mary was locked up by Elizabeth, or, to quote a more analogous case, since the youthful King of France was captured by the German Emperor Charles V., on the battle-field of Pavia.

LOVELY SURROUNDINGS.

Beside the château stands the theatre built by Jerome Bonaparte when King, and in which he himself used to act. Just behind it is the highest fountain in Europe (except that at Chatsworth), which throws up its fairy spray twelve inches in diameter and 180 feet high.

Farther up is an artificial waterfall, descending from a tall aqueduct over beds of stone arranged in exquisite taste, and on Sundays and Wednesdays, when the waters play, great crowds flock to see them.

The Aquatic Staircase and the Octagon Temple of the Winds, with the Statue and other extravagances connected with it, are reported to have employed 2000 men for fourteen years. When their labors were completed, the cost was found to be so enormous that the accounts were burned, to destroy all records of it.

The Cascade of the Karlsburg, is another of the many wonders of the place — a flight of stone steps, 900 feet long, over which a stream of water is at times permitted to fall. Half way up the stairs is the Giant Euceladus, rudely represented lying on his back, with a mountain of rocks heaped upon his breast. The artist intended a jet of water fifty feet high should spout from his mouth, but none plays there now. The staircase of this "Château d'Eau" is surmounted by an octagon building 1312 feet above the Fulda, surmounted by a pyramid serving as a pedestal to the colossal Hercules, thirty-one feet high, of beaten copper. Nine persons, it is said, can stand at one time in the hollow of the club, and enjoy a charming view out of a little window formed in it.

IN THE MIDST OF THE PARK

is a toy castle — "Luxemburg" — built to imitate a stronghold of the middle ages, with draw-bridges, battlements, towers, and ditches. Among the rusty suits in the armory is one which belonged to the great Condé. There is also a very curious collection of drinking-glasses, a series of portraits of the Tudors and Stewarts, and a library filled with romances alone.

FRERE (LATE PERE) HYACINTHE TO MINISTER WASHBURNE.

SIR: Detained in the country for more than a month by the state of my health, which has suffered so many and cruel ordeals, I much regret that it is not in my power to grasp the hand that has just written a letter so noble and sympathetic toward my country.

That letter is a page in the history of liberty in the two worlds. It revives the recollections of Washington and Lafayette, and proves that if despotism had succeeded in dividing two governments, liberty had not delayed an instant to unite two peoples. Europe, where the blood of our defeated heroes has flowed, is still silent, but America, despite the ocean which separates us, has made her voice heard. She affirms that neither distance nor diversity of race will make strangers of nations which have the same soul, and that she demands for her young sister that right which it appertains to her to define, because she was the first to know how to practise it — the inalienable right to live toiling for the happiness of all.

I am happy that such sentiments have found their official interpreter in one whom I love and esteem so much, and I pray you to accept with the expression of my patriotic gratitude the homage of my respectful and deep attachment.

BOULIAC, *September* 10, 1870. HYACINTHE.

METZ.

Prince Frederick Charles, who fired a salute of 101 guns of shot and shell upon it on Saturday last, the 10th of September, in honor of the victory gained by the Prussians at Sedan, has commenced the work of destruction. The whole of the troops now around Metz, amounting to nearly 200,000 men, are under the entire command of Prince Frederick Charles, Steinmetz having been relieved from the command of the First Army, (First, Seventh, and Eighth Corps). They have at present no large siege guns at Metz, they being all employed at Strasburg. The heaviest guns used there at present are twelve-pounders. Bazaine is now thoroughly hemmed in in his fortress, the Prussians having entirely surrounded it, and opened rifle-pits. Two days ago Bazaine sent out of Metz all Prussian prisoners that he had captured, and also all the wounded.

SUNDAY, *September* 11. — The Prussian army advances. Destruction of bridges by the French.

PRUSSIAN ARMY.

The Eastern Railway is still open to Nogelet, but the Prussians are at Château-Thierry, advancing on La Ferté sous Jouarre. The rolling stock of the road is withdrawn as the Prussians advance, and the bridges and culverts are destroyed before the track is abandoned. The Prussian scouts are reported at Villiers, Acron, Verneuil, Châtillon, Montmesnil, Vailly-sur-Aisne, Sezanne, and Lehauny. They maintain strict discipline, and commit no depredations. The Prussian force was at Compiégne on Saturday.

BISMARCK HAS SAID

that he will have such a tremendous force in France as will crush resistance, and especially prevent everywhere the organization of new forces. But for the national clamor for Alsace and Lorraine, it is certain that Bismarck would be content with Metz and Strasburg as national fortresses.

THE DUKE OF MECKLENBURG,

with the Seventh Division of the First and a division of the Ninth Corps, heretofore in Schleswig-Holstein, and two divisions of reserves and landwehr, constituting the (Sixth) army lately formed at Homburg in the Palatinate, is on the way to invest Toul and Soissons.

MONDAY, *September* 12. — Demonstration in Marseilles in favor of the United States. Count Bismarck proposes to recognize any *de jure* government in France. Russia and Austria reject overtures in favor of the Republic.

HONOR TO THE UNITED STATES.

An imposing demonstration was made in Marseilles in honor of the United States. Twenty thousand people assembled in front of the American consulate, and the city authorities, through M. Esquiros, presented an address to Milton M. Price, the consul of the United States. Speeches were made, the bands played the national airs of America and France, and the immense crowd cheered with great enthusiasm the consul and the Government of the United States.

THE UHLANS ARRIVE.

The uhlans are at Nogent-sur-Marne, only five miles east of the city. Orders have been given by the German commanders forbidding the destruction of bridges behind the army, under dire penalties.

A large body of Prussian engineers is at Champigny, a few miles east of Paris. The German cuirassiers are still before Soissons. Twenty-five hundred Bavarians are at Vaucoulleurs.

The bridges at Corbeil and Creil were blown up by the French troops on the approach of the Prussians.

TUESDAY, *September* 13. — France desires peace. She makes an offer through England, and is willing to dismantle Metz and Strasburg, and pay Prussia the expenses of the war. Queen Victoria hates the Republic, and instructs Gladstone to tell Lyons not to show the slightest recognition.

FRANCE FOR PEACE.

QUEEN VICTORIA OPPOSED TO THE REPUBLIC.

M. Thiers arrived in England to-day. He looks careworn and ill, and shows a disinclination to conversation. He intimated that he knew no Republic — only the Government for the defence of Paris. Thiers is not so good a Republican as Favre, but he has the interest of France at heart. M. Thiers has the proposition of the French Government to make peace with Prussia, and asks England's aid. *Queen Victoria hates the Republic.* She sees in it the germ of the coming power which is to overrun England. "*How soon may not a Republic be declared in London, if we recognize this one?*" she has said to Gladstone. She has told Granville to tell Lyons, the English ambassador in Paris, not to dignify the Republic by the slightest recognition. Thus do the crowned heads hope to destroy the wedge which will one day split monarchy and make a wreck of thrones. Granville, in the kindness of his heart, first felt a warm feeling for the new Government, but now he is as cold as ice. Rumor says Gladstone has frozen Motley too.

It is strange how soon a few cold English dinners will freeze the blood of a weak Republican. Sumner ought to be in England now. But men get conservative as they get old, and you will see Sumner and Wendell Phillips one day standing in Reverdy Johnson's shoes. How warm is Washburne to that Puritanical aristocrat, Motley!

FRANCE OFFERS FOR PEACE.

through M. Thiers, as follows:

"Payment to Prussia of the war expenses; destruction of all the forts in

Alsace and Lorraine; temporary occupation of Metz and Strasburg by the German troops until the election of an authorized Government for France, and the ratification of the treaty by the proper authorities."

This is history: France asked Granville to be the means of communication with Prussia. Granville said "Yes, if Gladstone will let me." *The Queen and Gladstone said "No," emphatically.*

MONDAY, *September* 14. — It is officially announced in Berlin that the French Republic is a government *de facto* but not *de jure.* The advance of the Prussian army reaches Paris. French territory to be annexed to Germany.

THE REPUBLIC NOT *DE JURE.*

The following is officially announced in Berlin to-day:

"The National Defence Government in Paris, though existing *de facto*, is deemed of no validity *de jure*, and cannot and will not be treated with when Paris is taken. The Senate and Corps Législatif, with the Regency — the Government *de jure* — can and will, it is expected, resume their sessions, and appoint a commission to accept terms of peace, and the Empress can return. When peace is concluded, Napoleon will be released, and France be left free to have an empire or such other government as its people want."

FRENCH TERRITORY TO BE SEIZED.

The Prussian Government has formally notified Bavaria of its intention to annex to Germany a portion of France as a military frontier.

This notification calls forth the opposition of many distinguished German Democrats. Dr. Jacobi, of Königsberg, has been imprisoned for opposing the national will (Bismarck's?). The cry of France begins to be, "not one stone of our fortifications, not one inch of our soil."

The *Frankfort Gazette* is publishing a series of articles by Herr Carl Vogt, the great German naturalist, against the annexation of Alsace and Lorraine. Herr Vogt protests even against the annexation of such places as Metz and Strasburg. He advocates the dismantling of all fortifications between Paris and Berlin, if it be necessary, and the exaction of a pecuniary indemnity; but he implores the people of Germany to beware of bringing down upon their country, in a moment of thoughtless military intoxication, a league between France, Russia, Italy, and Austria, which must end by obliterating not the unity only, but the very existence of the German nationality.

TUESDAY, *September* 15. — The forests about Paris fired by the French. Gen. Uhrich telegraphs despairingly from Strasburg. The Crown Prince passing to the south of Paris. Prussians within sight of Paris.

STRASBURG.

Gen. Uhrich sends this telegram to the Minister of War:

"Situation worse; bombardment without intermission; overwhelming (*foudrogante*) artillery. I shall hold out to the last. How could I cross the Rhine without a bridge and without a boat? Abandon this impracticable idea. An honorable but costly sortie this morning, and with no result except the respect forced on the enemy."

FRANCE BURNING.

PARIS, *September* 15 (*Evening*).—For miles about Paris the country is on fire, burning like an American prairie. The forests of Maisons, Montmorency, St. Prix, and the woods of St. Gratian, all in flames. Human ingenuity must have had a hard struggle with the rain, in trying to set the trees ablaze. But as science in our time is pretty nearly sold to the devil, the tears which Heaven wept are of no avail in saving the sylvan beauties of the environs of Paris.

The Prussians were to make their appearance around Paris to-day, and this is the fire which is to dart its flaming tongue and frighten them away. Alas! I fear the damage is more to France than to Prussia. The flames lick up many a pretty château, and the begrimed walls of many an elegant villa will be seen to-morrow.

The estimable M. de Villemessant, who for his health's sake now finds it expedient to remain in the country, and M. Emile de Girardin, who was thought to be at Florence with his friends, but who is in the flesh at Limoges with Ollivier and Plon Plon, must inevitably suffer from the vast conflagration to the north of Paris. But who can pity them if their sumptuous country-houses are licked up by the flames this moment raging round these abodes of luxury? They were the foremost men in supporting the bands organized by M. Pietri to cry *à Berlin* last July.

"The gods first make mad whom they would destroy."

INTO THE CRUCIBLE OF FIRE,

it would seem, will be thrown the château of the Princess Mathilde. The woods and copses of the St. Prix, St. Gratian, and Montmorency have been fired by means of petroleum and gas tar, which it would have been dangerous to have in a city that in a few days may be exposed to the terrific fire of a bombardment. Dealers in these combustibles received notice a few days back that they must surrender to the Committee of National Defence what they could not take to a seaport out of the reach of Prussia.

GRAVE-YARDS BURNING.

The firing of that part of Bondy visible from Montmartre at eleven o'clock last night was a still more awful spectacle. The trees were perfectly dry, so that oil and petroleum, which were spilt about in the brushwood, had no obstacle to contend with. Isolated columns of flame and clouds of smoke suddenly rose, and, before half an hour, were lost in one general blaze, which stood out like a fiery wall against the sky. In the light of this vast furnace, hideous objects were last night rendered visible on the Martyrs' Hill — yawning graves, dug to hold three or four hundred persons, reminded the lookers-on of the impending destruction of human life.

LOOKING FOR THE ENEMY.

PARIS, *September* 14. — Every hour the Prussians are expected to come within gun-shot of the forts. If we are to judge from appearances, the enthusiasm of the 200,000 National Guards and Gardes Mobile, reviewed yesterday by Gen. Trochu, indicates a determination on the part of these civic legions to defend the city resolutely. The line extended from the Place de la Bastille to the Triumphal Arch. The French engineers have destroyed the bridge at Creil — an hour's distance from Paris by ordinary train — and since late last night, direct communication with England by the Northern line has been stopped.

THE ENEMY IN SIGHT.

PARIS (*Evening*). — About 600 Prussians appear at Clamart (five miles south-west of Paris), within gunshot of the fort of Vanvres. (See map p. 340.)

THEY CREEP — THE STEALTHY RABBITS —

under cover of the woods on the heights. These woods join those of Versailles by those of Meudon, Sevres, and Viroflay, and were too green to be more than imperfectly burned. The advanced guard also signals Prussians at Creteil, within shot of the fort of Charonne, and two and a half miles from Charenton. Barricades were erected by the Mobiles there. The population is gone.

FRIDAY, *September* 16. — Count Bismarck replies to Jules Favre's circular to the crowned heads. He declines to "mix in the internal affairs of France," but says, "Prussia will demand the price of her mighty effort." Russia declines further mediation. French strength in Paris, 268,000 : Prussian, 350,000.

PARIS FORTS, GUNS, AND MEN.

The forts around Paris contain the following number of guns:

Vincennes	118
Mont Valérien	79
Aubervilliers	66
St. Denis	99
Bicêtre	60
Issy	64

Ivry	70
Nogent	55
Romainville	49
Rosny	56
Vanvres	45
Noisy-le-Sec	57
Montrouge	43
Total	861

In this estimate neither the guns of the *enceinte* (interior) nor of the redoubts of Joinville and Lagavelle are included. Heavy guns, having a range of five miles, have been placed in position on the heights of Montmartre. General Trochu has made good use of the short time he has been in power in the way of improving the fortifications of Paris. Every commanding spot in the environs has been crowned by a redoubt, all the ground near being cleared so as to give full play to the artillery of the defenders. A redoubt has been erected on the hill of Courbevoie, on the west of Paris. The strength of the *enceinte* has been much increased.

IMPREGNABILITY.

Large earthen demilunes have been erected outside each gate, and the covered way has been rendered a formidable impediment by means of pallisades. At the foot of the glacis is a road made of planks studded with nails three inches high. Beyond these again are three rows of wires two feet from the ground and three feet apart. These successive obstacles, which cannot be easily destroyed from a distance, will render it impossible to attempt an assault until at least the foot of the glacis has been reached by regular approaches. A second line of fortifications following the course of the circular railway is in course of construction.

NUMBER OF MEN.

The number of men under arms, within the line of the forts at Paris, on the 16th ult., is estimated as follows by the French:

Regular soldiers	80,000
Sailors and marines	20,000
Douaniers and gendarmes	20,000
National Guards — including the New battalions	120,000
Parisian Gardes Mobile	18,000
Provincial Mobiles	180,000
Total	438,000

To estimate the effective force, throw out as useless 10,000 sailors and marines, 10,000 gendarmes, 80,000 new battalion guards, 10,000 Parisian Gardes Mobiles, and 60,000 provincial Mobiles, and we have 268,000 men, which is about the fighting force. If the French have 438,000 men, why not march out and attack the Prussians, who have only 350,000 men?

BISMARCK'S CIRCULAR.

Count Von Bismarck to-day sends this circular letter to German representatives abroad, in reply to M. Jules Favre's circular of the sixth. (See p. 278.)

MEAUX, FRIDAY, *September* 16, 1870.— Your Excellency is familiar with the circular which M. Jules Favre has addressed to the foreign representatives of France in the name of the men at present holding power in Paris, and who call themselves "Le Gouvernement de la Défense Nationale."

I have learned simultaneously that M. Thiers has entered upon a confidential mission to the foreign courts, and I may presume that he will endeavor on the one side to create a belief in the love for peace of the present Parisian Government, and on the other side will request the intervention of the Neutral Powers in favor of a peace which shall deprive Germany of the fruits of her victories, and for the purpose of preventing every basis of peace which would make the next attack of France on Germany more difficult.

FRANCE NOT SINCERE.

We cannot believe in the sincerity of the desire of the present Parisian Government to make peace, so long as it continues by its language and its acts at home to excite the passions of the people.

DON'T CARE WHO GOVERNS FRANCE.

We are far from any inclination to mix in the internal affairs of France. It is immaterial to us what kind of a Government the French people shall formally establish for themselves. The Government of the Emperor Napoleon has hitherto been the only one recognized by us. Our conditions of peace, with whatever Government, legislating for the purpose we may have to negotiate with, are wholly independent of the question how or by whom the French nation is governed. They are prescribed to us by the nature of things, and by the law of self-defence against a violent and hostile neighbor.

WANTS STRASBURG AND METZ.

The unanimous voice of the Germanic Governments and the German people demands that Germany shall be protected by better boundaries than we have hitherto had, against the dangers and violence we have experienced from all French Governments for centuries. So long as France remains in possession of Strasburg and Metz, so long is its offensive strategically stronger than our defensive, so far as all South Germany and North Germany on the left bank of the Rhine are concerned. Strasburg in the possession of France is a gate wide open for attack on South Germany. In the hands of Germany, Strasburg and Metz obtain a defensive character.

FRANCE ALWAYS THE AGGRESSOR.

In more than twenty wars we have never been the aggressors on France; and we demand of the latter nothing else than our safety in our own land, so often threatened by it. France, on the other hand, will regard any peace that may be made now as an armistice only, and, in order to avenge the present defeat, will attack us in the same quarrelsome and wanton manner as this year, as soon as it feels strong enough in its own resources or in foreign alliances.

CRIPPLE FRANCE FOR LASTING PEACE.

In rendering it difficult for France, from whose initiative alone hitherto the disturbances of Europe have resulted, to resume the offensive, we at the same time act in the interest of Europe, which is that of peace.

GERMANY WANTS PEACE.

From Germany no disturbance of the European peace is to be feared. Although France had been trying to force the war upon us for four years, we, by our care, and by restraining the feelings of our national self-respect, so incessantly outraged by France, had prevented its occurrence.

FORTIFICATIONS AND TERRITORY.

We mean now for our future safety to demand the price of our mighty efforts. We shall demand only that which we must have for our defence. Nobody will be able to accuse us of want of moderation if we insist upon this just and equitable demand.

Your Excellency will make these views your own, and advocate them in discussions.

BISMARCK.

SATURDAY, *September* 17. — The Czar of Russia shows his personal sympathies, by bestowing the Cross of the Order of St. George on the Crown Prince of Saxony and on the Prince of Hesse. The fort of Vincennes is abandoned and destroyed by the French. The blockade of the North Sea raised. French scouts blow up the locks on the Marne, and stick the Prussian siege guns in the mud. Herr Carl Vogt, and Dr. Johann Jacobi, of Königsberg, lead German Republicans in opposing the acquisition of Alsace and Lorraine. Jacobi arrested.

PRUSSIA BECOMES VINDICTIVE.

This they say in Berlin to-day: The fact that Paris is successfully invested, and that all its communications are cut off, seems to admit of no doubt, and if it is to fall, as it must, it had better fall soon, and thus escape the dreadful fate of poor Strasburg. The King himself seems to look forward to an easy capture, because he has actually summoned some of his old companions in arms, who entered Paris with him in 1815, to come to headquarters, and share with him in the impending triumphal entry, himself at the head of the victorious and conquering hosts. Certainly he is having a surfeit of victory and glory, and there are those who begin to believe that it would have been better for the people of Germany not to have had so much success.

PLYAING THE RÔLE OF FRANCE.

They are showing signs of losing their better judgment and their sense of right and justice under it, and of assuming the very *rôle* which France has played so long, and which they themselves have so strongly and justly denounced.

"WHIP THE WORLD."

Germany can whip the world now. What need we care for others? Such is the universal cry. If a wise and a good man among them dares to raise his voice, and utter words of wisdom and caution, as did Johann Jacobi at Königsberg, the military power lays hold of him, and drowns his voice behind prison doors.

WEAK DESPOTISM.

The arrest of that unswerving and single-minded patriot, one of the few, if not the only, consistent public men in Germany, for no other crime than raising his voice for peace, for the Republic in France, and against doing violence to the people of Alsace and Lorraine, is an act unworthy of a great Government. Germany is to be united, but not to be free, it seems.

SUNDAY, *September* 18.—The Prussians appear on the heights of Villejuif and Sceaux, in the environs of Paris. General Vinoy attacks the Prussians at Creteil. The French retreat. Foreign Ministers, except Washburne, leave Paris. The Prussians "*feel*" Forts Ivry and Charenton. The *Liberté*, *Constitutionnel*, *Gazette de France*, and some other journals heretofore printed in Paris, are printed in Tours. The Corps Diplomatique arrive in Tours.

WHAT WAR HAS DONE.

THE COMIC SIDE.

The war has undermined a good many errors. Before Sedan the French looked down upon the Germans. They made fun of German art, German music, and German philosophy. If there was a mean thing in Paris, it was called German. When the band squeaked in *La Belle Hélène*, with what irony Calcas exclaimed, "*C'est musique Allemande.*" They spoke about and got to look upon the German nation as Southerners were taught to look upon Northerners, before our war destroyed certain popular fallacies. The "Yankee" was found, after all, to be the true man—the leader of American civilization. Frenchmen have been puffed up and self-deceived. If the superior civilization of Prussia shall capture Paris, it will be a good thing for the French nation. They will commence again. Their eyes will be opened. The Mahommedan says "Christian dog" so much, that he gets to believe it. A crusade now and then would let a little truth into that Dead Sea of Eastern error.

"A bas Bismarck" and "A Berlin" were easy to say. By and by the French got to believe them. It would be well if the French would believe their war songs too. The "Chant du Départ," for example, is a song in which kings are attacked, and not with sugar-plums. Take these lines:

"Tremblez, ennemis de la France,
Rois ivres de sang et d'orgueil;
Le peuple souverain s'avance:
Tyrans, descendez au cercueil."

Kings drunk with blood and pride are images not exactly to the taste or adapted to the purposes of the Emperor. The revolution and its songs are useful, when trimmed to the pattern of Imperial democracy, and thus the above lines do service now in the following disguise:

"Tremblez, ennemis de la France,
Tous, ivres de sang et d'orgueil;
Le peuple souverain s'avance:
Tombez, descendez au cercueil."

The Zouaves sang when they marched out:

"Bismarck, si tu continues,
De tous tes Prussiens n'en restera guère;
Bismarck, si tu continues,
De tous tes Prussiens n'en restera plus."

And this:

'Quand t'es Francaise par le cœur,
Voudrais-tu devenir Prussienne?
Si tu veux rester Alsacienne,
Aime-moi, je serai vainqueur!
Grâce à toi, piquante Alsacienne,
La Prusse, ma parôle d'honneur,
En verra d'un, drôl' de couleur!"

The "drôl' de couleur" is that sallow tint of fear which is known to Paris couturières as the Couleur Bismarck.

Alas! the poor Zouaves were almost all captured at Weisenburg and Woerth. *Turcos, Turcos, Turcos.* It was all Turcos before the war. Nobody says Turcos in Paris now. The *mitrailleuse* is almost dead too. The Turcos and *mitrailleuses* were to kill Prussia, but the German King looks down on poor Paris from the Imperial palace of *St. Cloud.* War has done this.

SUDDEN CHANGES.

It is hard to keep up with the sudden changes in Paris. Fifty persons were arrested one day for crying "*Vive la République!*" and sixty the very next day for crying "*Vive l'Empereur!*" One hour it is "up with the Imperial eagles," and the next the mob goes shouting, with a dreadful irony, "à bas la volaille"—"down with the *poultry.*"

The French do not know what they do want. They are children. The balloon fever set the city in a frenzy one day. It was so amusing that they forgot King William. Everybody wanted to ride. Even Gambetta, the Minister of the Interior, took a diplomatic balloon ride over the walls toward Tours. The *bourgeoisie* are too ignorant to care for results. Rather than fight for Alsace and Lorraine, they would receive back Napoleon from the Prussians, and look upon him as a saviour.

Ask a Frenchman what he thinks of Jules Favre's proclamation to the crowned heads, and he will say, "It is too long, and not to the point." The point should be all in a nutshell, thus:

"King William! You said you fought against a man and not against the people. The man is gone, and the people are ready to make a peace. If you refuse reasonable terms, you are declaring fresh war, in which the sympathies of Europe must also be distributed afresh."

ALL SAVE HONOR LOST!

M. Arthur de Boissieu, who, alluding to the famous despatch of Francis I.: "*Tout est perdu hors l'honneur!*" remarks that Napoleon III. at Sedan had lost everything which the other had saved at Pavia!

MONDAY, *September* 19. — The Prussian army reaches Paris on the north. The Crown Prince passes the Seine at Villeneuve St. Georges, eight miles south of Paris, marches to the south of the city, and defeats three divisions of French under General Vinoy, near Sceaux. Immense Republican meeting in London, to express sympathy with France. Bismarck talks to Mr. Malet about having Metz.

PARIS.

THE BATTLE OF THE 19TH.

LOUIS BLANC WRITES:

"PARIS, 19th.

"There has been fighting to-day all around Paris, with alternations of success and disadvantage. The city is full of spirit, and yet calm. The National Guard has shown itself resolute, and the Garde Mobile, coming from all parts of the country, displays that careless gayety so characteristic of the French.

"We are sad, yet hopeful. Do not suppose that we expect to escape the consequences of a war into which we have been dragged in spite of ourselves. We desire peace on equitable and honorable conditions; if we cannot have that, we are ready to accept war to the knife."

KING WILLIAM TELEGRAPHS.

TO THE QUEEN:

The French abandoned their position near Pierrefitte, north of Fort St. Denis. At the same time the Prusso-Bavarian Corps, crossing the Seine near Villeneuve, attacked three divisions under the command of General Vinoy, on the heights of Sceaux, and captured seven guns and many men. Fritz directed the movements. The weather is superb.

WILLIAM.

(See map p. 340)

ACCOUNT OF THE GREAT SORTIE.

This most important battle of the 19th took place upon the southern side of Paris. Here General Ducrot, who escaped from Sedan, with 50,000 men fought the Crown Prince with about the same number. The heights of Clamart and Meudon were the scene of the engagement. (*See map, 25th Sept.*) The weak point of Paris is in front of these two villages, and they were for days the objective point of a besieging army.

THE MISTAKE OF FRANCE

was in first permitting the Prussians to occupy these locations. Not only this, but the Marne and Seine should also have been defended. Once with Krupp's guns planted behind earthworks at Clamart, *and the brickwork of Issy and Vanvres will fall like the walls of Sumpter*, and then the long-range guns will carry to *Notre Dame*. Then falls Paris. What wonder that Ducrot made a heroic effort? But before Clamart came the Marne and Seine. History will ask, "Why were not they defended before?"

It was along the Seine that former besieging armies met their severest trials, and more than one army has been nearly decimated in crossing those two rivers. But these positions were given up without a struggle, and the enemy made the passage of the Seine without opposition. Once in possession of the country about Juvisy, the way was open to the very forts around Paris, and no engagement took place until the redoubt of Châtillon was reached. This work was unfinished and only partially mounted, for the guns were to have been taken out two days ago, had not the bad weather stopped the work. As it was, the guns were spiked and left.

General Trochu explains the abandoning of these positions to the fact that the disasters of Woerth and Sedan had demoralized the French army to such an extent that it could only be trusted behind breastworks. For this reason, Gen. Trochu reluctantly gave up the defence of the Seine, and fell back to a point within supporting distance of the forts.

THE BATTLE FOR THE LOST GROUND.

At the very last moment Gen. Ducrot arrived, having escaped from the capitulation of Sedan. Gen. Trochu thought that if the troops would follow any leader, it would be one fresh from the smell of powder. It was then too late to defend the river, but Gen. Ducrot thought that he could hold Châtillon and the wood of Meudon, at least for some days. A reconnoissance, made on the evening of the 18th, showed that the enemy had already entered the wood, and while one portion of his force was pushing on toward Versailles, another had turned face toward Clamart. Troops were being rapidly pushed across the Seine, occupying positions near Juvisy, or were as far up as Villejuif, and twenty thousand were already sheltered in the wood beyond Châtillon. Gen. Ducrot decided to attack them on the morning of the 19th. At five o'clock the fire was opened. Before a Prussian was seen, the French began to fire into the wood with small arms, and this fire was kept up briskly as the force advanced, but without bringing a response. Presently a wreath of smoke rose among the trees, and a well-directed volley was poured into the advancing force. The cavalry immediately turned, and, as it was forced to do, broke through the infantry, leaving a bad impression upon the fresh troops. At this time Gen. Vinoy occupied the extreme left resting upon Fort Bicêtre, his force stretching along the plateau in front of Villejuif and his right resting upon Gen. Ducrot's left. The Second Zouaves was on the left of Ducrot's division, a regiment greatly cut up in the battles with MacMahon, and reorganized by incorporating young men from the city. The enemy, still under cover of the wood, sent another volley into this regiment, throwing it into the greatest confusion, and another volley caused a complete panic. The Zouaves broke, and in an utter rout, without having seen the head of a single Prussian, and in a terror-stricken panic, fled to the city. The panic also spread to some regiments near, and, in utter confusion, some fifteen thousand men fled to the forts, to announce that all was lost, and to say that the Prussians were close upon them. It was a case of pure fright, and in vain the chagrined officers tried to rally their men. Only a score or two responded, and the retreat was sounded. This was taken up by other regiments, and Gen. Ducrot, seeing his force leaving the field, was forced to order a retreat behind the guns of the redoubt. For the first time the enemy began to move, and, seeing that he was being flanked, the guns of the redoubt were spiked, and left to fall into the hands of the Prussians. The General and his staff, or the few men that remained of it, were the last to leave Châtillon.

THE FRENCH BULL RUN.

Meantime the fugitives had reached the city, and, throwing the forts into a state of alarm, the draw-bridges were raised and the men put in position to repel an assault; but as time went on there was a large collection of fugitives without, and, as no enemy appeared behind them, the bridges were again lowered. Instead of arresting these men upon the spot, and of sending them back under guard to find their arms, they were turned loose into the city, to spread consternation there by their tales of disaster and defeat. "We entered the fight this morning 116 strong," said a frightened Zouave, "and we eight are all who came out alive. We are the saved." Saved by their legs, as were all the rest, save two, that being the sum of their casualties.

It was the old story of Bull Run repeated. Did not the author meet a few straggling Ellsworth Zouaves at Alexandria, after Bull Run, who had the same tale? "We are all that are left of the Zouaves," they said sadly. Again at Fort Runyon, at the end of Long Bridge, were a hundred more. "The rest are all dead," they sighed. In Washington were still a few hundred more of the survivors, while a few weeks afterwards the regiment rendezvoused in New York 900 strong! *Brave Zouaves!*

THE BLAME.

But these raw French soldiers were not wholly at fault. Doubtless the older Zouaves were demoralized by the terrific battles before Sedan, and the new recruits had never before been under fire. Fortunately for all, the panic was stopped for a time by a brigade of Breton Mobiles, who could not be induced to fly before they had seen the enemy, and it was with some difficulty at last that their officers got these young men away, when to fight longer would have been useless. But the fact soon became apparent that an overwhelming force was massing for an attack. From the first the French officers have been surprised by the rapid marches of the Prussians, and by the rapidity of their concentrations. Trusting to the reports of the evening before, Gen. Ducrot still believed that he had had to do with a force of the enemy twenty thousand strong, and that he had the advantage of numbers; but during the night the Prussians had been largely reinforced from the corps of Gen. Vogel Von Falckenstein, which had crossed the Seine at Villeneuve St. Georges, and made a forced march to the wood of Meudon. It is probable that there were fifty thousand men before Gen. Ducrot, and that 25,000 were engaged.

EXCITEMENT IN THE CITY.

After these engagements the city was thrown into a great state of excitement by the *fuyards* from the army, who dispersed through the streets relating their false romances. Large groups of citizens surrounded these men, and listened with eager interest to their tales, while, in certain quarters already designated, real panics were caused. As the fugitives grew more numerous, the public began to understand the true state of the case, and a feeling of indignation arose. Some men were caught throwing their cartridges into the Seine. The stories told by these men were numerous, and far from ingenious. Some claimed to be the sole survivors of their regiments. Others had used all their cartridges, but a far greater number put themselves upon a high Republican sentiment, and said that their officers were traitors, sold to the King of Prussia, and whole regiments were about to be given up when the treason was found out. This cry drew immediate sympathy, and for a time the crowd cried, " Death to all Bonapartists," and was loud in accusing of treason every man who had ever served the Empire. Later in the evening, Gen. Ducrot's force entered the city, and the truth was known. Orders were given to arrest the fugitives, and the National Guard went about the task. Gen. Trochu issued an order, threatening the punishment of death to any soldier who throws down his arms in the face of the enemy. The same night countercharges were made, and the report spread that the old Zouaves, who had fought under the Empire, had really sold themselves to the enemy.

RESULTS.

The results of the day show that Gen. Trochu was right in his estimate of his men, for they would not stand against the enemy in the field. The disgrace of the Zouaves has had a good effect, however, and next time men will be more careful how they leave the field before the enemy come in sight. The position captured by the Prussians at Châtillon is a very important one, and one which they will use to great advantage as soon as heavy guns can be mounted upon the redoubt.

THE STATUS OF PARIS TO-DAY.

With the defeat of the French at Châtillon, and the occupation of the redoubt there, the Prussians gained a very important point. They now hold a height which dominates Fort Vanvres, and at a distance of about (I believe) 3800 yards. From that point Fort Vanvres can be reduced in a few hours. That battery is also only three and a half English miles from Vaugirard, and fire can not only be opened upon the main fortifications, but upon the city itself. Supposing that the troops are driven from Fort Vanvres, these guns can then be pushed forward, and an effectual fire opened upon the main works. No troops can be kept behind a mass of stones while these terrible projectiles are crashing against them; but, as for the assault, when the breech is made everything depends upon the spirit of the soldiers within the walls. As for the people, they can do nothing better than to give an example of coolness and bravery, for it may as well be acknowledged at once, that, before organized troops, an armed mob could render but little service, if it did not really embarrass the defence.

THE PRUSSIAN ENTRY.

Paris walls are made of stone and mortar. They cannot stand the fire from an earthwork. Delhi in India was breeched with field howitzers in two hours. Sumpter fell with one-half the firing which it took to reduce Fort Fisher. America has demonstrated that no reliance is to be put in stone and mortar. Stone and mortar fortifications will die with the siege of Paris. There is a belief in Paris that the Prussians will enter the city *at their first serious attempt.* Gen. Trochu issues the following order relative to the fight of to-day (19th), and prepares the army against future panics:

To the National Guard, the Garde Mobile, and the Troops in Garrison at Paris.

In the combat of yesterday, which lasted nearly the whole day, and in which our artillery, whose firmness cannot be too highly praised, has inflicted enormous losses on the enemy, some incidents have occurred which it is necessary, in the interest of the great cause which we defend in common, should be communicated to you.

An unjustifiable panic, which the efforts of an excellent chief of the corps and of his officers were unable to prevent, seized the regiment of Zouaves which held our right wing. From the commencement of the action the most part of the soldiers were thrown into disorder, producing there the greatest alarm.

In order to excuse their conduct, these cowards have declared that they were being led to certain destruction, although their effective was intact, and they were without wounds; that they wanted cartouches, although they had not used those with which they were supplied. I have ascertained myself, from what they still have; that they had been betrayed by their chiefs, etc., etc. The truth is, that these unworthy fellows have compromised an engagement, which, notwithstanding this panic, has produced considerable results due to others, soldiers of the infantry joined to them.

Already the misfortunes which have happened to us in the commencement of the war have caused to flow into Paris undisciplined and demoralized soldiers, who produce inquietude and trouble, and escape, through circumstances, the authority of their chiefs and all attempts at repression.

I am firmly resolved to put an end to such grave disorders. I command all the defenders of Paris to seize all men who, being regular soldiers or belonging to the Garde

Mobile, are rolling about the town in a state of drunkenness, thus bringing scandal and dishonor upon the uniform they wear.

The soldiers or Gardes Mobiles thus arrested will be conducted to the headquarters of the place — 7 Place Vendôme — the inhabitants arrested to the Prefecture of Police. They will afterwards be brought before a council of war, which, sitting *en permanence*, will adjudge the rigorous application of martial law.

Article 213 prescribes the punishment of death to every soldier who abandons his post in presence of the enemy or of armed rebels.

Article 218 prescribes the punishment of death, with military degradation, to all soldiers who refuse to obey when commanded to march upon the enemy.

Article 250 prescribes the punishment of death, with military degradation, to all who pillage food, merchandise, or effects, by soldiers in bands, either with arms or by open force, or with violence towards the person.

Article 253 prescribes the punishment of death, with military degradation, to all soldiers who destroy the means of defence, supplies of arms, victuals, or munitions of war, etc., etc.

It is as much the duty of the Government to defend Paris, which is just being subjected to siege, as it is to maintain order. By the present arrangements, it associates in the effort all men of heart and will, of which the number is great in the city.

The President of Government, Governor of Paris, GENERAL TROCHU.

Paris, September 20.

THE REPUBLIC IN LONDON.

LONDON, *September* 19. — The democratic demonstration of the people of London to-night, in Trafalgar Square, is one of the greatest popular assemblages ever seen in the British capital. For nearly two hours the streets leading to Clerkenwell, Bethnal Green, and Holborn were alive with the successive processions of the workingmen's societies, and the democratic associations of the metropolis.

The great wave that swept away the empire of France has reached England, and the throne of Queen Victoria totters to its fall.

In that great quadrangle at the base of Nelson's column are 50,000 Republicans. Trafalgar Square is filled with Englishmen carrying the flags of republican France and republican America, and the white flag of the British republic that is to come, and shouting, as Englishmen and Americans only can shout, for "Liberty, Equality, and Fraternity;" for the French republic that is, and for the British republic that is to be.

The meeting was called to sustain the new Republic of France. So eager were the people to respond to the notices of the meeting that had been issued, that although the proceedings were announced to commence at seven o'clock, the terrace in front of the National Gallery, and between that building and Nelson's Pillar, was filled at six o'clock, and when the processions from different parts of the city arrived, the assemblage became immense. These processions carried with them the American flag, the French tricolor, and the British flag, with the union down and draped in crape. Along their lines, also, were seen liberty-caps, borne on the ends of spears, and, most significant of all, a pure white flag, with the word

"REPUBLIC"

emblazoned in gold letters on its folds.

DIPLOMACY.

Mr. Malet, Second English Secretary of Legation, reports to Lord Granville the following conversation with Bismarck at the King's headquarters:

Malet asked "for France a Prussian ultimatum:"

"We must have Metz and Strasburg," said Bismarck.

"Dismantled?" asked Malet.

"No!" replied Bismarck, "stronger than ever."

"Then, suppose the French Government finds your terms impossible?"

"We shall invest and starve Paris; if that does not succeed, we shall try sharper means."

"Would you bombard the city?"

"Certainly; and burn it, if forced. The necessity is sad, but how is it to be escaped?"

Bismarck's observations about Gladstone and Granville, and their timid message-carrying, were the reverse of respectful, and he did not hesitate to let it be seen that he cared nothing for the efforts of outsiders, and was resolved to settle all questions with France alone.

MOTLEY'S OPINION.

Mr. Motley says:

"The statement that Prussia refuses to treat, except with the Regency, and intends to reinstate Napoleon as Emperor of France, is false. Prussia objects to recognizing the present Government, not because of the proclamation of the Republic, but on the ground that it is unauthorized, unstable, and incapable of giving lasting guarantees."

TUESDAY, *Sept.* 20. — The Prussian army arrives at Versailles. The Republic proclaims "not an inch of territory" to Prussia. The Italian army enters Rome. General R. Cadorna receives from General Kanzler the surrender of the Papal forces. Jules Favre is received by King William in Rothschild's château at Ferrières. Prussian forces skirmish toward Fontainebleau, and press the fortifications of Paris — Forts Ivry and Charenton.

PROCLAMATION OF THE REPUBLIC.

This important proclamation announcing the policy of France appears to-day:

TO THE FRENCH PEOPLE.

A report has been in circulation that the Government of the National Defence thinks of abandoning the policy for the carrying out of which it has been placed in the post of honor and of peril.

This policy may be summed up in these words:

Not an inch of our territory, not a stone of our fortresses. The Government will maintain this policy to the end.

Given at the Hôtel de Ville, the 20th of September, 1870.

GENERAL TROCHU,
EMMANUEL ARAGO,
JULES FAVRE,

JULES FERRY,
GAMBETTA,
GARNIER-PAGES,
PÉLLETAN,
ERNEST PICARD,
ROCHEFORT,
JULES SIMON,
The MINISTER of WAR, General LEFLO;
The MINISTER of AGRICULTURE and COMMERCE, M. MAGNIN;
The MINISTER of PUBLIC WORKS, M. DORIAN.

THE MILITARY STATUS.

The influx of troops into France still continues. 650,000 men are already on French soil. The Crown Prince of Saxony on the north, and of Prussia on the south side of Paris, hold the city in so tight a grip, that balloons and carrier-pigeons are the sole means of communication with the outer world.

Between Paris the Duke of Mecklenburg-Schwerin commands a large force for the reduction of Toul and Soissons.

To the southeast, through the Gap of Belfort, 65,000 Prussians and Bavarians are streaming into France, threatening Lyons and Dijon.

Prince Albert is moving towards Orleans on the south, and a large Prussian force threatens Rouen on the north.

All telegraphic communication with Paris has ceased. The Prussians have crossed the Seine at Choisy, near the confluence of the Marne, and advanced toward Forts Ivry and Châtillon, where skirmishes took place without serious loss on either side.

They now occupy Clamart, Meudon, Villeneuve, and Choisy-le-Roi and Sceaux. The French have constructed earthworks near St. Denis and Clamart.

A Prussian force has entered Fontainebleau, and made a requisition for 150,000 francs.

THE OCCUPATION OF VERSAILLES.

This morning an aide-de-camp of General Von Kirchbach, of the Fifth Corps (army Crown Prince), followed by a single cavalier, presented himself before the municipal authorities of Versailles. The aide-de-camp demanded a place for Prussian wounded, and the keys of the stores for fodder. He then returned to General Kirchbach for consultation. At eleven A.M. there arrived a captain of engineers, aide-de-camp also to

General Kirchbach. Two National Guards conducted him to the municipality to receive the surrender of the city.

Fighting was now going on between General Vinoy and the Prussians a little way to the right, beyond Sceaux, to the forest of Meudon. M. Ranraud, the Mayor of Versailles, mounted a stone before the gate of the Avenue of Paris, and read the whole text of the capitulation, signed by himself and the delegate of General Von Kirchbach:

1st. All property and every person will be respected, as well as all monuments and works of art.

2d. The confederates shall occupy all the barracks with their soldiers, but the inhabitants must lodge the officers, and in case the barracks are insufficient, the soldiers also.

3d. The National Guards will remain armed, and in the common interest will be charged with the duties of police inside the town, and in all the posts there situated. Only the confederates will occupy, as they require, the gates of the barriers.

4th. There shall be no contribution in money, but the town must furnish, at the market price, all that will be necessary to the armies passing through, as well as to those stationed in Versailles.

5th. The same day the gates of the city shall be opened to the passage of the Fifth Corps.

At a quarter past twelve, the Fifth Corps commences marching through Versailles, lasting until five o'clock in the evening. General Kirchbach is installed at the Hôtel des Reservoirs. The artillery has bivouacked on the Place d'Armes, in the Barracks of the Avenue de Paris, and others have gone to the Barracks of Saint Martin.

A CROWD OF ZOUAVE PRISONERS,

captured in the fight of yesterday, defile with the rest. The crowd silently uncovered as they passed; a few, however, raised the cry "Vive la France!" Another little incident — the first aide-de-camp, with the flag of truce, of which I have already spoken, was saluted as he passed along the Rue des Chantiers by an individual who said to him: "Vive la France!" The officer replied: "My friend, it is 'Vive la paix!' that you ought to cry." As soon as the great defile had passed, the requisitions began; twenty-six cattle were delivered by the town, ten "pieces of wine," etc., and all the forage of the war, worth 300,000 francs, which the military administration wished to burn, and which the town bought in view of actual events.

KING WILLIAM'S HEADQUARTERS

will be moved from Ferrières to Versailles, with his master, Bismarck. We say his master, as it would have been said in the past that Louis XIII. reigned under Richelieu. The Prussian army has tried to make a triumphal entry into the chief place of Seine et Oise, in full dress, playing the national German airs, as if for a parade. The Prussians are orderly. They are gotten up for a grand review, with their mustaches waxed and cleanly shaved faces.

VERSAILLES.

The city of Versailles is fourteen miles from Paris, and is the most charming spot in France. The author spent two days in the château and about the grounds in 1867. It was the fête day of Napoleon III. The magnificent fountains were illuminated, and all Paris was out to see the gorgeous spectacle. To call Wilhelmshöhe the Versailles of Germany, is to make the Emperor's residence a place of fairy enchantment.

THE OCCUPATION OF ROME.

The occupation of Rome by the Italian troops of Victor Emanuel, and the surrender of the forces of Pope Pio IX., is a part of the present war. It was absence of French troops which made the occupation possible. For years, Napoleon III. has bolstered up the Pope against the people of Italy. The author, who was a guest at the American College in Rome in 1867, can testify to the personal hatred of the Italian people to Pope Pio IX. The Church got to be a despotism — the Pope temporal King. Like Napoleon, he is in his chair days, old and imbecile. Infallibility is the result of religious despotism and imbecility.

THE ATTACK.

At five o'clock the Italian forces of General Cadorna opened the attack. The Pope had about 15,000 soldiers, mostly pardoned convicts and foreigners hired to do his fighting.

An Italian battery was aimed to open a breach on the right side of Porta Pia. General Ferrero's artillery assaulted Porta del Popolo (one of the principal gates of Rome), and Gen. Angelini, who had come from Naples only a few hours before, was opening breaches and doing hard work near St. Giovanni and St. Lorenzo.

The fire had been going for several hours, and long columns of black smoke rose in the blue sky. The breach was half effected, when in the rear it was discovered that a house belonging to the Bonapartes had taken fire.

ZOUAVE BAD FAITH.

At nine precisely, a bomb-shell fell on the roof of the St. Agnese Church, smashed the ceiling, and fell into the church. An order was immediately given to several soldiers to mount to the top of the tower, and hoist the white flag of the Geneva Convention. Several wounded men had already been brought in. At half-past ten a strong fire of musketry was heard.

The musketry fire ceased later, and the Pontifical Zouaves hoisted a white flag. The thirty-fifth battalion of Bersaglieri (sharpshooters) mounted the barricade, when the rascally Zouaves fired again, killing on the spot Signor Patelieri, the major of the battalion. A feeling of furious indignation seized every Italian soldier. Gen. Caseny, with his wounded arm, and his Staff, marched in front, sword in hand, to the barricade. The Fortieth and Forty-first Regiments of infantry followed. The first officer who advanced was Signor Valuziari, who had been exiled from Rome for eleven years, and was now rejoicing to see the place of his nativity again. Just as he reached the top of the barricade, he fell dead on the ground, struck by a bullet in the forehead.

ROME SURRENDERS TO ITALY.

The soldiers mount the barricade with gayety and laughter. The colonel of the regiment rides to the very top of the barricade, appears to look proudly on his soldiers, and to care little for the bullets whistling about him. The troops have occupied the gates, the Papal artillery surrenders, and firing ceases. On the left there is the tramp of horses, and a long row of carriages in splendid livery appears. This is the Diplomatic Corps, going in grand procession to the headquarters of Gen. Cadorna, to treat for capitulation. The barricade is strewn with wounded, and their comrades seize the opportunity to place them on litters and convey them to the hospital. There is much bloodshed, and the shrieks of the sufferers are appalling. Porta Pia is in ruins, and covered with mattresses which had been used as breastworks, and were now on fire. But hundreds of exiles, with tears of joy in their eyes, were happy in the prospect of entering again their native city.

ZOUAVES SURRENDER.

At the Piazza del Coeli, the Italians received the surrender of the Zouaves, and proceeded to the Piazza Colonna. The enthusiasm of their reception at this point was astonishing. Old men ran about with tears in their eyes, waving their hats and their handkerchiefs. Windows were filled with ladies waving tricolor flags and ribbons. The air was filled with cries of exultation. And now the *squadriglieri*, for fear of being massacred by the people, had intrenched themselves in the square of the capitol. They had made a barricade of mattresses, and had posted two pieces of artillery against the esplanade of the Piazza del Coeli. The bottom of the esplanade was occupied by *bersaglieri*, and the *squadriglieri* fired three times on them, but doing no harm. A regiment of infantry arriving on the square by back streets, had surprised the *squadriglieri*, and had made them all prisoners.

ENTHUSIASM OF THE ROMANS.

The General commanding was actually besieged by men, women, and children kissing his hands and the very legs of his horse, and crying, "Long live our liberators!" About fifty men ran up the staircase of the capitol, broke open the doors, ascended the towers, and hoisted the Italian flag. The event foretold by Cavour, and which had influenced every act of the Italian people for eleven years, was now fulfilled. Bells pealed. The military band played the Royal march. Thousands of people shouted, "Long live Victor Emanuel."

AN ILLUMINATION.

At nine P.M. the streets were brilliantly illuminated and crowded with people. Bands of 200 or 300 persons with tricolor flags and torchlights paraded the streets. Every Roman has one of the bersaglieri by the arm; the women beg the feathers of their hats, and kiss them. Old men and women are seen embracing the soldiers of Italy, holding them tight by the waist, and crying, "Don't leave us." The Corso looks like a fairy scene, with thousands of colored lamps, and houses covered with flags. Bengal fires illuminated the stately Coliseum, and voices of men and women cried vivas in the midst of the amphitheatre.

A PROCLAMATION TO THE ROMANS.

The following proclamation was posted up throughout the city:

"*Romans!* The excellence of our right and the valor of our arms have in a few hours brought me among you to restore to you liberty. Now your destinies, those of the nation itself, lie in your own hands. Strong by your sufferings, Italy will at least have the glory of solving that great problem which has been so terrible a burden to modern society. Thanks, Romans, also, in the name of the army, for the heartfelt reception you have given us! Continue to preserve, as you did to this day, public order, because without it there is no liberty possible. Romans! the morning of the 20th September, 1870, makes a memorable epoch in history. Rome is again restored, to be now and forever the great capital of a great nation. Long live the King! Long live Italy! R. CADORNA."

Gen. Cadorna addressed to the army an order of the day, in which he expresses his high satisfaction for their conduct during the attack.

TERMS OF THE SURRENDER.

Capitulation for the Surrender of the City of Rome, stipulated between the Commanding General of the Troops of His Majesty the King of Italy, and the Commanding General of the Papal Troops, respectively represented by the undersigned:

VILLA ALBANI, Sept. 20, 1870.

First: The City of Rome, except that part which is limited to the southern part of the walls of the Sante Spirito, and comprehends Mount Vatican and the Castle of St. Angelo, forming the so-called Leonine City, its complete armament, flags, arms, ammunition, and stores. All the material belonging to the Government shall be consigned to the troops of His Majesty the King of Italy.

Second: All the garrison of the city shall depart, receiving the honors of war, with flags, arms, and baggage. After the honors shall have been rendered to them, they will lay down flags and arms. The officers shall have a right to carry with them their swords, horses, and anything belonging to them. The foreign troops shall leave first; the others will follow, in the order of battle, with the left in front. The garrison will leave to-morrow morning at seven.

Third: The foreign troops shall be disbanded, and immediately sent back to their respective countries. They will leave to-morrow by railway. The Government has the right of taking into consideration the rights of pension which they might have stipulated with the Papal Government.

Fourth: The Roman troops will be formed at a depot without arms. The Government will take into consideration their claims as to their future situation.

Fifth: The troops will be forwarded to-morrow to Civita Vecchia.

Sixth: A mixed commission will be appointed, formed of an officer of artillery, one of the engineers, and a functionary of the Administration. The Commission will receive the consignment referred to in the fixed article for the City of Rome.

F. RANOLTA, Chief of Staff, Papal Army.
F. D. PRINCIANO, Chief of Staff, Italian Army.
F. CADORNA, General Commanding Italian Army.

Seen, approved, and ratified by the General commanding Rome. KANZLER.

A TOUCHING SCENE.

The men who were wounded the other day were brought into the city and carried to the hospital of San Giovanni. They were literally covered over with flowers, and it was with the greatest difficulty that the ambulances could advance, so great was the crowd. The people were shouting as loud as they possibly could, but when some one reminded them that their cries would do the wounded men harm rather than good, perfect silence ensued in an instant, and all *waved their hats and handkerchiefs without uttering a word.* The losses of the army are about 200 killed and wounded. Before signing the capitulation, Gen. Cadorna asked Gen. Kanzler whether he believed that the 200 men left with the Pope would really suffice to keep order. Gen. Kanzler's answer was so positive, that the terms were agreed to without any other observation.

RECEPTION OF THE LIBERATORS.

In the morning, Gen. Cadorna and his staff entered the city by the Porta Pia. The balconies bent under the weight of so many people. The very houses seemed to move, for the banners and the thousands of waving handkerchiefs hid every inch of wall and roof from sight. The soldiers seemed delighted at the universal ovation. As they passed an imposing structure, the soldiers nearest the crowd asked, in a hurry, "What's that?" "Colonna Trajana," was the answer, and that name was repeated by each soldier with an air of admiration and astonishment. Gen. Cadorna alighted at the Piazza Colonna. He witnessed from the balcony the defile of the whole division, and then retired, but the cheers of the thousands who filled the square compelled him to show himself to the people. Waving his handkerchief, he cried:

"LONG LIVE ROME, THE CAPITAL OF ITALY."

It was the first time that such words had been pronounced by a person of official station, and their reception by the people was indescribable.

THE PAPAL PRISONERS.

They were sixteen thousand in number, eight thousand of them good soldiers, the other eight thousand worthless. The conduct of the men was disgusting. Many of the Zouaves were quite drunk; the officers had cigars in their mouths, and as they passed Gen. Cadorna's horse, they blew smoke at him. The General was so indignant, that he called to one of them, and said, "We render you the honors of arms, though you do not deserve it; but it is your duty to bow to a superior. Take off your hat, sir!" As the French of the Legion of Antibes passed by, they looked up to the General with a provoking air, and shouted, "*A vous revoir*, villains!" "Italians, *a bientôt!*" and similar cries.

POPULAR DEMONSTRATION AGAINST THE POPE.

After the Papal troops had left the Leonine city, in a few minutes the space in front of the Vatican was full of people waving tricolored cockades, who, looking up toward the Papal residence, began hissing and howling in a frightful manner.

THE POPE BECAME ALARMED,

and sent immediately for Count Arnim. On the entrance of the Prussian Minister, the Pope came forward and begged that he would go at once to Gen. Cadorna, and ask him to send some troops to reëstablish order. The Pope, seeing no way to escape, wrote an autograph letter to Gen. Cadorna, asking him to send the Italian soldiers to protect him from the populace. Gen. Cadorna telegraphed to Florence for instructions, and the Pope's demand was complied with.

A CONTRAST.

Can a state of things last long, in which liberty and civilization are divided from ignorance and despotism only by a river, so that while men enjoy on this side all the blessings coming from an enlightened government, on the other side men as patriotic as they must serve and suffer under Papal rule; so that the soldiers of King Victor Emanuel in the morning defend Italian independence and in the evening Papal tyranny?

ROYAL HONORS ACCORDED TO THE POPE.

The Pope desiring to drive through the city, Cadorna gave orders that he should have the same honors paid to him as to the King, and the cardinals the same as those given to princes of the royal blood.

PEACE NEGOTIATIONS FAIL.

WEDNESDAY, *Sept.* 21.—Jules Favre returns to Paris from his consultation with Bismarck, and reports that the King of Prussia "*requires the cession of Alsace and Lorraine, and immediate possession of Metz, Strasburg, and Mont Valérien.*"

M. Favre concedes on the part of France "*an indemnity reimbursing Prussia for the cost of the war, the dismantling of Metz and Strasburg and other fortifications,* BUT NOT ONE INCH OF FRENCH TERRITORY."

The French Ministry proclaims war to the last extremity, and says, "Rather than give up French territory, Paris will bury herself beneath her own ruins."

Bismarck and Favre have a diplomatic dispute, and a question of veracity arises. The Crown Prince at Versailles.

NEGOTIATIONS FOR PEACE.

FAVRE AND BISMARCK MEET AND DISAGREE.

Lord Granville sought the interview between M. Favre, the Vice-President of the Republic, and Minister of Foreign Affairs, and Count Von Bismarck, to prevent further bloodshed. Bismarck, believing France was crushed, asked exorbitant demands. Had his demands been within reason, France would have accepted them, and there would have been peace in Europe to-day. If France made the war, the verdict of humanity is, that *Prussia has continued it.* History will dwell upon the failure of M. Favre's mission as a lamentable mistake in diplomacy, and from yesterday the burden of war will be upon the shoulders of Prussia.

Prussia may gain territory by a prolongation of the war, but at what a cost! The thirst of Bismarck is for territory — territory. As yet, no European nation has dared to criticise this desire. England is timid, Austria is powerless, and Russia is busy with her thoughts on Turkey and her eyes on the Bosphorus.

The first interview between Favre and Bismarck occurred on the 10th of September at Rheims, which is thus described by M. Favre in his report to his colleagues in Paris:

France having declared war in the beginning, our desire for peace did not look plain to the world. Our situation was untenable. It permitted the enemy to lay upon us the responsibility of continuing the struggle; it condemned us to ascertain her intentions for ourselves; it was necessary to escape from the position. I believed myself bound to obey an imperious necessity. One time I told you of the agitation of my mind, and I said that it would be at rest only when I had done everything that was possible for man to do to bring this horrible war to an honorable conclusion. Recalling the conversation which arose from this beginning, I feared some objections, and I was decided. I wished, in meeting M. de Bismarck, to be free from every engagement, in order to have the privilege of not making any. I make these acknowledgments sincerely. I make them to the country, in order to release you from a responsibility which I alone assume. If my mission be a mistake, I alone must bear the penalty.

THE JOURNEY TO THE PRUSSIAN HEADQUARTERS.

We moved toward the enemy by the Porte de Charenton. I suppress all the details of this unhappy journey, which was full of interest, but the incidents of which would not be in their place in this report. Conducted to Villeneuve-Saint-Georges, where was the General-in-Chief commanding the Sixth Corps, I learned rather late in the afternoon that the headquarters were at Meaux. The General proposed to me to send an officer as bearer of the following letter, which I had prepared for transmission to M. de Bismarck:

M. LE COMTE — I have always believed, that, before undertaking serious hostilities under the walls of Paris, it were possible that an honorable arrangement could be attempted. The person who had the honor of waiting on your Excellency two days ago has made me gather from his words the expression on your part of a similar desire. I have come to the *avant-postes* to put myself at the disposition of your Excellency. I expect you will let me know how and where I can have the honor of conferring with you for a few moments.— I have, etc.

JULES FAVRE.

We were separated by a distance of forty-eight kilometres. The next morning, at six o'clock, I received a reply of which this is a copy:

I have not received the letter your Excellency has had the goodness to write to me, and it will give me the greatest pleasure if you will come to see me to-morrow here at Meaux. Prince Biron, the bearer of this, will see that your Excellency is conducted across our lines.—I have, etc.

DE BISMARCK.

At nine o'clock the escort was ready, and I left with it. When we arrived near Meaux, about three in the afternoon, I was stopped by an aide-de-camp, who told me that Count Bismarck had left Meaux with the king, to go to Ferrières for the night. I went back, and proceeded to a farm which had been pillaged, as were all the houses which I passed on my route. At the end of an hour M. de Bismarck joined me. It was difficult for us to consult in such a place. One habitation — the Château de la Haute Maison, belonging to the Count de Rillac — was in the vicinity, and we proceeded thither. Our conversation took place in a saloon, in which *débris* of all sorts was lying about.

THE DIPLOMATIC TALK.

I at once specified the object of my mission. Having made him acquainted, by my circular [*see Sept.* 6. — p. 278], with the intentions of the French Government, I wished to know those of the Prussian Minister. It seemed to me inexcusable that two nations should, without previous explanations, continue a terrible war, which would inflict deep suffering on the conquerors, notwithstanding the advantages they had gained. *Caused by the power of one man*, this war had no longer a *raison d'être* when France had become mistress of herself. I pledged myself for her love of peace, but at the same time for her indomitable resolution not to accept any condition which should make that peace a brief and threatening truce. M. de Bismarck said that if he believed such a peace was possible, he would sign it at once. The Opposition had always condemned the war. But the power which that Opposition represented was no longer anything but precarious. If within a few days Paris were not taken, it *would be overthrown by the mob*. I interrupted him to say that we had not a mere mob at Paris, but a population which was intelligent and devoted, which knew our intentions, and which would not make itself an accomplice of the enemy in obstructing our defence.

FRANCE WILL NOT FORGET SEDAN.

As regarded our power, we were ready to place it in the hands of the

Assembly already convoked. "This Assembly," replied the Count, "will have designs which nothing can make us foresee. But, if it obey the sentiment of France, it will wish for war. You will no more forget the capitulation of Sedan than Waterloo, than Sadowa, which did not concern you." Then he insisted at length on the wish of France, the accomplishment of which had been prevented, to attack Germany, and to take away a part fo its territory. From the time of Louis XIV. to that of Napoleon III. her tendencies had not changed, and when war was declared, the Corps Législatif *had received the words of the Minister with acclamation.* I remarked to him that the majority of the Corps Législatif had some weeks before called out for peace; that that majority, chosen by the monarch, had believed itself bound to follow him blindly; but that the nation, which had been consulted twice, at the elections of 1869, and at the vote on the *plébiscite*, had persistently clung to a policy of peace and liberty.

BISMARCK WANTS FRENCH TERRITORY.

The conversation on this subject was prolonged — the Count maintaining his opinion, whilst I defended mine; and, as I pressed him strongly on these conditions, he replied in effect, that the security of his country commanded him to guard the territory which protected it. He repeated several times, "*Strasburg is the key of the house; I must have it.*" I then asked him to be more explicit. "It is useless," he replied, "since we cannot listen to you. It is a matter to arrange later." I asked him to do it at once. He said then that the two Departments of Bas Rhin and Haut Rhin, a part of the Moselle, with Metz, Château-Salins, and Senones, were indispensable, and that he could not give them up in the negotiation. I then remarked that the assent of the people of whom he was thus disposing was more than doubtful, and that the public opinion of Europe would not be satisfied with it. "I know well," he replied, "that they are not with us. They will impose an unpleasant job on us, but we cannot suffer it. I am sure that in a short time we shall have a new war with you. We wish to make it with all our advantages."

FAVRE PROTESTS.

I protested, as I should, against such solutions of the question. I said that two important elements of the discussion had been forgotten: Europe, which would find these proposals to be exorbitant, and oppose them; then the new right — the progress of civilization and manners — which was opposed to such conditions. I added that, so far as we were concerned, we would never accept them. We could, I stated, *perish as a nation, but we would not suffer dishonor;* besides, the country alone was competent to decide regarding a cession of territory. We have no doubt about its feeling, but we are willing to consult it. Opposite to it Prussia is arrayed; and, to be brief, it is clear that, influenced by the intoxication of victory, she wishes for the destruction of France. The Count protested, taking his position behind the absolute necessity of the national guarantee.

BISMARCK REJECTS AN ARMISTICE.

I continued: "If it is not an abuse of strength on your part — concealing secret designs — let us summon the Assembly. We will resign into its hands our powers. It will nominate a definitive Government, which will consider your conditions." "For the execution of this plan," replied the Count, "*an armistice would be necessary, and I do not wish for that at any price.*" The conversation took a turn even more and more painful. Evening approached. I asked M. de Bismarck for a second interview at

Ferrières, where he was going to stay for the night, and we left, each for his own destination.

MIDNIGHT TALK.

We then pursued the discussion, which was prolonged until midnight. I insisted particularly upon the necessity of summoning an Assembly. The Count appeared to become convinced by degrees, and to return to the subject of the armistice. I asked for fifteen days. We discussed the conditions. He expressed himself in a very qualified way, and reserved his privilege of consulting the King. He consequently postponed our conversation until the next day at eleven o'clock.

THE TALK ON THE 19TH.

I was at the Château de Ferrières at eleven o'clock. The Count left the King at 11.45, and I heard from him the conditions which were required for an armistice. They were contained in a text written in the German language, of which he gave me the sense verbally. (*See Bismarck's reply following.* — AUTHOR.)

He demanded as a guarantee the occupation of Strasburg, of Toul, and of Pfalzburg; and as to the demand of the previous evening, that the Assembly should meet at Paris, he desired in that case to have added a fort commanding the city — that of Mont Valérien, for instance. At this point I interrupted him by saying, "It will be much more simple to ask us for Paris itself. How can you suppose a French Assembly can deliberate under your cannon? I have had the honor of telling you that I shall faithfully transmit our interview to the Government; but I really do not know that I dare tell them you have made to me such a proposition." "Let us seek another combination," he replied. Then I spoke to him of the Assembly meeting at Tours, and of no material guarantee being given in the neighborhood of Paris. He then proposed to speak of this proposition to the King, and, returning to the question of the occupation of Strasburg, he added: "The city is about to fall into our hands — it is now only a question of days; so I ask that the garrison should surrender themselves prisoners of war."

FAVRE MOVED BY GRIEF.

At those words I was moved by grief, and, rising, I said, "You forget that you are speaking to a Frenchman, Count. To sacrifice an heroic garrison — the admiration of ourselves and of the entire world — would be a piece of cowardice; and I do not promise that I shall not say you attempted to impose such a condition." The Count replied that he had no intention to wound me — that he only conformed to the laws of war; and that, if the King consented, that article might be modified. He then went and saw the King, and, returning in a quarter of an hour, said His Majesty accepted the proposition with regard to Tours, but insisted on the garrison of Strasburg being retained as prisoners of war. My strength was now exhausted, and for an instant I feared it would fail me altogether. I turned to hide the emotion which nearly choked me, and, apologizing for my involuntary weakness, I took my leave with these simple words: "I was deceived, Count, in coming here; but I do not repent. I have suffered sufficiently for my own excuse, and, moreover, I only came in deference to a sense of duty. I will report to my Government all that you have told me; and if they think proper to send me back to you, however painful it may be to my own feelings, I shall have the honor of seeing you again. I am grateful to you for the kindness you have shown toward me; but I fear there is no other means remaining than to let events take their course. The population of Paris is courageous, and resolved to make any sacrifice. Their heroism may change the course of events. Even if you conquer, you will not make them submit. All France entertains the same sentiments. So long as we can find an element of resistance we will fight you. It will be a struggle between two peoples, who ought rather to join hands. I hoped for a different solution, and I do part deeply grieved, but, nevertheless, full of hope.

. . . .

Receive, my dear colleagues, the fraternal homage of my unalterable devotion.

The Vice-President of the Government of National Defence, and
Minister of Foreign Affairs.

Paris, Sept. 21. (Signed) JULES FAVRE.

THE FRENCH GOVERNMENT IN A FRENZY.

The report of M. Favre threw the Paris Government into a frenzy. The Bismarck propositions were indignantly rejected, and M. Favre immediately wrote the following note to the Prussian headquarters:—

M. LE COMPTE—I have faithfully expressed to my colleagues in the Government of the National Defence the declaration that your Excellency has been good enough to make to me. I regret to have to make known to your Excellency that the Government has not been able to accept your propositions. They will accept an armistice having for its object the election and meeting of a National Assembly, but they cannot subscribe to the contingent conditions. As to myself, I can say with a clear conscience that I have done my utmost to stop the effusion of blood, and to restore peace to two nations which would be so much benefited by that blessing. I have only been stopped by an imperious duty, which required me not to yield the honor of my country, which has determined energetically to resist such a sacrifice. I and my colleagues associate ourselves without reserve in that determination. God, our Judge, will decide on our destinies. I have faith in His Justice. I have, etc.,

(Signed) JULES FAVRE.

September 21, 1870.

This circular of M. Favre to his colleagues, describing his interview with Count Von Bismarck, brought out the following reply from the Prussian Vice-Chancellor, who in the mean time began to feel that his demands upon M. Favre were a little exorbitant, and calculated to alienate the friends of Prussia in Europe and America. The circular is addressed to the North German ambassadors:

BISMARCK'S EXPLANATION.

FERRIERES, *September* 27.—The report addressed by M. Jules Favre to his colleagues on the 21st instant, regarding the conversation he had with me, induces me to make your Excellency a communication which will enable you to form an accurate idea of the course these conversations took.

It must be acknowledged that, on the whole, M. Favre has endeavored to render a correct account of what took place between us. If he has not been always successful, it must be ascribed to the length of our conferences and the peculiar circumstances under which they occurred. I must, however, object to the entire tendency of his exposition, and insist on the fact that the principal subject we had to discuss was not the conclusion of a treaty of peace, but that of an armistice by which it was to be preceded.

In regard to the demands we should advance, before signing a definite treaty of peace, I expressly stated to M. Jules Favre that I declined to enter into the subject of the new frontier claimed by us till the principle of a cession of territory had been openly acknowledged by France. In connection with this declaration, the formation of a new Department of the Moselle, containing the circumscription of Saarburg, Château-Salins, Saargemund, Metz, and Thionville, was mentioned by me as an arrangement in consonance with our intentions; but, at the same time, I in no way renounced our right to make additional stipulations in a treaty of peace, in proportion to the sacrifices which should be imposed on us by lengthening the war.

Strasburg, a place described by M. Favre as the key of the house — an expression which left it still doubtful whether France was the house in question — was expressly declared by myself to be the key of our house, which we therefore did not desire to leave in foreign hands.

"TAKE OUR GOLD, BUT LEAVE OUR COUNTRY."

Our first conversation, in the castle of Haute Maison, near Montry, did not go beyond an academical disquisition on the present and the past, the pith and marrow of which were contained in a declaration on the part of M. Favre of his readiness to yield *tout l'argent que nous avons*, while he refused to entertain the idea of a cession of territory. When I spoke of such a cession as being indispensable, he declared that negotiations for peace would have no prospect of success, and maintained that to part with any portion of her territory would be humiliating and dishonoring for France. I was not able to convince him that conditions, the fulfilment of which France had obtained from Italy and demanded of Germany, without having been at war with either of these countries — conditions which France would no doubt have imposed on us had we been conquered, and which had been the inevitable consequence of nearly every war, even in modern times, would not be ignominious to a country which had succumbed after a brave resistance; and besides that, the honor of France was not something essentially different from that of all other nations. I was equally unsuccessful in persuading M. Favre that the restoration of Strasburg no more implied dishonor than the cession of Landau or Saarlouis, and that the violent and unjust conquests of Louis XIV. were not more closely bound up with the honor of France than those of the first Republic or the First Empire.

A QUESTION OF VERACITY. — AN ARMISTICE.

Our conferences took a more practical turn in Ferrières, where we exclusively discussed the question of an armistice — a fact *which refutes the statement* that I declared I would accept an armistice under no circumstances whatever. The manner in which M. Favre represents me as saying with reference to this and other questions: "*Il faudrait un armistice et je n'en veux à aucun prix*," and other things of the same kind, obliges me to rectify his statements, and add that in similar conversations *I have never made use, and never do employ such phraseology* as that I personally wish or require or approve of anything. I constantly speak of the intentions and demands of the Government whose representative I am.

In this conversation both parties agreed in considering the necessity of giving the French nation an opportunity of choosing who alone would be in a position to grant the present Government powers sufficient to enable them to conclude a peace sanctioned by international law, as the reason of an armistice. I called attention to the fact that an armistice was always a military disadvantage for an army engaged in a victorious advance ; that, in the present case, it was a most important gain in point of time for the defence of France and the reorganization of her army ; and that we, therefore, could not grant an armistice, unless military equivalents were offered. As such I mentioned the surrender of the fortresses which impeded our communications with Germany, for, as a truce would prolong the period during which we had to support our army, concessions facilitating the transport of supplies must be the preliminary condition of granting it. Strasburg, Toul, and some smaller places were the objects of this discussion. With respect to Strasburg, I urged that since the glacis had been crowned, its capture must shortly be expected, and we therefore thought the military situation demanded the surrender of the garrison, while those who held the other fortresses would be permitted to march out with the honors of war.

PARIS CONSIDERED.

Another difficult question referred to Paris. Since we had completely surrounded the city we could only permit the admission of new supplies on the condition that the new provisioning of the town did not weaken our own military position, and protract the period necessary to reduce the city by hunger. After consulting the military authorities, I accordingly offered, at the command of his Majesty the King, the following alternatives with respect to Paris : Either the position of Paris must be conceded to us by the surrender of a commanding part of the fortifications, in which case we are prepared to permit free intercourse with Paris, and not to hinder the new provisioning of the city.

Or the position of Paris need not be conceded. In which case, however, we could not consent to give up the iuvestment, but must insist on the continuation of the military *status quo* before that city as the basis of the urmistice, as otherwise at the end of that period we should be opposed to Paris being provisioned and armed anew.

M. Favre distinctly rejected the first alternative, containing the surrender of a part of the fortifications of Paris, as well as the condition that the garrison of Strasburg should be made prisoners of war. On the other hand he promised to consult his colleagues as to the second alternative, containing the retention of the military *status quo* of Paris.

The programme which M. Favre took back with him to Paris as the result of our conversation, and which has been discussed there accordingly, did not contain anything whatever as to the terms of the future peace, but only the granting of an armistice of from a fortnight or three weeks to prepare the way for the election of a National Assembly under the following conditions:

I. *The continuation of the status quo in and before Paris.*

II. *The continuation of hostilities in and around Metz for a certain distance, the extent of which was still to be determined.*

III. *The surrender of Strasburg, the garrison of which were to be made prisoners of war, and of Toul and Bitche, their garrisons being permitted to march out with the honors of war.*

I believe that our convictions that we made very conciliatory offers will be shared by all neutral cabinets.

If the French Government has resolved not to use the opportunity offered of proceeding to the election of a National Assembly, even within the parts of France occupied by us, it shows its resolution not to get rid of the difficulties which prevent the conclusion of a peace in accordance with international law, and not to listen to the public opinions of the French people. That free and general elections would lead to results favorable to peace is a conviction which forces itself upon us here, and which can hardly have escaped those in power in Paris.

I take the liberty of requesting your Excellency to bring the present circular to the notice of the Government to which you are accredited.

VON BISMARCK.

NAPOLEON III. ESTIMATES THIERS, FAVRE, AND BISMARCK.

The ex-Emperor at Wilhelmshöhe gives the following estimate of the three men who hold the diplomatic destinies of Europe in their hands. Said the ex-Emperor to an English gentleman:

"Jules Favre has not ability enough to conduct a discussion with the Minister of King William. He will wind him round his finger. I have been quite duped by him—I, to whom everybody agrees in attributing penetration and taciturnity. How, then, will it fair with M. Favre, whose strength lies in his too great fluency of speech? All these words will be turned against him in the form of an agreement with his pacific intentions. M. Bismarck will throw the responsibility of a refusal on his august Majesty. The talent of this diplomatist consists in his knowing how to throw on others the responsibilities of resolutions that have been taken. I was without this talent when at the Tuileries, and I paid dearly for this defect. The Chancellor of the North is bent on making all Europe think that it was the French people who demanded the war, whereas in reality it was he and I who alike wished it. If I had been able to persuade the French that they urged me to this war I should still be at Paris, or I could have returned without fear. The contrary occurred, and my fall and the capitulation of Sedan are the consequences of that failure."

Shortly afterwards, speaking of M. Thiers, he said: "I was beaten at Boulogne [see p. 85.—AUTHOR], because, in my simplicity at that time, I confided in *this* Minister of Louis Philippe, who had promised me his assistance, but only to drag me into the net. I troubled him in England. He attracted me to Boulogne in order to confine me at Ham."

"Count Bismarck," the ex-Emperor said, in conclusion, "is an able man, but it is his audacity that makes him so. This is what distinguishes him from Cavour, the greatest politician I have ever met. If Cavour had been the Minister of King William, the German empire would have been completed, and that without a shot."

THE TOURS GOVERNMENT EXCITED.

The Tours branch of the French Government were as highly exasperated at M. Favre's report of Von Bismarck's demands as the officials in Paris, and the Ministry immediately issued the following proclamation:

TO THE PEOPLE OF FRANCE.

Before the siege of Paris, Jules Favre desired to see Count Von Bismarck, to know the intention of the enemy. The following is the declaration of the enemy:

Prussia wishes to continue the war in order to reduce France to a second-rate power. Prussia demands Alsace and Lorraine, as far as Metz, by right of conquest. Prussia, before consenting to an armistice, demands the rendition of Strasburg, Toul, and Mont Valérien. *Paris is exasperated, and will rather bury herself beneath her ruins.* To such insolent pretensions, we can respond but by *resistance to the last extremity.* France accepts the struggle, and counts upon her children.

TOURS, *Sept.* 24.

CREMIEUX.
GLAIS-BIZOIN.
FOURICHON.

BISMARCK'S DENIAL.

The Proclamation of the Tours Government brought out the following denial from Count Bismarck, the chronology of which would come on the 6th, but it is placed here the more readily to explain events :

FERRIERES, *Saturday, Oct.* 1, 1870.

From reports in the public journals it appears that the delegation of the French Government in Tours have officially announced that I had declared to M. Favre that Prussia would continue war in order to reduce France to the condition of a Power of the second rank. Although such an expression could only be intended to influence a circle unacquainted with the language used in international negotiations, and ignorant of the geography of France, still the circumstance that this official announcement bears the signatures of Messrs. Crémieux, Glais-Bizoin, and Fourichon, gentlemen belonging to the Government of a great European power, induces me to request your Excellency to put it in a proper light in your official intercourse.

In my interview with M. Favre, the question of peace was not formally considered. At his repeated request I communicated to the French Minister, in general outline, the same views which formed the principal topic of the circular dated Meaux, September 16. [*See* page 296. — AUTHOR.] *Demands exceeding those therein contained have never yet in any way been made by me.*

The cession of Strasburg and Metz, which we seek, in territorial connection implies a reduction of French territory equal in area to the increase through Savoy and Nice; while the population of these provinces obtained from Italy has made that of France 750,000 larger. When it is considered that France, according to the census of 1866, numbered 38,000,000 inhabitants without Algiers, and with Algiers (now furnishing an essential part of the French war forces), 42,000,000, it is palpable that a decrease of 750,000 changes nothing in the importance of France as against foreign countries, while we leave to this great Empire the same elements of power, possession whereof, in the Eastern and Italian wars, enabled it to exercise so decisive an influence on the destinies of Europe.

These few points will suffice to successfully oppose the logic of facts to the exaggeration of the proclamation of the 24th of last month. I only add, that in communication with M. Favre I expressly directed his attention to these views; and I need not assure your Excellency that I refrained from every offensive allusion to the consequences of the present war in respect to the future position of France as a great power of the world.

BISMARCK.

BISMARCK NOT OPPOSED TO THE REPUBLIC.

VERSAILLES, *October* 6, 1.30 P.M.—I do not hold the opinion that the Republican institutions of France constitute danger for Germany, nor have I, as asserted in a letter of the 17th ult., published in the London *Daily Telegraph*, ever expressed such a view to Mr. Malet, or any other person.

BISMARCK.

BISMARCK DEFINES PRUSSIA'S POSITION.

The following memorial, in regard to the fatal consequences to which the population of Paris are exposed by a prolonged resistance, has been sent by Count Bismarck to the Embassador of North Germany:

The conditions of an armistice offered to M. Jules Favre, intended as the basis for the reëstablishment of order in France, have been rejected by him and his colleagues. They thereby decree the continuance of a struggle which, according to the course of late events, appears without any chance of success for the French people. Since then the prospects of France in this war, so full of sacrifices, have still further declined. Toul and Strasburg have fallen. Paris is closely surrounded, and German troops are advancing by the Loire. The large forces heretofore engaged near the above fortresses are now at the free disposal of the German commanders. The country has to bear the consequences of a war *à outrance* decreed by the French authorities in Paris. Its sacrifices will be unnecessarily increased, and its social condition suffer a more and more dangerous decomposition.

The command of the German armies does not find itself in a situation to counteract this; but it perceives clearly the consequences of the resistance chosen by the Powers in France, and feels compelled to call general attention to one point, namely: the special condition of Paris.

The heaviest attacks heretofore made from this capital (on the 19th and 30th of September), in which the *élite* of the armies collected in that city have not been able to throw back the first line of the besieging forces, led to the conviction that the capital will fall sooner or later. If the time of surrender is postponed by "The Provisional Government for the National Defence" until the threatening want of provisions necessitates a capitulation, the most terrible results must follow.

The unwise destruction of railways, bridges, and canals within a certain distance around Paris by the French has not been able to stop for one moment the advance of the German armies. All communications by land or water needed for military operations have been reëstablished in a very short time. These repairs naturally regard military interests exclusively, while the other destructions, even after a capitulation, will prevent for a long time the communication of the capital with the provinces. It will be an absolute impossibility for the German commanders, when that case occurs, to provide one single day's rations for a population of nearly 2,000,000. The environs of Paris, to the distance of several days' journey, since all stores there are necessarily required for the use of the German troops, will then offer no resources, and will not permit the inhabitants of Paris to evacuate by the roads into the country. The inevitable result would be the starvation of hundreds of thousands.

The persons in power in France cannot fail to discern these consequences as clearly as the German commanders, and since to the latter nothing is left but to carry on the war proffered, the rulers of France are responsible for forcing such extremes.

THE CROWN PRINCE IN FRONT OF PARIS.

The Crown Prince to-day visits the captured redoubt which was carried yesterday while the Fifth Corps was taking possession of Versailles. The view of Paris from this position is charming. In front is the Tuileries, with the Louvre behind it; yonder is the dome of the Invalides, where Napoleon I. lies buried.

After a long look at Paris and a careful examination of the ground immediately before his troops, the Crown Prince returned to where the escort of lancers had halted, and quitting the main *chaussée*, crossed some fields toward the edge of the woods above Meudon. There were many traces of the battle of the previous day, though it was evident that the fighting had not been nearly so severe on the northern as on the southern side of the road to Châtillon. Several dead horses lay in the track of the French retreat, fearfully mangled by shell fire; and a dead soldier could be seen here and there among the tops of the beet-roots, his scarlet trousers contrasting vividly with the prevailing color around him. At the edge of the wood there had been a longer stand made by the French before they abandoned altogether the high ground near Le Petit Bicêtre. Many men had fallen where the road dipped from the brow to the slope of the hill, and many bodies were being collected for burial, both from the open fields and from the wood itself.

A DUSTY RIDE.

Clouds of dust flew up along the road as the Prince trotted toward Versailles. The staff became very dusty, or rather much more dusty, for it had been in a similar atmosphere for hours past. Now there was a Prussian battalion halted by the wayside, and ringing cheers burst as His Highness was recognized by the troops.

THE CROWN PRINCE ENTERS VERSAILLES.

The royal cavalcade came to the gates of the town, and rode along a paved street for some distance before reaching the Avenue de Paris. Thousands of the good people of Versailles were assembled to witness the entry of the Crown Prince of Prussia and his staff. No demonstration of any kind was made; the people accepted the event in logical silence. Loud swelled the notes of the military band, drawn up to receive the Prince. The Prussian anthem in Versailles! The needle-gun in the Avenue of the "Grand Monarque!" We are carried back nearly sixty years, to the disasters of another French empire. Yes; there they are — the spiked helmets, and the strong, sturdy wearers of the same. There is King William's only son, the commander of the Third German Army, the victor of Weisenburg and Woerth, riding into the court-yard of the Versailles Prefecture, to establish his headquarters at the Hampton Court — the old Philadelphia State House of the French capital. He does not enter the stately palace of the Bourbon Kings, because that palace is used as a military hospital, and has the red cross flag waving over it. But he has good quarters for a fighting prince in the handsome Prefecture on the Avenue de Paris, with his carriages drawn up in the court before the entrance, ready to march at half an hour's notice.

MORE TROOPS.

The Second and Third Corps from Prince Charles' Metz army are on their way to Paris. Prince Charles' army before Metz comprises the First army (Steinmetz) and the Second army consolidated. Steinmetz is relieved from duty in the field, and appointed to a semi-military position. No reasons are assigned for the change; but it is well known in the Prussian army that there is a difference of opinion between Prince Charles and Steinmetz, the last mentioned being too hard a fighter, and not relying enough on his artillery. "Signal for close action," the motto of Farragut, has always been the ruling order of the "Lion of Skalitz." Spicheren and Courcelles, bloody and glorious victories, are the only *charges against him.* Prince Charles has the First, Seventh, Eighth, and Tenth Corps; the Eighteenth Division of the Ninth Corps; the Twenty-fifth division of Hesse-Darmstadt; the division of Gen. Kummer, composed of regiments of the line, formerly the Mayence garrison, and not technically connected with any corps; and sundry landwehr divisions — making the whole force 180,000.

Many Prussian and Bavarian troops are now armed with captured chassepôts. The reserve army forming in Berlin is designated as the Thirteenth Corps, with marching orders for the seat of war.

A large German force is already passing through Alsace toward Lyons.

SEPTEMBER 21 — PARIS PROCLAMATIONS.

To-day in Paris is the anniversary of the Proclamation of the Great Republic, and Paris is in a very manifesting mood.

Gambetta issues proclamations every half hour, calling upon Parisians, as Minister Washburne says, "in more or less flowery language, to die for their country." This is the last one issued:

"CITIZENS: This is the Twenty-first of September! On this day seventy-eight years ago, our fathers founded the Republic, and took an oath to themselves, in the teeth of the foreigner, whose presence polluted the sacred soil of their country, to live free or die fighting. They kept their oath. They conquered, and the Republic of 1792 has survived, in the memory of mankind, as the symbol of national heroism and grandeur. The Government installed at the Hôtel de Ville, amidst enthusiastic cries of '*Vive la République!*' could not allow this great anniversary to pass, without hailing it as a great example. Let the mighty impulse which animated our forefathers inspire our souls, and we, too, shall conquer. This day let us honor our fathers' memories; to-morrow let us, as they did, secure victory by facing death. *Vive la France! Vive la République!*"

M. Arago, the Mayor, followed suit, heading his manifestoes with the old rallying cry, "*Liberté, Egalité, Fraternité.*" The French are so constituted that they cannot really exist without processions, bouquets to statues, and grand phrases.

The Parisians parade the streets like children, sometimes weeping, and sometimes breaking out in patriotic lunacy. The statue of Strasburg is covered with flowers. Among the patriotic outbursts we have —

VICTOR HUGO'S PRIVATE PROCLAMATION.

"TO THE PEOPLE:

"The Prussians have decreed that France shall be Germany and Germany Prussia. That I, as a Lorrainer, am a German; that the Nile, the Tiber, and the Seine are affluents of the Sarre; that the city which for centuries has irradiated the globe is superfluous, Berlin henceforth being capable of answering every measure; that Montaigne, Rabelais, Pascal, Molière, Diderot, Rousseau, Danton, and the French Revolution never existed; that, having Bismarck, we do not need Voltaire, but the universe belongs to the conquered of Napoleon the Great and the conquerors of Napoleon the Little; that henceforth thought, conscience, poetry, art, will begin at Potsdam and finish at Spandau; that, moreover, it is not established that our existence is necessary; that we are Sodom and Gomorrah, and they, the Prussians, are the fire of Heaven; that it is time to put an end to this state of things, and that henceforth the human race will be a power of the second order. This, dearest Parisians, they are executing upon you. When they suppress Paris they mutilate the world; their attack is aimed *urbi et orbi*. Is such a future possible? We answer only by a smile."

M. Victor Hugo proceeds to show the nature of this conflict:

"It is the old one between the Archangel and another Dragon, and it will have the old predestined end — Prussia will be overthrown. The war has hitherto only been a small war — it is about to become grand."

M. Victor Hugo calls to the Prussians to come forward like men:

"No more forests, no more thick fogs, no more tortuous tactics, no more gliding along in the dark. The strategy of the cat will not avail when you meet the lion. In vain you will step softly. The very dead will hear you. Paris is watching you — the thunder in her hand. Come out of the shadows; advance, show yourselves. Your facile successes are over, and you must fight foot to foot and hand to hand. You are about to meet a great soldier, whose name was Gaul when you were the Borussians, and who calls himself France now that you are Vandals. Miles Magnus said curses of France; soldier of God said Shakespeare. We are going to put your General to the test, and shall see whether your Moltke's ability is really better than the crepitude of Le Bœuf."

M. Victor Hugo then discusses famine and bombardment as means of reducing Paris, and proceeds:

"Attack Paris, then; blockade, bombard her. Try it; but while you are about to unite will come snow, sleet, hail, rain, frost, ice. Paris will defend herself. Paris, which has been accustomed to amuse mankind, will now terrify it. The world will be amazed when it sees how grandly Paris can die. The Pantheon is already asking itself where next it is to put the amount of power who are about to acquire a title to the shelter of its dome. 'O Paris! thou hast crowned the statue of Strasburg with flowers; history will crown her with stains!'"

Notwithstanding all this humbug, a large portion of them mean to fight it out. They have taken it into their heads that Paris can be successfully defended, and if it be not, they are determined that it shall not be their fault. It is intended to keep well beneath the cover of the pits, not to risk engagements more than is necessary — gradually to convert the Garde Nationale and the Garde Mobile into good soldiers, by accustoming them to be under fire; and then, if things go well, to fall on one or other of the Prussian armies.

THURSDAY, *Sept.* 22. — Russia moves troops mysteriously towards Turkey. The Czar moves to control the Black Sea and the Dardanelles. Sorties from Paris and Metz.

SORTIE FROM PARIS.

The division of Gen. Mand Luy, at three o'clock this morning, attached the heights at Villejuif, on the south of Paris, which were occupied by the Prussians. The attack resulted in no advantage. At the same time a force of French made a reconnoissance, and drove the Prussians from the village of Drancy; and Gen. Bellamère, the commander of St. Denis, attacked the Prussians in the village of Pierrefitte, the small detachment of Prussians retiring. (*See map*, *Sept.* 25.)

METZ.

Another balloon from Marshal Bazaine's headquarters at Metz has fallen within the territory controlled by the French. The balloon contained 137 letters. From these it seems butcher's meat is very dear at Metz, and the army is consequently eating horse-flesh. There is plenty of other provisions.

The Germans have armed the captured Lunettes, 52 and 53, with mortars. Other batteries have been erected on the heights. The German suffered a heavy loss at the capture of Lunette No. 52. Among the killed was Gen. Quitzon.

A SORTIE.

The French have been in the habit of coming out of Metz and of digging potatoes in the fields in the neighborhood of the villages which form the suburbs of Metz; to-day was the first time they have been prevented, for no sooner did they make their appearance than the Prussian outposts, who had been previously strengthened, opened fire. The French then withdrew, but only for a few moments. In half an hour's time the French, much to the astonishment of the Prussians, opened a smart fire from the earthwork of St. Privat. (*See wap, p.* 154.) This work is situated about 3000 yards from the suburb of Montigny, and 3500 yards from the village of Augny, occupied by the Prussians. Into this work the French had brought some field artillery, and they opened a heavy fire upon the village of Augny, the Prussian foreposts in that direction, and also upon the village of Marly, to the left of Augny. While this was going on, the enemy, evidently determined to have potatoes, made an advance, supported by cavalry, in the neighborhood of Mercy le Haut, driving back the Prussian outposts, and occupying that village and the village of Peltre, both under protection of the guns of Quelen. They were, however, after some sharp skirmishing, driven out, and, having no doubt accomplished their object of foraging, they retired into Metz by way of Le Sablon. The cordon is now to be drawn tighter than ever; the best shots are to be supplied with French chassepôts, and to do duty on the outposts close to the beleaguered city.

RUSSIA AND TURKEY.

The news of the fall of Napoleon was received with great rejoicings by the Russians, among whom he has long been universally detested. The Government, however, shows no disposition to recognize the Republic. The Prussian party, which consists of such influential men as Count Stackelberg, Baron Meyendorff, and Gen. Milutyn, is led by no less a personage than the Czarewitch.

When the Czar made the two Crown Princes members of the Order of St. George, it was to show his sympathy out and out for Prussia. The treaty of Paris was signed by Russia after the Crimean war *on compulsion.* France was up then; now she is down; and Russia desires to break it, and move her armies again against the Sultan, to make a seaport for herself on the south.

The author could see that it was the religion of Russia to go to the Mediteranean, when in Moscow in '67. "We must have a front door. The back door, frozen up seven months in the year, left us by Peter the Great, is not enough. It is the *manifest destiny* of Russia to go to the Mediterranean," said the Moscow *Gazette* in 1867.

THE TREATY RUSSIA WANTS ANNULLED.

This treaty was forced upon Russia by France and England at the close of the Crimean war.

All the Russian newspapers are discussing the Eastern question, and urging the abrogation of the said treaty, which, the St. Petersburg *Diplomatist* says, Gortschakoff has resolved to speedily annul. The contracting Powers of this treaty were France, England, Russia, Sardinia, and Turkey, and the following is a synopsis of the points of most interest in it at present:

Art. 9. Mentions that the Sultan grants reforms in regard to his Christian subjects.

ART. 11. The Black Sea is neutralized. While open to the mercantile marines of all nations, its waters and ports are formally and in perpetuity interdicted to vessels of war, whether belonging to nations having territory bordering on it, or otherwise.

ART. 12. This article prescribes that all regulations respecting trade in the Black Sea shall be conceived in a spirit favorable to the development of commercial transactions.

ART. 13. The Black Sea being neutralized by a foregoing provision, Russia and Turkey engage neither to construct nor maintain any naval or military arsenal upon its coast.

ARTS. 20 and 21 concede a portion of Russian territory, to be annexed to the Principality of Moldavia.

ART. 22. The Principalities of Wallachia and Moldavia are to enjoy under the suzerainty of the Porte, and under the guarantee of the contracting Powers, the privileges and immunities of which they are in possession. No exclusive protection shall be exercised over them by any of the guaranteeing powers. There shall be no private right of interference in their affairs.

ART. 23. The Sublime Porte guarantees to the aforesaid Principalities an independent and national administration, as well as full liberty of worship, legislation, commerce, and navigation.

ART. 28. The Principality of Servia will continue to be dependent upon the Sublime Porte, and subject to stipulations nearly similar to those named for the other Principalities.

ART. 30. Russia and Turkey are to retain in their full integrity their possessions in Asia to the same extent as before the war. Commissioners are to be appointed to settle the boundaries.

THE RUSSIAN ARMY.

The land forces of Russia are formed of two descriptions of troops, different from each other in many respects — the regular troops, properly so called; and the feudal militia of the Cossacks and similar tribes.

The nominal strength of the Russian army, according to the returns of the Ministry of War, is as follows:

Regular Army.	Peace-footing.	War-footing.
Infantry	364,422	694,511
Cavalry	38,306	49,183
Artillery	41,731	48,773
Engineers	13,413	16,203
Total	457,875	808,670
2. *Army of First Reserve.*		
Troops of the line	80,455	74,561
Garrison in regiments	80,455	23,470
Garrison in battalions	19,830	29,862
Total	100,285	127,925

3. *Army of Second Reserve.*		
Troops of all arms	254,036	199,380
General total	812,096	1,135,975

Among the irregular troops of Russia, the most important are the Cossacks. The country of the Don Cossacks contains from 600,000 to 700,000 inhabitants. In case of necessity, every Cossack, from fifteen to sixty years, is bound to render military service. The usual regular military force, however, consists of 54 cavalry regiments, each numbering 1044 men, making a total of 56,376. The Cossacks are reckoned in round numbers, as follows:

	Heads.	In Military service.
On the Black Sea	125,000	18,000
Great Russian Cossacks on the Caucasian Line	150,000	18,000
Don Cossacks	440,000	66,000
Ural Cossacks	50,000	8,000
Orenburg Cossacks	60,000	10,000
Siberian Cossacks	50,000	9,000
Total	875,000	129,000

Russia, as may be seen by the foregoing, controls in time of war an army of more than 1,000,000 soldiers, while she has a navy capable of obstructing commerce and inflicting extensive injury on an enemy. The annual expenditure for the army is $80,000,000, and for the navy $15,000,000.

THE NAVY.

According to an official report, the Russian fleet consisted last year of 290 steamers, having 38,000 horse-power, with 2205 guns, besides 29 sailing vessels, with 65 guns. The greater and more formidable part of this navy was stationed in the Baltic. The Black Sea fleet numbered 43; the Caspian, 39; the Siberian or Pacific, 30; and the Lake Aral or Turkestan squadron, 11 vessels. The rest of the ships were either stationed at Kronstadt and Sweaborg, or engaged in cruising in European waters.

Included in the iron-clad fleet are three floating batteries of 14, 16, 27 guns respectively, one frigate of 18 and one of 24 guns.

The largest of the iron-clads are two armed frigates, the Sevastopol and Pojarski. The Sevastopol nearly equals the British iron-clads Black Prince and Warrior in her dimensions, and exceeds those of the French Gloire and Normandie.

The Imperial navy was manned at the beginning of 1868 by 60,230 sailors and marines, under the command of 3791 officers, among whom are 119 admirals and generals.

THE TURKISH ARMY.

The military force of Turkey is divided into — 1st, the regular army, called Nizam; 2d, the reserve, or Redif; 3d, the contingents of auxiliaries; and 4th, the irregular troops.

The regular native army consists of six corps, under command of a field marshal, with their headquarters at Scutari, Constantinople, Monastir, Karbrout, Damascus, and Bagdad. Each corps consists of two divisions, commanded by a General of division. The corps comprises eleven regiments, namely: six regiments of foot, four of horse, and one regiment of artillery.

In the last war with Russia the number of auxiliaries amounted to about 75,000 men, namely, 30,000 from Bosnia and the Herzegovina, 20,000 from Upper Albania, and 25,000 from Egypt.

The total of the military forces of Turkey are officially estimated as follows:

	Regiments.	War-footing.	Peace-footing.
Infantry	36	117,360	100,300
Cavalry	24	22,416	17,280
Field artillery	6	7,800	7,800
Artillery in fortresses	4	5,200	5,200
Engineers	2	1,600	1,600
Detached corps	10	16,000	16,000
Total	80	170,376	148,680
Reserve			148,680
Auxiliaries			75,000
Irregulars			87,000
Total military strength			459,360

The 87,000 irregular troops are calculated to consist of the following:

Kavas or gendarmes on foot	30,000
Tartars	5,000
Hungarian and Polish volunteers	2,000
Moslem volunteers	50,000
Total of irregulars	87,000

The total strength of the Turkish army in the last war with Russia was 216,893, of whom about half were of the reserve.

THE TURKISH FLEET.

The fleet of war of Turkey was composed, at the commencement of this year, of 163 vessels, carrying a total of 2283 guns and manned by 30,000 sailors and 4000 marine troops. The largest iron-clad in the navy is the Osman Ghazy, armed with 24 guns. The next two powerful vessels are clad in heavy armor of an average thickness of five and a half inches, and carry four 12-tun rifle Armstrong guns in a central battery.

THE RUSSIAN FLEET NEAR CONSTANTINOPLE.

The Russian squadron, Admiral Boutaroff, has arrived in Greek waters. The interpretation of the appearance of the fleet is, that Russia is in no degree prepared for the rapid course the Franco-German war has taken, and sees herself obliged to do hurriedly now what she had hitherto determined to accomplish at her own time and convenience — viz., a strong demonstration of naval force before Constantinople, while demanding a revision of the treaties of 1856, and a new arrangement of the right of Russian war vessels to traverse the Black Sea. As the possibility of a Congress is not altogether excluded from men's minds, this action on the part of Russia is by no means unlikely.

FRIDAY, *September* 23.— Surrender of Toul, with 109 officers, 2240 men, and 197 guns. Bloody sortie from Metz. The Berlin war-office ships supplies to Paris for a protracted siege.

CAPTURE OF TOUL.

At the capitulation of Toul, 109 officers, 2240 privates, 120 horses, 1 Garde Mobile (standard), 1 eagle, 197 bronze cannon, among which 48 are rifled, 3000 muskets, 3000 sabres, 500 cuirasses, a very considerable quantity of ordnance, quartermaster, and commissary stores, fell into our hands.

VON KREUSKI.

THE SIEGE.

The siege commenced on the 14th of August. On the 16th an assault was repulsed. On the 23d of August a regular bombardment commenced, lasting one month.

The Bavarian railroad directors, who run the line from Weisenburg through Nancy to Paris, offered to build a branch road around Toul in a fortnight; but Moltke said, "No; we shall have Toul long before that time." The straggling attack, however, was of no avail. The fortress had a double escarpment with full bastions, and was fully casemated. There was no glacis, but a double moat, each ditch being thirty feet wide all around the fortress. It was defended by seventy-five guns, of which twenty-six were heavy rifled pieces from Strasburg, brought thence while yet France intended an earnest defence of Toul.

Within the last fortnight heavy siege guns, which had arrived from Germany, were put in position on a spur of Mount St. Michael on the north, on the heights opposite the Faubourg St. Egare on the southwest, and at Dommartin-les-Toul on the southeast.

THE SURRENDER.

Nothing serious was then attempted until last Friday, when at daybreak a concentrated bombardment of the works was begun by twenty-four-pounder batteries of the Second and Fourth Artillery regiments, supported by troops of the Thirty-fourth Infantry brigade. All these form part of a new independent command, under the Grand Duke of Mecklenburg-Schwerin, embracing all the forces lying between the armies of Frederick Charles and the Crown Prince ; that is, all the troops of the invasion not engaged in the sieges of Metz and Paris.

The firing continued all Friday, with an active but very ineffective reply from the garrison. In the evening, the town being on fire in twenty-three places, the pressure of the inhabitants upon the commander induced him to hoist the white flag, and offer to capitulate. The offer was immediately accepted by Colonel Manteuffel, commanding the siege corps, and the town was entered at seven P.M. The conditions of surrender were precisely those of Sedan. A council of the Municipality, held on Friday, decided not to favor a surrender ; but the urgent representations of individuals who feared useless destruction completely overcame the belligerent determination of the military and civil authorities.

HOW TOUL LOOKS.

Many houses are destroyed. The condition of things is worse than at Sedan, but not so bad as at Bazeilles. The Gothic chapel of St. Gengoult is almost ruined, but the ancient and very imposing cathedral has only a window arch demolished and its outside battered by a score of shells. The town and environs have a picturesque appearance, and are built very much in the old German style. There are but few wounded, no sick, and but little disorder in Toul. Only two battalions of the Nineteenth Infantry remain as garrison. The prisoners of the native Garde Mobile were released under parole not to serve again during the war. Of the Garde Mobile 500 were trained during the siege to serve the guns; they alone performed the artillery service; but in repulsing the assault of the 16th ult., all the male inhabitants that could procure arms participated.

SORTIE FROM METZ.

At noon to-day (23d), the forts surrounding Metz opened a tremendous cannonading, under cover of which the French forces sallied forth in considerable strength on the Prussian right, and immediately began a vigorous attack. The assault was so impetuous and well-sustained, that the Prussians were thrown entirely upon the defensive, and were, in fact, compelled to take advantage of the woods to check the French advance.

From midday the battle raged until nearly seven o'clock in the evening. At this hour the Germans were heavily reinforced, when they promptly assumed the offensive, and advanced upon the French. For a brief while the struggle was quite fierce, but finally the forces of Bazaine were driven back within their lines.

SUNDAY, *September* 25.—King William announces the complete investment of Paris. The only communication with the French capital by balloons. Bazaine keeps Prince Charles engaged at Metz.

THE GERMAN ARMY AROUND PARIS.

The royal headquarters of the combined German armies, and the temporary residence of the King of Prussia, with Count Bismarck and General Moltke, are at Ferrières (ten miles east of Paris); the headquarters of the Crown Prince at Versailles, eight miles southwest of Paris; and those of the Crown Prince of Saxony at Grand Tremblay, ten miles northeast of Paris. The two armies now form a cordon around Paris, the strongest front being on the south and southeast. The advance positions of army corps are as follows—the corps themselves being about three miles in the rear of their advance positions given in the map:—The Fifth Corps, the extreme left, extends from Bougival, on the Seine, in front of Mont Valérien, to Meudon, in front of Fort Issy. The Second Bavarian continues the line in front from Fort Issy to Fort Vanvres, in front of Clamart. The Sixth (Silesians) from Vanvres past Châtillon, Montrouge, to Bicêtre, in front of Villejuif; the

Eleventh (Nassauers and Hessians) completing the line from Fort Ivry to the Seine on the south-east, in front of Vitry. The Würtemberg contingent, consisting of two divisions of cavalry and a division of infantry, with a proportion of guns, is stationed in the fork between the Seine and Marne. The First Bavarian Corps is in reserve between the Second Bavarian

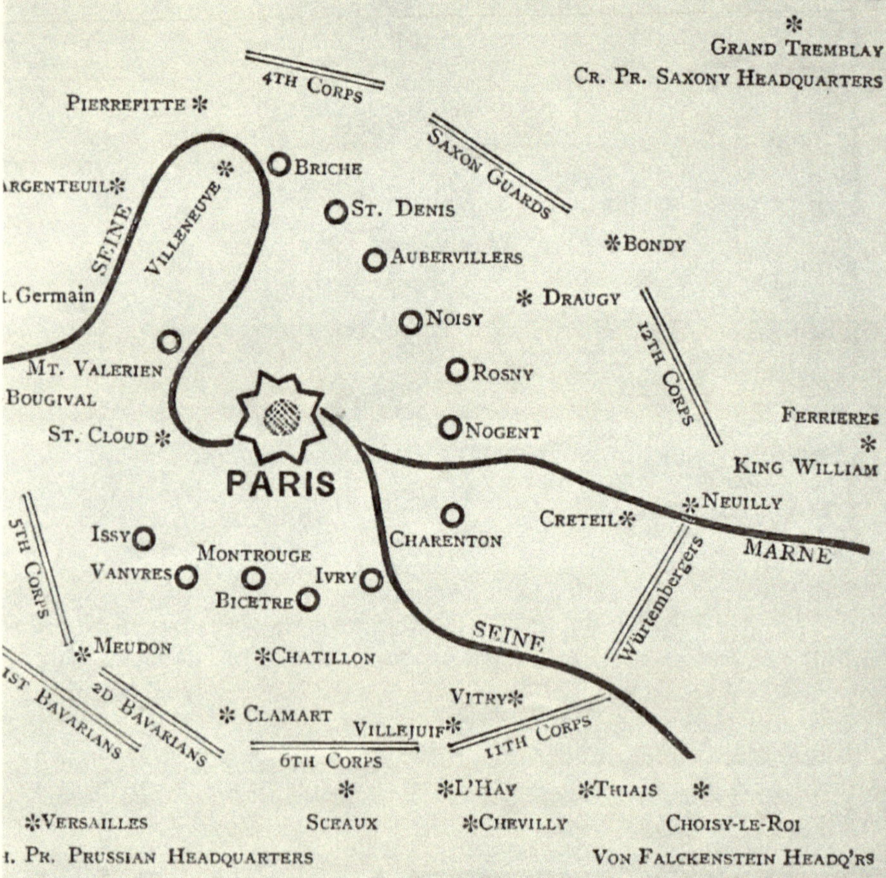

and Versailles. The army of the Crown Prince of Saxony, now called the Army of the Marne, consists of the Twelfth Corps, which joins the Würtembergers at Neuilly, on the Marne; the Guards in front of Rosny and Noisy, and the Fourth Corps, completing the chain past Aubervillers beyond St. Denis on the north. The cavalry connects the links between the corps, making a continuous living wall of men from Bougival on the Seine to the left front of Versailles, to St. Denis on the north. Gen. Von Falckenstein (the Moltke of the Crown Prince) is at Choisy-le-Roi, superintending the grand siege of South Paris. The Prussians have seized a small hill between Enghien and Argenteuil, from which they can shell the advanced works of St. Denis. They have fortified this hill, and will place about twenty siege guns in it as soon as they come up. The French have already abandoned many of their outworks near this fort, which were thrown up to guard the passage of the Seine. All the bridges have been broken up to the St. Germain railway bridge, which is still passable. The wooden-topped bridge at St. Germain has been burned by the French, and the Prussians have made a boat bridge near Port Marly.

STRATEGY.

When the Prussian army of 350,000 arrived before Paris, a division of counsel arose. Von Moltke was in favor of immediate bombardment, while King William and the Crown Prince were in favor of the starve-out process. The King's views were finally accepted. The Prussian army now sits before Paris, only doing a moderate amount of digging, while large Prussian detachments are moving through France towards Rouen, Amiens, Tours, and Lyons. The Duke of Mecklenburg, freed from Toul, is besieging Soissons. One by one the French provincial towns are surrendering to King William. French recruiting is stopped, and the machinery of the French Government is idle. The strategy of King William is to let time decide the fate of Paris, while the army in detachments demoralizes France as Sherman demoralized the South in his "march to the sea."

THE DAILY SKIRMISHING.

All along the chain is heard the rattling fire of the skirmishers, or the bursting shells as they hiss and explode in mid air. Destroying war is everywhere. Follow a by-road and it leads plump into a field where a battery is to be seen with its guns unlimbered and pointed enemy-wards — precautions at given points against sudden surprises on the part of the enemy. Sentinels stand at all the cross-roads and at close intervals along the routes converging on Paris, and they stand surveying certain directions with fixed gaze. Those great routes are all strongly barricaded with huge trees cut down from the wayside, where they have towered aloft for many years; and such barricades have been prolonged and assisted on the flanks by hastily built earthworks. The air is one of readiness.

THE GARDEN — A DESERT.

Did the reader ever pass over the aqueduct bridge from Georgetown in war time? Go back to 1862, and see that desolate country from Fort Corcoran, Fort Runyon, and the old headquarters of Blenker, and around Fairfax Seminary, to Alexandria. History repeats itself to-day in front of Paris. Oh the scourge of an army of occupation! Around beautiful Versailles the fairy gardens are macadamized by the dress parade, and sweeping lawns are cut by the zigzag paths of the Prussian scouts. Begrimed walls of once beautiful châteaux stand silent sentinels to the devastations of war. Houses become suggestions of houses, windowless, doorless, deserted. Hedges are browsed away, and become leafless and gray. Soldiers who have followed our armies in Virginia can see this zone deserted in front of Paris, and still alive with a strange, moving mass of armed humanity. Luxuries have ceased. The poultry have been massacred, and the cows have been butchered for beef. Within sight of the beautiful Louvre, with its miles of marbles, and gems of art, not so much as a pin can be bought. These are the facts which look down upon the once lovely capitol of France — look down upon the column of July, the tomb of the first Napoleon and his sublime "*arch of triumph to the stars!*"

VIEW FROM MEUDON.

How beautiful in all this desolation is the night view in front of Paris. A thousand encampments with their illuminated tents spread out to the right and the left, and a flood of light radiates against the clouds till the sky is all aglow with mellow light. At nine the lights of the soldiers go out, and at eleven darkness draws a veil over the scene. Not yet. Away over a zone of darkness Paris throws skyward a halo of light like the milky way. Standing against the sky is the grand arch of Napoleon, the Madaleine with its Greek inspiration, and the dome of the Paris Pantheon, after which our capitol was designed. I pray God that an enemy may never look down upon that capitol as 350,000 Prussians look down on Paris to-night.

SORTIE FROM METZ.

Bazaine shows great activity at Metz, and by his energetic movements holds in front of him an army twice the size of his own. Not knowing on what *radius* Bazaine may advance,

Prince Charles is compelled to close a line around Metz at least twenty-five miles long. To-day Bazaine made another sortie on the Thionville radius, north of Fort St. Eloy. Covered by the cannon of the fort, which opened a severe fire, the French attacked vigorously the left of the Prussian line, a little east of the Thionville road. Regiment after regiment rushed upon the solid line of defences formed by the Prussians, who held their ground with an iron-like tenacity.

Once the French gained an advantage, which, though it proved but temporary, made the situation grave while it was held. They succeeded in carrying an outwork of the Prussian lines and in turning the flank of another position. They were, however, promptly met as they pushed on by heavy masses of Prussian reinforcements, and driven back, though slowly, as they gallantly contested every inch of ground they were forced to yield.

At length, after a bloody and protracted struggle, they were forced to retire to the protection of the forts. The display of heroism and stubborn determination on both sides was great and often thrilling, and has never been excelled in modern warfare.

TUESDAY, *September* 27. — Strasburg surrenders with 10,000 men to General Werder (Thirteenth Corps). General Uhrich paroled, and goes to Tours. General Von Terten appointed Governor. The Prussian besieging garrison (17,000 men) forms a new army operating along the Vosges and against Lyons.

THE FALL OF STRASBURG

TO THE QUEEN:

FERRIERES, *September* 27, 11 P.M. — Strasburg capitulated at five this afternoon. WILHELM.

THE BOMBARDMENT.

Since the 24th the bombardment has been terrific and almost incessant, and the breach in the walls became large enough to warrant an assault. It became evident that storming was inevitable in a few hours, unless stayed by a capitulation.

THE WHITE FLAG!

On Tuesday, the 27th, near four o'clock in the afternoon, the joyful sight of a white flag was beheld flying from the Cathedral.

This was speedily followed by the same welcome token of surrender from the citadel. A young lieutenant of the Thirty-fourth Regiment was the first to discover the flag, and the firing instantly ceased. Then general attention was called to the flags by an universal cheer which rose from one portion of the besieging lines, and was soon caught up and echoed throughout the entire army.

JOY.

The scene which followed was indescribably exciting. Officers sprang to their feet and embraced each other, clasping hands. The men followed the example, and some actually cried with joy. This joy is a relief to the impressive sadness in the city.

TERMS OF CAPITULATION.

Colonel Von Leczynski, General Werder's chief of staff, entered the town and arranged the following terms of capitulation. The mildness of the terms of surrender is only accounted for by the fact that the Prussian authorities have been instructed, in the Departments of Alsace and Lorraine, to win over the inhabitants by kindness, and prepare them for becoming a part of Prussia.

The Royal Prussian Lieut.-Gen. Von Werder, commander of the corps besieging Strasburg, solicited by the French Lieut.-Gen. Uhrich, commander of Strasburg, to put an end to the hostilities against the fortress in consideration of the honorable and brave defence of the place, agrees to conclude the following capitulation:

ARTICLE I. — At 8 o'clock in the morning on September 28, 1870, Lieut.-Gen. Uhrich evacuates the citadel, the Austerlitz gate, the Fisher gate, and the National gate. At the same time the German troops will occupy these positions.

ART. II. — At 11 o'clock on the same day the French garrison, including Gardes Mobiles and National Guards, leave the fortress through the National gate, take up position between lunette No. 44 and redoubt No. 37, and there lay down their arms.

ART. III. — The troops of the line and the Gardes Mobiles become prisoners of war, and march out with their luggage. The National Guards and Francs-tireurs are released on parole, and by 11 o'clock A.M. surrender their arms at the Mayor's office. The list of the officers of these troops at the same hour to be furnished to Gen. Von Werder.

ART. IV. — The officers of the French garrison of Strasburg are at liberty to depart and chose their own place of residence on parole; the form of the parole is attached to these articles of capitulation. Those officers who do not sign the parole proceed with the garrison as prisoners of war to Germany. All the French military surgeons remain until further notice in their functions.

ART. V. — Lieut.-Gen. Uhrich, immediately upon the surrender of arms, agrees to deliver over, through the proper officers, all the military material on hand. Officers and officials charged with this duty assemble on the 28th, at 12 o'clock, upon the Place de Broglie.

This capitulation is executed and signed by the following plenipotentiaries: On the German side, by Lieut.-Col. Von Leczynski, chief of staff of the Corps besieging Strasburg, and Count Henckel Von Donnersmark, Captain of Cavalry and Adjutant. On the French side, by Col. Ducasse, Commander of Strasburg, and Lieut.-Col. Mangin, Sub-Director of Artillery.

Read, accepted, and signed,

VON LECZYNSKI,
COUNT HENCKEL VON DONNERSMARK,
DUCASSE,
MANGIN.

Affirmed, Mundolsheim, September 28, 1870.

VON WERDER, Lieutenant-General.

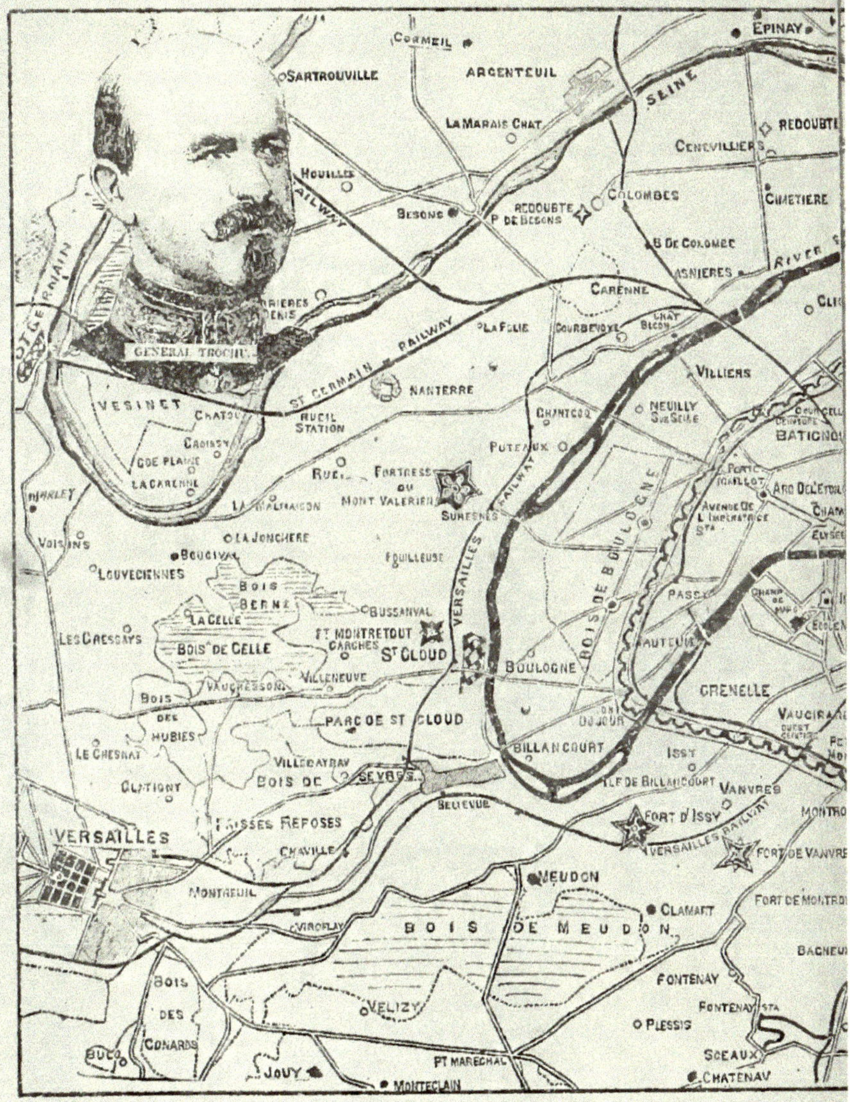
GENERAL TROCHU.
CORMEIL
EPINAY
SARTROUVILLE
ARGENTEUIL
SEINE
REDOUBTE
LA MARAIS CHAT
HOUILLES
RAILWAY
BESONS
REDOUBTE
P DE BESONS
COLOMBES
CIMETIERE
B DE COLOMBE
ASNIERES
RIVER S
CARENNE
LA FOLIE
COURBEVOYE
ST GERMAIN RAILWAY
NANTERRE
VILLIERS
VESINET
CHATOU
RUEIL
STATION
CHANTCOQ
NEUILLY
SUR SEINE
BATIGNO
PUTEAUX
FORTRESS
OU
MONT VALERIEN
SURESNES
BOIS DE BOULOGNE
ARC DE L'ETOIL
MARLEY
LA MALMAISON
LA JONCHERE
BOUGIVAL
LOUVECIENNES
FOUILLEUSE
VERSAILLES RAILWAY
PASSY
BOIS
BERNE
BUSSANVAL
LA CELLE
LES GRESSAYS
BOIS DE CELLE
FT MONTRETOUT
GARCHES
ST CLOUD
BOULOGNE
AUTEUIL
VAUCRESSON
VILLENEUVE
GRENELLE
BOIS
DES
HUBIES
PARC DE ST CLOUD
LE CHESNAY
BILLANCOURT
ISSY
VILLEDAVRAY
BOIS DE SEVRES
ILE DE BILLANCOURT
VANVRES
BELLEVUE
FORT D'ISSY
VERSAILLES RAILWAY
FAUSSES REPOSES
VERSAILLES
CHAVILLE
FORT DE VANVRE
MEUDON
MONTREUIL
CLAMART
FORT DE MONTRO
VIROFLAY
BOIS DE MEUDON
BAGNEU
BOIS
DES
CONARDS
FONTENAY
VELIZY
FONTENAY STA
PLESSIS
BUC
PT MARECHAL
SCEAUX
JOUY
MONTECLAIN
CHATENAY

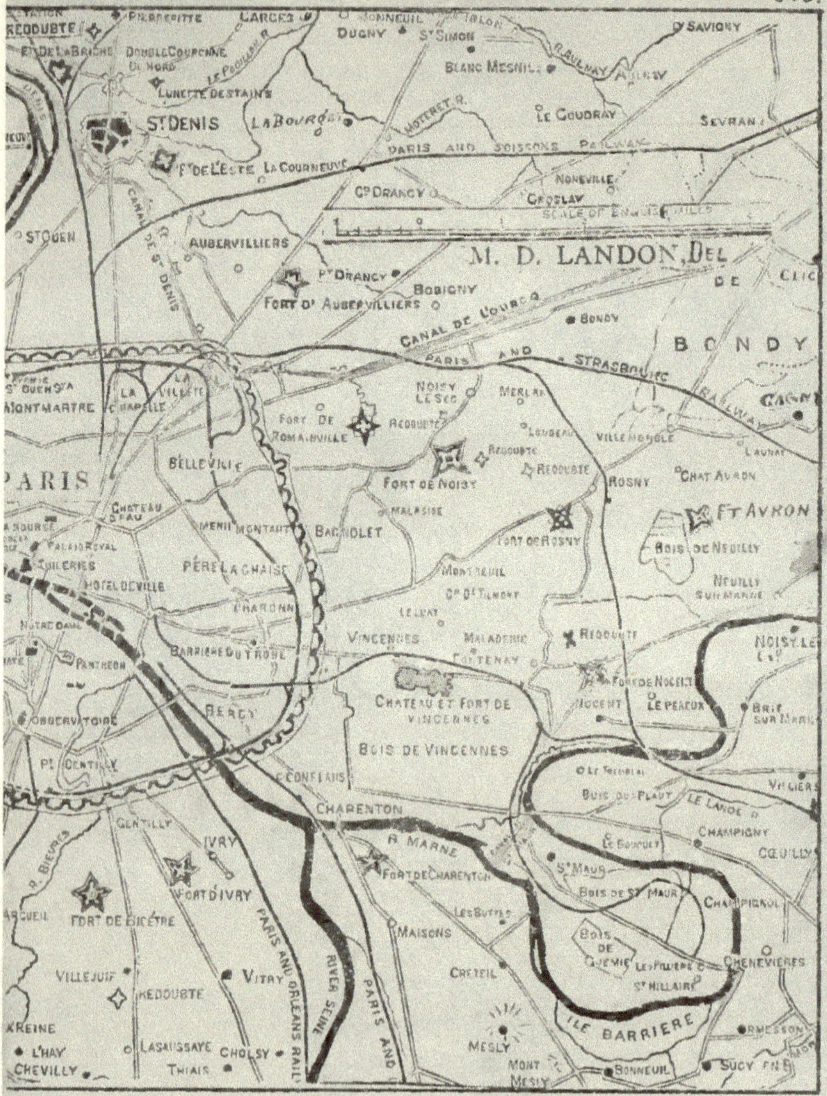
REDOUBTE
PIERREFITTE
GARGES
DUGNY
ST SIMON
BLANC MESNIL
SAVIGNY
LE GOUDRAY
SEVRAN
ST DENIS
LUNETTE DE STAINS
FT DE L'ESTE
LA COURNEUVE
PARIS AND SOISSONS RAILWAY
NONEVILLE
CD DRANCY
SCALE OF ENGLISH MILES
M. D. LANDON, DEL
ST OUEN
AUBERVILLIERS
FT DRANCY
BOBIGNY
FORT D' AUBERVILLIERS
CANAL DE L'OURCQ
CANAL DE ST DENIS
BONDY
B O N D Y
PARIS AND STRASBOURG RAILWAY
NOISY LE SEC
MERLAN
FORT DE ROMAINVILLE
REDOUBTE
LA VILLETTE
LA CHAPELLE
MONTMARTRE
BELLEVILLE
PARIS
FORT DE NOISY
REDOUBTE
ROSNY
CHAT AVRON
FT AVRON
BOIS DE NEUILLY
NEUILLY SUR MARNE
CHATEAU D'EAU
MENIL MONTANT
BAGNOLET
MALASISE
FORT DE ROSNY
PALAIS ROYAL
TUILERIES
PERE LA CHAISE
HOTEL DE VILLE
MONTREUIL
CHARONNE
VINCENNES
FONTENAY
REDOUBTE
FORT DE NOGENT
NOGENT
LE PERREUX
PANTHEON
BARRIERE DU TRONE
BERCY
CHATEAU ET FORT DE VINCENNES
BOIS DE VINCENNES
OBSERVATOIRE
CONFLANS
CHARENTON
BOIS DU PLANT
CHAMPIGNY
GENTILLY
IVRY
R. MARNE
ST MAUR
FORT DE CHARENTON
FORT D'IVRY
FORT DE BICETRE
BOIS DE ST MAUR
LES BUTTES
MAISONS
CRETEIL
CHENEVIERES
ST HILLAIRE
VILLEJUIF
VITRY
REDOUBTE
RIVER SEINE
PARIS AND ORLEANS RAIL
PARIS AND
ILE BARRIERE
L'HAY
CHEVILLY
LASAUSSAYE
CHOISY
THIAIS
MESLY
MONT MESLY
BONNEUIL
SUCY EN B

UHRICH AND WERDER MEET.

The commanders of the two forces, Gens. Werder and Uhrich, met for the first time after the terms of capitulation had been arranged. The meeting took place just inside the gate, on the east side. Gen. Uhrich advanced to Gen. Werder, and, with a voice much agitated, said:

"I have yielded to an irresistible force, when further resistance was only a needless sacrifice of lives of brave men. I have the consolation of knowing I have yielded to an honorable enemy."

Gen. Werder, much affected, placed both hands on Gen. Uhrich's shoulders, and said:

"You fought bravely. You will have as much honor from the enemy as you can have from your own countrymen."

LOSSES.

Gen. Von Werder, the Prussian commander, reports that the besiegers lost from the 21st of September to the capitulation of the place, 30 killed and 195 wounded. During the entire siege the Germans lost 906 killed and wounded, including 113 officers.

CAPTURES.

By the capitulation 10,000 men, eleven hundred guns of all sorts, twelve thousand chassepôts, three tons of ammunition, and fifty locomotives of the Paris and Strasburg Railroad, which had been collected there, fall into Prussian hands.

THE DAMAGE.

One house standing at a corner was propped up lest it should topple over. A cannon ball had swept a large piece out of the corner, and had cut through one of the beams which supported the two upper floors. In the Place Kleber, one of the largest and finest open spaces in Strasburg, the signs of destruction were most striking. The handsome building which filled the north-eastern side of the square, and in which was a valuable museum of ancient and modern works of art, is now represented by empty walls. Nearly every house has been pierced with shot or shell.

THE CATHEDRAL

is uninjured. The spire is as attractive a spectacle as ever, but it has been struck in more places than one. The cross on its summit appears to have been touched by a projectile. It leans to one side. Some of the ornamental work has been carried away, and in one of the side towers a portion of the stone stairway has been destroyed. The outer roof of the nave has been burned; the windows have here and there been pierced with balls, but the famous clock has escaped destruction, and the Cathedral is on the whole in excellent condition. To this place the German soldiers hastened as soon as they arrived. They ascended the tower; they explored the interior. The officers were as eager as the men not only to see the renowned Cathedral, but also to learn the truth as to the damage done it. All expressed their satisfaction at the comparative unimportance of the injury inflicted. They would have lamented the destruction of the Cathedral quite as sincerely as the Strasburgers themselves. More than one German artillery officer says that orders were daily given to carefully avoid firing in such a way as would either damage or endanger the Cathedral. Other public buildings, however, have not escaped. The Prefecture, the theatre, and the church library, the latter of which is world renowned, are now represented by bare walls.

THE CITY OF STRASBURG.

The venerable city of Strasburg was founded in the time of Augustus. It has indeed had a checkered existence. It has been sacked by the Romans, pillaged by the Huns, seized by the Germans, captured by the French, and it now falls back to Germany, its natural ally. In turn it has been made Catholic and Protestant. Its fortifications were completed by Vauban in 1684. They consist of five massive bastions and five demilunes, and were considered impregnable until the invention of the latest rifled artillery of heavy calibre, such as the foundries of America, and the workshops of Krupp, at Berlin, can furnish.

MONUMENTS AND BUILDINGS.

Strasburg is full of monuments and objects of interest, among which is the bronze statue of John Guttenberg, the modern inventor of printing.

The Public Library, near the Temple Neuf, or New House of Worship, has 110,000 volumes, and among them some of the rarest works and missals of the middle ages, with Gothic and Byzantine illuminations; and some rare imprints of Bibles and classic authors by Faust and by Egglestein, of 400 years back date. Along with these is a collection of Roman antiquities found in Alsatia, and precious specimens of curious stained glass. The Académie, founded in 1538 and made a University in 1621, was the scene of Goethe's completion of his collegiate course, and his graduation as a doctor of laws in 1772; while such illustrious names as Oberlin, Schoepflin, and many of scarcely less note, are on its records. The great German poet eloquently refers to his student days there in his autobiography.

THE GREAT CATHEDRAL

was founded by Clovis in A.D. 504; reconstructed by Charlemagne, who built the grand choir; nearly ruined by lighting in A.D. 1007; and again remodelled, as it now stands, in 1015. The body of the edifice was finished in 1439.

It stands there, the embodied thought of pious generations, struggling upward toward heaven, and crystallized beneath the sun into a perpetual memento — a never-ending prayer. How grand and touching a growth to spring from the graves that enrich the soil below — a passion flower, blooming forever in colored glass, in glittering metal, and in granite etchings!

THE ASTRONOMICAL CLOCK

is the mechanic miracle of this unrivalled Gothic fane. At noonday, with clang of bells and organ music, the mechanism of the dial moves, and the busy throngs in the streets below look up with awe at the personified legends of the faith that governs life and death.

WEDNESDAY, *September* 28. — General Bourbaki leaves Metz for England, with a message for the Empress. Grand parade of Prussian troops at Versailles.

PARIS. — COMIC RADICALISM.

The news of the fall of Strasburg becomes known in Paris. A proclamation, dated Hôtel de Ville, and signed by all the Ministers, is issued, acknowledging the noble resistance of the city, and declaring that the siege had only drawn closer the bonds which attach Alsace to France. Then follows an enactment:

"That since the siege of Strasburg the national feeling of the people of Paris had not ceased to lavish testimonies of patriotism upon the statue of Strasburg, and, in order to perpetuate the sentiment, the statue now standing in the Place de la Concorde should be cast in bronze, and have an inscription added to it commemorating the occasion."

VOICE OF A RADICAL ("RED").

M. Felix Pyat and his friends take the matter very differently, and his paper, the *Combat*, which appears with a heavy black mourning border, contains an article signed by him, apostrophizing the Government in this style:

"What a confession! But we expect such failures from your imbecility. Yes, these heroic cities (Toul and Strasburg) have held out, as you say:

glory to them, but for you they have only a cry of malediction. No more phrases, discourses, and placards. Since September 4, you have had the fate of France in your own hands — what have you done? Nothing. You go on your knees to Bismarck, and immediately after Toul and Strasburg surrender. If only half of those who carried flowers to the statue had carried arms and provisions to the town, they would have held out until to-day. And so you are going to recast the statue. You will have the bronze, and Prussia the town. It is in this way that you reinforce the Prussians. Toul is a frontier lost; Strasburg is a gate of Paris. And you find time to scatter the flowers of rhetoric and to stick up placards, and no time to make the commune, the Revolution, and the arming of the people. Take care; you are for the Empire under the disguise of the Republic (*l'Empire Républicaine*). Sedan killed your predecessors; Strasburg will kill you. Begone! your deposition is pronounced."

RADICAL TWADDLE.

The Red Republicans in Paris are doing great mischief. They *mean* well enough, but they seem to have no sagacity. They are Jacobin agitators. Trochu has controlled them by setting them at *useless* work — as in the navy, the marines, to keep them out of mischief, are kept holystoning the deck. Thus M. Blanc and M. de Jonvielle, and a host of Jacobin fellows, have been made officers of barricades. Such complete *twaddle* is all this barricade business! How wise M. Blanc looks at every street paved with cobble-stones! They have just torn up the street in front of the Pantheon; and now these foolish fellows are wisely discussing how to build the barricade. Why, one of Krupp's guns would send a whole barricade flying like grape-shot amongst the citizens. They are positively a good thing for the Prussians. They are good to kill women and children with — splendid for the destruction of innocent dogs and unsuspecting dray horses. Well, *they amuse the "Reds"!* At night, when the "Reds" are unable to work at their barricade nonsense, they meet in clubs and pass startling resolutions. In the morning these "*Wendell-phillips* fellows" (as Minister Washburne calls them) display their resolutions as if they proceeded from a constituted authority. Last evening the following atrocious resolutions, radical enough to startle the bones of the agrarian Grachii, were passed:

Resolved, That the demolition of the column Vendôme, this useless monument of despotism, of which the material could be converted into money, would be a public good.

(Little did the first Napoleon think his shocking idea of melting the silver disciples into money, "that they might go about doing good," would one day come back with such dreadful irony against his own statue.)

Resolved, That the people demand that all of the population of Paris shall henceforth be rationed with all the necessaries of life.

Resolved, That the property of those who have cowardly (*lâchement*) fled from Paris shall be confiscated for the benefit of the defenders of the Republic.

Resolved, That from this time every person shall be provided with a card *civique,* indicating his name and surnames, his age, his address, his signature, and the kind of service which he performs in the national defence. This card to be shown at the demand of any citizen.

Resolved, That all the property, real estate or personal, furniture and houses of those who have been accomplices in the depredations of the Bonapartes, be sequestered.

Hugo and Louis Blanc have written letters against the "Reds."

M. Rochefort has become exceedingly conservative in his expression. He advises his friends the "Reds" to behave themselves, to be patriotic, and above all things not to make Prussians of themselves. The more violent of the "Reds" whisper to themselves that Rochefort has turned traitor to the cause, and they threaten even to "whip off his head" the very first chance which they can obtain; they do not say whether they mean his head corporeal or his head political.

IMPERIAL SECRETS.

The story and correspondence of the Marguerite Bellanger scandal is published. The paternity of Mlle. Bellanger's little boy is attributed to the Emperor, and the secret comes out that the lady (?) was caused to disavow the Imperial paternity through the intriguing of President Devienne (First Judge of the Empire). The Emperor kept Marguerite in the style of a princess. Dogs, carriages, jewellery, and a magnificent palace on the Avenue de la Reine Hortense, were her portion given by the Emperor.

THE STORY OF MARGUERITE.

At a time when the Prince Imperial was in very bad health he was under the impression that he was the father of Marguerite Bellanger's boy. Imparting his grief to her at the prospect of being deprived of posterity, she, in melting moments, got him to listen to her complacently, when she said that her son was his, and that, apart from social conventions which he might overrule, the direct line of the Napoleons was in any event assured. The Emperor might very well have caressed the idea over a cigarette, that, if he lost his legitimate son, his power and might would be equal to the achievement of a plebiscite conferring his adoption on an illegitimate one. This is the man who was the hero of Strasburg and Boulogne (see biography), and who was once received in the best society of Bowling Green and Bleecker Street. Later, the Prince Imperial got better; the Empress rebelled against the Marguerite Bellanger scandal; and a moment came when the Emperor thought it expedient to obtain a disavowal from Miss Marguerite of his paternity of her child at any price. M. Devienne, at the time when he soiled his ermine with this dirty business, was First President of the Imperial Court, *i.e.*, the Second Judge of the Empire. As a reward for service which the lowest pettifogging attorney would have been ashamed to own, he was promoted to the highest judicial office in the gift of the Crown, namely, the Presidency of the Court of Cassation. He is now impeached for disgracing the bench.

HOW NAPOLEON MADE FRIENDS.

The Tuileries correspondence reveals the fact that both Cassagnac and Jérôme David were regular pensioners on the civil list. The cost of the Prince Imperial's baptism amounted to $180,000. The cousins, male and female, of the Emperor, received $250,000 per annum. The Duc de Persigny received in two months $12,000; Prince Sablonowiski, the Countess Gajan, Madame Claude Vignon, Gen. Morris, and many others, are down for various sums.

PRUSSIAN LOSSES AND CAPTURES.

The Prussians have captured up to to-day, one marshal, 39 generals, 3577 officers, 123,700 privates, 10,280 horses, at least 56 eagles, 102 mitrailleuses, 887 field and fortress guns, more than 400 wagons, several pontoon trains, magazines, railway train, and almost incalculable quantities of supplies of arms, ammunition, clothing, equipments, forage, and provisions.

The number of French prisoners in Germany does not fall short of one hundred and seventy thousand men. One hundred and ten thousand and twenty are within the territory of Prussia, sixty thousand and sixty of whom are in the several fortresses, and the others are in open camps, which are well guarded by the landwehr. At a council of the Prussian Cabinet, it was decided that the prisoners may be employed by persons not connected with the military departments.

The official tables of the Prussian losses since the war began place the casualties at 1690 officers killed and wounded, and 38,151 men.

FRIDAY, *September* 30.—Sortie from Paris. French defeated and driven back by the Fifth and Eleventh Prussian Corps.

THE PARIS SORTIE.

KING WILLIAM'S DESPATCH.

TO THE QUEEN: FERRIERES, *September* 30.

Early this morning, the French troops of the line made a sortie against the troops of the Sixth Prussian Corps, while the Prussian Fifth Corps was attacked by three battalions. At the same time a brigade made a demonstration against the Eleventh Corps. At the end of two hours the French took shelter under the guns of the forts. The Crown Prince commanded the Prussians. WILLIAM.

TROCHU'S REPORT. (*See Map*, p. 340.)

TO THE PEOPLE: VITRY, *September* 30.

Our troops, in a vigorous sortie, successively occupied Chevilly and L'Hay, and advanced as far as Thiais and Choisy-le-Roi. All these positions (on the south of Paris) were wholly occupied. After a sharp artillery and musketry engagement our troops fell back on their positions with remarkable order and coolness. The Garde Mobile was very firm. Our losses were considerable; those of the enemy probably as large. As a whole, the day was very honorable. TROCHU.

The following is the longer report of the battle of Villejuif, issued by General Trochu:

"After the concentration of the positions adjacent to Villejuif by the division of Gen. Mand Luy, the enemy remained master of the villages of L'Hay, Chevilly, Thiais, and Choisy-le-Roi, thus protecting his line of communications with Versailles. For several days past he has been constructing works on this line, throwing up earthen mounds, completing its bounds, and walls of the villages, etc. The Germans thought, indeed, that a combined action on the two banks of the Seine should be contemplated in order to reconnoitre exactly the forces of the enemy on these positions. With this object the troops under General Vinoy were last night massed toward the forts of Ivry, Bicêtre, and Montrouge (these forts forming a chain on the south of Paris). At daybreak they quitted their lines, and were at once received with a brisk fire of musketry and cannon, to which they replied with energy. The engagement soon became general upon the entire plateau of Villejuif, and lasted not less than three hours. While the troops under General of Brigade Guilbein (Thirty-fifth and Forty-second) pushed the enemy back with vigor out of Chevilly, the bulk of General Blaine's column (divisions Mand Luy) penetrated as far as the village of Thiais and took a battery in position, the guns of which batteries it could not carry off, having no horses. At this juncture the enemy brought up heavy reinforcements concentrated within call, and could not have numbered fewer than 30,000 men. Géneral Vinoy, judging that the enterprise had been pushed far enough, ordered the retreat. It was effected under fire, with a calmness most remarkable, and which does the troops infinite credit. The artillery throughout steadily and effectively supported the movements by the accuracy of its fire, and the battalions of the young Mobiles, following the example of the infantry of the line, on their side, showed an admirably firm bearing. In the engineers, who attacked the enemy directly in front, in their fortified positions, our losses, not yet estimated, were heavy. We have to regret the loss of General Guilbein, a valiant officer, who has deserved well of his country. General Exea, who with a single brigade marched upon Creteil, on the adverse right, although strongly enfiled, appears to have had only thirty men wounded. This general officer greatly praises the attitude of his troops. The fire from the mitrailleuses greatly tried the enemy, who, thrown on the plateau of Villejuif, lost heavily. The military intendence and the services at its disposal, and the International Society for the Help of the Wounded, fulfilled their mission with much devotedness. To resume, the combats of September 30 have proved to our soldiers how much they are worth, to their chiefs what they may expect of them ; and this day is honorable to the efforts of the defensive bourgeoise.

THE FACTS OF THE SORTIE

are as follows: The French made the sortie for two reasons: First, Trochu desired to try his raw troops in the presence of the enemy; and, second, to find out the extent of the *spade* work done by the Prussians. It was a sortie in force, the French advancing from behind Forts Ivry, Bicêtre, and Montrouge in large masses, upon the Sixth Prussian Corps, occupying the right centre of the army of the Crown Prince. A little later in the day, General Exea advanced on the extreme French left towards Cretéil, assaulting the Würtembergers between the Seine and Marne. The French advance was all along the south of Paris, from the junction of the Marne and Seine rivers to St. Cloud. After the action began, the Crown Prince, accompanied by his staff, hastened from his quarters at Versailles to the battle-field, and assumed immediate command of the troops. The French troops advanced steadily upon the Prussians under cover of a heavy fire of artillery. Pushing forward vigorously they struck the advance posts of the Prussian Sixth Corps, compelling them to fall back upon the main line. This they immediately assaulted. After nearly three hours of severe fighting, during which the Prussian lines remained unshaken, the French gave way before a heavy fire of artillery, and commenced retreating rapidly towards their forts.

The Germans now took the offensive, and vigorously following the retreating French, succeeded in breaking their retreating columns into great disorder, and capturing 400 prisoners. The German loss was between four and five hundred. The Paris *Temps* says:

"Our loss was about 500 wounded and 400 killed. The object of the sortie was to blow up a bridge over the Seine, and arouse the courage of the Parisians by obtaining a success where the Prussians were not supposed to be in force. Neither end was attained, and Paris is consequently greatly depressed."

SATURDAY, *October* 1.— French blockade raised. Falckenstein orders lights and buoys replaced. Bavaria and Würtemberg become members of the German Confederation. Russia announces neutrality, and adds: "*A Turkish war would have no connection with the present conflict.*" Balloons from Paris.

BALLOONS FROM PARIS.

TOURS, *October* 1.— M. Tissander, the aeronaut, has arrived here from Paris. He publishes in the journals an interesting narrative of his balloon trip, and the situation of affairs in Paris at the time he left. He started from that city at two o'clock yesterday afternoon. No Prussians were to be seen near Paris.

A complete silence reigned about the city. There were no people to be seen on the roads leading to the city, and no boats of any kind on the river. On nearing Versailles, the Prussians were observed in great numbers in camp. M. Tissander dropped among them great numbers of the proclamation of the Government officers, which had been printed in the German language for that express purpose. The Germans opened a sharp fire on the balloon, but the range was too long, and no damage was done. On arriving over Houdon, fifteen miles south-west of Mantes, the balloon began to fall, and M. Tissander was obliged to throw out "ballast." Fortunately, he had several packages of newspapers, which answered the purpose, and he was not obliged to throw over his letters or sacrifice anything valuable. The balloon then rose rapidly, and was carried along to a point near Dreux, in the Department of Eure-et-Loire, many miles west of the Prussian lines.

M. Tissander descended slowly until he came within hailing distance of a few peasants, whom he now saw for the first time. These assured him that there was no danger of capture, as no Prussians had yet been seen in the neighborhood. M. Tissander therefore alighted on reaching an open spot favorable to his project. The balloon was properly secured, and the letters, *twenty-five thousand* in number, were placed in sacks and taken to the post-office at Dreux, whence they will be forwarded in all directions, wherever the lines of communication are not interrupted. A special locomotive was placed at the command of M. Tissander, at Dreux, in which he came forward to Tours with a large number of despatches to the Government. Still another balloon from Paris passed over Evreux to-day.

A BALLOON BATTLE.

A balloon battle, the first in the history of the world, occurred over Paris to-day. The balloon seems to be especially adapted for communicating with beleaguered cities. In the American war, the author frequently saw Union balloons in front of Fredericksburg, and on one occasion he had the pleasure of taking a balloon trip to the height of a thousand feet, while the balloon remained tied to the ground. It was left for the French to use the balloon at Metz and Paris as a means of communication. The balloon battle occurred to-day in this manner. M. Nadar left Tours for Paris, with Government despatches, to-day at six A.M., in the "Intrépide," arriving in view of Paris at eleven A.M. While M. Nadar was floating about 3000 metres above Fort Charenton in the "Intrépide," a second balloon was observed in the horizon. Nadar was seen to display a streamer with the French national colors. Immediately another national flag floated from the car of the other balloon. Vigorous hurrahs and cries of "C'est Durouf!" proceeding from the garrison of the fort, greeted the appearance of the two aeronauts, whose balloons gradually approached. When they were within a short distance of each other, suddenly a loud report was heard in the air, followed by a series of explosions. These were at first thought to be demonstrations or signals of victory, until Nadar was seen to fling himself into the network of his balloon and to cling to its sides. During this time the other aeronaut continued discharging shots at Nadar, which were traced in the sky by their luminous effects. The "Intrépide" descended rapidly, and it appeared to the spectators below that some incomprehensible events had taken place above. But mark what the French flag in the neighboring balloon had come to. It had been removed, and a black and yellow standard was observed to be floating in its place. Then all was explained. "Treason! It is a Prussian balloon! He has fired on the 'Intrepide!' Nadar is lost!" were the cries that burst simultaneously from the French people. But Nadar was safe; for he was seen to descend rapidly in his car, and the balloon to nearly reach the earth. He cast out the ballast, and reascended, having stopped the hole made in his balloon by his adversary, Then shots were rapidly fired from the "Intrépide" into the Prussian balloon, which one, losing all power, descended to the earth with giddy velocity. A detachment of uhlans who were in the plain, and who had been following the aereal combatants throughout this exciting struggle, rushed forward, and surrounding the balloon, received their champion, and then all hastened off at full speed to the Prussian advanced posts. In the meantime Nadar descended safely at Charenton.

EXTRACT FROM A FRENCH LETTER.

PARIS, *October* 1. — There have left Paris since Thursday, September

29, no fewer than three balloons. The two first were tied together at the top and at the *nacelles*, and a smaller one was placed between them, so as to keep them steady. They were mounted by M. Godard and by M. Courtin, an army contractor. Those gentlemen descended the same day, near Evreux, and arrived in Tours the next evening.

They started from La Villette and passed over Mont Valérien, being then about 2600 feet above the ground. It was only after they had gone a mile at least beyond the fort that they could see the Prussians. Some shots were fired at them, but without effect. They then rose to 5000 feet, and were for some time becalmed, or nearly so, over the Forest of St. Germain, where they were again fired at. It was somewhere near Mantes that they began to descend. When they were nearing the earth, and, indeed, had cast anchor, and were being driven along the ground by a low wind, they saw a troop of horsemen riding upon them at great speed. They thought they had unluckily fallen among Prussians. They were very much relieved on finding these horsemen were free cavalry of M. Estancelin, who escorted them to their destination.

EXTRACT FROM A GERMAN LETTER.

VERSAILLES, *October* 1. — A balloon went over this place this morning in a westerly direction, quite out of shot. Indeed, hardly a day passes without one or more balloons escaping from Paris. Yesterday, at St. Germain, two, fastened together, came out from Paris, and, when directly over St. Germain, dropped a heavy packet into the town. This fell directly into the Ursuline Convent. Away went the Prussian officers in pursuit; but lo! when they succeeded in obtaining admittance to the Convent, no packet was forthcoming, the Sisters unanimously declaring that they had seen nothing of the kind. "Very well," said the officer, "I shall quarter twenty hussars here to-night, if the packet does not appear, and twenty more to-morrow, and so on, until the letters are found." Last night, as I passed the Convent on my way to dine with a French banker, I saw one of the green hussars on guard at the lowest door — a sight somewhat unusual. This morning the packet must have appeared, as, on driving by the Convent door, I saw no sentry on duty. The balloon which brought this much-sought-after packet had some half-dozen shots fired at it as it went over the Seine — of course without result, as it was at least 2000 yards above the river. "Ah, if we had only a chassepôt, we would bring it down," said an aide-de-camp to me. But it sailed on unmolested, the object of a hundred glasses.

A few days ago, at Argenteuil, a balloon was not so lucky, as it was hit by three shots and came toppling over, and its contents, two French officers and some 3000 letters, fell into the hands of the Eighty-sixth Regiment, quartered at Argenteuil.

THE BLOCKADE.

As the raising of the blockade has now been made known officially to the neutral States, the navigation of the Elbe and Weser has again commenced, and a considerable number of neutral vessels have already arrived at Bremerhaven and Hamburg. Efficient steps are also making to replace the buoys and beacons without delay all the way down the river, and the lightships have been sent down, and will again resume their stations at the mouth of the Elbe either to-day or to-morrow. German vessels have to run the risk of capture. The blockade lasted one month. The French papers valued the damages done to the German commerce at 5,000,000 francs per day. This admission is the more important to German shippers, as the damages of about $1,000,000 per day to be assessed for this item *the Germans expect France to pay.*

SUNDAY, *October* 2.—Sortie at Metz, and the village of Nouilly burnt. Provisions in Paris becoming scarce.

MONDAY, *October* 3.—Admiral Fourichon resigns the French portfolio of war, but remains in the cabinet at the head of the navy. General De Caen dies of wounds in Metz.

General Schmeling crosses the Rhine at Mulhouse with the Fourth Division of landwehr, to join General Werder in operations against Lyons and Besançon.

AMERICAN GERMANS ON ALSACE AND LORRAINE.

At a large meeting in St. Louis the following address is adopted and cabled to Count Bismarck:

TO THE GERMAN PEOPLE:

BRETHREN: The struggle which French audacity forced upon you is closing. Marching with your leaders, under the holy banner of the Fatherland, with a bravery unequalled and discipline which can only be obtained by a high civilization, you entered France and your cause was victorious. *We ask that you will make the fortresses which have heretofore menaced you the guards of your border; that you will retain Alsace and Lorraine, of which you were robbed; and demand reimbursement for the expenses of the war.* Let German unity and a full and free representation of the people in parliament be the reward of your bravery.

WEDNESDAY, *October* 5.—King William moves the royal headquarters from Ferrières, and holds a grand review at Versailles.

KING WILLIAM IN VERSAILLES.

The entry of the King into Versailles to-day was a great historical event. The Crown Prince, attended by General Von Blumenthal, Count Eulenberg, Colonel Von Gottberg, and a certain number of the members of his staff, left Les Ombrages early in the afternoon, in order to meet the King on his way to the confines of his command.

At 5.35 the cheers of the troops who lined the Rue de Chantiers heralded the arrival of the King at last. The officers in front of the Prefecture formed front. The cheers sounded nearer. A *peloton* of lancers with their lances lowered swept round the corner, and took post on the right front of the Prefecture. These were followed by a small body of dragoons or gendarmerie. Then came the Stahlmeister and some mounted equerries, closely followed by a General or field-officer, at whose heels clattered a troop of lancers, with lances raised, who wheeled round and halted on the flank of the rest of the squadron. Next, in an open carriage, appeared the King. He was covered with dust, but he looked wonderfully well and strong. On his left was the Crown Prince, dusty, and vigorous-looking also. The troops cheered, the colors were lowered, the band burst into a wild triumphal blare of drums and trumpets, and the whole crowd of officers, with upraised casques and caps and shakos, shouted lustily. The calèche drew up some thirty yards in front of the Prefecture, and the King bounded rather than stepped out of it, followed by the Crown Prince. His officers pressed forward to greet him, and, with that peculiar mixture of profound respect and heartiness which we cannot imitate, thronged close to the King. He shook hands most warmly with Generals Von Kirchbach, Voigts Rhetz, and others, and then, with the Crown Prince a little behind him, strode off to inspect, according to custom, the color company, drawn up on the left of the Palace, which received him with the usual honors. His Majesty walked along the front of the line, and as he went, the crowd of Princes, Dukes, Generals, and officers broke from their places and followed him, being in turn hemmed in by the crowd, to whom in general the gendarmerie were very indulgent. There was no space cleared, no border kept, and the people got quite close to the person of the royal conqueror. The excitement was great. As the King turned he shook hands with the members of the great German Confederation, whose soldiers fight under his banners, stopping now and then to talk to some old soldier servant or some familiar friend, and, followed by the Crown Prince, General Blumenthal, Colonel Gottberg, and his Staff, he strode at last, vigorous, straight, and strong, into the courtyard of the Prefecture, turned round and saluted the uniformed multitude, and then passed into the hall, over the portal of which was waving the royal standard. The crowd slowly dispersed, but it was long before the groups of citizens were broken up, and they stood in front of the Prefecture in the moonlight, talking of their new visitor. "*C'est un bel homme, ce vieux Guillaume; mais jes serais très content, pourtant, de n'avoir pas vu le bon Roi de Prusse à Versailles.*"

Count Bismarck came into the Hotel des Reservoirs at 6.30, dusty and hungry, with a few officers of the Royal Staff, and ordered dinner in the *salle à manger*, which was crowded with the *habitués* of the place. Recognizing General Burnside, who was seated at a table with General Sheridan, General Forsyth, and Mr. Forbes, he took a chair beside them, and spoke for some time in the easiest and pleasantest way possible with the former respecting his visit to Paris.

STRANGE REILGIOUS CELEBRATION AT METZ.

METZ, *October* 5.— To-day is the Jewish Feast of the Tabernacles. The Jewish Kippur is being celebrated by 1200 Jews in front of Metz. It is a strange scene to see these devoted Jews praying in their uniforms and cloaks, while their Christian brothers stand guard over them to prevent an assault from Bazaine.

There is a very liberal religious sentiment in Prussia, and this nation, which once legislated against the Jews, confiscated their lands and persecuted them with fire and sword, now forms around them a wall of Christian soldiery while they pray the great prayers of their faith. It is a beautiful, *a Christian sight*, to see this little band of the children of Israel thus protected in their religious rights. *It is the Old Testament watched over by the New.*

THURSDAY, *October* 6.— Defeat of the new French army of the Rhône at Epinal, forty miles south-west of Strasburg, by General Werder. Bazaine commences his four-day sortie from Metz.

THE FIGHT AT EPINAL.

To-day, for the first time, the veteran Prussian troops met the newly-organized troops of Southern France — the forlorn hope of the Republic. The French army which fought to-day near Epinal (St. Remy) was organized in Dijon, Saône, and Haute Marne, and was the advance of the new southern army. The troops engaged in the fight were chiefly Mobiles, under General Dupré. The Prussian forces were under General Werder, with General Von Dagenfeld, chief of the Baden division, and General Schmeling commanding the landwehr. The battle lasted from nine A.M. until four P.M., and was hotly contested between 10,000 Germans and about the same number of French. The German loss was 410 men and twenty officers killed and wounded, and of the French 2000 were placed *hors de combat*, the Germans capturing sixty officers and 600 men. The Badeners bivouacked upon the victorious field, and the remaining French retreated toward Dijon.

The battle is of consequence, as the first of a series planned and executed by the released garrison of Strasburg under Von Werder against the southern French Army of the Rhône. War Minister Von Roon says in an official report that the German troops need have no farther fear of French opposition in the south.

THE KING AND THE FOUNTAINS OF VERSAILLES.

To-day all the grand fountains of Versailles played in honor of his Majesty, King William, who showed himself to the good people of Versailles for more than an hour in the palace gardens. The town is very gay, as two headquarters are now concentrated here, and princes are as common as blackberries.

Yesterday the Grand Duke of Saxe-Coburg, brother of the late Prince Albert of England, said, "The French must be thoroughly beaten, for I am afraid that they will want to go to war again as soon as the recollection of their present disasters has in the least degree passed away. We must therefore take away from them the power of hurting us. We are now sending an army to Lyons, and so the south of France will learn what a terrible thing war is, and will wish for peace as earnestly as do the inhabitants of the East."

VON MOLTKE AND BISMARCK.

What a change? In 1867 the author saw nothing but light-hearted gayety in the alley of the three grand Versailles fountains. Now crowds — German crowds — clad in the grim armor of war line the lovely walks. Yonder comes a quiet, thoughtful walker, unattended, absorbed in deep thought. There is a buzz of voices. "Is that really Von Moltke?" "Where?" "You see that tall, thin man, without any moustache or whiskers, his hands behind his back — the officer with the grayish hair, very short, and a face cut with many fine lines, his head slightly stooped, the eyebrows pronounced, and the eyes deep set? There is the man whom the Junkers of Berlin called 'the old schoolmaster.' What a lesson he has taught the Austrians and French!" "Is that the strategist who caught Benedek in a vice at Königgrätz, mouse-trapped Bazaine at Metz, and netted an Emperor, a Marshal of France, and 150,000 men at Sedan, and who is now angling for such an enormous prize as the capital of France?" "He looks very grave." "He is always so. But there, you see, striding through this crowd, is a very different-looking person." "Yes! who is that frank, smiling major of dragoons? He comes this way — the officer in the white cap and yellow band, dark blue or nearly black double-breasted frock coat with yellow collar, taller than the tall officers around him?" "That is Count Bismarck." There is a stir wherever he goes — caps touched and hats raised. He makes straight for a little knot of Americans — General Burnside in plain clothes, General Sheridan, General Hazen, and General Forsyth, in uniform, but without swords. You hear his laugh above the murmurs of the crowd, and the wave of sound in which his name, "Bismarck," is borne. How heartily he shakes hands with them, buoyant and free, elated as some officer might be who had just won promotion on a battle-field. All the world knows the soulless likeness out of which even photography has failed, however, to take all expression; but one must have actual experience of the peculiar vivacity, or rather penetration of his glance, as it is emitted from under those tremendous shaggy eyebrows, to measure the power of his face — the one grand overwhelming force of which is, to my mind, intrepidity — an immense, audacious courage, physical and mental, and a will before which every obstacle must yield or be turned. The people were never tired of looking at him, and Grand Dukes and Princes were of small account as long as he was to be seen, the Prince of Hohenzollern being, however, an exception to the remark — "the fair pretext of the war," as a lady called him, alluding to his blonde complexion and hair; and indeed, to use Scott's words of Claverhouse, his face is such an one "as limners love to paint, and ladies to look upon." There were men of note there, too — Generals of renown and the owners of names which history will make famous; and there were Princes, Grand Dukes, and Dukes waiting for the King and his staff — the reigning Duke of Coburg, the Prince (Béritier) of Würtemberg, the young Erbprinz of Mecklenburg-Strelitz, two Royal Dukes of Würtemberg, the Duke of Augustenburg, Prince Adalbert and Prince Albrecht, General Voigts Rhetz, General Von Kirchbach, Col. Von Gottberg, and hosts of others, coming "to see the waters play before the King." Amid the galaxy of uniforms and orders you look in vain for some feeble representative of France. Where is the gorgeous hussar of the Empress — the splendid dragon-vert, with his leopard-skin helmet? Gone — gone the way of earthly glory. A few mob-capped women, nurses, and children, an old woman with cakes, and a wounded soldier, represent France to-day before the gorgeous fountains of Versailles.

FRIDAY, *Oct. 7th.* — Gen. Garibaldi arrives in Marseilles, and joins the Republican forces. Bazaine makes a grand sortie from Metz.

BAZAINE'S SORTIE OF THE 31ST AND 1ST.

Bazaine, true to his private despatch to MacMahon on the 22d of July, has made unceasing efforts to escape from Metz. The first grand sortie was on the 31st of July, while MacMahon was fighting at Sedan. This sortie was toward the north and east, — Nouilly, Servigny, Grimont, Malroy, Colombey, Retonfay — and against the forces of Manteuffel and Kummer, under the direction of Gen. Stiehle, chief of staff, Second army. This sortie was grand and bloody, the Germans losing in the two days (31st and Aug. 1st), killed, 17 officers, 314 men; wounded, officers, 96; men, 855; missing, 1490. (*See* p. 233)

GENERAL STIEHLE'S DESPATCH TO PRINCE CHARLES.

From the morning of August 31, to mid-day of September 1, Marshal Bazaine has almost unceasingly attempted, with several corps from Metz, to break through toward the north. General Manteuffel, under chief command of Prince Frederick Charles, has repulsed all these attempts in glorious battles, which may be united under the name of Battle of Noisseville. The enemy were again thrown back into the fortress. The First and Ninth Corps, Kummer's division (line and landwehr), and the Twenty-eighth infantry brigade, took part in the battle. The principal fighting took place at Servigny, Noisseville, and Retonfay. Night surprises were repulsed with East-Prussian bayonets and clubbed muskets. Our losses not yet ascertained, but not very large proportionally; those of the enemy heavy.

THE GRAND SORTIE OF OCT. 7TH.

To-day the greatest battle around Metz since Gravelotte has been fought in the valley of the Moselle — that portion extending like a basin northward towards Maizières. Bazaine, with

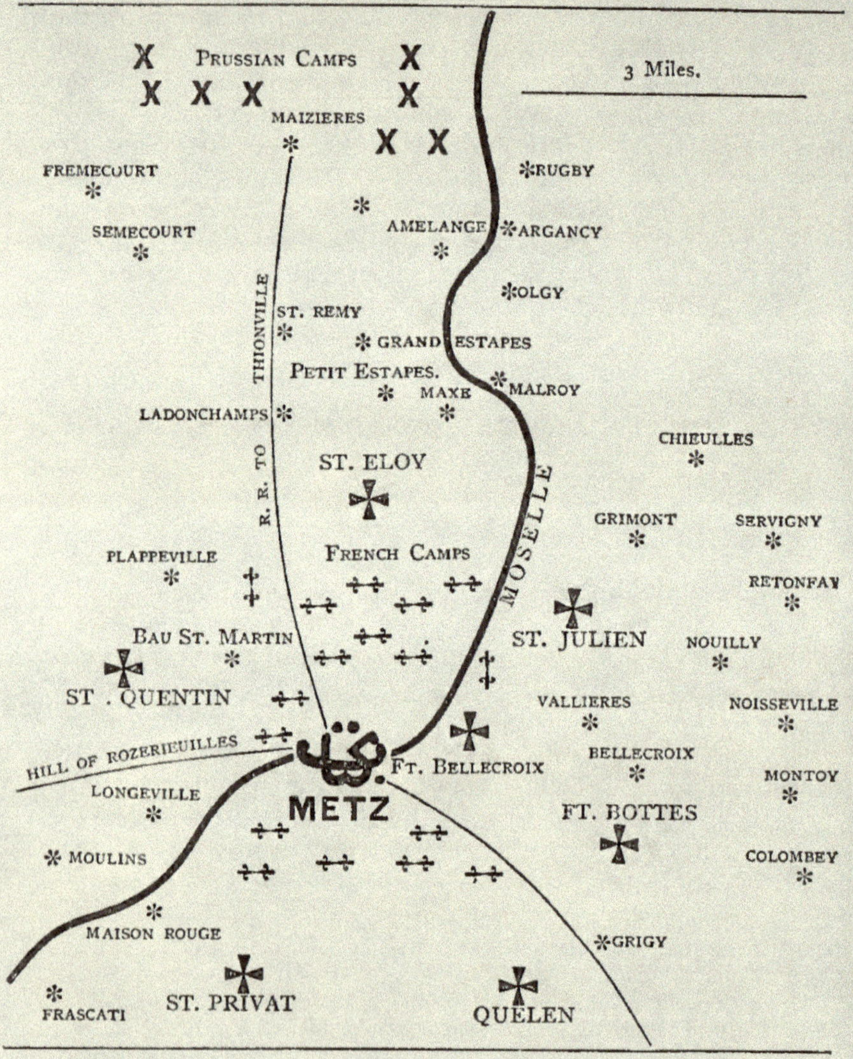

50,000 men, threw himself against the Fifth Corps (Kirchbach), Tenth (Voigts Rhetz), and three brigades of landwehr. Bazaine's design was to push back the Prussian army and regain his communication with Thionville, seventeen miles to the north.

The following is a picture of the position before the engagement. On the northeastern outskirt of Metz is Fort Julien; a mile farther, in the sweeping valley of the Moselle, is Fort Eloy; and just out of the range of her long guns, five miles to the north, is Maizières. On the west bank of the Moselle, along the high hills, are Semecourt and Fremecourt, near Maizières, and nearer to Metz, St. Remy, and Ladonchamps. Along the banks of the water are Maxe, Olgy, Argancy, and Amelange, within range of Fort Julien.

The Prussian guns from Fremecourt and Semecourt, overlooking the grand valley of the Moselle, prevented French communication with Thionville. The Prussian Tenth Corps was stationed on the east bank of the Moselle, near Argancy; while the Fifth and landwehr divisions held the plain from Argancy across to Semecourt, in front of the guns of Maizières. (See map.)

THE COMMENCEMENT.

From these several positions the bombardment of Fort St. Eloy had been going on, and also a shell-fire into the village of Ladonchamps, some little distance nearer Metz than St. Remy, and on the line of railway.

On the 6th, nearly one thousand shells having been thrown into Ladonchamps and around it, the French, late in the evening, had evacuated the shattered ruins of the once smiling village. The Prussians at once threw forward troops in the direction of the village, establishing their reserves in its rear, and sending forward sergeants' squads to occupy it and the villages of Grand Estapes and Petit Estapes, to which its possession was the key, St. Remy constituting the chief support. There lay the Fifty-ninth Regiment of the landwehr. Maxe, close to the river and considerably in advance, was occupied by outposts sent forward from the Tenth Army Corps, on the other side of the Moselle.

The two divisions of the landwehr stretched athwart the valley from the bridge at Argancy, where they touched the Tenth Army Corps, to near Merange, where they met the Fifth Army Corps, and to them was confided the duty of holding the flat alluvial tract on the western bank of the Moselle.

At Maizières was the headquarters of General Von Kummer, who commands the landwehr. The guns of the Prussian batteries by Semecourt began to be heard.

The roar of the guns grew louder and louder, and there came first one heavy "boom," and then another from the big

backs to the walls and their faces to the foe. The other battalions of the same regiment suffered terribly.

So far, then, Bazaine had succeeded. He had occupied the chain of villages athwart the valley, and had placed a few batteries of artillery out on their front to reply to the Prussian fire. But this *statu quo* he neither wished to nor could maintain. The Prussian artillery, throwing their projectiles from three sides of the parallelogram, interfered with the comfortable realization of such a conception. It seems clear that Bazaine would not have done what he did, if he had not contemplated something more. That something, I have not the remotest doubt, was a sortie to establish communications with Thionville. His tactics were well conceived. From St. Remy and the two Estapes he kept the Prussian fire engaged with musketry and artillery. He sent forward from Grand Estapes great swarms of sharpshooters, who fared extremely ill at the hands of the landwehr. Besides this, he massed a great body of men, nearly 30,000 in all, on the bank of the Moselle, under cover of the houses of Maxe, and sent them forward to cut through the Prussian environment where it was weakest, close to the river.

The moment was a critical one. The landwehr had all been sent forward against the villages, with the exception of one brigade that was in reserve, but the Tenth Army Corps had been crossing the pontoon bridge, and was massing between the river and Amelange. There General Von Voight was in command of the back operations, and he gave the order for several regiments to advance. The movement was a sight not easily to be forgotten. First came the fusileers, extending at a rapid run into skirmishing order, and covering the whole plain with their long, thin lines. Then came the dense columns of companies of grenadiers, the bands playing and the colors unfurled. But all the work was not left for the infantry to do: the artillery entered the village alone, and concentrated their fire on the French columns advancing by the Moselle. Bazaine is singularly weak in field artillery, and the only reply to the Prussian fire was from the sullen sides of Fort St. Julien or from the ramparts of St. Eloy. But the mitrailleuse venomously sounded its angry whirr, making the skirmishers recoil narrowly as they crossed the line of fire, and tearing chasms in the fronts of the solid masses of which they were the forerunners.

The artillery and the skirmishers were enough for the French.

Their dense columns staggered, and then broke apart. They ran pell-mell into the village of Maxe; but when once they had walls of stone and lime between them and the Prussians, they became obstinate, and would go no further. In vain the Prussian artillery fired upon the village, advancing closer and closer in alternate order of batteries, with a precision and rapidity that could not have been exceeded on parade. That obstinate battery in front of Grand Estapes would not be silenced, and the French sharpshooters still lined the highway in its front. By this time it was nearly four o'clock.

ADVANCE IN FORCE.

As the Prussians stood in this suspense, a staff officer galloped along the front line, with orders for a general advance, to take the village by storm. The advance was to consist of four brigades of the landwehr, with two brigades of the Tenth Army Corps supporting. In a few minutes more the command came sounding along the line, and the men sprang from their cover and went forward with that steady, quick step, so characteristic of the Prussian marching. The shells from the battery of Grand Estapes tore through the line; the mitrailleuse and chassepôt bullets poured against it their leaden hail; but still the landwehr, silent and stern, marched steadily to the front. I never knew a more furious fire than that to which the centre of this line was exposed. General Von Brandenstein, commanding the Third brigade of landwehr, was shot down as he rode, and several of his staff were wounded. At length the entrenchments were reached, behind which were lying the shattered remnants of the Fifty-eighth and Fifty-ninth landwehr. The fraternization consisted of "*Hurrah Preussen!*" and then, "*Vorwarts! Immer vorwarts!*" and the line threw itself to the front in a run. The gunners from the battery drove on. The stubborn French had barely time to run around the corner before the landwehr were upon them.

The French left their guns perforce. They made a last stand in the villages, but it would have been better for them had they run away at first. The landwehr, with less of the conventional warriors in them than the line, are not so much inclined to give quarter as are the professional soldiers. With many a Frenchman this afternoon, the first shock consisted of a bayonet thrust. The French fought "like devils" in the narrow streets of the villages, and used the mitrailleuses with fair judgment and effect. But there came upon them the steady, inexorable forward stride of the landwehr. The bayonet obtained force from that strength of back and thigh which is the leading athletic characteristic of the Prussian, and the villages were cleared of all, save the victors, the dead, and the wounded. To the landwehr must be conceded the honor of the fray. They it was who checked the rush of the French advance, by holding the villages till they had not a man left who could stand upright and fire the needle-gun. To them was entrusted the grand final advance which swept the French out of the villages.

SATURDAY, *October 8th.* — An extraordinary session of the American Cabinet approves a proclamation enforcing American neutrality. Gambetta, the French Minister of the Interior, leaves Paris for Tours in a balloon, amid great excitement. Food begins to be scarce in Paris.

THE BALLOON VOYAGE OF MINISTER GAMBETTA.

The event of Paris to-day was the departure of Gambetta, the Minister of the Interior, on his balloon voyage for Tours. The trials of the siege were forgotten for the moment, and all Paris was wrought up to a high pitch of excitement. What a change has sixty days wrought! Sixty days ago, and the Paris press were talking about carrying on the war for the repossession of the Rhine boundary; now 350,000 Prussians frown down upon Paris, and the Minister of the Interior flees the Capital in a balloon. Unfortunate Gambetta! Let the reader but imagine our Secretary Fish or Mr. Boutwell, or the ex-Premier Seward, sailing from Washington in a balloon.

THE START.

M. Nadar had the balloon ready at 11 A.M. The Minister of the Interior appeared at this moment. The vast crowd experienced great relief as he donned his cap and fur coat, and entered the car. Gambetta is a man of nerve, but he is unaccustomed to the queer sensation incident to a balloon trip. He clutches the shrouding convulsively, and his color becomes almost livid. An additional line of rope is thrown around the shrouds of the car, to prevent the delicate Minister from falling out. Following Gambetta come two secretaries, bags of letters and baskets of carrier pigeons.

M. Nadar gave the order, "*Laches tout!*"

The balloon rises majestically from the earth, amid cheers from the crowd. Handkerchiefs wave all over Paris, and "*Vive la République*" is shouted forth by thousands of tongues as the aerial travellers unfurl the French flag.

AN ALARM.

Near Montmartre, a steep hill rises abruptly from the Place St. Pierre. As the balloons pass over the spot they appear to descend rapidly. Everybody is petrified with fear. Horror is depicted on the faces of the people. The appearance at the moment is beyond the power of the pen to describe. The Minister of the Interior contracts his arms, and it is thought that the letter bags, the contents of which are expected to convey hope and new life to thousands of persons, will fall into the hands of the Prussian soldiers.

What a relief?

The balloon sails steadily onward and upward, Paris shouts again and again, "*Vive Gambetta*," and the scene is over.

OUTSIDE OF PARIS.

Gambetta descends at Mont Dizier. His voyage was full of adventure. As the balloon came near the ground, just outside of Paris, the secretaries threw out ballast, and rose, passing slowly over the Prussian lines. Again the balloon descended near Creil, and espying a force of Prussians, the voyagers throw out shawls and travelling-bags. They arise slowly again — a .shot just grazing the hair of Gambetta. Striking among the trees at Mont Dizier, the balloon becomes torn, and falls to the ground, when the diplomatic party take a conveyance for Amiens, while a party of uhlans pursue them from the other side of the wood.

SUNDAY, *October 9th.* — Gambetta arrives at Tours in a thunderstorm, and is warmly received at the station. Garibaldi arrives, and is received by Crémieux. The Francs-tireurs request M. Glais-Bizon to embrace Garibaldi for the regiment.

VON ROON ON THE SIEGE OF PARIS.

The impatience of the German people at home, on account of delay in the fall of Paris, has led War Minister Von Roon to dictate the following semi-official note, published in the *Berlin Staatsanzeiger:*

Experience has taught us, that in a war with France no satisfactory peace can be obtained unless dictated at Paris. All our operations are necessarily aimed at this one object. Had Paris been in possession of an army fit to undertake its defence, a long resistance might have been offered in front of and between the various forts of the *enceinte.* To deprive it of this resource by annihilating one-half of the French troops and shutting up the rest, was the result of the first portion of the campaign.

Having thus robbed Paris of the army which might have turned its fortifications to account, the efficiency of the defences was considerably diminished. Notwithstanding, however, the damage inflicted upon the enemy, the moral and material resources remaining to him are of no contemptible kind, and *having been placed at the disposal of an energetic commander, render the task of our armies one of the most difficult recorded in the military history of the world.*

Considered as an object of attack, Paris can be scarcely regarded as a fortress. It is rather a fortified battle-field, with forts covering every point of access. Among these forts, some are strong enough to rank as citadels of themselves; while others, as for instance Mont Valérien and St. Denis, are well known to exceed the strength of many a fortress. Behind the forts there is a continuous rampart nearly six geographical miles in circumference. It would take no less than twelve hours to visit the forts in succession, the sphere of their efficiency actually extending over eighteen hours.

Directly our generals recognized that, owing to the unavoidable incompleteness of the investment and position of affairs in the interior, reduction by mere enclosure would not lead to prompt result, preparations were begun to bombard and regularly besiege the place. Although in a city of 2,000,000 inhabitants the steady decrease of provisions and the progressive disorganization of society alone may be regarded as guaranteeing ultimate surrender, still, as the inclement season is drawing near, *a partial bombardment, accompanied by an attack upon those of the advanced forts whose possession may be indispensable in certain contingencies, will be an effective means to accelerate the catastrophe.*

We must not omit mentioning that the portion of the environs from which a bombardment can be directed, not alone against the main rampart and several suburbs, but against the very heart of the city, is the most hilly and impracticable of all.

It is, however, probable that the bombardment of the city will not be proceeded with until the fire of several forts has been silenced. Great as might be the impression made by a bombardment, it cannot be our object to aim at a partial result. To secure all we want, and secure it safely, we require the forts. We may confidently expect that we shall not be long in conquering some. The investing army has the means to protect itself from rain and cold, and as the winter at Paris is, as a rule, much milder than in Germany, we may hope to brave the rigors of the season without any very sensible suffering. Paris, on the other hand, will get weaker every day the siege lasts. Provisions will become scarcer and scarcer, and the *proletariat* is likely to rise ultimately against the wealthy — a contingency hastened on by our hindering any fresh supplies from reaching the beleaguered town. Our numerous cavalry is quite competent to carry this out.

The French Minister of the Interior, in his latest circular of the 9th inst., assures his countrymen that Paris can neither be taken by force, nor surprise, nor famine, nor rebellion. His self-delusion, it must be admitted, is complete. He enumerates the very calamities which will compel surrender, and in his blind confidence draws a false conclusion.

Our task is to possess ourselves of the French capital with as little loss of time and life as possible. We are sure to master the uncommonly difficult problem, but shall scarcely succeed so very rapidly as the anxious expectation of our countrymen would desire.

TUESDAY, *October 11th.*—The French Army of the Loire defeated at Artenay (25 miles north of Orleans) by General Von der Tann. Von der Tann pursues the French, captures Orleans, and 8000 prisoners. The Army of the Loire totally defeated. The Badeners under Schmeling enter Epinal, on the Moselle.

BATTLE OF ARTENAY.

The first of a series of battles by the Prussian General Von der Tann occurred to-day at Artenay, twenty-five miles north of Orleans. The German force consisted of the First Bavarian Corps, reinforced by one Prussian division of infantry and two Prussian cavalry divisions. For the past week the cavalry division of Prince Albrecht has been scouring the country south of Paris, towards Orleans, from whom the Francs-tireurs have fled in every instance, being outnumbered, as the French have been in every engagement since Saarbrück. The French forces were immediately under the command of General Lorgnell, reinforced by about 10,000 disorganized Mobiles and a new organization known as the *Partisans.* The French had about 20,000 men, while the Prussians had about 25,000, General Von der Tann having been reinforced by the twenty-second division of the Eleventh Corps. The battle commenced by heavy skirmishing on the 8th at Etamps, when the French fled towards Artenay, on the road to Orleans. The French had no artillery, and after the Prussians opened with batteries on the town on the 10th, they became demoralized, and fled in precipitate confusion. The Prussian artillery destroyed the railroad depot, and quite a number of citizens were killed by the *flying stones from the barricades.* The Prussians came across the new order of French troops called Partisans for the first time to-day. For these men the Prussians have the most supreme contempt. These new levies are the body-guard of the Tours Government, and are thus described in the Prussian official report:

"In the account books they had with them their pay and other emoluments from the Republican authorities were accurately stated. They were mostly men above 40, or youngsters between 16 and 18; those between these two extremes having been previously drafted into the Mobiles. They were indeed unable to defend themselves, being totally ignorant of everything military, and, moreover, armed with Minie rifles, which cannot compete with modern weapons. In reply to our questions, they said they knew nothing of the service, and altogether represented their situation as pitiable. The peasants would not give them anything to eat, nor even direct them how to find their way across the country. The fear of the Germans was so universal in those parts, that everybody shunned intercourse with the indigenous troops. The costume of the Partisans consists in a short black coat, black trousers, gaiters, and a red sash round the waist. They wear hats with broad brims, those of the captains being about four times as large as those worn by the privates. The commander-in-chief of the body taken prisoners at Angerville was a private gentleman from Nantes. Most of them had the words *Partisans de Gers* on their hats. The Departement de Gers being 400 miles south of Paris, and only 150 miles north of the Pyrenées, their presence in the Orleannois would seem to prove that the central Departments are already drained of most of the people that can be induced to join."

The entire French army of the South seems to be demoralized at the overwhelming numbers of the Prussians, and are flying disastrously towards Orleans.

THE BATTLE OF ORLEANS.

KING WILLIAM'S DESPATCH.

To the Queen:

Versailles, *Wednesday*. — Thousands of prisoners fell into our hands as the result of Von der Tann's victory near Orleans. The battle lasted from nine o'clock in the morning to seven in the evening, and was fought on difficult ground. The capture of Orleans followed. The losses of the French were heavy; ours were small.

Wilhelm.

DESPATCH FROM THE FRENCH GENERAL MOTTEROUGE.

La Feste St. Aubin, *October* 12. — Yesterday the enemy continued to advance towards Orleans. Our troops, *who were on the road to Paris*, and had taken part the day before in the battle at Artenay, gave way. A brigade of the Third division, who tried to oppose the enemy's advance, being constantly opposed by forces more numerous, and a superior artillery, had to fall back on Orleans, disputing the ground foot by foot. I was obliged, in order to check the enemy's progress, to go forward personally with three battalions of the reserve, belonging to the Second division. The enemy was checked for three hours, but at last we were broken and overcome by their shells. After very sharp fighting, which does honor to our army, I determined to evacuate Orleans, and to withdraw to the left bank of the Loire. Our retreat, which was not molested, was effected with coolness and in good order.

THE BATTLE OF ORLEANS.

The French forces had fallen back from Artenay like a disorganized mob. The superior artillery of the Prussians had pounded the life out of Lorgnell with his 12,000 men, at long range, and the morning of the 11th found him in the forest behind Cercottes, in front of Orleans. General Motterouge having relieved Polhes, was in supreme command at Orleans, over an army of 40,000 French, disorganized, gunless, ammunitionless. Every moment the terrible Von der Tann, with 30,000 organized Prussians, splendidly served with artillery, was expected in front. What was to be done? Motterouge sent couriers to Tours pleading for arms, went himself to Blois, and his aides galloped to every township and rummaged in every military store where it was thought the muzzle of a field-piece might be hid. A trophy gun or two was found in some of the out-of-the-way places — an old Spaniard, still bearing on its carriage an inscription to the effect that it had been presented to some long since dead and forgotten mayor, in commemoration of the eternal glories of France; and a very ugly Russian, which had made the long journey from Moscow in 1812, and which rumbled and bumped and creaked along on its axles, as if it were anything but pleased to be roused from the slumbers of age to kill more men. Rewards were offered to any one who could discover the whereabouts of a field-piece. There were no more to be found; but the public necessity stimulated the invention of a patriotic brass-finisher of Blois, who laid his stock-in-trade of chandeliers under contribution, and, by dint of much bellows-blowing and no little swearing, produced a tubed something, which looked like the wooden guns of Manassas. It was an enlarged gas-pipe.

With this atrociously shabby artillery, Motterouge decided to make a stand against Von der Tann. General Reyau was sent forward to reinforce Lorgnell with 12,000 more troops, while the General commanding sat down and *hoped for more guns from Tours and Blois.* The French encamped in front of the innumerable Prussian watch-fires last night, and sang and told stories to keep up their courage, while not an eye was closed in Orleans. As the Prussians unlimbered their guns this morning, the French fell back on Orleans; but not until Reyau had asked for the last time for guns to fight with. The French outnumbered by 10,000 the whole Prussian force. But what of that? Without artillery they were little better than a disciplined mob without arms. Guns, guns, guns, was the cry of the soldiers in the ranks and the tacticians in the cafés. As each train was signalled, they ran to the edge of the platform and peered into the darkness, in the hope of catching a sight of a black muzzle, and when instead of that they saw but countless white faces of men, their welcome almost took the form of a malediction. And whenever they turned away with this disappointment at their hearts, there would be sure to be some poor bedraggled wretch from Reyau's quarters at the door of the railway station, to ask the ordnance officers for the love of God to tell him "if they had come?"

THE FIGHT.

At 7 A.M. the Prussians threw 30,000 organized men and a hail of balls on the unfortunate French in the woods, compelling the last Frenchman to fall back on Orleans. They now rushed forward in hot haste, and seized on Mont Joie. Mont Joie is a high plateau visible from Orleans, and as Motterouge sent an orderly to the station to inquire if the guns had arrived from Tours, he had only to lift his eyes to this eminence to see the Prussians preparing to give him an answer from the throats of eighty guns. It was too late to talk of getting ready now. There was nothing for him to do but to evacuate the town; for to have advanced without artillery to the capture of that height, would have been to rush on to an irreparable disaster.

BLUNDER AGAIN.

At 8 A.M. the guns from Tours and Blois arrived, but *too late*. A whole railroad train filled with *what might have saved Orleans!* Eighty Prussian guns in orderly lines looked down upon Orleans, and here, in inextricable confusion, were piles of arms, heaps of knapsacks, tons of provisions, cases of surgical appliances, and bodies of men. Blois had roused itself at the last moment, and with one spasm of energy had cleared out its stores, its magazines, and its barracks, and bundled them all together — goods, guns, and men — into the lap of Orleans. For all or any of these things to be of the slightest use to Motterouge, they must be sorted and rearranged, and that was a half-day's labor for a competent staff.

If the Prussians now, by a superior chivalry, would give the French ten hours to prepare — but they will not. France is always just ten hours behind.

THE ARMY RETREATS.

Reyan had fallen back, and while General Arago, with 3000 guards, held the Prussians in check (for Mont Joie only commands the suburbs of Orleans), the French army commenced moving out of the town. In about half an hour from the commencement of their march, and when the advance had barely got clear of the town, a loud roar of artillery from Mont Joie shook earth and air, and the first shower of an iron storm that was to beat unceasingly for over eight hours fell on the devoted guard at Banien, in the suburbs of Orleans.

The retreat was splendidly covered by Arago with his faithful 3000, but at what a cost! There was no plan of battle, but to stand behind houses and walls, and shoot. There was not even organization enough to surrender, and so they stood each, and fought for his life for eight hours.

The Prussians simply fired until they judged that the breaches in the living fortress warranted an assault, and then they dashed at their men with cavalry and infantry, only to be driven back in ruin by the chassepôt. The failure of repeated attempts of this kind at length taught them to rely exclusively on their artillery.

THE ENCOUNTER OF DEATH.

This enabled the French to find shelter behind the walls of Banien and the Gare des Autrais. The Foreign Legion, composed mainly of young men of pleasure from Paris, and not a few Americans, held Banien while Autrais was held by the French Pontificals.

The point of honor between the two corps was which should surrender last; or to put it differently, since each had the certainty of death before it, which should raise the last shout of defiance to the foe. Neither won; it was a dead heat of glory. Of 1500 of the Foreign Legion, 36 came back to Blois, and of 370 Zouaves but 17 left the field alive.

The shelter of houses, though they saved their lives for the moment, did but prolong their agony; and it must have proved a far severer test to their fortitude than even the stand in the open field, where death comes too swiftly to permit them to reflect on its terrors. Those in the railway station sought the shelter of the trucks and the waiting rooms; those in the faubourg hid themselves in the cellars of the houses, ready to spring forth the moment an enemy could be found to face them. They lay thus, and perished slowly one by one. The Prussians had got the range of the railway station and the range of the faubourg, and every half minute or so a shell came crashing though wall or roof, and its *débris* buried a man. The Legionaries for the most part bore their fate with a calm, despairing fortitude; the Pontificals showed less patience, and ever and anon some dust-begrimed wretch, mad with fury and blind with his own blood, dashed forth to shriek and shake his fist towards the pitiless cannon, till a new discharge swept him into eternity.

Hours elapsed, and still the situation in all its essential features remained unchanged. The Army of the Loire — for it was really the bulk of the army, although there were divisions at Bourges and at Tours — defiled out of Orleans. The Prussians pounded the positions in front of them, in order to be able to push forward and cut the retreating force in half. The three thousand held the positions. No message came from their comrades, and no answer to their own message asking for reinforcements to enable them to make a dash on the heights. Three o'clock, four, five came, and though by this last hour every man and every gun had passed out of Orleans, no word was brought. The bloody drama was yet to linger out in representation for two hours more. At 7 o'clock the artillery fire suddenly ceased, and the Prussians made their fifth advance in force. Not a shot was fired against their heavy masses as they deployed in the open field; but as they swarmed into Banien and into the railway station, about a hundred and fifty ghastly creatures in the military garb rose up to meet them in the longed-for embrace of death. The Prussians captured from Arthenay to Orleans about 8000 stragglers.

THE INHABITANTS.

The inhabitants were divided. Some were for defending the town, but a far greater number entreated that no defence should be offered. It was this defence which caused the Prussians to burn the railroad depot. It was a battle in utter confusion, without orders, without officers. During the onset in the faubourg, the peasants seemed beside themselves, some with alarm, others with rage. Women were wringing their hands as they were sent off to some safer place. Men were preparing to hold out against the enemy, or to disperse in the fields and fire at them in isolated parties. No plan was yet made. The drum was beating *La Générale*, and bells were sounding.

AFTER THE BATTLE.

An excited multitude was flying towards Beaugency, a few miles to the south of Orleans. It was a headless caravan of peasants, nobility, and soldiers, with women and children. Soldiers knew not where to go. The Zouaves had orders to retreat at Bull Run, and they continued it to New York. So the French Zouaves seemed making a demoralized run for Tours. At Meung, a few miles nearer Orleans, the excitement was still greater. Officers of the *Garde Mobile* rode by in consternation. They had no idea where their commands were. About's description of MacMahon's flight through Saverne is a faint attempt to portray the sickening scenes in Meung. Many men who had been fighting were gentlemen of position in the neighboring country districts. There was an indescribable terror everywhere. In Tours there was the most complete ignorance. Even Gambetta knew nothing of the occurrences. It would seem that the Republic must now make peace, or continue to fly before the advancing Prussians, for, disorganized, however patriotic its votaries may be, it cannot fight the organized legions of a Monarchy. *The Army of the Loire has disappointed the expectations of the world.*

PRUSSIAN OFFICIAL ESTIMATE OF ORLEANS.

Orleans is one of the wealthiest cities in France. The region north of it, the so-called Beauce, is certainly the most fertile district we have as yet entered. It provides Paris with enormous quantities of excellent wheat, ground by the steam and water mills in the province. It also abounds in oats (which will be a great acquisition for our cavalry), and produces grapes and every variety of fruit in such plenty, that, in addition to supplying Paris, its choice articles are exported to foreign countries. The possession of the Beauce will sensibly diminish the number of our provision trains from Germany.

The occupation of Orleans is also important from a strategical point of view. Situate on the right bank of the Loire, and being the point of junction for the Central Railway, and the lines from Nantes, Bordeaux, and Toulouse, it protects our army from attack from the south, and all but prevents our enemies in the North holding communications with the south. By blowing up a single arch of the two magnificent bridges over the Loire, each of which has cost 2,000,000f., we render it difficult for a southern enemy to penetrate north, the next two bridges at Jargeau and Beaugency not being strong enough for artillery to pass over. Gien, higher up the river, is already ours, and the Sologne, which is the name of the country lower down, beyond Blois, is so barren and destitute of roads, that it serves as a natural safeguard from that side. Orleans is known for the pacific disposition of its inhabitants, and has large barracks and other buildings, which will be useful should the campaign be prolonged.

EPINAL, ON THE MOSELLE, CAPTURED.

General Schmeling, with his victorious Badeners, marches on from St. Remy and captures Epinal. The citizens (15,000) make a stout defence, but the German artillery begins to destroy the town, when it surrenders.

TOURS.

Minister Gamebtta issues an excited proclamation relative to sorties from Paris to-day.

The new French coat of arms makes its appearance. It consists of a figure of Liberty, with the legend, "In the name of the French people." On the reverse is a garland of mixed oak and olive, with a wheat ear in the centre. There is also the inscription, "*Républiquc Française Democratiquè, Une et Indivisible.*" Around the periphery are the words, "*Liberté, Egalité, Fraternité.*"

THURSDAY, *October* 13*th*. —The French guns from Mont Valérien destroy the Palace of St. Cloud. Amiens, St. Quentin, and Rouen, on the north, threatened by the Prussian forces under Prince Albrecht. General La Motterouge, the French Commander of the Loire, is superseded by General Aurelles De Palladines.

THE PALACE OF ST. CLOUD DESTROYED.

St. Cloud falls a tribute to the power of modern artillery, while its destruction marks the barbarism of war. This beautiful palace, about five miles south-west of Paris, has recently been the rendezvous of Prussian officers, and to-day it was decided in Paris to destroy it. The structure itself is not of much importance, while the grounds are laid out in profligate magnificence. The fountains in front, with their thousands of colossal frogs, lizards, and other reptiles, each spurting a stream high into the air, are only equalled by those of Versailles and Wilhelmshöhe.

FRENCH ACTIVITY.

The terrible artillery fire of Fort du Mont Valérien has literally swept the country round about. For a circuit of six kilomètres, the Prussian works have been delayed, and their advance lines have fallen back.

The Château of Meudon has also been destroyed. The Prussian engineers have been driven from Clamart, Meudon, and Montretout. The French scouting parties have advanced as far as Villejuif and Vitry.

The Prussian circle around Paris is therefore expanding daily instead of contracting, and the Parisians are greatly encouraged.

The Prussians have decided in war council to abide the starvation process, rather than to reduce Paris by active siege. Bismarck's idea is, that internal dissensions, idleness, and hunger will reduce Paris sooner than Krupp's guns. However, many guns are arriving, and the Prussians are planting them within range of Paris.

FRIDAY, *October* 14.—Bazaine makes another sortie from Metz, capturing 193 wagon loads of provisions, and retires behind Forts Bellecroix and St. Julien.

SATURDAY, *October* 15*th*.—Bismarck expresses a desire to treat for peace. Correspondence is opened with Lord Granville, M. Thiers, and Minister Washburne. The French continue to fire on the Prussians, who have not fired a gun. Trochu protests against Paris impatience.

PARIS IMPATIENCE.

General Trochu, being sadly disturbed with the impatience of the Parisians, who demand an attack on the Prussians, writes as follows to the Mayor of Paris:

PARIS, *October* 15.

MONSIEUR LE MAIRE—In the month of July last the French army, in all the splendor of its strength, passed through Paris, amidst shouts of "*A Berlin! A Berlin!*" *I was far from sharing their confidence, and alone, perhaps, among all the general officers, I ventured to tell the Marshal Minister of War that I perceived in this noisy manner of entering upon a campaign, as well as the means brought into requisition, the elements of a great disaster. The will which at this period I placed in the hands of M. Ducloux, a notary of Paris, will one day testify to the painful and too well-grounded presentiments with which my soul was filled.*

To-day, in the presence of the fever which has rightly taken possession of the public mind, I meet with difficulties which present a most striking analogy with those that showed themselves in the past. I now declare that *I will not cede to the pressure of the public impatience.* Animating myself with the sense of the duties which are common to us all, and of the responsibilities that no one shares with me, I shall pursue to the end the plan which I have traced out without revealing it, and I only demand of the population of Paris, in exchange for my efforts, the continuance of that confidence with which it has hitherto honored me.

Receive, Monsieur le Maire, the assurance of my high consideration.

GENERAL TROCHU.

SUNDAY, *October* 16.—Soissons, fifty miles north-east of Paris, surrenders, with 99 officers, 4633 men, and 132 guns, to the Grand Duke of Mecklenburg-Schwerin.

SOISSONS.

Soissons is another link in the chain of connection between the Prussian forces in front of Paris and their home base of supplies. Laon, Toul, and Soissons are of inestimable value to the Prussians. There only remain now between Paris and Berlin, Metz and Verdun. When these shall fall, King William will be master of the two great railroads which connect Berlin with Paris.

THE SIEGE.

The Grand Duke of Mecklenburg commenced the bombardment of Soissons on the 12th. His force consisted of the Würtemberg foot, the Pomeranian, Hessian, and Magdeburg artillery, the Schleswig engineers, eight battalions of landwehr, and the Halberstadt horse. The investment lasted three weeks, and the bombardment four days.

Few houses were damaged, and the German army occupied the town without disorder. Beside the 99 officers and 4633 men, captured, the Germans took 132 guns, 70,000 bombs, 150 tons of ammunition, and a military chest containing 92,000 francs.

THE EFFECT OF THE SURRENDER.

The effect of the surrender of these military keys of France begins to drive the French people to desperation. They feel as did the Confederates when General Sherman was marching his army victoriously to the sea. The base of an army is not Paris or Washington or Berlin—it is the cornfield, the vineyard, and the pastures of fat cattle. Capture these, and an enemy will soon starve. When Sherman once got into the corn-cribs of the South, the Rebellion became a hollow shell. So it is becoming to-day in France. With a Prussian army moving towards Lyons from Strasburg, towards Tours from Orleans and Paris, towards Rouen on the north from Soissons, capturing towns, disorganizing labor, and destroying the agriculture of

France, what hope is there in a continued war? There is no organization in France — no head. Favre is a timid man; Gambetta is full of fire, but people have no confidence in him; and Trochu is sealed up in Paris. 40,000,000 unconquered Frenchmen are as powerless as were 8,000,000 Confederates with Richmond, Charleston, Nashville, and Columbia captured, and the head, Jeff Davis, like Napoleon, a captive. *France is in the iron vice of Prussia.* Every battle only screws the vice tighter and makes Bismarck more exacting.

MONDAY, *October* 17. — General Napoleon Boyer, Bazaine's chief of staff, visits Versailles to negotiate the surrender of Metz. He desires to surrender the army to Prussia, but would leave a garrison to hold the fortress for France. King William insists on a similar capitulation to Sedan. The forces of the Duke of Mecklenburg-Schwerin move from Soissons towards Paris.

TUESDAY, *October* 18. — The French in front of General Werder, at Epinal, retire towards Dijon and Lyons, in the Rhône Department. 8000 Prussians capture and nearly destroy Châteaudun, a few miles north of Orleans, Department of the Loire. Bismarck declares a continuation of the same policy and demands by Prussia.

BISMARCK'S PRUSSIAN POLICY.

Bismarck declares to-day that —

The position of Prussia has never changed, from the hour of the declaration of war by France to the present. Compelled unwillingly to draw the sword, he declares that his countrymen would never sheath it until Germany was safe from future cruel assaults, and from the ambition and insolence of her unprincipled neighbor. He makes the same declaration now, confident in the justice of the cause.

Said Bismarck: "We anticipated victory, but it was left to the experience of war to teach us what guarantees would effectually accomplish the object we had in view at the commencement. The blood, treasure, and suffering it cost us to win our past victories convince the Prussian nation that they can hope for no full security without reclaiming those provinces wrenched from Germany for the purposes of aggression, lust, and conquest. Prussia earnestly desires peace, but peace only which will give full security for the future."

"Germany can stand a long campaign. We have large resources at hand,

and the hardest work is over. While we are anxious for peace, we have no fear for the future. Continued war complicates negotiations for peace. Prussia is willing to listen to proposals seeking an end of the war from any quarter likely to lead to practical results, in view of the disorganized state of France, no matter whether it comes from the ex-Empire or the present Provisional Government; but an armistice is useless, unless made so as to lead to peace."

WEDNESDAY, *October 19th.* — Large Republican meeting in London, in favor of the French Republic, and censuring Gladstone and the Queen.

NEW MILITARY DIVISIONS OF FRANCE.

The following new military divisions have been formed in France:

Division of the North — General Bourbaki, commanding; headquarters at Lille.

Division of the West — General Fiereck, commanding; headquarters at Le Mans.

Division of the Centre — General Aurelles de Paladines, commanding; headquarters at Bourges.

Division of the East — General Ernest (Cambriels, resigned), commanding; headquarters at Besançon.

FRIDAY, *October* 21. — St. Quentin, sixty miles to the north-east of Paris, surrenders to the Grand Duke of Mecklenburg. Chartres, thirty miles south-west of Paris, surrenders. General Boyer returns to Metz with King William's ultimatum, that the surrender of the fortress can only be "on the same terms as Sedan." General Boyer desired permission for Bazaine to remove the women and children, surrender the army, but hold the fortress with a regular garrison.

SATURDAY, *October* 22. — Besançon, the headquarters of the French General Ernest, occupied by the Prussians. The French Army of the Rhône falling back. Earl Granville opens negotiations with the Government at Tours, Berlin, St. Petersburg, Vienna, and Florence, in the interests of peace or an armistice. A suspension of hostilities favored by Bismarck, who desires to treat on same terms offered to Favre, September 21st. The armistice is to allow the convocation of the General Assembly, and the holding of a general election.

SUNDAY, *October* 23.—The natives and Jews of Algeria are decreed citizens of France. The Provisional Governor withdrawn, and M. Henri Didier appointed Governor-General over the Prefects. Garibaldi at Dole, between Dijon and Besançon, at the head of 5000 Spanish, Italians, and French, without discipline. The Empress takes up her abode at Chiselhurst, The Army of the Grand Duke of Mecklenburg evacuates St. Quentin, and marches towards Paris.

GARIBALDI.

On account of Garibaldi's anti-Catholic prejudice, his presence at Dole, a few miles south-east of Dijon, does not harmonize French sympathy. The General has under him only about 5000 men, without discipline or organization. Like Napoleon III., the once powerful patriot is in his chair days. The "old fire is up in his eye," but rheumatism has drawn up his fingers, and he will be useless in the field. All the confidence placed in him by poor fallen France will depart the first time he meets the organized armies of Prussia. Garibaldi has with him his son-in-law, Canseo, chief of staff. The grand old patriot, who paved the way for the entry of the Italian troops into Rome (see 20th September), and who has made Northern Italy almost a unit against the Pope, is better calculated to organize a people than an army. His last order is more like an address to the world than an order to his band of 5000 rangers. In this order, Garibaldi reproaches republics for their failure to act for mutual defence. Switzerland, he says, is kept down by the cash boxes of her great bankers. Referring to the United States the General says: "President Grant, by lifting his finger, might have sent Prim's soldiers in Cuba back to Madrid, but he allows the murder of the entire population of Cuba, who are part of Washington's great family; barely permits the Republic to fling a word of sympathy to the brave descendants of Lafayette. Thou, who first proclaimed the emancipation of races, classical land of liberty, home of the exile, wilt thou abandon in the struggle of giants thy sister nation, who marched and will again march at the van of human progress? Heroic struggle!" he continues; "France is in ruins, because her army of braves were led by the stupidest of tyrants. But the nation is here. It has risen as one man, and will make the old autocrat of Prussia repent his inhuman butchery."

The order closes with an appeal to the soldiers, declaring that their courage is unquestionable, but that they want coolness and discipline, so indispensable in war.

MONDAY, *October* 24.—The Spanish candidature of the Duke of Aosta, in place of Prince Leopold of Hohenzollern, approved by five European powers, including Prussia. The French war loan of $10,000,000 taken in the English market. M. Schneider says France will hold as sacred all debts incurred in saving her existence. The Empress Eugenie denies Imperial intrigues at Chiselhurst, and asserts that she could never entertain the idea of peace based on a cession of Alsace and Lorraine to Prussia.

THE SPANISH THRONE—PRUSSIA'S VINDICATION.

To-day Prussia vindicates herself against the accusations of the Hohenzollern intrigue by approving, with the other European powers, the candidature of the Duke of Aosta for the Spanish throne. In the case of Prince Leopold, treated of in the first seventy pages of this volume, Prussia announced strict non-interference. Constant to this idea, she now as quickly and generously approves the candidature of the Duke of Aosta, while Prince Leopold fights with King William before Paris. This act of approval makes the position of Prussia as splendidly logical as Mr. Seward made our policy of non-interference when he applied the case to our own country, and rendered back Mason and Slidell to the flag of England. "Do to others as ye would—" is the sublime foundation of sound law, personal and international. Napoleon III. declared war because King William would not interfere, as King, *vi et armis*, against Prince Leopold's candidature. Just as well might France declare war to-day against Victor Emmanuel, compelling his interference against the Duke of Aosta's candidature; and this, no doubt, she would do, had not Sedan broken and captured her *personal* ruler, the war-declaring Cæsar, who has kept Europe armed, through an empty threat of bloodshed, for eighteen years. The Duke of Aosta is elected to the throne, November 16.

TUESDAY, *October 25th.* — Bazaine makes known to his officers that Metz is about to capitulate to famine. General Coffinières, commanding the city and fortress, desires to cut his way through the Prussian lines, but is overruled. This afternoon, General Changarnier passes through the lines to Prince Charles's headquarters, south of Metz. An hour's conference is held, relative to the surrender of the fortress, when Changarnier returns to Metz. The Prussians around Paris have in position, to open on the city, 225 siege guns.

METZ.

Metz, the virgin city, is about to surrender to famine. After General Changarnier returned from a conference with Prince Charles to-day, there was a second consultation at Frescati Château, three miles south of Metz. There, in solemn conference, met Changarnier, Bazaine, Coffinières, and Humbert, second in command of the fortress, on the part of the French; and General Stiehle and Colonel Von Herzaing, chief of the German staff, on the part of the Germans. The main points of the capitulation were discussed and agreed upon substantially the, same as at the capitulation of Sedan. Matters are so far understood to-day, that the Second Corps (General Fansecki's) moves to the assistance of Paris this evening. As yet, the French troops have no knowledge of the intended surrender of Metz. The Prussian forces are moved forward to prevent French desertions — Bazaine's last means of prolonging the struggle in Metz. There is a defiant air in Metz among the inhabitants. Little do they suspect the truth of the situation, and that, while the troops are clamoring to cut their way out, the terms of to-morrow's surrender are already being discussed.

The army is generally demoralized. The troops have lost confidence in Bazaine, and he has no longer any command over his men. If Bazaine should attempt to cut his way through the Prussian lines to-day, he would undoubtedly be shot by his own men. This is his great fear, — personal safety, which impels him to surrender. This is the first time in the history of the world that 150,000 men are surrendered against their will. Oh, if they had a leader! But there is no leader. Changarnier is old and useless, a relic of the military past; and Bazaine is timid, and too proud to put a second and braver man in command. He has not shown himself to his men for weeks. The *esprit* of 150,000 Frenchmen is dead, and to-morrow the virgin city of Metz will be *virgin* no more. "The Old Guard dies, but never surrenders," was said of that terrible reserve which the first Napoleon threw upon a wavering field, but in a day, that proud Imperial Guard, as prisoners to superior military genius, will pass in review before the great Captain of Germany.

WEDNESDAY, *October 26th.* — The Prince and Princess of Wales pay a state visit to the Empress at Chiselhurst, and are received by the Prince Imperial in Camden House.

METZ continues to negotiate for a surrender. Bazaine asks Prince Charles for another conference. General Stiehle, Chief of Staff of the Second army, and General Wartensleben, Chief of Staff of the First Army, have a three hours' interview at Frascati with the French Commissioners. Bazaine desires that his officers shall be allowed to retain their side-arms. Prince Charles telegraphs the King at Versailles for instructions.

THE LAST OF A GREAT ARMY.

To-morrow will be surrendered the last man and the last officer, with the exception of Bourbaki, of the proud force which made up the Imperial army of France. The *right*, MacMahon, the *left*, L'Admirault, and the *centre*, Bazaine, besides sub-commanders Canrobert, De Caen, Frossard, and Lebœuf, the Imperial ex-secretary of war — all are now prisoners to King William. The list of fortresses now surrendered to Prussia comprises Herny, Toul, Laon, Soissons, St. Quentin, Strasburg, and Metz. Only the little fortresses of Thionville, Neuf Brisach (south of Strasburg), Verdun, and Bitche, remain. These will soon fall, and with the last regular soldier captured, the last marshal paroled, and the last fortress in the hands of Prussia, the picture for France is dark indeed. Metz is the Gibraltar of France, — her fancied impregnable centre. Her military heart is in the Prussian vice. France wants a leader shrewd enough to see and bold enough to act on the situation. Perhaps M. Thiers, in his projected conference with Bismarck at Versailles, will be that man. It is idle for France longer to cope with the overpowering military force of Prussia.

THURSDAY, *October* 27.— The surrender of Metz completed. 173,000 men, 6000 officers, 66 generals, and 3 marshals of France, lay down their arms. King William telegraphs the surrender to the Queen.

METZ SURRENDERS.'

TO THE QUEEN: VERSAILLES, *Oct.* 27.

Bazaine's army and the fortress of Metz have capitulated. There are one hundred and fifty thousand prisoners, of whom twenty thousand are sick and wounded. This is a most important event. God be praised!

WILLIAM.

PARTICULARS OF THE SURRENDER.

Prince Charles received a telegram from the King this morning, granting the French officers permission to retain their side-arms. This was the only obstacle which prevented the signing of the articles of surrender last evening.

At eight o'clock, Bazaine's Chief of Staff, General Jarras, and Major Samuel, on the part of General Coffinières, commanding the fortress, met General Stiehle and General Wartensleben, Chiefs of Staff of the First and Second German armies, at Frascati (see map, p. 156), within the Prussian lines, and completed the act of surrender.

The following paper was now agreed to, and signed by Colonel Jarras and General Stiehle:

First — The French army under General Bazaine, including 3 marshals of France, 66 generals, 6000 officers, and 173,000 men, are declared prisoners of war.

Second — The fortress and town of Metz, with the forts and munitions of war, provisions and everything else found in the place, which may be the property of the State of France, shall be given up to the German army, and delivered in the condition in which it was found the first day of the capitulation.

Third — On the Saturday next following, at midday, the forts at St. Quentin, Plappeville, and the remaining forts and port Moselle, shall be surrendered to the German troops.

Fourth — At the hour of ten o'clock, the same day, Prussian officers of the artillery and engineer corps shall be admitted into all the forts in order that they may take possession of and occupy the magazines, and draw all charges from the mines.

Fifth—The French arms, all army material, flags, eagles, cannons, mitrailleuses, fourgon and ammunition and artillery equipages left at Metz and in the forts under military commission of France, to be given immediately to the German commissioners.

Sixth—The French troops in Metz, after surrender, to be conducted, without arms, by regiments or regimental corps, in military order, to some fixed place, to be indicated by the Prussians.

Seventh—The French officers in command of the men, after their arrival at this fixed place, to be at liberty to return to the intrenched camps or to Metz, on giving their word of honor not to quit either place without an order of permission from the German commandant.

Eighth—The troops after surrender to be marched to bivouac, the French soldiers retaining their personal effects, cooking utensils, and so forth.

Ninth—All the French generals and other officers, with military employes who rank as commissioned officers, and who engage by written promise not to bear arms against Germany, and not to agitate against Prussian interests during the war, not to be made prisoners of war, but be permitted to retain their arms and to have their personal property in recognition of the courage displayed by them during the campaign.

Tenth—The French military surgeons will remain in the fortress to take charge of the wounded. They will be treated according to the rules of the Convention of Geneva, and considered as being attached to the hospitals of Prussia.

Eleventh—All questions of detail, such as concern the commercial rights of the town of Metz and the interests and rights of civilians and non-combatants, will be considered and treated subsequently in an appendix to the military paper of capitulation.

Twelfth—Any clause, sentence, or word used in the present draft of arrangement, the reading of which may present a doubt as to its exact meaning, shall be interpreted hereafter in favor of the people of France.

THE SCENE IN THE CITY.

This completed the tragedy of Metz without the citadel. Within, a different scene was being enacted. The actual surrender of the troops did not take place until Saturday, as per the third article; but in the meantime, the terms of capitulation were discussed in Metz.

When the particulars of the capitulation became known, the people were furious. The National Guards refused to lay down their arms. On the afternoon of the 28th inst., a captain of dragoons appeared at the head of a body of troops, who swore that they would sooner die than yield. Albert Collignon, the editor of an ultra-Democratic daily newspaper, the *Journal de Metz*, rode about on a white horse, firing a pistol, and exhorting them to sally forth and seek victory or death, to escape impending shame. He was followed by a lady singing the Marseillaise. This produced terrible excitement. The doors of the Cathedral were burst open, the tocsin was sounded, and the bell rung nearly all night.

When General Coffinières appeared to pacify the people, three pistol shots were fired at him. Finally, by the aid of two regiments of the line, he quietly dispersed the mob; but all night the sounds of grief, indignation and terror continued. Respectable women ran about the streets, tearing their hair and flinging their bonnets and laces under their feet, seeking their friends, and asking wildly, "What will become of our children?" Soldiers, drunk and sober, tumbled hither and thither in irregular groups, with their caps off and their sabres broken, sobbing and weeping like children, and crying, "*Oh pauvre Metz! Oh ma pauvre Metz! Tout est perdu!*"

The people were totally ignorant of anything which had transpired in France since the 18th of August. The City Council detained an English gentleman, one of the first strangers to enter Metz, for two hours, to ask all manner of questions — some childish in their uncertainty and terror — as to what the Prussians would do, how they would do it, and how they must be met. It was as if they had never seen or known a Prussian. They demanded to know whether their already destitute larders must still supply the troops, and whether they would be personally maltreated if unable to furnish what was required. They were relieved by hearing that a thousand wagons were ready at Courcelles to bring provisions hither, and also that there were funds in London ready to be applied to their relief, in response to the appeal of the Mayors of Briey and other communes, published in English and American journals, saying, "Help is needed quickly."

IMPERIAL INTRIGUES.

General Von Zastrow, who held the woods of Vaux on the morning after Gravelotte, expresses the decided opinion that Bazaine could have avoided being enclosed in Metz. After he was thus enclosed, he could have, according to Metzian statement, made a sortie and joined MacMahon more easily by far than MacMahon could reach him. After most of Bazaine's cavalry and artillery horses had been eaten, this proceeding was of course more difficult; still his movements are said to have lacked determination, and in the last two sorties (see Oct. 7th) to have been even frivolous. This is charged to a plot in behalf of the Regency, by which this army was to try to remain in *statu quo* until the conclusion of the war in Western France, and then was to become available, with Prussian consent, for Bonapartist purposes. Bazaine himself expected in that case to be the Governor of the Prince Imperial, and the virtual Regent.

"Nearly all the Metzians seem to believe this," says a writer in the *Pall Mall Gazette*, "and their most influential people have avowed such belief." * After the time of the investment, Bazaine was never seen in the camps except on extraordinary occasions; never at all in the hospitals, which are in part constructed in numerous railway box-wagons, on the Place Royale. Equally seldom was he seen in the city. The civil authorities had to find him at Bon St. Martin; he did not appear at the City Hall once. He rarely, if ever, said a word to encourage his troops. Canrobert sometimes cheered their hardships a little, and then they would cry "*Vive Canrobert! A bas Bazaine.*"

Towards the last, Bazaine dared not show himself to his own men for fear of assassination, and the terribly relaxed discipline is assuredly the cause of the hasty capitulation, when a week's rations for all were on hand. On the morning of the 29th, five soldiers lay dead of starvation at Montigny, while the staff still indulged in luxurious meals. Four days' rations were given to the entire army that morning (29th), but for two days previous they had received none. No beef nor pork had been obtainable at any price for a week; but on that morning, *before anything had arrived in town, the shops had plenty thereof*, which goes to prove the charges current in the town, that *a quantity of food had been withheld from the troops, that*

---

* Said Bazaine in conversation, after the surrender, while a prisoner of war in Cassel:

"*I have sworn loyalty to the Emperor and the constitution. The Emperor is a prisoner, but the constitution is in force; and neither I nor any of my comrades will ever acknowledge any other government until we shall have previously obtained a discharge from our oath at the hands of the Emperor himself.*

"I proposed to march out with the army, and to pledge our honor that we would not fight again in this war, but that we should be permitted to convene and protect the French Chambers against the mob, or, as Bismarck called them, the street loafers. I detest politics. We only wanted to do what Gambetta claims that he wishes to do—that is, to re-establish legality, by calling together the Representative Body.

"*Even had we not been forced by hunger, I should have opened negotiations on the day when I learned that it was not the Republicans, but the mob, who governed at Paris, Lyons, and Marseilles—on the day when I learned that the army was insulted, that the memory of men whom I venerate was reviled.* But, as the case really stood, it was hunger, and nothing but hunger, that compelled my surrender."

through starvation they might agree to the terms of surrender. It is not plain to any one yet, that Bazaine did not hasten the surrender through deception, and in obedience to a known wish of the Emperor, understood and connived at by the Prussian authorities at Versailles. A strong suspicion attaches to the integrity of this surrender. The real truth lies buried in the hearts of Bazaine, Canrobert, and the Emperor. The interpretation placed upon the surrender in Metz, and I chronicle the fact for the future historian, is this: The Republic had refused to hold an election, to make the present Republican *de facto* government a government also *de jure.* Bismarck knew he must treat with both a *de jure* and *de facto* government; Napoleon III. must either become *de facto* or the Republic *de jure.* To make Napoleon III. *de jure* was simply to end the war, and place the Emperor or the Prince upon the French throne. The surrender of Metz is the Emperor's part of the bargain, and it remains to be seen whether King William will fulfil his portion of the contract.

CASUALTIES.

The French have lost, since Gravelotte, 24 generals, 2140 officers, and 42,339 men; and on the morning of the surrender 19,000 men lay sick in Metz. For three weeks the meat used has been horse-steak, without salt. Sugar was sold for $6 per pound; salt, $3; a ham, $60; one potato, nine cents; and a little pig, caught near Gravelotte, sold for $150.

DEMORALIZATION.

Bazaine himself declined the Prince's generous proposal to let all the troops lay down their arms outside of the works in view of their conquerors, instead of laying them down in the arsenal, saying that he could not guarantee their behavior. The Imperial Guards alone had preserved discipline sufficiently to be trusted to pass in armed review. The inhabitants had never ceased to hope for the appearance of Bourbaki's army from Lille, or of the Army of the Loire, or of some other relieving force; but the troops themselves during the last few weeks could no longer be deceived, as they got better information through the German outposts.

Their demoralization, due largely to hunger, was bitterly and openly complained of by their officers.

THE PRUSSIANS OCCUPY METZ.

SATURDAY, *Oct.* 29. — According to the terms of the articles of capitulation, the Prussian officers of the artillery of the

Seventh Corps entered the fortifications and withdrew the charges from the mines.

At one o'clock the Third Division (which will depart towards the southwest) and the Fourth Division were reviewed in splendid pageant by the Prince, on the Nancy-Metz road, near Tournebride. Thereupon the (French) Imperial Guards marched out of Metz, bearing their arms, which they subsequently laid down at Frascati, and passed in review before the Prince. This honor was accorded to them alone. All the rest laid down their arms in the Metz arsenals, and then marched to their cantonment outside the town, to await transportation. The Imperial Guards were received by the Prussian troops with respect; not a jeering syllable was heard, nor an improperly exultant look seen. Previously, at the Prince's review of the German troops, the cheering was loud and long-continued.

At 4 P.M. General Zastrow, of the Seventh Corps, as military Governor, took possession of the city and fortress of Metz.

THE CHIVALRY OF WAR.

The entire besieging army voluntarily gave up their bread rations yesterday to feed their French captives. This deeply touched the Metzians, and did much to relieve their fears. On the faces of all the German soldiers was to be seen a look of quiet satisfaction — nothing more. Not one of the French officers and soldiers who swarmed all about, even when intoxicated — which was surprisingly unfrequent — wore any other expression than a look of sadness or defiance, the latter not being common, and occurring chiefly among the younger officers.

A good deal of suffering was experienced by the soldiery on account of the hoarding of provisions, and, when given out, on account of unequal distribution. For many days only four ounces of bread were served to each man, and even this many thousands failed to get. Horse-flesh, in small quantities, was distributed, but the sickly, emaciated condition of the horses occasioned much sickness among the troops.

THE CITIZENS OF METZ.

Many of the citizens were so highly incensed at Bazaine for surrendering, while he yet had a stock of provisions locked up, that a conspiracy originated to ignore the surrender, and seize the arms in the arsenals, and make forcible resistance to the entry of the Prussians. General Déligny, on the part of the French officers, even desired to make a sortie after the surrender was known, but the consummation was defeated by the Imperial Guard. To pacify the citizens, a supplementary protocol was published, in which the Prussians granted

"the right to the French civil officials to remove or remain, at their option, undisturbed in person or property. None of the inhabitants, either in their civil or military capacity, are to be interfered with, or held responsible for any previous acts, or for their political opinions. The sick and wounded are to have every care, and families of officers or soldiers serving in the armies of France are not to be molested in any of their rights. The public property, with archives, moneys, and papers, are to have protection. The mode of disposing of wounded prisoners is also prescribed."

The municipal authorities seemed to be more pacified on reading the kind intentions of Prussia, and with the Prussian authorities they counselled quiet submission. Fearing a repetition of the Laon disaster, the city authorities issued a pacificatory address to the citizens, exhorting them to patience under misfortunes for which they are not responsible, and promising that France and history will exonerate the people of Metz from any share in the ignominy of her surrender.

In order to win over with kindness the citizens of Alsace and Lorraine, the German authorities have given orders that the soldiers from Alsace and Lorraine, captured at Metz, as well as those who may hereafter be taken, be separated from the other prisoners, as such will be regarded as German, and not French.

HATRED TOWARDS BAZAINE.

To-day at 4 P. M. (Oct. 29) Bazaine passed through Ars, on his way to Wilhelmshöhe, in a closed carriage, marked with his name, escorted by several officers of his staff on horseback.

The women of the village had heard of his coming, and awaited him with cries of "Traitor!" "Thief!" "Coward!" "Loafer!" "Brigand!" "Where are our husbands whom you have betrayed?" "Give us back our children, whom you have sold!" They attacked the carriage, and broke the windows, and would have lynched the Marshal but for the intervention of Prussian gendarmes.

The people now admit that the last hope of France is extinguished. Generals resign, because the people have no confidence in them; and the old Imperial officers, with occupations gone, proceed with the Empress to Wilhelmshöhe, to intrigue against the Republic. It were better for the Republic to hold an election at once, become both *de facto* and *de jure*, and make peace with the victorious Prussians, even with the surrender of Alsace and Lorraine. This the Emperor will do, if, out of patience, the King turns to him; and then the Republic will be strangled by a King and an Emperor.

THE DETAILS OF THE SURRENDER.

By the capitulation of Marshal Bazaine, 53 eagles, 541 field-guns, ammunition for more than 85 batteries, 800 siege-guns, 66 *mitrailleuses*, 300,000 rifles and sabres, 2000 military carriages, a powder-factory, etc., fell into the hands of the Prussians.

Including the garrison surrendered, the army originally comprised 221 battalions of infantry and 162 squadrons of horse. The original numerical strength was 210,000 infantry, 21,450 cavalry, 690 guns, and 102 mitrailleuses.

Besides the foregoing, there were three marshals — Bazaine, Canrobert, and Lebœuf; three corps commanders — Frossard, De Caen, and L'Admirault; 40 division generals; 100 brigadier-generals; of sound prisoners, 90,000 sent to North Germany and 50,000 sent South; the sick and wounded being distributed in the same proportion.

DISPOSITION OF THE METZ ARMY.

The First Army, under Manteuffel, including the First and Eighth Corps (Goeben), goes northward, and will occupy Picardy and Brittany, maintaining connection with the Fourth Army, under the Crown Prince of Saxony, north of Paris, and accomplishing the reduction of Verdun Mézières, Amiens, and Rouen. The Seventh Corps (Zastrow) is to garrison Metz and reduce Thionville. Prince Charles' Second Army, except the Second Corps (Fansecki), which proceeds to Paris, goes south, establishing connection with the right wing of Gen. Werder, moving on Lyons, and with the left of Gen. Von der Tann, at Orleans. Kummer's landwehr division, which covered itself with glory in repulsing the great north sortie towards Maxe and Ladonchamps on the 7th of October, returns to Germany with the prisoners.

As Prince Charles prepares to leave Metz, the scene of his great triumph, he issues the following:

SOLDIERS — I recognize your bravery, obedience, and calmness. Your cheerfulness and devotion in the dangers and difficulties of the situation were incalculable. You proceed to new triumphs. For the present, farewell!

As the German troops separate to go to new fields of glory, there are many scenes of grief, and promises of speedy reunions in the Fatherland.

GENERAL CHANGARNIER ON THE SURRENDER OF METZ.

"No, sir!" said the venerable old general, in giving his opinion as to the cause of the surrender, "there was no treachery. Bazaine did not sell himself to the enemy. He had no need of money. His work was far from being an act of treason to France. Mon Dieu ! There was no treachery ; it was absolute necessity. Bazaine was driven into Metz on the 19th of August. He could have escaped soon after had he marched boldly out with his entire army during the thirteen remaining days of the month of thirty days to September 1, and for fifteen days of October. This is an absolute certainty. Any man possessing a sound knowledge of military affairs will tell you the same thing. Look at the facts. There were fifty-eight days elapsed with Bazaine shut up in the strongest fortress of France, where her 150,000 of the bravest and most experienced soldiers could merely exist. Once in the field with such an army, there would be no more Sedan. Sedan was made notorious for this — that the troops insulted their officers; were insubordinate, as well as inefficient. What sort of an army is that ? Look, however, sir, in Metz ; the soldiers remained entirely obedient to orders. Every order was executed on delivery. They did not have in Metz another army — an army of 'Reds' and radical republicans.

" But," continued the General " Bazaine was selfish. He wanted to be a hero. Imagining that peace would be concluded, he thought that the world at large would say, 'Bazaine held Metz after France had dropped stronghold after stronghold into the hands of the enemy.' During the last ten days of the investment of Metz, French sorties had been rendered impossible. No attack on the Prussians, no attempt at escape, could be made. Bazaine had really no artillery, no cavalry mounted, and only, in fact, 60,000 infantry. He could do nothing against these three branches of the Prussian service in force and well equipped.

Bazaine at the surrender had 135,000 men. Of these there were twenty-five thousand disabled by wounds, and ten thousand laid up with sickness of different forms. The cavalry and artillery were useless — there were no horses to render them available. Bazaine was thus reduced to sixty thousand infantry. There you have it, sir. Were we not in a bad state at the moment of the capitulation ? Mon Dieu ! All our fine horses had been eaten up. Our bread and breadstuffs were gone. We had no salt. Horseflesh, Monsieur, is not bad as an article of food when it is eaten with bread and salt, and when the animal had been in good condition and fat before slaughter ; but our horses in Metz were not fat, and we had neither bread nor salt. The taste of the horse meat was horrible. Could troops thus fed stand well in any great battle ? The world must have reason, sir. You must understand, do not forget, that during the last ten days of the Prussian investment, the soldiers of France walked in mud deep enough to reach almost to their knees. The heavy rains and sheer starvation forced us to surrender. But, as I have told you, there were fifty-eight days when Bazaine could have taken this fine army out and saved France. How unhappy !"

BAZAINE'S SORTIES.

" Look, in his sorties ! Bazaine never made a decided, serious effort to escape from Metz. Every sortie was merely a pretended movement, made for appearance' sake, and nothing else.

" There were, sir, four officers of high rank in Metz, as well as Bazaine. They were all in favor of a system of inaction. I had an opportunity of observing all the military movements. They were all shams, every one. Bazaine and the generals and officers, his friends, were not acting as soldiers. They were only seeking and working for their own public future.

"Bazaine's sorties were always with a small force, and evidently with no preconceived idea that they would be successful, although every sortie was finely executed. True history must speak well of the French troops as fighting above all examples of heroism, but small sorties are useless measures. Let me say more about Bazaine. He was not at the battle of the 18th of August. He was far from the field. So also was King William, who sent a bombastic account to Queen Augusta, stating he was on the field. I was there myself, and I slept under a historic tree, one that might now be known as the *arbre des morts.* In the fight of the 18th of August 300,000 Prussians were opposed to 150,000 Frenchmen. Let me tell of the surrender. Four outlets were fixed for the exodus of the French troops. The morning they defiled out of Metz I shall never forget. Old man as I am, and old soldier too, the sight I witnessed will never pass from my memory. It moved me more than any event of my long life. Soldiers kissed and embraced their officers. There was one universal shout of '*Vive la France!*' It was something grand to see 100,000 men in tears for their country.

"Bazaine ought to have moved toward Nancy, where the country was rich, and the fields were covered with products."

In regard to Napoleon, the venerable General said, "*He is dead.*" The Prussians may put him back on the throne, but Paris and France will not recognize him. The restoration of the Orleans family will bring peace to France. Orleans in Peace. It must come."

COFFINIERES ON THE SURRENDER.

Gen. Coffinières, the commander of the fortifications of Metz, thus avows his difference with Bazaine in a letter to the *Independence Belge:*

. . . .

Every time that I was called upon to give my advice, I firmly advocated: That the place of Metz ought to have interests totally distinct from those of the Army of the Rhine, and that all political predilections should be avoided in order only to think of the necessities of the defence. After long and excited discussions, in which I was alone in my opinions, after each time having given in my resignation, I only yielded to the contrary opinion, when it entirely prevailed in the council of war, to the complete exhaustion of all our alimentary resources, and, above all, to the formal order of the general-in-chief. As to provisions, it suffices in order to prove that they were sufficient, to say that Metz, which ought in a normal condition to contain only ninety to one hundred thousand souls, including the garrison, was able to feed nearly 240,000 men during two months and a half. I shall certainly prove later, by sufficient evidence, that I fulfilled loyally my duty as citizen and soldier. In the meantime I beg you to discard all perfidious insinuations, and to insert my letter in one of your approaching numbers. Accept, sir, etc.

General COFFINIERES DE NORDECK.

FRIDAY, *October 28th.*—Great joy at Versailles and consternation in Tours. King William appoints Prince Charles a Field Marshal of Prussia. Gambetta pronounces the surrender of Bazaine a crime.

JOY AT VERSAILLES.

An overwhelming joy has seized the armies about Paris. There are enthusiastic scenes of congratulation at the King's headquarters, while a carnival of gladness seems to seize the troops. Officers embrace, and the soldiers sing songs of victory. The King, Von Moltke, and Bismarck do not conceal their supreme satisfaction, and express openly their belief in the near approach of peace. The King appoints the Crown Prince and Prince Charles Marshals of Prussia, and the telegraph carries the following note of thanks from the King to Prince Charles, before Metz:

VERSAILLES, *Oct.* 28—1.10 P.M.

TO PRINCE FREDERICK CHARLES:

I awaited the news, which was received during the night, of the completion of the capitulation of Metz, before sending you my heartfelt congratulations and acknowledgments for your circumspection and endurance before the victory which your command has shown during the long and tedious environment of Bazaine's army. The same acknowledgment is due to the brave troops who, by their intrepidity and the privations they have endured, have set examples without parallel in the history of the world. The occurrences before Metz constitute an imperishable epoch of honor and glory for our army. My thanks should at once be conveyed to the troops. To honor you and your command for such signal services, I have appointed you General Field Marshal, a distinction which I have also conferred upon my son, the Crown Prince. WILHELM.

THE KING TO THE ARMY: VERSAILLES, *Oct.* 28*th.*

Soldiers of the Confederate armies:

When, three months since, we took the field, I said God would be with our just cause. That this confidence has been fully realized—witness Woerth, Saarbrück, Metz, Sedan, Beaumont, Strasburg—each a victory for our arms. To you belong the merit and the glory. You have maintained all the virtues which especially distinguish soldiers. With Metz, the last army of the enemy is destroyed. I take this opportunity to thank you all, from the General to the soldier. Whatever the future, I look forward to it calmly, because I know that with such soldiers victory cannot fail. I honor you all to-day, by appointing as Field-Marshals my son, the Crown Prince of Prussia, and Prince Frederick Charles, who have repeatedly led you to victory. WILLIAM.

CONSTERNATION IN TOURS.

A profound impression was produced at Tours by the news of Bazaine's capitulation. The news was a bomb-shell in the camp of the Army of the Loire, demoralizing the troops, and creating a feeling of abject hopelessness. To revive the spirits of the people, Gambetta, always sanguine and hopeful, issued the following circular:

TO PREFECTS OF DEPARTMENTS: TOURS, *October* 28*th*, 1870.

I have received from all sides grave reports, the veracity of which, in spite of all efforts, I cannot establish officially. It is said that Metz has capitulated. If so, it is well that you have the opinion of the Government on the matter. Such an event could but be the result of a crime, the authors of which should be outlawed. Be convinced that, whatever may arise, nothing can abate our courage in this epoch of rascally capitulations. *There exists one thing which neither can nor will capitulate, that is the French Republic.*"

GAMBETTA, Minister of the Interior.

M. Gambetta issues another proclamation to stimulate the forlorn hope of the French Republic at Tours and Lyons, but it falls almost without effect upon the troops. It is almost the last call upon the patriotic, but demoralized armies of France:

SOLDIERS — You have betrayed no dishonor. During three months, fortune has been unfavorable to you, owing to incapacity and treachery. You are now rid of unworthy chiefs. If you are prepared under proper guidance to wipe away outrage, forward! You no longer struggle for a despot, but for a country, for houses burned, for families outraged. France is delivered up to the fury of an implacable enemy. You have a sublime mission, requiring every sacrifice, to shame the calumniators who render the army responsible for infamy. Your chiefs having justly incurred the stigma of treason at Sedan and crime at Metz, I tell you to avenge your honor, which is that of France. Your brothers in the Army of the Rhine already protest against the cowardly *attentat*, and withdraw from the accursed capitulation. It is for you to raise the standard of France, soiled by the last Bonaparte and his accomplices, and recall victory. But practice republican virtues — discipline, activity, and contempt for death. Bear in mind the danger of the country. The time of treachery and weakness is past. The destiny of the country is confirmed, you having restored France to serenity. Then be free and peaceful citizens of the Republic. GAMBETTA.

THE FEELING IN BERLIN.

The feeling in the Prussian capital is happy indeed. Every little German town has put out its colored light, and indulged in a jollification in honor of the surrender of the "Virgin City." From Stuttgart, the court city of Würtemberg, the author's sister (Mrs. Wm. H. D.) writes of enthusiastic festivities. Every house is illuminated, and a speedy peace is predicted. That the French should talk of continuing the war, is beyond Prussian comprehension; and the utmost contempt is felt for the helpless party who would prolong the struggle.

Herr Wachenhusen comments in the Cologne *Gazette* on the impossibility of reasoning with the French:

They know that it is all up with them, and console themselves with the belief that in five years they will revenge their shameful defeat; but in the same breath they protest that they are not conquered, and are deceiving themselves to the last with the absurdest reports of victory. The "genius of the defence of Strasburg" is invoked by Gambetta. A patriot, but a fool, expects by barricades to repel a million practised soldiers, and by a mob of

Mobiles and Francs-tireurs to annihilate the enemy in the provinces. The townspeople and peasants, with their excitable temperament, are stirred up by babblers and dreamers to deeds of so-called heroism; and while a handful of the enemy fall victims, the localities implicated are punished by destruction or contributions. Emissaries and proclamations are sent about inciting a guerilla war, directing people to assume to-day the Franc-tireur's blouse, to-morrow the peasant's smock, so that they are to blame if peasants and Francs-tireurs are fusiladed. The barricades and obstructions placed in the roads are not, however, defended; and behind the costly railway bridges and tunnels, which are shattered to pieces, there stood not one man to prevent the passage of the Moselle by the enemy on a bridge of boats. Will the well-to-do effeminate Paris tradesman or the artisan display more bravery than the army? Will he not throw away his musket as soon as the first shells fall into the city, like the people of the large provincial towns? To talk of dying under the ruins of Paris is the very fudge which has talked France into destruction.

EXCITEMENT IN PARIS.

The news of the capitulation of Bazaine created intense excitement and dismay. *Le Combat*, Felix Pyat's newspaper, charged the Government with knowing the fact and withholding it from the public. The citizens, incensed at this accusation, destroyed all the copies of Pyat's journal they could find, and sought to arrest the editor. The *Journal Officiel* published an indignant denial, the Government not deeming it possible that Bazaine could betray his trust.

SUNDAY, *Oct.* 30. — General Werder occupies Dijon, after the capture of the French position on the heights, by William of Baden. M. Thiers, the French ambassador, has his first peace interview with Bismarck at Versailles. The Republic proclaims against the treachery of Bazaine. Von Moltke receives the title of Count. England is distressed at the Russian movement of troops towards Turkey.

KING WILLIAM TO THE QUEEN.

VERSAILLES, *Oct.* 29, 1870.

The defeat of the two hostile armies which recently marched against us, warrants me in conferring on our two commanders, Fritz and Frederick Charles, the batons of Field-Marshal — the first instances of such appointments in our family history.

WILLIAM.

CAPTURE OF DIJON.

The Prussian forces under Gen. Werder capture Dijon today. The French forces under Garibaldi and General Ernest make a weak fight, and retire towards Dole. William of Baden crossed the heights on which the French forces were posted. Dijon is a city of 50,000 people, in the department of Côte d'Or, one hundred and sixty miles southeast of Paris, and is celebrated as being the birthplace of Bossuet. The Prussians were twelve thousand strong, and were well provided with artillery. They attacked the city at nine o'clock in the forenoon of Sunday, and the bombardment was continued till nearly nightfall. The town was not fortified, and the commander of the French, not able to resist with his small force, was compelled to retreat.

MONDAY, *Oct.* 31.—Peace negotiations (commencing 31 Oct. and ending Nov. 5) between M. Thiers and Count Von Bismarck fail. Bismarck will not allow the revictualling of Paris. Radical revolution in Paris. Pyat and Flourens imprison the members of the Government, and seize the Hôtel de Ville.

Napoleon issues a pamphlet on the conduct of the war up to Sedan, throwing the blame of disaster upon the Ministry in Paris.

THE REPUBLIC.

The Republic, in her dire distress, looks dismal enough. While M. Thiers is negotiating for peace at Versailles with Bismarck, the Tours Government issues the following to the disheartened French people :

"LIBERTY—EQUALITY—FRATERNITY.

"PROCLAMATION TO THE FRENCH PEOPLE.

"FRENCHMEN :—Raise your spirits and resolution to the fearful height of the perils which have broken upon the country. It still depends on us to mount above misfortune and show the world how great a people may be who are resolved not to perish, and whose courage increases in the midst of calamity.

"Metz has capitulated. A General, upon whom France counted, even after Mexico, has just taken away (*vient d'enlever*) from the country in its danger more than a hundred thousand of its defenders. Marshal Bazaine has betrayed us. He has made himself the agent of the Man of Sedan and the accomplice of the invader ; and, regardless of the honor of the army of which he had charge, he has surrendered, without even making a last effort, a hundred and twenty thousand fighting men, twenty thousand wounded, guns, cannon, colors, and the strongest citadel of France—Metz-Virgen ; but for him, to the contamination of the foreigner, such a crime is above even the punishments of Justice !

"In the disasters of the country in less than five months 250,000 men have been delivered over to the enemy, a sinister sequel to the military *coup de main* of December.

"It is time for us to reassert ourselves, citizens, and under the ægis of the Republic, which we have determined not to allow to capitulate, within or without, to seek, in the extremity even of our misfortune, the renovation of our political and social morality and manhood.

"However tried by disaster, let us be found neither panic-stricken nor hesitating. No illusion is now left. Let us no longer languish or grow weak, and let us prove by our acts that we can ourselves maintain honor, independence, integrity — all that makes a country proud and free.

"Long live the Republic, one and indivisible!

"Cremieux.
"Glais-Bazoin.
"Gambetta."

RADICAL REVOLUTION IN PARIS.

To-day, Oct. 31, has occurred in Paris one of those queer revolutions, so incident to the French existence. While M. Thiers was negotiating an armistice with Bismarck at Versailles, the Republican Government, captured by a wild mob, were held prisoners in the Hôtel de Ville.

Rumors of the armistice, the Prussian recapture of La Bourgat, east of St. Denis, and the surrender of Metz, had created intense agitation, and at 11 A. M. about 200 people assembled in the Place de l'Hôtel de Ville. The members of the Government suspected the gathering storm, and the crowd was harangued by M. Arago and M. Jules Favre, and finally by M. Jules Simon; while other members, including Gen. Trochu, Picard, and Ferry, remained in the Legislative Chamber. The eloquence of Arago and the venerable presence of Favre quieted the crowd, which gave signs of dispersing; but at two o'clock, Flourens, Blanqui, Pyat, and others of the factious party, came at the head of their battalions, entered the Hôtel de Ville, and took forcible possession of the Council Chamber. As soon as the Radical mob gained possession of the Hôtel de Ville, they organized a committee of defence, throwing their bulletins from the windows to the excited crowd below. Their proclamations were all different, showing no accord among the rioters. Victor Hugo, Pyat, Ledru Rollin, Flourens, Louis Blanc, Rochefort, and Dorian were among the persons named as directors. The name of Rochefort was hooted, while Dorian refused to have his name used. While these elections were going on, Picard and Ferry managed to escape from the Council Chamber, and flew to sound the alarm, and organize the Gardes Mobiles and the Gardes Nationales, for the relief of their imprisoned colleagues. During the mock legislation of the mob headed by Flourens, Gen. Trochu, Jules Simon, Jules Favre, Garnier Pagés, and Arago were held prisoners around a large table, and were momentarily in fear of being assaulted. Jules Simon attempted to speak, but was silenced by a brutal wretch, who slapped him in the face. Garnier Pagès then rose and endeavored to speak, but, overcome with emotion, he fainted away, fell on the floor, and was trampled on by insurgents, who tore Gen. Trochu's decorations from his breast. The venerable appearance of M. Garnier Pagés would have imposed silence upon any but a ruffian set, respecting nothing. The insurgents, to cries of "Vive la Commune," "Déchéance," "Down with Trochu," greeted with cheers the proclamation of acts from Blanqui and Flourens, while M. Pagés was rescued, and carried to a window under the care of Messrs. Favre and Simon. Gen. Trochu retained his place in an arm-chair near the table while all this indescribable tumult continued.

Pyat and Blanqui now sent emissaries to the Finance Department, demanding large sums of money to defray the expenses of the new Government. These emissaries M. Picard arrested, and gained possession of the orders as evidence against Pyat and Blanqui. Rochefort tried to address the mob from without, but his voice was drowned by loud cries of "*Resistance à mort*," "No armistice," and "Vive la République!"

This imprisonment of the members of the Government lasted until six o'clock in the evening, when M. Jules Ferry, who had come to the Hôtel de Ville with an immense force, demanded their release. A messenger went up to Flourens to demand a reply. Ferry waited more than two hours for the return, rather than execute any violent movement. In fact, it was distinctly understood that at the sound of the first shot at the place, Trochu, Favre, Simon, Arago, and Pagés would be instantly murdered. In the meantime, however, the National Guard under Ferry had succeeded in pushing a mass of men up the stairs and into the Council Hall. One of the officers of the One Hundred and Sixth Battalion, a colossal fellow, made a sign to Gen. Trochu, edged his way round the table, and at a favorable moment, when protected by his men, seized the General in his arms, lifted him out of his chair backward, and without a word conveyed him down stairs. On the grand stairway his *kepi* (fatigue cap) was recognized, and a miscreant took deliberate aim at the General, fortunately missing him.

One of the men knocked off the General's cap, replaced it by his own, and thus saved him from further attempts.

As Trochu emerged from the rabble his staff greeted him, and the crowd shouted with enthusiasm, while, bareheaded, he faced the crowd, and addressed his rescuers as follows :

"CITIZENS — I thank you from my heart for coming to our rescue. Like you, we have but one great, controlling desire, and that is to save the Republic by saving France. In four hours you will meet in your local, district, and arrondissement committees, and take measures to elect a chief magistrate for this great city of Paris. Let us be united, and all will be well; and let our rallying cry, now and hereafter, continue to be '*Vive La France!*'"

"Down with the Commune," shouted the people; and all along the boulevards and in the Place de Vendôme the death of the Flourens Government was cried with enthusiasm. The long roll of the drums soon drew the National Guard to the Hotel in force, and the insurgents, finding themselves outwitted and outnumbered, dispersed ; but it was not before three o'clock in the morning that the fate of the Government of National Defence was decided. Ferry and Picard acted gloriously ; the latter, a man of sixty years of age, showed all the fire and energy of his more youthful coadjutors.

There is but one remark to make on this day's proceedings. This mob was in favor of no armistice. It was not a disloyal mob, but a mob so loyal, that they looked upon such men as Favre and Arago as lukewarm. They were like the abolitionists during our war—terribly loyal, and as radical as liberty itself. Had this mob been anti-Republican, it would have signified much ; as it was, it was simply hot-headed loyalty run mad. It was not like the anti-war riot in New York, which set up against the war and the Republic itself; but rather like a brigade of Wendell Phillipses, enraged because McClellan did not take Richmond, and because Lincoln delayed the proclamation of liberty to the slave.

THE THIERS-BISMARCK ARMISTICE NEGOTIATIONS.

Since the M. Favre peace negotiation failure on the 21st of September (see page 316), the war has been vigorously prosecuted. The fall of Toul, Strasburg, and Metz, and the vigorous repulse of every French sortie from Paris, made it proper and magnanimous in Prussia to treat for peace with France.

The initiatory steps were taken at the suggestion of England, Russia, Italy, and the other neutral powers. The Prussian Minister at Brussels, the Prince de Croy, forwarded despatches, on the 18th of October, to Count Von Bernstorff, the North German representative to England, which caused the latter to signify to Earl Granville the fact that Bismarck was not opposed to further peace negotiations. Earl Granville at once proposed a meeting between M. Thiers and Bismarck, the Prussian ambassador sending the French ambassador, through General Von der Tann at Orleans, a safe conduct from Tours to Versailles. The Tours Government concurred, and on the 21st authorized M. Thiers to undertake peace negotiations.

THIERS ARRIVES AT VERSAILLES.

On the 30th, after many delays, M. Thiers arrived at Versailles, having made the trip from Tours in a carriage drawn by Prussian artillery horses. Before treating with Bismarck, M. Thiers proceeded to Paris, where he held consultations with Trochu and the members of the Government, who expressed a strong desire for peace.

This morning (Oct. 31st), M. Thiers arrived from Paris to have an interview with Bismarck.

The Prussian Chancellor says in his report:

"This was the first time that a statesman enjoying such distinction and importance as M. Thiers does, had accepted plenipotentiary powers at the hands of the Paris Government. This fact induced me to hope that proposals would be submitted to us by him on the part of France, the acceptance of which would be possible."

"Bismarck opened the conference," says M. Thiers, "by remarking—

"'That the remains of the Government now at Cassel were the only one recognized by Europe. That he, however, merely made the remark to establish the diplomatic situation, having no intention to meddle with the internal management of France.'"

To this M. Thiers immediately replied—

"that the Government which precipated France into the abyss of a war so foolishly resolved upon, *had forever terminated its existence with its fatal career at Sedan, and would be for France but a semblance of shame and grief.*"

The two diplomats now examined the following questions of the armistice:

"France, in case an armistice is agreed upon, is to be furnished time for the expression of her will as to the government she should choose to have; entire freedom to be allowed for the elections during the armistice, and *also for the organization of the French armies*; lastly, *the revictualling of the besieged places, and especially of Paris, to be permitted.*"

To the first of these questions, there was an immediate

agreement. The present *de facto* Government of France was to hold an election, and become *de jure*, so as to be able to guarantee the execution of a treaty of peace. The German troops were to remain in the positions which they should occupy on the day when the armistice should be signed. Even the Metz troops, which were available for other operations, were to remain in their present camp, while France would, by the conclusion of an armistice, be enabled to develop its resources, and to complete the organization of the army corps then forming, and, after the armistice, confront Prussia with organized troops, which did not exist before signing the armistice.

THE QUESTION OF ALSACE.

In regard to Alsace, it was understood that the Prussians would *not insist on any stipulation which would call in question the right of the claim of France to the German departments before the conclusion of peace*, and that Prussia would not make or hold any of the inhabitants of these parts responsible for their appearance in a French National Assembly as the constitutional representatives of their countrymen.

THE VICTUALLING OF PARIS CAUSES A RUPTURE.

Up to this time negotiations had gone on smoothly; the two diplomats, formerly warm friends, being in perfect harmony. When the question of victualling Paris came up, Bismarck desired to consult with Moltke, and withdrew from the interview. The next conference occurred on the 3d. In the meantime, Bismarck had heard of the revolution of the Paris "Reds" — Gustave Flourens, Hugo, Pyat, and others — and, satisfied that Paris would soon fall through its own demoralization, Bismarck could not conceal his gratification on meeting M. Thiers. As M. Thiers entered, Bismarck looked up from his busy desk, and asked —

"Ah! M. Thiers, have you heard the news?"

M. Thiers. — "No."

Bismarck. — "Paris is in revolution, and a new Government is proclaimed."

M. Thiers. — "If disorder for the moment has triumphed, the people's love of order and patriotism will soon restore quiet."

The two diplomats now discussed the question of revictualling Paris, when M. Thiers said:

"In the name of my Government, I can accept no armistice which does not provide for the reprovisioning of the citizens and garrison of the capitol."

Bismarck.— "But the military authority of Prussia will not consent to the revictualling of Paris, unless a military equivalent is conceded in return."

M. Thiers. — "What do you mean by this?"

Bismarck.—"A fort—perhaps more than one."

M. Thiers (excitedly).—"Paris you want? Paris—our force, our hope—which you are not able to vanquish, after fifty days' siege?"

M. Thiers continued, that he was not able to make any military offer in return for the re-provisioning of Paris.

"In this shape," says Bismarck in his report, "I had to submit the result of our negotiations and conversation to his Majesty the King and his military advisers.

"His Majesty was justly surprised at these exorbitant military claims by France, and he was disappointed in his expectations as to the probable result of the negotiations into which I had entered with M. Thiers. The incredible demand that Prussia should give up the fruit of all the efforts which she had made in the field during the past two months; surrender the many advantages she had gained, and thus bring the situation back to the condition which existed at the moment when the investment of Paris was commenced, could only prove that in Paris they were merely looking for pretexts to deny the French nation the right of holding the election, and that they were not willing to give the people an opportunity to carry the voting out without interruption."

To this M. Thiers replies:

"Arrived here, we could go no farther. I saw the military spirit all powerful in the Prussian resolution against the peace policy, and asked Bismarck for leave to see M. Favre and advise with him. Bismarck charged me to declare that he would not interfere with the elections, even if there was no armistice, and would let Paris communicate with Tours on the subject. The Government was informed of what had occurred, and they desired me to break off the negotiations on the refusal of the revictualling, and leave Versailles, which resolution I imparted to Bismarck."

In conclusion, Bismarck remarks:

"The course of the negotiations with M. Thiers has impressed me with the conviction, that the present rulers of France did not, from the very beginning, sincerely wish to hear the views of the French nation expressed in a representative parliamentary body, constituted by a free and uncontrolled election, and that just as little has been their intention to bring about an armistice; but that they stipulated for a concession which they knew from the first to be unacceptable, and that they only asked for these conditions in order not to give to the neutral Powers, on whose support they count, a direct refusal.

On the 6th, M. Thiers, having received the final negative of Bismarck against the revictualling of Paris, retired to the outposts, to consult with Jules Favre and General Trochu, who by this time were frightened out of all idea of peace by the Paris mob. The Prussian propositions were rejected, and M. Thiers returned to Tours on the 7th.

THE CAUSE OF THE RUPTURE.

The cause of the rupture was the radical influence of a small minority in Paris, who rose against the idea, seized the Government, and intimidated the Paris authorities into rejecting an armistice which was *fraught with good to France, and which will stand an enduring monument to the magnanimity and chivalry of Prussia.* M. Thiers was unfortunate in being the bearer of the news of the sad surrender of Bazaine at Metz — a fact which made his very entry into Paris unpopular with the ignorant masses. A guard was even required for this grand old man, venerable with fifty years, service for France, and he finally left Paris, *protected by an escort of cavalry.* If Bismarck overreached in his demand of Jules Favre on the 21st, he made up the discrepancy by most mild and conciliatory demands of M. Thiers. If the burden of war was then left upon the shoulders of Prussia, *it now hangs like a dead weight upon the Republic.* The Republic has rejected an honorable armistice. She fears to go before the people, for fear that in choosing a new constituent assembly the present rulers shall lose their power. By refusing to hold an election, the verdict goes to the world, that they chose rather to stand *de facto* upon the result of a *coup d'état* than upon the *de jure* votes of the sovereign people. The "man of Sedan" fell from his high pinnacle for no less a crime than this. Eighteen years of possession crowned by a gilded plebiscite, could not varnish over this first usurpation of power.

THE EMPEROR'S APOLOGY.

The captive Emperor issues an address to the French people, giving the cause of disasters to France. He says France was taken by surprise, and that he was startled by the rapidity with which Prussia moved her troops. On the 14th of July the Emperor had no idea that Steinmetz and Prince Charles were in force around Metz. The Emperor tries to shift the blame of the declaration of war upon the people whom he represented, and refers to his manifesto (given at length on page 67), and to the misgivings with which he listened to the cry, "On to Berlin!"

He says his plan was to mass 150,000 men at Metz, 100,000 at Strasburg, and 50,000 at Châlons, and to cross the Rhine near Haguenau with a large force, in order to separate Southern Germany from the Northern Confederation. He hoped to win the first great battle, and secure the alliance of Austria and Italy with France in imposing neutrality on Bavaria, Baden, and Würtemberg. The defects in the French military system, and the delay in bringing up men and material, defeated this plan. He enumerates the difficulties encountered, but acquits the War Office of blame.

The Germans having had ample time to bring their forces into the field, the French were outnumbered and put on the defensive. A new plan was necessary, involving a retreat on Châlons. This the Regency disapproved as discouraging to the public, and the Emperor was urged to resume the offensive. Yielding his convictions, MacMahon's advice and plan were adopted. He alludes to his situation, after he had given up the command of the army, and when his name and authority were ignored at Paris, as exceedingly painful.

He acquiesced in the march for the relief of Metz, though conscious of the danger of that enterprise.

The pamphlet closes with the declaration that the German successes are due to superiority of numbers, improved artillery, rigorous discipline, respect for authority, and the military and patriotic spirit of the people, which absorbs all other interests and opinions.

It censures the loose habits introduced by the African wars in which the French regular troops have been engaged, which it enumerates as want of discipline, lack of cohesion, absence of order, carelessness of bearing, and the excess of luggage carried by the infantry. The efficiency of the army was weakened, too, by the excesses of the opposition in the Corps Législatif and the Republican press, introducing into it a spirit of criticism and insubordination.

The Emperor ends by this recommendation of Cæsarism to France:

May our unhappy countrymen, now prisoners, profit during their sojourn in Prussia by appreciating all which gives strength to the army — the powers that be respected, the law obeyed, the military and patriotic spirit dominating over all interests and opinions! To sum up, the army always reflects the state of society. When authority was exercised, France was strong and respected, and the constitution of the army presented a remarkable solidity; but when excesses of the tribune and the press were permitted, they enfeebled authority and introduced everywhere a spirit of criticism and insubordination, and the army felt the effect of it. God grant that the terrible drama now enacting may serve as a lesson for the future, and that our country may rise again from the catastrophe which now overwhelms her.

WEDNESDAY, *November* 2.— Garibaldi's position at Dôle becomes untenable. The French have no enthusiasm for Garibaldi, and secrete property and run away in a panic at every approach of the Prussians. General Cambriels, commanding the Department of the East, ignores Garibaldi. Neuf-Brisach, south of Strasburg, on the Rhine, besieged. An insurrection in Marseilles, and Alphonse Gent, Government administrator of the city, wounded. George Francis Train makes radical Republican speeches in Lyons — is arrested, and incarcerated in jail for one week, and then liberated by Gambetta.

FRIDAY, *November* 4. — Provisions become very scarce in Paris. The people eating cats, rats, and horse-flesh. General D'Aurelles de Paladines appointed commander of the Army of the Loire. The fortress of Belfort, on the river Savoureuse, 30 miles west of Basle, besieged by General Treskow with 40,000 Germans.

FAMINE IN PARIS.

While the besieging army outside of Paris is filled with joy at the steady stream of victories, until the German camps become carnivals of song and festivity, a different scene is being enacted within. Comedy changes to tragedy, and hunger holds the largest place in the households of Paris. The saying of the terribly earnest Victor Hugo, that "Paris, which has amused civilization, will now astonish the world," begins to prove true. Paris is heroic, and her very women and children seem to be imbued with patriotic fortitude. The whole population is now on scant rations.

Beef and mutton are served out at the rate of 50 grammes (or one ounce and two-thirds) per head. Horse is sold at 1f. 25c., per lb., ass and mule at 3f. per lb., and at these prices they are in such demand that the supply at the public markets runs short. Before the siege a good fat goose brought from 6 to 7 francs; at present the current price is from 25 francs to 30 francs; chickens fetch from 14 to 15 francs; a brace of pigeons is considered cheap at 12 francs; turkey is a very scarce article; there are none to be had at the markets — a few are to be seen in poulterers' shops. Ham is 8 francs per pound; charcoal has risen to $100 per ton.

The following private letter from a lady of distinction gives a succinct and graphic picture of daily life in the besieged capital:

PARIS, *Sunday, Nov.* 4, 1870.

MY DEAR ——: I am quite well, and trust you all are, but I often feel very anxious. Everything might happen, and I not know it. We have had, as you know, great riots. I could not imagine what all the drum-beating meant in the night. We manage to live somehow. I made up my mind at last yesterday to eat horse, and think I have got over my disquiet; I was really too hungry. I can't tell you how hungry we often are. No butter (19f. a pound), cheese, or bacon to be had for money; potatoes getting rare, and from 4f. 50c. to 8f. a bushel. Lots of coffee, but no milk. I am favored by the milkman — only soon he will have to kill his cows, as there is no forage. The fruiterer saved also a little oil for us. We have four tins of beef-tea left, and more than half the ham Mr. —— sent, and have not touched the two tins of meat I bought; so you see I have saved all I could. I fry the ham slice by slice, and save the grease to eat. Our rations of meat for three days we always eat in one meal, and desire more. I was two hours and a half getting my piece of meat (horse), and very much pushed; but it was nothing to the meat-crowd on Friday —

the barrier thrown down twice, and I very much hurt. I screamed awfully. I don't remember in the least how I was got out. The women are like devils. I quite understand the scenes of the Revolution. Yesterday Mr. —— was there three hours; one of the guards was nearly killed, and carried away on a stretcher. I don't think I can go again; but I had rather go there than that we should have none; for with bread and rice I am faint from morning till night.

No one can imagine what the privation from meat, grease, and cheese is, without they try. Donkey is from 4f. to 6f. a pound. I wanted some, but recoiled at the price. There are vegetables — very dear. No pulse whatever. Few eggs, 6d. each; apples, 8d. each. I have bought a little stove on which I cook, as there is no charcoal, and I think I have laid in coal enough for the whole winter. The price keeps going up, of course, and it is getting rare. There is very little gas now in Paris. Paris looks puny now, I can assure you.

I am so glad my little baby is in England. I fear she would starve in the arms of her mother here.

I pray God she is all right, and all of you. I hope you have had all my other letters. I am very well, and my impression is that I am not a woman, but a horse. I only require food, and then I am as well as possible. I must say I devoutly hope for an armistice, but as yet, I think, no one knows. E—— has a beautiful uniform, which I hope will never be deteriorated. There are quantities of things I might relate to you, but have no room. Lightest letters go first. With love to all near you, your very loving ————

One of the cleverest letter-writers from Paris shows a fund of humor when he writes:

I hope I shan't utterly horrify you and henceforward become a social outlaw, if I confess to having this morning eaten at one of the best restaurants in Paris — rats. Two months ago I should have been as much appalled at the bare idea of perpetrating such an atrocity as, perhaps, any other civilized Englishman. But, first, one's principles receive a dangerous shock in eating horse; then you meet friends, ordinarily decent, respectable people, who tell you that they have been avowedly eating cat; and that you have yourself already been served in the same way if you have ever, at no matter what restaurant, ordered rabbit. One's gastronomic conscience gradually hardens, I suppose, in an atmosphere of this kind; and so, when this morning I met a friend on the Boulevards just about breakfast time, who asked me to come with him to Hall's, as he had there ordered rats, instead of at once running away, or, perhaps, trying to knock him down, I agreed to go and just look at them. They looked very good, served up in a *salmi*, with gravy and toast, and my friend pronounced them "excellent;" and so I did eat, or rather taste, and am obliged to confess that I should have no objection to repeat the experiment to-morrow. The flesh was white and very delicate, like young rabbit, but with more flavor. We curiously inspected the bill to see whether the proprietor of the restaurant would venture to give the dish its real name; but there was only a significant blank space, and then 1f. 50c. On being remonstrated with for this unbusiness-like method of procedure, he wanted to write *Salmi du Gibier*, the word "rat" being quite impossible. As there were two rats in the *salmi*, each cost about 7d., but bought wholesale (I am told that they are now exhibited publicly for sale in some shops) and cooked at home, they would, perhaps, be cheap eating, even in time of siege; only, unluckily, the poor people, who want them most, would be the last to consent to touch them.

It is a question of the belly, nothing more. Our beef and mutton will be exhausted in a fortnight, perhaps sooner. Will Paris feed on horse, of which there is abundance? I believe it will, and those who, like myself, vow never to touch horse, will live on vegetables. For me, I am Shadrach. You remember the story of the three children who would not in captivity eat the flesh offered to idols, and fed on pulse. At the end of forty days they were very fat. I think I could get up in Paris the Shadrach, Meshech, and Abednego Club. When the siege of Paris is over you will see us as fat as pigs on our diet of pulse, peas, beans, and lentils.

Talking of pigs, let me end this letter with an anecdote. I took a friend to breakfast with me yesterday morning at Brabant's. On the bill of fare I found *cochon de lait.* Now, I have many weaknesses, but all are as nothing in comparison with my weakness for sucking pig. I at once said, "By all means, we shall have sucking pig." But I called back the waiter and asked him if it was a real sucking pig? He said, "Truly." Then I said, "A little pig?" He replied, "Surely." Again I said, "A young pig?" But this question floored him, and he hesitated. At last he confessed, "It was a guinea-pig.—*cochin d'Inde.*" Now, I ask you, are you equal to guinea-pig?

SUNDAY, *November* 6.—Garibaldi evacuates Dôle and moves to Autun, sixty miles to the east. Würtemberg, Baden, and Hesse-Darmstadt accept the North-German constitution and enter the North-German confederation. Fort Mortimer, one of the fortifications of Neuf Brisach, destroyed by Prussian shells.

GARIBALDI.

For the last ten days, Garibaldi has held his army at Dôle, in front of General Werder, with the Fourteenth Prussian Corps at Dijon and Vesoul, 5000 men of the former and 20,000 of the latter. On the 4th, General Bossak, commanding Garibaldi's advance, ten miles north of Dôle, fell back, his troops being somewhat disorganized. On the 6th, Garibaldi received an order from Gambetta to fall back to Autun. The same day a detachment from General Werder attacked the French advance a few miles north of Dôle, on the Saone river, driving them back. Menotti Garibaldi, with his brigade, joined his father the same day south of Autun, while Ricciotti joined his father on the north. Garibaldi made this movement to jeopardize General Werder's communication in his expected move on Macon and Lyons. Autun is a small town of 12,000 inhabitants, at the foot of the Vosges, and forming the western apex of a triangle with Dijon and Macon. It is a capital position, from which Garibaldi intends to make a sortie, falling on the German flank if they shall advance southward.

TUESDAY, *November*, 8.—Verdun capitulates, with 4000 men, two generals, and 100 officers.

VERDUN.

Verdun is a first-class fortress, its ordinary war garrison consisting of 4200 men and 700 horses. It is considered as the key to the Argonnes passes, which have long been in the possession of the Germans, but will now be more securely held, as numerous Francs-tireurs, relying on the fortress, infest them. Verdun is at present the terminus of the railway, which is to be continued in a direct line from Rheims and Châlons to Metz, but which will not be available for communication between Metz and Paris, owing to its considerable distance from the former. It has 18,000 inhabitants. The negotiations for its surrender were opened on the 3d inst., and an eight-days armistice was first concluded. The commandant, Baron Guerin de Waldersbach, who had previously protested that he would hold out as long as one stone remained on another, thought that after the fall of Metz resistance was useless, as relief was out of the question, while the besieging force might be largely strengthened. The fortresses now held by the French in the north-east are Mézières, Montmédy, and Longwy, the latter provisioned for a year. Verdun surrendered to General Von Gayl on the eighth, with several weeks' provisions. The town has been severely bombarded, the citadel suffering much from Prussian shells. Manteuffel, with the First Corps of Steinmetz' old army, released from Metz, was already on the march to assist in its reduction, but the soldiers divided themselves into Republican and Imperial parties, when an internal quarrel ensued. Baron Waldersbach goes a prisoner to Wilhelmshöhe, and Manteuffel, with Goeben, marches toward Amiens, in the north of France.

WEDNESDAY, *November* 9. — Gortschakoff's letter abrogating the treaty of Paris delivered in London, Vienna, Constantinople, Florence, and Tours. Immense excitement in England. The press and people clamor for war, and Earl Granville writes a threatening reply. A general European war threatened; but Queen Victoria discountenances war measures, milder counsels prevail, a congress of European powers convoked, and England covers up a broken treaty and wounded honor with the smoke of diplomacy. General Aurelles de Paladines defeats General Von der Tann at Coulmiers, south-west of Orleans, near Mer, capturing guns, ammunition, and prisoners. Von der Tann makes a precipitate retreat through Orleans and Artenay to Toury.

RUSSIA — PRUSSIA *vs.* TURKEY — ENGLAND.

THE BREAKING OF THE TREATY OF PARIS.

Preliminary to the breaking of the treaty of Paris (given page 331), Czar Alexander of Russia commenced cultivating friendly relations with King William. This friendly diplomacy met with great prejudice among the Russian masses, who are exceedingly jealous of Prussia, and who, as the author noticed in St. Petersburg and Moscow, in 1867, never lose an opportunity of showing their supreme contempt for the Germans. For months in Moscow, in the Russo-American family of his cousin, Robert Williams, the Russian railroad king, the author was thrown constantly in the society of representative Russians. They had one feeling — a hatred towards England and Prussia, and one political belief — which was to break the treaty of Paris and open up the Black Sea to the armed ships of Russia. When a Cabinet Minister asked Nicholas about the expediency of teaching German and English in the Russian school, he exclaimed, "No, no! teach them no English, but French and American." This hatred of Prussia is also indulged in by the Czarewich, who married Dagmar of Denmark; and the work of conciliating Prussia, as a necessary preliminary to the breaking of the treaty of Paris, devolved entirely upon the far-seeing Czar.

After the declaration of war by Napoleon on the 15th of July, Gortschakoff visited Berlin, and had several interviews with Bismarck and King William before their departure for war. Gortschakoff then made known Russia's intention to remain neutral, and asked as her reward the acquiescence of Prussia in the abrogation of those articles in the treaty of Paris which forbid Russia from keeping a fleet in the Black Sea. This Bismarck secretly agreed to do, but it was then mutually understood that the agreement should not be publicly promulgated until the conclusion of peace between France and Prussia. This bargain enabled Prussia to place in the war the two corps that had been left for the defence of the eastern province of Silesia. Russia also agreed secretly to restrain any interference on the part of Austria, and for this purpose mobilized her army toward the Austrian border.

To further conciliate King William, simultaneously with the mobilizing of 300,000 Russian troops in Southern Russia, the Czar conferred upon the Crown Princes of Prussia and Saxony the highest compliment of Russia — the Order of St. George. Was it not significant of Queen Victoria's kind wishes towards Napoleon III., when she conferred upon him the "Order of the Garter," and received his Imperial kiss on the Windsor staircase? That act did not signify more than this act of the Czar; for in the hall of St. George, that magnificent white chamber in the Imperial palace of St. Petersburg, only the especial friends of the Czar are allowed to banquet. Following in quick succession, the same Order was conferred upon the Grand Duke Mecklenburg-Schwerin; while numerous letters from the Czar, congratulating King William on his victories over the French, won the conciliation of the Prussian King. On the eve of the battle of Sedan a courier arrived from the Czar, congratulating his Majesty on the victories before Metz; adding, however, that he felt confident that Prussia would offer fair terms of peace, and would not require any cession of territory from France.

After the victory of Sedan and the proclamation of a republic in Paris, a second autograph letter came from the Czar, full of congratulations, but repeating the remark as to territorial acquisitions, which might alter the present position of the great Powers to the disadvantage of Russia.

The reply of King William was warm; the old man's heart was melted into complacency, and henceforth the friendship of Russia and Prussia went on increasing. Bismarck offered mild terms to Jules Favre and magnanimous terms to M. Thiers; while Count Von Moltke looked upon the mobilization of 500,000 Russian troops, showing his gratification in a smile.

GORTSCHAKOFF AND GRANVILLE.

Prussia was conciliated. If the rest of Europe could be induced to permit Russia to break the treaty of Paris, what chance would the 12,000,000 Turks stand against the 80,000,000 Russians? The odious articles in the treaty of Paris which are given in full on page 331, stipulate that,—

"The Black Sea shall only be entered by merchant vessels; that *no armed* vessel, of whatever nation, *shall ever enter her waters;* and that Russia and Turkey shall not construct any arsenal, naval or military, upon her shores.

The Russians claim that the treaty has been broken by the passage into the Black Sea of the Turkish, English, and American frigates of war, and that as one of the powers (France) which signed the treaty is not in a condition to meet in a congress of nations to abrogate the same, that Russia will take the initiative, and *peacefully break it*, by sending her squadron to winter quarters through the Bosphorus.

These war frigates, over which Russia makes such a serious complaint, were the pleasure ships of the Sultan, the royal ship of Prince Albert, the pleasure ship of Lord Lytton, and the frigate "Franklin," commanded by the late Admiral Farragut.

Another article of the treaty of Paris stipulated that there should be no union of the Danubian Principalities; whereas Wallachia and Moldavia have made a political union, and elected Charles as Hospodar, and this *with the connivance of Turkey, and the silent consent of England, France, and Austria.*

After Russia had allowed these infringements to go on quietly for several years, the present war made opportune the time for complaint and vigorous action. So, on the 19th of October, Gortschakoff addressed to the Russian Ambassador in London, for the benefit of Earl Granville, a letter setting forth the Russian intention to break the treaty. In this letter, after going over the ground complaining of the infringements on the treaty by other powers, Gortschakoff summed up the Russian intentions. He says in substance, "*a treaty broken in favor of other nations should not stand against the interests of Russia;* that the treaty has not withstood the test of time, and that Russia will not imperil her own security by keeping a treaty which has not been kept article by article by other nations:" therefore,—

"His Imperial Majesty can no longer consider himself bound by the obligations of the treaty of 18th (30th) March, 1856, so far as these limit his right of sovereignty in the Black Sea; . . . that he loyally gives notice of this to the powers signing and guaranteeing the general treaty, and that he restores to His Majesty the Sultan the full possession of his right in this respect, as he equally reclaims his own for himself. . . . .
It is by no means the purpose of his Imperial Majesty to raise the Eastern question upon this point. He has no other wish than the preservation and consolidation of peace. He fully maintains his adhesion to the general principles of the treaty of 1856, which settled the position of Turkey in the European system. He is ready to confirm its general stipulations or renew them or to substitute for them any other equitable arrangement which may be thought suitable to secure the repose of the East, and the European equilibrium. His Majesty, however, is convinced that peace and equilibrium will have a stronger guarantee when they shall have been placed on more just and solid bases than those resulting from a position which no great power could accept as a normal condition of existence."

This Russian note from Gortschakoff, written from Tzarskoe-Selo, October 19th, was delivered simultaneously at London, Vienna, Constantinople, Florence, and Tours, on Wednesday the 9th of November, creating a diplomatic stir throughout Europe. It was gravely written, to the point, and meant business. Divested of its diplomatic language, the Czar's note meant this: *You three strong powers strangled my father Nicholas after the Crimea, and made him agree to a foolish, unjust thing — never again to go in and out of his own front door. That front door is on the Black Sea, while his back door is on the Baltic, frozen up seven months in the year. Now one of you villains is dead — that is, France, and I have bought the other — Prussia, and I fear not the third — Great Britain, even though she can summon those little Bluebeards, Italy and Austria, to help her. I defy you, and to-day I go in and out of my front door left me by my father.*

On the 20th of October Gortschakoff addressed another note to Baron Brunnow, the Russian ambassador in London, couched in still stronger language, and throwing the blame of the first infringement of the treaty upon the shoulders of England and the powers of Europe.

THURSDAY, *November* 10. — Earl Granville replies to Gortschakoff's note.

On the 10th of November, Earl Granville delivered, through the Queen's messenger, Sir Andrew Buchanan, a firm reply to Gortschakoft's two notes, acknowledging the infringement by other powers against the treaty of Paris. Earl Granville maintained that these infringements by other powers were no excuse for Russia's breaking the treaty; that the question was not as to its justness or unjustness, but turned upon the issue of *who has the power to break a treaty.* The Earl maintained that *not one* of the treaty-signing powers had a right to break the treaty, but *all the co-signers* must agree together. If treaties are to be interpreted and broken at the will of *each* of the parties at discretion, the result will be the entire destruction of treaties in their essence. In a treaty each power surrenders a certain individual free agency for the benefit of the rest, but by the doctrine of Russia each power holds the right of the free interpretation of every article of a treaty — bringing back the entire subject to its own control. Earl Granville ended by saying:

"I need scarcely say that Her Majesty's Government have received this communication with deep regret, because it opens a discussion which might unsettle the cordial understanding it has been their earnest endeavor to maintain with the Russian Empire, *and for the above-mentioned reasons it is impossible for Her Majesty's Government to give any sanction on their part to the course announced by Prince Gortschakoff.*"

The Earl maintained that any infraction of the treaty should have been referred to the co-signers of the treaty for adjudication, and that such a proceeding would have the result of preventing future complication, and presented a very dangerous precedent as to the interpretation of international obligations.

PRUSSIA'S POSITION.

To the note of Gortschakoff, Bismarck's reply was conciliatory. "Russia's claims are natural," says the Chancellor; "and there should be an amicable settlement of the treaty question. Prussia can see no cause for alarm on the part of the co-signatory powers. Russia might have appealed to the co-signatories for a revision of the treaty, but one of them has at present no organized government, and is unable to take part in any congress that might have been proposed.

AUSTRIA'S POSITION.

Baron Von Beust, the Austrian Minister, has concurred since 1867 with Russia in the belief that the treaty of Paris was unjust to Russia, but he takes exceptions to the manner of abrogating it. *He says "had Russia submitted the treaty to the co-signors for a revision, a favorable result would have ensued."* His difference is only in form, but his letter to Gortschakoff is firm and pointed. He insists on the

"force of the obligations contracted in 1856, which are not to be evaded or annulled. The fact that Turkey can sustain a fleet where Russia cannot, is not sufficient for arbitrarily dissolving the treaty. The action of Russia endangers all existing and future treaties. Turkey is responsible for the union of the Principalities. Turkey asks that we shall not give our sanction to a breach of the treaty. The mere holiday excursions of frigates into the Black Sea, with princes on board, were perfectly harmless. Russia should have shown her dissatisfaction, and spoken at the proper time. Austria deplores Russia's determination, and expresses her surprise at it. She points out to Russia the inevitable consequences of the step she has taken.

RUSSIA REPEATS HER DEMAND.

Earl Granville's reply was received respectfully in St. Petersburg, the Czar having already had assurances that the Prince of Wales, representing the views of Queen Victoria, had represented to the Cabinet her disapproval of the Earl's previous hasty and warlike reply to Russia.

To Earl Granville's letter written on the 10th of November, Gortschakoff replied from the palace of Tzarskoe-Selo on the 20th. His tone was pacificatory, and he excused the action of Russia in breaking the treaty, on the ground that "*the attempts made at different times to assemble the powers in a general conference have invariably failed, and the prolongation of the present crisis and the absence of a regular government in France postponed the possibility of an agreement.*"

Gortschakoff still maintained that the abrogation of one article of the treaty did not abrogate the whole treaty, and that Russia would be glad of a peaceful adjustment of the matter, either by mutual explanations or by a congress of the signing powers. Without backing down, the Russian Premier, with Chesterfieldian diplomacy, poured oil on the troubled waters, and the political heavens, so full of stormy war-clouds, became quiet and serene. Milder counsels soothed the war feeling which ran high in England, and a great treaty was broken without bloodshed. The breaking of this treaty was a direct assault upon England, who first blustered, and then quailed and surrendered a great principle, glad to have the disgrace covered up in the smoke of diplomacy. A great amount of diplomatic smoke will surround the breaking of this treaty. Gortschakoff will be prevailed upon to withdraw his first note, and all that for form's sake; but in the mean time Russia sails her iron-clads in and out of the Black Sea, and Ignatief, the Russian ambassador, dines with the Sublime Porte, and convinces him by diplomatic logic that Russia will give Turkey better guarantees than the treaty of Paris. Luxemburg, Holland, Belgium, and Savoy, whose existences depend upon treaties and guarantees from the great powers, now tremble, not knowing when Bismarck, Von Beust, or Gortschakoff may take a fancy to blot out their feeble existences. Beyond the smoke of the Black Sea business, Bismarck already has his eye on trembling Luxemburg.

ROUMANIA BREAKS THE TREATY.

On the 25th of December, substantiating the logic of Earl Russell, the Roumanian Government repudiated the treaty of Paris and declared its independence. The Servians are also moving to establish an independent kingdom, like Hungary. Thus Turkey loses her Danubian provinces, Servia looks toward a Hungarian alliance, and the Roumanian Hospodar (ruler) who is a Hohenzollern, related to King William, and a brother of Leopold, the old Spanish throne aspirant, becomes an ally of the Czar of Russia. In the mean time it becomes known that Russia has been preparing since 1863 to break the treaty of Paris — that she has been building a substitute for Sevastopol, which could not be restored, according to the treaty of Paris, as an arsenal. The site chosen for the new naval harbor is the town of Poti, at the mouth of the river Rion, on the eastern coast of the Black Sea, a few miles distant from the Turkish frontier, which separates Circassia from the Russian province of Georgia. A railway has been constructed from Poti to Tiflis and the Circassian Sea, down the valley of the River Kur; and two million roubles have been expended by the Russian Government on its docks and piers, making Poti capable of harboring a large squadron of war ships.

THURSDAY, *Nov.* 10. — The battle of Coulmiers — the first French victory. Von der Tann retreats, with loss of guns and prisoners, to Toury. Paladines takes possession of Orleans. Earl Granville writes his famous war letter to Gortschakoff. General Treskow moves from Belfort to the assistance of Von der Tann, leaving force large enough to besiege Belfort. General Bressoles at Lyons orders the fortress to be provisioned for 70,000 men for two months.

THE BATTLE OF COULMIERS (*Nov.* 10).

The defeat and flight of Motterouge's command from Artenay, and its disgraceful retreat across the Loire at Orleans on the 11th of October, given on page 366, filled the Tours Government with grave apprehensions. The Republic was in danger — the terrible Von der Tann seemed almost to reach out his hands towards the Republican capital, and Southern France was fired again to deeds of danger and patriotism. It was the old terrible recoil of the North after Manassas, and a whole nation seemed to spring forward to wipe out the stigma of Motterouge's defeat. These were dark days for France. The magnificent army which moved out with a haughty Emperor had surrendered at Sedan, and the proud Imperial Guard, with a hundred and fifty thousand veterans, had surrendered at Metz. Manteuffel was moving upon Amiens on the north, Werder was pushing Garibaldi towards Lyons on the east; the Grand Duke of Mecklenburg was marching towards Le Mans on the west, and Prince Charles was sweeping down with an hundred thousand veterans fresh from the glories of Metz. France was fated to show one of those sublime efforts by which she has astonished more than once the centuries, and awed the world to admiration. Thousands of her sons were ready to fight—ready to die for France; but where was the leader—who the man to concentrate her dying energies? From the red furrows of battle sprang the young soldier of the Republic, Aurelles de Paladines. Paladines is a natural Republican. The Emperor lavished no honors upon him, but kept him constantly in the background, while decorations and promotions were held out to Bazaine, Bourbaki, and De Failly, the strong supporters of the Imperial *régime*. Born of the Republic, the very presence of Aurelles de Paladines seemed to organize victory from the military chaos left by Motterouge. South of Orleans he immediately reorganized the defeated Army of the Loire. Polhès was placed in command of the Fifteenth Corps, Lussac in command of the Sixteenth Corps, and Pallières in command of the Seventeenth Corps; while General Fierck, assisted by Kératry, that stanch Republican, who demanded the abdication of the Emperor in August, organized the Army of the West at Le Mans. Guns came from Tours and men flocked from Southern France, until, as if by magic, Paladines had 80,000 men, well supplied with artillery. Von der Tann was in front with about 25,000 men, but they were the First Bavarian veterans, who had fought with the Crown Prince at Weisenburg, destroyed MacMahon at Woerth, and formed the chain about Sedan which captured an Emperor.

On the 5th of November, Paladines commenced the movement against Von der Tann in Orleans, which was to give the first victory to France. General Lussac's Sixteenth Corps was advanced on the west of Orleans, threatening a flank movement across the Loire from Blois to Marchenoir, supported by General Polhès' Fifteenth Corps at Mer. Pallières threatened Orleans in front from the south bank of the Loire, while a force of 30,000 French marched up from Bourges to attack Von der Tann from the east.

On the 8th there was an unusual commotion in Von der Tann's camp at Orleans, and a grave apprehension that Paladines was about to move Lussac and Polhès against the German rear, to cut off communication with the Paris army. The whole German army, leaving only a regiment in Orleans, was marched westward to ascertain the intentions of the French. A Coulmiers between Orleans and Mer, on the morning of the

9th, the First Bavarian Corps, formerly with the Crown Prince, encountered Polhès, Lussac, and Pallières, eighty thousand strong. Polhès immediately commenced the attack with large masses of infantry, ninety guns, and seven regiments of cavalry. Though outnumbered, it would not do for the heroes of Woerth and Sedan to fall back without a fight; so all that day the Bavarians withstood the shock of twice their number. Four times Polhès advanced in fearful onslaught against the sturdy Germans. Von der Tann should have retreated early in the day, but it was a hard thing for men who carried Froschweiler to turn their backs for the first time upon a victorious foe. Surprised at his own success, the first hesitating advance of Polhès became a bold and bloody attack. The French began to fight again with something of hereditary renown. Suddenly the Germans yielded up the glories of a dozen victories, and after a bloodier day than Woerth or Sedan, night gave the first French victory to Paladines and the Republic. The First Bavarian Corps lost 70 officers and 3000 men, and the next morning the Prussian ammunition train fell into the hands of the French. In the midnight darkness Von der Tann fell back to Orleans, his personal luggage and camp carriage falling into the hands of the French. As the Germans fell back towards Orleans, Cathelineau, with the troops from Bourges, supported by Pallières with the Seventeenth Corps, fell upon the retreating Von der Tann. Strongly fortified positions were stormed and captured by the French, and the Germans were compelled to abandon to the French an immense amount of hospital stores, with sick and wounded. The Anglo-American Ambulance Corps was also captured by Paladines. On the 10th, Von der Tann made a stand at Baccon, a few miles north of Orleans, beyond the forest of Cercottes, where another sanguinary conflict ensued. Paladines' victorious troops stormed the German entrenched camp with a terrible impetuosity, throwing the Bavarians into a precipitate retreat through Artenay to Toury, where they were reinforced by the Sixth Prussian army, 40,000 strong, under the Grand Duke Mecklenburg, and the forces of Prince Ollrich, from Chartres. Their decisive victories filled the French troops with joy. Cowed by losing every battle since Saarbrück, they had lost all hope. Now, as they mounted guard around the captured caissons and guns, they looked proud and cheerful, and a new "fire was up in the eye." The victory of Paladines was complete, though his forces, as heretofore has been the case with the Germans, three times outnumbered the enemy. General Paladines, on taking possession of Orleans, issued the following order to his troops:

SOLDIERS: ORLEANS, *Nov.* 10*th*, 1870.

The action of yesterday was a glorious one for our army. Every position of the enemy was vigorously carried, and the enemy is now retreating. I have informed the Government of your conduct, and am instructed to return to you their thanks for your victory. Amid the disasters in which France is plunged, her eyes are upon you, and she counts upon your courage. Let us all make every effort, in order that this hope may not be mistaken. D'AURELLES DE PALADINES,
Commander-in-Chief.

General Paladines, in a dispatch to the Tours war minister, says:

We have taken possession of the city of Orleans, after a fight which has lasted two days. Our aggregate losses in killed and wounded do not reach 2000, while those of the enemy are much larger.

We have made more than 1000 prisoners thus far, and are continually adding to them as we follow up the fleeing enemy. Among the property captured are two cannon of the Prussian model, 20 ammunition-wagons, and a great number of vans and provision-wagons. The hottest of the fight took place around Coulmiers, on Wednesday, the 9th. Notwithstanding the bad weather and other unfavorable circumstances, the *èlan* displayed by the troops was remarkable.

The tidings of victory from the Army of the Loire roused the wildest excitement throughout France. Great numbers of troops were hurried up from the south to join Paladines in his northward march for the relief of Paris, while Minister Gambetta issued these ringing words of hope to the first victorious French army:

TO THE ARMY OF THE LOIRE:

Your courageous efforts recall victory to our cause. France owes her first ray of hope to you, and I offer you the public praise and gratitude for your reward. Recovering strength with discipline, you have retaken Orleans, inaugurating a glorious offensive. You are on the road to Paris, which awaits you; our honor hangs on your loosening the grasp of these barbarians; redouble your constancy and ardor, and you will overcome your enemies' superiority in cannon with French *èlan* and patriotic fury. So will the Republic issue victorious from the struggle. GAMBETTA.

The victory of Paladines placed the German besieging army in a grave situation. Prince Charles, marching from Metz by way of Toul, Bar-le-Duc, Troyes, and Montargis, was urged to quicken his march to the relief of Von der Tann, while King William acknowledged defeat in the following dispatch:

TO QUEEN AUGUSTA: VERSAILLES, *November* 11th.

General Von der Tann yesterday retired from Orleans to Toury before a superior force of the enemy. He fought the French, however, all the way. He has already been reinforced by General Wittich and Prince

Ollrich. The latter came up from Chartres. The Duke of Mecklenburg-Schwerin will also join his forces to those of Von der Tann to-day.

WILHELM

General Trochu received by carrier pigeon the following dispatch of victory from Tours, which arrived the same evening in Paris. As soon as the news was detached from the pigeon it was published by Jules Favre, and placarded throughout the city, causing immense enthusiasm :

GAMBETTA TO TROCHU : — The Army of the Loire, under the command of General D' Aurelles de Paladines, took possession of Orleans yesterday, after a combat which lasted two days. Our losses in killed and wounded do not reach two thousand men ; those of the enemy are much greater. We have taken a thousand prisoners, and the number is being augmented in the pursuit. We have taken two cannon of the Prussian model, twenty-six caissons of munitions, and great quantities of wagons and provisions. The principal action was concentrated around Coulmiers on the 9th. The spirit of our troops was remarkable, in spite of the bad weather.

TOURS, *Nov.* 11, 1870.

FRIDAY, *November* 11. — Capitulation of Neuf Brisach, with 5000 men and 100 guns.

SATURDAY, *November* 12th. — General Paladines made generalissimo of all the French armies outside of Paris, and General Pallières appointed Commander-in-Chief of the Army of the Loire. Immense activity on the part of the French in preparing the campaign for the relief of Paris. Death of M. Pietri, formerly Prefect of Police in Paris.

PIETRI — OLLIVIER — GRAMONT — BENEDETTI.

These haters of the Republic seem to have dropped into supreme contempt. Pietri, who, as chief of police in Paris played the atrocious *rôle* of chief Imperial spy, causing ignominious arrests and blind persecutions among the opponents of the Empire, has expired in a retired town in Switzerland. Ollivier, the blind tool of Napoleon, but whose political head was severed after Woerth, and his old shoes thrown to Palikao to appease the wrath of Paris, has wandered into Italian obscurity ; and Gramont, who made the speech in the Chambers, that waked the sleeping dogs of war, with as jaunty a nonchalance as if he were betting a hat on a horse-race, is lost in the London fogs. Baron Hausmann and Prince Napoleon have become as mythical as Slidell and Benjamin after the end of Appomattox ; while Schneider, the old President of the Chambers, who lost his hat getting out of the Chamber before the coming men of September 4th, occupies a retired chamber in Regent street. Benedetti, George Ripley's "little red pepper-pot of a Corsican," who stormed old King William at Ems, and then wrote puzzling dispatches of war and beer and barrels of treacherous Rhine wine to the Emperor, advises the surrender of France in demoralized articles in "*The Situation*," and writes from London how he was opposed to the war which the French people brought on, in spite of himself, Gramont, and a blundering Emperor! As ridiculous are these I-told-you-so pretensions of broken-down Imperialists as would be a claim on the part of Charles O'Connor that Sumner made him write about "just, wise, and beneficent slavery," and that all the time he was in favor of Lincoln's scheme of emancipation.

TUESDAY, *November* 15.—Prince Charles' advance arrives to the relief of Von der Tann. Von der Tann marches west to support Mecklenburg, while Prince Charles marches south, threatening Paladines. Kératry advances towards Mecklenburg at Dreux, to relieve Paris. Manteuffel moves towards Amiens. Thionville burning. The Berlin banker Gutterbach arrested for taking the French loan. Garibaldi falls back, and Werder in force occupies Dôle.

The treaty with the South German states Baden and Hesse for the establishment of the German Bund, signed. Bavaria and Würtemberg to sign on the 25th.

THE GREAT ARMIES MOVING.

After the fall of Metz the world looked for peace, but never since the first gun at Saarbrück has such energy been shown by both armies on the soil of unhappy France as to-day.

The Republic, born amid the convulsions of war and nursed amid bloodshed and defeat, seemed almost to surrender to despair, but the victory of Paladines fired to a flame her expiring hope. The vindictive power of the Prussian king was roused to a terrible energy, and it was thought to strangle in one grand sweeping German advance all the new armies of France. France with her 40,000,000 was gaining ground, while united Germany with her 39,000,000 could see only defeat in delay.

Trochu had reorganized his 320,000 effective men into three grand armies, under command of Thomas, Ducrot, and Vinoy, holding King William with 350,000 men around Paris. General Ernest, with Garibaldi in advance at Chagny, and with 40,000 men at Macon, stood in front of Werder's 55,000 at Vesoul and Besançon. General Farre's 30,000 at Amiens and Faidherbe's 20,000 at Lille were awaiting the arrival of Manteuffel's 70,000 veterans from Metz, while Kératry's 55,000 were at Le Mans, in front of Mecklenburg's 30,000 fresh from the fall of Soissons, supported by Von der Tann's 25,000; and Paladines' 180,000 were pressing up from Orleans to Artenay, against Prince Charles' 110,000 foot-sore veterans arriving to Von der Tann's relief from Metz.

The relative positions of the ten grand French and German armies of 800,000 men, from the 15th to the 18th of November, were about thus:

PARIS.

GERMANS, 350,000. *King William and Crown Prince.* — The Guards, Prince Augustus; Second Corps, Fansecki; Fourth Corps, Alvensleben; Twelfth Corps, Prince George of Saxony; Würtembergers, Von Obernetz; Eleventh Corps, Böse; Sixth Corps, Tumpling; Fifth Corps, Kirchbach; Second Bavarian; Twenty-third and Twenty-fourth Divisions, Infantry; Twelfth Corps, Artillery (Twelfth Cavalry Division at Creil, to support Manteuffel).

FRENCH, 320,000 (effectives.) *Trochu*, Governor of Paris, Commander-in-Chief; Gen. Schmitz as Chief of the Staff, Gen. Foyer second. Chief of Artillery, Gen. Ginod; Commandant-in-Chief of the Engineers, Gen. De Chaband la Tour; Chief of the Commissariat, Gen. Wolf.

First Army — Commanded by Gen. Clement Thomas, who also replaces Gen. Tamisier as the Commander-in-Chief of the National Guard. Chief of the Staff, Col. Montagut, 266 battalions National Guards. The Legion of Cavalry is commanded by Col. Quiclet, and the Artillery by Col. Schœlcher. In all about 100,000 effective men.

Second Army — Commanded by General Ducrot. Chief of Staff, Gen. Appert; Second Chief, Lieut.-Col. Warnet; Commandant of Artillery, Gen. Fróbauer; Chief of the Engineers, Gen. Tripier; General Wolf, Commissariat of this Second Army. *The First Corps* is commanded by Gen. Blanchard; the artillery by D'Uberi. The First Division is under Gen. De Malroy, the Second is commanded by Gen. De Mandluy, the Third by Gen. ——. Gen. Renault commands the Second Army Corps. The three divisions are under the orders respectively of Gens. Susbielle, Birthant — who has replaced Gen. De Bellemare at St. Denis — and De Maussion. Gen. D'Exéa commands the *Third Army Corps*, and the First and Second Divisions have for chiefs Gen. De Bellemare and Gen. Mattat. This corps also includes a division of Cavalryun der Gen. De Champéron. It consists of two brigades, and a regiment of mounted gendarmerie. In all about 150,000 men.

Third Army — Gen. Vinoy commanding. Consists of eight divisions, including one of cavalry, and seventeen brigades. Commanders of divisions, Gens. Soumain, De Liniers, De Beaufort, Correard, D'Hugues, Vice-Admiral De la Roncière, and Rear-Admiral Pothuan. In all about 70,000 men, 1000 guns.

North (*Amiens — Lille*).

GERMANS, 70,000. *Gen. Manteuffel.* — First Corps; Eighth Corps, Goeben.

FRENCH, 50,000. *Gen. Farre*, Amiens. — Gen. Faidherbe, Twenty-second Corps, Lille.

East (*Lyons — Dôle*).

GERMANS, 55,000. *Gen. Werder.* — Fourteenth Corps. Schmeling at Dijon.

FRENCH, 75,000.	*General Walsin-Esterhazy* at Lyons. — Army of the Vosges, Cambriels, Garibaldi, Menotti, and Ricciotti at Autun.
	WEST (*Le Mans — Chartres*).
GERMANS, 45,000.	*Grand Duke Mecklenburg.* — Thirteenth Corps, composed of the Seventeenth Infantry Division (Treskow), the Twenty-second (Wittich), and the Fourth and Sixth Cavalry under Prince Albrecht at Chartres, — and supported by the First Bavarian Corps under Von der Tann, at Etampes.
FRENCH, 65,000.	*Gen. Jaures* commanding, Twenty-First Corps — supported by Gen. Fierck and Kératry's Brittany Corps.
	SOUTH (*Artenay — Orleans*).
GERMANS, 110,000.	*Prince Frederick Charles* — arriving from Troyes with Third Corps, Alvensleben (2d); Ninth Corps, Manstein; Tenth Corps, Voigts Rhetz (supported by Von der Tann).
FRENCH, 150,000.	*General Paladines*, Commander-in-Chief of French armies outside of Paris. Gen. Pallières, Commander-in-Chief of Army of the Loire. Commander of Corps — Fifteenth Corps, Polhès; Sixteenth Corps, Chanzy; Seventeenth Corps, Sonis; Eighteenth Corps, Bourbaki; Twentieth Corps, Crouzat.

THURSDAY, *November* 17. — The Grand Duke Mecklenburg-Schwerin repulses Kératry's 7000 Brittany Mobiles at Dreux, while General Treskow captures the town. The Prussian bark *Hermann Helbmanns* blown up by a French frigate off the coast of Ireland. Amadeus, son of King Victor Emmanuel II. of Italy, and Duke of Aosta, elected King of Spain by the Spanish Cortes, in a vote 191 against 120.

FRIDAY, *November* 18. — General Wittich's division storms and captures Château Neuf, driving back Kératry's Brittany Mobiles towards Le Mans.

BATTLE OF DREUX (*Nov.* 17–18).

For a week there has been great uneasiness felt by King William lest the victorious army of Paladines should move northward, and, reinforced by Kératry, attack the Paris besieging army. Prince Charles, whose intention was to march to the assistance of Werder, was ordered to move forward in hot haste with the Third, Ninth, and Tenth Corps to the relief of Von der Tann, relieving Mecklenburg's Thirteenth Corps and Prince Albrecht's cavalry.

The 16th of November found Prince Charles' Tenth Corps at Sens, following up the Third Corps at Nemours and the Ninth at Etampes. While Paladines held Von der Tann and Prince Charles in front, Kératry was ordered to penetrate the Prussian investing line about Paris; and at the same time Trochu, supported by the fire from the forts south of Paris, was to co-operate with Kératry marching to the relief of Paris. News of Kératry's movement was sent to Trochu by carrier pigeon, and to the impatient Parisians Trochu had said, "Wait—deliverance is at hand—when you hear Paladines' guns to the south, then the garrison of Paris will march to battle." The watchful eye of Von Moltke, always cognizant of every French movement, through his cunning spies, saw Kératry's designs as soon as Trochu. He immediately ordered the Second Corps (Fansecki) of Prince Charles' old Third Army to the support of the Sixth Corps (Tumpling), south of Paris, despatching Mecklenburg from Etampes towards Dreux, with orders to attack any force approaching. On the 17th, Kératry's advance, 7000 Brittany Mobiles, reached Dreux, followed by the marching columns of Fierck and Jaures from Le Mans. The Bretons were met promptly by Mecklenburg's Seventeenth division (Treskow) at 2 P.M., the battle lasting until night. Kératry's raw levies could not stand the steady fighting of the German veterans. The Seventeenth and Twenty-second Prussian divisions stood like serried granite before the French advances. At 5 P.M. on the 17th, Treskow advanced impetuously forward with the Seventeenth division of the old Fifth Corps, which had smelt powder at Woerth under the Crown Prince. The Bretons now fell precipitately back upon Château Neuf, while Treskow swept the field, capturing two hundred prisoners, and the town. The French lost 150 in killed and wounded. On the 18th Mecklenburg made no advance, except to clear the woods and hills beyond Château Neuf. On the 19th, Wittich, with the Twenty-second division, advanced through Château Neuf to Digny on the way to Chartres, capturing 119 Mobiles, while the whole French force retreated beyond Chartres towards Châteaudun. Says an eye-witness:

The French troops were of the most irregular kind, many of them boys from fourteen to sixteen years of age, who, though armed with the chassepôts, did not know how to use them. They generally fought behind breastworks, but as the Germans advanced they discharged a few volleys and ran away pell-mell to a safe distance, discharging and running as before. Five hundred of these Mobiles ran from their breastworks at La Madelaine, took shelter in a house and fired from the windows. About seventeen were taken prisoners, when the rest threw away their guns and ran away. The Germans have become ferocious from this kind of warfare. The French having no uniform but a red strap sewed on the shoulder are treated as outlaws, and shot down with impunity. These occurrences have become sickening. An officer of the lancers, narrating these engagements, said he had heard a heavy musketry fire from a clump of trees, and was astonished to find that it came from a single old man.

"What did you do with him," said a bystander.

"I sent a lieutenant with four men to him; and then —," and he made

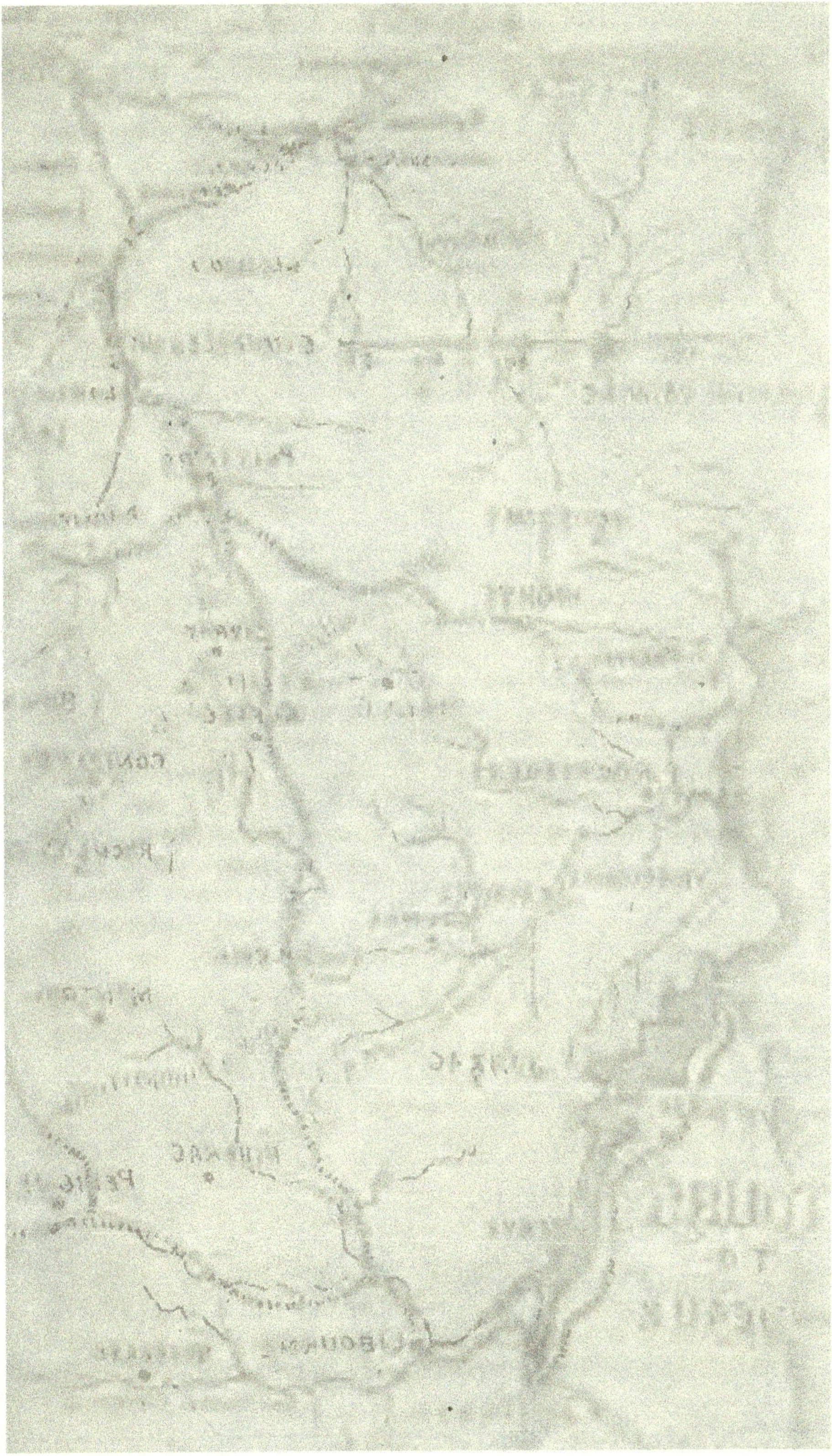

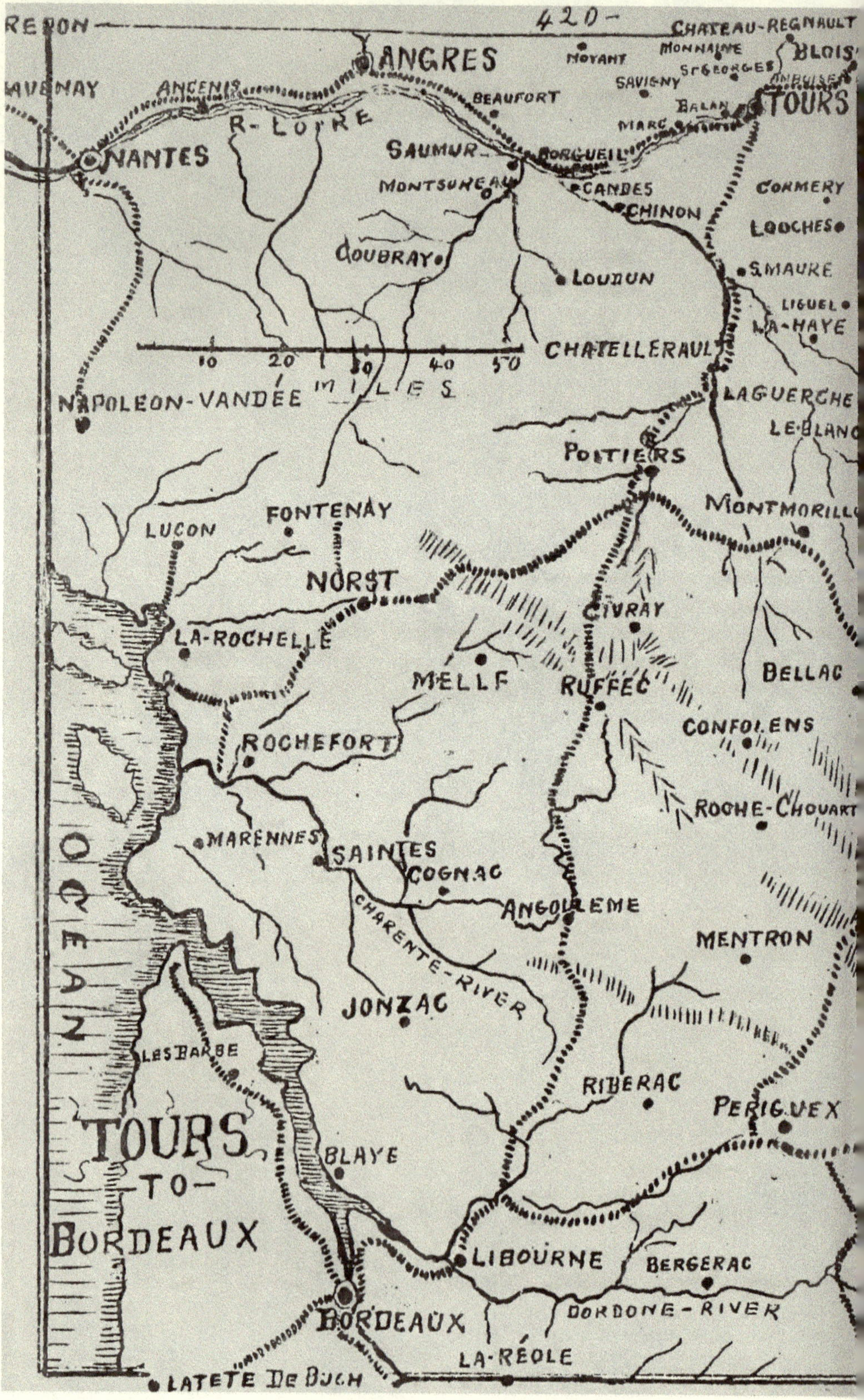
420-
CHATEAU-REGNAULT
BLOIS
ANGRES
NOYANT
MONNAIRE
ST GEORGES
SAVIGNY
ANCENIS
BEAUFORT
TOURS
R-LOIRE
MARC
BALAN
NANTES
SAUMUR
BORGUEIL
MONTSUREAU
CANDES
CHINON
CORMERY
LOCHES
COUBRAY
LOUDUN
S.MAURE
LIGUEL
LA-HAYE
10 20 30 40 50
MILES
CHATELLERAULT
NAPOLEON-VANDEE
LAGUERCHE
LE-BLANC
POITIERS
MONTMORILL
FONTENAY
LUCON
NORST
CIVRAY
LA-ROCHELLE
MELLE
RUFFEC
BELLAC
CONFOLENS
ROCHEFORT
ROCHE-CHOUART
MARENNES
SAINTES
COGNAC
OCEAN
ANGOULEME
CHARENTE-RIVER
MENTRON
JONZAC
LES BARBE
RIBERAC
PERIGUEX
TOURS
-TO-
BORDEAUX
BLAYE
LIBOURNE
BERGERAC
DORDONE-RIVER
BORDEAUX
LA-REOLE
LATETE DE BUCH

a significant sign of the lancers jabbing the man with lances. "He was lying on his back on the ground, and although one of them had bored him through with his lance in such a way that it took two men to withdraw it, he had strength enough to discharge his piece and kill one of the lancers, and after the lieutenant had shot him through the breast with his pistol, he once more discharged his gun, and it required three more shots to kill him. The Germans are rapidly becoming brutalized from this kind of work. At Dreux, on the 17th, no quarters was shown, and even the wounded Frenchmen were stabbed with the bayonet."

The Bavarians were in reserve the whole day. To those unacquainted with the character of the Bavarian troops, it will be a matter of surprise that they were so badly beaten by these irregular troops at Orleans on the 9th. There is a great deal of the brute in the common Bavarian soldier. In every town that they enter they pillage, plunder, and ruthlessly destroy. Their last act of this character was at Digny. So long as they know that there are Prussians to support them, they fight with brutal force; but where they are left to themselves they have not sufficient moral courage to carry them through, and to this fact is to be ascribed their defeat at Orleans.

The next day Mecklenburg advanced towards Le Mans, while Prince Charles moved his army towards Beaune-la-Rolande and Montargis, threatening a flank movement against Paladines. In Paris, Trochu listened in vain for the glad boom of Paladines' guns. Kératry thundered the attack, but the sound of his artillery died away long before it reached Versailles and the beleaguered capital forty miles away. So ended the first attempt of the Republic to succor Paris. A load of apprehension was lifted from the shoulders of King William, while Trochu continued to feed the Parisians on the feeble diet of hope. King William reports the victory at Dreux as follows:

TO QUEEN AUGUSTA: VERSAILLES, *Nov.* 18.

The Grand Duke of Mecklenburg yesterday repulsed the enemy along the whole line, near Dreux. Gen. Treskow at the same time captured Dreux. Many prisoners were taken. The enemy were pursued in the direction of Le Mans. WILLIAM.

AMADEUS, DUKE OF AOSTA.

Amadeus, elected King of Spain by the Spanish Cortes, to-day comes into quiet possession of the throne aspired to by Prince Leopold of Hohenzollern. At the same time, his father, Victor Emmanuel II., becomes King of united Italy, wresting temporary power from Pope Pio IX. The King is fifty years old, stout, and carries a red face, almost covered with an immense mustache. Amadeus is a tall, slender, verdant-looking youth of twenty-five.

Victor Emmanuel II., by his wife Adelaide of Austria, has had six children; Clotilde Maria Theresa, born 1843, wife of

Prince Napoleon; Humbert, Prince of Piedmont, born 1844; Amadeus (King of Spain), born 1845; Oddo Eugene, Duke of Montferrat, born 1846; Maria Pia, born 1847, and Charles Albert, Duke of Chablais, born 1851.

Amadeus accepts the Spanish crown at Milan on the 20th of November, and is crowned at Madrid January 1st, after the assassination of Marshal Prim, when he selects the following cabinet:

Marshal Serrano	President of the Council.
Cristinos Martos	Minister of Foreign Affairs.
Juan Ulloa	Minister of Justice.
Rear-Admiral Beranger	Minister of Marine.
Praxedes M. Sagasta	Minister of the Interior.
Don Zorilla	Minister of Public Works.
Francisco Ayala	Minister of the Colonies.

What a commentary on the land of Ferdinand, the patron of Columbus, and the glories of Charles the Vth! Spain has become a nation of children, and now the descendants of Cervantes and Murrillo, led by Marshal Prim, carry the Spanish crown on a begging trip to the verdant stripling of Milan. What a commentary on twenty centuries of civilization! With what disgust does a proud American democrat look upon the ignorant vanities of the old world despotisms! The new House of Italy, which now rules Rome and Madrid, and casts a covetous glance at stolen Savoy, promises to wield great future influence on the destinies of Europe. It is now Italy allied by ties of blood to Austria and Spain on the south, with Prussia and Russia on the north, and poor France struggling between.

SATURDAY, *November 19th.* — Ricciotti Garibaldi surprises 750 Prussians at Châtillon, in the Department of the Vosges, capturing 9 officers and 150 men. Prince Charles receives orders to prepare for a grand movement towards the south of France, for the purpose of flanking Tours and Le Mans.

RICCIOTTI GARIBALDI'S RAID.

From Dôle the Garibaldis (the General and his sons Menotti and Ricciotti) fell back to Autun. Here the General organized a camp of about 8000 mixed troops. There were old Garibaldians, Italian bandits, adventurers, rangers, and Francstireurs. Such a motley crowd was never seen before, unless it were in Jeff Thompson's Arkansas camp in '62. The work of this command was to continually hang on the flanks of the organized Prussians under Von Werder at Dijon, and for this purpose Ricciotti and Menotti have been kept constantly in the saddle. On the 12th Ricciotti organized a new command of about 800 rangers. Every man was full of dash, and as reckless of danger as the raiders of Kilpatrick. Dangerous spirits gathered around Ricciotti, without call, for they knew he would lead them to successful adventure. On the 18th, Ricciotti started on his long raid in the rear of Von Werder. From Autun he marched north 26 miles to Saulieu, then 25 miles north to the village of Motbard. Twenty-five miles farther north, at Châtillon, which is 50 miles north-west of Dijon, were 700 Prussians, awaiting reinforcements from Chaumont. With a dash the Garibaldians swept forward, and 5 o'clock on the morning of the 19th found them in front of the sleeping Prussian garrison. Ricciotti sent a company of 80 men to surround the Hotel of the Côte d'Or, and caught all the officers of the staff in bed. Fancy the surprise, the scramble, the struggle. Every officer barricaded his door. In that hotel only eight officers surrendered; two preferred to be shot. In another none would surrender; six were killed. Meanwhile the other corps went from house to house, making prisoners wherever they could. Sometimes a band of Prussians resisted: they were shot. While Ricciotti's officers were consulting as to whether they should attack, the news came that 1400 Prussians were arriving on the route to Chaumont. Ricciotti then gave the order to collect prisoners, horses, and spoil. They counted 100 dead on the Prussian side, among them one major and two colonels, one the commander of the garrison of the town, the other acting Prefect. They brought away 167 prisoners (among them nine officers), 62 horses, four carriages full of baggage, cases of cigars, papers, and quantities of rifles and ammunition, and arrived at Motbard, with three dead and twenty wounded, causing great enthusiasm, and an ovation from the French people of the town. Garibaldi heard of the success of the raid at Aignay-le-Duc, twenty-five miles northwest of Dijon, he having changed his quarters from Autun on the 20th. An eye-witness who gave him the news of the victory says:

I wish you could have seen his face, and the proud smile that danced in his eyes. "*C'est un joli petit coup de notre garçon*," was all he said. Then he read the letters I brought, and wrote off a concise account of the affair, recommending the prisoners to the generosity of the French, and warning the enemy to beware how they bring upon themselves reprisals.

Some one said, "I should think Ricciotti ought to be promoted." "Well," said the General, "I think we may make him major;" but a few lines he wrote to his youngest son he addressed Captain, whereas the Francs-tireurs have made him Colonel, and they have the right to name their officers.

Paladines' victory over Von der Tann could not have raised the hope of Tours more than this little *coup* of Ricciotti has raised the expectations of the Garibaldians. For this success the Tours government has made Ricciotti a "Member of the Legion of Honor."

The past movements of General Von Werder have been as follows: marched on Epinal, Oct. 12th; on Vesoul, Oct. 18th — the French withdrawing to Besançon and the fortress of Belfort. While General Werder was at Vesoul, General Cambriels made a threatening stand at Besançon, which place surrendered to General Werder on the 22d, Cambriels falling back on Auxonne and Dijon, the former place being burned by the Prussians, the flames lighting up the last steps of Werder's successful advance from Strasburg, with the victorious Fourteenth Corps.

For this French defeat Cambriels was released from his command, to which General Ernest succeeded; while Garibaldi, coming from Italy, was placed in command of the Francs-tireurs in the Vosges, assisted by his sons Menotti and Ricciotti. (See page 378.)

SUNDAY, *November* 20. — Amadeus, Duke of Aosta, accepts the Spanish throne. Gortschakoff replies to Earl Granville's war letter. (*See Nov.* 10.)

FRIDAY, *November* 25. — Thionville, seventeen miles north of Metz, capitulates. The Germans set 4000 prisoners free. Von Moltke, apprehensive of the vast numbers of Frenchmen rushing to arms from the south, abandons his contemplated southern movement, and concentrates the German armies to the support of the army of Paris. Manteuffel with the First Corps, and Goeben with the Eighth Corps, ordered to be ready to support the besieging army.

SURRENDER OF THIONVILLE (*map, p.* 65).

Thionville, a demolished city of 7000 people and 500 houses, surrendered, not from starvation, but to escape the terrible

Prussian bombardment. The inclosing fortifications are exceedingly strong, but, owing to the absence of exterior forts unlike Metz, the town was liable to a direct bombardment. On the 7th and 8th of October, when Bazaine made his great sortie, 121 wagon loads of provisions destined for Metz, from the French-sympathizing Luxemburgers, remained in Thionville, furnishing the city with six months' supply of food. This non-observance of neutrality on the part of Luxemburg will not be forgotten by the map-making Bismarck. On the 10th of October came the German investing army, and Thionville was hermetically sealed. The surrender of Bazaine sent Zastrow and the old Seventh Corps of Steinmetz, with 400 German guns, to Thionville, whose fortifications were strongly defended with 380 French guns, from sixteen to twenty-four pounders. After the 22d of November, the German fire became intense, the average number of shots being seventeen per minute. On Wednesday, the 23d, at 11 A.M., while the city was burning in many places from the furious German fire, General Zastrow demanded of the French commander the surrender of the town. The French commandant replied:

"So long as there remains one stone upon another, or one drop of French blood, the city will not be surrendered!" — a reply sufficiently heroic, but, unfortunately for its historic worth, not a stone of the fortifications was disturbed, nor a drop of French blood wasted. On Thursday, at 6 o'clock A.M., the French offered to surrender the city, on condition that the Gardes Mobiles were allowed to go free. After two hours' consideration of this question, the Prussians answered with six hours' bombardment. Finally, the French displayed the white flag, and offered to surrender on whatever conditions were granted them. At six P.M. of the 24th of November, the capitulation was subscribed. It was stipulated that on the morrow (the 25th), at nine o'clock, the Germans should enter the town. The time of entrance was, however, at the request of the French commander, made two hours earlier, on account of the insubordination of his troops, who were enraged at the surrender, and threatened even to explode the magazine. There was no danger on the ramparts, as all the German shells were directed against the city. The surrender was hastened by the appearance near the ramparts of women and children, who upon their knees besought the commander to submit, since all the cellars where they had sought concealment and safety were overflowed with water, one or two feet deep, on account of the rise of the Moselle. The whole number of prisoners was 6000. Of these, the regular line troops — about 2000 in all — were retained as prisoners. The remainder were taken to the first station and set free. There are 107 buildings totally destroyed; eighty-three so badly injured that they will have to be torn down; 250 houses will have to be built anew from the first story. The material loss is reckoned at $800,000, and the commercial loss at $4,000,000. Not one house is left uninjured. During the fifty-three hours' bombardment, the Prussians poured into the city from 30,000 to 40,000 bombs of eighty pounds weight.

The leniency toward the Gardes Mobiles was on account of their speaking the German tongue, and belonging in a district which the Prussians intend to appropriate.

SATURDAY, *November* 26. — General von Werder defeats Garibaldi near Presques, sixteen miles from Epinal. Generals Kératry and Carre-Kerresouet resign at Camp Conlie, a few miles north of Le Mans, and report to Tours. Kératry's Breton Guard turned over to General Jaures. All the Prussian armies south and west of Paris commence advancing — Mecklenburg towards Le Mans, Von der Tann towards Châteaudun, and Prince Charles from Toury, Pithiviers, and Montargis towards Beaune-la-Rolande and Orleans. The Prussian Tenth Corps (Voigts Rhetz) encounters the French, driving them towards Beaune-la-Rolande.

THE SKIRMISH AT PASQUES.

Garibaldi, emboldened by the success of Ricciotti at Châtillon, ordered his other son, Menotti, to commence a farther march in the rear of Von Werder. Menotti, in his movement north along the Vosges, reached Pasques, about twelve miles south of Epinal, late in the afternoon of the 26th. The Prussian outposts were completely surprised, for no knowledge of Menotti's rapid march had reached them, and they were attacked with great impetuosity. The Prussians were first compelled to fall back, but reinforcements coming up, the Garibaldians were in turn repulsed in disorder. The next morning General Werder ordered pursuit, overtaking the French rear-guard, when another engagement ensued, in which the Garibaldians lost 250 killed, wounded, and prisoners, Menotti having about 2000 men under his command. The last engagement occurred at Plombières, about sixteen miles south of Epinal, and famous for its warm baths. This repulse discouraged the Garibaldians, and for some time no more attempts were made against the Prussian rear.

SUNDAY, *November* 27. — Preparations for a grand battle at Beaune-la-Rolande. Prince Charles and Paladines face to face, skirmishing all along the line through Montargis, Pithiviers, and

Toury to Châteaudun. Trochu receives news of Paladines' intended battle by carrier-pigeon. Immense movement of troops in Paris. The forts commence a terrific cannonade. Manteuffel skirmishing before Amiens. Von der Tann moves towards Châteaudun and Mecklenburg threatens Le Mans.

PREPARING FOR BATTLE.

The great plain of Beuce, which spreads out between Toury and Orleans, is macadamized by the tramp of 350,000 soldiers manœuvring for position. The coil of 150,000 Germans slowly winds around the threatening French. Prince Charles' veteran Third, Ninth, and Tenth lie coiled up at Montargis for a dreadful spring, while Von der Tann quietly awaits at Toury, inviting forward the unsuspecting Paladines drawn up in a grand horse-shoe line in front of the Prussians, from Montargis through Toury to Châteaudun. As if to spur the 200,000 French to desperation, Mecklenburg, with his barbarous Bavarians, marched a week ago in reckless nonchalance southward, almost within shot of the hot-headed Corsican, Gambetta, at Tours; while Manteuffel fired his first shot into the camp of General Farre at Amiens, filling the region of Picardy with dismay and demoralization. Then suddenly the whole German army withdrew towards Paris. To-morrow will be a day big with events — events which will make a mark among the centuries, for the three great battles of Beaune-la-Rolande, Amiens, and Paris are to settle the weal or woe of the Republic and of France. On the 24th, the German armies were stretched over sixty miles of country, from Montargis to Le Mans; but on the 25th came orders for Mecklenburg and Von der Tann to fall back to Prince Charles' support. Von Moltke's official report, dated Versailles, November 6th, says:

Nearly the whole of the forces at the disposal of the French Government have been concentrated between Blois, Tours, and Orleans. If defeated they will probably retreat to Lyons, which is strongly fortified and provisioned.

All around Orleans the country people, instigated to fight by the priests, who have been ordered by Bishop Dupanloup to preach a crusade, have begun a guerilla warfare against the Germans.

Patrols are fired at from every building and every hedge. Officers carrying orders are shot down by laborers, seemingly working in the fields, but provided with rifles as well as spades. To avenge these assassinations, all non-soldiers carrying arms are immediately executed. Not a few priests are now awaiting trial. The towns of Sens and Nemours have been severely punished for conniving at the surprise of Prussian detachments by Francs-tireurs.

MONDAY, *Nov.* 28.—Prince Charles defeats Paladines and the French Right at Beaune-la-Rolande, taking 1600 prisoners. Manteuffel captures Amiens, the citadel, and 600 prisoners.

TUESDAY, *Nov.* 29.—Generals Trochu, Ducrot, and Vinoy commence their three-days sortie from Paris. Feint from St. Denis, Mont Valerien, and Mont Avron, and attack in force on Brie, Champigny, and Villiers.

WEDNESDAY, *Nov.* 30.—Ducrot makes a bloody attack with 100,000 French on the Würtembergers and Saxons across the Marne. The struggle for Villiers.

THURSDAY, *Dec.* 1.—General Chanzy defeats the Grand Duke of Mecklenburg, and drives back the Bavarians from Artenay towards Toury, capturing two guns and 300 prisoners. The French and German armies around Paris rest to bury the dead.

FRIDAY, *Dec.* 2.—Mecklenburg defeats Chanzy and the French Left, driving it south of Artenay, capturing eleven guns and 700 prisoners. The left wing of the Army of the Loire doubled up. Ducrot and Trochu continue the struggle around Champigny, Villiers, and Brie, losing 1800 prisoners. The French advance stopped, and Ducrot prepares to fall back to Paris.

SATURDAY, *Dec.* 3.—The Army of the Loire broken into three divisions, and driven by Prince Charles, Von der Tann, and Mecklenburg into the intrenched camps of Orleans.

Trochu's great sortie ceases, and the French army retire over the Marne.

Bismarck declines farther neutrality towards Luxemburg, and abrogates the treaty of London.

SUNDAY, *Dec.* 4.—Prince Charles defeats the Army of the Loire, breaking it into three retreating divisions. Chanzy falls back with the Left towards Tours, Pallières falls back with the Centre on Vierzon, and Bourbaki falls back with the Right on Bourges. Gambetta escapes capture at La Chapelle. Prince Charles captures seventy guns and 8000 prisoners.

Manteuffel defeats the French north-east of Rouen, capturing 400 prisoners. No fighting around Paris.

BATTLES IN FRONT OF ORLEANS, Nov. 28—Dec. 4.

On the 28th of November, commenced the gigantic wrestle of the giants Paladines and Prince Charles, on the plain of Beuce between Orleans and Paris. This immense plain spreads away from Paris sixty miles to Orleans on the Loire, and is one of the grandest battle-fields of Europe. The country is dotted with innumerable little French villages, formerly filled with a wealthy and contented peasantry. On the left of this vast prairie, looking southward, is the village of Beaune-la-Rolande, snugly couched at the feet of a grand elevation. Beaune is the strategetic key to the German Left, and no less a General than Prince Charles held the sentinelship of the location. Paladines looked cautiously at Beaune, and in its capture could see his army already pushing forward to the Seine and Paris. He did not think that a French repulse would bring down Prince Charles with the bloody Third and Tenth upon Orleans. Paladines had laid his plans with consummate strategy. His army had been reorganized, new general appointed, and, flushed with his last victory over Von der Tann, his hopes ran high indeed. The Republic expected much of Paladines, and Paris looked only for deliverance in success.

The French Centre, in front of Prince Charles, was commanded by General Martin de Pallières, with the old Fifteenth Corps of Polhés; the Right-Centre, the Twentieth Corps, was commanded by General Crouzat; and the extreme Right, the Eighteenth Corps, was commanded by General Bourbaki. The Left Centre, the Sixteenth Corps, in front of the Grand Duke of Mecklenburg, was commanded by General Chanzy; and on the extreme left was the Seventeenth Corps, commanded by General Sonis. The lines were about twenty miles long, extending from beyond Beaune-la-Rolande past Pithiviers, to Artenay in these relative positions:

Right. **MECKLENBURG.** Centre. **PRINCE CHARLES.** Left.

1 Bav's, Von der Tann's 13 C. and 17 and 22 div's. 9 Corps, 3 Corps, and 10 Corps.

* * * * * * * * * *

* * * [Battle-Field between.] * * *

* * * * * * * * * *

Sonis, 17 C. Chanzy's 16 C. Pallières' 12 C. Crouzat's 20 C. Bourbaki's 20 C.

Left. **GEN. AURELLES DE PALADINES.** Right.

Word had gone to Trochu that the Army of the Loire would deliver the beleaguered capital, and while Trochu, Vinoy, and Ducrot were moving to the bloody battle of the Marne, Paladines advanced upon the German left at Beaune. It was a day of battles, that 28th of November, and the day was freighted with the destinies of men and nations. Reorganized, the army of the Republic was to meet, face to face, the veterans of Metz; and Paladines, the hope and the right hand of the Republic, was to meet Prince Charles, the strong arm of Prussia and the king.

BATTLE OF BEAUNE-LA-ROLANDE — *Nov.* 28.

Sixty thousand Frenchmen had been manœuvring around the little village of Beaune to fall upon Prince Charles. All day long the 27th, Voigts Rhetz's old Tenth Corps, which stood the six-hours Balaklava assault at Mars-la-Tour, eyed in sullen silence from the quiet village the threatening Twentieth Corps, the Right Centre of Paladines' army. The cattle from the plains had vanished, the hamlets were deserted, and the peasantry had fallen to the rear.

The sullen gloom about Beaune was the quiet which precedes the shock of a great battle. During the forenoon of the 28th, scouts began to clatter back and forth from the fronts of both armies, the pickets were strengthened into a reconnoissance, and on each side the artillery limbered up and galloped hither and thither to good positions near the front. The strategy of Prince Charles was to tempt Paladines forward towards Toury, that the Prussian army might move by the flank on the enemy's rear, cutting him off from Orleans, and holding him in a vice between Von der Tann, Mecklenburg, and his own army.

At two o'clock, Paladines' first attack commenced. Covered

by artillery, the Twentieth French Corps made a terrific assault upon Voigts Rhetz. The advance was close to the Prussians, as the French artillery was of shorter range than the Prussian; and the last victory at Orleans had taught Paladines to move his artillery within range. At three the fighting became general around the village of Beaune, the French reinforcing with portions of the Eighteenth and Fifteenth Corps, while Voigts Rhetz was soon supported by the First and Fifth divisions of Alvensleben's veteran Third Corps. The onslaught of the French, who had regained something of their hereditary *éclat* by their victory over Von der Tann, was fierce; but the steady fighting of Voigts Rhetz's Hanoverians met every assault without flinching.

At five o'clock the French completely surrounded the village of Beaune, and opening with close artillery, a steady rain of iron hail poured upon and through the burning village. After a long and bloody infantry assault, the French demanded its surrender. It was refused, and again the battle grew hotter than before. It was the last struggle of the day; but the 50,000 French were met by fresh reinforcements from the Prussian Third Corps and driven back.

The Prussian forces holding the village of Beaune had now shot away all their ammunition. The situation was grave, indeed. "My children," said the brave Colonel of the Sixteenth Regiment to his ammunitionless men —

"We have been ordered by our Prince to hold this village at all hazards; in our efforts to do so we have run short of ammunition. This is a misfortune, but you must remember that there is one sort of ammunition which never fails — our bayonets. You must now trust to them. If the French attack the village, they must be driven back with the cold steel; we have no other means of stopping them."

The men answered this appeal with a cheer, and when ordered to bring their arms to the charge, did so with a good will which augured ill for the chances of the French should they attempt to storm the village.

The attempt was not made, for the Third Corps had already repulsed the advancing French, capturing 900 prisoners, and leaving the ground thick with 2000 French and German killed and wounded. The Prussians now advanced in force, covering the field, while the French fell back, leaving to the heroic Voigts Rhetz and Alvensleben the honor of bivouacking on the victorious battle-ground of Beaune. On the morrow, Paladines fell back into his entrenched camps before Orleans. On the result of this battle Gambetta was silent, while King William sent the following despatch:

TO THE QUEEN: TUESDAY, *Nov.* 29, 1870.

Frederick Charles reports the complete defeat of the Army of the Loire in the battle of Monday, in which the French had the Twentieth Corps, probably the Eighteenth, and portions of the Fifteenth and Sixteenth Corps, engaged. A thousand French were found dead on the field, 4000 were wounded, and 1600 taken prisoners. General Aurelles is reported to be wounded. The German loss was 1000; among them few officers.

WILHELM.

Thus ended the first effort of the Army of the Loire to succor the beleaguered capital, and the hope of Paris was fated to end in calamitous despair.

SKIRMISHING.

On the 29th both armies rested, Von der Tann occupying the extreme right of the German line, which extended from in front of Allaines to Nogent on the left, where the Third Corps were encamped. For twenty miles north-east of Orleans, between Nogent, Château Neuf, and Montargis, is an immense forest, and Paladines moved his army towards the entrenched camps at Artenay, fearing, in case of disaster, to be caught with no chance to retreat. The 30th was spent by both Prince Charles and Paladines in manœuvring for position. Both armies were concentrated, and ready to leap forward to battle.

Thursday, the 1st of December, found Paladines pressing forward from Artenay, while Prince Charles was awaiting patiently the results of Trochu's attempt to escape from Paris. The cavalry and Bavarian corps of Mecklenburg's troops were worn out with incessant marching. For days they had been marching and scouting away off towards Le Mans and south towards Tours. Ragged and shoeless, they were in no condition to fight. From the 9th of November to the 30th, the restless spirit of Mecklenburg had been marching his men on an average of 18 miles per day. He had been driving the armed peasants and Bretons from Dreux and Château Neuf, and menacing Tours from Vendôme. Thursday found his weary army and Von der Tann encamped on the same ground in front of Artenay, from which he had withdrawn on the 14th of November. The Bavarians occupied Mecklenburg's right. While the Duke was dining at the headquarters at Jeanville, a small village between Artenay and Allaines, the French under Chanzy were making a victorious attack on the Bavarians. The Bavarians were outnumbered and driven back towards Toury, with the loss of two cannon and a few hundred prisoners. It was the report of this victory which electrified the Tours Government, and caused the *Te Deums* to be chanted in the French churches. All that night the Germans concentrated for the attack on the morrow, while Chanzy sent a report of victory from his headquarters at Patay.

BATTLE OF DECEMBER 2.

December 2d opened cold and frosty. Mecklenburg (or his chief of staff, Gen. Stosch) had completed arrangements for the day's battle. At daylight the Duke with his staff dashed off to the front. Twenty villages were passed before the battlefield was reached. The attack of Chanzy commenced at eight o'clock. The first French onslaught was fierce and confident. The worn-out Bavarians met them stoically and without flinching. Chanzy pushed forward the entire Sixteenth French Corps against the Bavarians, who were four times beaten back, and at last were unable to resist any longer, and their place had to be supplied with the Seventy-fifth and Seventy-sixth Hanseatic Regiments of the Seventeenth Division, who entered the fight at about 11 o'clock. The fight gradually extended towards the east, and at 2 o'clock the whole line, from beyond Artenay to the Bavarian lines, was one continuous storm of shot and shell. The French stood their ground bravely. The Germans, weary and exhausted by long marches, made desperate efforts to beat back the French, who were largely superior in numbers, and had cannons, mitrailleuses, and chassepôts.

The Seventeenth Division (Prussian) had not seen a serious engagement before, and they did not fight like the veterans of Woerth and Metz. All day long the battle raged. Hundreds of houses were in flames from the bursting shells, and villages burned, victims of shot and sword. As night approached, on one side the moon shone brightly, and on the other the whole horizon was illuminated by the glare of burning houses and villages. The ground was very well adapted for cavalry charges, and opposite Artenay the Fourth Cavalry Division was very active. At one time along the road was to be seen a herd of over 100 riderless horses, which galloped along in great terror, most of them being very badly wounded, and covered with blood. A whole cavalry regiment had been met by a deadly mitrailleuse fire.

It was the death struggle of Chanzy and the French Left, the Right having flinched and fallen before Prince Charles at Beaune. The French do not yield with night, but as darkness comes on, victory seems to hang on the side of the Republic. The Bavarians, weary and decimated, cry loudly for Prince Charles, and tremble for the morrow. The battle is not ended. Von der Tann is wounded. 3000 French and German wounded lay upon the ground, and 1700 Frenchmen prisoners, and several dismounted and broken cannons are filing to the rear. To-morrow will tell whether German tenacity or French *élan* shall win the day; for to-night fate hangs breathless in the balance. To show how uncertain is the result of a great battle, we give the dispatches of Mecklenburg and Paladines, as night abruptly ended the fight. Seldom is a great army conscious *when* it has won a great victory. This was the case at the second battle of Bull Run, when, if Lee had known the status of Pope's army, a cavalry charge might have pushed back the Union army upon the capital in dismay. So at Gettysburg, when for twenty-four hours the author saw Meade stand motionless, while Lee was in precipitate retreat. The strategy of the German armies has been to push forward after a battle, striking terror to a hesitating enemy. Had Meade done this at Gettysburg, thousands instead of hundreds of prisoners would have fallen into his hands at Falling Waters, where Lee fled across the Potomac. On that night of the 2d of December, as the smoke cleared away, Paladines, flushed with the hope of victory, wrote to the Bishop of Orleans : "We have had a series of successes. I do not say victories; I reserve that word for to-morrow." Mecklenburg, as full of hope, thus telegraphs to King William :

"This morning a battle commenced near Bazoches-les-Hautes [to the north of Artenay]. After a hot fight the Fifteenth Army French Corps was defeated and driven back to Artenay, and the Sixteenth French Army Corps driven beyond Loigny. Several hundred prisoners and eleven guns were taken. The enemy's loss is considerable. Our loss is unknown, but it is much smaller than that of the enemy."

BATTLE, DECEMBER 3.

Last night was a sleepless night for the two armies. All night long the German artillery rumbled to the front, to be ready at the first gleam of light to open on the French. Prince Charles had pushed the Third and Tenth Corps along the forest of Cercottes towards Chevilly, almost in the rear of Chanzy, severing Bourbaki's corps, which had fallen back to the south-east, towards Château Neuf. As the first ray of morning lighted up the frosty battle-field, Paladines was startled to hear Prince Charles pounding away on his right, between Chevilly and Orleans; while Mecklenburg and the revengeful Von der Tann stood squarely in front. Soon the north wind wafted the smoke of sixty German cannon into the faces of the French, and red streams of shells went whizzing over their heads or ploughed the macadamized fields. Bourbaki had fallen back the day before with a dogged sullenness, giving up inch by inch the soil as purchased by the blood of the old Tenth Corps of Voigts Rhetz. Voigts Rhetz kept his eye on Bourbaki, while Alvensleben, with the Third Corps, opened with Mecklenburg and Von der Tann on Chanzy, in the triangle between Chevilly, Artenay, and Patay. The French seemed dismayed at the unexpected boldness of the Germans, and the hazardous situation of their army. Paladines had reserved "victory" for the Bishop of Orleans to-day, but that message was fated to tell of defeat. Chanzy sullenly fell back towards Orleans, abandoning the field to Mecklenburg; while Voigts Rhetz, hanging on his right flank, captured several hundred prisoners and eleven guns. The day was a fighting retreat, and the Germans did not advance, except against the savage fire of an army determined to sell its position with the price of hundreds slaughtered. The French army was doubled up.

The German advance was irresistible, and Paladines ordered the Left and Centre, with the Sixteenth Corps of Chanzy, the Seventeenth Corps of Sonis, and the Fifteenth Corps of Pallières, to fall back upon Orleans and the Twentieth and Eighteenth, under Bourbaki, severed from the main army, retreated over the Loire to the east of Orleans, near Château Neuf and Jargeau. Everywhere the Germans pushed forward their victorious columns with a dreadful rapidity, striking demoralization and terror among the retreating French. Night found Paladines across the Loire, surrounded by his sorrowful staff. Victory had been wrested from him, and the defeat of a day had thrown him from the high pinnacle of fame and trust to the low estate of a vanquished General. That night he advised the Government of the necessity of evacuating Orleans, and retreating to the left bank of the Loire. The Goverment, however, was of opinion that it would be better to hold firm at Orleans; but Gen. Paladines reiterating his views, the Government coincided, and Orleans was eventually evacuated.

The defeat of Paladines and the Army of the Loire was thus gently announced to the French people by Gambetta, who has always shown himself a conspicuous mouth-piece to cover up Republican disasters:

CITIZENS — The Army of the Loire has discontinued its forward movement owing to the resistance of the enemy, who has concentrated large masses of troops between Pithiviers, Artenay, and Angerville. The army occupies strongly intrenched positions, in which it will remain for the present, postponing its advance until a better opportunity is offered. In the meanwhile Gen. Ducrot, with the army which he led out of Paris, is disengaged, and will be able to act more freely, not finding before him the masses of the enemy which it was supposed were going to meet him, but which are really retained north of Orleans. GAMBETTA.

BATTLE — DISASTER — EVACUATION OF ORLEANS, DEC. 4.

Sunday morning, December 4, found the Army of the Loire ready to break into three divisions. Bourbaki, with the right, was already cut off by Prince Charles, and was retreating southeasterly, towards Bourges. Chanzy, with the Sixteenth and Seventeenth Corps, was ready to commence his struggle northwesterly towards Blois and Tours, and Pallières held Orleans with the Fifteenth. At noon, Paladines telegraphed Gambetta that he had changed his opinon, and would continue to hold Orleans. The impetuous Gambetta instantly started for Orleans. The train was ordered forward at lightning speed. At La Chapelle, a few miles south-west of Orleans, the engineer rang his bell in terror, and came to a sudden halt, while Mecklenburg's Fourth Cavalry fired a volley of bullets, filling the War Secretary with fear and consternation. "What is that?" exclaimed Gambetta; and then again came a flash, — a crash, and the Mecklenburg bullets tore through the car, while down towards Gambetta's carriage rushed the speechless railroad official, with his eyes wide open. "All right, Henri!" said the Minister in affected composure; "back to Beaugency—quick!" Like lightning buzzed the reversed wheels of the locomotive on the icy track. The moment's delay seemed an age, for in front was a squadron of terrible uhlans, galloping at breakneck speed after the flying Minister. At first the uhlans gained on the train and Gambetta fumbled nervously for his pistols, but in a moment more the light train sped away, and the last shots of the Prussians only brought a derisive screech from the locomotive. At Beaugency, Gambetta found himself surrounded by an excited crowd. "What news, — where are the rascals?" asked a dozen voices. "All is well" said the ever-sanguine Minister — "it is all v-e-r-y well; — my mind is relieved; my doubts are at rest. Our countrymen are defending Orleans as becomes true Frenchmen. At La Chapelle I heard the Orleans cannons, — I know we are victorious. I must now get a carriage for the south road to Blois as soon as possible; there good news awaits me. Take courage, my friends, — France shall yet be saved." So saying, he darted into a carriage, and his horses were soon trotting over the frozen ground towards Blois. On he flew, past the astonished villages. The night was now dark, and the roads were as slippery as when Dickens says:

> "There's frost upon the pathway and there's mud upon the track,
> And the ice it isn't water and the water isn't free,
> And you couldn't say that anything is what it ought to be."

No news! On sped the Minister. Now a messenger arrives on a panting horse with a dispatch. In a moment Gambetta caught its contents. "*Mon Dieu!* it is all lost. Freycinet says D'Aurelles has surrendered Orleans!" The Minister's eyes gleamed vengeance for a moment, and then hope seemed to come. "It is terrible," he said, but the Army of the Loire is still there; the Republic has yet 200,000 soldiers, well provided with the material of war. No one shall doubt—we will save the country yet." Back flew Gambetta to Tours, where, jaded and worn, in the early morning he found a despatch from Pallières announcing that Prince Charles had demanded the evacuation of Orleans under a threat that he would bombard the place, and that he had agreed, in the name of Paladines to comply with the demand. Accordingly the marine batteries were spiked, the powder destroyed, and while Chanzy marched towards Blois, pressed by Mecklenburg, Pallieres fell back to the south side of the Loire, and then farther on, southward to Vierzon. Before the evacuation of the city Manstein's Ninth Corps of Prince Charles' army assaulted and captured St. Jean, a railroad station in the north suburb of Orleans, with thirty guns and a thousand fleeing French; while the Third and Tenth Corps went after Bourbaki. Chanzy marched towards Tours, followed by the restless Mecklenburg, and with the Fourth and Sixth Cavalry everywhere hanging on his rear and flank. Thus on the 4th of December, was the new Army of the Loire,—the hope of the Republic, broken into three fleeing divisions, and its commander, Paladines, who gave the first victory to the Republic, relieved, and, be it said to the shame of France, disgraced. At midnight the Germans occupied Orleans, from which Von der Tann had been driven on the 10th of November. The re-occupation of Orleans was thus announced by King William:

TO THE QUEEN: VERSAILLES, *Sunday—midnight.*

After two days' battle, in which the army of the Grand Duke of Mecklenburg was mainly engaged, Manstein's Corps captured St. Jean, a railway station and suburb of Orleans. Thirty guns and 1000 prisoners were taken. The Prussian loss was moderate; Wrangel's division suffered most.

The Prussians found nine cannon and much ammunition on the field before Amiens. WILHELM.

TO THE QUEEN: VERSAILLES, *Dec.* 5.

The city of Orleans was occupied by our forces last night, without being stormed. The Third Corps took nine cannon and one mitrailleuse. The Eighth Corps of the First Army, on the 4th inst. defeated the French in several conflicts north-east of Rouen, taking one gun and 400 prisoners. Our loss was only one killed and 40 wounded. We have taken 70 guns and 10,000 prisoners in three days. WILHELM.

THE SPITE OF TOURS.

The excitement in Tours on the defeat of the army was intense. Paladines was blamed, abused, and finally relieved from command, and ordered to duty at Cherbourg, with as much vindictiveness as was displayed by Stanton when he ordered Fremont to the "Mountain Department." Chanzy, with Voillemont as chief of staff, was placed in command of the First Army, struggling towards Tours, while Bourbaki, with Borel as chief of staff, was placed in command of the defeated remnant at Bourges. Paladines refused to be "shelved" at Cherbourg, choosing rather to retire broken-hearted to his estate. Colomb succeeded Sonis, the captured commander of the, Seventeenth Corps; Ballot was placed in immediate command of Bourbaki's old Eighteenth Corps, and Jaurezibery succeeded to Chanzy's Sixteenth Corps.

So ever with war. It makes and unmakes a good many heroes. Much glittering tinsel becomes rubbish, and many unfortunate uniforms slide from the red furrows of battle to quiet nooks in domestic corners. Victory smiles and the world is awed; adversity frowns and back slide the heroes to their old rostrums and nostrums, to their old bar-rooms and bars. How many have sighed and died like Paladines, — how many have wept like the First Napoleon at Toulon!

THE CAPTURE OF AMIENS (*Nov.* 28).

Simultaneous with the attack and defeat of Paladines at Beaune-la-Rolande and the commencement of Ducrot's great sortie for the deliverance of Paris, Manteuffel, with the First and Eighth Corps (Goeben's) of Steinmetz' old First Army, attacked the French under General Farre at Villers-Bretonneux, ten miles south of Amiens.

The Mobiles made a weak defence, and though their force numbered about 50,000, they could not stand before the veterans who stormed the heights of *Spicheren* and swept L'Admirault and Frossard into Bellecroix after the battle of Pange. The French camp was captured, the Mobiles making a hasty retreat, after a short and bloody fight; while Goeben, who defeated Frossard at Spicheren, advanced upon the city. The Prussian losses were 74 officers and 1300 privates.

On Monday the Prussians threw some companies of infantry around the fortress, who quickly took possession of the houses in the neighborhood, and, under this cover, fired on every man who appeared on the ramparts. It was thus that the Captain intrusted with the defence, formerly in the army, but actually belonging to the artillery of the National Guard, was killed by a ball through the lungs. He had refused to surrender. During the night the Prussians placed eight batteries of artillery in position, commanding the citadel from three sides; and the citizens passed a very uneasy time of it, expecting to be shelled on all sides, with a great probability of being blown up in addition, as the defenders had sworn to explode the magazine rather than yield. However, soon negotiation was going on; the garrison was prepared to surrender if accorded the honors of war,— a demand at which Gen. Von Goeben laughed; finally the white flag was run up, and the victors entered, taking 600 prisoners, half of whom were quite sufficient to defend the fort. By the capitulation the Prussians were free to withdraw 6000 troops for operations against Rouen. The Prussians admit that the fort could have kept them occupied for thirteen days, the moat being very wide, and the walls, though only of brick, very high. Even when the brick would have been knocked about, the fallen earth would still form an incline very steep and difficult for a storming party. Excepting the French commandant, there were no killed or wounded on either side. Three civilians were wounded through their own imprudence, and a little girl killed by a shell. Considering the densely populated district where the citadel is situated, it is surprising more damage was not done.

The body of the commandant was handed over to his wife and four children, and, in deference to the wishes of the people, was "laid out" in the chapel of the Hôtel Dieu. The deceased will go down to posterity as the bravest of the brave, while the Prefect of Somme will be held in disgrace for abandoning his post with the following selfish speech:

CITIZENS: The day of trial has arrived. In spite of all our efforts, Amiens must fall into the enemy's hands. The Army of the North is retreating and the National Guards are disarming. I leave you, but will soon return. Be calm, be confident. France will be saved.

After German occupancy an eye-witness wrote:

It is quite a pleasure to notice the changed aspect of Amiens since it has been occupied. There is a quiet spirit of order everywhere pervading. The inhabitants are beginning to reappear, having discovered that the end of the world has not taken place. The conduct of the troops is most admirable, and it is amusing to note their appearance of complete indifference to the fact that they live among French people. Where they are billeted they offer to assist the owner in all kinds of work. They are the most willing of "aids." The shops are reopening. After a while we shall become accustomed to the invaders. As an example of how the French judge their unwelcome visitors, a shopkeeper complained that the soldiers robbed him. On being investigated, it appears a poor Saxon desired to buy a piece of sponge, and offered to pay for it in thalers, which money was declined, with a notice that it would never be taken in payment for French goods. The soldier explained that he wanted the sponge, tendered ready money for it, which, being refused, informed the shopkeeper he would retain the article. After a week's hard marching, and three days of fighting, coupled with the small pittance a German soldier receives, the offer to pay under the circumstances was creditable, and the marching away with the sponge no more than poetic justice.

Manteuffel and Goeben both occupied the city in person, and by their kind courtesy got to be looked upon as friends rather than as invaders.

King William thus announced the capture of Amiens:

TO QUEEN AUGUSTA: VERSAILLES, *Nov.* 29.

Yesterday General Manteuffel, with a portion of the First Army, defeated the French a few miles south of Amiens. The French lost 1000 in killed and wounded and 600 in prisoners. The Prussian loss was comparatively unimportant. WILLIAM.

The French field forces retired toward Arras and Lille on the north, blowing up the bridge at Albert on the Amiens and Lille Railroad; while Manteuffel received news of the threatening battle before Paris, and orders to fall back towards the French capital until after the result of the great battle should be decided, and then to continue his march on Rouen. Manteuffel detached a thousand men, who occupied Abbeville, an important town at the mouth of the Somme, and another force was sent to Albert. The result of Trochu's great battle of the 29th resulted favorably to the Germans, and Manteuffel abandoned the idea of succoring the besieging army. On the 3d, Manteuffel left Amiens to a small force, and marched on Rouen with the First and Eighth Corps of 70,000 men, capturing eight guns and occupying that town on the 8th of December with Goeben's corps. Rouen, being at the head of ship navigation on the Seine, is an important point for the shipment of supplies by water from Prussian seaports to the invading army.

LUXEMBURG EXPLAINED.

To-day (Dec. 3d) Bismarck writes a letter withdrawing Prussian neutrality granted to Luxemburg on the 17th of July (p.

52), and reserving "the right to claim compensation from the Duchy for losses sustained by Prussia on account of Luxemburg's non-observance of her neutrality." Bismarck claims that the Luxemburgers are responsible for the revictualling of Thionville; for omitting to stop French refugees, which, to the number of 2000 men were assisted through the resident French consul to rejoin the French armies. This letter of the map-making Bismarck simply means that the little garden spot of Luxemburg, a few miles north of Thionville and which almost upset the peace of Europe in 1856, is to fall with Alsace and Lorraine into the lap of Prussia; that treaties, unless backed by bayonets, are valueless; and that the once sacred parchments on which were written the treaties of Paris and of London have dwindled into cigar-lighters for King William and the Czar. This is a digest of Luxemburg's history: In 1815 Belgium and Luxemburg were placed under the sovereignty of Holland, and Luxemburg was also accorded a place in the Germanic Confederation. Luxemburg joined Belgium's revolt against Holland in 1830, and was only brought back to Holland and the Confederation in 1839, when the Great Powers united in guaranteeing the independence of the Duchy. Thus Luxemburg stood until after Sadowa in 1866, when Bismarck and Napoleon both looked to its absorption. Napoleon now secretly offered to buy the Duchy from the King of Holland, also Grand Duke of Luxemburg. The bankrupt King was about receiving Napoleon's gold, when the terrible Bismarck said no,— "Prussia is not in a position to consent to the separation, under any form, of Luxemburg from Germany, or the evacuation of the fortress." This resolution was modified, and at the conference which met in London, May 7th, 1867, all parties — the Grand Duchy, Prussia, Austria, Russia, England, France, Italy, Belgium, and Holland — signed the following "treaty of London:"

ART. 1. Affirms the rights of the King of Holland.

ART. 2. Enacts that Luxemburg shall be perpetually neutral, under the guarantee of Austria, France, Great Britain, Prussia, and Russia.

ART. 3. Stipulates that the town of Luxemburg shall cease to be a fortified place.

ART. 4. The King of Prussia agrees to withdraw his troops.

ART. 5. The King of Holland agrees to demolish the fortress of Luxemburg, so far as will comply with the intention of Art. 3.

ART. 6. Recognizes that the dissolution of the Germanic Confederation "led to a rupture of the bonds which united the Duchy of Limburg collectively with the Grand Duchy of Luxemburg."

The fortress of Luxemburg was evacuated by the Prussians and razed in 1867. Art. 2 of the treaty was declared by England and Russia to be a *joint* guarantee, and not an individual guarantee of neutrality. The situation is now changed. Napoleon is a prisoner at Wilhelmshöhe. France is almost at the feet of the victorious Germans, and Bismarck quietly breaks the treaty of London, keeping time to the symphony of Gortschakoff, who shatters the treaty of Paris. The next move of Bismarck will be to tempt the King of Holland into "turning an honest penny" by selling what he cannot defend, and whose existence is only guaranteed with the power and integrity of France. Austria is furious over the atrocious presumption of Bismarck, and England, not yet convalescent from the diplomatic stab of Gortschakoff, *dare not stand by her contracts* for fear of setting a whole continent in a blaze, and seeks now to cover up the dishonor of two broken treaties in diplomatic smoke.

How must feel the blundering "nephew of his uncle, who intended in July to push the French boundaries to the Rhine"? In the meantime the bought-and-sold Luxemburgers cry out to Prince Henry of Orange and King William of Holland, to chase away the terrible Bismarck.

King William wrote a letter to Prince Henry of Luxemburg on the 10th of January, advising the Luxemburgers to be prudent and cautious, and asserting that Prussia never intended to attack the independence of the Duchy. Let the world watch, and see how a King will keep his word.

TUESDAY, *November 29th.* — Gen. Trochu makes his great sortie from the south of Paris, towards Choisy-le-Roy, with Ducrot south-east towards Creteil and Mont Mesly, and Thomas north from St. Denis. A feint from Mont Valérien towards Bezons.

THE BATTLE OF THE MARNE.

Gen. Trochu waited in vain with his unhappy army for the hoped-for assistance from Paladines. The 28th was the day which Gambetta had appointed, and sent by carrier pigeon from Tours, as the day when the boom from Paladines' guns were to be heard in Paris. But alas for Paladines! the German lines were not pierced, and the battle of Beaune threw his army, defeated, broken, and demoralized, into the arms of Orleans. The smoke was still hovering over the battle-fields of Beaune and Amiens, when Trochu commenced the great and final sortie for the relief of Paris. The preparations of Gen.

Trochu were executed with deliberate care, for on this sortie depended the fate of Paris and of France. This gigantic death-struggle with the German hosts was fraught with solicitude, and the eyes of a world were turned toward the heroic endeavors of the army of the Republic. Trochu's well-conceived plan was to make feigned advances from Mont Valérien (see map, pp. 336 and 340) towards Bezons and Bougival on the WEST, from Fort Nogent towards Mont Avron on the EAST, and from St. Denis on the NORTH; while the great sortie was to take place on the SOUTH, towards Choisy-le-Roy, Mont Mesly, Bonneuil, Champigny, Villiers, and Brie.

THE FIRST ARMY, General Thomas, was to hold Paris with the National Guard.

THE THIRD ARMY, General Vinoy, was to make the feint east, west, and north, and towards Choisy-le-Roy and Chevilly on the south.

THE SECOND ARMY, General Ducrot, was to break through the Prussian lines at Villiers, Champigny, and Brie.

THE COMMENCEMENT.

The sharp ears of the Prussian sentries on Meudon and Châtillon heights caught the sound of French drum and clarion and artillery rumble at midnight. Von Moltke's active mind caught the omen, and immediately the telegraph to the right and to the left warned the besieging army to be on their guard. Had Von Moltke been permitted to look into Paris, he would have seen a sight which would have called the old Emperor trapper and the King to the front. The whole French army was moving. The *generale* had been sounded at nine on the evening of the 28th, and Paris was filled with caravans of *Mobiles* and *Nationals* and batteries of artillery moving through the city gates.

All Paris seemed to spring into a carnival of moving action. Newsboys shouted, and in the dusky twilight the busy bill-stickers bulletined the government proclamation of advance, while the people, full of hope, seized and devoured these burning words of Trochu:

CITIZENS OF PARIS, SOLDIERS OF THE NATIONAL GUARD AND ARMY: The policy of invasion and conquest means to complete its work. It has introduced into Europe, it pretends to establish in France, the right of brute force. Europe may submit in silence to this insult, but France means to combat it, and our brethren call us to go beyond our walls for the last struggle, despite all the blood spilt, and blood is going to flow again. Let the responsibility be on them whose detestable ambition tramples under foot the laws of modern civilization and of justice. Putting our trust in God, let us march forward for our country.

GENERAL TROCHU, Governor of Paris.

The Government of the National Defence fired the ardor of the soldiers and quieted city discords in the following address :

CITIZENS : The effort is making which the honor and the safety of France demanded. You waited for it with a patriotic impatience, which your military leaders had trouble to moderate. As determined as you to dislodge the enemy from the lines in which he is entrenched, and to hasten to meet your brethren of the provinces, it was their duty to prepare powerful means of attack. Those means are ready. Your leaders have begun the battle. Our hearts are with them. All and every one of us are ready to follow them, and like them, to pour out our blood for the deliverance of our country. This critical hour, while they are nobly exposing their lives, we owe to them the support of our firmness and our civic virtue. Whatever may be the violence of the emotions which agitate us, let us have the courage to keep calm. Whoever would foment the least disturbance in Paris, would betray the cause of its defenders and serve the cause of Prussia. As the army cannot conquer except by discipline, so neither can we resist except by union and order. We reckon on success. We shall not allow ourselves to be depressed by any reverse. Above all, let us seek our strength in the unshaken resolution to destroy, as a germ of ignominious death, every ferment of civil discord. Vive la France ! Vive la République !

Jules Favre, Vice-President of the Government ; Emmanuel Arago, Jules Ferry, Garnier-Pagés, Eugene Pelletan, Ernest Picard, Jules Simon, members of the Government ; General Le Flo, Dorian, J. Magnin, Ministers ; André Lavertujon, F. Herold, A. Dreo, Durier, Secretaries of the Government.

Fifteen hundred guns about Paris had been belching forth a terrific fire during the previous day, and the night had been made lurid with a thousand bursting shells. It was a chain of fire around the unhappy capital, and the deep boom from a thousand cannon sounded like the roar of Omnipotence.

ON THE WEST.

In the early twilight, on the morning of the 29th, the Jäger outposts of Kirchbach, in front of Versailles, saw General de Beaufort, of Vinoy's army, debouching a division of Frenchmen from behind Fort Mont Valérien, towards Bougival and the heights of Malmaison, on the road to Versailles ; while General De Liniers pushed rapidly forward a supporting division towards Bezon bridge, on the north-west. In both directions the French attacked with seeming vigor, while the guns from Mont Valérien covered them with a canopy of fire. Kirchbach now ordered up several Fifth Corps field-batteries, and a large force of line infantry, to support the Jäger companies now engaged. The Prussians moved forward with a stern resolve, not knowing but what the whole French army was in front, but making no response to the belching storm of shot and shell from the Seine gunboats and Mont Valérien ; Kirchbach's guns were shotted with grape and canister, for an anticipated infantry assault, and he was not to be deceived by a feint. Beaufort's men made a crude attempt to storm the Prussian works around Bougival and Montretout, but the assault failed from lack of support, the whole attack being a *feint* to cover the real attack of Ducrot and Vinoy on the south. After it was thought that the *feint* had drawn Von Moltke's attention, and called reinforcements from the investing Prussian corps on the south, Beaufort and Liniers marched back again from Bougival and Bezons, and debouched behind the guns of Mont Valérien. During the feint, the French officers exposed themselves to the Jäger fire, and many were killed or wounded during the skirmishing of the day.

ON THE NORTH.

Admiral Roncière had command of the sortie to the north, from St. Denis, towards Epinay, Drancy, and Le Bourget. His advance was met by Alvensleben's Fourth Corps, and a portion of the Saxon Guards under Prince Augustus of Würtemberg. The result was a defeat of the French, who lost several hundred prisoners; the Saxons losing twelve officers and one hundred men.

ON THE EAST.

The plateau of Avron was occupied by the marines of Admiral Saisset, sustained by the divisions of D'Hugues and a numerous long-range artillery, capable of menacing Chelles, Neuilly, Noisy, Brie, and Villiers.

DUCROT'S AND VINOY'S SORTIE ON THE SOUTH.

The great sortie was made on the south : Vinoy commanded the Right, towards Choisy-le-Roy, Thiais, L'Hay, and Chevilly, against Tumpling's Sixth Prussian Corps; while Ducrot commanded the Left, which crossed the Marne at Nogent, and attacked Champigny, Brie, and Villiers. About 9 o'clock on the 29th, twenty battalions under Vinoy marched from Villejuif and L'Hay, and advanced upon the position of Tümpling's Sixth Corps.

The guns of a new work at Villejuif supported the attack by an incessant fire, reaching mainly the right of the Second Bavarian Corps, and inflicting slight losses. The beginning of the movement on the part of the French was conducted with great energy, but they speedily became discouraged under the sharp fire of the besieging forces, who unmasked field-batteries which immediately proved exceedingly annoying to the French.

Notwithstanding the great exertions of their officers, the attacking battalions were thrown into disorder. Their supports failed to arrive. The affair was over in two hours. The estimated German loss is 100, of whom 30 were Bavarians; the rest Prussians of the Sixth Corps. The French loss was from 500 to 600, including 250 prisoners.

Vinoy was repulsed by Tumpling at 11 o'clock, who immediately telegraphed the result:

A great sortie has occurred. Vinoy moved out against the Sixth Corps and the Würtembergers early in the morning, supported by a heavy cannonade from Villejuif. The Sixth Corps repulsed the enemy at 11 o'clock, when they retired. Subsequently Ducrot attacked the Würtembergers (General Von Oberwitz) near Mont Mesly, at 3 P. M. The Würtembergers had been reinforced by cavalry and artillery, and soon defeated the French. The German losses were trifling.

As indicated in Tumpling's dispatch, Vinoy attacked the Würtembergers at Mont Mesly, between the Seine and Marne, at 3 P. M. The French were soon repulsed, and Von Oberwitz telegraphed the result to the King of Würtemberg:

"The Second and Third Würtemberg Brigades, with the Seventh Prussian Brigade, have just defeated a sortie of the French under Ducrot, made in the direction of Mont Mesly. After five hours' fighting the Germans took 300 prisoners. The German loss was as follows: six officers killed and 34 wounded, and 700 rank and file killed and wounded."

While Vinoy was being repulsed at Mont Mesly, Ducrot, with the Third Army, crossed the Marne in front of Fort Nogent, and engaged the Saxons and Würtembergers at Champigny, Villiers, and Brie-sur-Marne. In this engagement, Ducrot captured two guns and then retired from the advancing Saxons to the Marne, now spanned by eight pontoon bridges. Prince George, who commanded the Saxons, reported that:

The French were repulsed and driven over the heights between the two villages, leaving behind hundreds of prisoners. The French attacking force numbered 50,000. The loss of the Saxons was 12 officers and 100 privates.

As Ducrot and Vinoy withdrew, Fansecki moved towards Mesly and Choisy-le-Roy with the Second Corps, to be prepared for another sortie. The German troops were greatly elated at the prospect of active work; the camps were noisy with singing soldiers, and above the din the bands echoed the music of war. King William thus announces the day's actions:

TO THE QUEEN: VERSAILLES, *Nov. 30th.*

The Sixth Corps yesterday repulsed a sortie of the French near L'Hay, on the south of Paris. Over 100 French prisoners were taken, and several hundred dead and wounded were left on the field. The French also made sorties on the positions of the Würtembergers and Saxons at Bonneuil,

Champigny, and Villiers, to the east and south-east of Paris. The positions were taken by the French, but were subsequently retaken by the Prussians. At the same time sorties were made at the north and west, and at St. Denis against the Fourth Corps and the Guards.

The French were repulsed and driven back behind their works in all cases. I remained at Versailles, as it was the central point.

WILHELM.

THE BATTLE OF WEDNESDAY, Nov. 30 (*map, p.* 340).

The morning of Wednesday, the 30th, found Ducrot with his army well under cover of Fort Nogent, and ready for a furious assault. The Twelfth Saxons, commanded by Prince George, occupied a curved line from Noisy-le-Grand, past Villiers, around the curve in the Marne to Ormesson, where they joined the Würtembergers commanded by Oberwitz, who continued the line in front of Bonneuil, supported by Fansecki's Second Corps. Ducrot held Brie and Champigny after yesterday's battle. Brie, Villiers, and Champigny form a little triangle, Villiers making the projecting apex, held by the Saxons. In the morning the Germans had decided to retake Champigny and Brie, while Ducrot had decided to advance his forces to break the German cordon and capture Villiers.

As Ducrot marched his 70,000 to battle that morning, he fired his soldiers with the following stirring words:

SOLDIERS OF THE SECOND ARMY OF PARIS: The time has come to break the iron circle which has cramped us too long, and threatens to stifle us in a slow and painful agony! The honor has devolved upon you of attempting this great work. I am certain you will prove yourselves worthy of it. Its first steps, doubtless, will be difficult. We shall find implacable enemies, made audacious and confident by too many successes. To prepare the way for you, the foresight of our Commander-in-Chief has collected above four hundred cannon, at least two-thirds of which are of the heaviest calibre, which no physical object can resist; and to dash into this breach ye will be above 150,000 men, all well armed, thoroughly equipped, abundantly supplied with munitions, and, I hope, all animated with an irresistible ardor. Your success is certain if ye be victorious in this first period of the contest, for the enemy has sent to the banks of Loire river his most numerous and best soldiers. Therefore, courage and confidence! Remember that in this last struggle we are fighting for our honor, for our liberty, for the security of our dear and unhappy conntry; and if this thought be insufficient to inflame your hearts, think of your devastated fields, your ruined families, your sobbing sisters, wives, and mothers. May these remembrances make you share the thirst for vengeance, the pent-up fury which animates me and fills you with contempt for danger! As for myself, I am most determined. *I swear to it before you, before the whole nation, to return no more to Paris except dead or victorious.* You may see me fall. You will not see me retreat. Then do not pause in your onward march. Avenge me. Forward, then! Forward! May God be our helper!

A. DUCROT.

At daybreak Ducrot threw the First Corps (Blanchard) and the Second Corps (Renault) across the Marne, between Joinville and Nogent. Eight concealed pontoon bridges carried the French across. At nine o'clock 70,000 Frenchmen threw themselves upon the villages of Champigny and Villiers; while D'Exéa, with the Third Corps, advanced across the Marne in front of Brie-sur-Marne and towards Neuilly. Bellemare's division occupied Brie, and united with Renault in seizing the crest of the height in front of Villiers. Ninety thousand Frenchmen were now in that little triangle of Brie, Villiers, and Champigny not more than a mile square. Fort Nogent and Mont Avron threw their shells thick and fast among the advancing Germans, and they went hissing over and through the Saxon ranks, causing a carnival of death and destruction. Outnumbered, the Saxons were swept back from Brie towards Noisy, while Blanchard's right stood and died before the terrible German line at Champigny. Now came the terrible struggle of the war. The Germans determined to take Champigny, and the French determined upon the capture of Villiers. Blanchard's corps fought and lost in fearful numbers; but the hundreds slain were the price of victory; for the end found the French Right in victorious possession of Champigny, though subject to a terrible shelling from the Prussian guns at Cœuilly and Chenevières. Blanchard now began to entrench at Champigny, when the Saxons made a furious assault from Villiers upon the troops of Renault. Back and forth in front of Villiers swayed French and Germans, each resolved on the possession of the town. From twelve till two was a time of terrible slaughter, and the terrible crest in front of Villiers was made thick with the dead and dying. Here General Renault fell, severely wounded. The impetuous French again and again rushed forward upon the sullen Saxons, who only fell back or wavered to give room for reinforcement. Noon, twilight, dusk came, but the fight only ceased with the darkness. Night found Blanchard with his decimated corps in possession of Champigny, while the men of the wounded Renault stood hopeless before the sturdy Saxon wall in front of Villiers. Each army had been foiled. Each had advanced in the morning to take a coveted position, and each had failed in everything but heroic endeavors. On that awful Wednesday night Blanchard slept amid a thousand dead at Champigny, while the Saxons closed their eyes behind a wall of dead and dying at Villiers. Terrible were the losses in this day's battle. The sad tale of Mars-la-Tour is but a faint echo of the dreadful shock of death which came to two armies in front of Villiers. During the day Vinoy continued to make sorties towards Choisy-le-Roy and Thiais, while Susbielle advanced beyond Creteil, occupying Mesly until evening.

ON THE NORTH.

Admiral La Roncière occupied Drancy from Fort Denis while Ducrot was engaged on the south, and at two o'clock the Admiral advanced with fresh Paris troops against the village of Epinay. Out burst the French from St. Denis at double quick, while a gunboat coming down the stream, swept the banks clear of German outposts, and landed a force at Epinay, half surrounding the Seventy-first Prussian regiment.

The French force being overwhelming, the Germans fell back, fighting, and evacuated the village, reinforcements arriving near St. Gratien. The French then barricaded Epinay. The Germans sent the whole Fifteenth Brigade and the Seventy-first and Thirty-first Regiments — altogether six battalions — to retake the village. Advancing rapidly, the French were driven out. During the two hours the German lost was 200 men and 13 officers.

All day Fort Valérien kept up its dreadful thunder, and St. Denis on the north answered in sullen roar the deep-toned columbiads from Nogent and Noisy. Shells went crashing into Argenteuil and Bezons. The French lined the bank of the Seine with infantry, while the Germans kept up a faltering fire in anticipation of a French attempt to restore the bridge at Bezons. The double-crown of the North kept a stream of shells pouring into Montmagny, while Fort de l'East and Aubervillers paid their death compliments to Le Bourget and Drancy.

Another demonstration took place in the direction of Le Bourget, at a later hour. Dense columns of French troops showed themselves on the plain in front of the fort of Aubervillers, and advanced steadily towards Le Bourget. But they lost heart before they got nearer than the railway station, and never came within range. Bourget, already pounded with shells, was again bombarded.

THURSDAY'S BATTLE AND BURIALS.

While the four days' battle is commencing against Paladines on the south, both the French and German armies about Paris rest from the terrible struggle of the previous day.

In the sullen silence of an armistice both armies filled the plain between Brie, Champigny, and Villiers with burial parties. The casualties among officers had been great. The French officers had exposed themselves to rally their men; but they were no more reckless of danger than the Germans. Thousands were buried to-day, and the sickening sight was enough "to glut ambition for a thousand years." Yesterday it was poetry — to-day among the harvest of death it is prose indeed.

In German council of war, Von Moltke decided that Brie and Champigny must be retaken in the morning — that this was essential to the success of the Paris investment. Little do the thousands of living know that death awaits them in the last struggle of the giants to-morrow.

FRIDAY'S BATTLE (DECEMBER 2).

If Wednesday's battle was the Mars-la-Tour of Paris, Friday's struggle was the Gravelotte. The Saxons and Würtembergers at mid-day left Trochu as closely besieged in Paris as was Bazaine in Metz by the hermetical sealing of Prince Charles and Steinmetz. The battle-ground was in the old triangle between Brie, Villiers, and Champigny. When the curtain fell at the end of the bloody drama of Wednesday, the Saxons stood fast in Villiers in spite of all the French troops and forts could do to dislodge them, and as firmly in the grasp of the French were Brie and Champigny, under the guns of Fort Nogent.

THE FIELD OF BATTLE.

On the road that passes through Noisy, the south bank of of the Marne is low, with a gradual rise, furrowed by inconsiderable rectangular depressions. From Noisy to the southward, toward Brie and athwart the thick part of the curve of the Marne, is a broad, flat space, offering a favorable scope for military evolutions. From this plain toward Villiers there rises gradually a low but shaggy elevation, covered chiefly with copse-woods and vineyards. This elevation is not continuous to Villiers. There are occasional depressions, debouchments of which cause the trivial hollows that occur on the road to Noisy. The general tendency is, nevertheless, upward, so that the tableland at the back of which Villiers lies is higher than any ground between it and the plain. The ridge, therefore, though hampered by hedges and brushwood, would form no bad position for resistance to a force which, having deployed on the plain, should attempt to carry it, if it were not swept by the direct fire from Fort Nogent at easy range, and enfiladed at longer range, but still effectively, by batteries on Mont Avron.

Brie divided with Noisy the attentions of the French batteries, and Brie is more open to attack. The 107th Regiment had made a dash into Brie out of Rosny early in the morning. Could they hold the place under such ding-dong pelting? By 10 o'clock the question was resolved. First came a drove of French prisoners, red-breeched regulars, up toward Noisy, along the slight shelter afforded by the road; then Saxon soldiers and more prisoners; and finally the bulk of the 107th, in very open order, making the most of the few opportunities for cover. The 107th, in a rapid rush in the morning, had surprised the occupants of Brie, some asleep, others drinking coffee. There was a trifling resistance. Nearly 500 prisoners were taken, including eight officers. The prisoners looked like sturdy fellows, anything but ill-fed. They were hearty, and good to fight. Said a sergeant cheerily, "If any one indulges in the anticipation of the speedy capitulation of Paris, he is extremely out in his reckoning; food is plentiful." He said with a laugh, "The programme is sorties every day, in every direction." The prisoners were escorted back to Chelles.

The reason for the Germans relinquishing Brie was that the terrible persistent fire from the forts rendered it utterly untenable. What this advantage represented was simply that Brie gave the French a footing, so to speak, on the Saxon mainland, while Champigny formed a key to the peninsula of the Marne. The object of the day on the side of the Germans was to dislodge the French from Brie and Champigny. This task fell to the lot of the Saxons, Würtembergers, and a brigade of the Second Corps.

As the French prisoners filed in from Brie, a dense column of French infantry reinforcements, which had been bivouacked under the wings of Fort Nogent, appeared in view. The spectacle sprang up by magic. Right and left, across the railway, they formed, covered by the south guns of Nogent. Now they stood fast, closing up as the fronts of battalions halted. Then there was a slow movement forward as the head of the column dipped out of sight between the village of Nogent and the river. Then there seemed to be a final halt. The dense masses stood, their bayonets glittering in the sun, as if the men had come out for a spectacle. Presently the dense mass began to move towards the river, in the direction of Brie. The river passed, simultaneously the whole caravan sprang into life, and the plains south of Brie swarmed with an army. Suddenly another army deployed at double-quick from St. Maur, behind Champigny, and both armies made a wall of men across the neck of the loop of the river. From Champigny, at 8 o'clock, the Würtembergers had driven the French after a desperate fight, only to be repulsed in turn by the serried columns of another overpowering army. Back, pell-mell, fled the Würtemberg sharpshooters, and Champigny was again in the hands of the French. The impetuous red breeches did not stop here, but on they swept at double-quick to the front of Villiers, the objective point of the day's attack. Forty thousand Frenchmen came with a shock against Von Obernetz and his 2000 Wütembergers at Villiers, while 5000 French held Champigny. On the French left, another column of 20,000 assaulted the Saxons under Prince George at Brie, while Nogent rained a storm of projectiles over the head of Villiers, and into the advancing Germans behind. The French skirmishers were thrown out with as much regularity as if the day's work had been but a peaceful parade. The Germans were surprised at the magnitude of the French evolutions, and soon made up their minds that Ducrot intended not only to capture Villiers, but to sweep on to Noisy. Preparation was made to meet Ducrot in the open space between Villiers and Noisy. On came the French. From behind Villiers several German regiments came out to the right of the brow of the hill under the shell fire. As the French came up the gentle acclivity, the guns of the forts continued playing without interruption. So narrow was the margin between the combatants, that shells fell into the French ranks. Ten thousand Saxons now opened the terrible assault. It was sharp and bloody. The affair of Spicheren could not have been quicker or bloodier. In front of the One Hundred and Eighth Prussian regiment, two lieutenants shook hands with a hussar aid-de-camp, who brought the order to advance, and then swept forward with their commands. On went divisions, brigades, and regiments. French shells went crashing through the dense columns of the advancing companies.

Now the battle-line forms — rear files close up at double-quick, and in a twinkling, through the fifty yards of space, flies a storm of bullets. Now comes the firing by volley — then sharp firing by file. So close are the combatants that the field becomes a field of horrible slaughter. The Saxons had fought at Sedan, and the leaden hail had no terrors for them. Decimated, but not defeated, the brave French broke and gave ground, only to get back to the next dip of the ground, to let the guns of the fort go to work again. The Saxons had to find what cover they might. They fought on after the French with the bravery of veterans. What soldier thought of the rear in the battles of the Wilderness? As all thought of the rear ended at Gettysburg, so it ended with the Germans at Gravelotte. The belching shells from Nogent put a stop to the Saxon advance.

When the regiments came back — they had not been gone twenty minutes — thirty-five officers out of the forty-five had gone down. Neither of the blithe lieutenants were to the fore. Now there came a lull in the musketry fire, as a few moments before there had been a lull in the cannon. The Saxons could not get their artillery into action with advantage. The ground itself was unfavorable, while the fire from the forts speedily silenced their field guns; therefore this great advantage was lost to them.

THE LAST STRUGGLE.

All this took place before noon. After a little time the artillery fire from the forts slackened considerably. The French infantry made no demonstration.

On the German left about Champigny, General Vinoy was engaged with the Würtembergers, who, supported by Fansecki's Second Prussian Corps, repulsed every French advance. Fansecki had command of the German left, while Prince George led the Saxons on the right.

About one o'clock the French made another advance, having received considerable reinforcements. This onslaught swayed the Saxons a little, and crouching back for a forward spring, Trochu thought he was on the eve of victory, and immediately telegraphed to Paris:

BATTLE-FIELD, 1.45 P.M. — The Prussians with enormous forces attacked the French position at daybreak to-day. The fighting has lasted more than seven hours, and at the moment of sending off this report the enemy is giving way along the whole line and once more abandoning the heights. I have ridden along the line of skirmishers from Champigny to Brie, and have been received with enthusiastic cheers by the troops. I expect that the enemy will return to the attack, and that the battle will last all day.

The Saxons now sprang forward upon the French with a new vim, but a different policy was this time adopted. It was plain that the only escape from the thunderbolts of the forts lay in getting at close quarters with the French infantry — unless, indeed, a retrograde movement was to be made, and that was not to be thought of. So when the French fell back, the Saxons followed on, as if they would settle the question with the bayonet's point. It was the old cry, "*Vorwarts, immer vorwarts;*" but the *vorwarts* was very slow.

For the next hour it was a sullen fight all along the line. Both sides were decimated, and it was only a question of dogged grit. Germans tenacity prevailed, while from Fort Nogent, across the Marne, at 5.30 P. M,. Trochu thus announced the French defeat:

> The second great battle which I expected has been more decisive than its predecessor. The enemy attacked us at the *reveille* with fresh troops and reserves. We have fought three hours to maintain our position, and five hours to carry the positions of the enemy.

While the forts continued a furious cannonade into Champigny and Villers, the French slowly and stubbornly fell back across the north side of the neck of land, the Saxons pushing them hard. Now and then, as if exasperated at fate, the French rallied only to meet the same steady fire. On this portion of the plain, south of Brie, there was a prolonged struggle. The Saxons were striving to get at and cut the pontoon bridge; but this became an impossibility, when Fort Nogent went to work again with the frightful accuracy of which the short range admitted. The combatants parted about 3 o'clock, both sides falling back. The fire of the fort continued some little time longer.

THE END — LOSSES.

What is to be said of results? Not much have the Saxons gained. Was there much to gain? The Würtembergers hold one end of Champigny. Brie stands empty and desolate; there were French in it this morning; later, there were Saxons. That is all. But look at the bloody side of the picture.

The losses of the Germans during Wednesday's and Friday's battles were 6500, as follows: The Saxons, 2000; the Second Corps, 2800; the Würtembergers, 1700.

The French losses during the three days' fighting were thus reported by General Schmitz, General Trochu's chief of staff:

	Officers.		Soldiers.	
	Killed.	Wounded.	Killed.	Wounded.
Second Army	61	301	711	4,098
Third Army	8	22	192	364
Corps d'Armée of St. Denis	3	10	33	218
Total	72	342	936	4,680

ABSTRACT.

	Killed.	Wounded.
Officers	72	342
Soldiers	936	4,680
Total	1,008	5,022

Four regiments of the Saxon forces, the 104th, 106th, 107th, and 108th, lost 15 officers killed and 63 wounded. The total number of French prisoners taken was about 3000.

The total loss sustained by the Würtemberg troops in the battle of the 2d inst. is officially reported to be 848 killed and wounded.

Had it been possible for the Saxons to hold Brie, the French advance would have been impossible; its flanking fire would have prohibited breasting the slope toward Villiers.

At five, all was quiet except the sullen roar of the big guns from Fort Nogent. Brie was abandoned by both sides, the German line remained everywhere unbroken, and the French behind a wall of sturdy Saxons, are hermetically sealed in Paris. The official report of Trochu says:

Thursday was passed in burying the dead and succoring the wounded. On Friday morning the Prussians attacked with great impetuosity the French at Champigny and in front of Villiers. After seven hours' fighting the enemy failed to carry the positions of the French, and retreated, leaving their dead and wounded on the field. Their losses were from 15,000 to 20,000. On Saturday the French recrossed the Marne and took up positions. The enemy made no attempt to resist them.

General Ducrot greatly distinguished himself in the battle of Friday. Among the killed is General Lacharier, and General Renault was badly wounded.

After recrossing the Marne to the cover of the guns of Nogent, General Trochu issued the following address to his army:

SOLDIERS! — After two days of glorious battles, you have recrossed the Marne, having found that your efforts were fruitless. When the enemy has not time to concentrate, or to prepare to continue the vain sacrifice of life, let us renew the contest with increased animation, and raise our hearts to the level of the sacrifice demanded by the holy cause, for which we must not hesitate to sacrifice our lives.

Prince George, commanding the Saxons, telegraphs the King of Saxony:

"The enemy has retired behind the Marne, and other offensive operations on the part of the French are impossible. The total loss of the Saxons in the late engagements is — officers, 76; rank and file, 2100."

THE END OF THE SORTIE.

THE QUEEN: VERSAILLES, *Dec.* 4.

There was no fighting of moment yesterday at Paris. The French are massing troops from Vincennes. During the fight of December 2d, the French lost 1800 prisoners, including one general and 20 superior officers; also, seven guns. WILHELM.

MONDAY, *December* 5. — Bourbaki and Chanzy falling back

before Prince Charles and Mecklenburg. Von Moltke announces the defeat of the Army of the Loire to General Trochu.

VON MOLTKE TO TROCHU.

The defeat of the Army of the Loire brought the following Chesterfieldian note from Von Moltke to General Trochu:

VERSAILLES, *Dec.* 5.

It may be useful to inform your Excellency, that the Army of the Loire was defeated near Orleans yesterday, and that that town is re-occupied by the German troops. Should, however, your Excellency deem it expedient to be convinced of the fact through one of your own officers, I will not fail to provide him with a safe-conduct *to* come and return. Receive, General, the expression of the high considerations with which I have the honor to be, your very humble and obedient servant.

The Chief of the Staff, Count MOLTKE.

General Trochu, Governor of Paris.

On the receipt of this courteous note, several of the Paris authorities were disposed to surrender, but the opinion of Trochu prevailed, and the Governor promptly answered:

PARIS, *Dec.* 6.

Your Excellency thought it might be useful to inform me that the Army of the Loire was defeated near Orleans, and that that town is re-occupied by German troops.

I have the honor to acknowledge the receipt of that communication, which I do not think it expedient to verify through the means which your Excellency suggests to me. Receive, General, the expression of the high consideration with which I have the honor to be, your very humble and very obedient servant,

The Governor of Paris, General TROCHU.

To Count Von Moltke.

TOTAL LOSSES.

The losses by death in battle are always less than estimated on the field. When a regiment of one thousand men loses fifty in killed, the regiment is too demoralized and "cut up" to go into action without reformation. Fifty killed in the American army meant 200 wounded and 300 demoralized and frightened. The entire German losses up to this time, with the exception of the recent killed in the Würtemberg and First and Second Bavarian Corps, are as follows:

	Killed and Wounded.	*Missing.*
Generals	12	—
Staff Officers	206	1
Subalterns	2,691	25
Ensigns	909	15
Sergeants, &c	5,384	198
Surgeons, &c	100	5
Rank and file	53,541	6,858

This gives a total loss of 2,935 officers and 67,012 men for the twelve Prussian army corps, the landwehr, and the Baden division.

WEDNESDAY, *December 7.*—Mecklenburg defeats the French at Chambord with the Twenty-second Division, while the Bavarians skirmish to the west of Meung, capturing 260 prisoners and a mitrailleuse. Prince Charles' Third Corps defeats Bourbaki's rear-guard south of Gien.

CHANZY—MECKLENBURG.

After the evacuation of Orleans on the 4th, Mecklenburg continued to push General Chanzy towards Tours, while Prince Charles dispatched the Third Corps after the retreating army of Bourbaki at Bourges. Every day Chanzy gave battle, but every night his army bivouacked nearer Blois and Tours. On the 7th, the Seventeenth Division engaged Chanzy west of Meung, in a severe encounter, of which King William says:

TO THE QUEEN: VERSAILLES, *Dec.* 8.

There was severe and successful fighting yesterday near Meung. More resistance is expected there. One gun, several mitrailleuses, and 260 prisoners were taken. The sanitary condition of the army in the field has taken a very favorable turn.

This fight was by the Seventeenth Division, supported by the First Bavarians. At the same time, the Ninth Corps of Prince Charles' army marched towards Chanzy's rear from the pursuit of Bourbaki on the south, and captured Château Chambord, nine miles from Blois.

Chambord was prepared for defence, and held by 600 Frenchmen of the Fifteenth Corps, but instead of a fortress it proved a trap. So bad were the dispositions of the French commander, that the Germans completely surprised the place, and captured the greater part of the men. Approaching the place at dusk, the Ninth Corps, operating on the south of the Loire, drove before them a batch of prisoners, and the deception was so effective, that the Germans reached a striking point before a shot was fired.

The only brave act on the part of the French was done by a Mobile, who shouted to the sentinels, "We are prisoners. The German devils are behind." He lost his life. His warning was too late. Having thus readily gained the Château Chambord, Manstein was in possession of a sort of back entrance to Blois, where his appearance was expected hourly.

Opposite Blois, on the south side of the Loire, the little suburb of Vienne is connected with the city by a splendid stone bridge. A portion of the French troops and artillery had been fighting on the south side. They passed over the bridge on Friday night, and the engineers immediately commenced destroying one of the arches, but did not finish its destruction. Crowds gathered to witness and to bewail this operation. They abused the soldiers without stint. In fact, all the people of Blois seemed to care for was the bridge. Meantime thousands of half-clad soldiers stood shivering in the streets, while other thousands, all wounded, were being carried to the railroad station, where desperately working locomotives strove to convey them beyond reach of the Prussians.

FRIDAY, *Dec.* 9.—The Tours Government moves to Bordeaux. Gambetta goes to Blois. Continued fighting around Beaugency and Blois. King William accepts the title of Emperor Frederick William I. of Germany.

BATTLE OF BEAUGENCY.

On Friday evening the bridge south of Blois was cut, and the French forces, consisting of Pallières' Fifteenth Corps and the newly organized Twenty-first Corps, leaving a force in Blois, moved northward towards Beaugency, occupied by the worn-out forces of Mecklenburg. Chanzy, who had been fighting all the day before near Beaugency, was still engaged in a terrific encounter with the Grand Duke, supported by Voigts Rhetz from Orleans, and a part of Manstein's forces from Blois. This was the last bloody fight of Chanzy during his retreat upon Le Mans, and the Germans were left so crippled that he was allowed to continue his retreat almost unmolested. It was here that the Bavarians first began to break, and show that demoralization which ultimately compelled Mecklenburg to retire towards Paris. Voigts Rhetz did not arrive from Orleans in time to take part in the battle of the 8th, but the moral force of his presence prevented a demoralized retreat on the part of Mecklenburg on the succeeding day. Chanzy thus reports the battle of Beaugency:

We were attacked all along the lines, from Meung to St. Laurent, last night (8th). To-day the principal effort of the evening was at Beaugency. The Germans were very strong at that place, having no less than eighty-six cannon. Their forces consisted of two divisions of Bavarians, one division of Prussians, 2000 cavalry, and strong reserves. They were under the command of Prince Frederick Charles and the Duke of Mecklenburg. We sleep to-night on the positions we had this morning. The prisoners taken acknowledge that the Prussians suffered heavy losses. The battle lasted till night. I have not yet received a complete list of our losses. We may be attacked again to-morrow, but we are prepared to resist to the utmost. Three French corps were engaged.

SATURDAY, *December* 10. — On the morning of the 10th, Gambetta arrived at Blois from Tours. The War Minister ordered Chanzy to make another attack on Mecklenburg, and the Bavarians were startled on being attacked by an enemy whom they supposed to be on the retreat. It was the death-struggle of the worn-out armies, but the Tenth Corps soon came to the relief of Mecklenburg, by threatening the French right towards Blois. The battle ended in Chanzy's falling back towards Blois. Though Mecklenburg was not defeated, he had not the heart nor power to vigorously pursue the French. Both sides claimed the victory, and Mecklenburg wrote:

The enemy violently attacked us to-day, but were victoriously repulsed by the Seventeenth and Twenty-second Divisions, notwithstanding the superiority of his officers. Our losses were smaller than yesterday. Beaugency was occupied on the 8th inst., and Vierzon to-day.

At noon the Fifteenth French Corps, which had been fighting the Ninth Corps on the south side of the Loire, commenced retiring over the river, and through Blois, to the north. The river here is about the size of the Hudson at Albany. In spite of the protests of the citizens at Blois, the splendid bridge was blown up, and the French defied the advancing Germans who were in seemingly harmless positions on the south side of the river. Though almost defeated themselves, the Bavarians again took heart when they saw the French retreating, and soon the muzzles of Manstein's cannons frowned down on Blois from the German camp. Boom went the Ninth Corps' guns, and smash, crash went the piercing shells into the belfry, and through the spire of the magnificent Blois Cathedral. Now the shells go bursting over and into the Blois barracks, situated on the elevated point to the north of the city. The trembling citizens begged to surrender the town, for Manstein was now in front of the suburb of Vienne, blazing away at anything like a French uniform, utterly regardless of the city and its beautiful buildings. The Mayor had held up the white flag of surrender, when Gambetta, covered with dust, arrived from Chanzy's headquarters outside of the city. The one-eyed Minister immediately broke up the programme of surrender. The Prussians now saw that only the gap in the bridge prevented their advance into Blois, and they sent word to the Mayor, giving him twenty minutes in which to make the bridge passable. The cut in the bridge was but thirty feet wide, and there was plenty of timber at hand long enough to span it. Had the answer been left to the Mayor, the Prussians would have entered Blois the same night.

But Gambetta had no idea of surrender, and crash went the French answer over amongst the Germans. It was not "yes" from the mouth of the Mayor, but "no" from the mouth of a cannon, and a terrible "no," cast in the foundry at Toulouse. The next day Gambetta returned to Tours, and telegraphed to the Government at Bordeaux:

"I have returned to Tours, having left General Chanzy yesterday continuing his efforts to successfully defend the line of the Loire. I think the situation so good that I may go to Bourges to see what can be done with the Second Army."

The next day the whole Army of the Loire retire northward, when Voigts Rhetz occupied Blois, capturing a large amount of provisions, and several hundred straggling deserters, while Gambetta posted off to Bourges to re-organize Bourbaki's army.

BORDEAUX.

Bordeaux, the present seat of the Republican government, is a charming city, full of cultivation and art, and is the second seaport town in France. The river is wide at its mouth, the quay three miles long, and lined with beautiful buildings. It is the seat of the national court, of a university, and an academy. The city is in communication with the Mediterranean by the river Garonne and Canal du Midi. Its exports are wine, brandies, and fruits, and chemical products. Two hundred thousand hogsheads of wine — Medoc, Château Lafitte, Château Margeaux, and other brands of claret and Burgundy — are exported annually to the United States. Among the most remarkable public edifices of Bordeaux are the remains of the palace of the Roman Emperor Gallinus, a circle capable of holding 15,000 people, the Cathedral of St. Andrè, and the Church of the Feuillants, which contains the tomb of Montaigne. The city is fanned by delightful sea-breezes, and to the tourist is one of the most charming spots of Europe.

TUESDAY, *December* 13. — The fortress of Pfalzburg, the stronghold of the Vosges, surrenders with 52 officers, 1800 men, and 63 guns. Bourbaki marches eastward against Werder at Dôle and Besançon. Chanzy retires northward towards Le

Mans, to receive the support of Jaures and the Army of the West. Bourbaki goes to Bourges.

MOVEMENTS OF ARMIES.

Grand moves have been made on the checker-board of France within the last few days — moves which show the natural buoyancy of the French people, and which initiate the new species of strategy resolved upon by the French authorities. That buoyancy is the perpetual habit of the French to make almost instantaneous changes from defeat and despondency to victory and hope; and the new French strategy is the determination to offer no great battles, but to continually harass the invading forces. Bourbaki, with the Eighteenth and Twentieth Corps, leaves Bourges, and moves towards the valley of the Rhône, to fall upon Werder, destroy the German communications between Paris and Strasburg, and relieve the struggling garrison of Belfort. Prince Charles ceases to march towards Tours, and returns towards Paris, to cover the besieging army from any attack from the French army at Le Mans. King William telegraphs to-day to

QUEEN AUGUSTA: VERSAILLES, *Dec.* 13.

After four days' fighting around Beaugency, the French retired to Blois, Tours, and Le Mans. Their loss was severe. Many deserters came into our lines here and at Rouen. WILLIAM.

Every day the Germans are becoming less hopeful, and many troops, especially the Bavarians, are demoralized and despondent. Each defeat of the French has been thought to be the last, but still the end does not come. "What are we fighting for?" is now often asked in Mecklenburg's army; while around Paris the patience of the besieging army is exhausted. For ninety days have the heroic French held out, and still no signs of the surrender of Paris. Day by day the rations of the besieged have grown plainer and scantier. Black bread has taken the place of white; and salt provisions, with horse, rats, and cats, are eaten by the inhabitants, who defy the weary besiegers. Von Moltke has placed no guns in position, because he has daily expected the surrender of the capital. Now for the first time guns are to be mounted for the reduction of Mont Avron, a redoubt to the east of Paris, and about a mile from Nogent. This redoubt threw many shots into the Prussian ranks during the fight at Brie, Champigny, and Villiers on the 2d. After reducing Avron, the German guns will open on Nogent and Rosny, and against the forts on the south.

AMIENS — ROUEN — HAVRE.

After the capture of Amiens on the 28th of November, Manteuffel moved upon Rouen, which fell, with 400 prisoners and ten guns, on the 4th of December. Rouen is at the head of navigation on the Seine. From Rouen, Manteuffel turned his attention towards the seaport of Havre, fortified by the sea and harbor on three sides, and by strong fortifications on the other. On the 8th of December, General Goeben, with the Eighth Corps, took Dieppe, on the channel, about forty miles to the east of Rouen, but soon abandoned it. On the 13th General Goeben returned to Dieppe with 8000 men, which he billeted upon the inhabitants. Of this occupation says an eye-witness:

> The French submit very patiently and submissively to the indignities of the occupation, and the conduct of the Prussian troops is praiseworthy in the extreme; they are as friendly and sociable as their position will permit — giving alms to the little beggars, dividing their rations of sausage and biscuit with others, kissing their children, and doing all in their power to make their unwelcome presence as little galling as possible.

FRIDAY, *December* 16. — Prince Charles occupies Vendôme, driving Chanzy towards Le Mans with the loss of six guns. Mecklenburg withdrawing to Chartres to cover Paris.

All the German Princes and the Hanse towns concur in bestowing upon King William of Prussia the Imperial crown of Germany, under the title of Frederick William I.

EMPEROR FREDERICK WILLIAM I.

The hope of Bismarck, and the prayer of Prussia for German unity, is accomplished. First the South German states were lukewarm, then the unbearable insult of Napoleon III. made them allies against France. Once allies, fighting for the German Fatherland, and the tie of blood and language wove the woof of German unity and friendship. The German nations became one, and Frankfort, which so hated King William in '67, now begs the honor of being made the place wherein is to be held the crowning ceremony. That King William shall resume the title of Emperor of Germany, has been ratified by Bavaria, Saxony, Würtemberg, Hesse, Baden, and the free cities of Hamburg, Bremen, Lubeck, and Frankfort, and, sixty-four years after Charlemagne, the Imperial crown falls upon the white head of the capturer of Napoleon III. Germany is now great and powerful. Broken and divided in 1815, she fell an easy prey to the first Napoleon; but the blood of 1870 has healed her internal wounds, and made her one of the grandest powers in the Old World despotisms.

The new German Empire will be composed of 25 States, of which four are kingdoms, three free cities, and the remainder grand duchies, duchies, and principalities. Its total area at present is 204,700 square miles, or only two-thirds of the German Empire at the time of Frederick Barbarossa, and four-fifths of the German Empire at the close of the last century, and its population in 1867 amounted to 38,500,000. Both in point of territory and population it would still be nearly equal to France, which had 209,000 square miles and 38,100,000 inhabitants, not counting her colonies. The Constitution of the new Empire will bear more resemblance to that of the United States and Switzerland than with that of any other European State. The Federal House of Representatives is elected by universal suffrage, at the rate of one deputy for every 100,000 inhabitants; while the Federal Council consists of the plenipotentiaries of the several States — not, however, as in the United States and Switzerland, in equal numbers, but varying according to the population of the several States. Prussia, however, though she has more than one-half of the total population of the Empire, has only seventeen out of about sixty votes.

German unity means power and grandeur, but does it mean freedom and reform? Will not the thousand petty princes return from the war, where they have been bolstered up by brave and talented chiefs of staff, and rule over the common people with the hateful rod of a pedantic aristocracy? Germany, I fear, is to be great, *but not free.* King William goes not back to the desolate hearth of Germany as went Washington to Mount Vernon, or Cincinnatus to his neglected fields. Before him is the old desire of glorious conquest, and Luxemburg and the old German provinces of Austria must come back, or be deluged in blood. America can see no hope in all this aggrandizement of power, all this gluttonous absorption. Europe will not learn the lesson of Republicanism, but her free city of Frankfort claims to crown an Emperor; and Spain, weak with a blood-sucking nobility, *carries* her own cross, and journeys to Milan for a king!

CHANZY'S RETREAT.

From Blois, Chanzy moved his army northward towards Vendôme, threatening Mecklenburg's right flank. On the 15th,

Prince Charles left his splendid Third Corps of Brandenburgers to watch Bourbaki, and threw the Ninth and Tenth, with Mecklenburg's army, upon Chanzy. The fight took place a little north of Vendôme, at Frèteval, and lasted till the night of the 15th, when Prince Charles held the town, and Chanzy fell back towards General Jaures at Le Mans. On the evening of the 16th, a council of war determined that the safety of Chanzy's army required a retreat upon Le Mans.

SUNDAY, *December 18th.*—Gambetta sends dispatches from Bourges to Trochu, by carrier pigeon. Prince Charles occupies Vendôme, and Chanzy falls back on Le Mans. General Werder occupies Nuits, twelve miles south of Dijon, defeating General Creamer's force of 15,000 men and eighteen guns. The French loss was 1700 killed and wounded. Prince William of Baden and General Glumer were wounded.

CHANZY'S RETREAT.

On the 17th, Prince Charles placed the Third Corps in Beaugency, and ordered the Ninth and Tenth to march on Vendôme, while Von der Tann held the German left towards Gien with a Bavarian battalion. On the 18th, Chanzy retreating from Vendôme, Prince Charles marched his army to Orleans, to check an expected advance of Bourbaki. Ascertaining that Bourbaki's army was about moving towards Lyons, Prince Charles marches towards Le Mans, and determines with Mecklenburg to destroy the Army of the East.

PARIS AND GAMBETTA.

Gambetta found Bourbaki in a demoralized state, but he immediately sent this carrier-pigeon dispatch, buoyant with hope, to General Trochu in Paris:

GAMBETTA TO JULES FAVRE AND TROCHU: BOURGES, *December* 18.

I have been at Bourges for the last four days occupied with Bourbaki organizing the three corps, Fifteenth, Eighteenth, and Nineteenth, of the First Army of the Loire, which, owing to forced marches during frightful heavy weather since its evacuation of Orleans, were in a bad state. The positions occupied by Bourbaki cover Nevers and Bourges. The other part of the Army of the Loire, after the evacuation of Orleans, retreated on Beaugency and Marchenoire, where they withstood all the efforts of Prince Frederick Charles — thanks to the indomitable energy of General Chanzy, who appears to be the real man-of-war brought forth by last events. This army, composed of the Fifteenth, Seventeenth, and Twenty-first Corps, supported, according to the orders of General Trochu, by all the forces of the west, executed an admirable retreat, causing terrible losses to the Prussians. Chanzy prevented Prince Frederick Charles from executing a great movement on the left bank of the Loire, and the Prince vainly attempted to cross the Loire at Blois to Amboise, and menaced Tours. Chanzy is to-day in perfect security between Vendôme and Le Mans, ready to take the offensive so soon as his troops have had some repose. These troops have not ceased to fight most admirably against superior forces from the 30th of November to the 12th of December. You thus see that the Army of the Loire is far from annihilated, as is represented by the Prussian falsehoods. It is separated into two armies of equal force, ready to operate to the north of Paris, and the other to march on the south. Faidherbe is in Bosworth, and it is thought that he has retaken La Fere, with a great deal of ammunition, artillery, and provisions. But we are most anxious as to *your* fate. It is now more than eight days since we have received any news from you, or by the Prussians. The cable with England is interrupted. What is going on? Deliver us from these torments by sending balloon; the winds are favorable, and will take it to Belgium. The retreating movement of the Prussians is accentuated. They seem fatigued with the continuance of the war. If we can hold out, and we can do so with energy, our triumph is certain. According to the reports which reach me, the enemy have sustained enormous losses, and they provision themselves with difficulty. But we must make up our minds to make supreme sacrifices, not to complain, and to struggle till death. The most perfect order reigns in the interior. The government and the National Defence Committee is everywhere respected and obeyed.

(Signed) GAMBETTA.

This dispatch increased the despondency of Paris. The Parisians on the 18th were reduced to black bread and horse-flesh, and two-thirds of the Paris cab horses had been eaten. Market prices were as follows: Geese, 80 f.; turkeys, 100 f.; chickens, 25 f.; rabbits, 30 f. A Prussian bomb dropped inside the capital near the Point du Tour, the first warning of the coming bombardment; and the others went flying about the Pantheon, Luxembourg, and Church of the *Invalides*.

TUESDAY, *December 20th*.—Tours captured by Voigts Rhetz.

CAPTURE OF TOURS.

On the morning of Tuesday, December 20th, a division of Voigts Rhetz's Hanoverians encountered a division of the Twenty-first French Corps a few miles north of Tours. The Hanoverians opened with twenty-four guns, defeating the French, and marching upon the city of Tours, the recent capital of the Republic. Soon after Voigts Rhetz commenced bombarding the city, the Mayor surrendered the town, which was held for a few hours, when Voigts Rhetz received orders from Prince Charles to march the Tenth Corps back to Orleans, to watch the strategetic movement of Bourbaki.

WEDNESDAY, *December* 21.—Trochu makes a sortie towards La Bourget, and is repulsed by the Saxons.

TROCHU'S SORTIE.

A dispatch from Gambetta had prepared Trochu to expect succor from the outside armies on the 21st. Bourbaki, who was supposed to be marching against Werder in the valley of the Rhône, was to make a rapid turn, and in connection with Faidherbe attack the invading Germans on the north of Paris. Prince Charles discovered the intended movement, and immediately drew his army back on Orleans, to watch Bourbaki, whose designs were thus frustrated. Early on the morning of the 21st, Vinoy advanced with 50,000 men toward La Bourget east of St. Denis, while Ducrot fought a battle towards Gagny and Bondy. The unfortunate village of Bourget had been taken and retaken on a former occasion, and the place was looked upon with anything but kindly eyes. When the Saxons advanced to recapture it, a feeling of German hate caused its destruction. It was found necessary to storm house by house. At length a dwelling was reached, on the outside of which, in a prominent position, was scrawled with charcoal and in German, "The Prussians are dogs and cowards! We shall kill them all!" Then German ferocity showed itself. Scorning to fire a single shot at the enemy intrenched behind this barricade, the German soldiers broke open the doors and windows amid the fire from within, and killed every Frenchman there found with the butt ends of their rifles.

Ducrot was also compelled to retire with the loss of 900 prisoners, and, disappointed again, the army of Paris retired behind the forts, while King William sent this dispatch:

TO THE QUEEN:

The French made a sortie in the direction of Staines and Bourget, prompted by the mistaken idea that a French army of relief was approaching. Many French prisoners were taken in the assault on the Saxon position. The sortie was easily repulsed. The cold is intense.

WILHELM.

FRENCH HONOR.

Bismarck charges Generals Ducrot, Barral, and Cambriels with having violated their paroles of honor. Trochu defends Ducrot in a letter, in which he says:

"You gave your parole to surrender yourself as prisoner of war at Pont-à-Mousson, and that was all. And there having made yourself officially a prisoner, thus redeeming your parole, you conceived and executed, in the face of great danger, a bold escape, by which you hoped to assist Paris."

FRIDAY, *December* 23. — General Manteuffel defeats General Faidherbe near Amiens, driving him north toward Albert and Arras, and capturing 1000 prisoners.

FAIDHERBE *vs.* MANTEUFFEL.

Faidherbe and Manteuffel fought a series of engagements, in which both commanders claimed victories, but the fact that after the smoke of battle had cleared away Manteuffel occupied the ground from which Faidherbe withdrew, leaves the verdict of history in favor of Manteuffel. On the 23d, Manteuffel, leaving Goeben's forces at Rouen and Dieppe to look after Havre, arrived in front of Faidherbe, with about 40,000 men among the surburban villages of Amiens. The conflicting reports are given to illustrate a future complaint of Faidherbe as to German veracity. Faidherbe telegraphed:

"Manteuffel gave us battle on the 23d inst. near Amiens. The battle lasted from eleven in the forenoon until six o'clock in the evening. For the greater portion of the time it was an artillery duel, which was finally terminated by a charge by the French infantry along the whole line. The enemy were driven back, and the French troops remained masters of the field."

After sending this dispatch, Faidherbe *retired northward towards Albert*, and the following dispatch was sent by the King to

QUEEN AUGUSTA: VERSAILLES *Dec.* 24.

Manteuffel won a victory on the 23d near Amiens, taking 1000 prisoners, and commenced to pursue the French in the direction of Arras to-day.

WILLIAM.

Subsequent events proved that Manteuffel won the victory, though Faidherbe retreated in good order.

GEN. FAIDHERBE.

Louis Léon César Faidherbe, now Commander-in-chief of the French Army of the North, was born at Lille on the 3d of June, 1818. He was educated at the college in that place, entered the Polytechnic School in 1838, then went on to the military school at Metz, which he left in 1842, with a lieutenant's commission in the First Regiment of Engineers.

He fought in Africa from 1844 to 1845; returning there again in 1850, where he won the Cross of the Legion of Honor for distinguished service. In 1852 he was sent to Senegal, where he gave such proof of ability, that he was made Governor of the Colony in 1853. He now sought to renovate the colony. He fought the Moors of Furza, and conquered the Prophet El-Hadji-Omar, who undertook to expel the French and found a Mussulman empire in Central Africa. El-Hadji-Omar conquered, Faidherbe left Senegal to command the subdivision of Sidi-bel-Abbes, having been made Lieutenant-Colonel of Engineers in 1855, and Colonel in 1858. But his absence was soon felt in the colony: his policy was not maintained, his instructions were neglected, and everything retrograded. On the 20th of May, 1863, M. Faidherbe, raised to the rank of Brigadier-General, resumed the reins of government in Senegal. Two years after, his health requiring his return to a less murderous climate, he took the highest command in the subdivision of Bône. M. Faidherbe has written much on the manners, language, and history of the African nations, ac well as on the topography, geology, and archæology of the districts they inhabit. He is a member of the Geographical Societies of Paris, London, and Berlin.

Faidherbe is now the rising man in the north of France, and promises to do much for the Republic.

SATURDAY, *December* 24. — Skirmish before Havre. The French defeated, and driven into the fortifications with a loss of 200 prisoners.

SKIRMISH BEFORE HAVRE.

While Manteuffel was fighting Faidherbe at Amiens, the French commander at Havre organized an expedition of 3000 men, under Colonel Macmanard, to attack a force of about 1800 Prussians from General Goeben's force, stationed at Yvetot, a considerable town twenty-five miles north-east from Havre. The advancing French were met promptly by the Germans, and after an artillery and cavalry fight, driven back to the fortifications of Havre, which are considered to be impregnable to almost any investing force. A writer in *The London Standard* writes:

The defences of Havre consist of a line of forts and batteries running along the crest of a range of hills, commencing about a mile beyond Le Hive, on the sea coast, to Harfleur, on the River Seine. They are about three miles from the outskirts of the town of Havre, and are armed with about 100 heavy naval guns. These lines are about six miles in length, and can only be approached by two roads, both of which are well swept by batteries, and the position is so formidable by nature, that, with a flanking fire on both extremities from the men-of-war, they could easily be held by 10,000 good troops against all the Prussians in France.

The present French force in Havre numbers 40,000 men. So immense is the value of shipping and stores in Havre, that the city would not stand a bombardment, and no labor has been spared upon the outworks and redoubts, to make them strong enough to keep the Germans outside of shell range of the city. Havre has a population of 75,000. St. Romain is eight miles from Havre, and with Harfleur, four miles from the city, it will probably be destroyed when the regular investment of Havre commences.

TUESDAY, *December* 27. — The bombardment of Fort Avron commences. The German batteries throw twenty-four shots per minute, the French replying regularly. Bismarck apologizes for the scuttling of six English vessels near Rouen, by the German troops. Manteuffel advances in pursuit of Faidherbe, capturing French troops at Albert.

BISMARCK'S APOLOGY FOR SCUTTLING ENGLISH VESSELS.

On the 27th, the German troops, a few miles from Rouen, seized and scuttled six English vessels, turning the English crews adrift. The affair agitated England, and the English vice-consul at Rouen presented to the Prussian commander a formal protest. The Prussian commander claimed that he seized them for fear that the French would use them to land troops, and Count Bismarck apologized by this telegram to Earl Granville, through Count Bernstorff, the Prussian Minister:

VERSAILLES, *Jan.* 8, 1871.

The report of the German commander at Rouen respecting the sinking of the English colliers has not arrived, but the facts are known. Tell Lord Granville that we sincerely regret that our troops, to avert imminent danger, were obliged to seize the British ships. We admit the claim for indemnity. If unjustifiable excesses were committed, we regret them, and will call the guilty to account. BISMARCK.

THURSDAY, *December* 29.—The Germans capture Mont Avron, south of Paris. General Prim assassinated while proceeding from the Cortes in Madrid to his residence, by three villains in the Calla Alcala. Bourbaki reinforces the French in front of Nuits, and Werder falls back, evacuating Dijon, Gray, and Dôle, which are occupied by the French. The Roumanian Government repudiates the Treaty of Paris, and declares independence. The Crown Prince goes to Amiens to confer with Manteuffel. Mézières surrenders with 2000 men and 106 guns.

MONT AVRON.

The German guns in a curved line from Noisy le Grand to Gagny (see map, page 340) opened on Mont Avron on the 27th, at 9 A.M., throwing twenty-four shots per minute, and silencing the French guns on the morning of the 29th. The Crown Prince of Saxony entered the fort with his old Twelfth Corps, who stood with him at Sedan, and thus telegraphed his entry:

TO KING JOHN OF SAXONY: MONT AVRON, *Dec.* 29.

The Saxons have Mont Avron. When my troops entered, they found the work deserted. The French had removed their guns to Noisy. The German batteries were then ordered to open fire on Noisy, Merlan, and Bondy. The French subsequently withdrew from the village of Rosny, along the road to Paris.

While from the King came this dispatch:

TO QUEEN AUGUSTA: VERSAILLES, *Dec.* 29.

The bombardment of Fort Avron silenced the enemy's guns. The railway station at Noisy was shelled, and the French artillery at Bondy dislodged.

The Prussian loss was three men. The garrison of Fort Avron has fled into Paris.
WILHELM.

SUNDAY, *January* 1. — Manteuffel moving against Faidherbe on the north. Grand banquet at Versailles.

KING WILLIAM'S TOAST.

At the New Year's banquet at Versailles, the King gave a toast to "The German Princes," to which the Duke of Baden responded in a speech, rejoicing at the restoration of the old German Empire, and concluding with a toast to "William the Victorious."

MONDAY, *January* 2, 1871. — Manteuffel marches north from Amiens, past the fortress of Peronne, and fights Faidherbe near Bapaume.

TUESDAY, *January* 3. — Faidherbe is repulsed by Manteuffel, and retreats upon Arras.

BAPAUME AND PERONNE.

After the victorious encounter of Manteuffel at Amiens, the Germans commenced their northward march. The fortress of Peronne was invested, and the cavalry, light infantry, and artillery pushed on to Bapaume, about fifteen miles south of Arras, another fortified town, which, with Douai and Lille, forms an almost impregnable triangle, with a fortress at each angle. Faidherbe made his last stand at Bapaume before withdrawing to the neighboring fortified towns. He attacked Manteuffel on Monday, south of Bapaume. The contest was hot and bloody, and after an all-day fight, both armies rested on their respective fields. On Tuesday morning, Manteuffel ordered Goeben to advance upon the French again. After a sanguinary struggle, the French withdrew into the town of Bapaume, and commenced a retreat towards the north. The town was destroyed, and the Eighth Rhenish Cuirassiers pursued the retreating French towards Arras and Douai. A strange question of veracity again sprang up between Faidherbe and Manteuffel, but the *dénoûments* of a few days showed Faidherbe's pretensions to be groundless. The following dispatch from Faidherbe proved to be as false as General Pope's famous dispatch claiming the capture of 10,000 rebels south of Corinth:

We have fought a battle near Bapaume, which lasted from eight in the morning to six in the evening of Monday. We have driven the Prussians from all their positions and the villages occupied by them. The enemy's losses are enormous. Ours are serious. FAIDHERBE.

This question of veracity arose from the fact that Captain Von Maire's cuirassiers were at one time repulsed, and retreated in disorder before a superior force of French. The main battle was in favor of Manteuffel, who sent his uhlans scouring the country in all directions; some even crept up under the walls of Lille.

BATTLE ON THE SEINE.

While this fight was going on at Bapaume, General Von Bentheim sallied out from Rouen towards Havre, routing the French under General Roy, and capturing 1000 prisoners.

THURSDAY, *January* 5.—The fortress of Rocroy surrenders. Von Moltke orders the bombardment of the southern forts of Paris — Montrouge, Issy, and Vanvres.

FRIDAY, *January* 6.—Terrific bombardment of southern forts continued.

KING WILLIAM'S DISPATCH.

TO QUEEN AUGUSTA: VERSAILLES, *Jan.* 6.

The weather has moderated. We are now having a thaw. Our losses during the bombardment of Fort d'Issy, so far, are 17 killed and wounded. Large supplies were captured from the French at Rocroy.

SUNDAY, *January* 8.—Prince Charles commences his march against Chanzy at Le Mans. Manteuffel leaves the Army of the North to Goeben, Kummer, and Prince Albrecht, and prepares to take command of a new German army, to operate against Bourbaki's rear. German shells fall into the gardens of the Luxembourg, and around the Pantheon.

THE BOMBARDMENT.

TO QUEEN AUGUSTA: VERSAILLES, *Jan.* 8.

Frederick Charles continues his victorious advance on Le Mans. Our forces meet with resistance. Everything has beeu quiet in the North since the 3d. The bombardment here is proceeding favorably. The barracks in Fort Vanvres are on fire WILHELM.

MONDAY, *January* 9.—Bourbaki arrives in front of Werder

with his Orleans army, and is defeated by the Germans, with a loss of 800 prisoners.

TUESDAY, *January* 10. — The great battle of Le Mans commences. The Germans advance one thousand yards nearer Paris. The Parisians demand active operations, and blame Trochu. The fortress of Peronne capitulates with 3000 prisoners.

KING WILLIAM'S DISPATCH.

TO QUEEN AUGUSTA: VERSAILLES, *Jan.* 10.

Owing to a snow-storm and heavy fog, the bombardment is slower to-day.

Peronne has capitulated with 3000 prisoners.

Werder defeated Bourbaki on the 9th, south of Vesoul. He took 800 prisoners.

WILLIAM.

THE BATTLE OF LE MANS (*January* 10 *and* 11).

The last hope of France to succor Paris was dispelled to-day — a day rife with strategy and battles. Goeben, with the First and Eighth Corps, supported by Prince Albrecht's cavalry, already in possession of Peronne, held Faidherbe defiantly towards Arras. Manteuffel, with Fansecki's second corps, started post haste to threaten Bourbaki, now in front of Werder, near Belfort. While these grand movements were being made upon the checker-board of Eastern France, another and grander movement was going on in the west. Chanzy had withdrawn his defeated army from Vendôme to within seven miles of Le Mans, where, reinforced from Cherbourg and Bordeaux, he awaited with 150,000 men the attack of Prince Charles. The battle commenced at nine o'clock on the morning of the 10th. Chanzy located his Sixteenth, Seventeenth, and Twenty-first Corps, commanded by Admiral Jaurezibery, and Generals Colomb and Jouffroy, in a line extending from the village of Brette, about four miles from Orleans, along the railroad towards La Ferte, overlooking the valley of the Huisne. Jouffroy commanded the French Right covering Brette, Colomb the Centre on the plateau of Auvours, and Jaurezibery the Left. Prince Charles advanced with the Third, Ninth, Tenth, Fourteenth, and the First Bavarian Corps, about 150,000 veteran troops. Prince Charles first attacked the Right of the French, hoping to cut them off from Le Mans, and to prevent a retreat to the south, choosing rather to drive Chanzy towards Cherbourg and the sea.

Chanzy received the attack with his army well drawn up with artillery in front, and cavalry on the right and left. The battle-field was perfect, and the French line reflected the hereditary glory of France. Twelve inches of snow covered the ground. Between the two armies was a valley, and for the first hour it was a battle of artillery. At eleven o'clock, Prince Charles gave the order for an infantry advance, and the two armies met face to face in a bloody struggle. The French were fierce—the German veterans cool and determined. At twelve o'clock, the Third and Tenth German Corps made a terrible advance against the French centre. The French Mobiles wavered and fell back, and again Voigts Rhetz and Alvensleben covered a victorious field.

The snow was red with blood, and, as Chanzy fell back towards Le Mans, night came on and shrouded the dreadful scene. All that night Chanzy worked with a terrible energy to retrieve the fortunes of the day. Reinforcements arrived from Camp Conlie, and, after a night of anxiety, the morning dawned upon the French prepared for another conflict. Forward came Prince Charles at daylight—but the French had fallen back, and their position was not reached until ten o'clock. Again the attack sounded—this time on the French Left. A tremendous German force, under cover of a heavy artillery fire, struck Jaurezibery, who met the advance in a terrible struggle. The Germans carried the Left, capturing two guns, when Chanzy moved forward supports, checking a farther German advance. Here the French left stood like a wall against every German onslaught, and around La Ferte was a long and sanguinary encounter. An overpowering German force now massed and attacked Colomb in the centre. Colomb fell back to a position where the rising ground gave the French artillery an effective position. Here were stationed the marines, with a large park of artillery, shotted with shell and canister. Its terrible fire soon compelled the Germans to fall back. Now the battle stood still for two hours, with varying fortunes. The sun now came out warm, and the snow commenced rapidly to melt. As usual, the fighting had brought on an impending storm.

At four P.M. Prince Charles changed his tactics, and threw an overpowering force against the French Right beyond Brette. In front of Brette is a large wood. This was filled with Germans, who showered bullets and canister upon the unfortunate town. At dark, Chanzy ordered his right to fall back, and soon the streets of Le Mans, only a few miles to the rear, were filled with stragglers. At five, Prince Charles advanced his entire line, and Chanzy ordered his army to retreat. This was done in good order; the French deciding to renew the fight again in the morning. Prince Charles did not rest with night, but even in the darkness a tremendous assault was continued against the French Right, which gave way, the Gardes Mobiles from Brittany flying in disorder towards Le Mans. After a council of war, Chanzy decided to retreat towards Alençon on the north, and Laval on the west. Thus ended the hope of the Republic in the Army of the West. On the morning of the 12th Mecklenburg telegraphed:

We advanced to-day north of Le Mans, without fighting. Our van-guard has crossed the Sarthe.

The Third and Tenth German Corps occupied Le Mans, and Mecklenburg moved upon Jaurezibery toward Alençon. King William sent the following dispatch of victory:

TO QUEEN AUGUSTA: VERSAILLES, *January 12th.*

Prince Frederick Charles has fought and defeated the French at Le Mans. Chanzy's army is broken up, and is retreating on Alençon and Laval. Ten thousand prisoners and many guns are falling into our hands.

WILHELM.

LOSSES.

Since the 6th, the French losses have been, besides killed and wounded, 22,000 prisoners and twelve canon. The Prussian official losses were 177 officers and 3203 men killed and wounded; about the same number of French have been placed *hors du combat.*

FRIDAY, *January 13th.*—Prince Charles continues his pursuit of Chanzy. Trochu makes a sortie from the north of Paris. The bombardment continues. Montmédy surrenders. after its walls are breached with solid shot.

PARIS — A SORTIE.

To-day important sorties were made against the Eleventh German Corps at Meudon, the Second Bavarian at Clamart, and the Guards at La Bourget; all of which were repulsed. A rain of projectiles is pouring upon Paris. causing death and destruction in the region between the Invalides, where lie the ashes of the first Napoleon, and the Odeon. Two shells per minute drop around the Luxembourg and Church of St. Sulpice.

Bread is scarce, but still the heroic population resist surrender. To-day, a poor wretch, half-dead with fatigue, and wasted by misery, exclaimed: "Mon Dieu! que cela finisse" (My God! when will this end). Suffering women surrounded her, abused and hustled her about, till she fainted on the street. There is a mad class of stoics who propose absolute starvation, that the world may be stunned by an example of sublime self-destruction. A great cry is raised in Paris against Gen. Trochu, who has failed to organize victory. Gen. Vinoy, now seventy years old, is the favorite now in Paris. An American gentleman thus writes to-day:

General Trochu is a complete failure, and if he were out of the way there would be some hope of saving France. He has been so flattered for his supposed greatness that he believes his own safety paramount to that of Paris, and has talked of leaving Paris by balloon, to avoid capture when the city falls. When urged not to do so, and told that the French people would regard such an act as cowardice, he replied that his capture would be the ruin of France, and by his safety alone could the people expect to succeed in driving the Germans from the soil of France.

The price of provisions is enormously high; there remains only enough on hand to enable the city to hold out until the 20th of January — possibly a few days longer. Horse-meat has entirely given out, and is notto be found in the markets. Mule-meat sells for $2.00 per pound and upward, according to quality. Cats bring $4.00 each, dogs $1.50 per pound, and rats are $1.00 per pair. One turkey sold for $50.00.

The weather is fearfully cold, and fuel is exhausted. The people are burning fences and furniture. Oil is gone, and the city is in total darkness at night.

MONDAY, *January* 16. — Bourbaki attacks Werder south of Belfort, and is defeated. Prince Charles occupies Laval, and Mecklenburg Alençon, capturing four locomotives and four hundred wagons. Chanzy moving west, and Jaurezibery north. Faidherbe moves toward St. Quentin.

BOURBAKI'S DEFEAT.

After the defeat of Paladines, on the 3d of December, had broken the French Army of the Loire into three retreating forces, Bourbaki fell back upon Bourges with the Eighteenth Corps. While Prince Charles pursued Chanzy toward Tours, Bourbaki commenced the strategic movement of falling upon Werder at Dijon before reinforcements could reach him. On the 11th of January, Fansecki started in hot pursuit of Bourbaki with the Second Corps, while Werder fell back with his inferior force towards Belfort, garrisoned with four thousand besieged French. On the 16th of January, Bourbaki, with the other French forces, arrived in front of Werder, near Belfort, and immediately gave battle to the Germans, hoping, if successful, to raise the siege of Belfort. Bourbaki's forces, with the forces of Cambriels and Garibaldi, and with reinforcements from Lyons, amounted to 125,000 men. The encounter was bloody, and there was great solicitude at Versailles as to the result of the French attack. All day long on the 16th, both armies fought on the plain near Belfort, and the beleaguered garrison hoped, but in vain, for victory. At night both armies slept on the field. On the morning of the 17th, Bourbaki commenced a fresh attack. It was the last struggle of the Army of the East, and defeat meant the abandonment of the struggling garrison. Towards night Werder swept forward his entire army in one grand advance. The French wavered — then the centre broke, and Bourbaki was defeated. He commenced his retreat suddenly towards Dijon, hoping to reach Lyons before the flanking army from Paris, now under Mantueffel, should break his communications. Bourbaki's failure caused him such regret that insanity followed ; and a week afterwards we hear of his making an attempt upon his own life. Poor General ! If the writer threw a doubt about you in August, he now withdraws it ; for you *have* proved true to the Republic.

THURSDAY, *January* 19. — King William is proclaimed Emperor of Germany in the Hall of Mirrors at Versailles. Faidherbe defeated and driven into and through St. Quentin, where Goeben captured 2000 French wounded, 5000 unwounded troops, and six guns. Trochu makes his last sortie from Paris. General Glumer pursues Bourbaki towards the Swiss border.

THE KING BECOMES EMPEROR.

In the presence of all the German Princes, to-day, at Versailles, King William was proclaimed Emperor of Germany. The occasion was the scene of a great military pageant ; and while Napoleon III. is a throneless prisoner, the man who was to be besieged in Berlin receives the crown once worn by Charlemagne. The Emperor — Frederick William I. — appoints Bismarck chancellor of the German Empire, and issues the following proclamation to-day :

TO THE PEOPLE OF UNITED GERMANY:

In consequence of the appeal of the German Princes and of the free towns for us to restore the German Empire, after a lapse of sixty years, we announce that we consider it our duty to the Fatherland to accept the Imperial dignity. Henceforth we and our successors will bring to the title of Emperor of Germany the hope that God will vouchsafe a blissful future to the Fatherland, and that, under our auspices, its ancient splendor may be restored. We partake of the dignity, conscious of our duty to preserve with German fidelity the rights of the Empire, and of its members to maintain peace, and to support and strengthen the independence of Germany, in the hope that the German people will reap, in lasting peace, within our boundaries, the fruits of their bloody battles, and be safe against the renewal of French attacks. God grant that we and our successors may protect the Empire, not by warlike conquests, but by works of peace, freedom, and civilization.

WILLIAM, EMPEROR.

THE LAST SORTIE FROM PARIS.

On Wednesday evening the Government issued a fiery proclamation to the discouraged Parisians. It was the last hectic flush of a dying man. "To-morrow," read the eyes of Paris on a thousand bulletins, "we go forth against the foe which kills our wives and children!" All night long artillery rumbled to the west, under cover of Fort Valérien, and at the first dawn of light on Thursday, three *corps d'armée*—an hundred thousand strong—advanced upon the besieging Germans. The morning was beautiful and bright, and the French line was a historic tableau for the canvas of Doré and Meissonnier, who stood with Trochu in the centre. Ducrot commanded the right, occupying Bougival, in front of Kirchbach's Fifth Corps. General Vinoy took possession of the village of Montretout, and opened on the Germans with ten pieces of artillery. General Villemain subsequently took the line of battle on the Left towards St. Cloud. The fighting around Sevres and in the rear of St. Cloud was severe and bloody. Immense masses of the French threw themselves against that sturdy German wall; but it was all in vain. At three o'clock, the Second Bavarian Corps advanced upon the French Left, which recoiled, and broke towards Montretout. Trochu rallied his broken masses again, and placing himself at their head advanced upon the Germans, who pushed forward immense masses of infantry with heavy reserves of artillery. Trochu was driven back, and, abandoned by fortune, his unhappy army returned sullenly and sorrowfully to Fort Valérien, and the fiery proclamations of the morning were covered over with Trochu's terrible acknowledgment of defeat:

The day, which commenced successfully, did not terminate as we could have wished. The enemy were at first surprised, but subsequently concentrated great masses of artillery and infantry, and at three o'clock in the afternoon our left receded. We resumed at nightfall the offensive movement, but were unable to hold the heights which we had taken. The struggle was sanguinary. We have asked for an armistice.

The Emperor William sent the following telegrams:

To the Empress Augusta:

Versailles, *January* 19.—A sortie was made from Valérien to-day under cover of a heavy fire. It was entirely without result.

The Army of the North was beaten to-day before St. Quentin. Four thousand unwounded prisoners and two guns were captured.

Wilhelm.

Versailles, *Friday, January* 20.—Faidherbe will be pursued to-day.

The sortie from Valérien yesterday was made in great force. The troops are still outside of Paris. A fresh attack is certain to-day.

Wilhelm.

During the battle the Prussian shells went crashing into Paris, and that night, with defeat in the field and hunger at home,—with the skies raining shot and shell upon their beautiful capital, what wonder that Paris was the picture of despair!

William Emperor telegraphed at night:

To the Empress Augusta:

The enemy has entirely withdrew into Paris. Fifteen officers and two hundred and fifty men were captured at St. Cloud. William.

On Friday morning, Trochu, at a council held by the members of the Committee of Defence, announced that, as there was no hope for assistance from Chanzy or Faidherbe, it was his duty to surrender before the Germans destroyed the public buildings, and fired on the centre of the city. A quarrel ensued, when General Trochu offered his resignation; which was accepted, and Generals Vinoy, Frebault, and Clement Thomas were appointed a triumvirate to replace Trochu. Subsequently the council recoiled from the responsibility, and Trochu was sustained.

CAPTURE OF ST. QUENTIN.

The misfortune of Paris was not alone this day the misfortune of France. Faidherbe advanced defiantly beyond St. Quentin, where he was met by Goeben, defeated, and driven into and through the town with great loss. A general panic seized upon the people at Cambrai, while Faidherbe retreated to the fortress of Douai, with the loss of an entire division. The entry of the retreating army into the city of Cambrai was a sad scene of disorder. The troops were shoeless and in rags, and the army fragmentary to a great degree. General Goeben's losses at St. Quentin were 94 officers and 3000 men.

The Emperor William sent the following telegram:

To the Empress Augusta:

Versailles, *January* 20. — The number of unwounded prisoners captured at St. Quentin is 9000, beside 2000 wounded taken in the town. The total loss of the French is 15,000. The enemy has withdrawn to Valenciennes and Douai. We have again occupied Cambrai.

Fours Hours Later. — The latest estimate of the French loss at St. Quentin is 15,000 men, including 11,000 prisoners.

William.

With the French Army of the North defeated, with Bourbaki threatened by Manteuffel, with Chanzy flying disorganized before Prince Charles and Mecklenburg, and with Trochu driven into Paris, threatened with shells from without and internal disorders from within, the fortunes of France are unhappy indeed. It is folly longer to fight. Germany has fairly conquered.

Sunday, *January* 22. — Mob in Paris. Gustave Flourens released from prison. Three hundred National Guards attack the Hôtel de Ville, but are repulsed by the Mobiles. General Vinoy assumes command in place of Trochu. Emperor William accepts in an order the Imperial dignity, and praises his troops, charging them to remain the strong arm of the Fatherland. Gambetta at Lille. The Army of the North totally demoralized. The bombardment of Longwy proceeding.

Tuesday, *January* 24. — Paris concludes to surrender. Jules Favre visits Bismarck, and returns to Paris. The Bordeaux Government notified, and Gambetta accepts the action of the Paris authorities.

Wednesday, *January* 25. — The surrender agreed to. Longwy surrenders with four thousand prisoners and two hundred guns. Manteuffel crowds Bourbaki towards Switzerland.

Saturday, *January* 28. — An armistice of three weeks on land and sea agreed to.

FAVRE AND BISMARCK.

To-day, the German pickets were overjoyed at the sight of a flag of truce from Paris, and an unusual commotion, which indicated an important communication from the Capitol. A Prussian Captain advanced and received the French deputation, whichwas headed by a no less personage, than M. Jules Favre, the Minister of Foreign Affairs, who desired to be conducted directly to Count Von Bismarck's rooms in Versailles. The meeting between Favre and Bismarck was affecting — the voice of the former sometimes becoming gruff with emotion. After a few kind remarks, Bismarck, in the tenderest manner, remarked:

"My dear friend, I know the cause of your visit; you would stop the farther shedding of blood."

FAVRE (affected) — "Yes, yes, M. Bismarck; my object is to stop the terrible sufferings of my unhappy countrymen in Paris, for all hope of relief from without seems lost, and Paris must needs seek peace."

BISMARCK — "We respect the gallantry of the French nation, and we pity her sufferings. We will do what we can for peace, consistent with the safety and honor of Germany. This, my dear M. Favre, has been the desire of the Emperor William and his advisers since the unhappy war was forced upon him. What has Paris to offer?"

M. FAVRE — "If her soldiers were permitted to leave Paris with the honors of war, Paris would surrender."

BISMARCK — "It is not my province to refuse or accept your terms; but I will say, that personally, I do not approve them, and I feel confident that my august master will reject them. However, I will submit them to his consideration."

Count Bismarck now invited Favre to a repast, when the two spent an hour in social conversation. The Emperor firmly rejected Favre's proposition, and submitted the following, which Favre carried back to the Provisional Government:

The forts to be garrisoned by Germans.

The regulars and Gardes Mobiles to be sent to Germany.

Paris to receive no garrison for its protection — the city to be confided to the National Guards, who will not be disarmed.

As M. Favre rose to depart, the following conversation took place:

BISMARCK — "The surrender, M. Favre, should be signed by the entire Provisional Government, to make it binding in France."

FAVRE — "But we cannot bind the republic at Bordeaux.

The surrender is purely a military one, and the republic may reject every question outside of the garrison."

BISMARCK — "If the Republic rejects terms which will give peace, the Emperor is ready to accept them; and then France must choose between acceptance and a restoration of the empire."

M. Favre spent the evening of the 24th in Paris, but returned to Versailles on the evening of the 25th with the signature of the Paris officials to the articles of surrender. Bismarck now urged upon Favre the practicability of an armistice, that a *de jure* government might be elected by the people, whose representatives would have power to guarantee the execution of a :reaty of peace. Favre passed back to Paris again, returning :o Versailles on the 28th, when an armistice of twenty-one days vas agreed upon. The constituent elections to be held on the 3th of February, and the National Assembly to be convened ıt Bordeaux on the 15th. It was farther arranged that the orisoners of war were to remain in Paris during the armistice.

The National Guards and gendarmes to retain their arms, ıs were also the police. All Francs-tireurs to be disbanded. German prisoners to be exchanged. The public funds to remain in Paris.

The names of the French officers surrendering, are given in 'ull on page 418.

The Emperor sent the following telegram:

VERSAILLES, *January* 29, 2 P. M., 1870.

'O THE EMPRESS AUGUSTA:

Last night an armistice for three weeks was signed. The Regulars and Mobiles are to be *interned* in Paris as prisoners of war. The National Guard will undertake the maintenance of order. We occupy all the forts 'aris remains invested, but will be allowed to revictual as soon as arms are ırrendered.

The National Assembly is to be summoned to meet at Bordeaux in a ›rtnight. All the armies in the field will retain their respective positions, ıe ground between opposing lines to be neutral.

This is the reward of patriotism, heroism, and great sacrifices. Thank iod for this fresh mercy! May peace soon follow!

WILHELM.

Bordeaux agreed to the terms of this armistice, and decreed n election on the 8th of February, for members of the contituent assembly. The decree disqualified as candidates to ıe Republican election all Imperialists who have been Imperi-l candidates for, or held the offices of Minister, Senator, or Councillor of State under the Empire, and Prefects under Na-oleon III. To prevent the entire dissolution of the French rmies during the armistice, Gambetta issued the following roclamation:

FRENCHMEN: Prussia believes the armistice will dissolve our armies, and secure the election of a chamber ready to conclude a shameful peace. It depends on France to upset these calculations. It is necessary to make the armistice a period for the instruction of our young troops. Continue with unrelaxed vigor the organization for defence, and for war if necessary, while you instal a National Republican Assembly willing to make such a peace only as is compatible with the honor, rank, and integrity of France.

The surrender found Paris in a starving condition, and the railroads being broken, the German army was obliged to share its rations with the French troops. This was magnanimously done, causing much good feeling. Much damage was done to the old part of Paris and around the Luxembourg by the German shells, but new Paris escaped particular damage.

At the signing of the armistice —

Faidherbe's Army of the North (the Twenty-second and Twenty-third Corps) was in a demoralized condition in front of Goeben at Arras, Douai, and Cambrai.

Chanzy stood, defeated by Prince Charles, with the Army of the West at Laval.

Bourbaki (relieved by Clinchart) was fleeing into Switzerland before Manteuffel with the Army of the East, covered by General Billot.

Manteuffel was about capturing six thousand prisoners, which work was finished before news of the armistice reached him.

The success of the German armies is unprecedented in the history of warfare. Never in the world's history has an army, within six months, captured forces, the aggregate of which almost equal the capturing army. The following table gives the fortified places captured — time, and number of French prisoners of war:

Weisenburg	August 4	2,500
Lichtenburg	August 9	1,000
Herny	August 12	100
Vitry	August 19	500
Sedan	Sept. 1	110,000
Laon	Sept. 10	3,000
Toul	Sept. 23	2,240
Strasburg	Sept. 27	11,000
Soissons	Oct. 16	4,700
Metz	Oct. 27	200,000
Verdun	Nov. 8	4,500
Neuf Brisach	Nov. 11	5,000
Thionville	Nov. 25	5,000
Pfalzburg	Dec. 12	2,000
Montmedy	Jan. 13	4,000
Rocroy	Jan. 5	3,000
Peronne	Jan. 10	3,500
Le Mans	Jan. 11	10,000
St. Quentin	Jan. 19	8,000
Longwy	Jan. 25	4,000
Paris	Jan. 28	230,000
		614,040

PEACE!

The election on the 8th of February may provide a *de jure* government, and the world may look for peace between France and Prussia on the following basis :

1. France to cede Alsace and Lorraine to Prussia. Metz and Strasburg to become German fortfications.

2. France to pay Germany a war indemnity, and surrender twenty ships from her navy.

3. Both national armies to be reduced to a peace footing.

Tranquillity came with the surrender, but General Trochu feared far more the hatred of the Parisians than the Germans. He refused to become a candidate in the Provisional election, and retired to Brittany, a disheartened and disappointed man. The hatred for Gambetta was intense in Paris, and on the north. The people protested against his decrees, and against the idea of proscription, preventing a free election. Favre threatened to depose Gambetta, and appoint M. Herold in his place ; and Bismarck even interfered, and said the election should be free, and that Gambetta's decrees from Bordeaux, disfranchising the Imperialists, must be disobeyed. On the 5th, the differences of the dual governments became so great, that Favre resigned his position of Minister of the Interior, and Gambetta, intent on mischief, called a council of war in Bordeaux, "*to deliberate on the means of profiting by the armistice.*"

If the Constituent election was not held on the 8th of February, Gambetta and his hot-headed party from Bordeaux prevented it ; and all further anarchy or bloodshed will be on the head of this selfish, vain, and tyrannical republican despot. Germany will be compelled to organize a new Provisional Government for France, with the consent of England, Austria, and Russia.

If Napoleon III. made the war, Gambetta continued it, and even now jeopardizes the making of peace. The following is the list of Paris candidates for the Constituent Assembly, all true, but conservative men :

Jules Favre, Isaac Adolphe Crèmieux, Alexandre Glais-Bizoin, Louis Joseph Earnest Picard, Jules Simon, Pierre Clement, Eugène Pelletan, Emanuel Arago, Louis Antoine Garnier-Pages, Jules Ferry, Henri Rochefort, Admiral Saisset, Admiral de la Roncière de Noury, Admiral Pothouan.

WHAT MADE A NATION'S DISASTERS.

And so the end is come. Wonderful indeed is the sublime lesson taught by Divinity to the nations. The Coliseum has become the pigmy, and the scathing irony of Victor Hugo has become an awful truth. Voltaire has indeed surrendered to Bismarck, Versailles is but the shadow of Potsdam, the Lorrainer has become a German, and France — "the soldier of God" — stands trembling before the sword of the hated Teuton. What has caused this terrible change? History is full of explanation. Other nations have had their rise and fall — their period of prosperity; and then came the hectic flush, like the Paris frenzy for war in July, which proved the signal for the entry of political death. India taught the lesson of astronomy and architecture to Egypt — and died; Rome, with her Cæsar-palaces, bowed to the sturdy Vandals; and Napoleon the Great sharpened at Jena the Prussian sword which stabbed Napoleon the Little at Sedan. Imperialism rotted the political system of France. Military glory, ignorance, jealous suspicions, and official espionage culminated in the Imperial declaration of war against Prussia. It was the old assault of slavery against our Republic — and with the same result. The war declaration in July was but the blossom of Imperial decay. For ten years the nation has been dying, and nothing but a great national calamity could follow her rotten political system. The Emperor dazzled; but behind was a dark shadow — the ignorance and superstition of forty millions of subjects. In eighteen years America could applaud but one act in the reign of Louis Napoleon, and that act was the liberation of Lombardy. The Emperor astonished Europe on fête days, and covered over the corruption and decadence and the ignorance of a barbarous peasantry with the glare of luxury. The column of July was gilded at the top; but it looked down upon a capital full of intriguers, suspicious, and without manly confidence.

A nation cannot be great which gives five hundred millions of francs a year to its army in time of peace, and but forty millions to the education of her children. A nation cannot be great which spends four hundred millions of francs in fine barracks, imperial palaces, and grand opera-houses, but which looks in vain and in shame for a respectable school-house. Greatness will never come when the army officers ten times outnumber the schoolmasters. A nation cannot be great which carries on its shoulders that monster of decay, that vampire of Italy — the temporal power of a Pope; gives two hundred millions of francs a year to support a Papal imbecility, and refuses for years to contribute one hundred thousand francs to Gustave Lambert for an expedition in search of the north-west passage. Absolute power in one man and in one place — *Cæsarism* — will never expand the national mind. The effects of these eighteen years of despotism, of centralization, of luxury for the capital and ignorance for the rural districts, have shown themselves in blood, in shame, and in national disaster. Backward under the Empire, instead of *forward* to liberty, has been going the education of the people. A nation must be on the confines of barbarism when, unstartled, it sees the tax contributions of her half-starved rural laborers go to pay for the "pigeon wings" of M. Petitpas and Mlle. Fiocre on the boards of the Grand Opera. What hope is there for a people who pay sixty million francs a year from the state treasury to a half-naked dancer, and who refuse to pay more than forty francs a month to their school-teachers? It was a heathenish excuse that the dance-women brought strangers to Paris and enriched the people. Education and sound morality, and not money, among the masses, is a nation's only salvation. What hope is there for morality when opera-houses take the place of churches, and when an Emperor flaunts the soiled robes of a Marguerite Belanger in the face of the reigning Empress? Not the one-man education, but a broad and universal education will save a nation in her direst need. The Rousseaus, Pascals, Keplers, and Humboldts cannot save a people, but the great swaying masses must kneel at the fountain of wisdom and letters. First knowledge, then the Republic, and then GREATNESS; not first the Empire, then wealth, then ignorance, and then littleness!

Paris deceived the world. Her brilliancy, her splendid railways, and her dazzling soldiers were only masks covering an ignorant, superstitious, and priest-ridden peasantry. Such a people were incapable of great deeds. It was natural that the frugal, Protestant, educated Prussian should overrun her frontiers sooner or later, and teach France, by a visitation of fire and sword, the sources of her sickness and the remedy for her cure.

The Empire with its spy system made one man suspicious of another. This suspicious lack of confidence among citizens became a great social evil. Great deeds were betrayed, and affairs of state became intrigues of men. One half of France were watching the other half, and everywhere were a double set of sentries — one watching the other. M. de Persigny cautioned the Emperor in a letter against their mutual friend, the Prefect of Police. A whole nation became addicted to espionage — every man a natural policeman, stealing with the right hand and guarding with the left, and the people became two armies of parasites — the watchers and the watched.

The Empire died at Sedan; and then came the men of September 4th. The seeds of the Republic were faulty, and they fell on barren soil, worn out by imperial vegetation. It was the same old government with a plurality of rulers — Favre, Trochu, Gambetta, and Hugo, all pulling, but different ways. Each man became a Republican emperor, with the same love of decrees inherited from the Emperor. Every man who held a bit of power, from the Governor down to the lowest mayor or sub-prefect, must put into operation the abstract ideas he had been preaching in secret conclave to his disciples for the last twenty years; but fortunately for the state, they died as soon as launched. Arbitrary arrests continued, the people still belonged to the office-holders, and opinions were opposed by force and secret intrigues rather than by the ballot and free discussion. Men vote in a Republic, but do not decree; and when five or ten Republican emperors, like Gambetta and Trochu, decree themselves *de facto* rulers, refusing to go before the people in an election, they become despots. Gambetta could not trust the people; for the Empire had perverted humanity, and it must be born again before it could vote in a spirit of liberty. After the fall of Paris, Bismarck sent the defeated people to their ballot-boxes, and France did the first republican act since the *coup d'état* of Napoleon III. Months must elapse before we shall know the result. We do not despair of the Republic, for the war has been a blessing in disguise, pricking a visionary bauble, and placing a great nation in her true position, humbled, but in her right mind. By and by she may become a Republic. Republicans are born, not made; and only with thirty years of trial, and with a generation of born Republicans, can France be free from Imperial snares. America has passed through that dead sea of Imperialism; and every citizen, watched over by Republican parents and schooled in Republican schools, finds in himself that undying, unchanging Republican principle and thought, — that thought goes out in benedictions to struggling humanity — to Ireland, to France, to Hungary, and Poland, and beckons even among the thrones of depotism, saying, in a sweet voice, "COME TO US!"

THE END.

CPSIA information can be obtained
at www.ICGtesting.com
Printed in the USA
LVHW040742310323
742922LV00020B/30

9 783382 126797